THE IRON PIRATE

H.M.S. SARACEN

The Iron Pirate
H.M.S. Saracen

Douglas Reeman

BOOK CLUB ASSOCIATES
LONDON

To Dorothy, Frank and Stan—

from us, with love

This combined edition published 1987 by
Book Club Associates
by arrangement with Century Hutchinson Ltd
and William Heinemann Ltd

Set in 10/11 pt Compugraphic Paladium
Typeset by Colset Private Limited, Singapore
Printed in Great Britain by
Richard Clay (The Chaucer Press) Ltd
Bungay, Suffolk

Contents

The Iron Pirate

Chapter One

Charmed Lives

The sea's face that morning rose and dipped in an endless formidable swell. There were no crests, and the deep troughs gleamed in the early light like molten glass. A heavy mist drifted above the water, broken here and there into clearings while close by it barely skimmed the surface.

In a few days it would be August, but in the Baltic the dawn air was already like a knife, a threat of the winter which would soon grope down from the Gulf of Finland to torment ships and sailors alike.

Occasionally scattered groups of gulls and other sea-birds lifted on the successive swells like broken wreaths, pale in the dull light, unimpressed by the steepness of the troughs which in happier times could hide one fishing boat from another even when they lay less than half a cable apart. From end to end the Baltic had been one of the busiest waterways in the world where fishermen and coasters, timber ships and colliers created their own patterns and trails. Now, apart from a few wary neutral Swedish vessels, the waters were the hunting ground, and a burial place for friend and foe alike.

It was 1944 and for many, the fifth year of war. The sea noises were muted or dampened by the mist; it was like a wilderness, an abandoned place for a while longer on this particular morning. The gulls which floated silently and waited to begin their search for food were as usual the first to sense they were no longer alone. To begin with it was more of a sensation than a sound, not close enough to be a beat or throb, just a tremor through the water which soon made the birds rise flapping and mewing, disturbed, anxious yet unwilling to quit their territory.

Had there been an onlooker he would have been startled by the suddenness of the ship's appearance. First a great shadow, and then with a contemptuous thrust of her high, raked bows she swept through the mist, parting it, and cleaving the steep swell with impressive ease. Although her three screws were throttled

9

down to reduced speed she threw a sharp white moustache from her stem which spattered against her faded camouflage paint-work to give a hint of her true power. As she thrust across the grey water she grew in size and strength, but her four twin turrets and towering bridge structure did nothing to spoil the perfection of her lines. She was a heavy cruiser, one of the most powerful afloat, yet she retained all the dash and grace of a destroyer.

No figures explored her wet decks, and only occasional move-ments at gun mountings and on her bridge gave any sign of life. For a few moments she lay fully exposed in a clearing, like a graceful animal crossing a glade in a forest, and the reluctant dawn made her upperworks shine like glass and touched the flag, a solitary patch of scarlet with its black cross and swastika.

Before the mist closed in again the cruiser's secondary arma-ment seemed to come to life, the slender muzzles in their separate mountings around the superstructure training and lifting as if to sniff out a possible enemy. Each gun crew was fully aware of the cost of carelessness, the lack of constant vigilance. In these con-tested waters there was rarely a second chance.

Closed up at their various action stations, as they had been for most of the night, there were some 950 officers and men scattered throughout her armoured hull. Separated by the needs of safety, and yet welded into a solitary team to fit the demands of their ship, the wishes of their commanding officer.

At the rear of the open bridge, alone for a few more precious minutes in his spartan sea-cabin, Kapitän zur See Dieter Hechler sat at his desk, outwardly relaxed from long practice, but with his mind recording each movement and untoward sound beyond his small refuge. He rarely visited his spacious quarters below except in harbour, for time taken in running to the bridge in any emer-gency was time lost. He rarely thought about it. This was his world, and had been for the eighteen turbulent months since he had been given the honour of this command, one of the remaining crack cruisers in the German navy.

In a moment or so, Viktor Theil, his second-in-command, would call him on the red handset above the sea-cabin's crumpled bunk. Then Hechler would get to his feet, take a quick look round to ensure he had forgotten nothing, and walk to the bridge.

They would greet him with varied feelings. Relief, doubt, dis-like even, but all would accept him as their captain.

10

He sat back in the chair and stared unseeingly at the chart on his desk, the personal one he kept for his own guidance. When he joined the others of his team he would need to know everything, be ready to answer any question, even the stupidest one. He knew from hard experience that any man rebuked for asking something which in all truth he should have known, would never dare to ask another question, perhaps when it was vital.

His jacket hung from a rail beside the bunk, the four gold stripes glinting dully in the light from the desk lamp. His cap, like the medal ribbons on the jacket, showed his authority and skill at a glance, but any casual visitor would see him now as the man, not the commander. The cap and jacket were necessary trappings, just as banners and flags identified the old sailing men-of-war in the height of battle in another century. But for now, in his favourite roll-necked fisherman's jersey in thick grey wool, and the extra pair of flannel trousers beneath his uniform ones, he looked at ease. Hechler was thirty-six, the youngest captain to command such a ship as the *Prinz Luitpold*, and the responsibility was clear to see in the deep creases on either side of his firm mouth. His hair was dark and had remained unruly despite all the caustic comments of his superiors over the years. His strength, his qualities, the depth of the man himself showed mostly in his eyes. They were blue with the shadow of grey, like the sea itself.

In his youth he had discovered that his eyes had made him vulnerable. If they had showed his confidence, so too they had betrayed his doubts. He had taught himself to contain his inner emotions, and had seen the effectiveness of his control when he was dealing with his day-to-day life. A seaman to be punished, or to be promoted with a word of congratulation. A man to be told that his family had perished in an air raid. It was all part of his world, as was watching people die, sometimes horribly, knowing as he did that others would be looking at him to see his reactions if only to gauge their own fates.

Like last month when he had cleared the lower deck and had every officer and man assemble aft beneath the twin muzzles of Turret Dora, to tell them about the Allied invasion of Normandy. To most of *Prinz Luitpold*'s ship's company the other theatres of war had seemed remote and with little meaning. The Pacific, Italy, even the Atlantic, the bloodiest sea war of all, meant little. Their war had been here, or in the Arctic against the

11

Russians. Normandy had changed all that. The official news was optimistic, adamant that the British and their allies would soon be driven back into the sea and in turn leave England ripe for invasion. And anyway Normandy was a long, long way from the Fatherland.

But to many of the listening faces it seemed like a stab in the back, an enemy gnawing away at another front, which would make even greater demands on their own resolution and resources.

The deck gave an unexpected shudder and Hechler had to make himself relax again, muscle by muscle. Perhaps he was too tired. Maybe the war had pared away his resistance without his realising it. He smiled and ruffled his hair with his strong fingers. Then with a sigh he leaned forward and stared at the chart for the last time.

The coastline was familiar enough. It was useless to consider what might have been, to despair over the loss of ground in the past few months. Safe anchorages had come under constant air attack; now they lay in enemy hands. All the time, the Russian armies kept up their pressure along thousands of miles of savagely contested land. Up here in the North, the Finns, Germany's allies, were under terrible pressure and an entire German army was in danger of being cut off from retreat. Hechler's mouth moved in a wry smile. *Strategic withdrawal,* as the news reports termed it. The heavy cruiser always seemed to be at an hour's notice to get under way even after the briefest respite in harbour. Now with her escort of two destroyers divided on either beam, she was back in the same fiercely contested waters where she had once been able to rest; where she had been like a symbol to the army ashore.

As he ran his eye along the chart, or checked a measurement with his dividers, Hechler could see the coast in his mind's eye like a painting, a watercolour. Abeam was the northern coast of Lithuania, the gateway to the Gulf of Riga. During the night they had slipped past the low, sandy point, Kolkasrags, with its wooded darkness beyond, and would soon begin to turn in a wide sweep towards the land once more.

South-east and deep into the Gulf of Riga, where they had been ordered to supply artillery support to the beleaguered German army. Riga was the only point from which the army could retreat if the worst happened, and there had been nothing in the regular signals to suggest that the Russians were losing steam in spite of their horrendous losses in men and tanks.

It was always a risk, a ship against sited shore batteries. Those who gave such orders saw only the overall strategy, the latest necessity, and rarely considered the danger.

It was a task which *Prinz Luitpold* had carried out many times. Originally she had provided covering fire for their own landings, had supported a victorious army through one advance to the next. If winter closed in early there might be some respite on this front at least. Hechler pitied the poor devils who endured the bitter cold and privation, who would face it yet again with the added knowledge that the Allies were nearer their homeland than they were. *Unless.*

Hechler glanced up at the framed picture of his ship. The glass shivered in the frame to the gentle vibration from several decks below his feet. It made it look as if the photograph was alive. *Prinz Luitpold* was a lucky ship, and had become something of a legend in the tight world of the navy. Bombardments, hurling aside air attacks, or matching gun-for-gun with British cruisers of the North Cape, she had sustained only negligible damage, and had lost but two men killed. One of the latter had fallen overboard after slipping on an icy deck. Not a very proud death for his family to remember.

Hechler thought of other ships similar to his own. *Prinz Eugen*, another legend even in the enemy's navy, *Admiral Hipper* which had been rammed in a hopeless attack by a British destroyer early in the war – they were both fine ships. Another of the class, the *Blücher*, had gone to the bottom back in 1940, torpedoed by the Norwegians of all people. One more was still building.

But *Prinz Luitpold* seemed to lead a charmed life. Her launch, shortly after *Blücher*'s end, had been delayed by several fierce air raids. They had played havoc with the Blohm & Voss yard in Hamburg where her keel had been laid. And yet despite the devastation all around her, she had survived waiting patiently for the smoke to clear and the work to continue.

Hechler had been serving in a small, elderly cruiser when she had been launched by the Führer himself, her name chosen to cement Austrian friendship. He had seen her several times, and as his own advancement had progressed he had set his heart on her, this cherished command.

He stood up, his body balanced automatically to feel the strength of the ship beneath him. Fourteen thousand tons with the machinery to drive and sustain her every need, the weapons to fight anything faster or of equal size, she even carried three Arado float-planes, Hechler's eyes when he needed them.

Hechler was a tall man with broad shoulders, yet despite this he moved in the confined cabin with the ease of a cat as he slipped into his jacket and patted each pocket without really noticing this regular precaution.

He opened the drawer of his desk and placed the dividers and parallel rulers inside. As he did so he saw her face looking up at him from the worn leather case which he had always carried at sea. He sighed, his eyes distant. *Next to my heart.*

He heard a steel door slam shut somewhere below the cabin. A last bolt-hole sealed for anyone whose nerve might waver?

The ship, this ship, had helped him to get over even that, he thought. He could look at her face now, even study it without the old surge of bitterness and despair. Inger was not smiling in the photograph. When he thought about it now he realised that she had never smiled very much.

The red handset buzzed above the bunk, like a trapped insect. Hechler smiled and lifted it. Relieved at the interruption, to be freed from the sudden shadow, the depression. He closed the drawer as he spoke. Shutting her away, until the next time.

It was Theil, as he had known it would be. A man so dependable that Hechler had once found himself searching for flaws and mistakes. He had been in the ship since she had first commissioned at Hamburg and had served under the one other captain before Hechler. A competent officer in every way, one that commanded most people's respect and liking, qualities which rarely went hand-in-hand in a warship.

Theil should have had a command of his own; they were desperate for experienced captains in larger vessels. Each promising junior was snatched up and sent into submarines to combat the mounting toll in the Atlantic. Like cutting down a forest before the trees had had time to mature, as one elderly staff officer had complained.

Theil reported, 'Five minutes to the final change of course, sir.'

It would be. *Exactly.* Hechler replied, 'Very well, Viktor. I shall come up now.'

He put down the handset and reached for his cap and binoculars.

14

A glance in the bulkhead mirror made him grimace as he tugged the cap tightly across his thick hair. He looked calm enough. He examined his feelings as he would a subordinate.

Nothing. It was as if all pointless doubts had been worked out of him. He studied his image in the glass and saw the strain fall away. He was young again, like the day he had stood in church with Inger, had walked beneath an archway of drawn swords of his fellow officers.

The thought made a shutter fall across his blue eyes. Hechler snapped off the light and left the cabin. He never thought that each time might be the last. That too was a waste, an unnecessary burden on his mind.

He waited a few moments more in the deep shadows, his shoulder touching the damp steel plating, his eyes adjusting, preparing for the open bridge, and the sea. For the enemy.

Fregattenkapitän Viktor Theil, the heavy cruiser's second-in-command, stood on a scrubbed grating in the forepart of the bridge. His booted feet were wide apart so that he could feel the ship rising and slithering down beneath him, tasting pellets of salt spray as they lifted occasionally over the glass screen. A new hand aboard ship took days, longer if he was allowed, to grow accustomed to objects and fittings even in pitch darkness. Theil knew them all just as he could picture the faces of the intent bridge party on either hand and behind his back. Signalmen and petty officers, the massive, oilskinned bulk of Josef Gudegast, the navigating officer. Theil had some reservations about officers who were not regulars, but like the rest of the team he had cause to be grateful that Gudegast was the navigator. In peacetime he had earned his living in the merchant service and had been for much of the time the chief petty officer of a Baltic timber ship. Gudegast knew all the niceties and the perils of these waters like his own considerable appetite.

Theil analysed the captain's voice on the telephone. Calm. Nothing to worry about. Not like the previous captain who had cracked up when the ship had been under constant air attack for three whole days. Theil felt the old hurt like a physical pain. He had taken command, had got the ship back to Kiel when others had been less fortunate. He had dared to hope he would be promoted, and be given *Prinz Luitpold*. He had deserved it. He knew it. Instead, Hechler had stepped aboard to the trill of calls and the proud salutes. A man of excellent reputation who had since proved his worth a dozen times. But he was several years Theil's junior nonetheless.

Theil thought of the other faces, some of which were new to the ship. In the armoured superstructure above the bridge, the conning tower and fire-control stations, the officers he saw each day were waiting for the calm to shatter. Tired faces at the meal table, or flushed with drink after a trip ashore in some port or other. Faces which hid things or revealed too much. Like the youngest officer here on the bridge, Leutnant zur See Konrad Jaeger. A fresh-faced, green youngster of nineteen. He would be perfect on a recruiting poster. Apart from training, *Prinz Luitpold* was his first ship. He had a pleasant manner, and the confidence of one used to authority. His father was a much-decorated captain who had been put ashore after losing an arm and one eye in the North African campaign. Jaeger's father still had influence, Theil decided. Otherwise the youngster would have been a junior watch-keeper aboard a U-boat instead of serving a thoroughbred like this ship. It was rumoured that a junior officer's life expectancy in a combat U-boat was about that of a lieutenant on the Russian Front.

Theil shivered. It was best to leave it as a rumour these days.

He heard the steel gate at the rear of the bridge open, noted the way the dark figures around him seemed to come to life as the captain entered and touched his cap casually to the bridge party at large. Theil faced him, and recalled suddenly how he had resented, hated this man.

From beside the compass platform Jaeger watched the two senior officers, the men who between them controlled the ship and his destiny. They made a complete contrast, he thought. The captain, tall, powerful, yet with a calm unruffled tone. Theil, stocky, with short fair hair, given to angry outbursts if anything slipped below his very high standards.

Hechler could feel the youngster's scrutiny just as he could sense the navigating officer's indifference. The latter knew his charts with an uncanny accuracy; he was often known to scoff at the ship's new navigational aids, the first things to break down when you needed them, he proclaimed.

Beyond his long hours of duty as the ship hurried from one sea area to another, Gudegast rarely mixed with his fellow officers.

16

Another surprise about him was his skill as an artist. Despite his bluff seaman's appearance and colourful language he could paint and sketch everyday scenes with accuracy and compassion. Now he was rising on his toes to watch some circling gulls, one of his favourite subjects, like patches of spindrift against the mist. Another sketch maybe?

Hechler ducked his head beneath the canvas hood which hid the light of the chart-table and peered seachingly at Gudegast's neat calculations, bearings and fixes. Like his artwork, each pencilled note or figure was clear and delicate. Perhaps a frustrated artist from another age lurked inside his rugged frame. In his shining oilskin he looked like a sea-creature which had unexpectedly come aboard.

Theil joined him by the chart. 'The shore batteries are there sir. Our main armament is alerted and will be kept informed of any change of intelligence.'

From far beyond the hood's shelter Hechler heard the scrape of steel as the aircraft catapult was manoeuvred around ready to fire off the first float-plane. Each had a crew of two, and apart from cannon and machine-guns would today be armed with two heavy bombs.

Thinking aloud Hechler said, 'That is the railway station. We are ordered to destroy it. Ivan will bring up reinforcements by that route. We'll give him a headache.'

He withdrew from the hood and climbed on to the forward gratings to let the salt air sting away any lurking weariness. He thought of his men, sitting and crouching through his command. Some able to see the heaving water like himself, others confined to their armoured turrets, waiting to feed the big eight-inch guns, or down in the bowels of the engine- and boiler-rooms, deafened by the din of machinery and fans, watching dials or each other. Trying not to think of a shell or torpedo changing their roaring world into a merciless inferno.

In the streets of Kiel or some occupied seaport you would not notice many of them as individuals, Hechler thought. It was a pity the people at home could not see them here, in their environment. It might give them heart and perhaps some hope.

Theil said quietly, 'Time, sir.'

Hechler nodded. Glad they were committed. 'Alter course. Full ahead, all engines.' For a second his guise fell away and he added

17

softly, 'Another time, Viktor, but the same enemy, eh?'

Fifteen minutes later the ship surged away from the mist to greet the first weak sunlight like an enraged tiger.

As the four main turrets swivelled soundlessly on to the precribed bearing, all eight guns opened fire.

'Alter course, steer two-three-zero!' Hechler lifted his eyes from the gyro-compass repeater and tensed as the sea lifted and boiled into a solid cone of white froth some cable's length beyond the port bow.

He felt the deck tilt as the order was passed to the wheelhouse, the instant response as the raked stem bit into the glittering water. The forward turrets swung slightly to compensate for the sudden change of direction and then each pair of guns recoiled in turn, the shock-wave whipping back over the bridge, hot and acrid as the shells tore towards the land.

Hechler waited for the hull to steady and then raised his glasses once more. The land was blurred with smoke, the colour drained out of it by the hard, silver sunlight. Shell-bursts pockmarked the sky where the ship's three Arado float-planes ducked and dived over their targets, and the fall of the cruiser's shells was marked by great smokestains, solid and unmoving. They made the landscape look dirty, fouled, he thought vaguely.

Tracer lifted from the rubble of some dwellings near the waterfront, and he guessed that the army were using their fire to retake their old positions, the bitter house-to-house fighting which was an infantryman's lot.

Hechler thought briefly of his father, and the unexpected distraction disturbed him. He was unused to having his mind shifted off-course when he needed it most.

His father had been a soldier in the Great War, and had been wounded several times on the Western Front until he had been badly gassed and sent home, a coughing, broken wreck of a man. In clear moments he had described war at close quarters, and had chilled his family with tales of wiring parties in no-man's-land, raids on enemy trenches armed with sharpened spades, nailed clubs and long knives. No time to load a rifle, and a bayonet was next to useless in a hand-to-hand encounter, he had said. You could smell your enemy, feel his strength, his fear as you tried to kill him with the same methods they had used centuries earlier.

18

At sea you rarely saw the enemy. Gun flashes, the fall of shot, a shadow against the moonlight or fixed in a range-finder. It was better that way. Cleaner.

A great gout of fire, bright orange and tinged with red, erupted from the shore and Theil, who had a handset jammed beneath his cap, shouted, 'Railway station, sir!'

A seaman nudged his friend and they grinned at one another. The young officer, Leutnant Jaeger, shaded his eyes to look up at the control station with its narrow observation slits, like the visor of a massive helmet. He did not even duck as something whistled above the bridge and Hechler saw a seasoned petty officer glare at him behind his back. He probably wanted him to get down; any fool could die a hero.

'Aircraft, sir! Bearing red-one-one-oh! Angle of sight three-zero!'

The secondary armament were already swivelling round on their sponsons and in their small turrets, tracking the tiny, metallic dots which had suddenly appeared out of the smoky haze.

Hechler thought of Kröll, the gunnery officer, and was glad of his efficiency. Kröll, lean, tight-mouthed and devoid of any sense of humour, was a hard man to serve. Constant drills in every kind of exercise, switching crews around with loading numbers from the magazine and cursing any officer or seaman who failed to respond to his immediate satisfaction, had nevertheless made the ship a living example to many others.

The anti-aircraft guns and then the lighter automatic weapons clattered into life, the bright tracer streaking across the sea and knitting together in a vivid mesh of fire through which the approaching planes would have to fly.

One of the escorting destroyers was turning in a steep welter of foam, an oily screen of smoke trailing astern of her as she headed closer to her big consort, her own guns hammering sharply to join the din.

Prinz Luitpold's main armament recoiled again. Hechler had lost count of the number of rounds they had fired, and he heard the abbreviated whistle of the shells as they ripped towards the target.

'Alter course. Steer due west.' Hechler let his glasses drop to his chest as Gudegast passed his orders through the brass-mouthed voice-pipe by the compass.

'Two-seven zero, sir.' The rest of his words were drowned by the throaty roar of engines, and the increasing bang and clatter of gunfire as the enemy planes flashed over the water.

Hechler did not see which one straddled the destroyer, but the explosion just abaft her squat funnel made a searing flash and flung fragments high into the air even while the ship staggered round in another turn, her deck laid bare as she tilted over. Another great explosion blasted her from between decks and fire spread along one side like lava, masking her hull in steam and surrounding her struggle with bright feathers of spray from falling debris. Distance hid the sound of her destruction but it was clear enough for anyone to see.

Two of the Russian aircraft were weaving away, their own wounds revealed by smoking trails as tracer darted after them, and the sky around them was filled with drifting shell-bursts.

Gudegast said thickly, 'She's going! God, look at her!'

Hechler watched the destroyer as she began to settle down. One boat was in the water, but was carried away from her side by the swell with just a handful of men aboard. Floats were dotted about, but the first two explosions had obviously taken a heavy toll of life. Hechler had met the destroyer's captain at several conferences. It was a moment dreaded by every commander. *Abandon ship*. Even thinking the words was like a surrender.

Two more Russian planes roared over the listing vessel, and the sea around the solitary boat was torn apart by machine-gun fire. Hechler felt his stomach muscles contract, but made himself watch as the tiny, unreal figures clawed at the air or floundered in the swell before they were cut down.

Theil hurried to his side. 'One of the Arados is finished, sir!'

They looked at each other. Theil's voice was harsh; his words were not just a report. They sounded disbelieving, like an accusation.

Hechler strode across the bridge, his boots scraping on empty cartridge cases from a machine-gun, and watched the pall of smoke beyond the waterfront. The float-plane must have been hit just as she had released her two bombs and had exploded directly above them.

'Signal from escort, sir! Request permission to pick up survivors.'

Hechler glanced at Jaeger's handsome face. He had not yet

learned how to conceal his emotions, Hechler thought; his eyes looked wild, full of pain for the men who were dying out there.

It was an additional, unwanted drama. The remaining destroyer's captain knew better, even if the other one was his best friend.

It could have been his ship. The two after-turrets roared out again and sent a violent shock-wave through the bridge as if they had hit a sandbar. *Or it could have been us.* It would be no different. You must not even think about it.

He heard himself reply flatly, 'Denied. Discontinue action.'

He glanced quickly at his watch, aware of the tension around him, the shock at what had happened so swiftly.

His voice seemed to move them again, voices called into telephones and pipes, and Gudegast passed his prearranged course to the wheelhouse. Parts of a pattern. There were things to be checked, not least preparations for another air attack before their own covering fighters flew out to shepherd them to safety.

Hechler raised his glasses and stared at the mounting curtain of smoke where the railway station and surrounding streets had been under fire. It was already falling away as the cruiser swung on to her new course and threw spray over the forecastle like heavy rain. The signal would be sent, the army would be left to use whatever advantage and breathing space the bombardment had offered. Hechler moved his glasses and saw the stricken destroyer hard on her side, the swell around her smooth and stained with oil. A few heads bobbed in the water, but as the distance increased they seemed without meaning or purpose. Two aircraft shot down or severely damaged. A small price to pay for a destroyer and her company, he thought bitterly.

He lowered his glasses and moved to the opposite side to watch the other destroyer increasing speed to take station again. Nearby he could hear the watchkeepers whispering together while the voice-pipes kept up their constant chatter. Routine and discipline kept men from fretting too much. Later they would remember, but their pain would be mellowed by pride. The legend lived on. They had lost one Arado. Two absent faces at the mess table, telegrams to their homes, and later Hechler would write a letter to each family. Now, as he watched the drifting smoke he was dismayed to realise he could barely remember the faces of the dead airmen.

A messenger scrambled on to the bridge, wide-eyed and anxious, the first time he had left his armour-plated shell since the guns had opened fire.

Theil took the signal pad from him and after a quick glance said, 'Priority Two, sir. To await new orders.' Their eyes met.

Hechler nodded and removed his cap. The air felt clammy against his forehead. He thought suddenly of a bath, hot water and soap, an unbelievable luxury. He wanted to smile, but knew he would be unable to stop. It was madness. A helplessness which always followed a risk. He glanced up at his ship, the smoke trickling past her funnel-cap and the shivering signal halliards. She was not built to act as a clumsy executioner, a tool for some general who had failed to outwit the enemy's tactics. He thought of the destroyer which would soon come to rest on the bottom, how her survivors would still be floundering about and dying, but still able to see *Prinz Luitpold*'s shadow fading into the mist. Abandoned. In the twinkling of an eye they had become mere statistics.

He realised that Theil was watching him. Waiting, his features controlled and impassive.

The signal was brief, but said all that was needed. Fresh orders probably meant they would be ordered away from this battleground. The news would flash through the ship like lightning. It always did. Where to? What mission had been dreamed up this time?

Hechler gripped the nearest handrail and felt the ship respond to his touch. Like a great beast whose respect had to be constantly earned and won.

So many shells fired, and each selected target bombarded without damage and without cost to any man aboard. One aircraft was lost, and the others would be retrieved as soon as it was safe to stop the ship and hoist them inboard.

He felt suddenly angry, contemptuous of the fools who had risked the very survival of this ship for a gesture, one which would and could make no difference.

'Perhaps we shall be given bigger game to hunt, Viktor.' He looked at him searchingly and saw him flinch. 'Unless some politican has already thought up some wild escapade for us.'

Theil dropped his voice. 'I am a sailor, not a man of politics, sir.'

Hechler touched his arm and saw Jaeger relax as he watched

22

them. 'Sometimes we must be both!' Then he smiled, and felt a kind of recklessness move through him. 'This ship is a legend. She cannot remain one while she sniffs after fragments left by the army.'

The two Arados flew over the mastheads and rolled their wings. They had already forgotten. Survival was a great tonic.

Theil said, 'Normandy, do you think, sir?'

Hechler walked to the gratings again and rested his hands on the rail below the glass screen. The destroyer was already zig-zagging ahead of them, ready to seek out and depth-charge an enemy submarine, although it was unlikely there would be one in this area, he thought.

He considered Theil's question and pictured his ship charging through the invasion fleets and their supply vessels like an avenger. A proud but short-lived gesture it would be too.

No, it was something else. He felt a shiver run through him. A war on the defensive could not be won. He looked down at the forecastle, at the two pairs of smoke-grimed guns as they were trained forward again.

It was what he was chosen for, and why the ship had been built. To fight and to win, out in the open like *Scharnhorst* or the cruisers of his father's forgotten war.

Hechler nodded to himself. Nobody would forget his *Prinz Luitpold*.

Chapter Two

Faces of War

Kapitän zur See Dieter Hechler emptied another cup of strong black coffee and glanced around his spacious day cabin. Sunlight shone brightly through the polished scuttles, and he could hear some of his seamen chattering and laughing as they went about their work on deck.

The ship felt at peace as she swung to her cable, and it was hard to believe that they had been in action less than two days back, and had seen the destroyer go down.

Hechler stood up and walked to one of the scuttles. From a corner of his eye he could see Mergel watching his every move, his pen poised over a bulging pad as it had been for an hour or so since they had anchored. Mergel was a petty officer writer and would have made someone a fine secretary had he been a woman, Hechler often thought.

Even the weather was different. He shaded his eyes and looked towards the shore, the high shelving slope of green headland, the clusters of toy houses which ran all the way down to the water's edge. Untroubled – from a distance anyway.

Hechler was moved by what he saw. It was the east coast of Denmark, and the port which was set in a great fjord was named Vejle. He smiled sadly. He had visited here several times during the war, and earlier in a training ship, or to holiday with his parents and brother. Happy, carefree days. It gave him a strange feeling to be here again in *Prinz Luitpold*. Many eyes would be watching the ship, but how would they see her? Would anyone admire her lines, or would they see her only as an extension of the occupation forced on their peaceful country?

He saw a fuel lighter move away slowly from the side, men staring up at the ship, some soldiers with their weapons slung carelessly on their shoulders, a world apart from the Russian Front, he thought. With the taste of good coffee in his mouth he felt vaguely uneasy, as if he should be doing something useful. Another fuel lighter cast off and followed the first one towards

24

the fjord. Stück, the chief engineer, would run him to earth eventually to report on his department. Even in harbour there was no obvious rest from routine. Visitors came and went. Requests, demands, questions – it was like being responsible for a small town.

The thought of going ashore touched something in Hechler and made him eager to leave, if only to smell the land, feel the lush grass beneath his feet.

He sighed. It was not to be. Not yet anyway.

He looked at Mergel. 'Have the letters done first, and I'll sign them.' He tried to picture the faces of the two dead airmen. Did such letters ever help, he wondered?

Mergel gathered up his papers and moved to the door. 'May I ask, sir, will there be leave?'

Hechler shrugged. 'You will probably know that before I do.' He waited for the door to close. In the ship's crowded world he treasured the moments he could be alone. Alone with his ship perhaps?

He poured a last cup of coffee and ran his eyes over the pad of signals and news reports again.

There was some sort of security blanket on Normandy, he decided. Only one thing was certain. The Allies had not been flung back into the sea, but were pushing deeper into France. There was a mention of some possible secret weapon which would soon change all that, and enemy losses were still heavy in the Atlantic due to the aggressive tactics of the U-boats. Hechler bit his lip. Many words, but they said little.

The sentry opened the door and Theil stepped into the cabin, his cap beneath his arm.

Hechler gestured to a chair. 'It will be quite a while before the admiral arrives, Viktor.' He had seen the surprise in Theil's eyes, as if he had expected to find his captain unshaven and still in his seagoing gear.

Theil said, 'The upper deck is washed down, sir, and the boats are being repainted. The admiral will find no fault in the ship's appearance.'

Hechler looked away. There it was again. The defensive, bitter note in Theil's tone. As if the ship was his sole responsibility. Hechler pushed the pad of signals towards him. 'Read these, Viktor. They may amuse you.'

25

He put on his best jacket and buttoned it carefully. In his mind he could see the admiral very clearly. One of those round, ageless faces with wide confident eyes. He smiled. Unless you knew him. He was only a year or two older than himself and already a rear-admiral. One of Donitz's shining lights, everyone said, highly thought of even by the Führer himself. Or so it was claimed. Looking back it was not so surprising, Hechler thought. He had first met him when they had both been cadets, and then later they had served together in an old training cruiser which had unexpectedly been called to speed to the assistance of a burning cargo-liner in the Mediterranean. The event had captured the headlines, and in Germany had been blown up enormously to cover other less savoury news of attacks on Jews which had been giving the country a bad name abroad.

While others who had once been cadets in those far-off days had progressed or fallen by the wayside, he had always managed to seize the limelight. Now he was a rear-admiral. It would be interesting to see how that had changed him.

Theil said, 'Will there be leave, sir?'

Hechler looked at him and smiled. *You to?* 'I expect so. Our people can do with it. This kind of landfall makes the war seem far away.'

'It's not for myself, sir, you understand –'

Hechler nodded. 'We *all* need a break.'

Theil shifted in his chair. 'I hate not knowing. What is expected of us? I am not afraid of fighting, even dying, but not to know is like a weight on your back.'

Hechler thought again of his father. *Like waiting to go over the top.* Theil was right, but it was not like the man to express it so openly. Perhaps he should have looked for some additional strain earlier?

Hechler said, 'We both know that we cannot go on like this. The *Prinz* was not built to nurse an army. She was designed to fight.' He waved his hand towards the sunlit scuttles. 'In open water, like she did off North Cape.' The picture rarely left his thoughts. It had been the first battle he had fought in this ship. Up there off the Norwegian coast which had been shrouded in day-long darkness. Two British cruisers and some destroyers in a blizzard like the one last year which had covered the end of *Scharnhorst* in those same terrible seas. At the end of the day

26

Prinz Luitpold had won the battle, even though her escorts had been sunk, and another cruiser set ablaze. The British had hauled away, their losses unknown, and had left this ship almost unmarked.

Both sides had claimed a triumph, But Hechler knew in his heart that *Prinz Luitpold* was the only victor.

There was a tap at the door and after a small hesitation the executive officer, Korvettenkapitän Werner Froebe, stepped inside. Froebe was tall and ungainly, with huge hands which seemed forever in his way. Next to Theil he was responsible for the running of the ship and the supervision of the various watches and working parties.

Theil glared at him. 'Well?'

Froebe looked instead at his captain. 'I apologise for the intrusion, sir, but there is an officer come aboard from the town.' He dropped his eyes. 'A major of the SS, sir.'

Hechler studied him gravely. 'What does he want?'

'He wishes to load some stores on board, sir.' He held out a piece of paper. 'He has the admiral's authority.'

Hechler took it and frowned. 'It seems in order. Have the boatswain select a party of hands to assist him.'

Froebe said glumly, 'The major has some people, er, workers –'

Theil was looking from one of the scuttles. He said shortly, 'Civilian prisoners, more trouble!'

Hechler saw their exchange of glances. Civilian prisoners could mean anything in wartime, but with an SS major in charge it probably meant they were from a labour camp.

'Deal with it.' When Froebe had left he added, 'The admiral will be here soon, Viktor. I don't want the ship cluttered up with working parties when he steps aboard.'

Theil picked up his cap. 'I agree.' He seemed suddenly pleased to go, all thoughts of the next mission, even home leave forgotten.

Hechler examined his feelings. Like most of his colleagues he had heard stories of overcrowded labour camps, and the rough handling by the SS guards. But it was not his province; his place was here in the ship, or another if so ordered. It was what he was trained for, what he had always wanted.

He could almost hear himself saying much the same words when he had asked Inger to marry him.

He walked to a scuttle again, but the day was spoilt. It was like

27

having a bad taste in the mouth. Something you could not explain, and certainly something you could do nothing to change.

Somewhere overhead a speaker came to life, followed by the trill of a boatswain's call. The boatswain was already mustering a working party for the unexpected and as yet unidentified cargo. The deck gave a sudden tremble as one of the powerful generators was switched on, while down in the shining galley the chief cook would be ranting and cursing about having to delay the midday meal until the admiral had been piped aboard.

Hechler left the cabin and walked along the starboard side, his eyes on the choppy water, but missing nothing of his men who worked above or around him. They moved aside to let him pass, while petty officers saluted and called their men to attention if he caught their glance.

They respected him, he had brought them back to a safe anchorage, and that was enough.

He saw some seamen by the float-plane catapult, and Brezinka, the massive boatswain, wagging his finger as he explained what he needed done.

Froebe stood slightly apart with the SS major, a man who would have been utterly insignificant but for his uniform and the death's-head badge on his cap.

Something made Hechler pause. He asked, 'Is anything wrong?'

Froebe jerked to attention. 'N-no, sir. These hands will go ashore to man a lighter and bring it alongside –'

The major interrupted. 'They must be under my orders, Captain.'

Hechler glanced at him coolly. 'They are also under mine, Major. I will be pleased if you remember that.' He saw the man's flush of anger, but felt no pity for his embarrassment. He glanced at Froebe. 'Make it quick.' He saw a young acting petty officer who had been placed in charge of the party and thanked God for his gift of remembering names.

'You will be taking your final exam soon, Stoecker?'

The sailor had an open, pleasant face. One you could rely on. Stoecker smiled. 'Yes, sir. Three weeks' time if –'

Hechler touched his arm. '*If*, a word that carries much weight for all of us, eh?' He walked on, knowing that Stoecker would remember how the captain had spoken to him after snubbing the

28

major. Cheap? Possibly. But it *made* a ship's company.

With the warm sunlight across his shoulders Hechler walked alone right around his ship's upper decks. Past the towering bridge structure and capped funnel, beneath the long guns and over the white-painted anchor cables, his eyes missed nothing.

Germany had broken the treaty made by her old enemies to build the *Prinz* and her sister ships. Ten thousand tons had been the maximum which had been allowed, but secretly they were over 15,000 tons when they had been launched. From her raked stem to her handsome quarterdeck the heavy cruiser would make any shipbuilder proud.

The armament and gunnery controls in each of the class were unmatched anywhere. The ill-fated *Bismarck* had been given the credit for sinking the British battle-cruiser *Hood* early in the war, but it was believed throughout the fleet that *Prinz Eugen*'s guns had fired the fatal salvo.

Hechler looked at the two after turrets and forgot about his irritation over the SS officer.

Just given the chance. That word *if* again.

He smiled at the thought, and two seamen who were polishing the deck plate which bore the ship's name, where the admiral would step aboard, nodded to each other and grinned. There could be nothing to worry about.

Later, as the gleaming launch, with a rear-admiral's pendant streaming from it, curved in a frothing wake towards the accommodation ladder, Hechler, with the unaccustomed weight of a sword at his side, felt the same sense of pride.

For a moment at least the war itself had become a backcloth, and only the manned anti-aircraft guns, both here and ashore, gave any hint of possible danger.

The ship's company were dressed in their best blue uniforms, unlike their drab seagoing rig, and all but the duty officers were in ranks, with Theil, unsmiling and grim-faced, at their head.

The launch vanished beneath the rail and Hechler saw the top of the accommodation ladder give a tremble as the boat nudged alongside. He controlled the desire to laugh. All it needed was a band. But as they were always being reminded, there *was* a war on.

Konteradmiral Andreas Leitner lay back in one of the cabin's deep chairs and regarded the glass in his hand.

'Good, eh?' He chuckled. 'I find it hard to admit that only the Frogs can make champagne!'

Hechler tried to relax. Leitner was exactly as he had remembered him, youthful, confident, and so buoyant that it was impossible to imagine him ever being ruffled.

He had come aboard with a bounce in his step and after saluting the quarterdeck and side-party had faced the assembled company and thrown up a stiff Nazi salute which had seemed theatrical in spite of his gravity. An act? It was still difficult to judge. Hechler watched him while Pirk, his steward, refilled the glasses. Leitner must have brought a dozen cases of champagne aboard which his flag-lieutenant was now having stowed for future use.

Leitner had not mentioned their mission or his sealed orders; he was taking his time. In that repect too, he had not changed.

His hair was fair and well-groomed, and his skin had a kind of even tan, although Hechler had not heard of his being out of Germany for a year or more.

The admiral nodded to the steward. 'Well trained, eh? Pours it like a head waiter at the Ritz.' He grinned broadly. 'You have a fine ship, Dieter. I am quite jealous the way you are spoken of in the high command.'

He waited for Pirk to withdraw and said, 'I shall hoist my flag aboard very shortly.' He watched him evenly. 'A private ship no longer, how does that strike you, my friend?'

'I am honoured, sir.'

'You are not. I know you too well to accept that!' He laughed and showed his even teeth. 'No matter. You are the right captain. We shall do well together.'

'Shall we return to the Gulf, sir?'

Leitner became serious. 'I cannot discuss it yet. You and your ship have performed wonders, have given pride where it was lacking, a sense of destiny when some were only thinking of comfort and a quick end to the war.'

He wagged the empty glass at him and added, 'I have often thought of you, and the old days, believe me. Your parents, are they well?'

Hechler replied, 'They are managing.'

'I felt it personally when your brother was lost in *Scharnhorst*. A good ship too. He lies with a brave company, an honour to our country.'

30

Hechler tried to compose his features and his reactions. It seemed strangely wrong to hear Leitner, or anyone else, speak of his brother like a part of history. He could see him without difficulty, so full of life, excited at being appointed to so famous a ship.

Leitner was saying, 'Young men like Lothar are an example, part of our heritage –'

Hechler refilled their glasses, surprised that his hand was so steady. His young brother's name had come off the admiral's tongue so easily, as if they too had been close, and yet he knew they had never met.

He tried again. 'My people have had no leave, sir, and they deserve it. Whatever we are called to do –'

Leitner gave a mock frown. 'You will be told, but now is not the moment. I can only say that I am here for the same reason. You have earned a rest, albeit a short one, but the needs of Germany rise far above our own petty desires, eh?' He laughed lightly. 'When I watched your ship anchor, my heart was filled, I can tell you.'

Hechler realised he had drained another glass, but Leitner's mood was unnerving. For just a few seconds his pale eyes had filled with misty emotion, then they hardened as he continued, 'We shall have vengeance, Dieter, for Lothar and all the other fine young men who have died for our cause.'

The admiral stood up suddenly and paced about the cabin, touching things as he moved. He said, 'I have arranged some leave, but it will be short, I am afraid. I have my temporary headquarters in Copenhagen. It is not like Berlin, but it must suffice.' He shrugged. 'We do what we can.'

Hechler said, 'You were in America too.'

Leitner swung round, his eyes pleased. 'So you followed my career as I watched over yours, eh? That is good. Friendship is too strong to be parted by events. Yes, I was in Washington as a naval attaché. I learned a lot, mostly about American women. If their men fall on their backs as willingly this war will soon be brought to a successful conclusion!' He laughed and wiped his eyes. 'God, what a country. I was worn out!'

Hechler watched him as he moved about the cabin. Leitner had always excelled in sporting events, but he never recalled any great attachments with girls as a junior lieutenant. He had not married either.

31

Leitner paused by a bookcase and said without turning, 'I was sorry to hear about your marriage, Dieter.'

It was as if he had been reading his thoughts. Like a single bullet. 'It was a mistake.'

'I can tell by your tone that you blame yourself. I doubt that you have any cause, Dieter. An idealist, yes. A bad husband, I think not.' He sighed. 'Women are admirable. But never treat them as equals.'

Hechler relaxed slightly. Another problem solved. Was that how Leitner had gained flag rank, he wondered?

Leitner said, 'My gear will be sent aboard this afternoon. You have quarters for flag officers, that I do know.'

Hechler nodded. 'Had I known you were coming, sir, I would have had the quarters properly prepared. As it is –'

Leitner shrugged indifferently. 'Castle or charcoal burner's hut, it is the same to me. All I ask is a little luxury here and there.' He did not elaborate. Instead he said, 'Your last mission failed, I believe?'

It was so blunt after his affable chatter that Hechler sensed his own resentment rise to meet it.

'We carried out the bombardment, the objectives were all destroyed. We lost one escort because –'

'I know the hows and whys, thank you.' The smile broke through again like winter sunlight. 'But it was a failure nonetheless. I heard from OKM Operations Division an hour ago that we have at least a whole infantry brigade cut off surrounded.' He closed his fingers like a claw. 'They will fight to the death of course, but we lost a good destroyer for nothing.'

Leitner looked directly at Hechler but his pale eyes were faraway. 'No matter, my friend. The Führer has ordered the beginning of an aerial bombardment by rocket, the like of which will make Rotterdam, London, Coventry and the rest, seem like mere skirmishes. The first rocket was launched yesterday. I can say no more than that, but you will soon hear of it. There is no defence. The RAF had some success against our flying bombs over London, but against the V-2 there is *nothing!*'

Like most serving officers Hechler had heard about the much-vaunted secret weapons. They never seemed to appear. The fanatical confidence in the admiral's voice made him believe that this one was real, terribly so.

32

Leitner said, 'I know what you are thinking. War on civilians is foul. Perhaps it is. But to shield Germany from invasion any means are acceptable. God will always congratulate the winner!' It seemed to amuse him and he glanced at his gold wrist-watch before adding, 'We shall dine together tonight. In the meantime my flag-lieutenant will present a brief summary of immediate requirements.' His eyebrows lifted as the sentry's booted feet clicked together beyond the door. 'My aide is not blessed with all the arts, but he is ever punctual.'

There was a tap at the door and Hechler called, 'Enter!'

Kapitänleutnant Helmut Theissen strode into the cabin very smartly, a heavy file under one arm. Like his superior he had fair hair, and the same even tan. Maybe they had both been on a secret mission, Hechler thought, to Spain for instance, whose one-sided neutrality had often proved a great asset.

Theissen was young for his rank, with anxious eyes and a willowy figure which even his immaculate uniform could not disguise. At the sight of the admiral his confidence seemed to melt.

He said, 'I have brought the file, Admiral.'

Leitner glanced at him coldly. 'Don't stand there like a Paris whore, man, prepare it for the Captain.'

He looked at Hechler and winked. 'A mother's gift to a war-starved nation, yes?'

Hechler heard the harsh echo of commands and the clatter of the main winch. The mysterious lighter was about to leave. Froebe's men had done well. They had hardly made a sound.

He would escort the admiral to his quarters or wait until he was ready to go ashore again. He glanced briefly in the bulk-head mirror then looked away quickly. It was like uncovering a secret – worse, sharing it.

In those brief seconds he had seen Leitner and his anxious-eyed aide looking at each other behind his back.

There had been no animosity. Affection was the nearest description he could think of. He was surprised and troubled to discover how the possibility left its mark.

Later at the gangway before they exchanged formal salutes, Leitner said, 'I shall send my car to the pier tonight, Captain.' He glanced at the side-party and rigid guard of helmeted seamen. 'We shall speak of *old times*.'

Then he was gone, and Hechler saw his aide staring up from the launch, something like relief on his face.

Hechler nodded to the duty officer. 'March off the guard, Lieutenant.'

He watched them clump away, doubtless thinking of their delayed meal. It was a pity that life could not be that simple for us all, he thought.

When he looked again, the launch had vanished around an anchored freighter with the Swedish flag painted on her side. Her only frail protection against bomb or torpedo.

Life would not be quite the same again, he decided grimly.

A muffled explosion echoed against the superstructure and made several seamen come running, their faces taut with alarm.

Froebe panted along the deck and saluted. 'Captain, the lighter is on fire, an explosion in her engine, I think!'

Hechler thought suddenly of the young acting-petty officer's face. 'Call away the accident boat at once! Send help.'

It had been on the way back to the shore after unloading the mysterious cases.

Froebe watched men running for the main boom beneath which the duty boat was already coughing into life.

Then Hechler glanced at the placid shoreline. 'I want to know immediately what happened. Everything.' He strode away and wondered if the admiral's launch had seen the explosion, which must have been near the fjord's entrance.

In war you never accepted even the smallest disaster as an accident.

Hans Stoecker walked abreast of the lighter's long hatch-covers and turned to watch the cruiser, his home for about a year, as she drew astern, and her details and personality merged like a misty photograph.

Astern, *Prinz Luitpold*'s motorcutter kept a regular distance, her crew relaxed and unconcerned about the brief break in routine.

Stoecker was twenty-five and very conscious of his small authority. Even this rusty lighter represented *his* ship until he could gather the small working party together and return in the motorboat. He watched the SS major, hands in pockets as he chatted quietly with two of his men, machine-pistols crooked under their arm and not slung on their shoulders.

34

Stoecker glanced at the wheel, aft by the low guardrail. Künz was the helmsman. They had had a few rows since his acting rank had been awarded by the captain. Now he seemed to accept him. And he was a reliable seaman despite his foul mouth.

Stoecker walked along the side and kept the hatch covers between himself and the SS men. Locked down below there were ten prisoners who had carried the heavy steel boxes to the cradles to be hoisted up the cruiser's side. They had needed careful watching, for Stoecker knew that if just one tackle had been allowed to scrape the paintwork he would have felt Froebe's wrath.

He smiled and thought of his father who had been recalled to the navy after a few years' retirement. Too old for active duty, he was in charge of some naval stores in Cuxhaven. How pleased his mother would be after he qualified and they both went home in the same uniform!

Something touched his ankle. He glanced down, and saw a wiry hand reaching for him.

He looked quickly around the deck. The SS men were in deep conversation and peering at their watches, the few seamen who had not transferred to the motorboat were sitting on the hatch-covers, looking up at the sun, their eyes slitted with pleasure. Stoecker crouched down and peered through a narrow air vent at an upturned face.

He had mixed feelings about the prisoners. He did not after all know what they had done – they must have done something. They were dressed in clean, green, smocklike overalls, unnumbered, unlike some he had seen. They had been very docile, even cowed, and any sort of contact with the sailors had brought a scream of anger from the little major. There was one naval officer aboard, a pale, listless, one-striper who was said to be on light duties after his E-boat had been blown up in the North Sea. Stoecker and his companions had watched the young officer until his indifference and his sloppiness had made them bored.

He was up in the bows, his back to all of them, shutting them out.

Stoecker lowered his face. 'Yes, what is it?' He tried to be clipped and formal.

The man gazed at him, his eyes almost glowing in the gloom of the hold.

'I have a letter.' His German was perfect. 'Could you give it to

35

my family?' He paused and licked his lips. '*Please!*' The word was torn from his mouth.

'I can't – I don't see why –'

A dirty, folded letter was thrust through the hole, and Stoecker saw the man's thin wrist and arm beneath the green smock. It was raw, and covered with sores. Like something diseased.

The man whispered, 'I am going to die. We all are. In a way I am glad.'

Stoecker felt the sweat break out on his neck like ice. The address on the letter was Danish.

The weak voice said, 'I am, *was* a teacher.'

'Ah, *there* you are!' The major's boot glinted in the sunlight as he came round a hold-coaming.

Stoecker snapped to attention, his eyes on the sea alongside as the boots clicked towards him.

He knew that the prisoner's hand had vanished, just as he was sure that nobody had seen him in conversation. But he felt something like panic, the prickle of sweat beneath his cap.

He was a good sailor, and was secretly proud of the way he had behaved in the actions and bombardments which had been the cruiser's lot since he had joined her. His action station was high up above the bridge in the Fire Control Station, one of the gunnery officer's elite team. Kröll was a hard and demanding officer to serve, but Stoecker had noticed that he was rougher on his officers than the rest of them. Perhaps because he had once served on the lower deck and had had to build his own standards.

Stoecker knew what he should do, what he should already have done. But he could feel the grubby letter bunched in one hand, and anyway he disliked the major with his snappy arrogance. He doubted if he had ever been near the front line in his life.

The major snarled, 'The motorboat is falling too far behind. Tell it to draw closer!'

Stoecker climbed on to the hold cover and raised his arm until the boat's coxswain had seen his signal. What was the matter with the man? The boat was at exactly the right distance. The coxswain would not hold the job otherwise, Froebe would have made certain of that.

The major watched as the motorboat's bow-wave increased and said sharply, 'See that it keeps up!'

36

Stoecker saw the two SS men watching, the way they were gripping their machine-pistols. Afterwards he recalled that they had looked on edge, jumpy.

The explosion when it came was violent and sharp, so that the side-deck seemed to bound under Stoecker's feet, as if it was about to splinter to fragments.

The dozing sailors leapt to their feet, and even as the motor-boat increased speed and tore towards them, the lighter's engine coughed, shook violently and died.

Künz shouted, 'No steerage way!' He stood back from the wheel, his eyes fixed on a billowing cloud of smoke which was spouting up through a ventilator.

The major shouted, 'Get that boat here!' He glared at Stoecker. 'What are you gaping at, you dolt?'

Stoecker stared at the hatch coaming. Smoke was darting out as if under great pressure, and he could hear muffled screams, and the thuds of fists beating on metal.

The major flipped open his pistol holster and added, 'Sabotage! There may be another bomb on board.'

The motorcutter surged alongside, but when some seamen tried to climb aboard the major screamed, 'Get back, damn you! It's going down!'

Stoecker looked at the pale-faced naval officer and pleaded, 'We could get them out, sir!'

Over the officer's shoulder he saw one of the SS men swinging the clamp on the ventilator to shut off the dense smoke.

The officer stared at him glassily. 'Do as you are told. Abandon *now!*'

Stoecker felt his eyes sting as the smoke seared over him, and he peered at the little slit where the prisoner's arm had been. Only smoke, and even the cries had stopped. Like a door being slammed. He felt Künz grip his arm and hiss, 'Come *on*, Hans! Leave it!' Then all at once they were clambering into the motor-cutter, and when he looked again Stoecker saw that the lighter was already awash and sinking fast in the current.

The major said, 'Take me ashore.'

The boat turned towards the land again and Stoecker saw a naval patrol launch and some other craft heading towards the smoke at full speed.

He looked down at his fingers, which were clasped together so tightly that the pain steadied him. Some of the seamen sighed as the lighter dived beneath the surface, and one said, 'Lucky it didn't happen when we was alongside the old *Prinz*, eh, lads?'

No one answered him, and when Stoecker again lifted his eyes he saw the major was watching him. He appeared to be smiling.

They barely paused at the pier before turning and heading back at speed for the ship. It seemed important to all of them that they should be there, with faces they knew, and trusted.

There had been a black car waiting for the major and his men. He apparently offered a lift to the young naval officer, but the latter merely saluted and walked away.

Stoecker put his hand inside his jacket and touched the letter. The man had known he was going to die. He remembered the SS men looking at their watches. Most of all, he remembered the major's smile.

He looked up as the heavy cruiser's great shadow swept over them. He had expected to find comfort in it, but there was none.

Chapter Three

And So Goodbye

One day after the admiral's visit to the ship the news of leave was announced. It was little enough of an offering and brought a chorus of groans from most of the mess-decks and wardroom alike. Only seven days' leave would be allowed, and first preference for married men only. The rest of the ship's company, by far the greater proportion, was confined to local leave on Danish soil, with no sleeping-out passes below the rank of petty officer.

For the lucky ones seven days would be precious but pared away by the time taken to reach their destinations and return to the ship. It was rumoured that rail transport was always being delayed or cancelled due to day and night air raids.

As the men were lined up and inspected in the pale sunshine before rushing ashore to the waiting buses and trucks, Fregattenkapitän Theil reminded them of the seriousness of careless talk and the damage it could do to morale. Anyone who witnessed bomb damage or the like would keep it to himself, nobody would gossip about the ship, the war, anything.

Viktor Theil left the ship himself as soon as the others had departed. His home was in Neumunster on the Schleswig–Holstein peninsula, so he had less distance to travel than most.

As he sat in a corner of a crowded compartment in a train packed to the seams with servicemen and a few civilians, Theil reflected on the choice of a home. Not too far from Denmark. Now it seemed ironic, something to mock him.

The train crossed the frontier and clattered at a leisurely pace through the Hans Andersen villages, and the green countryside with its scattered lakes and farms. It was a beautiful part of the country, especially to Theil who had been born and brought up in Minden. At least, it should have been.

He thought of his wife Britta, their nice house on the town's outskirts, the perfect retreat for a naval officer on leave. He was known there, and certainly respected, especially when he was appointed to the *Prinz Luitpold*.

But he sensed people watched him, wondered what he really thought, if he cared. For Britta was Danish, and marriages from across the border were common enough before the war. It was often said that the Germans on the peninsula were more like Danes than they were. That too had a bitter ring for Theil.

When the German army had invaded her country Britta had tried to discover what had happened to her parents. Her father was a printer in Esbjerg, but he also managed a local newspaper. It had begun with letters and telephone calls, none of which had been answered. In despair she asked Theil to make enquiries but he had met with a stone wall of silence from the security offices. Eventually, when he was on a brief home leave, a plain-clothes police officer had called to see him. He was fairly senior and eager to be friendly and understanding.

'Your wife probably does not understand the need for security in these matters –'

Theil had tried to delve deeper and the policeman had said, 'You are a well-respected officer, a fine career ahead of you. Why spoil things, eh?'

When he had departed, Theil explained as well as he could to his wife. Perhaps her father had been in some political trouble, and was being kept out of circulation until things settled down. It had been the first time which he could recall when she had turned on him.

She had shouted, '*Settle down!* Is that what you would call it if the Tommies came here and started locking people in jails for wanting their country, their freedom!'

That leave had ended badly, and Theil had returned to his ship, which unbeknown to him was about to be called to action when the captain finally cracked under the strain and he himself by rights should have been promoted and given command. If not of the *Prinz Luitpold* then another of similar status. Instead, Hechler came.

Then Theil had received a message from a friend in Neumunster. He had not said much, but had sounded frightened, and it had been enough to make Theil hurry home after giving a vague explanation to his new captain. The ship was to be in the dockyard for a week, and anyway he knew that Hechler wanted to come to terms with his command on his own, and at his own speed.

The news had been worse than he had imagined. Britta had

gone to her parents' home alone. In spite of the strict travel restrictions, the impossibility of moving about in an occupied country without permission, she had managed to reach the port of Esbjerg.

When Theil had confronted her he had been stunned by her appearance. She had been close to a breakdown, angry and weeping in turns. That night when she had finally allowed him to put her to bed she had shown him the great bruises on her arms. The military police had done that to her when they had dragged her from the house where she had been born.

When he had tried to reason with her, to calm her, she had pushed him away, her eyes blazing, and cried, 'Don't you see? They've killed my mum and dad! Don't you care what those butchers have done!'

The doctor, another old friend, had arrived and had given her something.

When she had finally dropped into a drugged and exhausted sleep he had joined Theil over a glass of brandy.

Theil had asked desperately, 'What should I do? There must be some mistake, surely? The authorities would never permit –'

The doctor had fastened his bag and had said crisply, 'Keep it to yourself, Viktor. These are difficult times. Perhaps it is best not to know all the truth.' He had fixed him with a grim stare. 'You are a sailor. Be glad. At sea you *know* your enemies.' He had gone, leaving Theil with his despair.

As time wore on Britta withdrew more and more into herself. The local people tried to be friendly but she avoided them for the most part. She had been a pretty girl when he had married her; now she seemed to let herself go. Theil always regretted that they had no children, preferably boys to grow up in his footsteps and serve Germany. Once it had distressed her that she could not give him a child. The last time it had been mentioned Theil had found himself almost wanting to strike her.

'A *baby*! What would you give it? A black uniform and a rubber truncheon to play with!'

Theil walked the last part of the journey from the railway station. It had always been a pleasant little town but he noticed that the queues of people outside the provision shops seemed longer, and the patient women looked tired and shabby.

And yet the town had escaped the war apart from a few stray

41

bombs from homebound aircraft. The sky was empty of cloud as it was of the tell-tale vapour trails of marauding aircraft. It was almost like peacetime.

Theil was too deep in thought to glance at the bulletin boards outside the little church, and the people who were studying the latest casualty lists which like the queues were longer than before.

He thought of the case which he shifted from one hand to the other to return the salutes of some soldiers from a local flak battery. It was heavy and contained among other things, cheese and butter, Danish bacon and eggs which might bring a smile to her lips. She had enough to worry about without the damned shortages.

He had written to her several times since that last, unnerving leave. She had only replied once, a loose, rambling letter which had told him very little. Britta was never a great writer of letters. Their leaves spent together had always made up for that. He quickened his pace. This time it would be all right again. Just like all those other times. It *must* be.

Whatever his personal worries might be, Theil was a professional to his fingertips. He had noted all the recent happenings, not least the arrival of the rear-admiral, an officer whose face and reputation were rarely absent from the newspapers.

It might be his chance. The *Prinz Luitpold* was obviously earmarked for something important. That meant dangerous, but you took that for granted.

Perhaps he had been hard on Britta, or had written something in a letter which had upset her without intending it.

She had to understand, and be seen to be with him, no matter what. It was bad about her parents, but then he had never really got to know them. They should have considered her before they became involved with some political or subversive activity.

It was so unfair that because of it, his future might be endangered and her health also.

He thought of the ship lying up there in Danish waters. He knew the *Prinz* better than any of them. They would all need him when they were really up against it.

He turned on to the quiet road which led to his house; it was the last one in a line of five. Nothing was changed, and the flowers and shrubs in every garden made a beautiful picture after grey steel and the Gulf of Riga.

42

They would have three, maybe four days together. Then he would go back to the ship. As second-in-command he must be on time even at the expense of losing a day or so. But the leave would be just right. Like a reminder and a memory. A hope too for the future.

He thought he saw a woman in the neighbour's house, bending perhaps to pick up some flowers. When he looked again she had gone. He was glad. He did not want to loiter and discuss the war, rationing, and all the other complaints.

Theil reached the gates to his own garden and shifted his grasp on the heavy case. He squared his shoulders and wondered if anyone was watching. 'He's back.' He could almost see himself in his best uniform with the decorations and the eagle across his right breast.

He looked at the garden and hesitated. It was not like Britta to allow it to become so neglected. It was dry, and dead flowers drooped over the neat driveway, running to seed. It was unheard of. He held back a sudden irritation and strode to the main door. He fumbled with his key, expecting at any moment for the door to open and for her to stand there staring up at him. Her flaxen hair might be untidy but he would see it as before. Her dress would be for doing jobs about the house, but to him it would be like the silk one he had once brought her from France.

The house was so quiet that he stood stock-still within feet of the open door. Without looking further he knew it was empty. The sunlight which streamed through the back windows was dusty, and there were dead flowers in a vase near the framed picutre taken on their wedding day. He paused by it, off-balance, uncertain what to do. He stared at the photo, her arm through his, the faces in the background. That one was Willi, who was lost in the Atlantic two years back.

Theil put down his case and flexed his fingers. What did he feel? Angry, cheated, worried? All and none of them.

Perhaps she had gone away? He stared at the dead flowers. Where? He turned away, a sick feeling running through him. She had left him.

He walked about the house, opening doors, shutting them again, then went upstairs and looked out at the neighbours' house. So quiet and deathly still.

He opened a wardrobe and touched her clothes, remembering her looking up at him as he had undressed her.

What was she thinking of? He tried to contain it, as he would aboard ship when some stupid seaman had made a mistake. Did she think it could do anything but harm to behave like this? He touched a curtain which was pulled aside. Untidy. Again, out of character, or was it deliberate?

Theil went slowly downstairs and then saw some letters neatly piled on a hall-table where she kept her gloves.

He recognised the official stamps, his own writing. Unopened. She had not even read them.

He looked fixedly at his case by the front door. Abandoned, as if someone else had just arrived, or was about to leave.

What the hell had she done? There was no point in calling the police or the hospital. He would have been told long ago. An army truck rolled past, some soldiers singing and swaying about on the rutted road. How sad their song sounded.

He thrust the letters into his pocket and after a momentary hesitation picked up the heavy case once more.

He would ask the neighbours; they were decent people and had always liked Britta.

But he hesitated in the doorway and looked back at the silence. He thought of the future, the ship lying there waiting for him, for all of them, and was both apprehensive and bitter.

He *needed* her, just as she had once needed him, and she was gone.

Theil slammed the door and locked it and walked down the drive and then round to the next house.

Once he glanced over at his own home and pictured her in a window, laughing and waving. It had all been a joke, and now she wanted him.

The doorbell echoed into the far distance and he waited, knowing somehow that nobody would answer. But as he walked down to the road again he felt someone was watching him.

What should he do? He thought of his friend the doctor and walked all the way to his house, ignoring the weight of his case, his mind snapping at explanations like an angry dog.

The doctor was pleased to see him, although he had to leave for an urgent visit almost immediately.

He listened to Theil's story impassively and then said, 'I think

44

you must face up to it, Viktor. She has left you.' He raised one hand as Theil made to protest. 'She will be in touch, be certain of that, but she has to sort things out in her own way, d'you see? Women are like that. All these years, and they still surprise me!'

Theil made to leave. Britta had some other relatives somewhere. He would check through his address book. He looked at the heavy case. 'You take it, Doctor. For old time's sake, eh?'

The doctor opened it and gazed at the array of food.

'Thank you, Viktor. Some of my patients –'

Theil nodded and tried to grin. 'Of course.'

Outside, the shadows of evening were already making purple patterns on the road. Theil did not look towards his house. If he went back now he knew he would go crazy.

She had left him, had not given him a chance to make things right. He compensated by telling himself that she had no warning of his coming.

But all this time? Another man? He hastened towards the main road and did not even see two saluting soldiers as they went past. Never, not Britta. No matter what. Then back to Denmark? He looked at his watch. What should he do?

He felt his fingers touch the black cross on his jacket; like his other decorations it had always given him pride and confidence. For a few moments longer he stared unseeingly around him, hurt and then angry when he thought of what might have been, *could* have been. Because of Britta's anguish over her parents his own advancement and career had been scarred for all time. He had lost the *Prinz* because of it, because of her.

When she did come back, pleading for understanding, what would he do?

Theil turned towards the railway station. There was nowhere else he wanted to go now.

To some members of *Prinz Luitpold*'s ship's company the seven days' leave were as varied as the men themselves. To many of the lucky ones it was a lifeline, something precious and yet unreal against the harsh background of war. For others it might have been better if they had stayed with the ship, men who eventually returned from leave with the feeling they had lost everything.

Amongst those who remained aboard there was one who, after

a quick visit to a dockside telephone, made the most of each day and night in Vejle.

Korvettenkapitän Josef Gudegast, the cruiser's navigating officer, not only knew the ways of the sea and the landmarks which he had used in peace and wartime, he also hoarded a comfortable knowledge of harbours and what they could offer. When he had earned his living in timber ships he had often visited Danish ports, and Vejle was one of his favourite places for a run ashore.

On the last day but one of his leave he sat in a big chair, his reddened face tight with concentration as he completed a charcoal sketch of the woman who lounged opposite him, on a couch, her naked body pale in the lamplight.

The small house was quiet, more so because of the shutters and dark curtains across the windows. The place had always been his haven, stocked with food and drink, some of which he had carried with him from the ship to which he returned every morning, keeping an eye on his department and the work done by his assistants.

The room was very hot, and he sat in his shirtsleeves, his jacket with its three tarnished gold stripes hanging carelessly from the door, a reminder, if he needed it, that his time of freedom was almost over.

'There.' He sat back and eyed his work critically. 'Not bad.'

She got up and stood beside him, one arm around his massive shoulder. He could feel her body against his, her warmth and the affection which they had shared with passion and quiet desperation in turn. Soon they would lie together again and later they would sleep, wrapped around one another like young lovers.

Gudegast was forty, and felt every year of it. He tugged at his ragged beard and murmured, 'You're still a bloody fine woman, Gerda.' He gave her a squeeze. 'I've never forgotten you.'

She touched his hair. It was getting very thin, and without his uniform cap he looked his age, she thought. She could remember him as the bright-eyed mate of a visiting ship, the way that they had hit it off from the start.

She said, 'Get away with you. I'm sagging everywhere.' She peered at the picture. 'You've made me look nice.'

He covered it with some paper and said abruptly, 'It's yours.'

She stared at him. 'But you've never given –'

Gudegast stood up and glanced towards the bedroom door. 'I'll be off soon. Something to remind you of old Josef, eh?'

46

She gripped his arm, disturbed by his mood. 'It'll be all right, won't it?'

'*All right?*' He took his pipe from the mantelpiece and filled it with slow deliberation. It gave him time.

He was surprised that he cared that much. At the same time he did not want to alarm her.

He said slowly, 'No, I don't think it will, as a matter of fact.'

She sat on the couch and dragged a shawl over her naked shoulders.

Gudegast added, 'Did you see the way they buggered us about in the café this afternoon?'

She replied uneasily, 'They said they were full up.'

He frowned. '*Said.*' He lit his pipe and took several deep puffs. 'Little bastards. I had to put my foot down.'

She watched him and smiled. 'You got us a lovely table.'

'Not the point.' Puff, puff. 'They're more scared of the bloody Resistance now than they are of us, don't you see?' He studied her full mouth and barely covered breasts. She had been such a pretty girl. He should have married her, instead – he turned his mind away from his wife in Hamburg. It was all a mess. Like the bloody war.

He tried again. 'What will you do, Gerda, when it's all over?'

'I – I shall be here –'

He moved to her side and ruffled her hair. 'We're losing. Can't you face it either?'

'You mustn't say things like that, Jo! If anyone heard you –'

He grinned, his whole face crinkling. 'Christ, you care, don't you?'

'You know I do.'

'All these years.' He stroked her hair with one big hand while he gripped his pipe with the other. 'I know you're Danish, but there'll be plenty who'll remember you had German friends when it's all over.' He felt her stiffen and almost regretted saying it.

A few more days and he'd be off again. Probably for good, if the mad bastards at headquarters had anything to do with it. What sort of a war was it becoming? He was not even allowed to see his new charts. He felt angry just thinking about it so that when he spoke again his voice was unexpectedly hard.

'You must get out, girl. You've relatives in Sweden, go there if you can.'

47

She clung to his arm. 'Surely it won't come to that, Jo?'

He grinned, the rumble running through his massive frame. 'I expect our high command have it all worked out, some sort of treaty, a compromise. We've only wiped out half the bloody world, so who cares?'

She stood and looked up at him, her eyes misty. 'I never thought –'

He smiled at her gently. Too many German friends. No, they'd not forget. He had seen it in Spain after the Civil War. All the *heroes* who showed up after the fighting was finished. Brave lads who proved it by shearing the hair and raping girls who had backed the wrong side. It would be a damned sight worse here.

He held her against him and ran his big hands across her buttocks. Neither noticed that his fingers had left charcoal marks on her bare skin.

Their eyes met. He said, 'Bed.'

She picked up a bottle of schnapps which he had brought and two glasses. Gudegast stood back and watched her march into the other room with a kind of defiance. She would not leave. Perhaps she would find a nice officer to look after her when the Tommies marched in. He felt sweat on his back. God, you could get shot for even thinking such things.

He pushed through the door and stared at her, the abandoned way her legs were thrown on the crumpled sheets, unmade from that morning, and probably from all the rest.

He would do another sketch tomorrow. If he got time he might try and paint her in oils when he was at sea again. He shivered and then stepped out of his trousers.

She put out her arms and then knelt over him as he flopped down on the bed. He was huge, and when he lay on top of her it was like being crushed.

He watched her and said, 'I wish we'd wed, Gerda.'

She laughed but there was only sadness there. She took him in her hand and lowered herself on to him, gasping aloud as he entered her.

It was as if she knew they would never see each other again.

The cinema screen flickered and with a blare of trumpets yet another interminable newsreel began.

Hans Stoecker tried to concentrate but it was difficult to see

48

anything clearly. The air was thick with tobacco smoke. The cinema had been commandeered from the town, and he guessed it had once been a church hall or something of the kind. Between him and the screen were rows and rows of square sailors' collars, broken only ocasionally by the field-grey of the army.

The newsreel was concerned mainly with the Eastern Front and showed thousands of prisoners being marched to the rear of the lines by waving, grinning soldiers. The commentator touched only lightly on France, but there were several good aerial shots of fighter bombers strafing a convoy of lorries, and some of burning American tanks.

The major part of the reel was taken up with the *Bombardment of London*. The usual barracking and whistles from the audience faded as the camera panned across the great rocket, the V-2, as it spewed fire and dense smoke before rising from its launching gantry and streaking straight up into the sky.

The commentator said excitedly, 'All day, every day, our secret weapon is falling upon London. Nothing can withstand it, there is no defence. Already casualties and damage are mounting. No people can be expected to suffer and not break.'

There were more fanfares, and etched against a towering pall of flame and smoke the German eagle and swastika brought the news to an end.

Stoecker got up and pushed his way out of the cinema. Several voices called after him. There must be half the ship's non-duty watch here, he thought.

Outside it was dusk, with the lovely pink glow he had first seen in these waters. He thrust his hands into his jacket and walked steadily away from the harbour. There were plenty of German servicemen about, and they seemed carefree enough.

He thought again of the sinking lighter, the terrified screams of the prisoners trapped below. He had passed the place in one of the cruiser's motorboats when he had been sent on some mission ashore. It had been marked by a solitary wreck-buoy, but as one of the sentries on the jetty had told him, there had been no investigation, nor had any divers been put down. *Prinz Luitpold* carried her own divers but had not been asked to supply aid.

It was obvious, whichever way you looked at it. It was not sabotage. He thought of the SS major's face. It had been murder.

Stoecker crossed the street automatically and paused to peer into a shop window. He had done it merely to avoid three officers whom he would have had to salute. It was childish, but like most sailors he disliked the petty discipline which the land seemed to produce. He thought of the captain, how he had spoken to him, called him by name, from a company of nearly a thousand men. Hechler never laboured the point about discipline. He had his standards, and expected them to be met. Otherwise he was a man you always felt you could speak to. Trust.

A hand touched his sleeve. 'Hans! It *is* you!'

He turned and stared at the girl who was smiling at him. It all flashed through his mind in seconds, the brown curls and laughing eyes, school uniform, but now in that of a nursing auxiliary.

'What are you doing here, Sophie?' At home she lived just three doors from his mother. 'A nurse too, eh?'

She fell into step beside him, the pleasure at seeing him wiping away the tiredness from her eyes.

There is a big hospital not far from here.' She glanced away. 'Mostly soldiers who were in Russia.'

Stoecker thought of the jubilant newsreel, and of the ship's superstructure shaking like a mad thing when they had fired on the enemy position.

Later he had heard the deputy gunnery officer, Kapitänleutnant Emmler, say angrily, 'Ivan still smashed through and decimated a whole brigade! When will we hold the bastards?'

He said quietly, 'They are lucky to be in your care, Sophie.'

She put her hand through his arm. It was so simply done that he was moved.

She said, 'They have been in hell, Hans. Some of them are –' she shrugged and smiled, but there were tears on her cheeks. 'Now look what you've made me do!'

He guided her from the main stream of people and traffic and together they entered a narrow street, their footsteps their only company.

They talked about home, people they had known, and the last time they had seen some of them.

He said suddenly, 'I'd like to see you again.'

She looked at him gravely. 'I have every evening off unless –'

He nodded and gripped her hands. 'Tomorrow. Where we just met. I have to get back to the ship now.' His mind was unusually confused. If he had not gone to the cinema he would have missed her, would never have known.

50

'I'll be there.' She touched his face. 'You've not changed, Hans.'
She saw his expression and asked quickly, 'What is it?'

Stoecker stared past her, his hand on her arm as if to protect
her. The street name was faded and rusty and yet stood out as if
the letters were on fire. It was the same street as the one on the
letter. Almost guiltily he touched his pocket as if to feel it there.
He knew it was the house even though he had never been here in
his life. There was a shop beneath the living quarters, but the
windows, like the rest of the building, were burned out, blackened into an empty cave. But on one remaining door post he saw
the crude daubs of paint, badly scorched but still visible. The Star
of David, and the words, *Dirty Jew!*

The girl looked with him and whispered, 'Let's get away from
here.'

They walked down the narrow street towards the main road
again. Who was it, he wondered? Parent, wife, girlfriend? He
tightened his hold on her arm and could almost hear the man
whisper. *I am going to die. We all are.*

'Are you sick?'

He smiled, the effort cracking his lips. 'No. It is nothing.'

They looked at each other, sharing the lie as if it was something
precious and known only to them.

'Tomorrow then.'

He watched her hurry towards a camouflaged van with red
crosses painted on it.

Perhaps he had imagined it all. There was only one way he
would find out and he knew that he was going to read that letter,
no matter what it cost.

As darkness closed in over the anchorage, the boats which
plied back and forth from the shore ferried the returning sailors to
their ship. The duty officer with his gangway staff watched as
each returning figure walked, limped or staggered away to the
security of his mess.

Like a resting tiger the *Prinz Luitpold* was blacked-out, with
only the moonlight glinting on her scuttles and bridge-screens.

Almost the last launch to head out from the shore made a
broad white wash against the other darkness, her coxswain steering skilfully between anchored lighters and a pair of patrol boats.
Hechler seemed to sense that his ship was drawing near. He
climbed up from the cockpit and stood beside the coxswain, the

51

collar of his leather greatcoat raised around his ears, his cap tugged firmly down. Spray lanced over the fast-moving hull, but he did not blink as he saw the great shadow harden against the pale stars, and he felt a strange sense of relief. He saw the bowman emerge from forward, his boathook at the ready, heard the engine fade slightly as the helmsman eased the throttle.

The proud talk, the dinner parties, the uniforms and gaiety – he had had enough in the past few days to sicken his insides. Only here was reality. His ship.

A voice grated a challenge from the darkness and the coxswain shuttered a small hand-lamp.

The ship's raked bows made a black arrowhead against the sky and then they were turning towards the long accommodation ladder.

The captain is back on board. Maybe there will be news.

Hechler ran lightly up the ladder and folded back his leather collar so that the faint gangway light gleamed dully on the cross around his neck.

Prinz Luitpold's captain felt as if he had never left her.

Chapter Four

Maximum Security

There was a tap at the door to Hechler's day-cabin and then Theil stepped over the coaming and closed the door.

Hechler was glad of the interruption. His table was covered with intelligence files, packs of photographs and even vague news reports. In a matter of days he had soaked up everything he could find about the war so that he felt his mind would explode. It was the first time he had seen Theil since he had returned from leave, other than for the brief requirements of reporting aboard.

Theil looked paler than usual, and tight-lipped. Hechler had felt a change of atmosphere throughout the ship when the married men had returned from their brief escape. They might make laws about spreading gloom and despondency, but they could never enforce them, Hechler thought.

Several men had requested extra leave on compassionate grounds. Relatives killed or missing in the constant bombing. Unfaithful wives and pregnant daughters. The list was endless.

He waited for Theil to be seated and for Pirk to produce some fresh coffee.

Theil said, 'Everyone is aboard, sir, except for two seamen. I have posted them as deserters.'

Hechler frowned. A tiny fragment set against the war, and yet in any ship it was distressing, a flaw in the pattern.

Pirk opened one of the scuttles and Hechler saw some trapped pipesmoke swirling out towards the land. Gudegast the navigating officer had been one of his visitors; in fact Hechler had seen all of his heads of departments.

Gudegast never actually complained, but his dissatisfaction over the charts was very apparent. It was useless to tell any of them that he did not know the ship's new role or mission either. Nobody would have believed him. *Would I in their place?*

'They may have their reasons, Viktor. They won't get far.'

He thought of the news from the Russian Front. The enemy were making a big push, perhaps to gain as many advances as possible before winter brought its ruthless stalemate again.

Theil said, 'We sail this evening, sir.' It was a statement. 'The escorts have already anchored as ordered.'

Hechler looked at him casually. Theil sounded almost disinterested. It was so unlike him and his constant search for efficiency.

'Is everything well with you, Viktor?'

Theil seemed to come out of his mood with a jerk. 'Why, yes, sir.'

'I just thought – how was your leave?'

Theil spread his hands. 'The usual. You know how it is. A house always needs things.'

Hechler glanced at the papers on the table. So that was it. An upset with his wife.

'Anything I can do?'

Theil met his gaze. It was like defiance. 'Nothing, sir.'

'Well, then.' Hechler looked up as the deck trembled into life. It was a good feeling. He never got tired of it. The beast stirring after her enforced rest.

He said, 'Norway. We shall weigh at dusk and pass through the Skagerrak before daylight.' He studied Theil's reaction if any. 'I want to be off Bergen in thirty hours.'

Theil grimaced. 'I doubt if the escorts will be able to keep up.'

'So be it.' He pictured the jagged Norwegian coast, the endless patterns of fjords and islands. It would give Gudegast something he *could* grumble about.

'After that we shall keep close inshore and enter our selected fjord to await further intelligence.'

Theil nodded. 'Another fjord.'

Hechler guessed he was thinking of the great battleship *Tirpitz* which had been hidden in her Norwegian lair many miles from the open sea. Safe from any kind of attack, and yet about a year ago they had reached her. Tiny, midget submarines with four-man crews had risked and braved everything to find *Tirpitz* and to knock her out of the war by laying huge charges beneath her as she lay behind her booms and nets.

Hechler thought of his young brother again. *Scharnhorst* had been sunk a month later, the day after Christmas. The seas had been so bitter off North Cape that only a handful of survivors had been found and saved by the victors. His brother had not been one of them.

Hechler tried to push it from his thoughts and concentrate on what his ship would be required to do. The North Russian convoys again? Any pressure on the Russians and the destruction of much-needed supplies from the Allies would be welcomed by the army. Or was it to be still further north, and round into the Barents Sea itself before the ice closed in? Attack the Russian navy in its home territory. Hechler tightened his jaw. It might be worth a try.

Theil said, 'I had expected to see an admiral's flag at the masthead when I returned, sir.'

Hechler smiled. 'The admiral intends to keep us guessing, Viktor.'

He thought of the mysterious boxes which had been taken below. All the keys of the compartment where it was stowed had been removed from the ship's office. The admiral had one key, and Hechler had locked the other in his cabin safe. He was determined to get the truth about them out of Leitner.

He recalled Leitner's temporary headquarters in Copenhagen where he had been driven that first evening and almost every day since. Copenhagen was still beautiful. A war and occupation could not change that, he thought. The green roofs and spires, the cobbled squares, even the huge German flags which hung from many commandeered buildings could not spoil it.

Leitner seemed to have created another world of his own there. His HQ had once been an hotel, and the people, men and women, who came and went at his bidding seemed to treat it as one. There was always good food and plenty to drink, with a small orchestra to entertain his official guests with music either sentimental or patriotic to suit the occasion.

If Leitner was troubled by the news from the Russian Front he did not reveal it. He was ever-optimistic and confident and seemed to save his scorn for the army and certain generals whom he had often described as *mental pigmies*.

If any man was enjoying his war it had to be Leitner.

Theil watched him across the table, half his mind straying to the shipboard noises, the preparations for getting under way once more. But Hechler fascinated him far more. Was he really as composed as he made out? Untroubled by the weight of responsibility which was matched only by its uncertainty?

Theil thought of the rumours which had greeted his return. The arrival of piles of Arctic clothing on the dockside had added fuel to the fires of speculation even amongst the most sceptical.

He should feel closer to Hechler now. *His* wife had left him, although no one had ever discovered the whole truth. Did he fret about it and secretly want her back again? He watched Hechler's grave features, the way he pushed his hair back from his forehead whenever he made to emphasise something.

Theil tried not to dwell on Britta's behaviour. Perhaps she only wanted to punish him, as if it had all been his fault. He felt the stab of despair in his eyes. It was so unfair. Just when he needed her loyalty, her backing. If only –

Hechler said, 'I wonder how many eyes are out there watching us right at this minute, eh, Viktor?' He walked to a scuttle and rested his finger on the deadlight.

He looked more relaxed, more like a spectator than the main player, Theil thought desperately.

Hechler felt his glance, his uneasiness. It was not time for Theil to be troubled. Their first loyalty was to the ship, and next to the men who served her. After that – he turned, hanging from the deadlight like a passenger in a crowded train.

'We're going to fight, Viktor. I feel it. No more gestures, no more bloody bombardments with barely enough sea-room to avoid being straddled.' He looked at the nearest bulkhead as if he could see through it, to the length and depth of his command. 'Have you ever read about Nelson?'

He saw from Theil's expression that the change of tack had caught him off balance.

'No, sir.' He sounded as if he thought it was somehow disloyal.

Hechler smiled, the lines on either side of his mouth softening. 'You should. A fine officer.' He gave a wry grin. 'Misunderstood by his superiors, naturally. Nothing changes in that respect.'

Theil shifted in his chair. 'What about him?'

'The boldest measures are the safest, that's what the little admiral said. I believe it, never more so than now.' He eyed him calmly, weighing him up. 'We'll lose this war if we're not careful.'

Theil stared at him, stunned. '*Impossible!* I – I mean, sir, we can't be beaten now.'

'Beaten – I suppose not. But we can still lose.' He did not explain. Instead he considered Norway. The first part of their passage should not be too dangerous. Air attack was always possible, but the minefields should prevent any submarines from getting too close. He thought of the new detection gear which was being fitted. As good as anything Britain and her allies had. Kröll, the gunnery officer, had shown rare excitement, although he obviously disapproved of having civilian technicians on board telling him what to do. They would still be in the ship when they sailed; it was that sort of priority.

The unseen eye, one of the civilians had described it. The *Scharnhorst* had been tracked and destroyed with it even in a dense snowstorm. *Prinz Luitpold*'s was supposed to be twice as accurate, and they were the first to have it fitted.

Hastily trained men had been rushed to the ship, new faces to be absorbed, to become part of their world.

There was also a new senior surgeon, the original one having been released because of ill-health. It had been something of a cruel joke amongst the sailors.

Hechler considered discussing the surgeon with Theil but decided against it for the moment. The man's name was Stroheim; he was highly qualified and a cut above most naval doctors. The best were usually in the army for all too obvious reasons.

Hechler had skimmed through his confidential file, but only one part of it troubled him. There was a pink sheet attached to it. Hechler hated political interference. It was like being spied on. Nevertheless, Stroheim had come to him under a cloud. You could not ignore it. He held a mental picture of Oberleutnant Bauer, the signals and W/T officer. On the face of it a junior if important member of his team. Bauer too had a special form in his file. He was the ship's political officer, a role which even as captain Hechler could not investigate.

Hechler shook his sudden depression aside. 'I would like us to walk round the ship before the hands go to their stations for leaving harbour.' He forced a smile. 'To show a united front.'

Theil stood up and grasped his cap tightly to his side.

'It will be an honour. For the Fatherland.'

For a moment Hechler imagined he was going to add 'Heil Hitler' as Leitner would have done. He said, 'No one goes ashore from now on.' He thought suddenly about the explosion which had sunk the lighter. It was always unexpected when it happened. Vigilance was not always enough. *Sabotage*. They were out there watching the ship, the same people who had placed the bomb aboard the lighter. To damage the ship or to destroy Leitner's boxes, the reason made little difference. It could have been serious.

In London, quaking under the new and deadly rocket bombardment, a telephone would ring in some Admiralty bunker. *Prinz Luitpold is leaving Vejle.*

A brief radio message from some Danish traitor was all it took. He smiled again. Or patriot if you were on the other side.

Another more persistent tremor came through the deck plating from the depths of the engine-room.

He looked away from Theil's strained face. Like me, he thought. Eager to go.

The *Prinz Luitpold's* swift passage from the Baltic into Norwegian waters was quieter than Hechler had anticipated. They logged a regular speed of twenty knots and passed Bergen within minutes of Gudegast's calculations.

For much of the time, and especially for the most dangerous period in the North Sea when the Orkney Islands and later the Shetlands lay a mere 200 miles abeam, the ship's company remained closed up at action stations. Every eye was on the sky, but unlike the Baltic the weather was heavily overcast, with low cloud and spasms of drizzle which reduced visibility to a few miles. They were able to test some of the new radar detection devices, and Hechler was impressed by its accuracy as they plotted the movements and tactics of their escorts even though they were quite invisible from the bridge.

Further north and then north-east, still following the wild coastline which Hechler knew from hard-won experience. Past the fortress-like fjord of Trondheim and crossing the Arctic Circle until both radar and lookouts reported the Lofoten Islands on the port bow. To starboard, cut into the mainland itself lay Bodø, and an hour later the cruiser's cable rattled out once more and she lay at anchor.

A grey oppressive coast, with sea mist rising around the ship like smoke, as if she had just fired a silent salute to the shore. They were not alone this time. Another cruiser, the *Lübeck*, was already anchored in the fjord, and apart from their escorts there were several other big destroyers and some supply ships.

Some if not all of the tension had drained away on the passage north. To be doing something again, to accept that a sailor's daily risks put more personal worries into their right perspective, made Hechler confident that his ship was ready for anything.

With the ship safely anchored behind protective nets and booms, and regular sweeps by patrol boats, Hechler found time to consider the wisdom of his orders. Bodø was a good choice, he thought, if only for the enlarged, military airfield there. Bombers and fighters could supply immediate cover, as well as mount an attack on enemy convoys or inquisitive submarines.

Routine took over once again, and after the fuel bunkers had been topped up from lighters, they settled down to wait.

Less than twenty-four hours after dropping anchor Hechler received a brief but impatient signal. He was to fly immediately to Kiel. After the uncertainty and the mystery of his orders it was something of an anti-climax. But as he was ferried ashore and then driven at reckless speed to the airfield in an army staff car, the choice of Bodø as a lair for his ship became all the more evident. Everything was planned to the last detail, as if he had no hand in anything. He did not even know what to tell Theil before he left. He might even be going to Germany only to be informed he was relieved, that perhaps Theil was taking command after all.

The aircraft, a veteran Junkers three-engined transport, arrived at Kiel in the late afternoon.

Hechler had been dozing in his seat, not because he was tired but mainly to avoid a shouted conversation with an army colonel who spent much of the four-hour flight fortifying himself from a silver flask.

As the plane tilted steeply to begin its final approach Hechler got his first glimpse of Kiel through a low cloud bank. He had not returned there for about a year and he was unable to drag his eyes from the devastation. Whole areas had been wiped out, so that only the streets gave any hint of what had once been there. There was smoke too, from a recent air raid or an uncontrollable fire, he could not tell. He had seen plenty of it in five years of war. Poland, Russia, even in the ship's last bombardment he had watched the few remaining houses blasted into fragments.

Smokey sunlight glinted momentarily on water and he saw the sweeping expanse of the naval dockyard before that too was blotted out by cloud.

It was hard to distinguish serviceable vessels from the wrecks in the harbour. He saw fallen derricks and gantrys, great slicks of oil on the surface, black craters instead of busy slipways and docks.

In such chaos it was astonishing to see the towering shape of the naval memorial at Laboe, somehow unscathed, as was the familiar, gothic-style water-tower, like a fortress amidst a battle-field.

The drunken colonel peered over his shoulder and said hoarsely, 'We'll make them pay for this!' He wiped his eyes with his sleeve. 'My whole family was killed. Gone. Nothing left.'

The plane glided through the clouds and moments later bumped along the runway. Here again was evidence of a city under siege. Sandbagged gun emplacements with grim-faced helmeted crews lined each runway. Parties of men were busy repairing buildings and filling in craters. It seemed a far cry from *Prinz Luitpold*'s ordered world and Leitner's luxurious headquarters.

It felt strange to be here, he thought. More so to be amongst his fellow countrymen, to hear his own language in every dialect around him.

A camouflaged staff car was waiting and a tired-looking lieutenant seemed eager to get him away from the airfield before another alert was sounded.

No wonder some of his returning ship's company had seemed so worried and anxious. If all major towns and cities were like this – he did not allow his mind to dwell on it.

Naval Operations had been moved to a new, underground headquarters, but before they reached it Hechler saw scenes of desolation he had not imagined possible. There were lines of men and women queuing at mobile soup-kitchens, their drawn and dusty faces no different from those he had seen on refugees in Poland.

They drove past a platoon of marching soldiers who carried spades and shovels instead of rifles. They were all in step and swinging their arms. Some looked very young and all were singing in the staccato manner of infantrymen everywhere. But their faces were quite empty, and even their NCO forgot to salute the staff car.

The lieutenant saw his expression and said dully, 'It's been like this for weeks.' He dropped his eyes under Hechler's blue-grey stare. 'I – I'm sorry, sir.'

Another small cameo came and went as the car picked its way around some weary-looking firemen.

A stretcher was being carried from a bombed house, the front of which had tumbled out on to the street. Hechler caught a glimpse of some torn wallpaper and a chair hanging from the upper floor by one leg. An old man was being led to safety by a nurse, but it was obvious even at a distance that he wanted to remain with the blanket-covered corpse on the stretcher.

Hechler said, 'Night raids?'

The lieutenant shrugged. 'The Yanks by day, the Tommies by night.'

Hechler wanted to ask about Kiel's air defences but said nothing. *I am a stranger here.*

The lieutenant gave a sigh and wound down a window as some armed sentries blocked the road. The new headquarters was like a slab of solid concrete, not much different from the outside to one of the great U-boat pens, he thought.

But once inside, with the huge steel doors shut behind them, it was more like a ship than anything else. Steel supports, shining lifts which vanished into the ground like ammunition hoists, and even the officers and seamen who bustled about with briefcases and signal folders looked different from the embattled people he had just seen on the streets outside.

The lieutenant guided him into a lift and they stood in silence as it purred down two or maybe three levels. More doors and brightly lit passageways where the air was as cool and as fresh as a country lane.

Hechler had the impression that the lieutenant was taking him on a longer route than necessary in spite of his haste, perhaps to show him the display of businesslike efficiency. Hechler had not been in the bunker before and he looked into each room and office as they hurried past. Teleprinters, clattering typewriters, and endless banks of switchboards and flashing lights. There were several soldiers about too, and in one map-covered room Hechler saw that the Luftwaffe was also represented.

He felt his confidence returning, the dismal pictures he had seen on the street put momentarily aside. It was just that when you were involved in the fighting you never thought of those at home who had to stand and accept whatever was hurled at them. He thought of his parents and was glad they lived well away from the city.

The lieutenant pressed a button and another steel door slid to one side.

Several uniformed women were busy typing, while an officer was speaking intently on a telephone.

All of them jumped to their feet as Hechler appeared in the bright electric glare, and stared at him as if he was from another planet.

The lieutenant was relieved. 'The Admiral is waiting, sir.'

Two more doors, and each new room became less warlike. There were rugs, and pleasant lamp-shades, and the desks were of polished wood and not metal.

Leitner was sitting in a comfortable chair, a glass in one hand, his uniform jacket unbuttoned. He looked fresh and untroubled, as if he had just had a swim or a shower.

'Right on time, Dieter.' He gestured to another officer, a captain who was vaguely familiar.

Leitner said, 'Perhaps you know Klaus Rau? He commands *Lübeck*.'

They shook hands, and Hechler recalled the other captain who had once commanded a destroyer during the attack on Narvik.

He was a stocky, dark-jowled man with deepset eyes which seemed very steady and unblinking. Hechler sat down and pictured the cruiser which lay near to his own ship. *Lübeck* had been in the thick of it from the outbreak of war. The Low Countries, France and then in the Baltic against the Russians, she too had a charmed life despite being heavily damaged by gunfire and bombs alike on several occasions. *Lübeck* was an old ship, built in the early thirties and about half the size of *Prinz Luitpold*.

Leitner put down his glass and looked at them blandly.

'We shall be working together, gentlemen, just as soon as I hoist my flag. It will be a small but crack squadron, and the enemy will have cause to remember us.'

Rau glanced at Hechler. 'My ship has already given them reason enough.'

Hechler kept his face impassive. There it was again. Like Theil. He wondered briefly if it was coincidence or an accident that Rau had arrived here ahead of him. He had not been aboard the old Junkers. He smiled inwardly. It was unlikely that Leitner would ever permit a coincidence.

The rear-admiral added, 'You will receive your final orders

when you return to your commands. This is a maximum security operation.' He gave a quick grin, like an impish schoolboy. 'If it leaks out, I shall know where to come looking, eh?'

A telephone buzzed, and the flag-lieutenant appeared as if by magic through another door and snatched it up before his superior had time to frown.

Hechler could not hear what he said, but saw some dust float down from the ceiling; he would not have seen it but for the lights.

Leitner listened to his aide and said, 'Air raid. They are going for the harbour again.' He gestured for his glass to be refilled. 'Our fighters have brought down four already.'

Hechler looked at the ceiling. Was that all it meant down here? A tiny trickle of dust, and not even a shiver of vibration. He thought of the drunken colonel on the plane, his despair. How could a man like that lead his troops with conviction? He had been damaged as much as any man who loses a limb or his sight in battle. It was dangerous to cling to the past merely because he imagined he had no future.

Leitner glanced at his watch. 'We must see the head of Operations.'

Rau stood up. 'Until tomorrow then, sir.' He glanced at Hechler. 'A pleasure meeting you again.'

Hechler watched the door close. A man without warmth.

Leitner smiled. 'He is jealous of you. Nothing like envy to keep men on their toes.'

He walked to the other door. 'Come with me, Dieter. The time for cat-and-mouse with men like Rau can keep.'

Admiral Manfred von Hanke was an impressive figure by any standards. He was standing straight-backed in the centre of a well-lit map-room, his heavy-lidded eyes on the door as Leitner and Hechler were ushered in by another aide.

Hechler knew a lot about the admiral, although he had not found many people who had actually met him.

Von Hanke had been a captain in the Great War with a distinguished career ahead of him. He had been in the United States attached to the German Embassy where he had been engaged for several years in organising a powerful intelligence and espionage ring. In the final months of the war when America had abandoned her umbrella of neutrality, he had found himself arrested

63

as a spy. Even that, and the possibility of summary execution, had not broken him, and despite his aristocratic family background, something frowned on in Hitler's New Order, he had survived and prospered. Today he was second only to Donitz, while his grasp of strategy and naval operations took second place to no one.

He had iron-grey cropped hair, and because he had just come from an investiture was wearing his frock-coat uniform and winged collar. He could still be one of the Kaiser's old guard, Hechler thought.

Leitner began brightly, 'This is our man, sir –'

Von Hanke raised one hand in a tired gesture and Leitner fell instantly silent.

Von Hanke said, 'Be seated. This will not take too long, but of course if you have any questions?' He gave a dry smile. 'In that case –'

He pressed a button on his deck and several long wall panels slid away to reveal giant maps of each of the main battle areas.

Hechler stared at one of the Baltic and the Gulf of Finland where his ship had been mostly employed. It all seemed so long ago instead of weeks.

His eyes fastened on some red flags where one of von Hanke's staff had marked the various army units.

Von Hanke watched him steadily, his hooded eyes without expression. 'You have seen something, Captain?'

Hechler hesitated. 'The Twenty-First Division, sir. It is still shown south-west of Riga.'

'Well?' Not a flicker of emotion although Hechler could sense Leitner's irritation behind his back.

'It no longer exists. It was decimated weeks ago.' The admiral's silence was like an unspoken doubt and he added, 'I was there, sir.'

Leitner said, 'I expect it has been regrouped –'

The admiral clasped his hands behind him.

'I am glad you show interest as well as intelligence, Captain.'

Von Hanke gestured to the adjoining map which showed Norway and the convoy routes from Iceland to North Cape. It was pockmarked with pointers and flags, and Hechler felt a tightness in his throat when he saw his own ship's name on a metal pennant placed on Bodø. Pictures leapt through his mind. Theil's

64

anxiety, the straddled destroyer heeling over in a welter of fire and steam. Men dying.

The straight-backed admiral said in his slow, thick tones, 'The Allies are throwing everything they have into France. Even now there are advance units within miles of Paris, others breaking out towards the Belgian frontier. Our forces will blunt their advances of course, and already the army's pincer movements have taken many prisoners and valuable supplies. But the advance goes on.'

Hechler glanced at the flags nearest to the Belgian frontier. It was said that the new rocket-launching sites were in the Low Countries. The Allies would use every means to reach them before they could do their maximum damage in England.

Von Hanke continued calmly, 'Intelligence reports are excellent. The British intend to do something they have not attempted before and have two convoys in Northern waters at the same time. A loaded convoy routed for the Russians in Murmansk, and an empty but nonetheless valuable one on the reverse route to Iceland. The Normandy campaign has made the Royal Navy very short of escorts, that is their only reason.'

Hechler could see that too in his mind. The endless daylight, the convoys drawing further and further north towards Bear Island to avoid air and U-boat attack. It had always been a murderous battleground for both sides.

He examined his feelings. It was what he might have expected. An attack on two convoys when Allied warships were deployed in strength in the English Channel and Biscay. If they destroyed one or both of the convoys it might give a breathing space. Even as he considered it, he sensed a nagging doubt. Just to look at those probing red arrows, the British and American flags, made such an operation little more than a delay to the inevitable.

Much would depend on the army's counter-attacks in France. They had to hold the line no matter what if they hoped to gain time to break the enemy's determination with an increasing rocket bombardment.

Von Hanke said softly, 'You look troubled, Captain.'

Hechler faced him. 'I think it can be done, sir. My ship –'

'Your *ship*, Captain, is possibly the most powerful of her kind afloat, and she is one of half a dozen major units left in the fleet.' He glanced absently at the maps. 'Others are supporting our troops in the Baltic, as you will know better than most. Some are

65

marooned in ports on the Biscay coast. And there are those which are damaged beyond repair by air attacks.' He turned again and fixed his eyes on Hechler. '*Prinz Luitpold* is the best we have. If she is not properly employed, she may end up like her less fortunate consorts.'

Hechler glanced at Leitner. He looked bright-eyed; inspired would be a better description, he thought.

'At the right moment you will leave Bodø and seek out one of the convoys as directed by OKM.' His eyes never left Hechler's. 'And then, Captain, you will take full advantage of the disruption caused and –' He walked towards him and then gripped his hands in his. 'You will take your ship into the Atlantic.'

For an instant longer Hechler thought he had misheard or that the admiral was about to add something.

The Atlantic. A ship like *Prinz Luitpold* could create hell on the sea-lanes until she was run to ground.

Von Hanke said, 'You do not question it?' He nodded slowly. 'That is good. I would not like to give the ship another captain at this stage.'

Leitner exclaimed, 'It is a perfect plan, Dieter!' He could not contain his excitement. 'A tiger at large, with all the chain of supplies to make it possible!'

Von Hanke frowned. '*Later*.' He looked at Hechler. 'Surprise will be total. It will show the world what we can do.' He gripped his hands again. 'You will do it for Germany!'

A door opened and Hechler knew that the interview was at an end.

It was so swift, so impossibly vast he could barely think of it as a feasible plan. At the same time it was like a release, perhaps what he had always been looking and hoping for.

Von Hanke folded his arms. 'Nothing will be said beyond these walls. Only the Führer knows, and he will let nothing stand in your way.'

Hechler thought of the colonel on the plane, the frightened-looking people he had seen in the bombed streets.

Perhaps this *was* a way. Maybe it was all they had.

Outside the map-room Leitner said, 'Return to your ship. I will fly up in two days.' He shrugged. 'After that, who knows?'

Hechler found the tired lieutenant waiting for him and the car was ready to take him to the airfield.

He barely noticed the journey and was astonished that he could accept it so calmly.

The Atlantic. The vast Western Ocean. *The killing ground,* where every ship would be an enemy.

Leitner's words stuck in his mind. *A tiger at large.*

He touched the peak of his cap to a saluting sentry and walked out to the smoke-shrouded runway.

The waiting was over.

Chapter Five

Rank Has its Privileges

Dieter Hechler opened his eyes with a start and realised that his face was pressed on to his forearm. Two other facts stood out, that he had been writing a letter to his parents, but had been awakened by the clamour of alarm bells.

He jumped to his feet, his mind still refusing to grasp what was happening. He was in his day cabin, his jacket hanging on a chair, an empty coffee cup nearby. Normally the sound of those alarm bells would have brought him to instant readiness and it was likely he would have been in his tiny sea-cabin, or dozing in the steel chair on the bridge.

The telephone buzzed through the din of bells and running feet with the attendant slamming of watertight doors.

It was Theil. 'Red Alert, sir. Air attack.'

Hechler slammed down the handset and snatched his jacket and cap even as Pirk scampered past him to screw the steel dead-lights over the scuttles.

On deck the ship seemed deserted, and only abandoned brooms and paint brushes marked the sudden alarm.

He climbed swiftly to the upper bridge, aware that the anti-aircraft guns were already traversing towards the land, and men were putting on helmets and dragging belts of ammunition to the short-range weapons.

It was still a bright afternoon with just a few jagged clouds towards the open sea.

Hechler barely heard the quick reports from the officers around him but stared instead at the long stretches of camou-flaged netting which hung between the masts and above the main armament. It was the same aboard the *Lübeck*. It did not hide a ship from an inquisitive aircraft, but it acted as a disguise and broke up a ship's outline.

Theil took a pair of binoculars from a messenger and then handed them back with a terse, 'Clean the lenses, damn you!'

Hechler looked across the starboard screen. The airfield was invisible from here, but there ought to be some fighters scrambled by now, he thought.

He hated being at anchor. Like lying in a trap. The bait. The ship had been at short notice for steam since his return from Kiel, but not that short. It would take an hour to slip and work out to some sea-room.

He turned his attention to the other cruiser. All her secondary armament was at full elevation, and in his mind's eye he saw Rau, watching the heavy cruiser and probably comparing the times it had taken for both ships to clear for action.

Theil muttered irritably, 'Come on, get those planes airborne!'

He must be thinking much the same. Too many warships had been caught in enclosed fjords and damaged beyond repair by daring hit-and-run raids.

An inland battery had opened fire and every pair of glasses scanned the clouds as the shells left their familiar dirty brown stains in the sky.

Theil exclaimed, 'I can't see a bloody thing!'

The young one-striper, Konrad Jaeger, called suddenly, 'I see it! One aircraft, sir, at red four-five!'

Hechler sensed Theil's annoyance but concentrated on the bearing until sunlight shone like a bright diamond on the plane's cockpit cover.

Another voice hissed, 'Nowhere near the thing!'

Hechler watched the shell-bursts gathering in an untidy cluster while some earlier ones broke up and drifted downwind.

Hechler had to agree with the unknown sailor. The shooting was very poor and the tiny sliver of metal in the sky did not even alter course.

It was not a bomber anyway, and seemed to be quite alone.

Bodø was described as a safe anchorage and better protected than most. It was likely that enemy agents would know of *Prinz Luitpold*'s presence here, just as her departure from Vejle would be known and plotted in London. However, there was no need to invite some reckless reconnaissance plane to confirm everything.

Theil said between his teeth, 'Our Arado replacement is expected, sir.' He sounded anxious. 'I hope to hell that head-quarters have ordered it to stand away.'

Hechler looked over the screen and past the nearest gun-crews as they tried to track the aircraft, their anti-flash hoods making them look like members of some strange religious order.

The aircraft derrick was already swung out, the tackle prepared to hoist the new Arado inboard as soon as it landed in the fjord.

'Gunnery officer requests permission to use main armament, sir.'

'Negative.' Hechler knew that Kröll would shoot at anything just to exercise his men. But it was a waste of ammunition and with as much hope of hitting the reconnaissance plane as a bow and arrow. In fact the solitary aircraft was already heading away, flitting between the clouds, the shell-bursts too far away to catch it.

Theil said, 'Here they are! *At last*. Late as bloody usual!'

Two fighters streaked from the land, the echo of their engines roaring around the fjord with a throaty vibration. The sun shone on their black crosses as they tilted over and then tore towards the sea.

Hechler lowered his binoculars and glanced at Theil and the others. Theil was furious, too angry perhaps to notice the coincidence. The anti-aircraft battery had been haphazard, just as the fighter cover had been far too late to do anything.

It was as if they had been ordered to hold back. If that was so, it meant just one thing. Headquarters wanted the enemy to know they were here. It was like being in the dark. Being told only a part of von Hanke's strategy. Hechler tried to shrug it off. It was not the first time that air defences had been caught napping. He pictured the admiral in his winged collar, the dry grip of his hands. Von Hanke of all people would know each step before it was made. Just as he had known about the army division which existed only on his map. How many more divisions or battalions were represented only by coloured markers and flags? A million men lay dead from the last campaign. How many more were there now? He tried to dispel the sudden apprehension, the sense of danger.

'Aircraft at green one-one-oh, angle of sight one-oh!'

The gunnery speaker snapped into life. 'Disregard! Aircraft friendly!'

Some of the seamen grinned with nervous relief, but Hechler crossed the bridge to watch the float-plane as it left the land's protection and followed its own reflection across the flat water.

He snapped, 'I want to see that pilot as soon as he comes aboard! We may be short of a plane and the man to fly it, but by God I'll send him back double-quick unless he can explain himself!'

All the smiles were gone now. Even young Jaeger had enough experience to realise the cause of the captain's cool anger. If there had been a proper air attack, especially by carrier-borne torpedo bombers, the Arado replacement would have been right in the middle of it, and Kröll's flak gunners would have had to hold their fire or shoot it down with the attackers.

'Fall out action stations.' Hechler controlled his anger.

Moments later the guardrails were thronged with men again as the new float-plane made a perfect landing and then taxied towards the anchored cruiser.

Theil dropped his glasses. 'Extra passenger, sir.' He bit his lip. 'it looks like the rear-admiral.'

Even as the plane glided towards the side Hechler saw Leitner grinning up at them, before removing his flying helmet to don his oak-leaved cap.

He said, 'I don't care if it's Christ Almighty. That was a damn stupid thing to do!'

Hechler was as much concerned at his own anger as he was about the admiral's unorthodox arrival. Was it because there were so many questions still unanswered? If they engaged one of the British convoys for instance. Would Rau's *Lübeck* be able to withdraw safely? That, almost more than the mission itself, had filled him with uncertainty.

Followed by Theil he hurried from the bridge and down to the catapult, where a side-party had been hastily assembled.

Leitner pulled himself up from the Arado without waiting for it to be hoisted aboard. He was flushed and excited, and could barely stop himself from laughing aloud at Hechler's grave features. Together they watched the plane being hoisted up the side, water spilling from the floats as the handling party used their guy-ropes to sway it round. The Arado was brand-new, and bore no camouflage paint. As it came to rest on the catapult before being man-handled inboard Hechler saw the bright red stripe on the side. Like something from the Great War, he thought grimly.

Leitner stood with his arms folded, still dressed in a white flying suit, his cap at a rakish angle as he had appeared many times in the newspapers.

Hechler watched the pilot and observer climb down to the deck and then said, 'I'll see *you* later. You might have got your arse shot off!'

The pilot turned and stared at him and then pulled off the black helmet goggles.

Hechler stared as a mass of auburn hair tumbled over the other man's shoulders.

The admiral made a last effort to contain his amusement and said, 'Captain, may I introduce Erika Franke. One of the finest pilots in the Third Reich, I believe!'

She eyed him without curiosity, her lips slightly parted as she shook out her hair from her flying suit.

'Quite a welcome, Captain.' She did not offer her hand.

Hechler could feel the side-party's astonishment giving way to broad grins, and Theil's pink-faced disbelief that this had happened.

Hechler looked at the admiral. 'What I said still goes, sir.'

She was watching him, amused or merely bored he could not tell.

Erika Franke, of course. Her father had been an ace pilot who had died in attempting a lone flight across a desert in Africa. She had won several prizes within a year of obtaining her licence. And she had even made her name in the war when she had flown into an encircled army position in Italy to rescue one of the Führer's top advisers before the whole place had been overrun.

He said, 'I am not used to –' It sounded defensive, foolish.

She turned away to watch as the two fighters came roaring back across the water.

'Evidently, Captain. We must try to change that, mustn't we?'

Leitner clapped him on the shoulder.

'It will be a different war, Dieter.' He became serious again. 'For all of us, yes?'

The girl turned and looked at them calmly. 'I'd like to change and have a shower, if I may.' She touched her upper lip with her tongue. 'Even at the risk of getting my, er, arse shot off, eh?'

Hans Stoecker in his best uniform with a holstered Luger at his belt stood nervously outside the wardroom. He felt on edge, unable to concentrate on anything, even the prospect of meeting Sophie again.

72

It was all so strange and unreal, he thought, after the patrols and bombardments, the wild elation of watching from his position high above the bridge when the main armament had fired on the enemy.

The wardroom throbbed with music, and was packed from side to side with officers and visitors alike. Like the peacetime navy must have been, he thought, without fear of a sudden air-attack or torpedo.

With the rear-admiral's flag hoisted over the ship everyone had expected things to move swiftly, that the *Prinz* would head out to sea again.

He recalled seeing the girl pilot as she had climbed down from the catapult. Like most of the company he had read of her exploits, especially the last one when she had flown through enemy flak to lift off an important politician. Stoecker did not really like the idea of women in the firing line, but after meeting Sophie he was not certain of anything. She was not a schoolgirl any more. She was a woman, and had probably seen more results of war than he had.

Now he had two secrets to hold. One was the letter, still unopened. He had nearly destroyed it several times but something made him hold back. The other secret was what Sophie had told him.

She was ordered to a hospital in Norway. Suppose it was where they were based? They would meet again. Like that last time when they had kissed and clutched each other, hearts pounding while they had tasted a new and delicate love.

A curtain swirled back and Leutnant zur See Konrad Jaeger stepped over the coaming. He took a pistol from the rack and clipped it around his waist.

He grimaced as a great burst of laughter came from beyond him.

'Time for rounds, Stoecker. Others have all the luck.'

It would take all of an hour to go round the flats and messes, to check padlocks and magazine and to sign all the log-sheets. By the time they had finished some of the guests would have left.

Stoecker nodded to a boatswain's mate and messenger who were waiting to accompany the young officer on his rounds. There was a faint smell of schnapps in the damp air, and he hoped Jaeger had not noticed it. He was a good officer, for a one-striper

73

that was. But he'd come down on Stoecker if he found someone had been drinking on watch.

Jaeger was not aware of the acting petty officer's wary glance. He was thinking of the wardroom party, the first one he had ever attended in a real combat warship. The *Prinz* was famous; you could see the excitement, even awe, on the faces of the guests, and especially the women. The admiral must have a lot of influence even in that direction, he decided. There were lots of women aboard, and most appeared to be German except for the wives of some local officials.

Preceded by the boatswain's mate, Jaeger and his little party climbed to the cooler air of the quarterdeck, where Korvettenkapitän Froebe was waiting by the accommodation ladder to welcome guests below the shaded police lights.

It was a rare sight, and Jaeger paused to watch as two women in long, colourful dresses with some officers from the airfield stood by the guardrails, their hair moving in the evening breeze, their eyes exploring the ship.

Jaeger thought of the young girl he had met in the wardroom. It was unlikely he would get a look-in there, he thought. Hampe, the torpedo officer and a well-known womaniser, had been watching them, waiting for rounds to be called. For him to leave.

A figure moved from the shadows and Jaeger called his men to attention.

The captain touched his cap and smiled. 'Hard luck, Jaeger, but rank has its privileges, you see.'

Jaeger grinned. He could recall standing like a ramrod at attention for minutes on end in his last ship, where he had completed his training. That captain had been a tyrant, a bully you would never want to speak to even if it had been allowed.

Hechler was so different. Did he never have any worries or doubts?

Hechler saw the youngster's glance in spite of the gloom. He had also noticed the faint tang of schnapps. That would be the boatswain's mate. His mother and sister had just been reported killed in an air raid. He would let it pass. Hechler strode on, half-dreading the party and Leitner's exuberance. *This* time, he would say nothing.

Theil was waiting to meet him outside the wardroom and Hechler asked, 'All going well?'

74

Theil nodded. 'Like old times.'

Hechler stepped into the wardroom and moved through the packed figures. It was hard to see this place as it usually was, or used as a sickbay for wounded troops brought offshore from the fighting.

He sensed the glances and the occasional bold stares from some of the women. Why should he feel so ill at ease? This might be the last time for a long while that they could relax and drink too much. It could just as easily be the last time ever.

He heard a woman laugh and saw the auburn hair shining beneath a deckhead light.

Erika Franke wore neither a gown nor a uniform, it was something in between, dove-grey which set off her hair and her skin. She was speaking with Zeckner, a quarters officer, so that Hechler made to step aside before she saw him.

He was still uncertain what to do. Leitner had explained that the orders came from von Hanke and even higher. Erika Franke was to stay aboard. Incredibly, there was also a camera team. That in itself was not unusual in major warships, but with the prospect of immediate action it could put their lives at risk. Leitner seemed to treat the whole matter like a personal publicity operation.

She called, 'Why, Captain, so you have come amongst us after all!'

He faced her, surprised and angry at the way she got under his skin and made him feel clumsy.

He said, 'I hope you are being looked after?' She had long lashes and eyes which seemed to change colour as he watched. Hazel and then tawny.

She smiled. 'You are staring, Captain.'

Hechler took a glass of champagne which someone thrust into his hand.

'Yes. I'm sorry.' He raised the glass and lowered it again. 'And I apologise for the way I greeted your arrival on board.'

She touched her lip with her tongue as she had when she had faced him at their first meeting.

That must have cost you a lot, Captain.' She nodded, her eyes grave. 'I suspect you are not used to bending your knee.' The smile moved into her eyes again. 'Especially to a mere woman.'

Leitner joined them before Hechler could answer. He said,

'Good party. It will make everyone believe we are here as a part of a local squadron.' He beamed and showed his perfect teeth. 'Let them all relax and enjoy themselves, eh? Who cares about tomorrow?'

Theil was making signals from the door and Leitner remarked, 'A night full of surprises. As it should be.'

Hechler glanced past the noisy, laughing figures and saw her as she stepped over the coaming. He felt as if his breath had stopped, that even his heart was still.

Her hair was quite short so that her small, perfectly shaped ears were visible, as were the pendant earrings as she turned to look around.

Several officers stopped talking to stare, questions clear on their faces.

Hechler put down his glass. Inger had always commanded a lot of attention, like the first time he had seen her and lost his heart.

She had an escort, a much older man in an olive-green uniform, a political officer of some kind and obviously quite senior. That too was pretty typical, he thought bitterly.

Leitner was watching him, one eyebrow cocked. 'She asked to come.' He spread his hands with mock gravity. 'What must I do? How could anyone refuse her?'

'Your wife, Captain?'

Hechler looked at the girl with auburn hair. He felt suddenly lost. Trapped.

He said, 'Yes.'

'She is very beautiful.' But she was studying him, her eyes quiet with interest. 'You seem surprised?'

Leitner smiled. 'It is only right, Dieter.'

Hechler said, 'She has no place here.'

But she was coming across, men parting before her or trying to catch her glance.

She wore a red silk gown with thin shoulder straps. It was cut very low both front and back and Hechler guessed that she wore little if anything underneath it.

She presented her hand for him to take and kiss. Even that was perfectly done. The perfume on her skin, it too he could recall as if it were yesterday.

Leitner was shaking hands with her escort, but Hechler did not even catch his name. It was as if nothing had happened, that the fire still burned. The touch of her hand, the movement of her breasts which were barely concealed by the red silk, seemed to render him helpless.

He knew Theil and some of the others were watching. They were learning more about their captain every day. Why had she come?

She said softly, 'You look tired, Dieter. Doing too much.' She observed him calmly. 'As always.' Her eyes moved to the girl. 'And who is this?'

Erika Franke met her gaze, unruffled by the casual but faintly imperious tone.

She replied, 'I work here.' She gave a quick smile. 'I shall go and enjoy myself.'

Inger watched her leave and said, 'That's the flier. I thought I knew her.' She seemed to relax. 'She's been in some bother, I believe.'

Hechler did not want to discuss it. 'I was not expecting –'

'*That* is evident.' She smiled and touched his cheek but her eyes were quite cool. 'No matter. You are a man, a *hero*, some say.'

Leitner had moved away and was in deep conversation with her escort. The latter was staring across, unwilling to be shelved so soon.

Hechler felt the old anger again. Why should he have to put up with it?

Theil was watching too, although he was at some pains to cover it.

He heard himself ask, 'Why here and now, Inger? It's over.'

'You think so?' She rested one hand on his sleeve and touched the four gold stripes. 'You need me. You always will. Nothing's changed.' She seemed to become impatient and thrust her hand beneath his arm. 'Can we talk? In private?'

Hechler heard the lively dance strike up as another record was put on the gramophone and was grateful for the interruption. Voices grew louder and some of the guests began to revolve although there was barely room to move. Perspiring stewards and messmen pushed amongst the throng with laden trays of glasses. This evening was going to cost the wardroom a small fortune.

She said, 'Your cabin?' She looked up at him, her eyes steady, her lips shining, inviting.

77

They walked along the deck, the noise growing fainter as if the ship was reasserting herself, rising above them, grey steel and hooded guns.

Once she turned and looked across at the darkening water, the thin white line of a motor-launch's wake.

He asked, 'What about your friend?'

She shrugged. Even that motion stabbed him like a knife.

'Ludwig? He is head of a mission here, something to do with fisheries, I think. Don't worry about him.'

The cabin was quiet, with a tidiness which showed Pirk had been busy clearing up from the last official visitors. But there was some champagne and two glasses, as if it had all been planned. She saw his expression and said, 'Thank you, I should like some.'

He could feel her watching as he opened the bottle and wiped it free of ice. She never looked tired; he could not recall her ever refusing an invitation to a party or a reception. Like the time he had returned home with the knowledge he was being given *Prinz Luitpold*. He had been in bed reading when he had heard her come into the house, then the sound of men's voices.

When he had gone down he had found her in the arms of an artillery major, while another officer was on his knees beside a girl who had obviously passed out with drink. The man had been tearing the clothes off her, stripping her naked while Inger and her friend ignored what he was doing.

Somehow, he could barely recall how, they had made it up. She had even been excited when he had thrown the others out of the house, had pleaded for his forgiveness and then given herself to him with such wild abandon that he had surrendered.

Looking back he must have been mad. But he had loved her then. Hechler turned with the glasses. He still wanted her. Was that the same thing?

He sat beside her, feeling the longing and the pain of it as he studied her face and her mouth. When she took his hand and put it around her breast he could feel the drumming in his mind, could think of nothing but taking her, here and now. As Leitner had said, who cares about tomorrow?

She stretched out and put down her glass so that one shoulder strap slipped away and her breast was almost lying bare in his hand. She watched his face as if to test each emotion there and said, 'You are sailing soon. Why else would Andreas invite me?'

He should have guessed that Leitner was behind it. It was a game to him. He used people with little thought for what might happen.

'What do you want, Inger?'

She touched his mouth with her fingers. 'I need you to love me.'

It made no sense, but he wanted to hold her, tell her everything. Hopes, fears, all the things which were bottled up inside him . . . The telephone shattered the silence and she smiled as he reached out to take it.

It was Theil, his voice hushed and troubled. One of the guests had fallen down a ladder. It was someone important. He thought the captain should know.

Hechler watched her, the way she smiled as she slipped the other strap from her shoulder and allowed the red silk to fall about her waist. Her breasts were lovely, and she touched one, her lips parted, knowing it would provoke him.

He said quickly, 'Get the senior medical officer, Viktor.' He had not met the newcomer yet and as he watched the thrust of her breasts he could barely recall his name. 'Stroheim.'

He put down the phone and looked at her. She was staring at him, her eyes full of disbelief. 'What name?'

Hechler said, 'Karl-Heinz Stroheim. He's new on board. I –'

She struggled into her dress and knocked over her champagne without seeming to notice it.

Hechler stood up while she looked around the cabin like a trapped animal.

'You know him?'

She faced him, her eyes hot. 'Don't you *dare* question me! I'm not one of your snivelling sailors!' She recovered slightly and glanced at herself in the mirror. 'Take me back. I must go.'

He blocked her way. 'Tell me! For God's sake, you said you wanted me!'

She stared at him, and he could see her self-control returning, like a calm on the sea.

'What will you do, Dieter? Knock me down? Rape me?' She tossed her short curls. 'I think not – your precious Andreas would not care for *that*!'

Hechler could not recall walking back to the wardroom. More curious stares, her bright laugh as her escort lumbered over to claim her. He heard her say something about a headache, and

79

then as she turned to look towards him she said, 'It will be a relief to be alone.'

Leitner watched as she followed Theil towards the door. He asked softly, 'Not going with her, Dieter? Tch, tch, I am surprised.'

Hechler turned his back on the others, his voice dangerously calm.

'You did it deliberately, sir. For one moment I thought –' He shook himself angrily. 'I don't know what I thought.'

Leitner glanced towards his willowy aide who had just entered, his eyes everywhere until he had found his lord and master.

Hechler saw the brief nod. Nothing more.

Leitner picked up a fresh glass and watched the busy bubbles rising.

'I shall set an example and retire, Dieter.' He looked at him for several seconds as if making up his mind.' 'First-degree readiness.' He shook his head as Hechler made to speak. '*Not yet*. People are watching. We shall weigh tomorrow evening. As soon as the guests have departed, pass the word to the other commanding officers.' Some of his self-control slipped aside. 'You will brief your heads of departments as soon as we clear the anchorage.'

Hechler watched the crowd of guests thinning soon after Leitner had followed his flag-lieutenant outside. It was like an unspoken command, and he walked to the guardrails opposite Turret Caesar to watch the boats and launches queuing at the accommodation ladder to collect their passengers.

Perhaps he hoped to see the red silk gown. He did not know any more. But he could picture her sitting beside him, her lovely body naked to the waist. Then her anger – or was it fear?

Some of the departing guests were singing. The ship, deep in shadow, must look quite beautiful from the boats in the water, he thought.

First-degree readiness. Like the opening of sealed orders. Page one.

The squadron would slip away unseen in the darkness, but not a man in any of the other ships would know *Prinz Luitpold*'s true purpose. When they did there would be few who would wish to change places with them.

As one of the duty officers, Jaeger, with Stoecker standing close by, stood by the gangway and watched the visitors being guided and helped down the long ladder. The sailors were taking much greater care with the women than the men, he noticed.

He saw the girl pause and look up at him. Shad waited until he returned from rounds, and he had spent the rest of the time speaking with her.

He raised his hand in salute and saw her blow him a kiss.

He did not see the pain on Stoecker's face as he spoke her name aloud. *Sophie*.

By midnight as the watchkeepers changed round for the next four hours Hechler still walked the decks alone.

When he eventually went to his cabin he saw the glasses and ice-bucket had gone, the stain of her champagne all but mopped up from the carpet.

A light burned beside his bunk, some coffee in a thermos nearby.

He thought suddenly of the new medical officer, and her expression when he had spoken his name.

There was so much he wanted to know, so much more he dared not ask.

When Pirk entered silently to switch off the light he found the captain fast asleep, still fully dressed.

Pirk sighed and then swung Hechler's legs on to the bunk.

He thought of the newly installed admiral and what he had heard about him and his flag-lieutenant. If the other stewards knew, it would soon be all over the ship.

Pirk smiled with satisfaction and switched off the light.

The captain would see them all right. He always had.

Hechler slept on, and with his ship waited for the dawn.

Chapter Six

The Unexpected

Hechler slid from his steel chair on the port side of the bridge and stamped his feet on the scrubbed gratings to restore the circulation. One of the watchkeepers jumped at the sound, and Hechler noted the tense backs of the bridge lookouts as they peered through their powerful glasses, each man to his own allotted sector.

Hechler glanced at the armoured conning-tower and past it to the fire control position. Beneath and around him the ship vibrated and quivered but the motion was steady, and even some pencils on the chart table remained motionless.

He tried to dampen down his own anxieties. It was always like this when a ship left the land. For him in any case. Now, with the additional knowledge of what might lie ahead, he had to be certain of everything. *Confident.*

There had been no flaws, nothing serious anyway. He looked past two signalmen and saw *Lübeck* following half a mile astern, her faint funnel vapour streaming out abeam like her flags. The destroyers too were exactly on station, as if they were all on rails. They dipped their bows occasionally and Hechler saw the sea creaming over their forecastles before cascading down through the guardrails again. A small but powerful force, he thought, with air cover to make it easier. Every few minutes, or so it seemed, they sighted one of the big Focke Wulf Condors which acted as their eyes and escorts.

Two bells chimed out from below the bridge and the men relieved from watch would be having their lunch, the main meal of the day. It had been sixteen hours since they had weighed and with little fuss had steamed out of Salt Fjord, soon to lose Bodø in the gathering dusk.

Hechler had been on the bridge throughout that time, watching the cable clanking inboard with the usual chipped paint scattering to each massive link.

Westward to skirt the Lofoten Islands and then north, the ships closing in protectively on either beam.

All the captains had come aboard just prior to sailing, but Leitner had kept his comments on a general level. They all knew about the enemy convoys, each captain had an intelligence pack as big as a bible. The British might have a change of heart, or perhaps one of the convoys would be re-routed at the last minute.

Sixteen hours at a relatively gentle fifteen knots, although the destroyers were finding station-keeping hard work.

It was a strange feeling to be heading out into an ocean instead of sighting land every so often as in the Baltic. Now as *Prinz Luitpold*'s raked bows ploughed across the seventieth parallel nothing lay ahead unless you counted Spitzbergen or Bear Island. Scenes of other sea-fights, Hechler thought, before every eye had turned to Normandy and the Eastern Front.

He walked to the chart-table to give himself time to glance at the men around him. Most of them were warmly dressed, for despite the fact it was August, the air had a bite to it. Soon there would be no escape from the ice.

Their faces looked normal enough, he thought. That morning he had sensed the silence throughout the ship when he had spoken on the intercom to the whole company.

Leitner had been ready to make a speech, but Hechler had bluntly asked permission to speak to his men, in his own way.

He had pictured them as his voice had echoed around each deck and compartment like a stranger's. Gun crews and engineers, the damage-control men and those who cooked and served the hundreds of meals it took to feed the *Prinz*'s people.

'We are going out into the Atlantic –' There should have been rousing music, cheering; instead there was a silence which meant so much more to him, no matter what Leitner might believe.

Some had tried to tell him privately that they would not let him down. Others, like the huge Gudegast, had merely joked about it. *Good a place as any to lose a ship!*

He wondered what Rau would say if he knew.

Hechler shaded his eyes to look at the horizon. It was so eerie. A great, unbroken swell which roamed on and on for ever. And the sky, which was salmon-pink, painted the ragged clouds in a deeper hue, like copper. The ship's upperworks too were shining in the strange glow. Endless daylight, empty seas.

Another Focke Wulf droned overhead; a lamp winked briefly to the ships below.

The camera team had been on the bridge for much of the forenoon, but they seemed to have exhausted their ideas, and even the big four-engined Condor did not lure the cameras on deck again.

Oberleutnant Ahlmann, who was officer-of-the-watch, put down a handset and said, 'The lady flier wishes to come to the bridge, sir.'

Hechler thrust his hands deep into his pockets. He had not seen her since they had left Bodø, except once when she had been on the admiral's bridge with Leitner. Like the two girls who were in the camera team, her presence gave a sense of unreality. According to Leitner, they would be transferred before the ship headed deep into the Atlantic. Their films would be invaluable, he had said with all of his usual enthusiasm. A tonic to the people at home. It all depended on the first move. Von Hanke would decide after that.

Hechler had the feeling that the rear-admiral intended to use von Hanke as an excuse for almost everything.

He said, 'Very well.' He might get to the bottom of it by asking her what exactly she was doing aboard, in his ship.

Her voice came up the ladder and he pictured Inger, as he had a hundred times since the party. Her anger, her contempt, were so different from that earlier seduction. If it was to happen again . . .

He turned to face her as she was ushered into the bridge.

She wore a black leather jacket with a fur collar turned up over her hair. Her skin was very fresh from the wind and he guessed she had been exploring the upper deck.

'A wonderful view, Captain!' She climbed on to the gratings and peered through the salt-blotched screen. 'I should love to fly right now!'

Hechler watched her profile, her neat hands which gripped the rail as the deck tilted slightly to a change of course.

Ahlmann looked up from a voice-pipe and reported, 'Steady on Zero-Two-Two, sir. Revolutions one-one-zero.'

He turned and saw her watching him.

She shrugged. 'So different.' She gestured towards the upper bridge and radar, Leitner's flag leaping stiffly to the wind. 'So huge. You feel as if nothing would stop her, as if she could run away with you.'

Hechler nodded. 'When I was a young watchkeeper I often thought that. Especially during the night, the captain asleep, nobody to ask. I used to look at the stars and –'

'Gunnery Officer requires permission to train A and B turrets, sir.'

Hechler replied, 'Yes. Ten minutes.'

'It never stops for you, does it?'

He looked at her. 'I hadn't thought about it.' Together they watched as the two forward turrets swung silently on to the same bearing.

Kröll never missed a chance, which was why he had given him a time limit for this, another drill. At any moment, any second, the alarms might scream out. Men had to be clear-minded and not confused by too many exercises.

He thought of what Inger had said about this quiet-eyed girl. In some sort of trouble.

She said, 'Seeing those great guns makes me realise what your kind of war is all about.'

'Are you afraid?'

She seemed to consider it. 'I don't think so. It's like flying. There are only certain things you can do if the plane gets out of control.' She shrugged again. 'I don't feel I have any hold on things here.'

Then she laughed and one of the lookouts tore his eyes from his binoculars to glance at her.

'I *know* you are going to ask me, Captain, but like you, I am under orders. I am on board your ship because I have been so ordered. I am a civilian but I fly for the Luftwaffe.'

'I heard what you did.' Hechler tried to adapt to her direct manner. 'It's more than I'd care to do.' He scraped the gratings with his boot. 'Give me something solid . . .'

Theil appeared at the rear of the bridge and saluted, although his eyes were on the girl.

'The admiral sends his compliments, sir, and would you see him.'

'Yes.' Hechler was annoyed at the interruption. Being captain usually gave him all he needed, but he craved a conversation with someone who was not committed or involved with the same things. Leitner had probably seen them chatting, and was merely calling him away although it could hardly be from jealousy.

The thought made him smile and she said quietly, 'You should do that more often, Captain.' She turned away as the two forward turrets purred back to point fore-and-aft again.

Theil stepped forward so that he seemed to loom between them.

Hechler said, 'If there is anything I can do while you are aboard . . .'

She watched him, her eyes tawny in the strange light. 'Attend your ship, Captain. Her needs are greater than mine, I feel.'

Hechler turned away. The brief contact was broken. And why not? His own self-pity was a poor enough bridge to begin with.

He found Leitner on his armoured bridge, leaning with his arms spread wide on the plot-table.

Leitner glanced up, his neat hair glossy beneath the lights. 'All intelligence reports confirm my own thinking, Dieter. Tomorrow, we shall meet with the eastbound convoy. The British will know we are on the move. No matter, they will expect us to strike at the westbound one, to protect their friend Ivan's supplies, eh?' He nodded, satisfied. 'All working out. There are six U-boats in this area, and round-the-clock air patrols.' He stood up and clasped his hands at his sides. 'I can't *wait* to begin. Into the Atlantic, all that planning and von Hanke's preparations. God, it makes one feel quite humble!'

Hechler watched his emotion. It came and went like the wind. He thought of the reams of orders, the methods of fuelling, rendez-vous, and alternatives. This would be a million times different from previous raiding sorties.

Leitner said, 'I know it is important to you, Dieter, the close comradeship amongst your people. I heard it in your broadcast this morning. Saw it on their faces. Just boys, some of them, but the older ones who can be so hard and cynical –' he gave an elaborate sigh '– you had them eating out of your hand.'

Hechler replied, 'Comradeship is everything.'

'I *knew* it.' Leitner looked down at his plot-table again. 'Your second-in-command. I had a private signal about him.'

'Viktor Theil?'

'His wife has gone missing.' He sounded almost matter-of-fact. 'Of course I'm certain it will be all right. After all, ration books, identity cards, a civilian can't just vanish, eh?'

Hechler recalled Theil's face, the way he had parried questions about his leave.

Leitner said softly, 'I know what you're thinking, Dieter. *Don't!* He is a good officer, I'm sure, but he *is* the second-in-command. Should anything happen to you, well . . .' He shrugged.

'I trust him, sir.'

'Good. I shall remember it. But if he trips up on his mission, he goes, do I make myself clear?'

Hechler nodded. 'Very.'

Leitner yawned. 'Pretty girl, that Franke woman, eh? I wonder if she's as good in bed as in the cockpit.'

Fortunately a telephone rang and the flag-lieutenant appeared again like magic to answer it.

Hechler returned to the bridge. He felt strangely disappointed to find she was no longer there. Theil had gone too. For that at least he was glad.

He climbed into his steel seat and listened to the deep throb of engines, the occasional clatter of a morse lamp as signals were exchanged between the ships. Tomorrow that would all cease. He glanced over the screen at the same heavy guns. Moving targets, not rubble and houses, or a position on a range map.

He tried not to let Inger into his thoughts, to recall how she had looked, and shifted uneasily in the chair. He was getting rattled just when he needed every thought honed to a knife-edge. Tomorrow they would engage the enemy. Right now, at this very moment the convoy was being attacked by U-boats. Like sheep-dogs gone mad who were driving the convoy on a converging course.

He thought of Theil, then of himself. Two deserted husbands. It was laughable when you considered it. Was that all it meant? Voices muttered in voice-pipes, while guns moved in their mountings as the faithful Condor droned past the formation yet again. No, it was anything but laughable. He gripped the arms of his seat. Men would die, cursing his name, ships would burn.

Wives and petty squabbles were as nothing.

The bows dipped and he saw his reflection in the smeared glass. No, that too was a lie.

Hans Stoecker slammed yet another watertight door behind him and wedged the clips into place. Below the ship's waterline where one compartment was sealed from another the air felt cool and damp, the motion more pronounced. He passed the brightly lit door to the forward starshell room.

He had been carrying a message from the gunnery officer for one of the lieutenants but had purposely taken a roundabout route, and had parried not a few questions from sentries who guarded some of the vital bulkheads which in an emergency might prevent serious flooding. Stoecker glanced at the studded rivets and rough steel. It was best not to think of it, of those who might be trapped on the wrong side to face a terrible death by drowning.

He heard the familiar whistle and saw a grey-headed petty officer rummaging through a box of tools. Oskar Tripz was probably the oldest member of the ship's company. He had served in the Kaiser's navy, and when you got him going over a quiet glass of brandy or schnapps, would dwell with relish on the Battle of Jutland, and clashes with the Grand Fleet off the Dogger Bank. Even when he had quit the service he had been unable or unwilling to leave the sea and returned to it in the merchant marine and eventually in the famous Hamburg–Amerika Line. There again he could open the eyes of young sailors with his yarns of great liners, rich widows and randy passengers who chased the girls and sometimes the stewards with equal enthusiasm.

He was a rough, self-made seaman, and one of the gun-captains, despite his great age, great to younger men like Stoecker anyway. Stoecker was never bored by his stories of that other navy, another world, and was ever impressed by the man's knowledge of the sea. Tripz had even managed to teach himself at least three languages, with enough of some others to get him around in ports all over the world.

Tripz looked up and squinted at him questioningly. He had a round, crumpled face, as if that too had been carved from old ship's timber.

'You're a bit off-course, young Hans?'

Stoecker sat on a steel chest and eyed him awkwardly. Of all the people he knew he probably trusted the old petty officer the most. It had been due to his patience and private coaching that he had risen this far, with the hope of confirmation to petty officer in the near future.

With Tripz it was not learning. It was more like listening to well-told history.

'A job for the gunnery officer.'

Tripz wrinkled his nose. 'Oh, him.'

They both glanced up as the sea, muffled but ever-present, boomed along the outer hull. Thick steel and one of the great fuel bunkers separated them from it, but they both knew it was not enough to withstand a torpedo.

Tripz asked casually, 'Bit bothered, are you?'

Stoecker shrugged. Straight to the point. As always. This rough, outspoken man was respected by almost everyone, even if some of the young recruits made fun of him behind his back. God help them if his wintry eyes saw through them.

'It's the first time I've been in a battle with other warships.'

'Huh. Maybe it won't come to that. The Tommies might have other ideas.'

'When I heard the captain explain what we're going to do, I –'

Tripz grinned slowly. 'The Old Man knows more than *we* do, Hans.'

Stoecker bit his lip. It was usless to go on like this. He could barely sleep even when he got the chance, and he had been off his food since that day at Vejle.

Suppose he was wrong? Tripz might go straight to his divisional officer. He had been known to pass the time of day even with the captain, the Old Man as he called him, though Stoecker guessed that Tripz was old enough to be his father.

But he couldn't go on. He would certainly fail his exams and let down his parents unless – he made up his mind.

'I found a letter.' He hesitated as the petty officer's faded eyes settled on his. 'Somebody told me that –'

'Show it to me.' He held out one calloused hand. He saw the lingering hesitation. 'I'll make it an order, if you'd prefer it?'

Stoecker passed it across and momentarily the prospect of action, even death, faded into the background.

Tripz prised open the much-folded envelope and scanned the letter with great care.

He said, 'It's in Danish. But then you'd know that, right?' He did not look up to see Stoecker nod. 'One of those prisoners.'

'Yes.' He was surprised the admission came out so easily. 'Just before he was killed.'

Tripz eyed him grimly. 'Before the explosion.'

'Yes.'

'Told anyone else?'

Stoecker shook his head and thought of the others he had almost confided in. Even the young one-striper Jaeger. Until he had discovered about him and Sophie. That moment still gnawed at his insides like teeth.

'Good.' He folded the letter with great care. 'This is hot stuff.'

Stoecker found himself blurting out about the SS officer, then the ravaged shop.

Tripz grunted. 'Jews, eh.' He added vaguely, 'Well, they started it all, you know.'

Stoecker waited; at any moment Tripz might put him under arrest, take him to Korvettenkapitän Kröll. He could face detention barracks or much worse.

Tripz said, 'Best leave it with me.' He looked at him strangely. 'Just between us.'

'But I don't even know . . .'

'Better that way, my son.' Tripz placed the letter inside an oilskin pouch and buttoned it in his tunic.

He added, 'It could get both of us shot. Do I make myself clear?'

Stoecker nodded, glad to have shared his secret, moved by Tripz's confidence in him.

'When I've fathomed it out, I'll tell you.' His battered face split into a grin. 'Feel better?'

Stoecker gave a shaky smile. 'Much. I – I'm just sorry I got you mixed up in it.'

Tripz looked up quickly at the deckhead as if he had heard something. It was like an inbuilt sixth sense for at that moment the air cringed to the strident clamour of alarm bells.

Tripz was thickset, even ungainly, but he was through the steel door and on the rungs of a ladder before Stoecker had grasped fully what was happening.

Tripz peered down at him. 'Move it, boy! No time to hang about! You'll get a wooden cross, not an iron one, if you do! Remember what I once told you, one hand for the Führer, but keep one for yourself!' Then he was gone and would doubtless be in his turret before the bells had fallen silent.

Stoecker ran after him; he had further to climb than anyone. And yet despite the crash of steel doors he felt as if a great weight had been lifted from him.

*   *   *

90

'Ship at action stations, sir!'

Hechler returned Korvettenkapitän Froebe's salute and glanced briefly around the bridge. In war what a short time it took to know their faces, to forget them after they had gone.

Everyone stiffened as Leitner entered the bridge and strode unhurriedly to the gratings.

Hechler watched him curiously. The whole scheme might go badly wrong from the outset. There had been plenty of examples like *Graf Spee* and *Bismarck*, he thought. But Leitner looked very much at ease, even theatrical with a pure white silk scarf tossed casually around his throat, his rear-admiral's cap set at a rakish angle.

Leitner remarked, 'The stage is set, eh?'

Hechler could picture his men throughout the ship, as he had when he had told them their mission. Theil as second-in-command was down in the damage-control section, as far from the bridge as possible. Not too many eggs in one basket, as his father would have said. Did he ever hope a shell might fall on the bridge and give him the command he craved so desperately?

'I assume the engine-room is warned for full revolutions?'

Hechler nodded. It was almost amusing if you knew Wolfgang Stück, the taciturn senior engineer. He had been like a midwife to the *Prinz*, had been with her within weeks of her keel being laid, had watched over every tube and wire, valve and pump until her birth, when she had slid confidently into salt water at Hamburg.

So many miles steamed, thousands of gallons of oil, and a million day-to-day details. Stück would need no reminding. They got along well, allowing for the unspannable gap between bridge and engine-room, he thought.

Leitner was saying, 'Looking back, it all seems worthwhile now. Remember breaking the ice on those buckets with your head aboard the training ship before you could wash in the morning, eh? It would make some of these mother's boys puke!' His eyes were almost dreamy. 'And the electric shock treatment to test your reaction under stress at Flensburg Naval Academy. I'll bet we know more than those old has-beens ever did!'

Hechler raised his glasses and studied the nearest destroyer.

'Signal the first subdivision to take station ahead.' He glanced at Leitner. '*Now.*'

A lamp clattered and Hechler saw a young signalman staring at the admiral with something like awe. He had probably never been so close to a god before.

Hechler asked sharply, 'What are those people doing here?'

Leitner smiled. '*My* orders, Captain.'

The camera team huddled by a flag-locker, the two women looking ill-at-ease in their steel helmets.

Leitner added smoothly, 'A record. We must all take risks in war.'

Hechler watched the camera being mounted, the way Leitner was adjusting his scarf. But he thought of the battered streets in Kiel, the faces of his men who had lost their relatives and their homes.

The flag-lieutenant hurried across the bridge and handed Leitner his signal pad.

He took his time while the camera purred into life and all eyes watched as the scene was recorded.

Hechler thought for an instant it was an act, but Leitner said briskly, 'The attack on the convoy was a success. The one escort carrier was hit by torpedoes. She is out of the fight.' He returned the pad to his aide. 'Two U-boats were destroyed, but they carried out their orders. Brave men, all of them.'

Hechler tried to shut him from his thoughts. Voice-pipes and telephones kept up their muted chatter and he saw the two forward turrets turn slightly, the four big guns lifting and lifting until they appeared to be trying to strain themselves from their mountings.

The first subdivision of destroyers were tearing ahead and heeling over in a great welter of spray as they formed into line abreast, well ahead of their big consorts. The others were on either beam, with one solitary vessel lifting and plunging across *Lübeck*'s wake as she followed like a spectator. To sniff out any submarine, to pick up survivors, to stay out of trouble.

Leitner had made his name in destroyers; he was probably remembering it right now.

Froebe, the executive officer, tall and ungainly, his huge hands gripped around his binoculars, stood in Gudegast's place by the gyro-repeater. The navigator and his small team were up there in the armoured conning-tower, waiting to plot every manoeuvre and change of course, to advise, to take command even, if the main bridge was demolished.

Hechler could feel the youngster Jaeger standing as close as he dared to the steel chair. His action station was here too, and unlike the other junior officers he was privileged to hear and see everything. He was also more likely to be hit if the Tommies got too near.

Hechler thought suddenly of their sister-ship the *Admiral Hipper*. She too had carried out a raiding cruise in the Atlantic, and after a successful attack on a convoy and other ships had returned in triumph to her Norwegian lair.

But that had been in 1941. Things were different now.

Hechler examined his feelings again. What were their chances? His ship was the best there was anywhere. If skill and audacity counted they stood every chance of success.

It was strange to realise that *Hipper*, powerful though she was, had been rammed and severely damaged by the little destroyer HMS *Glow-worm*. A brave, hopeless gesture which had cost her captain his ship and most of his men. He smiled to himself as he thought of Theil's expression when he had mentioned Nelson. It was exactly what the little admiral would have done had he lived in this century.

The flag-lieutenant returned with his pad and Leitner said quietly, 'The British are concentrating on the eastbound convoy, Dieter. Von Hanke is a shrewd old devil. They have a battleship and two heavy cruisers as a covering force, but well to the north as expected.'

Hechler put one hand in his pocket and felt the familiar shape of his favourite pipe. It was somehow comforting, and he would have dearly liked to smoke it. It reminded him of Inger again. She had wanted him to give it up, change to cigars. Like Leitner who usually appeared in press photographs with a jaunty cheroot, although he had never seen him actually smoking one. Just for the record.

He walked to the rear of the bridge and peered aft past the funnel. The new Arado looked bright and incongruous beside one of the camouflaged ones. Was she really going to fly it as Leitner had vaguely outlined? He never gave the whole story about anything. Again, that was exactly how he had been as a junior lieutenant. A touch of mystery. He thought of the photographs Leitner had shown him prior to weighing anchor. The fjord at Bodø, shot from several thousand metres up. Even the camouflaged nets had looked the same. It could have been *Prinz Luitpold* lying there. But Leitner had explained, two old supply ships had been preparing for weeks. After this sortie they would be moored together in such a way that any reconnaissance aircraft would imagine the *Prinz* had returned to her anchorage. It was so simple, it was almost ridiculous. But if it worked it might give them the extra hours they needed.

Ahlmann, the lieutenant in charge of bridge communications, handed him a telephone.

'Gunnery officer, sir.'

Even the telephone could not disguise the satisfaction in Kröll's voice.

'Enemy in sight, sir. Bearing Green one-oh. Range two-one-five.'

Hechler wanted to turn and look up at the fire control station. The unseen eye reached beyond the empty horizon so that Kröll could already watch the enemy formation at a range of over 21,000 metres.

Leitner jabbed his sleeve. 'I am going to my bridge.' He grinned. 'This is a great day!' He brushed past the bridge party and Jeager said, 'They are almost within range.'

Froebe watched him over the gyro-repeater and muttered, 'So will we be soon.'

Hechler raised his glasses and stared past the leading destroyers. Even their wakes were salmon-pink, their shining hulls like coloured glass.

Intelligence had reported a dozen merchantmen in the convoy. Probably twice that number had originally set out for Murmansk, he thought. Homeward bound, and with all the heavy support groups to the north of them waiting for an attack on the other precious array of supply ships. He listened to the regular ranges and bearings coming over the bridge gunnery intercom and pictured the two converging formations in his mind as he had studied it on the chart and had planned for such a moment. As Leitner had said, all that training was bearing fruit now. *Observation, method, conclusion, attack.*

The forward guns shifted slightly, the muzzles high-angled for the first salvo. Astern, *Lübeck*'s gun crews would be ready too, but they would have to be patient a while longer

He wanted to glance at his watch, but knew such a move might be mistaken for doubt, anxiety.

94

Above the whirr of fans and the surge of water against the hull he heard the dull thud of an explosion. Far away, like someone beating an old drum. Another torpedo hit, one more ship gone to the bottom. Leitner did not seem to care about the cost in U-boats. To him nothing mattered but this moment.

Ahlmann asked, 'Permission to open fire, sir?'

'Denied.' He pictured the convoy again. Liberty ships for the most part. It would be a fast one, probably about fifteen knots. They would scatter if they fired too soon. It would be harder, and there was always the covering force to consider. A battleship and two heavy cruisers.

'*Aircraft*, sir!' Several of the men gasped aloud. 'Red one-five! Angle of sight one-oh!'

Froebe said between his teeth, 'Torpedo bombers, for Christ's sake!'

Orders rattled out from every side and the short-range weapons swung instantly on to the bearing.

Hechler stood in the corner of the bridge and levelled his Zeiss glasses, surprised that he should feel so calm, almost detached.

Two aircraft, so they had to be from the crippled carrier. They must have been flown off just prior to their being torpedoed. He considered it, weighing it up. Each pilot would know he had no chance of returning to his ship.

Like the little *Glow-worm* all over again, the unexpected factor. It would be the worst kind of attack – bravery or cold-blooded suicide, you could take your pick.

One of the aircraft might even be radioing a sighting report. So much for radar.

The British senior officer must have outguessed von Hanke, or was it just luck?

He tightened his jaw. 'Short-range weapons stand by. Secondary armament –' his eyes watered in the powerful lens as he saw the two small dots heading towards the ships. They were so low now they appeared to be scudding across the water. He knew their outdated silhouettes well enough. Swordfish, twin-winged torpedo bombers, like relics from the Great War.

He cleared his mind and shouted, '*Open fire!*'

The line of destroyers were already firing and the sky soon became pockmarked with shell-bursts. It would be tracer and cannon-shell soon, and then –

Ahlmann said thickly, 'The Admiral, sir.'

Leitner sounded faraway. 'The convoy may scatter. Increase speed. Signal the group to engage the enemy as ordered.'

Hechler saw the signalmen bending on their flags and said, 'Full ahead. Prepare to take avoiding action.' He saw Froebe nod. Then he forgot him and the others as the power surged up through the bridge like something unleashed until the whole structure quivered around them.

He had to shout above the sharp bang of the secondary armament, which poured acrid fumes over the bridge as the ship swept forward, faster and still faster.

'Main armament. *Open fire!*'

He barely had time to adjust his ear plugs before both forward turrets blasted the air apart to fire upon the target which was still invisible, below the horizon.

He looked for the two aircraft and saw them weaving amongst the shell-bursts while bright tracer lifted from the destroyers and crossed their path in a fiery mesh. One of the Swordfish was trailing smoke and it seemed impossible that either of them could survive the barrage.

One thing was obvious. *Prinz Luitpold* was their target.

Chapter Seven

Aftermath

Neither of the Swordfish torpedo bombers stood any chance of survival, and each pilot must have known it. As they pounded past the line of destroyers, the one trailing smoke seemed to stagger as tracer and cannon-fire tore into it.

Hechler jammed his elbows below the screen and stared at the weaving silhouettes as pieces of the damaged plane splashed into the glistening swell. Seconds later it exploded in a vivid orange flash. When the smoke drifted clear there was nothing to be seen. But the second aircraft was dodging the flak, and even as he watched Hechler saw the torpedo drop from the plane's belly and make a small feather of spray as it hit the water.

The plane continued towards them, shell-bursts, tracer, everything which would bear hammering into it. Perhaps the pilot and crew were already dead, but the Swordfish rolled over and then dived into the sea with a dull explosion.

'Torpedo running to port!'

'Hard a-port!'

At thirty knots the cruiser seemed to lean right on her beam, men falling and clutching anything for support as she thundered round.

'*Steady*. Hold her!' Hechler thought he saw the thin thread of white as the torpedo streaked towards the port bow.

The ship was steadying up, and Froebe croaked, 'Two-eight-zero!'

Leitner's voice broke through the din, distorted and wild on his intercom.

'Signal *Hans Arnim* to –' He got no further. The destroyer received the torpedo halfway down her port side even as she dashed protectively between it and the flagship.

At full speed the effect was instantaneous and terrible. Half of the forecastle collapsed and then rose in the air as the ship broke in two, the thrust of her screws driving her on and down as they watched.

Hechler said, 'Bring her back on course.' From one corner of his eye he saw the *Lübeck* surging past to take the lead into battle. He could picture Rau laughing as he watched the *Prinz* reeling from the line in confusion. His guns suddenly opened fire, and moments later he saw the tell-tale flash-flash on the horizon to mark the fall of *Lübeck*'s salvo.

Gudegast's voice intruded from his armoured conning tower.

'On course, sir. Zero-two-zero.' He sounded calm, even disinterested, even though the destroyer was turning turtle in a welter of smoke and foam.

The intercom reported dully, '*Hans Arnim* has sunk, sir.'

Hechler snatched up the gunnery handset. 'This is the Captain. I am turning to starboard. Bring the after turrets to bear on the enemy!' They had a better chance with four turrets in action.

He said, 'Alter course. Steer Zero-seven-zero.'

He raised his glasses again and winced as the fire-gong preceded the violent crash of the main armament. Kröll was using each turret in sequence, so that the bombardment seemed unbroken and deafening.

Jaeger wiped a smokestain from his cheek and gasped, 'The Admiral, sir!'

Leitner strode across the bridge, his silk scarf no longer so white.

He snapped, 'Can't see a damned thing up there. Too much bloody smoke.' He gritted his teeth as the two after turrets fired, gun by gun, the great shells shrieking past the ship and lifting towards the unseen enemy. They sounded like express trains.

Leitner shaded his eyes to look for the destroyer. If there were any survivors they were left far astern, forgotten.

Hechler waited for the guns to shift slightly and asked, 'Can I signal *Lübeck* to take station again?' He grimaced as the guns thundered out once more, their long orange tongues showing that Kröll was using semi-armour-piercing shells.

The intercom shouted, '*Straddling!* Two hits!'

Leitner scowled. 'Get up there, Theissen! I want to know what we're hitting today!' He seemed to realise what Hechler had said. 'No. Let Rau have his fun. He can take the lead.'

Flash-flash. Flash-flash. The blink of gunfire, partly masked by a mist along the horizon. It looked like copper-coloured smoke. The screeching hiss of a falling salvo and then the tall waterspouts which betrayed the fall of the enemy's shells made every glass turn towards the *Lübeck*.

Leitner said, 'Not even a straddle.'

The intercom shouted again. 'Another hit!' Somebody sealed behind thick steel was actually cheering. Or going mad.

'Gunnery officer, sir.' The lieutenant named Ahlmann looked pale, and was biting his lower lip as another salvo screamed out of the sky and burst into towering columns of spray. They seemed to take an age to fall, as if they were solid.

'Captain?'

Kröll said between explosions, 'We've sunk a wing escort and have hit two merchantmen. One ship is leaving the convoy, range closing. I would say it's a cruiser by her size and speed.'

More waterspouts shot from the sea, changing from white to copper in the weird light.

Hechler stared at the *Lübeck*, which was almost stern-on, her turrets trained hard round to bear on the enemy. Where his own ship should be. The bridge quivered again and yet again and Hechler could feel the din of gunfire probing into his ears like hot wires.

'Enemy in sight, sir! Bearing Red four-five!' Hechler lifted his glasses and scanned the distant mist. No longer empty. A dull, blunt silhouette suddenly wreathed in smoke as her guns fired at extreme range.

Hechler did not lower his glasses. 'Tell the Gunnery Officer to concentrate on the cruiser.' The forward turrets fired instantly, but it was too far away to see the results.

He heard the gunnery intercom mutter, 'Short.' Then Kröll's voice. 'Four hundred metre bracket!' A pause. *'Fire!'*

'Straddling!'

Leitner clasped his hands together. 'Signal *Lübeck* to go for the convoy. We'll take care of this upstart!'

'Two hits!' The rest was drowned by a violent explosion and as Hechler twisted towards *Lübeck* he saw smoke and flame burst from below her bridge and spread upwards and outwards in a fiery scarlet mushroom.

Lübeck was altering course again, her forward guns firing and recoiling as she concentrated on the convoy as ordered.

The British cruiser had been hit too, but there was no let-up in her gunnery or its accuracy.

99

The next salvo straddled the *Lübeck* as if she was smashing through columns of ice, and another fire had broken out aft, the smoke trailing astern in an oily screen.

Hechler saw a boatswain's mate start with shock, his eyes glow like twin coals as the *Lübeck* received another direct hit. She was slowing down, her bow-wave dwindling.

The speaker intoned, 'A hit!'

Hechler tried to keep his glasses steady. It was as if they were all struck by some terrible fever. Nothing would hold still, only the guns which fired again and again until thought became impossible. He saw the glow of fires amidst the smoke and knew that the enemy too had been badly hit.

Kröll announced, 'Convoy's scattering, sir. Cruiser's disengaging.'

Leitner snapped, 'What about the other escorts?'

'Some destroyers, I think, sir.' He sounded guarded, aware that he was speaking with his admiral.

The first merchantmen were now in view, ungainly and pathetic as they tried to head away from the oncoming warships.

The damaged cruiser was standing off with two of the destroyers closing around her to take her in tow if need be, or to make a last stand against *Prinz Luitpold*.

'Shift target! *Open fire!*'

The merchantmen had no hope of survival. One by one they were straddled and set ablaze until smoke stretched across the horizon like a dense curtain.

'Cease firing.' Hechler glanced at the conning-tower, knowing that Gudegast would be watching the helpless merchantmen burn and die. Would be recalling his own life in a peaceful timber ship. There were others in his command who would see beyond the destruction, who would feel disgust as their mindless companions cheered and slapped one another on the back.

The enemy cruiser had been outgunned from the start, but it only took a lucky shell. That was different. But merchant ships were vital to the enemy, who knew that each convoy route had to be kept open, no matter at what cost.

Hechler said quietly, 'In my opinion we should return to Norway, sir.' He stood his ground as Leitner stared at him. '*Lübeck* is down by the head. Even under tow –'

Froebe called, 'Signal from *Lübeck. Unable to make more than six knots. Request assistance.'*

Hechler watched his admiral. That must have cost Rau a lot, he thought.

Leitner shrugged. 'Signal the senior officer, destroyers, to escort *Lübeck* back to base.' He watched the lamp stammering, the young signalman's face white as he shuttered off the signal. The aftermath of battle. A convoy destroyed; God alone knew how many had died in the twinkling of an eye, or so it seemed.

Lübeck's signal lamp flashed again, almost hidden by the dense smoke which billowed from her lower bridge. Through his glasses Hechler could see the splinter holes in her funnels, the great crater left by a direct hit. But the fires were under control.

'From *Lübeck*, sir. *I require a tow.'*

Leitner said, 'Has the destroyer leader acknowledged?' He sounded more impatient than concerned.

'Acknowledged, sir.'

'Very well.' Leitner seemed to take a long breath. 'Discontinue the action, Captain. Phase Two, *if* you please.'

He turned as the smoke-grimed camera crew emerged from where they had been hiding.

Leitner went to the prettier of the two girls and pinched her chin.

'Warm work, eh, my child?'

She stared after him, still too dazed to understand any of it.

'Fall out action stations.' Hechler picked up the damage control telephone. 'Viktor? This is the Captain. Come up, will you. We have disengaged.'

Gudegast already had his orders. He spoke on his own intercom. 'On new course and speed, sir. Revolutions for twenty knots.' It was all he said, or had to say.

Even the men who had appeared on deck as they were stood down from first-degree readiness must have felt it, like a sickness as their ship turned away from the others, the strange light playing into shadows through upperworks and guns, leaving her wake in a wide, crisp arc.

Rau would be watching. Cursing them and their ship, Leitner most of all. But he was too good a sailor to speak out even with a bitter signal as the sea opened up between them.

Left to the wolves. The British would be out for blood, and

every aircraft which could be flown from the nearest carrier would be after Rau's *Lübeck*. And he would know it. In the same way that the captain of the *Glow-worm* had known, or the pilots of the two elderly Swordfish. Death or glory. It was no choice.

Gudegast came to the bridge and waited for Hechler to see him.

Hechler said, 'In ten minutes I'll join you in the chart-room.'

Gudegast nodded, his beard on his chest. He knew what Hechler meant. In ten minutes *Lübeck* and the others would be too far astern to matter.

He watched Hechler's grave features and did not know whether to pity him or to thank God he was in command.

He had seen one of the merchantmen die. A big freighter, high out of the water, in ballast. That feeling. *Going home.*

Gudegast decided to make a sketch of the unknown victim.

For the first time in his life he was suddenly afraid.

That evening as *Prinz Luitpold* steamed south-west into the Norwegian Sea she was greeted by a thick mist which cut down the visibility to two miles.

All signs of the brief attack on the convoy were cleared away, and ammunition racks and magazines were refilled and ready for instant action.

Every turn of the great triple screws carried them further and further from land, paring away the safety margin should they have to turn and run for home again.

Hechler had to admit there was some value in Leitner's confidence. Every radio message and intercepted signal was checked and plotted by Gudegast and his team, while high above all of them their new, triumphant radar kept up a constant search for unwelcome visitors. A pack of U-boats had forced home an attack on the big eastbound Russian convoy, and every available British warship was apparently engaged. The flimsy plan might just work, he thought, and *Lübeck* would reach Norwegian waters where she could carry out her repairs. Hechler could not accept that part. It stuck in his throat like a bitter taste. To leave *Lübeck* to her fate had been part of the plan, but at no time had Leitner allowed for such a spirited defence of the convoy by the lone British cruiser.

When he had voiced his opinion to Leitner the admiral had given him a dry smile.

'*You*, Dieter, of all people? I thought you had the stomach for this mission!'

There was no point in pressing the argument. It was said that an open row between the captain of the *Bismarck* and his admiral had sealed her fate as much as enemy gunnery.

Hechler considered it. They had destroyed the convoy, just as the enemy had tried to finish them in return. It was war. He thought of the radar and was glad of it. Apart from its vast superiority over anything else they had used, its range meant that they had some warning of possible attack by sea or air forces. It meant that the company need not stand at action stations all day and night. They could sleep for four hours at a time off-watch. It was little enough, but they were used to it. To lie down, even for a few moments, made all the difference. Escape.

Despite the frantic manoeuvring to avoid the torpedo, there had been no damage in the ship, apart from some broken crockery in the main galley.

There had been plenty of minor injuries, two men scalded in the boiler-room when they had been hurled from their feet, another with a broken leg after pitching down a ladder to the deck, and several other casualties.

One of the latter was Erika Franke, who had suffered a severe sprain to her wrist.

The medical report had been handed to Hechler with all the other items from the various parts of the ship. It was customary for the doctor to report in person, but he had sent a brief message to say he had too many casualties. Nervousness at meeting him, or a kind of arrogance, Hechler did not know. Yet.

Theil joined him on the bridge, his coat glistening as if it had been raining. The mist was wet and made everything shine in the failing light.

Hechler said, 'We seem to be clear, Viktor.' He spoke quietly. The men on watch were obviously straining their ears. Perhaps this lull after the roar of gunfire seemed like an anti-climax, or intimated that they had the sea to themselves.

He looked up at the sky, at Leitner's flag curling damply above the ship. 'We shall stand-to tonight.'

Theil looked away. 'Do you still intend to run south of Iceland, sir?'

Hechler nodded. 'Unless we're challenged, yes. At this time of

103

year there's no advantage in taking the northern route through the Denmark Strait. Too much daylight, too many air patrols. If we head between Iceland and the Faeroe Islands it will give us 150 miles on either beam to play with.'

Theil grunted. 'Do you think we'll get through, sir?'

Hechler watched two seamen carrying an empty stretcher into the shelter of the forward turret. It made him think of the girl. Theil was right to question him; he would be required to execute Leitner's wishes should anything happen to him. He looked strained, anxious. He was not worried about their mission, it would be out of character. He was a book man, and rarely trusted personal opinion. Maybe that was why he had never been recommended for a command. No, he was worried about his missing wife. That was bad. You could not afford that kind of diversion when you were at sea. It could be fatal. For all of them.

Hechler listened to the steady vibration, felt the confident power of the great engines. They had been doing thirty knots when they had made their turn. She could manage thirty-five if need be. Even a destroyer would find her a difficult one to outpace.

It seemed to get darker as they hurried to the south-west, the night an ally, their only friend in this hostile sea.

Hechler tried to contain the excitement. It was like heady wine. After the stark pictures of battle and burning ships, the prospect of actually getting into the Atlantic seemed suddenly real and clean.

Theil saw the lines at Hechler's mouth soften and wondered how he would have felt in his place.

Like all the senior officers in the ship Theil had studied their orders with great care. The plan was marked both by its audacity, and its very scale. The naval staff under von Hanke must have been working on it for many months just in case the chance presented itself. Perhaps too many people were already involved? Secrecy was vital; without it they might as well give up now.

Von Hanke's son was a U-boat commander, or had been until he had been lost in the Atlantic. Maybe he had first given the old admiral the idea. For two years at the beginning of the war, U-boats had been hampered by the length of time it took them to reach their patrol areas in the Western Ocean, with the same delay in returning to bases in France to refuel and rearm.

To counteract this a building programme had started to produce a flotilla of huge submarines which could stay at sea for
months. Their sole duty was to carry fuel and stores for their
smaller, operational consorts. In prearranged positions on a
specially charted grid, a rendezvous could be made or rejected
according to the needs of each U-boat commander. It more than
trebled their time at sea, and the enemy's losses had mounted
accordingly. Nobody ever mentioned what this extra time on
active service did to the morale of the submarine crews.

Now, these same supply submarines, milch-cows, were to be
employed as tankers for the *Prinz*. Daring it certainly was. Practical? Nobody knew, as it had never been done before.

None of the others had voiced any doubts, and after today they
might be glad they had not shown any lack of confidence. Once
again the ship had come through unscathed. It was a pity about
the *Lübeck*, but if it had your number on it, there was not much
you could do. *Lübeck* had got off lightly, Theil thought. While
she was in port, licking her wounds and enjoying all the glory, the
Prinz would be in the Atlantic, in the thick of it. It was some
comfort to know that a pin's head laid on a chart of the Western
Ocean represented as far as a man could see in any direction.

Hechler said suddenly, 'I was sorry to hear about your wife.'

Theil stared at him and then at the nearest of the watchkeepers.
He lowered his voice. 'The admiral?'

'He had to tell me, Viktor. I would have been informed anyway
if Leitner was not aboard. What's the matter, did you think I'd see
you as a lesser man?'

Theil felt the colour draining from his face. 'It makes no difference to my ability. None whatever, and anyone –'

Hechler slid from his chair and moved his legs to get rid of the
stiffness.

'I'm going to the sick-bay while it's quiet. Take over.' He eyed
him calmly. 'Shake the load off your back, Viktor. I just wanted
you to know that I am concerned for you, not your bloody
ability!'

Theil was still staring after him as he clattered down the
internal ladder.

It felt strange, wrong to be off the bridge while the ship was
at sea. Hechler saw the surprise on the faces of his men when
he passed them while he made his way down two decks to the

sick-bay. As a boy he had always hated hospitals, mostly because he had had to visit his gassed father in one; that was when they had promised there was still a good chance of a cure.

His poor mother, he thought, facing up to those daily visits, passing all the other veterans. No legs, no arms, gassed, blinded, some would have been better off lying in the mud of Flanders.

And always the bright cheerfulness of the nurses. *Coming along nicely. As well as can be expected.* It had all been lies.

He wondered how his father was managing now. He would soon be reading about the *Prinz* and their exploits.

His father, so sick but quietly determined to stay alive, was beyond pride. Love would be a better word, he thought.

The sick-quarters were white and brightly lit. Two medical attendants were putting bottles into shelves, and there was a lot of broken glass in a bucket. The same violent turn had done damage here too.

Some of the injured men were dozing in their cots, and one tried to sit to attention when he saw his captain enter, his plastered arm sticking straight out like a white tusk.

Hechler removed his cap and forced a grin.

'Easy there. Rest while you can, eh?'

The new doctor was not at all as he had expected. He was forty years old but looked much older. He had a heavy, studious face with gold-rimmed glasses. A lawyer, or a school teacher, you might think if you saw him as a civilian.

He made to stand but Hechler closed the door of the sick-bay and sat down. Then he pulled out his pipe and said, 'Is this all right?'

Karl-Heinz Stroheim watched him warily, one hand plucking at the three gold stripes with the Rod of Aesculapius on his sleeve.

He said, 'I have dealt with all the casualties, Captain.'

Hechler lit his pipe. A good feeling, almost sensuous, after being deprived on the bridge.

'I thought we should meet, so –' He blew out some smoke. 'So, Mohammet and the Mountain, you see?'

'I'm honoured.'

'You'll find this a different appointment from your last. The barracks at Wilhelmshaven, right?'

The man nodded. 'Before that, well, you know about it too.'

'You were in trouble.'

A flash of anger came and went in Stroheim's brown eyes. 'I

106

was too valuable to be thrown out. They put me in uniform instead.'

'No disgrace in that.' Hechler tried not to listen to the engines' beat. So much closer here.

He asked casually, 'Abortions, wasn't it?'

Stroheim's jaw dropped. 'How did you know?'

'I didn't. I guessed.' He smiled gravely. 'And I shall put down your lack of respect to the suddenness of your appointment, right?'

Stroheim thrust his hands beneath the table. 'I – I am sorry, Captain. I went through a lot. One day they will accept my views. Too late for many, I fear. But I have always believed –' he hesitated, as if he expected. Hechler to stop or reprimand him – 'a woman must have the right to choose.' His voice was suddenly bitter, contemptuous. 'There should be a better reason for having a child than producing soldiers and more mothers for Germany.'

Hechler stood up, his eyes on a bulkhead telephone. 'We'll talk again.'

Stroheim got to his feet. 'I'd enjoy that.'

Hechler glanced round the little office. A pile of records and a portable gramophone, some books, and a box of chessmen.

Hechler said, 'Don't make this too much like home. Mix with the others. It's not good to be cut off.'

Stroheim took off his glasses and held them to the light.

'Like you, do you mean, Captain?'

Hechler turned away. 'I don't need a consultation just now, thank you!'

He paused by the door. 'Take good care of my men. *They* did not ask to be here, so you see, they are like you, eh?'

He made to leave and almost collided with Erika Franke, her left hand bandaged and in a sling.

She gave a wry smile. 'Next time you change direction, Captain, please let me know. I need both hands for flying, you know!'

He looked past her at the doctor. 'I was sorry to hear of your injury.'

She laughed. It was the first time he had seen her really laugh.

He said, 'Can I see you to your quarters?'

She became serious, and gave him a mock scowl.

'So correct, so proper, Captain.' She relented. 'I shall walk with you. I find the ladders a bit difficult at the moment.'

107

They reached the upper deck, the passageway in shadows, the steel doors clipped shut.

She said, 'I would like to visit the bridge again. I hate being shut away down here. I feel trapped.'

'Any time.' He watched her, the way she moved her head, the colour of her eyes. He had hoped to see her. The doctor had been an excuse.

A messenger skidded to a halt and saluted. 'There is a message from the bridge, Captain.'

Hechler strode to a handset which was clipped to the grey steel and cranked the handle.

He heard Theil's voice, the muted sound of the sea and wind.

Theil said in a hushed voice, 'The admiral had a signal, sir. *Lübeck* was sunk.'

Hechler replaced the handset very slowly.

She watched him, her eyes concerned. 'May I ask, Captain?'

He looked at her emptily. '*Lübeck's* gone.'

He could see it as if he was there. As if it was now.

She said quietly, 'You didn't want to leave her, did you?' She saw the question in the brightness of his blue eyes.

She shrugged and winced; she had forgotten her injury. 'I was told. Everyone knew. They're very fond of their young captain, you know.'

He rested his hand on one of the door-clips. 'There are no secrets in a ship, no matter what they say.' He faced her again. 'Yes, I wanted to stay with her. Now she's gone.' He thought of the burning convoy.

They had had their revenge. He touched the girl's sound arm. 'Later, then.'

He opened the heavy door and stepped out into the damp air. *Lübeck* had been sacrificed. He quickened his pace to the first ladder, oblivious of the watchful gun crews.

It must not have been in vain.

Chapter Eight

Flotsam

The South African naval base of Simonstown was packed to capacity with warships of every class and size. It was like a melting-pot, a division between two kinds of war made more apparent by the vessels themselves and their livery. The darker hues of grey and garish dazzle paint of the Atlantic, at odds with the paler hulls of ships from the Indian Ocean and beyond.

Powerful cruisers which had the capacity and range to cover the vast distances beyond the Cape of Good Hope seemed to make the greater contrast with a cluster of stubby Canadian corvettes which had fought their convoy all the way from Newfoundland.

Freighters and oilers, ammunition vessels and troopers. There was even a cleanly painted hospital ship.

The largest cruiser in Simonstown on this particular afternoon lay alongside the jetty, her White Ensign hanging limply in the harsh sunlight.

She was HMS *Wiltshire*, a big, 10,000-ton vessel, typical of a class which had been constructed in accordance with the Washington Treaty in the late twenties. She was heavily armed with eight, eight-inch guns in four turrets, with many smaller weapons to back up her authority. An elderly Walrus flying-boat perched sedately on the catapult amidships, and her three tall funnels gave the ship a deceptively outdated appearance. She stood very high from the oily water, and because of her comparatively light armour plating her living quarters were both airy and spacious when compared with other men-of-war.

It was Sunday, and apart from duty watch and men under punishment *Wiltshire* was deserted. Officers and ratings alike took every opportunity to get ashore, to visit Cape Town and enjoy the colourful sights, untouched by war.

In his day cabin Captain James Cook Hemrose, Distinguished Service Order, Royal Navy, sat beneath a deckhead fan and regarded his pink gin while he wondered if it was prudent to take another. On one chair lay his best cap which he had worn for Divisions and prayers that morning. Beside another stood his golf clubs, a reminder of the match he had had to cancel.

He was a heavy man, and in his white shirt and Bermuda shorts looked ungainly. There were dark patches of sweat at each armpit despite the fans and he hated the oppressive heat.

He was in his late forties, but service life had been hard on him. He looked older, much older, and what was worse, he felt it.

The door opened and the ship's commander entered quietly.

Hemrose gestured heavily to the sideboard. 'Have a pink Plymouth, Toby. Do you good.'

The commander looked at the signals on the table and said, 'It's all true then, sir?'

'Pour me one while you're at it. Not too much bitters.'

The commander smiled. As if he did not know his ways. He had been with him over a year. The Atlantic, convoys round the Cape, Ceylon, India. It suited the commander. Routine, and often boring. But you could keep the Atlantic and Arctic runs. Let the glory boys do them if that was the war they wanted.

'Yes, it's true.' Hemrose's eyes were distant. 'The Jerries have put one of their big cruisers to sea. They think it might be *Prinz Luitpold*.' His eyes hardened into focus. 'I hope to God it is.'

The commander sipped his gin. Just right. 'She won't get down here. Not at this stage of the war.' When Hemrose remained silent he added, 'I mean, it's just not on, sir.'

Hemrose sighed. The commander, Toby Godson, was a well-meaning fool. He ran a smart ship, and that was enough. Until the signal had arrived anyway.

Hemrose recalled his excitement, although he would die rather than display it. The war might indeed end soon, maybe even next year. Being captain of a big cruiser, a ship well known as any of her class, was some compensation. But he had seen himself, still in command when the war ended. Then what? Passed over for promotion again, or merely chucked on the beach like his father before him.

They had some saying about it. 'God and the Navy we adore, when danger threatens, but not before!'

He looked at the lengthy signal from the far-off Admiralty. As from today he was promoted to acting commodore, to take upon himself the command of a small squadron. To take all necessary steps to seek out and engage the German raider should she manage to penetrate the defences and come to the South Atlantic.

It was unlikely, as Godson had said. But it had given him a well-needed boost. *Acting commodore,* a temporary appointment at the best of times. But it was his chance. The all-important step to flag-rank. It was not unknown in this war. Harwood, who had commanded the little squadron which had run the raider *Graf Spee* to earth, had made flag-rank immediately afterwards. It was something to think about.

One of his new squadron was already here in Simonstown. She was the small Leander class cruiser *Pallas* of the Royal New Zealand Navy. She looked like a destroyer compared with the *Wiltshire,* but her captain and her ship's company were well trained, and had been together since she had commissioned.

He heaved himself up and walked to one of the scuttles, one which faced away from the glare.

He thought vaguely of his home in Hampshire. His wife Beryl would be pleased when she heard. There were too many naval officers' wives who lived in the county whose husbands seemed to have been promoted ahead of him.

Acting commodore. He nodded. It sounded good. Old world; he liked that. He was distantly related to Captain James Cook and was proud of it, although it did not seem to have helped him over the years.

The commander asked carefully, 'I'd forgotten, sir. You crossed swords with *Prinz Luitpold* before. North Cape, wasn't it?'

'*I* don't forget.' He stared through the scuttle. Two sailors in a dinghy were calling up to some black girls on the jetty. A bit of black velvet, as his father would have said.

The commander ignored the warning signs. 'They say that Rear-Admiral Leitner's in command.'

Hemrose glowered. 'I don't give a bloody damn about *him*. Her captain's the man – Hechler. He was in command at North Cape, when –'

The commander said, 'She's a miniature battle-cruiser, sir. Makes our armour plate look like cardboard.'

Hemrose ignored him. 'Came out of the snow like a cliff. It was gun-for-gun.' He looked around the pleasant cabin, remembering it as it had been. 'This place was riddled, like a bloody pepper pot.'

The commander had lost his way. 'She made off anyway, sir.'

'Aye, she did that. Just as well. It was a right cock-up, I can tell you.' He saw the sailors paddling away. They had probably seen him looking at them. 'I hope it *is* Hechler in command. I'll get him this time.' He gave a rueful grin. 'Now he's like I was at North Cape.'

'How so, sir?'

Hemrose laughed out loud. 'He's got his fucking admiral breathing down his neck, that's why!'

The commander downed his gin. He was used to the captain's coarse speech and blunt manner. Perhaps his temporary promotion would mellow him. But it could not last. The fleet would catch the German raider before they got a look-in.

Hemrose rubbed his hands. 'Recall all the senior officers. I want 'em aboard by the dog watches.' He eyed his golf clubs. 'See how *they* like it.'

The commander nodded. 'I see –'

'You don't, Toby.' He became grave. 'I meant what I said. For the first time in my life their bloody lordships have given me a free hand, and by God I intend to use it.' He clapped him on the shoulder. 'Make a signal to *Pallas*. Captain repair on board.'

Godson said unhappily, 'He's playing cricket with the South Africans, sir.'

Hemrose beamed. 'Good. I want us out of harbour by this time tomorrow and I'll need you to form your own team to monitor all despatches and signals. Every damn thing.' He slammed his fist into his palm. 'So get that Kiwi aboard, *chop, chop!*' He bustled to the sideboard and groped for some ice, but it had all melted. He slopped another large gin into his glass.

'*Lübeck*'s gone to the bottom anyway. That's one less. Scuttled herself when our lot were almost up to her.' He frowned. 'I wonder if Hechler knows?' He turned. 'Somehow I doubt it.'

But he was alone.

Kapitän zur See Dieter Hechler closed the conning-tower's steel door and pushed through the fireproof curtain.

Outside it was dusk, but in here it was like night, with only the chart-table lights and automatic pilot casting any glow on the thick armour plate.

Hechler could sense the tension as well as the controlled excite-

112

ment. Gudegast was leaning on the vibrating table, his face in shadow, only his beard holding the light. His team stood around him, boys most of them, in various attitudes of attention as Hechler joined them.

Hechler looked at the chart, the neat calculations and pencilled fixes. Then at the plot-table which told him all the rest. Course, and speed, time and distance, variations, fed in by a dozen repeaters from radar, gyro and log.

'We're through.'

Gudegast nodded. Then he pointed his dividers to the chart where the course had crossed the Iceland-Faeroe Rise, where the seabed rose inexplicably like a hump. To U-boats and blockade-runners alike it was known as the *meat grinder*. Not a good place for a submarine to run deep to avoid a depth-charge attack, and no scope for a surface vessel to manoeuvre.

And yet they had made it. This great ship had passed through the 300-mile gap without opposition. Not a ship, not even a distant aircraft had been sighted.

Luck, a miracle, or a direct result of von Hanke's decoy, it was impossible to tell.

The curtain swirled aside again and Leitner strode in with his aide behind him.

He stared unwinking at the chart and said, 'We did it. As planned.'

He looked at the darkened figures round him. 'Two days since the convoy, and now we are here!' He slapped the chart with unusual fervour. 'The Atlantic, gentlemen! They said it could not be done!'

Some of the men were shaking hands and grinning at each other; only Gudegast remained unmoved and grim-faced.

He said, 'I should like to alter course in fifteen minutes, sir.'

Hechler nodded. 'I shall come up.'

A seaman called, 'From the bridge, sir.' He held out the telephone.

Hechler shook himself. Fatigue or anxiety, which was it? He had not heard it ring.

It was Froebe, who was in charge of the watch.

'Radar has reported a faint echo at Red one-oh, sir. About five miles.'

That was close. Too close. Hechler calmed himself. 'What is it, man?'

He could picture Froebe shrugging his gaunt shoulders. 'Very small, sir, barely registers.' Someone shouted in the background. 'It will be dark very soon.'

Hechler said, 'Alter course to intercept.' He felt Gudegast brush past him to adjust the chart.

Leitner muttered, 'Something small, eh? God damn them, it might have been a submarine's conning-tower. At five miles anything might happen!' Another flaw. The unseen observer.

Froebe spoke again, relieved. 'We've identified it, sir. It's a boat.'

Hechler hurried from the conning tower, not caring if Leitner was in agreement or not.

On the main bridge it was quite cold, and the clouds had thickened considerably.

He raised his glasses and felt the deck tilt very slightly as the helm went over.

Then he saw it and felt his taut muscles relax. There would be no attack from this lonely boat. It was a common enough sight on the Atlantic, but new to most of his company, he thought.

Theil had arrived on the bridge, panting hard as he snatched some binoculars from a messenger.

He said, 'A boat full of corpses.' He sounded angry, as if the drifting boat had wronged him in some way.

Hechler watched the boat. Would their journey ever end, he wondered?

'Slow ahead, all engines.'

Theil was peering at him with disbelief. 'You're not going to stop?'

Hechler said, 'Boatswain's mate, call away the accident boat.'

The boat would automatically have an experienced petty officer in charge. He glanced at young Jaeger. 'You go. Keep your wits about you.'

Theil said between his teeth, 'In the name of God, sir, we're a sitting target.'

Hechler said quietly, 'Keep your voice down, Viktor.' He gripped his glasses more tightly. A trick of the fading light, or had he seen a movement amongst the silent, patient figures in the listing boat?

'Stop engines!' He hurried to the side as the motorboat hit the water and veered away on the dying bow-wave. Jaeger had only just clawed his way aboard in time.

He remarked, 'Someone's alive out there.' When Theil said

nothing he added coldly, 'Would you have me fire on the boat?'
He raised his glasses once more, sensing the rift between them. He
saw the motorboat speeding across the swell, Jaeger looking
astern at the cruiser and probably wondering what would happen
if there was an attack.

He knew Leitner was beside him, could smell his cologne. But
he kept his eyes on the little drama as the motorboat hooked on
and Jaeger with a petty officer scrambled over the gunwale. The
petty officer was old Tripz. He was used to this kind of work. He
saw Jaeger lean on the gunwale with a handkerchief to his mouth.
Jaeger was not.

A signalman lowered his glasses. 'Two alive, sir.'

'Call the sick-bay.'

More feet on the ladder and he heard her thank a seaman for
helping her through the gate. She was wearing her black leather
jacket again, her hair ruffling in the breeze.

Theil moved aside so that she could stand between Hechler and
the admiral.

How huge the ship looked as the long forecastle lifted and then
fell again very slowly, the motion increasing as the last of the way
went off the hull.

She asked, 'Just two?'

Hechler nodded. She was probably thinking of its futility.
*Ships sunk and men killed, two aircraft shot down, and we
stop because of these living dead.* The unwritten law of the sea
perhaps? Or to make up for those they had already left to die.

He saw her right hand grip the rail beneath the screen so tightly
that her knuckles were white through the tanned skin.

When he glanced at her he saw moisture in her eyes, or were
they tears?

Leitner remarked, 'Flotsam of war, my dear.'

She said huskily, 'My –' She tried again. 'I knew somebody
who died at sea.'

Hechler glanced down at her. She looked sick. The motion was
getting worse as the *Prinz* rose and dipped like a huge juggernaut.

'Sit in the chair.' He took her elbow. 'Take some deep breaths.'
Then, so that the others should not hear he added quietly, 'Stay in
the air, little bird. The ocean can be a dirty place.'

He glanced across her head. 'Take over. I'm going to the sick-
bay.'

115

Someone yelled, 'Boat's hooked on, sir!'

The motorboat rose swiftly on its falls, and Froebe asked, 'The lifeboat, Captain? Shall I have a shot put into it?'

'No.' He raised his glasses once more and knew she had turned in the chair to watch him. 'They have found their harbour. Leave them alone.'

A great tremor ran through the deck and he felt the men sighing with relief as the great screws began to beat out their track of white froth again.

Leitner called sharply, 'Find out what you can, eh?'

Hechler ran down the first ladder and paused, gripping it with both fists.

What is the matter with me? Is it that important?

He found Jaeger and Petty Officer Tripz already outside the sick-bay.

'All right?'

Jaeger made an effort, but he looked ghastly.

'All the rest were dead, sir.' He was reliving it. 'Bobbing about together as if they were really alive. The gulls had got to some of them –' he retched and old Tripz said, 'Easy, sir. You'll get used to it.'

Jaeger shook himself. 'We brought two of them aboard.' He stared at the deck for a long moment until he could continue. 'One of them is an officer. The other –' he shook violently. 'He wouldn't leave without the cat.'

'Cat?'

Tripz said, 'The animal was dead, sir. We left it in the boat.' He looked despairingly at the young officer. 'Must have been adrift for weeks.'

Hechler said, 'You did well.' He gave Tripz a meaning glance. 'Both of you, go to my steward. He'll give you something to warm you up.'

Tripz gave a sad grin. 'It was worth it then, sir.'

The doctor was wiping his hands on a towel, and Hechler saw that both blanket-wrapped survivors were lying in bunks inside the office and away from the injured sailors.

An armed seaman stood outside but it seemed unlikely their passengers would create any problems.

One, the young officer with two tarnished stripes on his sleeve, was conscious, but only just. Hollow-eyed and filthy,

116

he was staring at the white deckhead with shock and disbelief.

The other man was much older with a white beard. Perhaps he had already seen and done too much when his ship had been blasted from under him. He had his arms wrapped into a cradle, as he had been when Jaeger had found him, clutching the ship's cat to his body to protect it.

The doctor said, 'I've given them something, Captain. They'll sleep. I shall get them some hot soup later on.' He nodded to the pathetic belongings on the glass table. 'They were aboard the *Radnor Star*, a freighter.'

The officer was probably the second mate. He was too young for much else, Hechler thought. In charge of a lifeboat, perhaps the only officer to get away when the torpedo struck. Watching them die, one by one, until he was alone but for the old man with his dead cat. Some last thread of discipline had made him hold on. He had been in charge. What else could he have done?

The doctor took off his glasses and polished them as he had done at their first meeting.

He said, 'So this is the Atlantic, the *killing ground* they warned me about?'

Hechler looked at him. 'Don't be clever with me, Doctor!' He jerked open the door as the sentry snapped to attention. 'Report when they recover enough to speak.'

He waited outside, breathing hard, angry with the doctor, more so with himself for dropping the guard he had built up so carefully. When he reached the bridge he was greeted in silence. He looked for the drifting lifeboat but it had already disappeared into the darkness astern.

He walked to the gratings, and with a start realised she was still sitting in the tall chair, wrapped about with somebody's heavy watchcoat.

She did not say anything and he was grateful. He saw Jaeger return to his place on the bridge, the way Gudegast moved across to pat his arm. That would mean more than anything to Jaeger just now. He was accepted. One of them.

And what of me? The captain without a heart? Do they imagine I have no feelings?

He stared down with surprise as she placed her hand on his wrist. She did not move it or grip with it. It lay there, separate, as if to listen.

117

She said quietly, 'I am here, Captain. I shared it with you. I saw it through your eyes.'

Hechler looked at her neat hand and wanted to seize it, press it against himself. She had understood, as if he had shouted aloud.

He said, 'I would like to talk –' He felt her hand move away very slightly. 'Later, afterwards –' He was lost for the right words.

She said. 'Afterwards may not be ours, Captain.' She slid from the chair and handed the coat to a seaman with a quick smile. Then she melted into the shadows and he heard one of his men assisting her on the ladder.

He touched the chair; it was still warm from her body. He climbed into it and wedged his feet against the voice-pipes.

She would probably laugh in his face if he even laid a hand on her. What about the man who had been lost at sea? She had nearly said something else. 'My lover' perhaps?

Afterwards may not be ours. Her words seemed to linger in his mind. His head lolled and he was instantly asleep.

The *Prinz Luitpold*'s petty officers' mess was in complete darkness apart from shaded blue lamps and one light above one of the tables. A different story from an hour before when the men off watch had been watching a film in the other part of the mess, one of the luxuries which went with their status. The film had been a noisy display of German armed strength, backed up between the excited commentary by rousing music from *Tannhäuser.*

The air had been electric, and had remained so since the intercom announcement from the bridge that they were forging deeper and deeper into the Atlantic, unchallenged as they were unbeaten.

Hans Stoecker sat in the pool of light, sipping a mug of bitter coffee, restless, unwilling to sleep although he had only just come off watch.

Opposite him, his grey head nodding in a doze, was old Oskar Tripz. His chin was covered in grey stubble so that he looked almost ancient.

His eyes opened and he stared at Stoecker, his gaze searching. Trying to discover something, to make up his mind.

'Why don't you turn in?' Tripz sniffed at the coffee and shuddered. 'What do they make this muck from – acorns?'

A dark shape shrouded in blankets called irritably, 'Hold your noise! Think of the watchkeepers!'

118

Tripz grinned. In harbour the mess housed a hundred petty officers, the backbone of the ship, as of any other. Now, with many of them on watch it seemed quiet, deserted by comparison.

Stoecker lowered his voice. 'I keep thinking about *Lübeck*.'

'You're always thinking about something. You should keep your mind on your exams. Do you more good. Let the bloody officers think. It's what they're paid for.'

Stoecker persisted, 'I mean, *Lübeck* should have been with us surely? Together we'd have made a stronger force.'

'Easier to find too.' Tripz rubbed his chin with a rasping motion. 'I reckon she was meant to return to base.'

Stoecker stared at him. 'We wouldn't just leave her!'

Tripz shrugged. 'Who knows anything any more? They'd sell their mothers for a bit of glory.'

'You don't mean that.'

Tripz became impatient. 'I've got more important things on my mind at present.' He leaned across the table until their faces were only a foot apart. 'Those boxes, for instance.'

They both glanced along the silent bunks like conspirators, then Stoecker asked, 'Do you know what's in them?'

'It's all in that letter. If half of it's true, and I see no reason why that prisoner should lie about it, our gallant admiral is carrying a bloody fortune with him, though I can't imagine why.'

Stoecker blinked. 'What kind of fortune, I – I mean, how much?'

The man watched him grimly. 'Do you know how much the *Prinz* cost to build?'

Stoecker smiled. 'You're joking –'

Tripz tapped his arm with a thick finger. 'You could build three ships like this one with what he's got tucked away.' He dropped his voice again to a hoarse whisper. '*If* that letter tells the truth.'

Stoecker thought of the man's face in the air vent, his despair. He often thought about it, also the man's quiet courage in the shadow of death. *Murder*. The word was fixed in his mind.

Tripz seemed satisfied with the young man's acceptance; he had never doubted his sincerity.

He said, 'It seems that the prisoner was writing to some friends. To warn them that the boxes were being moved.'

Stoecker recalled the burnt-out shop, the crude insults.

Tripz continued, 'His friends were Jewish, right enough. One of them was a jeweller. Probably why he was still at large.' He dropped his eyes. 'Or was.'

'I still don't understand.'

Tripz's gaze softened. 'You wouldn't, Hans.' He hurried on. 'All I do know is that we're probably carrying a bloody great fortune. If so, my guess is that Rear-Admiral Leitner's no more entitled to it than we are.' He changed tack before Stoecker could speak. 'What will you do when this lot's over, Hans? Always assuming you're still in one lump, of course?'

Stoecker hesitated. 'The navy. A career, I thought –'

The finger jabbed his arm again. 'Suppose we lose? D'you ever think about that?' He did not wait for an answer. 'Me? I'll be good for nothing, no matter who wins. I saw it after the last war. You couldn't even sell your bloody medals for a crust of bread. No, peace will be hard, even for the kids.' He shook his head. 'They'll toss me out like so much waste.'

Stoecker felt vaguely uneasy. 'Anyway, we'll probably never know. The boxes are locked away, under guard.'

'I know. The admiral's got one key, the captain's got the other.' He tapped the side of his nose. 'But there's a duplicate, my young friend.' He saw his astonishment and grinned, showing his uneven teeth. 'You've caught on. It's mine.'

A figure, naked but for a lifejacket, lurched past on the way to the heads.

Tripz stood up. 'Say nothing, or we'll both end up on the wrong side of a firing-squad. And that would be a pity, eh?' He leaned over and patted his shoulder. 'Thought you should know. In case I stop a bit of the Tommies' steel. After all, we're partners, right?'

He walked away, leaving Stoecker alone beneath the solitary light.

The *Prinz Luitpold*'s senior medical officer looked up from his book and saw the girl standing in the open door.

'Can't you sleep either?'

She walked to a chair and glanced at the two motionless survivors, swaying gently in their white cots.

'My wrist. It's bothering me. If I lie on it –'

He took her hand and reached out for some scissors. The girl was very attractive. It was hard to think of her as the professional

120

flier, as good as any Luftwaffe ace, they said. It seemed wrong that she should be here, in this iron machine.

'You're new aboard the ship?' She had a direct way of asking. As if she was telling him.

He looked at her. She seemed strained, and there were shadows under her tawny eyes.

'I am. Lost amongst strangers.' It seemed to amuse him.

She said, 'Call me Erika. If you like.'

He cut the last of the bandage. 'I do like.'

Her skin felt hot, feverish. He remembered all those other women. The scandal which had almost got him into prison, a ruined man. But the women who came to him 'in trouble' were people of influence, or those who had powerful friends. Curious that such power could be smashed because of an unwanted baby, he thought.

Like the captain's wife, for instance. Well-bred from an old family, she was always in the centre of society, that jungle which was safe only for the privileged few. It was strange how the high party members, *men of the people* as they liked to be known, were so in awe of women like her.

He wondered if the captain really knew what she was like. One of his colleagues had once described her as a thoroughly delectable whore. That doctor had been indiscreet in other ways too. Then one day he had simply disappeared.

He said, 'It is a bit stiff, er, Erika.'

She watched him, unsmiling. 'I have to fly in a day or so.'

'It will be all right by then.' What were they thinking of? Flying? They would meet up with the enemy at any time now. The British would not give up until they had brought them to action.

She glanced at the gramophone and the pile of well-used records. She raised her eyebrows. 'Handel? You surprise me. Is it patriotic?'

She smiled then, at some private joke perhaps.

'I like it.'

'You always do what you like?'

'I try to.' He looked at her, and tried not to think of her on his examination couch, naked.

She said, 'I wanted to talk. I knew you would still be awake. It's not like a ship down here.'

He chuckled. 'I suppose not. I shall attempt to keep it that way.'

'I was with the Captain when these survivors were brought aboard.'

He said nothing and waited. So that was it. There was certainly nothing wrong with her wrist which could not wait until daylight.

She said, 'He is different from what I expected.'

'An enigma perhaps?'

She smiled at him. 'You are leading me.' She added, 'He seems to care so much about people. How can he do his work?'

Stroheim spread his hands. 'Perhaps it is tearing him apart. I do not know him that well. Yet.'

'But you know his wife, don't you?'

He started. 'How do you hear these things?'

'A friend told me.' She had been going to say *a little bird told me*. But at that instant she remembered his face, the concern in his voice as he had said so quietly to her, 'Stay in the air, little bird.' To use the expression loosely would seem like a betrayal, like sharing a secret.

Stroheim said vaguely, 'She is very beautiful.'

'I met her.' She thought of the other woman's searching stare, her arrogance giving way to caution when she realised who Erika was. Because she was a flier and had carried out a mission for the Führer, people often thought she too had influence. Yes, she recalled that stare, her perfect body, so carelessly displayed in the cutaway gown. Try as she might, she could not see her and the Captain together. Maybe they had both changed.

'Well, you know what she's like.'

'Are they still married, or anything?'

He warmed to her. '*Anything* would be closer, I believe.'

She opened and closed her left hand, her face expressionless as she tested the pain, the discomfort.

Stay in the air, little bird.

'I'll say goodnight then.' She looked at the two sleeping figures. Flotsam, Leitner had called them. 'Or, good morning now, I believe?'

He watched her leave and then reopened his book.

Every so often, even in the midst of danger and death there was one small light. Like a flower in a forest, a lone star.

He sighed and crossed his legs. She had made him feel human again.

Chapter Nine

Viewpoint

Apart from the regular swell the sea's face was like glass, blinding bright in the sunshine. There was a fine haze which never seemed to get any closer, so that there was no break between sea and sky. For the Atlantic it was unusual, even this far south.

The two ships stood close together as if for support, which was true, and at a greatly reduced speed appeared to be almost motionless above their quivering reflections.

The SS *Port St Clair*, a freighter of some 8,000 tons outward bound from Sierra Leone, had the second vessel in tow. It was a slow, painful passage, with the other ship yawing out clumsily until she seemed to be overtaking, before veering back again with all the maddening alterations of course and speed until they were under command once more.

The first mate of the leading ship watched his captain, who was standing out on the bridge wing, staring astern at their companion. It was almost funny, when you thought about it. Both the captains were rivals of many years, and yet that same rivalry seemed to join them more persistently than any tow-line.

The other ship, the SS *Dunedin Pioneer,* had joined the convoy with them at Freetown, but after a few days had broken down with engine trouble. It was hardly surprising, the mate thought, she was probably older than he was.

The convoy escorts had been unwilling to leave them astern of the main body of twelve ships on passage for Liverpool. At any other time the senior naval officer would have ordered the *Port St Clair*, with her precious cargo of rice, New Zealand butter and meat, to keep station and leave the other ship to fend for herself until a tug could be sent from somewhere, or a hungry U-boat had found her.

But the rivalry, which over the years had often been akin to hatred, had carried the day.

The mate considered the news. A German raider at large in the Atlantic again. The navy had probably got it all wrong. The enemy warship had either returned to base, or had already clashed with Allied patrols.

It was a strange feeling to be out here, alone, on such a fine day. Soon the Atlantic would show its other face, but by then they would have turned round, and be on their way back to the sunshine and New Zealand.

He walked out on to the bridge wing and waited for the master to notice him. The latter had his stained cap tilted over his eyes as he watched the tow lift from the water, hesitate and then dip into it again.

He remarked, 'Bloody old cow.'

The mate replied, 'What about the raider?'

The master rubbed his bristled chin. He would not shave until they crossed the Liverpool Bar. There was no point in shaving while there was a chance of being blown up.

They had passed the Cape Verde Islands to starboard in the night, and tomorrow, or maybe the next day, would meet with ships of the screening squadron. Cruisers from Simonstown, it was said.

Half to himself he said, 'Should have left the old bugger.' He turned and eyed the mate cheerfully. 'If there *is* a raider, and that I doubt, it's a comfort to know that the convoy will run smack into it before we do! Justice for leaving us behind!' He chuckled.

The mate agreed and rested his hands on the rail, but withdrew them instantly with a curse. The bridge was like an oven. But you could keep Liverpool. A sailor's town, they said. Blackouts, air raids, and tarts outside the clubs who looked as if every one of those sailors had had a go at them. You could keep it.

Steam spurted from the ship astern, wavered around her poop and then faded away.

The master said unfeelingly, 'If his Chief can't get her going, I'll tow the sod all the way. That'll give him something to bite on!'

A whistle shrilled and the mate walked into the wheelhouse and hauled a little brass cylinder up the tube from the radio-room.

He returned to the glare and said sharply, 'Intercepted a signal. Convoy's under attack. German raider.' They stared at each other and the master hurried to the chart-room abaft the wheelhouse and snapped, 'Give it here. Where the bloody hell are they?'

124

He did not speak again until he had plotted the convoy's approximate course and bearing on the chart. 'Call up *Dunedin Pioneer*.' He held him with a grim stare. 'On the lamp. Tell him. He may not have picked it up on that relic he calls a receiver.'

Alone in the chart-room he stared at the chart. It was worn and stained. So many convoys, too many risks, and always a target for torpedoes and bombs.

It must be serious, he thought. He pictured the other ships as they had weighed anchor and had formed into two lines with the destroyer escorts bustling around them like sheep dogs.

The mate came back, breathing hard. They were all used to danger, and both the master and mate had already been torpedoed in other ships and knew the margin of survival. The U-boat, the most hated and most feared of any war machine. The unseen killer.

The master looked at his second-in-command. 'Rouse the lads, Bob. Have the gun manned, and set two more lookouts.'

The gun was mounted aft on the poop, an elderly four-inch weapon from another war.

This was something else, he thought. A raider, one of their bloody cruisers. How could she get through the patrols at this stage of the game, he wondered? The invasion was said to be going better than anyone had dared to hope – a newspaper in Freetown had proclaimed big advances all along the front. No longer beachheads, not just another wild hope; they were going all out for a grand slam.

He heard some of his men clambering up ladders and protesting at the call to arms. He gave a tight smile. They might soon have something to moan about.

He looked at the sky. A few clouds, but it was clear, washed-out blue. And it was another eight hours to dusk. He glared at the ship astern through the chart-room scuttle. Six knots. Without her dragging along like a sick elephant, they could increase speed, go it alone if need be. They would stand a better chance.

The mate and the second mate entered the chart-room and watched him without speaking. The second mate was just a kid, wet behind the ears, but he was learning.

'Look.' The master eyed them gravely. 'This bugger might come our way. But she's more likely to stand off before the screening squadron comes down on'em like a ton of bricks.' He stared hard at the chart. 'It's like being blind and deaf.'

The mate asked, 'Can't we make a run for it?'

'Is that what you'd do?'

The second mate said, 'We could turn back, sir.'

The master smiled. *Sir.* That showed how green he was.

He said, 'Can't leave the *Dunedin Pioneer*. He wouldn't cut and run if it was us.'

They looked at each other for support while the ship noises intruded. Usually they gave confidence. Now they seemed to represent their sudden vulnerability.

The master exclaimed angrily, 'No, sod 'em, we'll keep going as we are.'

There was a clang from aft and he strode out to the sunlight again to watch as the four-inch gun trained round on its mounting. Fat lot of use that would be against a bloody cruiser, he thought. But some of the seamen saw him and grinned up at the bridge. For some peculiar reason the old captain wished he had shaved, that his cap cover was crisp and white like those bloody RN characters.

The second mate clambered on to the bridge and said, 'Call from the tow, sir. Will be getting up steam in fifteen minutes.'

They all breathed out and the master said, 'Tell the silly bugger to get a move on.' He hid his relief from the others. 'And about bloody time!'

It was just minutes later that a seaman called, 'There's a plane, sir!'

'What? Where away?' The master strode through the wheelhouse and out on to the other wing. 'Why can't you learn to report the thing properly?' He ignored the lookout's resentment and raised his massive binoculars.

An aircraft. Out here. Hundreds of miles from anywhere. It could not be hostile. Maybe they were looking for them? To tell them to alter course, or to rendezvous with a tug. They'd get a surprise when the other ship cast off the tow and began pouring out her usual foul smoke, the bane of every escort commander.

He saw the sunlight glint on the little aircraft and stared at it until it misted over.

He said flatly, 'It's a Jerry.'

The second mate said, 'But it's too far –'

The master turned away. 'From the raider. Call up *Dunedin*

126

Pioneer right now. Then tell Sparks to prepare the emergency signal –'

But it was already too late even for that. As the little toylike aircraft cruised back and forth against the pale sky, the horizon's mist seemed to raise itself like a frail curtain.

They saw the blurred flashes, almost lost in the fierce sunlight. The master waited, counting the seconds, until with a terrifying screech the salvo fell close astern, the white columns bursting high above the ships before cascading down in a torrent of spray and smoke.

The old captain shouted, 'Send that signal! Plain language, tell the bloody world! *Am under attack by German raider!*'

The next salvo shrieked down from the sky and he felt the hull shake as if it had run aground. He staggered to the rail and peered aft. It was almost impossible to see anything through the smoke, but the other vessel was still there, standing away at right-angles. The tow must have been slipped, or had parted in the explosions.

Then he stared incredulously at a solid, black shape as it rolled over and began to sink. It was their own stern, the useless four-pounder pointing at the sky, its crew nowhere to be seen.

He seized the rail and yelled, 'Sway out the boats! Abandon ship! What the hell is Sparks doing?'

Glass shivered from the wheelhouse windows and men fell kicking and screaming under a fusillade of glass and wood splinters. The ship had stopped, her holds already flooding as bulkheads burst open and turned the engine-room into an inferno of scalding steam.

Another earsplitting screech, and the shells burst alongside and on the foredeck.

The master slid down the bridge wing, his eyes glazed with agony while he tried to call out. His mind recorded the crash of falling derricks, the savage roar of water through the hull below, and the fact he could not move for the pain. He was still staring at the top of the bridge canvas-dodgers when the sea boiled over the edge and swamped the wheelhouse as the ship plunged to the bottom.

Then there was silence, as if the whole world had been rendered speechless.

Aboard the other ship, the men on the bridge and along her rust-streaked decks, stared dumbly across the empty sea towards the horizon. Like beasts waiting for the inevitable slaughter for their own execution.

But nothing happened. Even the tiny aircraft had disappeared.

The master crossed the bridge and peered at the carpet of oil, the rising litter of fragments which spread across the swell in a great obscene stain.

Around him his men stood like statues, shocked beyond words or movement.

Then the master said, 'Lower a boat. Mister. Fast as you can.' He made himself stare at the floating pieces, all that was left of his old enemy. His best friend. He added brokenly, 'Seems they've no time for us, the bastards!'

As if to mock him the engine began to pound again.

'Stop engines!' Acting-Commodore James Cook Hemrose sat stiff-backed in his bridge chair and surveyed what was left of the convoy. A battlefield. A junk yard.

The commander stood beside him as the way went off the ship, and the endless litter of wreckage, bodies and pieces of men parted across the *Wiltshire*'s high stem.

Half a mile astern, her signal lamp flashing like a diamond eye, the New Zealand light cruiser *Pallas* followed reluctantly amongst the remains.

The convoy had scattered at the last moment when the first salvoes must have come crashing down. Hammers of hell, Hemrose thought bitterly.

'Stand by to lower boats!'

Hemrose trained his binoculars across the sea, hating the stench of escaping fuel oil and burned paintwork. A few figures floated or splashed amongst the filth, their bodies shining and pitiful in the oil. There were more corpses than living, but it was worth a try.

'Signal *Pallas* to cover us, Toby.'

The lamp clattered again. Even it sounded subdued.

A distant voice called, 'Lower away!' That was one of the whalers. The motorboat was all ready to slip from her falls, the surgeon in the cockpit with one of his SBA's.

He looked long and hard at a black line which lifted and dipped above the water like a crippled submarine. It was the keel of one of the escorting destroyers. Of a corvette there was no trace at all.

128

Another destroyer had escaped without a scratch and was now lashed alongside a listing tramp-steamer, hoses dousing some fires while men passed back and forth with stretchets and inert bundles. An oil tanker was awash, but still afloat, her engines and pumps working manfully to keep her going. Some wag had hoisted a Union Flag on the stump of her remaining mast.

The commander returned and watched the light cruiser increasing speed to circle around the scene of pain and death, her pale hull streaked with oil like an additional waterline.

Hemrose said savagely, 'Whole convoy wiped out except for these pathetic remnants!' He pounded the arm of his chair with his fist. 'All they needed was another day. The escort group was on the way from Gib, and three destroyers from Bermuda and us.'

The commander stared at the drifting filth and spreadeagled corpses. Some of them wore naval uniforms, or bits of them. It was like being with them, part of them. He resisted the urge to shiver. Even Hemrose must know that they would have stood no chance either.

The Admiralty had confirmed that the raider was *Prinz Luitpold*, and fresh details came in every hour. He watched his superior, suddenly glad that he did not share his responsibility.

Hemrose watched the boat coxswains signalling to one another with their shortened, personal semaphore. He knew what the commander was thinking. It made it worse. If *Wiltshire* had been on the spot, she might have scored a lucky hit, enough to cripple the bastard, or at least slow him down.

Now the German could be anywhere. He thought of the signals, and the information from the lone freighter *Dunedin Pioneer* which had been left untouched. Somebody aboard that poor ship, a spectator to the total destruction of the one which had been towing her, had kept his head. Had reported seeing the enemy's faint silhouette as she headed away at full speed to the south-west.

The commander had asked, 'Give chase, sir?'

Hemrose had studied his charts with the navigating and cypher officers for an hour while they had steamed at full speed towards the convoy's last position.

The raider had steamed away without sinking the *Dunedin Pioneer*. There had to be a reason. Now as he watched the oil-streaked boats picking their way amongst the human remains, he went over it again for the hundredth time.

Give chase. To where? To the coastline of Brazil, or back along the same course?

It had certainly put the cat amongst the pigeons, he thought. Every available ship was under orders. A nightmare for the Admiralty and the Allied Command. There must be no let-up in the lines of supply to the armies in France. The Channel was filled with vessels of every kind, carrying fuel and ammunition, transport and the precious cargo of men to replace the convoys which passed them on the way back. The wounded and the dying.

According to the latest intelligence there were seventeen major convoys at sea. Well escorted for the most part, but to resist U-boat and bombing attacks, not a bloody great cruiser like *Prinz Luitpold*.

Hemrose still could not fathom how it had happened. The RAF recce boys had reported that after the battle near Bear Island, *Prinz Luitpold* had been seen and photographed back at her lair in Bodø. It did not make any sense. Somebody's head would be on the block over it, but it offered no satisfaction for all this horror. He pictured the pandemonium in Whitehall. It made a change for them to be under siege. First the flying-bombs, then the massive V-2 rockets. The Allied HQ which controlled the Normandy invasion would be worried too. You could not ignore a raider, any raider. Convoys had to be diverted, held up, cancelled altogether.

Hemrose glanced around the open bridge, the intent figures and anxious faces. A midshipman was retching into his handkerchief as he stared at the bobbing remains which surrounded the tall hull.

Hemrose rasped, 'Get off my bridge, damn you, until you can act like a man!'

It was cruel and unfair. Hemrose knew it but did not care.

There was a third cruiser coming at full speed to join his little group. They should meet up with her in two days, unless . . . He said to the commander, 'I want a full team on this, Toby. The paymaster-commander, even the bloody chaplain. See to it.'

The man's words came back to him and he heard himself say, 'Give chase – I don't think so, Toby. He had a reason for letting the *Dunedin Pioneer* stay afloat. He wanted her to see him steam

130

away, to report his course.' It felt easier now that he had decided. 'No, I reckon he changed direction as soon as he was clear of all this. Get the convoy lists, and we'll study the chart. Outguess the bastard.' He eyed him grimly. 'It's up to us. As I see it, Toby, we'll get precious little advice from their lordships just now.' He wrinkled his nose. 'Signal a recall to the boats and we'll get under way. That destroyer can stand by the survivors until the escort group turns up.'

He heard one of the boats creaking up to the davits and felt the commander let out a sigh. No U-boats were reported in their vicinity. But if they could miss a big cruiser there was no point in adding to the risks.

The deck began to tremble and the *Pallas* headed round to take station astern again.

When the third cruiser joined them it would make all the difference. He looked down from the bridge and saw the first survivors being led away, wrapped in oil-sodden blankets. There did not seem to be many of them, he thought.

'Resume course, cruising speed, Toby.' He settled back in the chair. 'Send for a brandy. I need to *think* about this one.'

Astern, the listless ships, and the great span of oil and fragments seemed to fill the horizon.

For Hemrose the war had suddenly become a personal one.

It was like fighting free from a nightmare, only to discover that it was real. Even the overhead light, although it was partly screened by some kind of curtain, had a hard, unreal shape. Cold and still. Like death.

The man lay motionless, his hands balled into fists at his sides while he waited for his senses to return, or to fade again and leave him in peace.

In tiny fragments his mind recorded that he was suspended in some kind of cot, high-sided and white. He felt the surge of panic. A coffin.

He tried again and groped for clues, explanations, like piecing together parts of a puzzle.

He made his taut limbs relax but kept his hands pressed against his sides. His body was naked, but warm beneath a sheet and a soft blanket. Again, he felt the surge of hope. A nightmare after all. He could feel the pulsating tremor of engines through his

131

spine, the gentle clatter of unseen objects. But he felt despair close over him once more. It was not his ship. He closed his eyes tightly as if to shut out the stark, leaping pictures, the great fountain of searing flames, exploding metal as the torpedo, maybe two, had exploded into them. He tried again, and in his reeling thoughts seemed to read the vessel's name, as he had once seen it at the dockside. The *Radnor Star*. An old ship, then part of an eastbound convoy from St John's to Liverpool, packed to the gills with engine spares, bridge-building equipment, armoured vehicles, all heavy stuff. The poor old girl must have gone down like a stone afterwards.

He opened his eyes wide and stared at the solitary light. *Afterwards*. What then?

It was almost painful to work it out. He had been in the open, something in his hand. Had to see the captain. Then the explosion, wild faces, mouths open in silent cries, smoke, dense choking smoke which he imagined he could still taste.

Then the boat, water swilling over his feet and thighs as someone had fought it away from the ship, the terrible suction as she had dived for the last time. Why had nobody seen them? It was coming back, sharp and hard, like heart-beats, the panic of a child who wants to hide under the blankets.

It had been at night. That was it.

He felt the sweat break over his chest and stomach. The lifeboat then. Why did his mind refuse to examine it?

He heard a distant bell, the clatter of feet somewhere. *Where the hell am I?*

He tried again. *My name is Peter Younger*. He wanted to laugh, but was closer to weeping. He had a name after all. He could not be dead.

It was difficult not to cry out as another picture loomed through the mist.

Men bailing and working at a handful of oars, a great sea which lifted and flung the boat like a sodden log. Later still, the deathly quiet, the silent figures, some seared by fire, others who had died of exposure, a few eyeless, victims of seabirds. *They were all dying*. He vaguely recalled the hoarse voice of Colin Ames, *Radnor Star*'s second mate, close against his ear. He must have been dying too. The whole bridge had collapsed, and it was a miracle he had made it into a boat.

132

'Take the tiller, Sparks.' That was all he had said. Sparks? It was coming back. He had been the radio officer. Had been on his way to the bridge with a signal when the world had exploded. He recalled the other man wrapping his jacket around him. He must have lost his own. Younger examined his body limb by limb without moving a muscle. He ached all over, but he was whole. Then more distorted faces, alien voices, hands hauling him into another boat, a huge ship away in the distance. He tensed. This must be the one.

He remembered that he had been too weak to protest or struggle, but knew that in some strange way he had not wanted to leave his dead companions, and the boat he had steered until the last oar had drifted away.

All dead. Like the old ship, nothing left.

Another twist of terror as he pictured his mother reading the telegram. God, there had been plenty of those in their street. He could not remember its name, or that of the town. A seaport. Pictures of his father and uncles, all in uniform. Sailors.

Feet scraped on metal and he tested his strength, tried to raise his head above the side of the cot.

His eyes would not focus at first. All glaring white, bottles and jars on neat shelves, like a hospital, while nearby lay a pile of gramophone records.

Perhaps he had gone mad?

Bit by bit, section by section, like a complicated, coded message over the receiver.

He stared uncomprehending at two uniform jackets which hung from a brass rail. One with three stripes, the other with two, with some odd insignia above them, and – he caught his breath, the Nazi eagle on the right breast. He had seen enough of those. Again the urge to laugh. But only in films.

Then he saw the other cot, the untidy white beard, the ancient face creased with pain or some terrible memory.

He held on to what he saw. Like a life-raft. It was Old Shiner. A bit of a character in the *Radnor Star*, listed as boatswain but one who could do almost anything. He had been at sea since he was twelve. *A bit of a character.*

He caught a brief picture of him in the boat, his pale eyes wild while he had clutched the cat against his scrawny body.

Younger attempted to bridge the gap between the boat and

here. All he could remember was warmth, the fact that he felt no urge to hold on, even to live.

He imagined he had heard a woman's voice too, but that was impossible. A part of something else maybe.

So he and Old Shiner were in a German ship. Prisoners. Survivors. But not a U-boat. He recalled the misty silhouette of the ship. He also remembered a needle going into his arm, oblivion, but not before the world had begun to shake and thunder to gunfire. He had wanted to scream, to escape; instead there had been nothing.

He winced as a shadow fell across the cot and he saw a man in gold-rimmed glasses looking down at him.

'Well, now, Herr Ames, are you feeling better?'

Even his voice made him shake with silent laughter. Shock.

The man must be a doctor, and he spoke like one of those Germans in the movies.

He prised his lips apart, or so it felt, and tried to explain that his name was Younger. Then he saw the crumpled, oil-stained coat with the two tarnished stripes lying on a table. Ames's jacket, the one he had used to shield him from the wind and drenching spray. It flooded through him like fire. Anger, hatred, and an overwhelming sense of loss.

The doctor leaned closer and took his wrist. 'You had a narrow escape, young man.'

Younger moved his dry lips again. 'What ship?'

'*Prinz Luitpold.*' He lowered the wrist. '*Kriegsmarine.*'

Younger was not sure if the name meant anything or not.

'How is Old Shiner?'

'Is that his name?' The doctor gave a sad smile. 'He will live, but I fear his mind may be scarred.'

Younger heard himself shouting, but the words sounded wild, meaningless.

A door opened and he saw an armed sailor peer in at them, his eyes questioning. *Just like the movies*, a voice seemed to murmur. It must be his own, he thought despairingly.

The doctor waved the sailor away and said, 'You must try to eat something soon. You are young, it will pass.'

Younger could feel his strength draining away, and twisted his face to the pillow to hide the tears which spilled down his cheeks. They were all dead. He saw the needle glinting in the overhead

134

light and tried to struggle, but the doctor's grip was like steel. 'You killed them!' He saw the needle hesitate. *'Bloody murderers!'*

Stroheim felt the fight go out of the young officer and stood back to watch his face lose its anguish, its hate.

He moved to the other cot where the old man still cradled his lost cat in his arms.

They had no part in their ship's destruction, but the fact gave no comfort.

He thought of the guns thundering and shaking the ship from deck to keel, the muffled shouts of the intercom as one by one the convoy had been decimated.

Karl-Heinz Stroheim examined his hands. They were surprisingly steady.

He had been sent to the *Prinz Luitpold* as a punishment or a reprieve. All things considered it seemed likely they would come to rely on his skill.

The twist of fate which had brought these two strangers to his care was like an additional challenge. The oldest and the youngest in the lifeboat had survived.

He put on his jacket and gestured to the sentry. If hate was a reason for survival, the young officer named Ames would outlive them all.

Chapter Ten

Beyond Duty

Hechler wriggled his shoulders deeper into his watchcoat and felt the damp air exploring his bones. By leaning forward in his tall chair he could see much of the *Prinz Luitpold*'s long forecastle, which glistened now as if from a rain squall. But there was no rain, and as the high bows sliced through the Atlantic swell he saw the spray drift over the anchor-cables and breakwater to make the angled gun turrets shine like glass.

It was afternoon, and the sky was almost hidden by dark-bellied clouds. He heard Gudegast's rumbling tones as he passed another helm order before checking his ready-use chart again. How many times had he done that, Hechler wondered?

He saw the rear-admiral appear around Turret Anton, head high despite the misty spray, his face flushed and youthful in the distance. He was walking in step with Oberleutnant Bauer, the signals and communications officer. They could be brothers, he thought. Bauer was also the political officer and had been having a lot of private conversations with Leitner. What did they discuss? The *Prinz*'s captain probably.

Gudegast called, 'New course, sir. Two-one-five.'

It was a strange relationship, Hechler thought. Leitner had been as good as his word for the most part, and had let him handle the ship in his own way.

As they had steered south-west away from the broken convoy and the additional freighter which the radar had plotted with unnerving accuracy, Leitner had only once questioned his judgement.

Hechler had answered, 'The British will look for clues. By heading south-west in view of that ship which was under tow, they will assume it was a ruse, and expect us to alter course immediately to throw them off the scent. I think I would.'

Leitner had considered it, his eyes opaque, giving nothing away.

'But if *not*, Dieter? Suppose the British admiral thinks as you do?' Then he had nodded and had given his broad grin. 'Of course, that other convoy – they will think we are after it.'

OKM Operations Division had signalled more information about a vast troop convoy which was scheduled to head around the Cape of Good Hope en route for England. Commonwealth soldiers with all their equipment and vehicles, life-blood for the armies in France. A prize which would draw every U-boat pack in the Atlantic, and which would have a massive escort to match it.

Heavy units of the Home Fleet would be hurrying at full speed to meet it and swell the defences. Suicide for any attacking surface raider, but with such high stakes, the end might justify the means. Because of that risk no admiral would dare leave the convoy underguarded.

It was one of the biggest of its kind, too large to turn back, too vital to stop.

So the *Prinz Luitpold* had carried on as before. Nothing further had been sighted. If anything showed itself now they would have to forego their first rendezvous with a milch-cow. They had plenty of fuel, and Leitner intended it would remain like that. A little and often, as he had termed it.

It was too early to expect enemy submarines in their path. The simplicity of von Hanke's strategy had worked perfectly, and there had been no time to deploy submarines from their normal inshore patrols in the Baltic and the North Sea.

Hechler watched the two windswept figures until they vanished beneath the bridge. He thought of Leitner's broadcast that morning to the ship's company. Rousing, passionate, compelling. It was all those things, if you did not know the man.

Hechler had watched him as he had stood with the handset close to his lips in the armoured admiral's bridge. The flag-lieutenant and Bauer had also been present while Leitner's clipped tones had penetrated the ship above and below decks.

He had spoken of *Lübeck*'s loss at some length. Her sacrifice. 'We must not fail her, can never forget they fought for us, to give us the freedom to break out into the Atlantic! For *us* and our beloved Fatherland!'

Hechler had watched as one hand had darted to his cheek as if to brush away a tear. An act? He was still not sure.

Of one thing he was certain, however. There were two faces to the youthful admiral. After the attack on the convoy Leitner had walked around the upper deck, chatting to the jubilant gun crews, lounging against the mountings or slapping a seaman on the shoulder to emphasise his satisfaction.

Then, on the bridge, almost in the next breath, he had snapped complaints about this man or that, and had ordered Theil to deal with their slackness. So the reprimands would come from the bridge, not from their popular and untiring rear-admiral.

Then there had been the flash of anger over Leitner's mysterious boxes.

Hechler had requested permission to move them deeper in the hull, so that their space could be used to store additional short-range ammunition.

Leitner had snapped, 'They belong to me! I will not be questioned! I am entrusted to this mission, to carry it out in *my* way!' He had been almost shouting, his voice trapped inside the armoured bridge. 'It is a mark of my trust in this ship's ability, surely? If we are crippled or sunk in battle, my boxes will go to the bottom too!'

So they were that valuable, Hechler thought.

He heard Theil's footsteps on the gratings and shifted round to look at him.

'All well, Viktor?' Things were still strained between them, although Theil had shown his old pride and excitement when the enemy convoy had been destroyed.

Hechler had thought about that often enough. It had been so easy, he had found no satisfaction from it. It had been slaughter, the careering merchantmen and their escorts falling to their massive bombardment like targets in a fairground.

He had told himself that they would have done the same to *Prinz Luitpold*, would have cheered like his own men, if they had been left to burn and drown.

It was their war. What they had trained for. What they must do.

Theil shrugged and stared moodily at the grey ocean, the lift and dip of the raked bows.

'Yes, sir. I have just questioned the prisoner, the officer named Ames.' He shrugged again as if to sum up his irritation. 'The other one is raving. I can't imagine how he ever got to sea.'

Hechler eyed him thoughtfully. The old sailor should have been ashore with his grandchildren, not fighting for his life in an

138

open boat. They had been adrift for five weeks. How could the human body stand it? But it was pointless to say as much to Theil. It would sound like one more disagreement. Perhaps he was more worried about his missing wife than he would admit.

Hechler tried not to let his mind stray to Inger, but even in distance her will seemed too strong to resist. In that low-cut gown, when he had held her, had seen her perfect breasts. In another moment – he sighed. She could never be kept out of his thoughts for long. Her betrayal and her contempt were like deep scars.

He had felt clumsy by comparison, and she had scorned his reserve as being stuffy, and dull.

Maybe she had been right?

Theil said abruptly, 'The Englishman knows nothing. Just that the torpedoes hit his ship in the forward hold. She sank in minutes, apparently.'

Hechler glanced at his watch. The rendezvous was in twenty minutes' time. If it happened at all. It seemed impossible that two such diverse vessels could meet on a pinpoint in this ocean.

There was a coughing roar from amidships and Hechler stirred uneasily in his chair. He wanted to walk aft and watch the brightly painted Arado as it was tested on the catapult. Leitner had told him that it would be launched without further delay. The camera team would be down there too, waiting to record their audacity as they flew off their new aircraft, indifferent to the enemy and what they could do.

Hechler had seen the girl when he had left the bridge to visit the various action stations while the ship had steamed away from the last fall of shot. She had been in the hangar, where her new Arado had been housed throughout the bombardment, its wings detached and stowed separately rather than folded, like a toy in a crate. They had faced one another awkwardly like strangers; perhaps each was out of his or her depth.

Hechler had heard himself enquiring how she had accepted or endured the din of salvoes, the hull's shaking to each ear-shattering crash of gunfire.

She had watched him as if to see her own answers without asking the questions. How small she had seemed against the wet, camouflaged steel, and the smoke-blackened gun-muzzles.

Now she was down there with the aircraft-handling party.

Ready to fly off, so that some lunatic's desire for patriotic realism could be filmed.

Theil said dourly, 'I think it is madness to put that plane in the air. Suppose –'

The word hung between them. There were no enemy carriers anywhere in this part of the ocean if the OKM's reports were to be believed. Submarines, then? Even the hint of a plane would be enough to make them increase speed and head away. The Arado might fly after them, like a fledgling abandoned by its parents, until it ran out of fuel.

Theil whispered, 'He's coming up, sir.'

Leitner strode on to the bridge, the familiar silk scarf flapping in the keen air, but otherwise unprotected by a heavier coat. He smiled at the bridge-party and then returned Hechler's salute.

'According to my watch –' He frowned as Gudegast called, 'Permission to alter course for take-off, sir?'

Hechler nodded. 'Warn the engine-room.'

Leitner's good humour returned. 'See, the sky is brightening. It will do our people at home a lot of good to see these films.' He glared at his willowy aide as he clambered on to the bridge. 'Well?'

The flag-leiutenant eyed him worriedly, hurt by his master's tone. 'The camera team would like you to join them, sir.' He glanced shyly at Hechler. 'I have a list of the questions you will be asked.'

Leitner clapped one hand across his breast and gave an elaborate sigh. 'What we must do in the name of duty!'

Gudegast lifted his face from the voice-pipe as the helmsman acknowledged the change of course. He watched Leitner march to the after-ladder and then looked over at Jaeger, who shared the watch with Korvettenkapitän Froebe.

He said softly, 'Does he fill you with pride, young Konrad? Make you want to spill your guts for your country?' He grimaced. 'Sometimes I despair.'

He thought of the painting he had begun of Gerda. Just imagining the softness of her body, the heat of their passion, had helped him in some strange fashion to endure the massacre of those helpless merchantmen. Bomber pilots who nightly released their deadly cargoes over Germany did not care about the suffering they created; the U-boat commander did not see ships and

140

sailors in his crosswires, merely targets. Any more than an escort captain spared a thought for that same hull being crushed by the force of his depth-charges as the sea thundered in to silence the submariners' screams.

Hechler heard him, but let it pass. Gudegast was releasing the tension in his usual way.

'Ready to fly off aircraft, sir!'

'Slow ahead all engines.'

Hechler walked from his chair and leaned over the screen, the damp wind pressing into his face.

He saw the camera team down aft, some sailors freshly changed into their best uniforms, outwardly chatting to their admiral. Hechler looked at the vibrating Arado on the catapult, trained outboard ready to be fired off.

He saw the girl's helmeted head lowered to speak with one of the deck crew before she closed the cockpit cover and waved a gloved hand.

He felt his stomach contract and was stunned by the sudden concern. There was nothing that they could do or share. What was the *matter* with him? Was it Inger's fury or his own loneliness?

He tensed as the shining Arado roared from the catapult and without hesitation climbed up and away from the slow-moving cruiser.

Leitner returned to the bridge, his eyes squinting as he watched the little plane weaving and circling over the water.

He said, 'I hope she flies nearer than that. It's a camera down aft, not a bloody-gunsight!'

Hechler lifted his binoculars and watched the weak sunlight lance through the clouds to pick out the plane's thin silhouette.

'Five minutes, sir!'

Gudegast's voice made him pull his thoughts together.

Leitner remarked, 'Now we shall see, eh?'

It was more like a shoal of fish than a surfacing submarine. Long flurries of spray and frothing bubbles, so that when the hull eventually appeared some half-mile distant it rose with a kind of tired majesty.

Jaeger exclaimed, 'God, she's *big*!'

Leitner heard him and turned to look. 'Another idea with vision and inventive skill!'

The huge submarine surfaced and lay on the heaving water like

141

a gigantic whale. Unlike an ordinary combat U-boat she lacked both menace and dignity. Even as they watched, men were swarming from her squat conning-tower, while from her casing, untidy-looking derricks and hoses were already rising from hidden compartments like disturbed sea-monsters.

The tannoy blared below the bridge, and men ran to the pre-pared tackles and winches, ready to haul the fuel lines to the bunkers. Hechler saw the men waving to each other across the water. It must be a heartening sight to see such a big warship at large in enemy waters, he thought.

There would be no news from home as yet, but his own men could send their letters across while the two vessels lay together. It might be many weeks before those letters were read by wives, mothers and girlfriends. He wished now he had a letter written for his own parents. But they would understand. Without effort he could see the photographs of himself and his dead brother in the neat, old-fashioned house where he had been born. His mother preparing the evening meal early, in case there was an air raid, although they had been mercifully spared most of those where they lived. His father, reading the newspaper and coughing quietly at painful intervals.

A telephone buzzed and Jaeger called, 'Chief engineer reports hoses connected, sir.'

'Very good. Warn the wheelhouse to hold her steady.' It was probably unnecessary to warn anybody. Severed hoses might take hours to replace, and every minute exposed like this was too much.

Hechler watched the oily hoses jerking busily as the fuel was pumped across the gap of heaving water. What a strange war it was becoming. He glanced down at the deck below as an armed seaman walked past beside the captured English officer. The latter was downcast, and did not appear to be looking in any direction as men scurried to tackles to release the strain or to take up the slack.

A victim and a survivor.

Theil said, 'I think it unwise to let him walk about like that.'

Hechler smiled. 'He is hardly a threat, Viktor.'

He looked up to seek out the Arado, but the sky seemed empty. She would be feeling free right now, he thought. Unlike the sad-faced prisoner who walked alone despite all the seamen around him.

But the young officer who wore another man's uniform jacket

was anything but despairing. On his way to the upper deck, with his guard sauntering beside him, a machine-pistol dangling from one shoulder, he had heard the one sound which was so familiar that it pulled at his reserve like claws.

The urgent stammer of morse and waves of hissing static. The radio-room with at least three headphoned operators at their bench was like a laboratory compared with anything he had been used to. But the idea had formed in his mind even as they had passed the open door.

It was his one chance. His life would be forfeit, but he found it surprisingly easy to accept that. He had died back there in the open boat with his gaunt, eyeless companions.

When the time was right. It would take just one signal to bring the navy down on this bloody German like a force of avenging angels. He looked up and thought he saw the captain framed against the low clouds.

It would all be worth it then, even if he was dead when the first great salvoes came roaring down on the raider.

The armed guard saw him give a wild grin and sighed.

It could be no joke to be adrift in this ocean, he thought.

The girl named Erika Franke adjusted the clips of her safety harness and peered to starboard as she eased the Arado into a shallow dive. She had flown several of these flat-planes when she had worked for a while as a delivery pilot, before she had been asked to serve with the special section of the Luftwaffe.

She watched the grey wastes of the Atlantic tilt to one side as if it was part of a vast sloping desert, the occasional white horses where the wind had broken the swell into crests.

The cruiser had already fallen far away, and it was hard to picture her as she had first seen the ship. Huge, invulnerable, and somehow frightening. But once aboard it had seemed so much smaller, the great hull broken up into small intimate worlds, faces which you sometimes saw only once before they were swallowed up again. She watched the ship in the distance, her outline strangely broken and unreal in its striped dazzle paint. Beyond her was the austere shape of the great supply submarine which Leitner had described to the ship's company.

She saw the perspex screen mist over very slightly and adjusted her compass accordingly. They were too high for spray. The looming clouds said *rain*.

She bit her lip. If the visibility fell away she must return to the ship immediately.

She touched the microphone across her mouth. 'Rain soon.' She heard the observer, Westphal, acknowledge her comment with a grunt. A thickset, bovine man, he obviously resented being in the hands of a woman. She ignored him. It was nothing new in her life.

She deliberately altered course away from the ship and the motionless submarine. If only she could fly and fly, leave it all behind, until – she checked herself as Hechler's grave features intruded into her thoughts.

A withdrawn man, who must have been badly hurt and not just by the war. She remembered his voice, his steady blue eyes when he had visited her after the encounter with the enemy convoy. His presence had calmed her, like that moment when you fly out of a storm into bright sunlight.

During the bombardment she had felt no fear. There had been no point in being afraid. Her father had taught her that, when he had first taken her flying, had given her a taste for it. If you could do nothing, fear had no meaning, he had often told her.

But the feeling of utter helplessness had been there. The ship, powerful though she was, had shaken like a mad thing, with every plate and rivet threatening to tear apart, or so it had felt. Then Hechler, his voice and his quiet confidence had covered her like a blanket.

The Arado swayed jerkily and she quickly increased throttle until the blurred propeller settled again into a misty circle. The plane was unarmed, or at least it carried no ammunition. Just as well, she thought. That was one kind of flying she had not tried.

She thought of the two survivors who had been brought to the ship by the young officer, Jaeger. He was a nice young man, she thought, and she had seen him looking at her when she had joined the others in the wardroom for meals. It made her smile within the privacy of her flying-helmet. She was twenty-eight, but far older in other ways than Jaeger would ever dream. Why did they have to be so predictable? Those who saw her only as an easy victory, a romp in bed. Others who saw her reserve as a coldness, like something masculine.

144

When she glanced down at the endless, heaving water, she recalled another face with sharper clarity. Claus had loved her, and she him. He had been married, but the war had brought them together in Italy.

Had they ever really decided to take a step beyond the endless anxiety of being lovers? He had promised; she could almost hear his voice in her hair as he had held her, had pressed down to that delicious torment when he had entered her.

She had learned of his death through a friend. After all, she had no *rights* to him.

His ship had been torpedoed, lost with all hands. It was over.

She came back with a start as Westphal's surly voice intruded into her memories.

'Time to turn. Visibility's down.'

They would fly back now, she thought, and the camera crew would film her landing near the ship, and again as she stepped aboard to be greeted by Andreas Leitner. Strange how people of his kind always professed to be such men of the world, with an eye for every pretty girl.

She had met plenty like Leitner. It was surprising that the war machine attracted so many who might have been happier as women. She considered Hechler again. Dominated by his wife? Hardly. What was it then with women like Inger Hechler? She had seen her occasionally at those staid parties in Berlin which so often had changed into something wild, repellent.

She moved the controls sharply so that the plane tilted over to port. She could feel the pull of her harness, the pain in her breast as the Arado went over even further until it appeared as if the wingtip was cutting the water like a fin.

The changing light, the endless procession of unbroken waves, or was it a shadow?

'Dead ahead!' She eased the throttle with great care. 'Do you see it?'

Westphal had been deep in thought, watching her hair beneath the leather helmet, imagining how she would fight him, claw at him, when he took her.

He exclaimed, startled, 'What? Where?'

She found that she could watch the submarine quite calmly, for that was what it was. It looked dark, blue-grey, like a shark, with a lot of froth streaming from aft, and a faint plume of vapour above the conning-tower.

Westphal had recovered himself, his voice harsh as he snapped, 'Enemy boat! Charging batteries and using her *schnorchel!*'

He reached forward to prod her shoulder. 'Back to the ship, *fast!*'

The girl eased the controls over to port. Westphal had seen what he had expected to see, but had missed something vital. The submarine was trimmed too high – most of them would be almost at full periscope depth to charge batteries, and in their own waters it was unlikely they would submerge at all.

The submarine must be damaged, unable to dive.

Thoughts raced through her mind, and in her imagination she could hear Hechler's voice, then see the cruiser and the supply submarine lying somewhere back there, totally unaware of this unexpected threat.

Damaged she might be, but her commander would not hesitate when *Prinz Luitpold*'s silhouette swam into his crosswires.

Erika Franke had learned quite a lot about the navy, and one of the things which stood out in her mind was something which Kröll the gunnery officer had said about his new radar. That a submarine on the surface nearby could interfere with accuracy, and that was exactly what was happening right now.

She thrust the controls forward and tilted the Arado into a steep dive. She felt the plane quivering, the rush of wind rising above the roar of the BMW engine.

Westphal shouted wildly, 'What the hell are you doing? They'll see us!'

Sure enough there were tiny ant-like figures on the submarine's deck. They might have picked up the supply boat's engines on their sonar, or even the heavier revolutions of the *Prinz Luitpold*, but the sight of a brightly painted aircraft must have caught them on the hop.

She laughed. 'Scared, are you?' The Arado's shadow swooped over the water like an uneven crucifix, and then tumbled away as she brought the nose up towards the clouds.

It was responding well; she could even smell the newness in the fuselage and fittings.

She shouted, 'By the time we made contact with the ship it would all be over!'

146

Then she winced as several balls of livid green tracer floated past the port wing, and the plane danced wildly to shell-bursts. The clouds enfolded the aircraft and she peered at the compass, her brain working coolly but urgently as she pictured the other vessels, the enemy submarine's bearing and line of approach. She was probably American, one of their big ocean-going boats, which she had studied in the recognition books. She held her breath and pushed the stick forward, and felt the floats quiver as they burst out of the clouds into a great span of watery sunlight.

Just right for the camera team, she thought vaguely. Then more shell-bursts erupted on either side, and lazy balls of tracer fanned beneath her, so that she instinctively drew her legs together.

The plane jerked, and she heard metal rip past her body. But the engine was behaving well. It was time to turn back. They must have heard the shooting. There was still time.

She twisted round in her seat to yell at Westphal, but choked on a scream as she saw his bared teeth, his fists bunched in agony at the moment of impact. His goggles were completely filled with blood, like a creature from a nightmare.

The plane rocked again, and she almost lost control as more bursts exploded nearby. She felt as if all the breath had been punched from her body, and when she looked down she saw a tendril of blood seeping through the flying suit and over her belt.

Then the pain hit her like a hot iron, and she heard herself whimpering and calling while she tried to find the compass and bring the plane on to the right bearing.

She felt the pain searing her body, so that her eyes misted over. She dared not turn her head where her hideous companion peered at her, his teeth set in a terrible grin.

Nor could she call up the ship. Dared not. The submarine would know instantly what he probably only suspected.

'Oh, dear God!' The words were torn from her. 'Help me!'

But the engine's roar drowned her cries and every vibration made her swoon in agony.

There were no more explosions, and for a brief moment she imagined she had lost consciousness, was dying like the men in the lifeboat. Clouds leapt towards her and then writhed aside again to bathe the cockpit in bright sunlight.

She cried out, then thrust one hand against her side as blood ran over her thigh and down into her flying boot.

There was the ship, the supply submarine almost alongside, with tiny lines and pipes linking them like a delicate web.

She saw the ship begin to turn anti-clockwise across the windshield, revolving faster and faster, blotting out everything until it seemed she was plunging straight for the bridge.

Her mind recorded several things at the same time. The lines between the two vessels were being cast off, and a great frothing wash was surging from beneath *Prinz Luitpold*'s bows as she increased to maximum speed.

The girl fought to control the spin, to bring the aircraft's nose up and level off.

All she could think of was that she had warned him. She would never know if she was in time.

Chapter Eleven

The Truth Can Wait

Hechler joined Gudegast at the compass platform. It was going well, but any sudden cross-wind might bring the unmatched vessels too close together.

'Alter course to two-two-zero degrees. Signal the submarine's commander yourself.' He touched the big man's arm. 'Don't want oil spilled all over the ocean.'

He walked back to the gratings and imagined he could feel the fuel coming through those long, pulsating hoses.

His ship was the best of her class for performance, and with the additional bunkers she had been given last year could cruise over 7,000 miles unless she was called to offer full speed for long periods.

He thought of the girl in her brightly painted plane. It worried him more than he cared to admit to have her aboard. At the same time he knew he would miss her when she was ordered to leave. Maybe she did not have a genuine mission? Perhaps after all she was only a piece of Leitner's public relations puzzle.

Theil lowered his glasses. 'The Arado's a long time, sir.' He eyed him worriedly. 'Completely lost sight of it.'

Hechler peered over the rear of the bridge wing. One of the regular float-planes in its dappled camouflage was already standing on the catapult, the handling party lounging around with nothing to do.

Hechler contained his sudden impatience. One thing at a time. It was the only way. The collection of charts with their plotted rendezvous marks were all in the future. Nobody could say how much future they still had.

Leitner strode on to the bridge, his mouth set in a tight line. 'Where the *bloody hell* is that woman?' He moved this way and that, almost blindly, so that men on watch had to jump out of his path.

Theil suggested, 'Perhaps we should send up another aircraft, sir?'

Leitner stared at him. 'Don't be such a bloody idiot!'

Hechler saw the seamen nearby exchange glances. Some worried, others pleased that a senior officer was getting a choking-off for a change.

Hechler said, 'I agree with him, sir.'

Their eyes met. Hechler felt very calm and relaxed even though he wanted to yell at Leitner. *Go on, tell me I'm a bloody idiot!*

Leitner recovered his composure somewhat. 'It's taking too long,' he said mildly.

Hechler looked at Theil and winked. The admiral had climbed down. For the moment anyway.

Then Hechler moved to the opposite side of the bridge to watch the fuelling operation. In the Great War, German raiders had been tied down to coaling stations, built up in readiness for such a dangerous form of sea piracy. He smiled in spite of his anxiety for the girl. *Piracy. Is that what we have come to?*

He glanced at his team, the watchful faces, the occasional padding of an order for helm and engines.

And yet, in spite of the quiet discipline, or perhaps because of it, there was something not quite right. Like a fault in a painting. He knew it was not Leitner's outburst, or Theil's embarrassed confusion at being reprimanded like a first-year midshipman in front of the watch. You got used to the petty whims of superior officers. *Maybe I am like that myself now?*

No, it was a feeling of uneasiness.

He made up his mind. 'Warn the milch-cow, then sound off action stations.'

Leitner heard him and glared from the other corner of the bridge. 'It'll make them jumpy!'

Hechler forced a grin. 'I *am* jumpy, sir.' He heard the clamour of bells, muffled and far away beyond the thick plating.

To Theil he said, 'You stay here.' He shrugged. 'It's just in case.'

Leitner climbed on to the bridge chair and tugged his cap down over his eyes. When one of the camera team requested permission to come to the bridge, Leitner snapped, 'When I'm ready, damn him!'

Hechler lowered his voice. 'Pass the word to the catapult, Viktor. Prepare to launch aircraft.'

A telephone buzzed and seconds later the Arado's engine spluttered, then bellowed into life.

150

Leitner swung round. 'Of all the bloody useless –'

He got no further as the gunnery control intercom filled the bridge.

'Gunfire to the north-west!'

Hechler moved like lightning to the compass platform. 'Discontinue fuelling!' He snatched up the red handset and waited, mentally counting seconds. Then he heard Stück's voice from the depths of the engine-room, machinery sighing in the background like some insane orchestra.

Stück began, 'I'm sorry about the delay, Captain, but we're almost topped-up. I –'

Hechler said, 'Stop immediately, Chief. Maximum revolutions when I give the word.' He slammed down the handset. There was nothing to add. Stück better than most knew the narrowness of their margin.

He waved his arm. '*Cast off!* Take in those wires!'

Leitner was beside him, peering at him wildly. 'What the hell's going on?'

'Gunfire means an enemy, sir.' He swung round as a lookout yelled, 'Aircraft, Red four-five, angle of sight four-oh!'

'Stand by, secondary armament!' Without looking Hechler pictured the twin turrets along the port side already lifting and training. But for what?

He levelled his glasses and found the Arado almost immediately. It was rolling from side to side, but apparently intact. He felt his heart throbbing as he followed every painful movement.

Theil called, 'Clear that breast-rope, damn you!'

Hechler lowered his glasses and saw the remaining wire dragging the heavy submarine dangerously close alongside.

'Cut that line! *Now!*'

He turned back again but the plane had plunged into some low clouds.

The gunnery intercom intoned, 'Submarine on the surface, bearing Red two-oh. Range four thousand!'

Leitner was almost beside himself. 'How can it be?' He peered over the stained screen. 'In the name of Christ!'

Hechler called, 'Full ahead all engines!' He felt the sharp tremble through the deck plates. Now or never. If that wire refused to part they would take the milch-cow with them.

The port lookout was leaning against his mounted binoculars,

151

his legs braced behind him as if he was taking the whole weight of the ship.

'Aircraft in sight again, sir. Closing. Shift bearing to Red six-oh!'

Hechler gripped the rail as the deck seemed to rise and then surge forward beneath him.

'Line's parted, sir!'

'*Open fire!*'

The three twin turrets along the port side opened up instantly, their sharper explosions making men grope for ear-plugs, others crouch down away from their savage back-blast.

Theil called, 'Supply boat's diving, sir!' He sounded breathless.

Great fountains of spray shot from the milch-cow's saddle tanks as water thundered into them, and her wash indicated a frantic increase in speed.

Hechler tore his eyes from the Arado as it reeled over the ship and then appeared to level off on an invisible wire. Not before he had seen the bright, starlike holes in the paintwork, some of which appeared to cross the cockpit itself.

'Port twenty!' He wrapped his arms around the voice-pipes with such force that the pain seemed to steady his mind, the ache which that last sight had given him.

She had drawn enemy fire. There was no other possible reason but to warn the ship.

He felt the deck going over. Like a destroyer. '*Steady!* Hold her!'

Voices yelled on every side and then the secondary armament recoiled in their mountings yet again, their shells flinging up thin waterspouts against the horizon where the enemy lay hidden in the swell.

'*Shoot!*' Again the urgent cry, and again the sharp, earprobing crashes.

'Torpedoes running to port!'

Theil jumped to the voice-pipe but Hechler snapped, 'As she goes!'

He looked quickly at the supply-boat. Her bows were already under water, her squat conning-tower deserted as she prepared to run deep and head away. She would not even be a spectator, let alone wait around to pick up survivors.

The explosion was like one great thunderclap which rendered

152

men blind and deaf in a few seconds, as if shocked from every known sense.

Dense black smoke billowed across the water, so thick it seemed solid, then it rolled over the decks and through the superstructure and masts, and for a while longer it was like the dead of night. Through it all the intercom kept up its continual babble.

'Short!' Then, 'A straddle! Got the bastards!'

Hechler groped to the forepart of the bridge and almost fell over a young signalman. He could barely remember the boy's name as he was their newest addition. Logged as seventeen years old, Hechler guessed he was a good deal less.

He dragged him to his feet by the scruff of his tunic and shouted, 'Hold on, Heimrath!' He could hear his gasping and retching in the foul stench and dense smoke. 'It's not us this time!'

The torpedoes must have hit the big submarine just as she made to lift her tail and dive. There could be nothing left. Fuel, ammunition, spare torpedoes, they had all gone up together, scattering fragments for half a mile, while some had clattered across *Prinz Luitpold*'s forecastle and maindeck.

'Target is diving, sir.'

Diving or sinking, it made no difference now. That last salvo would put her out of the fight. It was far more likely that she was falling slowly into the depths, blacker than any death pall, until the weight of water crushed her and her crew into a steel pulp.

'Slow ahead.' Hechler dabbed his mouth with his sleeve. The smoke was streaming over and around them, and men were peering for one another, dazed and with eyes running while they sought out their friends.

Hechler gripped the rail with both hands. 'Tell the accident boat to stand by.' He saw Theil's disbelief, his eyes bulging in his smeared face. 'Lower to the waterline. Now!'

Reluctantly almost, training and discipline reasserted themselves. Like a great beast, rising and shaking itself before it had time to consider the fate which had taken one and spared another.

Leitner wiped his binoculars and glared through the fading smoke.

'Another minute and we'd have shared the same end, Dieter.'

Hechler steadied his glasses as the Arado's bright paintwork gleamed through the smoke. It was settled on the water, and rocking like a wild thing in the powerful rollers.

He said, 'Stop engines. Slip the boat!'

He raised his glasses once more, thought held at bay while he searched for the aircraft, made himself ready for what he might find.

A voice murmured on the intercom, 'Sounds of ship breaking up, sir.'

It must be the enemy submarine. There was not enough of the milch-cow to disturb their sonar.

He flinched as he saw the horrific face in the rear of the cockpit. Eyes of blood, hands in raised fists behind the slumped figure at the controls.

'Get the doctor on deck!' There was a new harshness in his tone.

Jaeger looked up from the voice-pipes. 'He's already there, sir.'

The motorboat ploughed into view across the lens, familiar faces he knew and respected leaping past his vision.

Leitner seemed to speak from miles away. 'It's afloat anyway. Good thing.'

Another voice said, 'The boat will tow it to the hoisting gear, sir.'

Was that all Leitner cared? Was it perhaps unimportant to him when so many men had died horribly just moments ago?

He gripped the binoculars harder as the motorboat's bowman clambered on to one of the plane's floats and hauled himself on to the fuselage. He wrenched open the cockpit and faltered. It must be a hundred times worse close to, Hechler thought despairingly.

Then he saw the man turn and signal. One dead.

She was alive. *Alive.*

He lowered his glasses to his chest and made himself walk slowly to the chart-table.

Around him, smoke-grimed and dazed by the cruel swiftness of destruction, the watchkeepers watched him dully.

Hechler said, 'As soon as the boat is hoisted inboard, get under way and alter course as prearranged.' He saw Gudegast nod. 'I want a complete inspection of hull and upper deck. We could have sustained some minor damage.' He touched the rail again. Even as he said it, he sensed that the *Prinz* would be unscathed.

He looked at Theil. 'Take over.' He half-turned to the rear-admiral. 'With your permission of course, sir?'

Leitner looked away. 'Granted.'

Bells jangled softly and the ship gathered way again.

Hechler hesitated at the top of the ladder to watch as the Arado was swung over the guardrails on its special derrick. The doctor and his assistant were there, and some men with stretchers. He hesitated again and looked into the bridge. His world. Now he was sharing it. Hopeless? Perhaps it was. But she was alive. Because of what she had done, they had all survived. He glanced at the admiral's stiff shoulders. He had made an enemy there, but it no longer mattered.

He nodded to Theil and then hurried down the ladder. This world could wait. The *Prinz Luitpold*'s spacious wardroom was almost deserted. It was halfway through the first watch, and the officers who would be called to stand the middle watch were snatching all the sleep they could. Then the hand on the shoulder, the unfeeling voice of boatswain's mate or messenger, a mug of stale coffee if you were lucky, and off you went to the wretched middle watch.

A few officers sat in deep armchairs, dozing but unwilling to leave their companions, or quietly discussing the explosion which had destroyed the supply submarine and everyone aboard. One man suggested it was lucky they had pumped off most of the fuel. Otherwise both ships might have been engulfed in the same inferno. But most of them, especially the older ones, were thinking of the miles which were hourly streaming away astern. The ship had made a violent turn and was now heading south-east, further and still further from home. If they continued like this, even at their economical speed of fifteen knots, they would cross the Equator in two days' time, and into the South Atlantic.

Viktor Theil as the senior officer in the mess stood with his back to the bar, a glass of lemon juice in his hand. He was conscious of his seniority, the need to set an example at all times in a wardroom where the average age was so low. His immediate subordinate, Korvettenkapitän Werner Froebe, tall, ungainly, and unusually solemn, clutched a tankard of something in one of his huge hands and asked, 'Do you think it went well today?'

Theil eyed him warily. An innocent enough question, but the delay in casting-off from the doomed milch-cow had been his responsibility. It could have been a criticism.

He replied. 'We saved the new plane anyway. Only superficial damage. Pity about the observer.'

Froebe grimaced. 'And the woman. Caught a splinter, I'm told.'

155

Theil swilled the juice around his glass. 'Could have been much worse.'

He looked at the red-painted bell on the bulkhead. Like an unblinking eye. As if it was watching them, waiting for them to relax, lose their vigilance even for a minute. Then the clamour would scream out here and in every watertight compartment throughout the hull. You never really got used to it.

Even in his bed at home, sometimes in the night – he gritted his teeth. He must not think about it. It would all solve itself. He tightened his jaw. But Britta would have to come to him. She had been in the wrong. He could see it. In the end he would forgive her. They would be reunited as never before.

Froebe watched him dubiously. 'I just hope they know what they're doing.'

'Who?' Theil wanted to finish it but something in Froebe's tone made him ask.

'I don't know. The staff, the high command, OKM, everybody who doesn't have to pick up the bloody pieces!'

Two of the very junior officers hovered closer and one said, 'At home, our people will know about us, and of *Lübeck*'s great sacrifice!'

Theil smiled. 'Of course. We are honoured to serve in this way.'

A figure moved heavily into the light. It was the doctor, jacket unbuttoned, his tie crooked.

He looked at them each in turn, his eyes tired. To Theil he said, 'There are ten casualties below. All doing well.'

Theil nodded. They were the men who had been cut or injured by falling debris on the upper deck after the explosion.

The same young officer exclaimed, 'They are lucky to be free of standing their watch!'

The doctor looked past him. 'The *Lübeck* didn't go down gallantly with guns blazing, by the way.' He returned his gaze to Theil. 'She was scuttled.'

Theil felt as if his collar had suddenly become too tight. Figures in nearby chairs were stirring and turning towards the small group by the bar. From torpor between watches the air had become electric.

Theil exploded, 'What are you saying? How dare you tell such lies in this mess!'

Stroheim gave him a sad smile. 'I was in the W/T office. One of the operators broke a finger when he lost his balance as the supply boat blew up. They were monitoring an English-speaking broadcast, from Bermuda it may have been. But that was what they said.' His voice hardened and he leaned forward, his eyes on Theil's outraged face. 'And something else to fill your pipe with. The Tommies and their allies are up to the Rhine, *do you hear me?*' He swayed and glared around the wardroom at large. 'Ivan is coming at us from the East, and *they're* up to the Rhine!' He looked at Theil again. 'Don't you see, man? We're on the bloody run!'

Theil snapped, 'Keep your voice down! How dare you spread –'

Stroheim made a sweeping gesture. 'What is the matter with everyone? It was the W/T office! What are they in there, a separate navy, or something?'

Froebe interrupted unhappily, 'Easy, Doctor – this won't help!'

Stroheim removed his glasses and massaged his eyes savagely. 'Then what will, eh?' He stared at the sideboard at the end of the bar, Adolf Hitler's profile in silver upon it with the ship-builder's crest and launch-date underneath.

'All lies. Raised on them, led by them, and now going to hell because of them!'

Theil said sharply, 'I must ask you to come with me.' He could feel his grip returning, although his anger was matched by a sense of alarm.

The doctor laughed, a bitter sound. 'Follow you? Of course, *sir*. Does the truth disturb you that much?'

Froebe saw another figure rise from a chair and then slip through a curtained door.

It was the flag-lieutenant. He suppressed a groan. In about three minutes the admiral would know all about this.

The doctor moved after Theil and said mildly, 'Don't any of you get sick until I return!'

Froebe leaned on the bar and stared at the steward. 'You didn't hear that.'

The man bit his lip. 'No, sir.'

Froebe saw the curtain sway across the doctor's back. The poor sod was drunk too. God, what a mess.

Suppose it was true. If it was, would it make any difference if they held up another convoy, or two dozen of them, *really* make a difference in the end?

157

He thought suddenly of his wife and two children. Near the Dutch frontier.

He felt like a traitor as he gave silent thanks that the Allies and not the Russians would reach there first.

Hechler clipped the door behind him and stood inside the admiral's bridge. It was illuminated only by the light immediately above the main table against which Leitner was leaning, his hands flat on the chart.

'You sent for me, sir?'

Leitner glanced up. 'I like to know where you are. At all times, eh?'

Hechler watched him as he peered down at the chart again. He had expected Leitner to lose control, to scream at him. It was obvious that he must know about Theil and the doctor.

Hechler had been in his quarters when Theil had come searching for him, his eyes ablaze with anger and indignation. Hechler had closed the door to his sleeping cabin where the girl lay drugged and unconscious after being treated by the doctor. One of Stroheim's attendants had sat nearby, and Hechler had stood beside the bunk, not moving, hardly daring to breathe as he looked down at her. She had seemed so much younger, like a child's face, eyes tightly shut, beads of perspiration on her upper lip and forehead.

A splinter had hit her in the side, just above the left hip. Stroheim had explained that she had lost a lot of blood, and a bone had been chipped, how badly he did not yet know.

Hechler had turned down the sheet and stared at the neat bandages, a small red stain in the centre. She was dressed in a pyjama jacket, and he pulled it across her breasts, one of which was exposed in the bunk light.

He remembered the touch of her skin against his fingers as he did so. Burning hot, like some inner fire, or fever. Otherwise, apart from bruising from her harness when she had made a desperate attempt to steady the aircraft as it had smashed down in a deep trough, she was unmarked. It was a miracle.

He thought of Theil's outrage, and Stroheim's apparent indifference. He was still not sure what he would have done, but the telephone had called him here. It might give him time.

Leitner was saying, 'Lieutenant Bauer just brought me a new

158

batch of signals. I have been working on them, plotting what we shall do.'

Hechler studied his glossy head and waited. So it was Bauer.

He said abruptly, 'He is one of my officers, sir, and as captain I expect to be informed of every signal which affects this ship.'

Leitner looked up, his eyes cold. 'His first responsibility is to me. I will decide –'

Hechler could feel the armoured sides of the bridge closing in, just as he could sense his rising anger and disgust.

'So it's true about *Lübeck*?'

Leitner straightened his back, his face moving into shadow as he snapped, 'Yes, I knew about it. What had happened.'

'You told our people she had gone down in battle.'

Leitner replied, 'Do not adopt that tone with me. It was the right decision. Afterwards, they can believe what they like!'

'I can't believe it.'

Leitner smiled gently. 'Because Rau was another captain, is that it? Death before dishonour? I can read you like a book. You've not changed, you with your outdated ideals and fancies!'

Hechler met his eyes. '*Graf Spee* would have fought back. Her captain was ordered to scuttle too. It did more damage than losing the ship to the enemy. It was madness.'

Leitner banged his hand on the table. 'I believe he shot himself after that, eh? Hardly the act of a *gallant captain*!'

He moved back into the shadows, his voice barely under control. 'I will be questioned. I command here, so remember it. And if that idiot Theil cannot keep order in his own wardroom, and shut the mouth of any foul, defeatist rumour, I will have him removed!' He strode about the small bridge, his shadow looming against the grey steel like a spectre. 'God damn it, I could order a man shot for such behaviour!' He swung round and said, 'After all I did for him, the ungrateful bastard!'

Hechler said, 'He brought the doctor to me, sir.'

'And I suppose you gave him a pat on the back! He can do no wrong, not one of *your* officers, oh no! Ingratitude, that's what it is. I am betrayed on every side –'

'I'm sure he acted as he thought right, sir.'

'Not before half the ship's officers heard what Stroheim said.' Leitner paused by the table, his chest heaving with exertion. 'I

159

should have known, should have overridden your belief in the man, damn him. No wonder his bloody wife was taken away –'

He paused at that point, his eyes staring, as he realised what he had said.

Hechler pressed his hands to his sides. 'When was that, sir?' He leaned forward. 'I must know!'

Leitner ran his fingers through his hair and replied vaguely, 'When we were at Vejle.'

All that time, while Theil had gone around the ship like a man being driven mad by some secret worry, Leitner had known.

'What had she done?'

Leitner took his calm voice as some kind of understanding. 'She had been making trouble. Her parents were arrested. Terrorists, I expect.'

'Is she in prison, sir?'

Leitner's gaze wavered. 'The Gestapo took her.' He looked at the chart without seeing it. 'That's all I know.'

Hechler thrust his hand into his pocket and gripped his pipe. He felt sick, unable to believe what he had heard. *Gestapo.*

Leitner picked up a telephone and added, 'Well, you wanted the truth, Dieter. Sometimes not an easy thing to share, is it?'

'Does Bauer know about it?'

'Yes.' It sounded like *of course.*

'Anyone else?'

Leitner smiled very gently. 'Only you.'

Leitner spoke into the telephone and asked for the navigating officer to be awakened and sent to the bridge.

He put down the telephone and said, 'The war goes on, you see. Within the week we shall carry out an attack which will throw the enemy into utter confusion.'

'Are you going to tell me about it, sir?' He was surprised that he should sound so level. If he had had a Luger in his hand instead of a pipe he knew he could have killed him.

'When I have decided.'

'Then I should like to leave, sir.'

Leitner watched him by the door. 'It is up to you whether you tell Theil about his wife. The ship comes first, you told me so yourself. If Theil is told, what good can it do? He is like the rest of us. A prisoner of duty until released, or killed. As it stands, stupid as he may be, he is a competent enough officer. I will not tolerate interference with my plans because of him, or anyone else, do I make myself clear?'

'Perfectly, sir.'

'Then you *are* dismissed.' He bent over the chart again.

Hechler opened the door and groped his way through the darkness, the night air clammy around him.

On the forebridge all was quiet, the men on watch intent on their various sectors, although Hechler guessed that Theil's confrontation with the doctor would by now be common knowledge.

He thought of the men he commanded. The ones who had trusted him, who had listened to Leitner's passionate speech about the *Lübeck*. Her sacrifice, he had termed it. Rau must have been ordered to scuttle his ship by no less than the Führer. Was there no room left for honour?

He knew Theil was waiting for him, could see his dark outline against the pale steel.

Theil said in a fierce whisper, 'I have sent him to his quarters, sir.'

'Good.' Hechler walked past him. 'I will have a word with him in the morning.'

Theil persisted angrily, 'He was raving about the *truth* all the time! Why should we be told everything, when security must come first! I did not believe him anyway – we would have been informed if –'

Hechler did not hear the rest.

What would you do with the truth, I wonder? If I told you here and now that your wife had been taken by the Gestapo?

He looked over the screen and allowed the spray to refresh his face. She was probably in some terrible prison. She might even be dead. God, it did not bear thinking about.

Theil finished, 'Duty first, I say. The truth can wait.'

Hechler slipped into the chair and touched his arm. 'If you say so, Viktor.'

It was as if Theil had decided for him.

Chapter Twelve

Doubts

Konteradmiral Andreas Leitner appeared to shine as he stood in the entrance of the conning-tower and waited for Hechler to receive him.

'All present, sir.' Hechler touched the peak of his cap and noted that Leitner was dressed in white drill, with a freshly laundered cap-cover to set it off.

Inside the conning-tower it was already stiflingly hot despite the fans, and the sunlight which cut through the observation slits seemed to add to the discomfort of the ship's heads of department who were crowded around the chart-table.

Leitner stepped over the coaming and nodded to his subordinates. For the next few moments at least *Prinz Luitpold* would be in the hands of her junior officers.

They were all there, Theil, beside the towering Gudegast, Froebe, and Kröll, even Stück, immaculate in a white boiler suit and somehow out of place. Oberleutnant Meile, the stores officer, who could at any time tell you how many cans of beans or sausages were being consumed per every nautical mile steamed, and of course Bauer, the smooth-faced communications officer.

Hechler saw the new doctor's shape wedged in one corner, as if he was trying to stay out of sight.

Leitner cleared his throat and glanced at his side. 'Very well, Helmut, we will begin.'

Hechler saw Gudegast raise an eyebrow at Froebe, and the latter's brief grin. Leitner's familiarity with his flag-lieutenant was unusual in public.

Hechler felt their interest as the aide laid a new chart on the table. It was covered with arrows and estimated positions where Lietner had plotted the ceaseless stream of information gathered by the W/T office.

He thought of the hasty Crossing the Line rituals that morning as the ship had reached the Equator, the makeshift ceremony on the forecastle while the anti-aircraft guns had sniffed at the clear sky, and every lookout had scanned his allotted piece of ocean. There was no carrier within a hundred miles, nor had any more submarines been reported. But the spies and the intelligence network which had been built up into an efficient world-wide machine during the past ten years or so, could not be expected to have all the answers.

Hechler had been on the bridge and had watched the boatswain, Brezinka, dressed in a false beard of spunyarn and a flowing robe made of bunting. His cropped head had been topped by a convincing crown, as he had challenged the cruiser's right to enter his domain. The rough ceremony was like a tonic after the strain and uncertainty, and even the young officers who were subjected to the 'bears' ' rough handling and ducked in a canvas bath, took it all in good part.

He thought of the girl who was confined to his own quarters, of his last, short visit there. She had been propped on a bank of pillows, dressed in another pyjama jacket which Stroheim's assistants must have found somewhere. She had greeted him with a smile; once again it had been an awkward greeting. Not as strangers this time, but like those who have been parted for a long while. 'Are they taking care of you?' Even that had sounded clumsy. He had wanted to tell her how he had touched her, had later sat on the bridge chair and thought about her, when the words had flowed so easily through his mind.

She had smiled and had tried to struggle up on her elbows. He had seen the sudden pain in her eyes, and helped her to be comfortable again.

She had said. 'You came to me when I got back.'

'Yes. We were all so proud of you.' He had looked at his hands. 'I was very proud. I thought when I saw the damage –'

She had reached out and their hands had touched. 'I knew you'd wait for me. Somehow I thought you'd pick me up.'

She had lain back, her hand still against his. 'How is the plane?' she had asked.

Then they had laughed together. As if it mattered.

Hechler looked up as Leitner's voice brought him into the present.

'It has been confirmed that the major convoy of enemy troops is going ahead.' He waited for his aide to rest a pointer on the chart. 'Around Good Hope, then escorted all the way to Gibraltar to change to an even larger protective screen with all the air cover they need.' He eyed them calmly, and Hechler wondered if the others were thinking of the doctor's outburst about the Lübeck, the Allied successes in France and Holland. Equally, if Leitner was searching for doubt or disloyalty amongst them.

Hechler glanced at Theil. He looked very calm, but the hands which gripped the seams of his trousers made a lie of his composure.

Leitner continued, 'If the British have a weakness it is their overriding interest in protecting life rather than the materials of war. They do not seem to realise that without such materials, they can lose everything, including the lives of those they intended to defend. It is a false equation, gentlemen, and we shall prove just how futile it is.'

The pointer moved on past the Cape, where the Atlantic met the power of the Indian Ocean.

'In moments of crisis, whole armies have been forced to a halt by the inability to keep up a supply of fuel. Even our own forces in Russia have often been in a stalemate because of holdups, flaws in the supply-line.'

Hechler thought of the great battleship *Tirpitz*, confined in her Norwegian fjord while her fuel had been earmarked for the tanks on the Eastern front. Because of her inability to move, the British midget submarines had found and crippled her. It was unlikely she would ever move again. Hechler still believed that the precious fuel would have done far more good in *Tirpitz*'s bunkers than in a squadron of snow-bound tanks in Russia. She was the greatest warship ever designed. If she were here now, they could have taken on the troop convoy and destroyed it, no matter what escorts were thrown against them.

Leitner said, 'There is just such a convoy, two days behind the troopships. A fast one, of the very largest tankers.' He allowed his words to sink in as the pointer came to rest on the Persian Gulf. 'It was assembled here. Twelve big tankers. Think of them, gentlemen. The life-blood of an army!'

Then his tone became almost matter-of-fact, bored even, as he said, 'Except for any unforeseen factor there would be little chance of surprise. My information –' his gaze rested only lightly on Hechler '– is that the enemy has no idea where we are at present, nor how we are obtaining our own fuel supply.' He nodded slowly. 'Planning, gentlemen – it far outpaces sentiment and outmoded strategy.' He jerked his head at his aide. 'Show them.'

The pointer rested on a mere dot in the Atlantic, just north-west of Ascension Island.

Leitner watched their faces as they all craned forward. 'The island of St Jorge.'

Gudegast said, 'A rock, nothing more. Like a pinnacle sticking up from the ocean bed.'

Leitner gave him a thin smile. 'I shall ignore your scepticism. You are, after all, more used to trading your wares around the sea ports than practising the arts of war, eh?'

Gudegast flushed, but when he opened his mouth to retort, Froebe touched his arm.

Hechler saw it, but doubted if anyone else had noticed the warning.

Leitner said, 'There is a Cable and Wireless station there which was built just before the outbreak of war.' His eyes flashed. 'Before we were forced as a nation to defend ourselves against British Imperialists and the dictates of Judaism!'

His aide said nervously, 'The wireless station has a powerful transmitter, more so even than those in the Falklands.'

Hechler asked, 'Shall we destroy it, sir?' He felt he had to say something, if only to snap the tension, to release his officers from being addressed like unreliable schoolboys.

'I spoke of *surprise*.' Leitner was very relaxed. Only the eyes gave away his triumph, the sense that he had them all in the palm of his hand. 'Provided we are not detected or attacked by some untoward enemy vessel, I intend not to destroy that radio station, but to capture it!'

They all stared at each other, their incredulity giving way to sur-prised grins as Leitner explained, 'We will *fly* our landing party ahead. By this method the enemy will have no chance to warn their patrols and raise the alarm. Down here, in mid-Atlantic, it would be the last thing any sane man would be expecting.' He turned his face very sharply to Hechler. 'What do you say?'

Hechler pictured the lonely Cable and Wireless station. An outpost in the middle of nowhere. No real loss to the enemy if some long-range U-boat surfaced and shot down the radio masts. But absolutely vital if they could signal the *Prinz*'s whereabouts.

165

Hechler said, 'Capture it and make a false signal.'

Leitner said, 'Yes. When – er, we are ready.'

He sounded irritated, disappointed perhaps that Hechler had not waited for a full explanation of his plan.

Hechler said, 'It is a wild chance.' He looked at Theil's blank face. 'And I think it might just work.'

What did it matter now anyway? Any risk, almost, was justified this far from base. Keep the enemy guessing, leave no set or mean track, and then they would continue to hold an advantage. A final confrontation could be avoided if their luck held out.

Leitner said, 'We will have another conference tomorrow.' He eyed them for a few seconds. 'Early. I will not abide laggards in this command!'

He swung on his heel and left the conning-tower.

Gudegast exclaimed, 'Aircraft? Better them than me!'

Theil crossed to Hechler's side. 'What do you really think?'

Hechler looked at the chart. If they failed to mount a surprise attack it would be an open invitation to every enemy squadron and patrol to converge on the tiny island of St Jorge. Hechler pictured the *Lübeck* as she must have been, heeling over, her guns silent while the enemy watched her final moments.

Suppose a signal was handed to him? The order to scuttle rather than meet an honourable fate; what should he do? What *could* he do?

He said, 'It is a daring plan, Viktor. It would mean leaving some volunteers on the island. For them, the war would be over, but we will cross that bridge when we come to it. After the war they might be heroes.' He watched for some sign of a smile or even disagreement. But Theil said fervently, 'For Germany. *Any* man would volunteer!'

'Perhaps.' He heard Gudegast give a snort of anger at something Froebe had said and when Theil turned to listen he watched his profile. Did he suspect, he wondered? Surely no man could love someone and not feel her anguish, her need?

For all their sakes, the ship had to come first. And yet, had he been informed earlier, when Leitner had not been aboard, would he have told Theil about his wife?

Suppose it had been Inger?

He saw the doctor making for the door and called, 'I want to talk to you.'

166

The doctor faced him warily. 'Sir?'

'Come to the bridge. I should like to ask you something.'

Theil watched them leave and ground his teeth. Thick as thieves, even after what had happened.

It was because of that girl. How could the captain behave so stupidly? Any officer, let alone one given command of a ship like this, had to be above such things. He stared after the others as they hurried away to their various departments. It was all so unfair. *I should have command here.* Perhaps it had all gone wrong a long time ago without his knowing? Britta may have said or done something indiscreet. It would go on his record, not hers. He clenched his fists together until he felt sick with the realisation. It had been her fault. When the war was over, he would be overridden by younger men; he might even be discharged! He thought of the friendly way Hechler had spoken to the doctor.

A new strength seemed to run through him. This was his chance to show Hechler, to prove to everyone what he could do, how much he was worth.

Gudegast rolled up his chart and watched his superior grimly. What was the matter with everybody, he wondered, if they could not see that Theil was cracking up?

He glanced at his watch. He would work on his charts and then retire to his cabin. The painting was coming along well. He gave a great sigh. Gerda was probably fixed up with another man already. He grinned. The painting would have to do instead. But for once he was unable to lift his apprehension.

Hechler felt the arm of his chair dig into his side, remain there, and then slowly withdraw as the ship swayed upright again. They had reduced speed to twelve knots and the *Prinz* was finding it uncomfortable. She was more used to slicing through every kind of sea with her cutaway Atlantic bow.

Despite the clear blue sky it was chilly on the open bridge after the heat of midday. The sun looked like a solid bronze orb, and was already laying a shimmering cloak down from the hard horizon line. Hechler turned up the collar of his watchcoat and saw his reflection in the glass screen. Hat tugged over his forehead, the old grey fisherman's sweater protruding through his heavy coat. Not everyone's idea of a naval officer, he thought.

A seaman handed him a mug of coffee and another to the

doctor who had joined him, somewhat uneasily in that corner of the bridge. Hechler said, 'It will be another clear day tomorrow.'

'Is that good, sir?' He watched Hechler's strong profile. A face with character and determination. No wonder Erika Franke was so interested. She had not said as much, nor had he asked her directly, but Stroheim knew enough about women to recognise the signs.

Hechler sipped the coffee. It must have been reheated for a dozen watches, he thought. But it was better than nothing.

'It could make things easier for our pilots.' He thought of the girl in his bunk. It might have been Leitner's intention to send her with the others, perhaps with a film camera as her sole protection. She had at least been spared that. He thought too of his answer. Another clear day might also bring an unexpected ship or aircraft, detection and the beginning of a chase.

Hechler added abruptly, 'You were stupid to speak as you did in the wardroom. I should punish you, but –' He turned in the chair and glances at the doctor curiously. '*But,* that word again.'

Stroheim smiled awkwardly. 'Perhaps I was wrong. I'm sorry. But I was angry at the time, incensed. Not that I could do anything.'

Hechler turned away to watch the horizon as it began to slope to the opposite side once more. *In another moment he will ask me what I think, if what he heard is true.*

He said, 'You are a non-combatant, but out here you are at risk like the rest of us.'

Stroheim made himself look at the ocean and shivered despite his thick coat.

He would be glad when night fell. The ship became more dominant, invulnerable, just as his own quarters and sick-bay had become personal, an escape.

He watched the bronze reflection and knew he would never be at home on the sea. Up here, on one of the highest points in the ship, it was all the more obvious. A vast, shark-blue desert, endless in every direction, horizon to horizon, so that the great ship seemed to shrink to something frail and unprotected. He thought of Gudegast, a man he liked although the navigator fought off every kind of close contact. He was at home out here, could find his way as others might grope through a city fog.

A man of peace, no matter what he proclaimed openly. A true

sailor, not a professional naval officer like Theil and most of the others. He glanced at Hechler again. And what about the captain? One who was not of any mould he knew. A loner, who accepted leadership without question.

Stroheim asked, 'Do you ever have doubts?' For a moment he thought he had gone too far, that the small contact was broken.

Hechler swung round in the chair, his eyes very blue in the strange light.

'Doubts? What do you think? You are the expert, surely!' He became calm again, angry perhaps that his guard had been penetrated so easily. 'My day is full of them. I must question the weather, my resources, the strength and weakness of every man aboard. The ship is like a chain. A weak link can cause disaster.'

He forced a smile. 'Satisfied?'

Stroheim grinned. 'I am glad you are in command. I hate the sea, but if I must be here, then so be it.'

Hechler did not look at him. 'You are a man of the world. While I have been at sea, learning my profession, you have seen and done many things. You must have found the war very difficult.'

Stroheim replied, 'I thought at first it was the end of life as I had known it. You on the other hand would have seen the war as a culmination of things, a suitable theatre to practise the arts of battle, to exercise all that training.' He looked at the captain's profile again. 'But I learned to live with it. People always need doctors.'

Hechler heard the bitterness. 'I know you were in trouble with the authorities.'

Stroheim grimaced. 'The whole world seems to know that.'

He recovered himself and added, 'But I am a good doctor, surgeon too. Otherwise I would be in field-grey on the Russian front instead of here on a cruiser.'

'You see, I am ignorant of that kind of life.' Hechler waved his hand over the screen. 'This is what I know best.'

Stroheim's eyes gleamed behind his gold-rimmed glasses. The captain was working round to something which was troubling him. He had experienced it many times, the patient in his plush consulting room, the roundabout approach to what was really the problem.

Heachler glanced round at the watchkeepers, familiar faces, men and boys who trusted him.

He lowered his voice. 'I knew someone who got into trouble, too. He was arrested, in fact.'

Stroheim held his breath. 'Easy enough to do.'

Hechler did not seem to hear. 'I was wondering, what sort of process does it involve?' He changed tack immediately. 'Here, in my command, justice is swift but I hope fair. I would never punish a sailor just to prove my authority. I am the captain, that is all the proof they need. The rest is up to me.'

Stroheim made himself look abeam where some large fish were leaping from the swell and flopping down again. He could feel Hechler watching him, could sense the importance of his casual questions. 'It depends on which security force is involved.'

Hechler said, 'Suppose it was at the top, the Gestapo. I mean, they have a job to do, but they must surely tread carefully too?'

Stroheim clenched his hands in his pockets. Gestapo. The *bottom*, he would describe them.

He said tightly, 'They are scum.' He felt the same recklessness as when he had spoken to Theil of the British broadcast. 'They are a machine for creating terror.' He faced Hechler suddenly and said, 'If your friend is in their hands, he can expect as much mercy as a heretic facing the Spanish Inquisition!' He turned away and stammered, 'I – I am sorry, sir, I had no right –'

He started as Hechler gripped his arm. 'Do not apologise. I asked for your help. You gave it.' He retained his grip until their eyes met. 'I have been in the dark.'

Feet clattered on ladders, and the watchkeepers shifted their bodies about, impatient to be relieved so that they could go below to their other world.

Stroheim flinched as Hechler said, 'I will not *ask* you this other question.' He tried to smile, but his eyes were very still and cold. 'You knew my wife. She had come to you for an abortion before, but this time you could not help.'

Stroheim stared at him. 'You knew?'

'*Guessed*. She came to my ship as you know. I should have realised why she had come, I ought not to have had *doubts*, eh?'

Stroheim said quietly, 'You would not be the first one to be deceived, Captain. She would have claimed that the child was yours.'

Hechler looked away. How could anyone hate the sea?

He said, 'Thank you for your company.'

170

Stroheim moved away as Kapitänleutnant Emmler, the assistant gunnery officer, clumped on to the bridge to take over the First Dog Watch.

As he reached the internal companion ladder he heard Hechler call after him. He turned and said, 'Captain?'

Hechler merely said, 'Between us.'

Stroheim nodded, suddenly moved by the man's quiet sincerity. 'Of course. Until the next time.'

Hechler faced the ocean again and wondered why he had spoken so freely with the doctor.

He had not needed to demand an answer from him about Inger, it had been plain on his face. But in his heart he had also known it, and that was what hurt the most.

The tiny cabin was more like a store or ship's chandlery than a place to live and sleep. There were shelves, jam-packed with wire strops, spare lashings and blocks. Mysterious boxes were wedged beneath the bunk, and the air was heavy with paint, spunyarn and tobacco smoke.

Rolf Brezinka sat cross-legged on the bunk, a huge pipe jutting from his jaw. The cabin was very hot, the air ducts switched to a minimum flow, and he wore only his singlet and some patched working trousers. As boatswain he stood alone, between wardroom and petty officers' mess. One of a dying breed, he often said, a man who could turn his hand to any form of seamanship, who could splice wire or hemp with equal skill, and who knew the ship's hull like his own battered face.

Opposite him, a cigar jammed in one corner of his mouth, was Oskar Tripz, the grey-haired petty officer. They were old friends, and although both had given most of their lives to the navy, they had each served in the merchant service between the wars, and more to the point in the crack Hamburg–Amerika Line.

When Brezinka had been drafted to the *Prinz Luitpold* he had pulled strings to get his old comrade and fellow conspirator posted to her too. The strings he pulled were unorthodox, but carried no less power than the brass at headquarters.

'It's asking a lot, Oskar.' *Puff, puff.* The big, crop-headed boatswain eyed him grimly through the smoke. 'We've taken a few risks, but I don't know about this one.'

Tripz grinned. At first he had thought of ignoring it, of telling

171

young Stoecker some cock-and-bull yarn to set his mind at ease. Then, the more he had thought about it, the less of a risk it had become. Those cases contained loot, there was no other word for it. Tripz had served in a destroyer in the Norwegian campaign and had seen senior officers shipping their stolen booty back to Germany. They came down like an avalanche on any poor sailor who so much as lifted a bottle of beer without permission. It was all wrong. Leitner must be in it up to his neck, although a ship was the last place Tripz would have stored it, unless he could not trust anybody.

He said, 'Suppose we're wrong? Maybe all the boxes are full of papers, secret files and the like.' He could see that Brezinka did not think so either. 'If we are, we'll drop it right there.'

Brezinka removed the pipe and shook it at him. 'You bloody rogue!' He grinned. 'How *could* we have a look-see? The place is guarded, day and night, and we don't want half the ship's company getting involved. I'm an old bugger, but not ready for the firing party just yet, thank you very much!'

'Nor me.' Tripz rubbed his chin. 'The only time the place is left without a sentry is –'

The boatswain frowned. 'I know. When the ship is closed up at action stations, you in your turret, and me in damage-control. No, mate, it just won't work.'

Tripz sighed. 'What about Rudi Hammer?'

The boatswain stared incredulously. 'Mad Rudi? You must be as crazy as he is!'

Hammer was a petty officer with the damage-control party and on the face of it, the obvious choice. He was no boot-licker, not even a Party member, and although he said very little, was liked by almost everyone, perhaps because of his eccentricity. His hobby was glass. He was determined to retain his skills as a glazier, in spite of all his mechanical training, and nothing could deter him. His divisional officer had had him on the carpet several times about scrounging glass and cluttering his mess with it; he had even taken him in front of Theil because of it. Glass was dangerous in a confined space, especially if the ship was suddenly called to action.

It made no difference. Some hinted that Rudi Hammer's apparent dedication was his way of staying sane, not the other way round.

Brezinka persisted, 'You couldn't rely on him, Oskar, he might blow the whole plan to the executive officer.'

Tripz shook his head. 'He hates officers, you know that, Rolf.'

'But, but –' Brezinka grappled for words. 'It makes me sweat, just thinking about it. No, we'd best forget the whole idea.'

Tripz said, 'If Rudi has any doubts, you know who he goes to?'

The boatswain swallowed hard. 'Well, *me*.'

'Exactly.' He leaned over to stub out the cigar. 'I'll put it to him. The rest is up to you.' He knew that his friend was wavering. 'Look, Rolf, we've been through a lot together. Remember the time we sold that fishing boat to a Yank, when it belonged to the harbour master?'

The boatswain grinned sadly. 'It would have meant jail in those days, not the chop.'

'They'll dump us when this lot's over. Like last time. I don't want to end up on the scrap heap, begging for bread, do you?'

Brezinka nodded firmly. 'No. You're bloody right, old friend. Let's just have a peep at the boxes.' He winked. 'Just for the hell of it.'

They both laughed and then solemnly shook hands.

'Mad Rudi it is.'

She lay as before propped up on pillows, her face pale in the bunk light.

Hechler heard Stroheim's orderly leave the cabin and after a slight hesitation sat down beside the bunk.

She watched him and said, 'You look tired.'

He saw that she had placed her hands under the sheet. In case he might touch one, he thought.

'How are you feeling?'

She smiled. 'The motion is awful. I was nearly sick.' She saw his concern and added, 'I'm feeling better. Really.'

Hechler heard the dull clatter of equipment, the buzz of a telephone somewhere. Perhaps for him. No, the red handset by the bunk was silent. Mocking him.

He explained how the ship was moving slowly to reach their rendezvous at the right time.

She listened in silence, her eyes never leaving his face.

'Don't you get tired of it?' She reached out from beneath the sheet and gripped his hand. 'It never ends for you, does it?'

173

He looked at her hand, as he had on the bridge that first time. Small but strong. He found he was squeezing it in his own.

'You know about the plan to fly off our Arados ahead of the ship?'

She nodded. 'Yes. The admiral came down to see me.' She seemed to sense he was about to withdraw his hand and said, 'No. Stay like this, please.'

Hechler grimaced. 'I am behaving like an idiot again.'

She returned his grip and smiled at him. 'A nice idiot.'

He asked, 'Can it be done?' He had pictured the two pilots missing their way, flying on and on before they fell into the sea.

She seemed surprised, touched that he should ask.

She replied, 'Yes, they could find it. After that –'

Hechler pushed it from his thoughts and said, 'I want you to be well again very soon.' He studied her face, feature by feature. 'My little bird belongs up there, where she is free.' He smiled and added, 'I wish –'

She saw his hesitation and asked softly, 'You wish I was not here, is that it? You are going to fight, sooner or later, and you are afraid for me?' She tried to raise herself but fell back again. 'Do you think I cannot tell what is going on in that mind of yours? I have watched you, listened to what your men say, I gather fragments about you, because it is all I have!' She shook her head against the pillow. 'Don't you *see*, you stupid man, I want you to *like* me!' She was sobbing now, the tears cutting down her cheeks and on to the pillow. 'And I look a mess. How could you feel more than you do?'

Hechler placed his hand under her head and turned it towards him. Her hair felt damp, and he saw a pulse jumping in her throat, so that he wanted to press her tightly against him and forget the hopelessness of it, the drag of the ship around them. He dabbed her face with the corner of the sheet and murmured, 'I dare not use my filthy handkerchief!' He saw her staring up at him, her lips parted as he continued quickly, 'You do not look a mess. You couldn't, even if you wanted to.' He touched her face and pushed some hair from her eyes. 'And I do like you.' He tried to remain calm. 'More than I should. What chance –'

She touch his mouth with her fingers. 'Don't say it. Not now. The world is falling down about us. Let us hold on to what we have.' She pulled herself closer to him until her hair was against his face.

174

'You came for me. I shall never forget. I wanted you to know.'

It was more than enough for her and he could feel the drowsiness coming over her again as if it was his own.

He lowered her to the pillow and adjusted the sheets under her chin. In the adjoining cabin he heard the orderly humming loudly, a warning perhaps that the doctor was on his rounds.

Then he bent over and kissed her lightly on the mouth.

A telephone buzzed in the other cabin and he turned to face the door as the white-coated orderly peered in at him.

'The Admiral, sir.'

Hechler nodded and glanced down again at her face. She was asleep, a small smile still hovering at the corners of her mouth.

Hold on to what we have.

He found he could accept it, when moments earlier he had believed that he had nothing left to hold on to.

Chapter Thirteen

Revelations

Acting Commodore James Cook Hemrose trained his binoculars towards the oncoming cruiser and watched as she started to swing round in a wide arc, in readiness to take station astern of the *Pallas*.

It should have been a proud, satisfying moment. The newcomer was the third ship in his squadron, the *Rhodesia*, a graceful vessel armed with twelve six-inch guns. Fast, and fairly new by wartime standards, she was commanded by Captain Eric Duffield, a contemporary of Hemrose; they had even been classmates at Dartmouth. Hemrose grimaced angrily. That felt like a million years ago.

He saw the diamond-bright blink of her signal lamp, heard his chief yeoman call, 'From *Rhodesia*, sir. Honoured to join you.'

Hemrose would have liked to send a witty reply, but the moment had soured him. Duffield would hate being ordered here, to serve under his command. They had always been rivals. Even with women.

He snapped, 'Acknowledge.' It was strange, these *Mauritius* Class cruisers were in fact slightly smaller than his own ship, but they appeared larger, more rakish.

The destruction of the convoy by the German raider had been hard to take, when so many warships were out searching for her. But it had put an edge to their purpose; he had felt it too when he had visited the New Zealander, the *Pallas*. A spirit of determination, a need for revenge.

Now there would be a sense of disbelief, anti-climax even, with the obvious prospect of being returned to general duties. He tried not to face the other important fact. It would also mean dipping his temporary promotion. He ground his teeth. *For all time.*

He lowered his glasses and watched the new cruiser continuing to turn in a great display of creaming wash. The weather was quite faultless. Clear blue sky, sunshine to display *Rhodesia's* square bridge and raked funnels, her four triple turrets. When

Duffield had finished buggering about, getting his ship perfectly on station, he would doubtless make another signal. To say he was sorry that the hunt was over. Meaning exactly the opposite.

Hemrose saw the commander hovering nearby and said, 'What time is our ETA at Simonstown?'

The commander watched him doubtfully. Hemrose had been even more difficult since The News, as it was termed in the wardroom. He could sympathise with Hemrose, although in secret Commander Godson was not sorry to be spared from crossing guns with a ship like *Prinz Luitpold*.

'We go alongside at sixteen hundred tomorrow.'

Hemrose had thought about it until his brain throbbed.

They had received a lengthy signal from the Admiralty, and an even longer top-secret intelligence report. It was quite plain. He should swallow his disappointment, even his pride, and accept it. A United States submarine had made a brief emergency signal to announce that she was in contact with the raider. There had been a shorter one, too garbled to decode properly. It was her last word.

When US warships had finally reached the search area, they had found nothing for a full day, except for a two-mile oil slick, and some cork chippings of the kind used in a submarine's internal paintwork to diminish condensation. Then later, as another darkness had closed in, one of the ships had picked up some human remains. To all accounts there had been little enough to discover in the grisly fragments, except that they were German.

The American submarine was known to have collided with a freighter which had failed to stop after their brief contact. The US commander had signalled that he was returning to base only partly submerged because of the damage to hull and hydroplanes.

Hemrose had considered the signals with great care, and had called the New Zealand captain, Chantril, across for a conference.

The Kiwi had accepted it philosophically.

'So the Yank got in a lucky salvo. Beat us to the punch. But it cost him dearly for doing it.'

Hemrose slumped in the bridge chair and said, 'Get a signal off to Simonstown, Toby. The squadron will refuel on arrival. But *lighters*, not alongside.' He slammed his hands together. 'I want to be ready for sea at the first hint of news.'

The commander opened his mouth and closed it promptly. It was obviously going to drag on until the boss accepted the inevitable. He ventured, 'They won't like it, sir.'

Hemrose slid from the chair and snapped, 'Plotting team in the chart-room, chop chop. I've got a *feeling* about that bloody German.'

In the cool shadows of the spacious chart-room Hemrose glared at his team. A mixed collection, he thought. But he had to admit that they had done well in their new role. Even the chaplain, who had devised a special file of sighting reports and information from neutral sources. It had all come together far better than he had dared to hope. Until the news about the submarine.

He knew they were watching him, gauging his temper. That suited him. He had always found that fear was the best prop to naval leadership.

The navigating officer had updated the charts daily, adding known convoys, escort groups, and isolated strangers in the vast sea area which touched two continents.

Even the progress of a solitary hospital ship was noted. They were always at risk. A U-boat commander might put one down because he had not taken the time to identify the markings, or the brightly lit hull at night-time. Or another, who was on his way back to base, might do it because his search for victims had been ill rewarded.

Hemrose pictured his German captain. No, he was not the sort to sink a hospital ship with its cargo of sick and wounded survivors. Hemrose held no admiration for Hechler whatever. He did not even know much about him, other than the intelligence reports and some newspaper articles, but he knew his worth as a fighting sailor. He could still remember the ship reeling over to the aggressive mauling of those eight-inch guns. Hechler was a man who took risks, who would not damage that reputation by killing wounded men.

He said, 'What do we know, gentlemen, *really* know?' They remained silent and he added, 'Some Jerry remains were picked up but we cannot be certain they were from *Prinz Luitpold*. Or if they were, she might be damaged, steaming away to put it right, preparing to come back into the fight when she's good and ready.'

178

The navigating officer, a fresh-faced lieutenant who had proved his ability even to Hemrose's satisfaction, said, 'My guess is the latter, sir. She was damaged, and is making for home base again.' He looked at the others as if for support. 'And why not? She's wiped out a convoy and other ships besides – she'll likely get a hero's welcome if she makes it back to Norway or wherever.'

Hemrose nodded, his heavy features giving nothing away. 'Good thinking, Pilot. In which case the Home Fleet will catch the bugger this time.' He looked round. 'Ideas?'

The chaplain cleared his throat. 'But suppose the raider is still at large, sir. Where will she go next? How does she find fuel?'

'Fucking good question.' He saw the chaplain wince at his crude comment, as he had known he would. 'She'll likely go for the big troop convoy, although my guess is that she's left it too late. The escort has already put down two U-boats, and they've not lost a single ship as yet.'

The navigating officer tapped the chart. 'There's the iron-ore convoy, sir. It should be near the Falklands about now.' He lifted the chart to peer underneath. 'Two more off Durban, both destined for the UK, and of course the fast oil convoy from the Gulf.'

Hemrose pictured the network of convoy routes in and out of Britain. In two great wars those same lifelines had almost been cut. Had that happened, the country, and therefore her dwindling allies would have been brought down. So many times, the convoy losses in the Atlantic had outpaced their ability to build replacements. It had been a raging battle from the first day, and the casualties had been awesome. Yet still men went back to sea, again and again, with only a handful of clapped-out escorts to protect them or die too.

He tried to picture himself in *Wiltshire*, a lone raider like Hechler's ship. *At large*, as the chaplain had described it. He would. But the man of God had a point about fuel supplies. It had to be something big before *Prinz Luitpold* could run for home. Iron-ore? He peered at the chart, his shadow across it like a cloud. Once it could have been vital, but not now. Not unless Mister Hitler pulled another rabbit from his hat. The Russians were still advancing, and the Allies were about to burst across the Rhine. It was still almost too hard to believe after all the retreats and stupid mistakes.

The Durban convoys then? He examined the navigator's typed

179

notes. Times, dates, weather, and already some hint of the escort. He said bluntly, 'I'd go for the big prize.' He thrust the upper charts aside. 'The oilers. Still the most valuable convoy, no matter what the newspapers blather about.'

The commander said, 'It would be a terrible risk, sir.' He flinched under Hemrose's red-rimmed stare. 'For the krauts, I mean.'

'Of course it would.' He stood back and decided he would have a Horse's Neck in a few moments to settle his thoughts. 'He could get cut off on the wrong side of the Cape of Good Hope if he decides to go looking for the convoy too soon.'

The commander said, 'But if their lordships and the C-in-C have already considered this, then surely –'

Hemrose beamed at him. Godson's stupidity was somehow reassuring. He had not missed the fact that none of them had further suggested that the *Prinz Luitpold* had been destroyed, or that they were all wasting their time.

He nodded, his mind made up. 'Did you signal Simonstown?'

The commander sighed. 'All agreed, sir.'

Hemrose rubbed his hands. 'Captains' conference immediately we anchor.'

The navigator looked up from the chart and asked simply, 'But if we're wrong, sir?'

Hemrose did not reply at once. 'You mean if *I'm* wrong, Pilot?' They all laughed politely.

Hemrose picked up his cap and studied it. It would look good with another row of oak leaves around the peak, he thought.

He said, 'My wife won't like it a bit.'

Not one of them realised that he actually meant it.

Korvettenkapitän Josef Gudegast stood with his hands on his hips and waited for the two Arado pilots to scribble a few more notes on their pads. It might be another warm day, but the dawn air in the conning tower was cold and dank. The massive steel door purred open on its slide and Gudegast saw the captain framed against a dull grey sky.

'Nearly ready, sir.'

Hechler glanced at the two pilots who had sprung to attention. 'At ease.' He knew Gudegast would take care of everything. He had done it often enough, but the pilots had to be certain of their orders. Both float-planes had been stripped of unnecessary weight, and would carry no bombs.

As Leitner had replied testily when this had been mentioned, 'We want to use the radio station, not blow its bloody mast down.'

He was up there now on his bridge, impatient, eager to get moving.

Hechler went over it again. Both aircraft would land in a tiny sheltered strip of water, and the landing party would go ashore without delay in rubber dinghies. The planes would be packed like cans of sardines, he thought. He lingered over the officer in charge, Oberleutnant Bauer. An obvious choice as he was a communications specialist. But he had done very little field training, so a good petty officer had been selected as second-in-command. Eight men in all, excluding the pilots. The intelligence reports were definite about the radio station. It was never fully operational and reliable reports stated that it was about to be adapted as a giant radar beacon. The invasion of Europe had made that an unwanted luxury. There were only three men on that lonely pinnacle of rock. Gudegast had said, 'What a way to fight a war. The poor bastards might never be told if it's over, or who's won!'

Theil had snapped at him, 'The war will end for *them* if they try to sabotage the station!'

Poor Theil, he was looking more strained, with deep lines around his mouth.

Hechler said, 'Met reports are good.' He looked at each of the fliers and recalled Leitner's angry outburst when he had suggested that the new Arado should be sent, and so keep a fully operational one on board, just in case.

Leitner had shouted, 'That is defeatist talk, Captain! For a man of action you seem beset by caution! The new plane will be employed *when I say so!*'

He too seemed more on edge. The prospect of action, the apparent lack of enemy signals. It was like steaming into an impenetrable fog.

Hechler glanced at the bulkhead clock. 'Five minutes.' He nodded to the pilots. 'Good luck.' He recalled his letters to the parents of the men lost in the Baltic. Their faces already wiped from his memory. He resisted the urge to shiver.

He made his way to the forebridge, and noted the lookouts and gun crews huddled together at their defence stations.

There goes the captain. he could almost hear the whispers. *Does he look worried?*

He waited for a seaman to wipe the moisture from his chair and then climbed into it.

Korvettenkapitän Werner Froebe had the morning watch, his face red in the chilled air, his huge hands wrapped around the gyro-repeater so that it looked no larger than a coffee cup. Young Jaeger was nearby, ready to relay orders, watching and learning. He seemed to have become suddenly mature after the lifeboat, and the convoy.

Hechler thought of their two survivors. The aged boatswain was still in a kind of daze, and Stroheim said that he rarely paid attention to anything that was happening. The other one, the young mate called Ames, had made a complete recovery. Hechler pictured the drifting corpses. If anyone ever got over that sort of experience.

Theil joined him on the gratings, his fingers busily adjusting his powerful binoculars.

Hechler glanced at him. 'After we find the convoy, Viktor, we can turn for home. Fight our way right through the British Fleet if need be.'

The first Arado coughed into life and he tasted the sharp tang of high-octane fuel. Surprise was everything. It was unlikely that the crew of the radio station would even guess what had hit them. After all, it had never happened before.

A phone buzzed and the seaman who picked it up yelled, 'Ready, sir!'

Hechler could imagine Leitner peering down from his armoured nest. But he did not turn to look. 'Go!'

The plane roared along the short catapult, dived clumsily towards the water, rallied and then climbed away from the slow-moving ship.

Voices muttered by the starboard ladder and Jaegar said, 'Visitor, sir.'

Hechler glanced across in time to see Theil's frowning disapproval and a signalman's quick grin.

She crossed the bridge very carefully, her hair rippling over her coat collar while she rested on a stanchion for support. Hechler took her hand and guided her to the chair. Once, he glanced up to

Leitner's bridge and thought he saw the admiral's cap move back quickly out of sight.

He asked, 'How are you?' He noticed the way she was holding her side and wondered why she had come. All those ladders, and she was still weak from losing so much blood.

She settled down on the chair and tucked her chin into a scarf. 'The doctor said it was safe.' She watched the second Arado as it roared away from the side, the camouflage dull against the dark, heaving water. 'I feel better already.'

Hechler heard Froebe say, 'The camera is cranking away, I see! God, we'll all be film stars yet!'

Hechler looked at her and found he was able to shelve his immediate problems. The next fuelling rendezvous. The convoy. The cost in ships and men. Perhaps after that, Leitner would be content. He ought to be.

He offered, 'You look fine. You've got your colour back.'

She looked at him, and for a few moments it was like a bond, a physical embrace although neither of them had moved.

A seaman called, 'From W/T office, sir. They are monitoring a broadcast and request instructions.'

Hechler nodded. 'You go down, Viktor. It may be nothing, but we need all the news we can get.'

He thought of Froebe's sarcastic comment, and then of the supply submarine's hideous end. Leitner had said originally that the women of the camera crew would be transferred to the supply boat with their cans of film. The milch-cow had been due to return to base to replenish stocks of fuel. He did not imagine that the two women would be very pleased at being made to wait for another rendezvous, with the prospect of a battle before-hand. With luck, the risk of damage should be minimal. All the enemy's heavy escorts were with the big troop convoy, and other units were still sweeping to the North for some reason. It was likely that valuable though it was, the convoy of oil tankers would rely on speed and a small, local escort until the last long haul of Biscay and beyond.

She was still watching him, her tawny eyes very bright in spite of the misty dawn reflections.

She said, 'It is like going on and on for ever.' She placed her hand on the rail below the screen so that it was just inches from his.

Another voice called, 'Lost contact with aircraft, sir.'

'Very well.' Hechler looked at her hand. It was almost a physical pain. But it was no longer ridiculous, even though any kind of future was nothing more than an idle dream.

She dropped her voice. 'Do you still miss her?'

Hechler stared. 'No. I – I'm not sure. To say I have wasted my other life beyond this ship, is like a betrayal – a deep hurt.'

The words seemed to burst out of him, yet he could not recall ever being so open with anyone. Like being stripped naked, left without any defences.

She said, 'I know what you're thinking, Dieter. You are wrong. I think all the more of you because of your frankness, your sense of honour.'

Hechler was only half aware that she had called him by name, that for just a few seconds her fingers had rested on his wrist.

She added, 'I have never met anybody like you.' She withdrew her hand and shrugged. 'Will you make me say it? Would you despise me if I told you?'

He looked at her. The figures around the bridge seeming to mist over like moisture on metal fittings.

He heard himself say, 'I will not make you. Let me say it, no matter what the rights and wrongs are.'

She said, 'We can decide.'

'Yes.' He looked away, afraid she would change her mind because of his inability to find the words. 'I want you.' It sounded so flat, so crude that he looked at her, expecting to see anger, or contempt. He was shocked by the happiness in her eyes, a new brightness there like the moment in his quarters.

She whispered, 'It's all I needed to hear. I've known there was something, I think from the beginning.' She shook her head as if she barely believed it. 'We must talk.'

Jaeger said, 'W/T office, sir.' He held out the telephone, his eyes on the girl.

'Captain?'

It was Theil. 'It was just some Brazilian radio station, sir.' He sounded petulant, as if he thought a junior officer could have been sent to deal with it.

Hechler looked at the horizon. The light was strengthening all the time. He tried to picture it in his mind. One hundred miles to the Cable and Wireless outpost. They should have arrived by now. Give them another five minutes, then full speed ahead. The *Prinz* would be there in three hours. By that time – he glanced at the chair but it was empty. He looked at Jaeger who said, 'She went below, sir.' He sounded very calm, but his young face asked a million questions. Something to tell his hero father about, if they ever got home again.

He heard Theil, humming quietly in his ear. A nervous sound. Hechler said, 'Never mind, Viktor. Check it through. You might glean something, eh?' He put the telephone in Jaeger's hand. 'Ask the navigating officer to come here.' He smiled, glad of something to distract him as he saw Gudegast already present, stripping off the canvas cover from the ready-use chart-table after a quick glance at the clear sky.

'What do you think?'

Gudegast stuck out his lower lip so that his untidy beard sprouted over his uniform, mottled with grey like frost on a bush.

'Now, sir.'

Hechler nodded. The W/T office would have picked up any alarm call from the island if the mission had gone rotten on them. There was always the chance of course that the two pilots had lost their way. He saw Gudegast's expression and knew it was less than likely.

'Take over. Full speed. Warn radar, and tell the Gunnery Officer to muster his landing party.'

Hechler would not be able to step ashore. Nothing was safe any more. But it would have been like a release to tread on firm ground again. With her. Her fingers inside his. Just a few moments of make-believe. He had said it to her. *I want you.* He examined his feelings, and the words seemed stronger than ever. It was true. He climbed into the chair. She had been loved, perhaps even married. He took another glance at his thoughts. Nothing changed. It was not a dream after all.

Theil watched the stooped shoulders of the radio operators, and listened to the endless murmur of morse and static over the speakers. The junior officer in charge, Leutnant zur See Ziegler, stared at him anxiously and said, 'I am not certain, sir. My superior has left no instructions –'

Theil glared. 'I'll deal with it!' He gripped the handle of Leutnant Bauer's private office and then rattled it angrily.

Ziegler stammered, 'It's locked, sir.'

'I can see that, you dolt!' He knew he was being unreasonable, but somehow he could not contain it. Perhaps seeing Hechler with that girl had done it. He was married. What was he thinking of?

'Give me the key!'

The young one-striper wrenched open a desk and handed it to him. Theil saw that it had a red tag on it. To be used only in a final emergency. He ground his teeth. It was unlikely that anyone would bother about colour tags with a ship on her last nose-dive to the bottom.

He slammed the door behind him and slumped down in Bauer's chair. It was curious that he had never set foot in here since the ship had been handed over by the builders. A secret place. A nerve centre.

He was growing calmer again and took several deep breaths.

There was a framed photograph of a young naval officer on the desk. Theil picked it up and grunted. It was Bauer himself. Typical of the man. He thought of Stroheim's outburst in the wardroom, the stares of the other officers while he shot his mouth off about some enemy propaganda. Naturally the British would claim all sorts of victories for themselves and their allies. They would hope for fools like Stroheim to listen in and spread the poison.

There was another key on the tag, a much smaller one.

Theil listened to the busy radio-room beyond the door. Back to normal, each man thinking of the one-striper's embarrassment when he had been told off. Serve him right, he thought savagely. We all went through it – he pushed the key into a steel drawer and held his breath as it clicked open.

He was the second-in-command. In battle he stayed with damage-control, whereas Hechler usually stood firm on the open bridge and disdained the massive armour plate of the conning-tower. Theil had thought about it often. He guessed that many officers in his position would consider the very real possibility of stepping into a dead man's shoes.

Even Leitner might fall in battle. Theil suddenly saw himself returning to his home in Schleswig-Holstein, to be decorated by the Leader.

His hand faltered on a pale pink folder with the eagle crest and

186

stamp of naval intelligence emblazoned on the cover. He flicked it open and felt his heart stop. His own name was at the top. Serial number, rank, date of commission, everything. There was his original photograph when he had joined this ship. His fingers felt numb, unable to turn the page. He wanted to lock the drawer, leave now, and to hell with the Brazilian broadcast. There was a freshly typed signal flimsy under the first page. His eyes blurred as he scanned the bottom first where Leitner's signature had been counter-signed by Bauer.

The name at the top was Britta's. Apart from a file reference there was little else except for the line which stood out like fire. *No further action by naval intelligence. Subject arrested by Gestapo.*

Theil did not remember locking the desk drawer, or even groping his way from the office.

The young officer snapped to attention and said, 'Nothing more from that station, sir. I –' He stared after Theil as he blundered past him and out of the W/T room.

Theil fought his way to the upper deck and clung to the safety rail by a watertight door for several minutes.

Britta arrested? It could not be. For an instant he was tempted to rush back there and read the file again. But it was true. It had to be.

Britta arrested. He squeezed his eyes tightly shut to find her face as he had last seen her. But all he could see was the empty house and dead flowers, the neighbours watching behind their curtains, the doctor's calculated advice.

He wanted to scream it out aloud. They all knew, must have done. Leitner, and that crawling Bauer. He thought of Hechler, his mind reeling like a trapped animal. He would know too, had probably been told weeks ago.

He allowed his mind to rest on the Gestapo. He had always avoided contact with them like most people. Secrecy had not always worked, and he had ignored that too.

But he had heard things. Torture, brutality for the sake of it. He thought of her face, her pleading eyes, the bruise on her body after she had tried to find out about her parents.

Gestapo. It was not just a word any more. It was death.

The ship began to shake and quiver around him and he knew they were increasing speed towards the tiny islet.

What should he do or say?

He turned his face this way and that, clinging to the rail as if he might otherwise fall.

Britta was dead, or was she even now screaming out her pleas to her torturers?

'No!' His one cry was torn from him, but rebounded against the iron plate as if it too was trapped and in agony.

Chapter Fourteen

'Auf Wiedersehen . . .'

Oberleutnant Hans Bauer strode down the steep, rocky slope and stared at the two float-planes as they lifted and swayed in the swell. They were safe enough, moored with their small anchors, and each with its pilot aboard in case the sea should get up.

Bauer stood with his feet planted apart, his fine black boots setting off his uniform to perfection. The heavy pistol at his waist, like the silk scarf thrown casually around his throat, gave him a dramatic appearance, or so he believed. He had enjoyed every moment of it, the culmination of surprise and excitement when the two rubber dinghies had been paddled furiously ashore and his men rounded up their prisoners.

It had gone almost perfectly, but for one unexpected development. There had been two extra people at the radio station. He now knew they were mechanics who had been left here for some maintenance work.

Bauer considered what he would say to the rear-admiral. Leitner would give him the praise he was due for his quick thinking. He shaded his eyes to watch the cruiser's shortened silhouette as she headed towards the small islet, only her bow-wave revealing the speed she was making through the water. After she had topped the hard horizon line in the early light she had seemed to take an age to gather size and familiarity, he thought. He went over the landing, the exhilaration giving way to sudden alarm as the two additional men had appeared. Yes, Leitner would be pleased. He frowned. He was not so sure about the captain.

He turned, his boots squeaking on the rough ground, and surveyed the desolated station. A long, curved corrugated building which the British called a Nissen hut, and two radio masts, one small, the other very high and delicate. It was a wonder it could withstand the gales.

He saw two of his men, their Schmeissers crooked in their arms, and congratulated himself on his choice. Hand-picked, and all good Party members. It was right that they should profit by this small but obviously vital operation.

Closer to the building lay a corpse, covered by a sheet which was pinned down by heavy rocks.

One of the visiting mechanics. He had seen the landing party, and had turned, blundering through his astonished companions, and run towards the building. To send a message, a warning, or to sabotage the equipment, Bauer did not know even now.

He remembered his own feeling as the heavy Luger had leaped in his grip, the man spinning round, his eyes wide with horror as he had rolled down the slope kicking and choking. The second bullet had finished all movement. After that, the others had crowded together, shocked and frightened, seeing only the levelled guns, the sprawled body of the dead man.

Bauer had told them to obey each order without hesitation, and after the building had been thoroughly searched, the radio transmitter checked for demolition charges, they had been locked in a storeroom and left under guard.

Bauer adjusted his cap at a more rakish angle, rather as the rear-admiral wore his. Such a fine officer, an example to them all.

He saw the petty officer, a grim-faced man called Maleg, coming down the slope, two grenades bouncing on his hip. He was not one of Bauer's choice for the raid. He thought of Theil who had detailed the man for the operation. Bauer was suddenly grateful he had never cultivated Theil as anything more than a superior officer. He had had everything within his grasp, and had been stupid, instead of taking full advantage of his position. He owed everything to the Fatherland, everything. How could such a man become involved with a subversive, a traitor? He should have known his own wife better than anyone. He sighed. Instead –

The petty officer saluted. 'About the burial, sir?'

Bauer eyed him coldly. 'The prisoners will do it. It should dampen anyone else's foolishness!'

Maleg stared past him at the distant cruiser. They had found no weapons, no demolition charges either. Even the prisoners were harmless civilians. It was all the lieutenant's fault, but any aftermath would be shared amongst them. Bauer had enjoyed killing the man, he decided. Given half a chance he would have gunned down all the rest. Maleg knew about officers like Bauer. Why had he been the one to get saddled with him?

190

Later as the prisoners stabbed at the rocky ground with picks and spades, Bauer entered the makeshift radio station and looked with disdain at the garish pictures on the walls, the nudes and the big-breasted girls in next to nothing. Decadent. How could they have hoped to win the war, even with the Yanks as allies?

He pictured his family home in Dresden, the paintings of his ancestors, proud, decorated officers. A heritage which was a constant reminder of his own role and his promising future. Leitner had promised him an immediate promotion with an appointment to the naval staff as soon as they returned to a safe harbour. Bauer was not so blind that he did not know about the rear-admiral's relationship with Theissen, his flag-lieutenant, but nothing could mar his qualities as a leader and an inspiration.

Maleg watched him and was glad that the ship was getting nearer. The *Prinz* was something he could understand and work in. He had good comrades in the petty officers' mess. He sniffed at the aroma of fresh coffee from the hut's spindly chimney. It was quite amazing. They had proper coffee and piles of tinned food which he had almost forgotten. He would take some back with him to the mess, he thought. He tried not to dwell on an old newspaper called *Daily Mail* he had found in the sleeping quarters. He could read English fairly well, but even if he had not been able to, the war maps and photographs with their screaming headlines would have told him anyway. The Allies were said to be through France and Belgium, and the only German resistance was in isolated pockets in Brittany and the Pas de Calais. The sites of the rockets and flying-bombs, the much-vaunted secret weapons, were said to be overrun, their menace removed for all time. It could not all be true. There was mention of some 400,000 German troops being taken prisoner. That could not be accurate, surely?

And the newspaper was not new. What had happened while they had been attacking the convoy? He considered himself to be a good petty officer, and he had destroyed the newspaper before the others could see it.

He looked round as he heard Bauer reading crisply from a small prayer book while the others stood leaning on their spades. Maleg wanted to spit. Kill a man, then send him off with full respects. He watched as Bauer threw up a stiff Nazi salute, then pocketed the prayer book with the same detachment he had shown when he had reholstered his Luger.

The spades moved again and Bauer marched towards the hut.

He said, 'Duty is duty, Maleg, no matter what.'

The petty officer sat down on a rock and waited for one of the men to bring him his coffee.

Suppose. The word hung in his mind. Just suppose they lost the war. It was unthinkable of course, but if the *Prinz* was down here in the South Atlantic, what then?

He turned and peered out at the ship, which in the last minutes seemed to have doubled in size.

Hechler would get them home somehow.

The first Arado was being hoisted up from alongside, many hands reaching out to boom it away from the hull as the ship dipped heavily in the surrounding current.

Leitner had come down to the forebridge, and his cigar smoke drifted over the screen like perfume.

Leitner said, 'Like clockwork. What did I tell you, eh?' He was almost jocular. 'God, what a coup it will be.'

Hechler trained his binoculars on the lonely station. They would land a small party with two of the ship's wireless telegraphists. They would have all the right codes, and even if they had been changed by the enemy, no one would question their one frantic call for help. Several things could go wrong, of course. A vessel might unexpectedly arrive on a visit to the islet. If that happened, a prearranged alarm signal would be made, and the *Prinz* would be on her own again. Or the fuel convoy might be delayed or rerouted. That was so unlikely it could almost be discounted.

What else then? They might meet with enemy warships, be held down to an engagement until heavier forces arrived to join the battle. He had gone over the rendezvous points with Gudegast; there were three possible choices, and the supply submarines would be on station whatever happened.

He glanced at Leitner. The admiral was nobody's fool, and would want to return to Germany as soon as the next convoy was destroyed. They might fall upon other ships on the return passage, small convoys, single fast-moving troopers too.

There was a blackout on Allied radio communications, or so it seemed. The enemy must be puzzled about their sources of fuel supply, and it was likely that all other convoys in the Atlantic

192

had been held up in their ports until the raider's position was verified.

Hechler was a practical sailor but had never ruled out the value of luck. Theirs simply could not last, and he had often imagined some special task force fanning out from Biscay for a sweep south in pursuit. They would have carriers, or at least one. Just a single sighting report was all the enemy admiral needed.

Feet clattered on the ladder and Theil entered the bridge, his eyes concealed by dark glasses.

He said, 'I've sent a double anchor party up forrard, sir, and given orders to break the cable if need be.'

Leitner's shoulders shook in a small chuckle. 'More caution, eh?'

Theil ignored him. 'Have you selected the men to remain on the islet, sir?'

Hechler looked at him. 'I have spoken to the doctor, Viktor. Three are still in sick-bay after being thrown from their feet.'

Theil replied, 'I have their names, sir. I did think they were malingering.' His voice was quite flat and toneless.

Hechler turned so that Leitner should not hear. 'Are you all right?'

Theil straightened his shoulders. 'I am.'

Hechler nodded. 'Good. We can land the two survivors also.'

Leitner turned. 'When they are picked up eventually, nobody can say we were not humane!' It seemed to amuse him.

Theil stared past him. 'A man was killed over at the radio station.'

Hechler exclaimed angrily, 'When? Why was I not told immediately?'

Leitner said, '*I* was informed. You were busy anchoring the ship, remember?'

Hechler recalled Bauer reporting aboard when a landing party had been sent to relieve him. An hour ago? It seemed like minutes.

Theil had a hand to his chest as if he was in pain but dropped it as he explained, 'Bauer shot one of the mechanics.' He waited and added harshly, 'A civilian.'

Leitner swung round again. 'In God's name, man, what do you expect? I will not have our people put at risk for any reason! Bauer acted as he thought fit. I will uphold his decision. Millions

193

have died in this war, and millions more will follow, I have no doubt!' He was shouting, ignoring the men on watch nearby. 'One bloody shooting is not my paramount concern, thank you, *sir*!'

Theil eyed him blankly from behind the dark glasses.

'Evidently, sir.' He turned and hurried from the bridge.

'Now what the *hell* was that all about?' Leitner grinned, but his eyes remained like cold glass.

Hechler thought he knew Theil. Now he was not sure of anything. He said, 'Nobody wants to see non-combatants killed, sir. I'll grant that it may have been necessary in this case. However –'

Leitner sniffed. '*However* sums it up, I think!'

Hechler was suddenly sick of him, even of Theil. When the latter discovered – he raised his binoculars to watch the party on the beach to hide his sudden apprehension. Suppose Theil already knew? How could he? As captain he had been told nothing until Leitner's anger had let the news spill out about Theil's poor wife.

Strain, combat fatigue, the yearning for a command of his own, of this ship most of all – moulded together they could have this effect on him.

Leitner said, 'You can speak to the men you have detailed. It will come better from you.' He was calm again, but as their eyes met Hechler could sense the spite in his casual remark.

Tell them you are leaving them behind. Why? For Germany? Would it be enough this time? He gritted his teeth. It was all they had.

He said, 'Tell the sick-bay I am coming down.'

Jaeger picked up a handset and watched him walk past.

Command – was this what it meant? Was this what it might do to the man who held it?

Leiter snapped, 'Don't gape! Do as you're told! By God, I intend to produce a full report on all this when we get back to Germany!'

A messenger called nervously, 'Camera team request permission to come to the bridge, sir.'

Leitner moved away from the side and loosened the collar of his white tunic.

'Of course.' He glanced at the others, Gudegast brooding by the chart-table, the petty officer of the watch, young Jaeger, and the rest of those subservient faces.

'All honour will be shown to this ship, gentlemen. A film which our children will remember!'

194

Gudegast watched him march to the rear of the bridge. Children? The admiral would have no problems there, he thought.

The ship was still in a state of immediate readiness, if not at action stations. On the petty officers' mess-deck, the air was hissing out of the shafts, compressed and smelling faintly of oil. The deadlights were screwed shut, and most of the watertight doors clipped home. The ship was stopped but only resting, and even the fans and muffled generators sounded wary and ready to switch to full power.

The small cluster of men at the end of one of the tables appeared to be engrossed in the one who was seated, his fingers busily arranging a pattern of coloured glass under an overhead light. Acting Petty Officer Hans Stoecker watched the man's hands working nimbly with the newly cut pieces of glass. Rudi Hammer was putting the finishing touches to yet another small box, a present perhaps for a wife or girlfriend. It was nerve-racking, unbearable, and yet Stoecker knew he must not break the silence. Opposite him, his grey head bowed with no outward show of impatience, Oskar Tripz also watched the box taking shape.

The fingers eased a fragment over and snipped a rough edge away. The man nicknamed Mad Rudi was pale in every respect, hair and lashes, even his skin; he was not far removed from an albino.

Stoecker tried not to think of that day when an unknown hand had given him the letter. The rest was a nightmare.

He glanced at the other petty officer named Elmke, a dour, humourless man whose only friend in the ship, it seemed, was Tripz.

Stoecker wanted to wipe his face. It felt wet with sweat. The sealed air perhaps? He knew otherwise. It was uncontrollable fear and disgust at what he had begun.

It had all seemed like a daring exploit when he had shared the letter with Tripz. He was friend and mentor all in one. But it had got out of hand. Even the boatswain Brezinka was implicated, and now Mad Rudi and Elmke.

He concentrated on the pattern of glass. What would his mother say, and his father when he found out? It had all been so simple, so right. As if it was a kind of destiny. Even meeting with

195

Sophie. He turned the thought aside. She had been with Jaeger. An officer.

Tripz said, 'Well, come along, old fellow, spit it out!' He was grinning, but the tension was clear in his voice. 'We have to know, God damn it!'

Hammer put down the flat-jawed pliers he used for snapping off excess glass. 'I nearly broke that piece!' He shook his head. 'After the war they will need all the glaziers in the world to put the cities together again, you'll see!'

Tripz patted his shoulder. 'God, man, if it's true what we think, you can buy your own glass factory!'

Hammer smiled. He was always such a gentle, reserved man. In his petty officer's uniform he looked like an imposter.

He said severely, 'Well, it wasn't easy, I can tell you.'

Elmke said roughly, 'Come *on*, man!'

Tripz shot him a warning glance. 'Easy, Ludwig! Give him time!'

Hammer smiled. 'It is true. I opened just two of the boxes.' He spread his hands. 'Jewels by the thousand, gems of every kind. Gold too. A factory, Oskar? I could buy a whole town with my share.'

The others stared at each other but Stoecker felt as if his guts were being crushed.

They were speaking of a *share*. It was all accepted, decided even.

He heard himself say in little more than a whisper, 'But if we're found out?'

Surprisingly it was Hammer who spoke up. 'In this ship we can die in a hundred different ways, Hans. I do not believe in miracles. We have fought a just war, but we are losing.' He seemed surprised at their expressions. 'Face it, comrades, it is not so bad when we have discovered an alternative to oblivion, yes?'

Tripz produced a bottle of schnapps. Drinking on duty would cost him his rank, all of them for that matter.

Very solemnly he filled four mugs and they clinked with equal gravity together.

'To us.'

Only Stoecker felt that he wanted to vomit. But the nightmare had already grown in size and power. It had been too late when he had taken that letter.

*   *   *

196

Hechler walked along the port side beneath the elevated barrels of the anti-aircraft weapons, nodding occasionally to familiar faces, pausing to speak briefly with the petty officer in charge of a working party.

There was no difference from being here at this rock and out on the high seas. The great ocean was the enemy, and yet being anchored made him feel vulnerable, unprepared.

A rising plume of smoke from the funnel showed that Stück and his engineers were equally impatient to move. Men off duty hung about in groups, nervous and not far from their action stations.

A lieutenant crossed the deck and saluted. 'The boat is ready, sir.'

Hechler stared past him at the small landing party, three of whom were still showing signs of their injuries.

It had been a difficult thing to tell them what was required. Hechler knew better than to make a speech. About Germany, the great sacrifice that others had made already.

He had explained simply, 'It is for us, comrades. The ship.'

A senior wireless telegraphist was in charge, with one other assistant, while the remainder were from the sick-bay.

'I shall come back for you if I can.'

He had sensed their efforts to be brave, not to let him down. It was, he thought, one of the hardest things he had ever asked anyone to do.

He walked with the lieutenant to the side, where a motorboat was waiting to transfer the small party to the radio station and bring back the others. After that – he sighed. It was best not to think of how they would feel when they watched their ship speeding away to disappear eventually below the horizon.

They were assembled by the accommodation ladder. Hechler shook hands with each one. He had entrusted a letter to the senior telegraphist to hand to the British or whoever arrived. Under normal circumstances he knew they would be well treated. But with a civilian lying buried on the islet, the letter might ease the situation.

He saw the two prisoners already in the tossing motorboat. The old boatswain had stared at him blankly when he had told him he would soon be released. The other one named Ames had met his gaze, not exactly hostile, but strangely defiant. He had warned the senior telegraphist about him. He was probably safer off the ship, he thought. As a mate, he knew about navigation and would have the *feel* of the sea like Gudegast. You could not watch a man all the time unless he was in irons. He might have been able to escape and sabotage the steering gear or something else vital, even at the cost of his life.

He said, 'I shall send aircraft for you if I can. If not –' He had almost shrugged but had seen the pain on their faces. 'It is the war. Our success rests in your hands.'

He looked round and saw the sunlight flash on binoculars from the upper bridge, and guessed that Leitner was watching each magnified face and reaction.

He thought of Theil. He should be here too. Something would have to be done before they met the enemy again. When their luck ran out.

Hechler saluted as they climbed down the side, one with a plaster cast on his arm swinging round to stare up at his messmates who waved to him. Suddenly, as if at a sign, one of the sailors at the guardrails began to sing. He had a rich, mellow voice, and as Hechler watched he saw many of his men leaning over the rails, their voices joining and rising above the sea, and the splutter of the boat below the ladder.

'*Auf Wiedersehen – until better days!*'

Hechler watched the boat until it vanished around the high bows then walked slowly aft. He remembered his brother Lothar joining with his fellow cadets and singing that same, lilting song when he had gained his commission.

'That must have been dreadful for you.'

He saw her standing by a screen door, one foot on the raised coaming. How long she had been watching he did not know, and yet in some strange way he had been aware of her.

'It was.' He stood beside her, shielded from the rest of the ship by the heavy, steel door.

She said quietly, 'If the war is won they will be free very soon. If not –' She did not continue.

He took her hands in his. 'I have been thinking about you.' He felt her return the squeeze. 'Maybe too much. But I have not forgotten our words up there, in my eyrie.' He saw her smile.

She said, 'People, your men, think you are made of iron. An iron pirate, did you know that?'

198

He looked down at her, studying her mouth, imagining how it would feel trapped in his.

She watched his face, his indecision. 'But I know the *real* man.'

He said, 'After we leave here –' He tried again. 'When we meet with the enemy – I want you safe. No matter what happens, I need to know you are spared the true danger. After the war –'

Her eyes left his face for the first time. 'I will not wait that long, Dieter.' She looked down and there was fresh colour in her cheeks. 'You think that is cheap, shameless?'

He touched her hair. 'No. I only feel shame for letting you say what I am thinking.'

The junior communications officer, Ziegler, appeared round the door and stared at them blankly.

Then he said, stumbling over the words, 'I have to report that the shore party has tested the signal, sir.' His eyes blinked quickly at the girl as he continued, 'No further enemy broadcasts intercepted.'

'Thank you.' They watched him march off and she said, 'We frightened him, poor boy.'

He knew he must go. 'Later on –'

She stepped back over the coaming, one hand to her side.

'I shall be there. Have no doubt of it.'

Hechler climbed to the bridge and walked to the fore-gratings. Voices hummed up and down the pipes, and messengers and boatswain's mates stood with handsets to their ears and watched the steam from forward as the cables clanked up and through the hawse-pipe.

'Stand by.'

Bells jangled and Gudegast said, 'Course to steer, one-three-five, sir.'

He heard someone murmur behind him, 'See the poor buggers on the beach, Max? I'd hate to be left –'

A petty officer snarled, 'I shall *personally* maroon you if I get the chance! *Stand to*, damn you!'

Hechler felt the sun warming his face through the toughened glass screen. The cable was coming in more quickly now. *Clank-clank-clank*. Would they ever drop anchor again? He smiled despite his anxieties. The Flying Dutchman. He smiled again and seemed to hear her voice. *Iron pirate*. The enemy probably had a less colourful name, he thought.

He craned forward and saw Theil with Leutnant Safer who was

in charge of the forecastle, although in action he was quarters officer in Turret Anton. Theil had his arms folded, as if he was hugging himself. Perhaps when they got into open water again he would snap out of his mood.

How would I feel? It was strange that he did not compare Theil's wife's plight with Inger. He pictured Erika's face. Her defiance. And her defeat.

'Anchors aweigh, sir!'

Hechler glanced at the lieutenant of the watch. It was as if the man had had to repeat it before he had understood.

'Slow ahead together.' He felt the deck vibrate gently, the ugly hump of land begin to move past. 'Starboard ten.'

Gudegast crouched over the gyro to check a last fix on the tall aerial.

'Steady. Steer one-three-five.' He picked up the telephone and noticed it has been newly cleaned. 'Chief? This is the Captain. Revolutions for twenty-five knots in half an hour.'

Stück sounded surprisingly close. 'You told me.'

Hechler grinned. 'Getting old, Chief.' He put down the telephone and saw Jaeger talking with Stoecker, the youngster who should have taken his final exam for petty officer but for this raiding cruise. He was obviously worried about it, for his eyes looked quite red. Lack of sleep probably.

Theil came into the bridge. 'Anchor secured, sir. Hands dismissed.'

He stared round the bridge. 'I'm not sorry. Not in the least.'

'Is there something you want to tell me, Viktor?' He glanced past him. 'Now, while we're alone.'

'*I am worried about my wife.*' He seemed to be staring, although the dark glasses made it hard to gauge his expression.

'I can understand that.'

'Can you?' Theil watched two sea-birds rise above the screen, their raucous cries suddenly loud and intruding.

He added calmly, in an almost matter-of-fact tone, 'You didn't have to consult with the doctor about the landing party, sir. I had it in hand, you know.'

Hechler tugged out his unlit pipe and jammed it in his mouth. 'It was my responsibility.'

Theil nodded very slowly, his dark glasses like two sockets in a skull.

'I see that, sir. A commanding officer must shoulder every burden when it concerns those who have to trust him.' He saluted. 'I must go to damage control and exercise the fire parties.' He added vaguely, 'Might help.'

Hechler made to climb into his chair but walked instead to the opposite side.

Theil was right. *I must tell him.* But Theil's words, his erratic behaviour, held him back, like a warning.

He turned and saw Gudegast watching him from the compass platform. The navigator dropped his gaze immediately, but not before Hechler had seen the concern there. Did he believe that Theil was falling apart? Even his bitter comment about asking the doctor. He was still angry about the scene in the wardroom, and Leitner's offhand indifference.

He raised his binoculars and trained them over the quarter towards the radio tower, but it was already blurred and indistinct. He thought of the unknown seaman's words. *I'd hate to be left.*

Korvettenkapitän Froebe, the executive officer, stamped on to the gratings and saluted.

'Well?' Hechler felt the warning again but could not recognise it.

Froebe shifted his long, ungainly legs.

'I hate to bother you, sir, but one of my divisional officers has made a complaint. He has threatened –'

Hechler stopped him. 'Nobody threatens you, Werner. You are part of my authority, a most important one.' He saw the words go home, some relief on the tall officer's features.

'The communications officer –'

Hechler kept his face impassive. It would be Bauer. A man of great conceit. He had certainly displayed no remorse over killing the civilian.

Leitner had given him his blessing. Was that all it took, after all? *I did my duty, nothing more.*

Froebe continued, 'He claims that the second-in-command entered his private office after forcing the watch-officer to give him the key.'

It hit Hechler like a steel bar.

So that was it. It was so obvious he could not understand how he had missed it. He had even ordered Theil to go there himself.

'You have told me, Werner. Leave it with me, eh?' He smiled, but his mouth felt like stiff leather.

Froebe bobbed his head, satisfied and relieved.

'And tell Bauer to mind his manners. Tell him from me.'

He heard Froebe clattering down a ladder and then bit hard on the pipe-stem.

Theil knew. Who would blame him? What might he do?

When the sun dipped towards the empty horizon he was still sitting in the chair, and his questions remained unanswered.

Chapter Fifteen

Middle Watch

Gudegast crouched over the chart-table and rubbed his eyes to clear away the weariness. It was two in the morning, but he could not sleep, and wanted to make sure he had forgotten nothing. He read slowly through his neatly written notes and paused again and again to check the calculations against his two charts. The ship was quivering violently beneath him, but he had grown used to that. She was steaming at twenty-eight knots, south-east, over an unbroken sea.

On deck it was easier to understand with a ceiling of bright stars from horizon to horizon. Here in the chart-room, it was all on paper. Noon sights, and careful estimations of tide, speed and weather. It was vaguely unnerving, with only the chart lights for company, but for a while longer he needed to be alone.

He tried not to think of a hot bath, scented with some of that Danish stuff he had picked up in Vejle. So long ago, he thought wistfully. He scratched himself beneath his arm as he pictured the voluptuous Gerda in her little house above the fjord. There would not be many baths from now on. Water was strictly rationed, and it would get worse unless they turned for home. Home? Where was that?

He heard feet scrape against steel and guessed that the watch was changing its lookouts yet again. An empty ocean outside, and yet in here you could see the inevitability of the embrace, the savagery of the approaching battle.

It would have to be a salt-water shower. He grinned into his beard. He must be getting soft as well as old. In the merchant service, where the owners counted and begrudged every mark spent, you got used to faulty fans, bad food, and machinery which went wrong at the worst moment. It had taken him a long while to get used to the navy, its extravagance at the tax-payers' expense.

The door slid open and he turned with an angry challenge on his lips. Instead he said, 'I've been over it all again, sir.' He watched Hechler by the table, his body shining in an oilskin. So he could not sleep either. *If I were captain* – he stopped it there. Gudegast would not have taken command of a warship if she were ballasted with gold bricks.

Hechler compared the charts. 'At this rate, fifty-seven hours.' He pictured the desert of ocean, their solitary ship heading swiftly on a converging course. There had been no signals from Operations Division, and silence in this case meant that the convoy was on course, and should now be around the Cape and steering north-west. Fifty-seven hours was too long. He peered closer at the pencilled lines and crosses. To increase speed would dig deeply into their fuel supply. To risk a late confrontation might invite disaster. He said, 'Thirty knots.'

Gudegast regarded him gravely. The cruiser could go faster, but she was not on sea trials, nor was she within reach of help if something failed.

Hechler smiled. 'I have just spoken with the Chief.' He saw him in his mind, cautious as ever, but quite confident. 'He agrees.'

Gudegast watched him, feeling his disquiet. 'After this, we can refuel at one of the rendezvous.'

Hechler glanced at him and smiled. It had sounded like a question, a challenge.

'My admiral favours the second rendezvous, 2,500 miles to the west.'

Gudegast dragged the second chart closer. The bright cross marked the exact grid position only; dates and times were safely locked in Hechler's safe.

Gudegast pursed his lips. 'The last thing the enemy would expect.'

'What you really mean is, we could be heading further north to the other rendezvous, and cutting off some 900 miles, right?'

Gudegast showed his teeth. 'Something like that, sir.'

'Fuel economy is not always the answer.'

Gudegast picked up his parallel rulers. 'I'll work on it for a while. An alternative might come in handy.'

Hechler nodded. 'I shall be increasing speed in two hours when the watch changes. Let me know what you find in your search.' He paused, one hand on the door clip. 'But get some sleep. I depend on you. You know that.'

The door slid shut and Gudegast stared at it with quiet astonishment. He both liked and respected the captain, but he had never thought that his feelings had been returned.

He grinned and turned back to his charts. He would do a sketch of the captain at the first opportunity. Just him with the ocean behind his back. It was something to look forward to.

Hechler did not remember much about leaving the chart-room, nor did he feel the usual guilt at not being on the bridge or in his little sea-cabin.

The charts, Gudegast's finality over the converging ships, had cast a cloak over all else. There was nothing, could be nothing beyond this ship, he told himself. Even if his suspicions about Theil were correct, he could not reveal it now or Leitner would have him arrested, humiliated and disgraced before everyone. God, it was bad enough as it was. Theil loved the *Prinz* as much if not more than all of them. He would not do anything to destroy that loyalty. But if the shock of his wife's arrest had acted as a twist of guilt, he might not even be the man he had once known.

He almost smiled. He was the one who had told Theil about a captain's responsibility.

An armed sentry stiffened at attention as he clipped a water-tight door behind him. He stared at the passageway with its shaded emergency lights, the blank-faced doors, the racks of fire-fighting gear laid out like an omen.

Hechler walked past the sentry and knew the man was staring after him. It was strange but he did not care. Not about that anyway. The whole ship had probably made up its mind long ago. Then he paused and listened to the movements about him, the gentle rattle of equipment, the shiver of metal as the great ship sliced through the water. Nearly a thousand souls were contained within her graceful hull. Men as varied as Theil and Gudegast, young Jaeger and the acid-tongued Kröll. On and on forever, she had said. With a start he realised he was standing outside the door of his own quarters. Perhaps he had known what he was doing, or had he allowed his heart to steer him?

He felt it pounding against his ribs, a terrible uncertainty which made him hesitate and stare at himself like a stranger. Tomorrow was the day which would tell. After that, their future could only be measured by hours and by luck.

But that was tomorrow.

He tapped the door and opened it.

The day-cabin was in total darkness and he saw her sitting beside the bunk in the adjoining one, staring towards him so that the door's rectangle stood out like an intimate photograph.

She wore his dressing gown, the one with his initial on the pocket, which his brother had given him on that last birthday together. It was shabby, but he would never part with it.

He walked towards her as she said, 'I have worn it several times.' She moved her arms beneath it. 'It helped.'

He rested his hands on her shoulders and drew her to her feet. They stood together for a long while until he pulled her against him. She had not resist, nor did she respond as he stroked her hair, and pressed his hand against her spine.

He murmured, 'I had to come, Erika.'

She lowered her face against his chest. 'I *willed* you to be here, with me.' She leaned back in his arms and studied his face. 'Welcome to our new home.'

She smiled, but he could feel the tension like a living thing, the nervousness which stripped away her outer confidence. Hechler sat her down on the bunk and knelt against her, his head pressed into her body. He felt her hand in his hair, moving back and forth, gentle and yet demanding, speaking for both of them.

She said softly, 'You won't stay, Dieter. I know you can't.' When he tried to look up at her she gripped his neck and held him more tightly.

'No. Hear me. You said you wanted me. We cannot wait.' He tried to free himself but her arm was like a band around his head. 'I – I feel so shy now that I have said it. But it means so much –' He took her wrist and lifted his face to watch her, to share the emotion her eyes revealed.

Hechler said, 'I love the way you are.' He felt her shiver as he untied the dressing gown and pulled it open. He kissed the warm skin and then dragged the dressing gown down until her shoulders, then her breasts were naked. He kissed her hard on each breast, felt her gasp as he pressed each nipple in turn with his lips, until neither of them could stand it.

He laid her on the bunk and undressed her. It was without gentleness, but she reached out to help him, until she lay watching him, her naked body shining in the solitary light above the bunk.

Hechler did not even glance at the telephone above them – it

206

could shatter their moment with the ruthless power of a torpedo. He saw the livid scar on her side, as if some beast had sunk its jaws into her body. She seized his head as he placed his mouth over the wound.

It seemed as if life was compressed into a single moment. There had been nothing before, and ahead was only uncertainty like an empty horizon.

He wanted her so much that it hurt, and yet he needed this moment to last forever. Even when he took her limbs, stroked and kissed them, or ran his fingers around and deep into the dark triangle of hair, he clung to each precious second as if it was the last. She was no longer passive, she was dragging at his clothing, pulling him over and against her until she could find and hold him.

For just a fraction of time more they looked at each other, their faces almost touching, and then, with her hand urging and guiding him into her, they were joined. Then, as they fell together, with love and in passion, Hechler knew that no matter what lay ahead, life without her would be pointless.

Hechler slumped in the tall chair, his face stinging with salt and spray, his ribs seemingly bruised by the pressure as his ship crashed through the long Atlantic swell. Was it lighter? Were those millions of stars smaller? It was said that only at sea, on an open bridge, could a man truly understand the reality and the power of God.

He rubbed his eyes with the back of his glove and heard a man move with alarm. It could be no fun to stand the middle watch with your captain always present. He thought of the friendly glow of the reading light above the untidy bunk in his sea-cabin. At any other time he would have dived into it, fully dressed, needing a shave as he did now, not caring for anything but escape. Not this time. He had wanted to stay awake, had needed to, in case he lost something of those precious moments.

It was so clear in his mind, her body thrusting against his, her cry of pain, the instant pressure of hands on his shoulders when he had made to draw away. He had hurt her. It had been a long time. How right. The same for them both.

He touched his face and decided he would have a shave. He looked into the black shadows below the chair, both happy and shamed. His face must have been as rough as the clothes which he had worn, when he had felt her beneath him, sensed her legs

207

spread out and over the side of the bunk. He could not recall anything like it, so complete, like a frankness which had pitched all barriers aside. And afterwards it had remained between them. More than just a bond, far more than a momentary passion for sex.

He glanced at the lieutenant of the watch; it was Ahlmann again.

Hechler wanted to touch himself beneath the oilskin, as if he was still sharing it. For he could still feel her. As if it had just happened.

Figures moved behind him and he heard the boatswain's mate of the watch ask politely, 'Some coffee, Captain?'

Hechler glanced down at him and nodded. Whatever it was, it would taste like champagne.

He said, 'I shall go to my sea-cabin for a shave afterwards.'

He peered at his luminous watch. When the time came to increase speed and alter course perhaps for the last time before – he did not dwell on the possibilities. They were all behind. Only this moment was real and important.

He thought of the small landing party he had left at the Cable and Wireless station. What would they be doing? Playing cards, writing letters, something sailors usually did without the slightest knowledge of when they would be sent on their way, let alone read by their loved ones.

His mind strayed to the convoy. It would make a big hole in the enemy's fuel supplies. For how long? Two weeks – ten? Even a few days could make all the difference to the embattled armies while they waited for winter, their most needed ally.

He thought of the meeting in Kiel with von Hanke, the way he had looked at him when he had disputed the German army strength on the Russian Front. An oversight? It seemed hardly likely. In his great command bunker was the Führer also deluded by the maps and victorious arrows and flags? Could it be that *nobody* dared to tell their leader the terrible truth? That half of his finest divisions were buried by their thousands in the mud and snow of Russia? It was stupid to think of such things. The ship was only a part of the whole; nobody, not the General Staff, Donitz, not even the Führer could see the complete picture.

Someone coughed behind him and several voices whispered pleased or sarcastic greetings to the morning watch as they

208

changed places with those who had stood the past four hours.

Froebe stooped beneath the chart-table's protective hood and spoke briefly with Ahlmann and his junior assistant. Then he stood up, glanced at the captain as if to ascertain whether he was awake or dozing and said, 'The watch is relieved.'

Feet shuffled on wet steel, and the smell of coffee drifted amongst the newly awakened officers and seamen like a welcome drug. Between decks the watchkeepers threw themselves into their blankets, some in hope of sleep, others merely to find solitude when surrounded by so many.

Thoughts of home, worries about shortages there, bombing, the next leave and the last one. It was all part of a sailor's life.

In the great engine-room and adjoining boiler-rooms the men on watch in their blue or white overalls shouted to each other or sang their bawdy songs, all unheard in the roar of machinery, but to one another. The duty engineer officer stood on his shining catwalk beside the little desk with its telephone and log book. Old Stück would be down again soon. He had led all of them from the moment the first machine parts had been installed in this great hull. And yet he trusted nobody completely when important orders had to be executed.

The engineer officer, whose name was Kessler, could feel his shoulders ache as he gripped the rail with his gloved fingers. He felt the ship, too, thundering around and beneath his feet. She was the finest he had known. He grimaced. Down here anyway. What he had heard about their gallant admiral hardly inspired anyone. Kessler stared at the quivering bilge water far below the catwalk, blue-green in the harsh lights; it reminded him of the Christmas tree at his home as a boy. The first glimpse of it on that special morning, the presents, his father's huge grin. He had made himself go there on that last leave. The house had gone completely. He had known about it of course, just as he had sensed Hechler's compassion when he had seen him after the town had been bombed; he had asked for leave when the RAF had gone after the ball-bearing plant there. But as Hechler had explained, had there been a dependant, a wife, children, then perhaps –

The captain had been right, of course. But Kessler had gone home all the same when his time for normal leave had come up.

He still did not know what he had expected, a gap in the houses, all that was left of his boyhood and his family memories.

209

It had not been like that at all. The whole street had gone, and several on either side of it too.

He squeezed the rail until his fingers ached. Would he *never* get over it?

The telephone made a puny rattle above the chorus of engines and fans.

He pictured Hechler up there in the open bridge, the air and the ocean which seemed endless.

He said, 'Ready, sir.'

Over his shoulder he heard Stück's voice and turned to see his figure framed against the bright pipes and dials, almost shining in a fresh suit of overalls.

'The Old Man?'

Kessler glanced at the shivering clock. 'Yes, Chief.' Stück was even earlier than usual. But Kessler was glad without knowing why.

Stück leaned his buttocks against a rail and folded his arms. He could see through the haze of steam and moisture, and his keen ears told him more than any log book.

He looked at the lieutenant and guessed what his assistant had been brooding about. He toyed with the idea of mentioning it, but sentiment found little comfort in lip-reading, in competition with their sealed, roaring world.

His eyes came up to the dials above the deck as a bell rattled again, and the three speed and revolution counters swung round with expected urgency.

Stück grinned and pretended to spit on his hands. His lips said, 'Come on, Heinz, feed the beast, eh?' Seconds later, the three great shafts gathered speed, so that even the men on watch had to make certain of a ready handhold.

Stück watched the mounting revolutions. A thoroughbred.

Here we go again.

Theil lay on his back and felt the increase of speed creating a new rhythm as it pulsated through the bunk and into his body. He had tried to sleep, but had been wide awake since he had left the bridge. His eyes felt raw, and despair dragged at his mind and insides like some creeping disease.

If he went to the admiral and pleaded for him to make a signal through the next refuelling submarine, would it make any difference? He knew immediately that it would not. Leitner could have told him about the arrest before the ship had weighed anchor, might even have intervened on his behalf. He did not want to, did not care; it was that simple.

Theil rolled on to his side and stared desperately at his clock. He would be called by a messenger very soon, then he would have to put on an act again, or go mad under this terrible weight. The ship was beginning to shake more insistently, so that objects in his cabin clattered together, as if to drive him out. Very soon now the ship would need him more than ever before. But for that sure knowledge he knew he would kill himself. Over the side in the night watches, lost in seconds in their ruler-straight wake. Or a pistol to the temple, a moment's fearful uncertainty – then nothing. The thought of the pistol which hung from his bunk made him violently angry, sick with it, until every limb trembled like the ship.

He saw himself in that cabin again, Bauer's stupid, handsome face exploding like a scarlet flower as the bullet smashed him down.

See if *he* could take it as well as he could shoot an unarmed civilian.

The thought brought no comfort. Unarmed civilian, like Britta. Perhaps she was released now, back at their house, putting right the damage to her beloved garden.

He buried his face in the pillow and found that he could not stop himself from sobbing aloud.

Two cabins away, Oberleutnant zur See Willi Meile, the stores and supply officer, lay on his side and stared at the naked girl who was clutching her breast and gasping with exhaustion.

Meile was no fighting sailor, his world was food and drink, paint and cordage, everything which fed and sustained his ship.

He had worked on one of the camera team ever since she had come aboard. She was certainly no beauty, but she was young and had a fine body. To Meile it was like being in heaven. Nothing like it had happened before, nor could occur again.

The executive officers and U-boat commanders had all the glamour. They were more than welcome to it, he decided. It was said that half of Hamburg was owned by ex-pursers of the Hamburg-Amerika Line, just as naval bases like Wilhelmshaven were profitable investments for retired supply officers like Meile.

211

No, after the war, those who controlled the food and drink would be the new heroes.

He leaned on one elbow and felt her breast. He had left lights switched on as he did not want to miss anything. Her bare shoulders were quite red in places where he had squeezed, even bitten them. She gasped out that she could take no more. 'You are more than a man –' The rest was silenced as he kissed her hard on the mouth, his hand reaching for her, exciting her despite all exhaustion. Neither of them noticed the sudden increase of engine noise, nor considered what it might mean.

Meile dragged her wrists over her head and held them tightly. He said, 'Don't fight me. I'm going to take you. *Now!*'

In the next cabin, young Jaeger switched on his light and squinted at his wristwatch. He would not wait to be roused, but would have a shave before they tested action stations to start another day. He thought he heard the girl's stifled cry through the thick steel and shook his head. That Meile was like an animal where women were concerned. He tried not to think of the gentle Sophie; it was wrong even to picture her in his mind with all that was going on in the next cabin. The sooner they dropped the three women off in the next rendezvous supply-boat, the better. He thought of Hechler's face when he had been speaking with the girl pilot. No, perhaps not her.

He stood up and felt the carpet tremble beneath his bare feet. Then he looked at the disordered bunk. It was not so difficult to see Sophie here after all.

On the opposite side of the ship the girl gathered up her things and pushed them unseeingly into a small grip. She would return to her allotted cabin, which she shared with one of the camera girls. Like Jaeger, she switched on some lights and stood, swaying to the heavy motion in front of a bulkhead mirror. Where he adjusted his uniform before going to speak with his sailors. She pouted at herself. Or, in the past, leave to see his unfaithful wife.

She opened her shirt and watched herself touch the scar on her side. It still hurt. Her hand drifted slowly across her skin as his had done. She could still feel him; her body was both elated and sore from their need for each other.

She had not realised how it was possible to be both loved and possessed, to feel victor and conquered at the same time. She buttoned her shirt and looked very slowly around the empty

212

cabin. She would not come back again. Not ever, unless they were together.

She heard quiet movements from the captain's pantry. Poor Pirk, his servant and guardian angel. In some strange way, his acceptance of her here had seemed like a blessing.

She supported herself in the doorway and listened to the mounting rumble of power. Like something unleashed, which would never be cowed until satisfied, or destroyed.

Her fingers rested hesitantly on the last light switch. She would remember everything. The rasp of his clothes against her nakedness, the thrust of his body which was like love and madness together.

The cabin retreated into darkness and she closed the door.

As she walked past the dozing sentry at the end of the passageway she knew she would regret nothing.

Chapter Sixteen

The Signal

Peter Younger, one-time radio officer of the SS *Radnor Star*, drew his knees up to his chin and shaded his eyes with one hand. He was still unused to being on dry land again, and for hours after his arrival with the small party of German sailors he had been light-headed, unsteady on his feet like some dockside drunk. When the raider had weighed anchor and had headed away from the tiny islet Younger had almost expected that each minute was to be his last. He had seen the rough grave, and had heard what had happened from one of the station's crew. It was curious, but the resident crew had been as withdrawn as the Germans from him, and of course Old Shiner. He glanced at the white-bearded boatswain who was sitting with his back to a rock, facing the sun, eyes closed. He could be dead, he thought.

He idly watched one German who was strolling up and down the slope, a machine-pistol dangling from his shoulder. Younger had heard the senior rating telling him off for not wearing his cap; it was absurd, when you knew you would soon be changing places with your prisoners.

Mason, the man in charge of the small station, had whispered to him that the place was no longer properly operational. So no regular monitoring or signals would be missed or expected. The enemy had worked it out very well. The man had said that when the German operator made his false signal, someone on the receiving end might realise it was not the usual telegraphist. He had added somewhat condescendingly that only a radio man would understand that. Younger had contained his impatient and irritation. *You can say that again*, his inner voice had answered.

Younger had decided not to share his plan with anyone just yet. The station crew seemed too dazed and shocked by what had happened to their companion. Cowed was putting it mildly, he thought angrily. The Germans would not want to kill anyone for no purpose. If the British or American warships arrived to find more graves, they might forget the Geneva Convention, so far from home, and take their own revenge. The krauts would think that anyway.

It would have to be after the false signal and without giving them time to destroy the transmitter. Younger had measured up the distance he had to cover, had even selected the sailor he would overpower to reach the radio-room. The German sailor in question was often on guard duty; he was apparently useless as a cook or anything else with one arm in plaster. He could not therefore carry more than a pistol, and he usually kept that buttoned in his holster. And why not? They had no means of escape, nowhere to run to. They were all prisoners now. He tried to gauge their feelings, those of the senior operator in charge anyway. He could see him now, standing by the ladder to the radio-room, his cap dangling from one hand as he shared the frail sunlight.

He was young but prematurely bald, a fact made more obvious by the dark hair on either temple. He was a thoughtful-looking man, introspective, with the sensitive features of a priest. He was probably brooding on his own predicament, which had been thrust on him in the name of duty.

Younger licked his lips and tried to relax his body, muscle by muscle. When he considered what he intended to do he was surprised at his strength and conviction. There was no fear at all. He thought of the torpedo which had blasted the old ship apart, men screaming and on fire, others being carried away by the suction to the same Atlantic grave.

This would be for them. The Old Man, Colin Ames, all of them.

With a start he realised that the old boatswain had opened his eyes and was watching him without recognition. His eyes were washed-out blue, so pale in the glare that they were like a blind man's.

Younger smiled. 'Okay, Shiner?' He wondered if he knew where they were. How they had got here.

The boatswain opened and closed his hands. They lay on the rock beside him, as if they were independent of their owner.

He said huskily, 'Wot time we goin' to eat, Sparks?'

Younger shot a quick glance at the two Germans, but neither had noticed.

He hissed, 'Don't call me that, mate!'

215

The eyes did not blink. 'You're Peter Younger, that's who.' He nodded, satisfied. 'Sparks.'

Younger sighed. 'Ames is dead. I've taken his place.' He could feel his plan running out like sand. 'The krauts wouldn't let me within a mile of this lot if they knew.' He gripped his arm fiercely. Through the ragged jersey it felt like a stick. 'Help me. To even the score for the lads and the old *Star*, eh?'

He saw understanding cloud the pale eyes for the first time. He said shakily, 'All gone. The lot of 'em. Jim, Colin, and –' he stared round, suddenly desperate – 'where's –'

Younger gripped his arm and said quietly, 'It's all right, Shiner. The cat didn't feel anything. He's buried with the lads now.' He watched the sentry's shadow reaching across the rough slope. 'Because of these bastards.'

The old man closed his eyes. 'Dead, you say?'

Younger looked down. *Please help me. In God's name, help.*

He said aloud, 'It was a U-boat. But they're all the same. The crew here don't understand like we do. They seem to think a war's for someone else to fight.' He steadied himself, knowing he would break down otherwise. 'Will you give me a hand?'

'Just tell me what to do, Sparks.' He smiled but it made him look even sadder. 'Sorry, I mean *Mr Ames*.'

Younger sat back on his haunches. It was suddenly crystal-clear what he would do. As if he could see it happening in slow motion, something already past.

He considered what the man Mason had told him about one operator being familiar to another. He had always known it, and the radio officer who had taught him had described how you could often recognise the sender before the actual ship was identified.

Did that mean Mason or one of the others would make the signal to keep in with their captors?

It made him sweat to think of it. The raider was off to attack the biggest prize yet. It must be really important to leave some of their own people behind. None of them seemed to know where the attack might be launched. In case they were captured and interrogated before the raider could make good her escape. The stark picture of the drifting lifeboat, the moments when he had been almost too terrified to open his eyes when he had drowsed over the tiller. They had all been waiting for him. The nightmare

216

had never gone away. They had died one by one, mostly in silence with a kind of passive acceptance.

It would not be much, but his actions might help to save other helpless merchant seamen. He hoped his old mother would find out that he had died this way. His dry lips cracked into a smile. Might get the George Cross. Something for his Dad to brag about down at the Shipwright's Arms.

Another shadow fell across them. 'We eat soon.' It was the senior operator, apparently the only one who spoke English. He would, of course.

'Thanks.'

The German glanced down at the old boatswain. 'He okay?'

Old Shiner did not open his eyes. 'Right as bloody ninepence, ta.'

The German turned away. That last sentence had thrown him.

He walked down to the water's edge and stared at the dark water. It shelved away steeply after that. Just a pile of rock in the middle of nowhere, he thought.

His name was Ernst Genscher and his home was in Leipzig. It would be cold there now. Winter always came early to that city. He tried to see it as in his boyhood, the spires and fine buildings. Not as on his last leave. The bomb debris, Russian prisoners working to clear the streets of corpses and rubble. The prisoners had looked like human scarecrows, and had been guarded by units of the SS. He thought of his divisional officer. Leutnant Bauer. They had never got on together. He smiled bitterly. That was why he had been detained for his final job. Bauer would have been right at home in the SS.

How much longer would the war last, he wondered? He and the others would end up in some prisoner-of-war camp in England or Canada. It might not be too bad. It was like their situation here in this damnable place, he thought. Neither side wanted to antagonise the other in case the wrong one came out victorious.

He thought of his companions. They were more worried than they admitted. Some even expected the *Prinz* to come back for them. A tiger had never been known to come back to release a tethered goat.

Genscher replaced his cap and smiled at his earlier show of discipline with the sentry.

217

He looked at his watch. He would send the signal in a few hours' time, just before sunset. His priest's face brightened into a smile.

It was somehow appropriate.

The three captains sat in Hemrose's deep armchairs and held out their glasses to be refilled.

Hemrose crossed one leg over the other and plucked his shirt away from his body. The air was hot and lifeless, and even with the scuttles open it was hard to ease the discomfort. The glass seemed steady enough, Hemrose thought, but it smelled like a storm. It was all they needed.

He watched his steward pause to take Captain Eric Duffield's glass to be topped up. *Rhodesia*'s captain was a big, powerful man, whose face had once been very handsome. A bit too smarmy for Hemrose's taste. Always excelled at sport and athletics. Not any more, Hemrose thought with small satisfaction.

He had forgotten how many Horse's Necks he had downed, nor did he care much. It was getting more like a wake than a relaxed drink in harbour with his captains, with a good dinner to follow. They would not be *his* captains much longer. He shied away from the thought.

With an effort he stood up and crossed to the nearest scuttle. The lights of Simonstown glittered on the water like a swarm of fireflies, while here and there small boats moved through the dusk between the anchored warships. It could be peacetime, he thought. Well, almost.

He heard Duffield say, 'Good place to settle down, South Africa. I'd think about it myself after this lot's over, but you never know.' Hemrose gritted his teeth together. He meant that he would be staying on in the service, promoted probably to end his time in command of a base, or with a nice staff job in Whitehall.

The New Zealand captain, Chantril, replied, 'We've not won the bloody war yet.' His accent took the edge from his words. He was feeling it too. The chance to meet and destroy the raider. Become a part of the navy's heritage.

Hemrose turned and signalled to his steward. 'I still can't believe it, you know.'

Duffield smiled. 'Believe or accept? There's a difference.' Hemrose ignored him. 'A whole ship gone west, not even a scrap of wreckage discovered?'

218

Chantril said, 'It happened to HMAS *Sydney*. Her loss is still a mystery.'

Duffield glanced at his watch. He could not wait to eat up and go. Get back to his own ship and tell them all how Hemrose was taking his unfought defeat.

He said, 'The backroom boys at the Admiralty know more than they let on.'

Hemrose glared. 'Bloody useless, most of them!'

Duffield coughed. 'We'll probably never know.'

Hemrose pushed a strand of hair from his eyes. He was getting drunk. 'That Jerry is still around. I'll stake my reputation on it.'

The others remained silent. They probably considered his reputation had already slipped away.

'I've had my team working round the clock.' Hemrose pictured the charts, the layers of signal pads and folios. All for nothing. 'We had a damn good try anyway.'

They both stared at him. It was the nearest he had ever come to an admission of failure.

The thought of sitting through dinner with them made Hemrose feel slightly sick. Chantril was all right, a real professional, but tonight was not the time. He had a letter to write to Beryl, and a report to complete for the Admiralty. After that, he could almost feel the carpet being dragged from under him. Perhaps they would both accept an excuse, go back to their ships instead –

He looked up, angry and startled, as if he had spoken aloud.

'Well, what is it now?'

The commander nodded to the seated officers and then handed a signal pad to his superior.

Hemrose had to read it twice, his face shining with sweat, as if he had been running.

He said slowly, 'From Admiralty, gentlemen. Thirty minutes ago a signal was received from the Cable and Wireless station on St Jorge.' He could tell from Duffield's expression he hadn't a clue where that was. 'It reads *Am under attack by German cruiser.*' He lowered the pad and eyed them grimly. 'There was no further transmission. We may draw our own conclusions.'

Chantril exclaimed. 'I know the place! Christ, it's nor'-east of Ascension. What the hell is he –'

Duffield said, 'And all the time –'

Hemrose remained grave and under control even though he

219

wanted to yell out loud. It was like having a great orchestra or band pounding into your ears, shutting out all else but those vital words.

He said, 'Yes, all the time we thought the German was destroyed.' He could not resist it. 'Some of us, anyway.'

Chantril stood up and knocked over a glass without even seeing it.

'What is he trying to do?'

Hemrose smiled gently. '*Do*? Who really cares? He probably intended to carry out a last attack before running to some friendly South American bolthole, *Graf Spee* all over again. *Kapitän Hechler* –' he spat out the name '– will know that heavy forces are to the north of him.' He nodded. 'He will head south after this, then scuttle, whether *he* likes it or not.'

'Can we rely on that signal, sir?'

Hemrose looked at him and beamed. 'What? Can you doubt your *backroom boys* at the Admiralty? Tch, tch!' It was like a tonic.

Commander Godson shifted from one foot to the other. The signal had knocked the breath out of him. It was like opening a door and expecting to meet an old friend, only to be confronted by a maniac.

Hemrose looked at him, but saw his own expression as it would be remembered after this day. Grave and confident.

'Make a signal to Admiralty, Toby. *The squadron is leaving without delay*.' Thank God he had insisted on fuelling from lighters; it would have taken another hour to clear the port otherwise. He took his time to look at the gold wristwatch which Beryl had given him.

'Pipe special sea dutymen to their stations in one hour.' He looked at the others as poor Godson fled from the cabin. 'Another drink, eh?' He grinned. '*Afore ye go*, as the man said.'

He watched their faces, each man thinking of his own ship's readiness for sea. Hemrose added gently, 'Call up your ships from here.' He recalled the *Rhodesia*'s great display of speed and swank when she had joined the squadron. 'I don't want to leave here alone!'

Later he said, 'It must be fate. I knew we were destined to meet. Right from the beginning, I always knew.' He glanced round the cabin affectionately. 'Settle the score.'

220

At the prescribed time, as watertight doors were slammed shut and men bustled to their stations for leaving harbour, Hemrose mounted the *Wiltshire*'s bridge and looked towards the lights of the shore. The raider had not allowed for anyone making a last desperate signal, any more than they would expect three British cruisers to be ready, and in the right place.

In his mind he could see the chart, south-west. Close the trap which the German had sprung on himself.

He touched his cap to Godson as he reported the ship ready to proceed.

It was no longer just a remote possibility. There soon would be two lines of oak leaves around his peak.

It was a proud moment. There should be a band playing.

He turned and looked at the chief yeoman of signals.

He said, 'Make to squadron, Yeo. *Weigh anchor and follow father.*'

The sort of signal they always remembered. He could not stop grinning. The fact that Duffield would hate it, was a bonus.

Hechler came out of his dream like a drowning man fighting up for a gasp of air.

Even as he propped himself on one elbow and jammed the telephone to his ear he knew what it was. The only surprise was that he had been able to sleep at all.

It was Froebe. 'W/T office has reported the signal, sir.' He sounded cheerful. 'Right on time.'

Hechler stared around the tiny sea-cabin, his things ready to snatch up, the place in total disorder.

'Thank you. You know what to do.' He thought of the wild dream which had been driven away by the telephone's shrill call. Her nakedness, her desire, the way she had writhed beneath him as if to postpone the conquest.

He said, 'I'll be up shortly.' He hung the phone on its cradle above the bunk and wondered what she was doing now. Thinking, but not regretting? Hoping, but not allowing it to reach out too far. He slid from the bunk and suddenly craved a shower. Even that was already too late.

He thought of the senior operator, Genscher, he had left on the islet. He had obeyed orders, no matter what he thought about the need or the futility of it.

Even now the signal would be flashing around the world. The raider had been verified and slotted into one section of this great ocean. Brains would be working overtime as staff officers rearranged their thinking and defences, like drawing the strings of a huge bag. Except that the *Prinz* was nowhere near the small islet, and was speeding in the opposite direction.

Hechler deliberately stripped himself to the waist. The narrow door opened slightly and he saw the faithful Pirk peering in at him with a steaming bowl of water for his shave. He had understood. But Pirk always had. Ice, sunshine, bombardments or dodging enemy aircraft, Pirk's world ran on quite different lines.

The telephone rang again and Pirk handed it to him.

Hechler said, 'Captain?'

This time it was Theil. 'Exercise action stations, sir?'

'Not yet.' He thought surprisingly of Nelson. 'Let them have one more good meal. It may be the last for some time.'

Theil grunted. 'Dawn attack, sir?'

'Yes. As planned, Viktor. Let me know when the admiral is on his bridge.'

He turned to the mirror and touched his face. As she had done. 'It's going to be a very long night, old friend.' But Pirk had left. He lathered his cheeks with care and though of each last detail. The Arados would have to be prepared well before dawn. Every station and gun-mounting checked and visited by a senior officer. The last meal for some time. Forever, if things went badly wrong. He searched through his mind for flaws. His landing party had played their part. Now it was up to them. He grimaced at his image in the mirror. At one time he had nursed doubts. He had imagined then that the enemy had some secret strategy which neither he nor Operations had recognised.

Now he knew differently. There was no secret plan. Once again, the *Prinz Luitpold*'s luck had won through.

Shortly after midnight Hechler made his way into the bridge. That last cat-nap had driven the tiredness away. Or was it the prospect of action?

In the darkness figures moved towards him, or held motionless at their positions. As if they had never shifted. It was a beautiful night, bright stars, and a deep, unbroken swell again. Gudegast had already reported that there might be rain with a southeasterly wind. He never sounded as if he trusted the signalled broadcasts as much as his own intuition.

Leitner's pale outline glided through the watchkeepers, and Hechler could smell his cologne as he groped his way to the forward part of the bridge.

'A good beginning,' he said calmly. 'They'll not forget this day.'

Hechler was glad when the admiral had departed for his quarters. To prepare himself, or to share the last hours with his aide, he did not know or care.

As the time dragged on, the weather began to change. It grew much colder, and the steep swell became visible on either beam as a rising wind broke the crests into ragged, white lines. The *Prinz* was built for this kind of weather, and as she dipped her forecastle until spray burst over the stem or spouted through the hawsepipes she seemed almost contemptuous.

More signals came in a steady stream. It must be strange for those far-off operators, Hechler had thought many times, to send off their instructions and messages, while the recipient had no way of risking an acknowledgement.

Operations Division sent one signal about a small British cruiser squadron leaving Simonstown. Agents there must have started a chain of messages almost as soon as the Tommies had hoisted their anchors.

It was hardly surprising, he thought. Germany had many friends in South Africa. When the Kaiser had been forced to surrender in the Great War, it was said that black flags had been raised over Johannesburg to show where their true feelings had lain.

Hechler said, 'Action stations in ten minutes.' He felt his pockets in case he had forgotten anything. He remembered as he had left the sea-cabin how he had seen Inger's familiar picture in the drawer. He had looked at it for the first time without feeling, even bitterness.

'Tell the supply officer to keep the galley on stand-by. I want soup and coffee sent around every section until the last moment.'

A winch clattered loudly and he knew the aircraft handling party were at work with the first Arado preparing for launching. If the launch misfired, the plane would be left to fend for itself. He thought of the girl's own aircraft, dismantled and folded into its nest. A last display for the cameras? Or did Leitner have some other scheme in mind?

Gudegast stood beside his chair. 'Time to increase to full speed in twenty minutes, sir.' He sounded calm enough.

'Good.' Hechler peered at his Doxa watch. 'Sound off.'

The alarm bells clamoured throughout the ship, followed by a few thuds as the last of the heavy doors were clipped home. Voice-pipes and handsets muttered around the bridge, an unseen army.

'Anton, Bruno, Caesar and Dora turrets closed up, sir!'

'Secondary and anti-aircraft armament closed up, sir!'

From every gun, torpedo and magazine the reports came in.

Hechler pictured his men within the armoured hull. Down in the sick-bay, Stroheim and his assistants would be waiting, their glittering instruments laid out, waiting for the pain and the pleading.

As it must have been at Coronel and Falklands, at Dogger Bank and Jutland. Hechler jammed his pipe between his teeth and smiled. Trafalgar too probably.

He heard himself ask, 'What about Damage Control?'

Froebe replied, 'Closed up, sir. Some delay over a lighting fault.'

Theil was there entrusted with saving the ship if the worst happened. Or taking command if the bridge was wiped out.

'The admiral, sir.'

Hechler took the handset. 'Sir?'

Leitner said, 'I want another flag hoisted today. See to it, eh?'

He meant another rear-admiral's flag.

Hechler said, 'Ship at action stations, sir.'

'I shall come up presently.' The line went dead.

Hechler said to the bridge at large, 'I'm going to the plot.' He walked to the ladder as Gudegast picked up a chart and followed him. He could visualise it clearly in his mind. Training, experience, skill. He heard Froebe telling a signalman to fetch another flag and take it aft. He wondered if the camera would record that too.

While their captain climbed to the conning tower, the men throughout the ship went grimly about their preparations. Ready-use ammunition in place, magazine lifts sliding smoothly up and down their shafts, gun crews testing training and elevation gear, the gleaming breeches open like hungry mouths.

Above them all, Kröll the gunnery officer sat in his small steel chair and adjusted his sights while he studied the radar repeater. His team, hung about with stop-watches, earphones and the tools of their trade, watched him, keyed up like athletes under the starter's gun.

The most junior member of the fire-control team, Acting Petty Officer Hans Stoecker, stared at his empty log, one hand wrapped around his telephone.

They had all worked together so long that there were no hitches, nothing to bring Kröll's wrath down on them.

It was like a small self-contained world. Essential to the ship's firepower, but entirely separate, so that when the heavy guns roared out, they too seemed like something apart.

He tried not to think of Rudi Hammer's mild features just as the bells had sent them all racing to their action stations.

He had smiled almost shyly and said, 'A very good time for our little plan, yes? Everybody minding his own business!'

They would be found out. Stoecker gripped the telephone with both hands, his eyes misty as he stared at the log book. It was madness, a lunacy which would cost them their lives.

The speaker intoned, 'Main armament, semi-armour piercing shell, *load!*'

Stoecker felt his seat tilt under him as the helm went over. The ship was increasing speed. Sometimes it felt as if their steel pod would tear itself away from the bridge superstructure as every strut and rivet shook violently in protest.

Kröll twisted round in his chair and glanced at the intent figures below him, lastly to Kapitänleutnant Georg Emmler, the assistant gunnery officer. Together they held the reins. Beyond here, quarters officers, gun captains, and even individual sailors strapped in their rapid-fire automatic weapons, waited for the word. *Bearing, range, target.*

Kröll bit his lip. Another convoy. One day he would get his chance to pit his skills against a powerful enemy warship.

'Loaded, sir.'

Kröll scowled. Ten seconds too long. He thrust the watch into his pocket. He would soon put that right.

On the bridge once more Hechler looked at the stars. Fainter now. He felt spray cutting his face, heard it pattering over the chart-table's canvas cover to make puddles in the scuppers.

A voice said, 'First-degree readiness, sir.'

The galley was shut; the cook and his assistants would be sent to help damage-control and the stretcher parties.

Hechler gripped the rail below the screen and stared into the darkness.

They should hold the advantage with the convoy framed against the dawn. The escort had not been identified, which meant that it was nothing important. They were holding that for the next leg. He looked at the stars. But that would be denied them.

'Port fifteen!' Hechler heard his order repeated, almost a whisper, lost in the clamour of fans, the great writhing bank of foam which surged down either side.

'Steady! Steer zero-four-zero!'

The bows plunged into a deeper trough than usual and the sea boiled up and over the forecastle as if a broadside had fallen silently alongside.

As the ship turned, the two big turrets below the bridge trained across the starboard bow. Without turning Hechler knew that the two after ones, Caesar and Dora, were also swinging round in unison, until all four guns were pointing on the same bearing, the long muzzles like wet glass as they steadied over the side and the great surge of spray.

The sea was still in darkness, so that the leaping crests looked like birds, swooping and falling to appear elsewhere in another guise.

'Admiral's on his bridge, sir.'

'Very well.' Hechler tightened the towel around his neck as more heavy spray burst over the screen and pattered against their oilskins.

Leitner had made a suitably timed entrance. Hechler thought of the girl. She had shown no fear, but being sealed below behind massive watertight doors would test anybody.

Somebody whispered and was instantly rebuked by a petty officer.

Hechler kept his binoculars sheltered beneath the oilskin until the last moment to keep them dry. But he had seen what the look-out had whispered to a companion.

A thin pale line, like polished pewter, cold and without colour. Dawn, or nearly so. Hechler thought suddenly of his father. How he had described his horizon of that other war. It had been first light on the parapet of his trench. That had been the full extent of his world in that horrifying arena in Flanders.

'*Radar – bridge!*'

They all tensed.

Then the speaker continued, 'Target in sight. Bearing Green four-five. Range twelve thousand!'

Hechler tugged his cap more firmly across his forehead. The peak was wet and like ice.

He stood up and let the spray dash over him as he peered towards the starboard bow.

They had found them. Now it was up to Kröll.

'*Open fire!*'

Chapter Seventeen

Blood for Blood

The paired explosions from the after-turrets were deafening, and with the wind thrusting across the starboard quarter, the down-draft of acrid smoke made several of the men duck their heads to contain their coughing fits.

Hechler held the binoculars on the bearing and watched the tiny pale feathers of spray as the shells fell on the horizon. Harmless, without menace, although he knew that each waterspout would rise to masthead level. The explosions sighed through the water and faded again.

The speaker said, 'Twelve ships in convoy, estimate three escorts.'

Froebe called from his bank of handsets, 'W/T office reports signals from enemy, sir.'

'*Shoot!*' Kröll sounded quite different over the speaker, his words drowned by the immediate response from all four turrets.

Hechler watched the sky. After the previous days it looked threatening. There was cloud there too. He imagined signals beaming away to the enemy's supporting squadrons and to London.

He tensed; a bright flash lit up the horizon and several of the ships for the first time. They looked low and black, but in the spreading glow of fire he could just determine their course and speed.

The speaker again. 'One escort hit. Sinking.'

Hechler could picture the gunnery team's concentration on the radar screens. One tiny droplet of light falling out of station, dropping further and further astern of the fast tankers. It would vanish from the screens altogether.

The guns roared out again. Surely the tankers would scatter soon? He held his breath as a straddle of shells fell across one of the ships below the horizon. She was instantly ablaze, but it was made more terrible by distance as the fire seemed to spread down from the horizon, like blood brimming over a dam.

'*Shoot!*'

Hechler waited and winced as the eight big guns thundered out.

'Slow ahead!' He crossed the bridge and saw a signalman watching him, a handlamp at the ready.

'*Now!*' The first Arado lifted from the shadows and circled quickly round and above the mastheads.

'*Shoot!*'

The whole bridge structure shook violently and Hechler had to repeat his order to the engine-room to resume full speed. He would launch the second plane if there was time.

Someone was yelling, 'Another hit! God, two of them are on fire!'

Hechler glanced round to silence the man, but all he saw was Leitner's second flag breaking out from the mainmast truck, the only patch of colour against the sky. It was raining more persistently now, but even that tasted of cordite. It was hard to believe this same sky had been full of stars.

Hechler moved across the bridge, half-listening to crackling static as the Arado pilot reported back to the ship.

It was a sea of fire. The great shells must have come ripping down out of the darkness without the slightest warning. He saw lazy balls of bright tracer rising from the sea and guessed that the Arado was already near the convoy. How slow it looked. How deceptive. He hoped the pilot had his wits about him.

'Convoy breaking up, sir! Kröll's voice cut through the murmur of orders and instructions behind him. It was as if the fire-control position, the pod, was alive and speaking of its own free will.

Kröll added, 'Two lines diverging, sir.'

Hechler lowered his glasses and wiped them with fresh tissue.

'Acknowledge.' He pictured the convoy; they would need no encouragement to break away. *We must close the range.*

'*Shoot!*'

'*Cease firing!*' It was Kröll but he sounded momentarily confused.

Hechler picked up the fire-control handset. 'Captain. What is it?'

Kröll must have been leaning away to study his radar; when he spoke he seemed angry, as if he no longer trusted what he saw.

'A ship turned end-on, sir. Rear of second line.'

'Wait!' Hechler pushed his way aft and into the tiny steel shack which had been added to the bridge to house a radar repeater

229

alongside that of the sonar. He bent over the screen and as his eyes accustomed themselves to the flickering symbols he saw the complete picture as seen by *Prinz Luitpold*'s invisible eye. The diverging ranks of ships, and then as the scanner swept over them, the motionless blobs of light, ships burning and dying in the spreading flames. Then he saw the isolated echo. A large one which had until now been mistaken for one of the tankers. But it was much bigger and was not standing away, but coming straight for the *Prinz*. Hechler had to force himself to walk back to the bridge.

'Can you identify it?'

Kröll sounded very wary. 'There are no major warships listed with the convoy.'

Hechler turned away. 'Carry on. Tell the conning-tower to alter course. Steer zero-six-zero!'

The bridge quaked again as the after guns bellowed out, their bright tongues lighting up the rain-soaked superstructure and funnel. A figure stood out in the flashes and Hechler heard Jaeger call, 'Captain, sir! Message from Arado pilot! The ship is a merchantman!' He hesitated, baffled. 'A liner!'

For an instant longer Hechler thought she might be a hospital ship, one which was trying to keep clear of the convoy, or which had been damaged and was out of control.

A figure in shining oilskins brushed Jaeger aside and Gudegast exclaimed, 'Steady on new course, sir. Zero-six-zero.' He clung to the safety rail, his body heaving from exertion.

Hechler said, 'Do you know what it is?'

Gudegast nodded jerkily. 'It was in the recognition despatches, sir. Oh, yes, I know her all right! He ducked as the guns fired again. Flashes rippled along the horizon. Kröll was ignoring the solitary ship in case the heavy tankers might escape.

Gudegast stared at him, his eyes wild in the reflections. 'She's the old *Tasmania*. Used to come up against her when she did the Scandinavian cruises in the thirties.' He pounded his fist on the rail and shouted, 'They've made her an Armed Merchant Cruiser, for Christ's sake!'

Hechler snatched up the handset. 'Gunnery Officer! Shift target to the big liner – she's the *Tasmania*, armed merchant cruiser!'

'Immediately, sir.'

Gudegast was staring at him. 'She won't stand a chance! You

230

know what they're like! No plating at all and just a few guns from the Great War!'

Hechler called, 'Warn the secondary armament, then call up the Arado.'

He swung on Gudegast and said, 'Have you forgotten the other AMCs, man? *Jervis Bay*, an old cargo liner, but she held off *Admiral Scheer* nonetheless! An old merchantman too, set against a battleship! She was sunk, she knew it was hopeless when she turned to face the *Scheer*, but by God, her sacrifice saved her convoy, and *don't you ever forget it!'*

He turned back to the screen as the four forward guns edged round, paused and then fired in unison.

The sky was brightening, although with all the smoky rain it seemed to have taken them by surprise. Hechler watched the exploding shells, the ice-bright columns of water. Then he saw the oncoming ship. In her dull paint she still looked huge, with her three tall funnels overlapping as she turned still more to steer towards the heavy cruiser. The next salvo fell right across her path, and for an instant, Hechler thought she had been hit.

Jaeger called thickly, 'She mounts eight-inch guns, sir!'

It was ironic. The same armament as the *Prinz*, in size and numbers only.

'Speed?'

Jaeger replied, 'Twenty-eight knots maximum, sir.' He faltered as the after turrets fired, paint flaking down from the upper bridge fittings because of the blast. 'In peacetime.'

Hechler stared at her dull shadow while he wiped his glasses again. They were on a converging course, approaching each other at the combined speed of some sixty miles an hour. Old she might be, and to all intents she could not survive, but just one lucky shot was all it took to delay them, while the convoy clapped on speed to escape. Spectators would remember this day if they were fortunate enough to survive.

'Shoot!'

A straddle. The liner was hidden by falling spray, and at least one shell had smashed into her unarmoured side and exploded deep inside the hull. It was like a glowing red eye.

. Hechler heard Jaeger shout, 'That should stop her!'

Gudegast seized his arm. 'Take a good look, *boy*!'

Jaeger stared with disbelief. 'She's hoisting flags to each mast!'

Gudegast stared past him at Hechler's shoulders, shining in the grey light as the rain bounced down on them.

'They're *battle ensigns*! They sent the poor old girl to fight, and by God she's about to!'

'*Shoot!*'

It was a controlled broadside from all four turrets, the heavy shells straddling the tall hull, and blasting one of the outmoded, stately funnels overboard, like paper in a wind.

Jaeger gripped the chart-table as it tried to shake itself from his fingers. He wanted to screw up his eyes as a great scream of shellfire shrieked over the bridge and exploded in the sea, far abeam.

He wrote in the log. 'The enemy opened fire at –' The rest was a blur.

Hechler turned to watch the falling spray. 'Tell our pilot to take a fly over that ship. He might get a lucky hit.'

He did not let himself blink as two flashes lit up the liner's side. Her armament was divided out of necessity. At most she could train only three or four guns at a time.

He bit his lip as Kröll's next salvo erupted on her waterline. Smoke and fire seemed to roll across the waves, and he guessed that one shell had burst deep inside her.

But she was firing back, the old guns sounding strangely hollow when compared with the *Prinz's*.

A messenger handed him a telephone, his face ashen as a shell screamed past the bridge.

It was Leitner. 'What is the matter with your gun crews!' He was almost screaming. '*Kill them! Stop that ship!*'

Hechler handed the phone to the seaman and watched a livid flash fan out from beneath the liner's bridge. A mast was falling, but the white battle ensigns still seemed to shine through the rain, and her bow-wave was as before.

Froebe shouted, 'She's on fire aft, sir! What's holding her together?'

Hechler let his glasses fall to his chest. The range was dropping rapidly so that she seemed to tower over the sea like a leviathan.

He said, 'I shall have to turn to port. It will give our spotters a chance.' It would also expose the whole broadside to the enemy, but speed was essential now. It was all they had.

'She's slowing down!' A man's cheer was cut short as the liner's two most forward guns fired together. It was all confused, and even the thundering crash of the explosion was muffled.

Half-deafened by the shell-burst Hechler dragged himself along the rail to the starboard side. A man was screaming, his face cut to ribbons, and Hechler saw that most of the glass screen had been fragmented by the burst. There was a lot of smoke, and he could smell the stench of burning paintwork and cordite.

'Steady on zero-six-zero, sir!' The voice-pipe from the wheel-house was unattended and Hechler saw a petty officer lying dead against the flag lockers. There was not a mark on him, but his contorted face told its own story. Hechler thrust a man into his place.

'Tell the wheelhouse to remain on course.' He slipped on blood and trained his binoculars on the other ship. She was listing badly, flames bursting through her side as if from jets. The last internal explosion had found her heart.

'Engine-room request permission to reduce speed, Captain!'

'What is it, Chief?' Hechler pressed the phone under his cap.

Stück's voice was very steady. 'Pump trouble. Nothing we can't fix. I'm still waiting for reports. That last shell –'

Hechler did not wait. 'Half speed, all engines.' A massive explosion rolled across the water, and fragments of steel and timber rained down until every trough seemed full of charred flotsam.

A man cried, 'She's going!'

Some smaller shells exploded close to the capsizing ship, and Hechler snatched up the gunnery handset, suddenly remembering Gudegast's despair. 'Shift target to the convoy!' It was not a rebuke for the gunnery officer, but it sounded like one.

The two forward turrets were already training round, seeking their targets. But the ships were scattering in several directions; each one was a separate attack.

In the armoured conning tower Gudegast had his face pressed against an observation slit. The *Prinz* had been hit, how badly he did not know. He could hear the intercom chattering, the stream of demands and orders as the damage-control parties swung into action. Gudegast had felt the explosion come right through the deck plates. As if they had hit a reef. Now all he could see was smoke, some small running figures by a dangling motorboat, cut in halves as it hung from its davits.

All he could think of was the sinking liner. The old *Tasmania*, of the Cunard White Star Line. He had seen her many times when she had been taken off her Atlantic runs to do some cruising in and around the lovely fjords of Norway. He had even been on board her once for an officer's birthday.

He could see her clearly, so different from his own timber ship. Spotless, well-laid decks, passengers drifting about with cameras, the elegance, the style of the liner and what she represented. He watched, sickened, as she rolled heavily on to her side, another funnel tearing adrift. There were more explosions, and Gudegast thought for a moment that Kröll was still directing guns on her.

He shouted wildly, 'Leave her! She can't hurt you now! Leave her alone, you bloody bastard!'

His assistants watched anxiously from the rear, their eyes glowing in the reflected explosions through the narrow slits.

Gudegast pressed a button and felt icy rain on his face as the massive steel door slid to one side.

He clambered out on to the little catwalk and then without realising what he was doing, removed his cap.

A ship had just been destroyed because fools had sent her to war.

He wiped his face with his sleeve. And she died with that same old dignity he had always admired so much.

Peter Younger knelt on the floor of the storeroom where the prisoners had been locked up for the night, and pressed his eye to a hole in the wall where a bolt had rusted away.

It was early morning and he heard some of the German sailors calling to each other. He found it hard to tell if they were angry exchanges or not.

Old Shiner sat with his narrow shoulders against the wall, idly watching the young radio officer's eyes in the filtered sunlight. 'They'm makin' a bloody row,' he said irritably. 'Couldn't sleep 'cause of it.'

Younger ground his jaws together as he concentrated on his tiny view of the station.

He said, 'They broke open a stock of booze, that's what all the racket's about.'

He should have guessed that something of the sort might happen. As soon as the false signal had been made, the prisoners had been herded together. It was as if the Germans had to let off steam, now the reality of their position was out in the open. Celebrating their part in the plot, or commiserating together at the prospect of early captivity he did not know, but he cursed himself for not taking precautions.

Mason, the man in charge of the station, dropped down beside him.

'It's too late then?' He sounded wary after Younger's outburst during the night, when he had told them what he was going to do. Mason had asked then, 'How do you know all this anyway?' Younger had exploded. 'We were bloody prisoners aboard the raider, that's how!'

He said, 'I must try. There's still a chance we might save a few lives, or call our blokes down on the krauts.'

Old Shiner said, 'If they don't open the bloody door I'm goin' to drop my trousers right now!'

Younger closed his eyes and thrust his forehead against the warm metal until he could think properly again. Poor old Shiner was halfway round the bend. He looked at Mason. 'When the guard unlocks the door we'll grab him and get his gun.'

Old Shiner remarked, 'Accordin' to the Geneva Convention we should 'ave proper toilet arrangements. I seen it in a book somewhere.'

Mason stared at him. 'God Almighty!'

Younger persisted, 'Are you with me?' He nearly said, *or are you like your chum over there who sent the signal under the German's supervision?* But he needed Mason. He was the only one now.

Mason nodded unhappily. 'It'll be the end of us, you know that?'

Younger shrugged. 'I'm not going to think about it.'

He stood up and walked to the corrugated door. The others would probably let him get on with it, watch him gunned down to join the dead mechanic.

Like the shutter in a camera he saw the drifting lifeboat for a split second. The patient, eyeless faces. The very horror of it. He glanced at Old Shiner. Poor bastard. He had been torpedoed and sunk so many times it was a wonder he was still breathing.

Mason said quietly, 'I'll *try*.' He sounded terrified, as if he could barely get the words out.

Younger touched his arm. 'Once inside the transmitting-room

235

I'll have a signal off before you can blink.' He was amazed he could speak so confidently, when he had not even seen inside the place. It might already be out of action, smashed by the Germans after raising the trick alarm. He decided against that. Germans or not, they were all sailors. No sailor was ever keen to sever a possible lifeline.

Mason exclaimed, '*He's coming!*' He pressed himself to the wall and whispered, 'Jesus!'

Younger tested the weight of the makeshift club in his hand. It was a length of firewood, probably left at the station for the winter months. It was not much, but the guard might be half-cut from the night's drinking. He thought of the balding senior operator. Obviously his sense of discipline was no longer shared by his companions. He held his breath until his temples throbbed as the man fumbled with the padlock and tried several times to insert a key. Younger heard him curse, and the clatter of the padlock as it fell on the rock floor.

Please God, let it work! He flung his weight against the door, it flew back and thudded heavily against the guard's skull as he stooped down to recover the padlock.

It all happened in seconds, and yet it lasted forever. The man's face squinting up in the sunlight, blood seeping down his face from the blow, then jerking back as Younger slammed his sea-boot into his gaping jaw. He did not recall how many times he brought the heavy piece of wood down on his head, but it was running with blood and torn skin as he threw it aside and wrenched the sub-machine gun from the man's shoulder.

Then he was running towards the rough ladder, expecting at any second to hear a challenge, feel the agony of a bullet between his shoulders. He heard Mason panting behind him, sobbing and muttering to himself as he followed.

At the top of the short ladder Younger turned for a quick glance. The shutter again. The sprawled sailor, and some terrified faces peering from the storeroom. Younger felt his heart breaking as he looked at the sea. So vast and impersonal, and suddenly without hostility.

It was all over. His ship, his friends, everything.

With a cry he kicked open the door and saw the German with the plastered arm staring at him, a mug of something in his free hand. Several things happened at once. The German lunged for his holster, which was dangling from a chair; Younger squeezed the trigger, but stared aghast as the gun remained silent. *Safety catch*. He fumbled for it, dimly aware that the German had dragged out his pistol, and that Mason was on his knees behind a packing case, burbling incoherently and in tears of terror. Something blurred across Younger's vision and he saw a heavy iron bar smash down on the man's plastered arm to crack it like a carrot. The German dropped his pistol and fell to the floor, his lip bitten through as the pain exploded in his shattered arm.

Old Shiner, his washed-out eyes blazing wildly, stepped further into the room and swung the long bar once more. It must have taken all his strength, but the German lay quite still, probably dead. Old Shiner tossed the bar aside and snatched the sub-machine gun from Younger and snorted, 'Yew'm never took a DEMS course like me. 'Ere, I'll keep them buggers off!'

With a gasp Younger sat down before the transmitter, his heart pumping as with a purr of power he switched it on. It was not so different from the one he had trained on. He dashed the sweat, or were they tears, from his eyes, and concentrated every fibre on the key. He knew most of the abbreviated codes issued by the navy. They needed to in Atlantic convoys, with ship after ship falling out of line, falling astern for the wolves. He blinked hard. Like *Radnor Star*.

He pressed the headphones over his ears and managed to hold the new sounds at bay. Sudden shouts, the blast on a whistle.

He came out in a rush of sweat. *The signal was already being acknowledged.* He grinned uncontrollably at the key. *You're the one who's too late, Baldy!* He was thinking of the senior operator, who probably wondered what the hell was happening.

There was a rattle of machine-gun fire and a line of holes punched through the wall, so that dusty sunlight cut across the room like thin bars.

Old Shiner had the door open just an inch and the room filled with smoke as he fired a long burst down the slope.

'Got one o' the buggers!' He was laughing as he crossed to the opposite side. Neither of them even noticed that Mason, the unwilling volunteer, had already been killed by the first shots.

Younger heard Old Shiner cursing as he snatched up the other German's pistol. He must have emptied a whole magazine in one go.

Younger winced as more shots crashed through the room and some exploded the dials and fuses at the top of the transmitter.

Too late. Too late. The words seemed to deafen the clatter of small arms fire, the occasional heavy bang as Old Shiner took a potshot at someone below the building.

More crashes, and the transmitter went dead. Younger threw the earphones on the bench and swung round. *'We did it!'* But the old boatswain did not hear him. He sat lopsided against the wall, blood seeping through his tattered jersey. His eyes were tightly closed, like those last moments in the lifeboat.

A window shattered and he stared without comprehension at a heavy cudgel-shaped object as it fell at his feet. He had not, of course, ever seen a German hand-grenade before.

His mind had just time to record that Old Shiner even had his arms cradled, as he had been when he had nursed his cat, when the grenade exploded and there was only darkness.

There was less smoke now and Hechler guessed that the fire-fighting parties had doused most of the flames between decks.

Voice-pipes chattered incessantly until Froebe shouted, 'Damage-control, sir!'

Hechler jammed the telephone to his ear while he watched the dead petty officer being dragged away. The man with the glass-flayed face had already gone; only his blood remained, spreading and thinning in the steady rain.

Theil said, 'A fluke shell, sir.' Someone was screaming in the background. 'A shot in a million.'

Hechler watched the smoke spiralling above the broken screen. 'Tell me.'

Theil explained in his flat, impersonal tone. One of the armed merchant cruiser's last eight-inch shells had plummeted down to pierce the battery deck between the bridge and Turret Bruno. As Theil had said, it was a chance in a million. It had struck the air shaft of a mushroom ventilator and been deflected through the armoured deck before exploding against a magazine shaft. Sixteen men of the damage-control party there had been killed. In such a confined space it was not surprising. But it was a double disaster. The explosion had severely damaged the training mechanism of Turret Bruno. Until the damage could be put right, the whole turret was immobile. It could not even be trained by manual power.

238

Hechler considered the facts as Theil described them. The engine-room was confident that all pumps would be working again at full power within the hour. Casualties elsewhere were confined to the bridge, and two seamen who had been putting out a small fire below the funnel. They must have been blasted over the side without anyone seeing them go.

'Report to me when you have completed your inspection.'

Froebe whispered, 'The admiral, sir.'

Leitner seemed to materialise on the bridge like a white spectre.

'What the *hell* is happening?' He glared through the trapped smoke, his shoulders dark with rain. 'I am not a bloody mind-reader!'

Hechler looked at him coldly. 'B Turret is out of commission, sir. We've lost nineteen men killed, and three injured.' He glanced at the blood. It had almost been washed away now. 'One man was blinded.'

'*I do not hear you*! What are you saying?' Leitner strode from one side to the other, his shoes crunching over broken glass. 'We have lost the convoy – don't you understand anything?'

Hechler looked up as Froebe called, 'New course is two-three-zero, sir.'

Hechler said, 'We have to turn, sir. Radar reports three tankers sunk and two, possibly three escorts as well.'

'*I don't care!*' Leitner was beside himself with rage, and did not even notice the astonished watchkeepers around him. 'Three tankers! A pinprick! We should have taken the whole convoy.'

Jaeger waited for Leitner to rush to the opposite side and stammered, 'W/T office has picked up a signal from the radio station, sir.'

Hechler eyed him calmly, although his nerves were screaming. 'Well?'

'They are not sure, sir. But it seems as if another operator has disclaimed the first signal. Now there is only silence.'

'Steady on two-three-zero, sir. All engines half-speed ahead.'

Leitner was suddenly facing him, his face streaming with rain.

'What was that? Am I to be told nothing by these idiots?'

Hechler replied, 'The information will doubtless have been sent to your bridge, sir.' He tried to contain his patience, when all he wanted to do was discover how badly the *Prinz* was damaged.

'It means that somebody on St Jorge took over the transmitter.

239

Had it been any earlier we would have had to abandon the whole convoy. I –'

Leitner thrust his face so close he could smell the brandy. 'I don't want your snivelling excuses! I'll have those men court-martialled and shot, and I'll personally break the officer responsible for the landing party!'

Hechler stood back, sickened. 'It was a risk. We knew it. It might have been worse.'

'Worse? *Worse*?' Leitner waved his arms at the bridge. 'I don't see that! A relic of a merchant ship stood against *Prinz Luitpold*, and because of someone's incompetence we had to withdraw! By God, Hechler, I'll not be a laughing-stock because of it! Do you know what I call it?'

Hechler pressed his hands to his sides. He wanted to hit Leitner, to keep on hitting him. A laughing-stock, was that all he saw in it? Men killed, and this fine ship isolated and at bay because of his haphazard orders.

'I call it cowardice! In the face of the enemy – what do you think of *that*?'

'I can only disagree, sir.'

'Can you indeed.' He stared around the bridge. 'There are some who will live long enough to regret this day!' He stormed off the bridge and Froebe hissed, 'I'm no coward, damn him!'

Hechler ignored him. 'Recall the Arado. Tell W/T to monitor every signal. We have roused a hornets' nest.'

He looked round, surprised, as sunlight broke through the dull clouds. 'And I want the navigating officer here at once.'

There was no point in wondering about the hand on the transmitter. It was probably as dead as the men trapped below when the shell had exploded amongst them.

A messenger handed him a telephone. Leitner's voice was quite controlled again. It could have been someone else entirely.

'We will rendezvous at the *second* grid-point. It will be safer than heading north right away.'

'Very well, sir.' *Why don't I argue with him? Tell him that we are wasting sea miles and precious time. Steer north and take the risk.* It would be 900 miles closer to home. But even as he thought it, Hechler knew it was fruitless. Leitner was unstable in his present mood. All he could think of was their failure to destroy the whole convoy, the effect it might have on his own reputation. He

240

had made it quite clear that he would see that all blame would rest elsewhere. On the captain's shoulders, no doubt. Hechler was quietly surprised that the realisation did not touch him.

What they had achieved this far, they had done well. The courage and sacrifice of that one old liner had shifted the balance, from offensive to the need for survival. That was war. It was also luck.

He heard Gudegast's seaboots crunching over the glass and turned to face him.

'You've heard about St Jorge?'

Gudegast met his gaze, troubled and wary. 'Yes, sir. The whole ship has.' He seemed to expect anger, even dismissal.

Hechler said quietly, 'You were right, Josef. She *was* a fine old lady.'

Gudegast's bearded features softened. 'No, I was a fool to question your actions. It was not my place to speak as I did.'

Hechler looked up at the rain. A man had died here, another had been blinded, just feet away. *It could have been me.*

He said, 'My guess is that the Tommies are on their way to St Jorge, or were until that last signal was sent. It will give us some sea-room, I think. Maybe our admiral is right to head for the second rendezvous. It will keep us out of the air patrols, and I think that the hunters will be expecting us to head for the North Atlantic without further delay.'

Gudegast shrugged. 'Home then, sir.'

'Yes. But we'll not reach Germany again without a fight.'

Theil entered the bridge and eyed them grimly. 'I have done my rounds, sir.'

Hechler nodded. 'Tell me the worst, Viktor.'

Theil looked at the broken screen. He had heard the blinded man screaming before he had been silenced by Stroheim's staff.

'One of my petty officers, Hammer, is trapped in the empty, ready-use room, sir. The mechanism was broken in the explosion.'

Gudegast said, 'But he should not have been in there surely?'

He saw the petty officer in his mind, a mild man, yet one who always seemed to be against authority in his mad desire to keep stocks of glass in any vacant space.

Hechler said, 'I have the key in my safe, Viktor.'

Theil faced him. 'Yes. And the admiral had the other. I am fully

241

aware of the security arrangements in this ship. I –' He seemed to check himself with a real effort.

'Well, he's trapped inside. With the admiral's boxes.'

It would have to be solved, but against what had happened it seemed trivial.

He would go round the ship as soon as the Arado had been hoisted inboard. With more and more enemy ships being homed either towards the broken convoy or the silent radio station, they would need all their eyes to avoid discovery.

'See what you can do.' Hechler looked at each of them in turn. 'And thank you.'

He felt utterly drained. Yet he must inspect the immobilised turret, see his heads of department, and bury their dead.

He thought of the girl's face so close to his own, the need to see her. It might be the last time.

He thought too of the unknown hand on the transmitter key, and the captain of the old ocean liner as she had charged to the attack. His men could and would fight like that. He pictured Leitner's insane fury and felt a sudden anxiety.

The legend and the luck were no longer enough.

Chapter Eighteen

No Hiding Place

Acting Commodore Hemrose moved restlessly to the starboard side of the *Wiltshire*'s bridge and fastened his duffle coat more tightly. The rain was getting heavier, he thought irritably. They could do without it.

He peered through a clearview screen and watched the long arrowhead of the cruiser's forecastle begin to shine through the darkness. Dawn soon. He felt like rubbing his hands but it was too wet for that. Since leaving Simonstown the three ships had maintained almost their full speed, and each had been closed up at action stations since midnight. Exciting, exhilarating, it was much more than either, Hemrose thought. Gone was the boredom and the nagging suspicion that the German raider was cocking a snook at them. For two days they had pounded through the heavy ocean swell, gun crews exercising without all the usual moans. This time it was in earnest.

Hemrose could picture his ships clearly despite the darkness. The *Rhodesia* was half a mile astern, while the light cruiser *Pallas* was way ahead in the van. If the German's radar was as good as the experts had implied, it was better to have the smallest ship in the lead. The *Prinz Luitpold* was a powerful and formidable opponent, but they would dart in to close the range, singly, while the others maintained covering fire to halve the enemy's resources. Hemrose thought of their old Walrus flying boat, the Shagbat as it was affectionately known in the navy. One engine, a *pusher* at that, with a ridiculous maximum speed of 130 odd miles per hour. But it only needed one sighting report, and the ancient Walrus could do that just as efficiently as any first-rate bomber.

Hemrose glanced at his bridge staff. The first lieutenant and officer-of-the-watch, the navigating officer, two junior subbies, and the usual handful of experts, signalmen and the like. As good a ship's company as you could find anywhere, he decided.

He licked his lips and tasted that last mug of cocoa, *pusser's*

243

kye. It had been laced with rum, his chief steward had seen to that. Just the thing to meet the dawn.

He heard the OOW answering one of the voice-pipes, then turned as he said, 'W/T office. Chief telegraphist requests permission to come up, sir.'

'*What*?' Hemrose dug his hands into his damp pockets. 'Oh, very well.'

The chief telegraphist was a proper old sweat. Not the kind to make fruitless requests when at any moment they might make contact with the enemy.

The man arrived on the bridge and paused only to nod to his messmate, the Chief Yeoman of Signals.

'What is it?'

The man had a signal pad in his hand but did not seem to need it.

He said, 'From Admiralty, sir, repeated Rear-Admiral commanding Force M.' He swallowed hard. 'The signal from St Jorge was a fake, sir. The northbound tanker convoy is under attack by the raider. HMS *Tasmania* is engaging.'

Some of the others had heard what the chief petty officer had said and were watching Hemrose, waiting for him to explode. Hemrose was surprised that he should feel so calm. And yet he had never expected this to happen. Not in a thousand years.

The chief telegraphist added, 'Also, there was one further transmission from that radio station, sir. Someone there was apparently trying to warn us.'

Hemrose looked up sharply as the first lieutenant murmured, 'Brave bastard!'

'Get the commander up here.' He had to think, but all he could see was the convoy, the shells ploughing amongst those heavily laden oil tankers. 'Call up the squadron. Remain on course. Reduce to cruising speed.' He hated to add, 'Fall out action stations. I'll speak to our people presently.'

'More kye, sir.' His chief steward had appeared by his side.

'Thanks.' He tried to grin, but his face felt rigid. 'I bloody need it.'

Godson clattered up the ladder and exclaimed, 'I just heard, sir. Bad show.'

Is that what you really think? Aloud Hemrose said, 'We'll be getting our marching orders soon, hence the signal repeated to Force M.'

Godson remained silent. Force M was one of the fleet's powerful independent groups, a battle-cruiser, a big carrier, with all the support and escorts they needed. It would be the end of Hemrose's little squadron. He would become a small fish in a much grander pool. Godson hated himself for being pleased about it. But it would be a whole lot safer.

The navigating officer murmured, 'When it's convenient, sir –' He hesitated as Hemrose turned towards him.

Hemrose said, 'We shall maintain this course for the moment, Pilot.'

Godson offered, 'Someone will have to lie off St Jorge and pick up the Germans if there are any.'

Hemrose said harshly, 'Well, not me. Leave that to some errand-boy!'

His sudden anger seemed to tire him. He said, 'I shall be in my sea-cabin. Call me if –' He did not finish it.

Alone in his cabin abaft the bridge he lay fully clothed, staring into the darkness.

When the telephone rang he snatched it up and snapped, 'Well?'

It was Godson. 'Signal from Admiralty, sir.' He cleared his throat as he always did when he was about to face something bad. 'The Armed Merchant Cruiser *Tasmania* has been sunk. One escort reported seeing a shell-burst on the raider. Most of the convoy has survived. We are to await further instructions.'

Hemrose slumped down again. Poor old *Tasmania*. It must have been the last thing her captain had expected too. He clenched his fists with sudden despair and anger. What was it he had learned when he had been a cadet at Dartmouth? *God and the Navy we adore, when danger threatens but not before*. How bloody true it had been proved over and over again in this war. Pleasure boats and paddle steamers used for mine-sweeping, Great War destroyers fighting the Atlantic and anything the krauts could fling their way. And it would be the same in any future conflict. Spend nothing, but expect a bloody miracle, that was John Citizen's battle cry.

He heaved himself up and stared at the luminous clock. What was the matter with him? Was he so overwhelmed by the German's trick that he had missed something so obvious? No ship as good as *Prinz Luitpold* would be deterred by the second signal from St Jorge. Not at that stage, with helpless tankers falling to her broadsides. The old AMC had scored one hit, they said. Well, it might only take one. It must have been bad enough to make Hechler break off the action.

He seized the telephone and heard the OOW reply, 'Bridge, sir?'

'Get me the commander.'

Godson sounded alarmed. 'Something wrong, sir?'

'*Tasmania* hit the raider, Toby. The *Prinz Luitpold* must be in trouble.'

Godson stammered, 'One shell, sir – well, that is, we don't know –'

'Shut up and listen. I want the attack team mustered in the chart room in ten minutes.'

There was no comment and he snapped, 'Are you still there?'

Godson replied weakly, 'Are you going after the raider again, sir?'

Hemrose touched his face. He would shave, and meet his little team looking refreshed and confident.

He said, 'We needed a bit of luck, Toby. That poor, clapped-out AMC may have given us just that.'

Godson persisted, 'The Admiralty will probably decline to –'

'Don't be such a bloody old woman.' He slammed down the phone.

It was so obvious he wanted to shout it at the top of his voice. The US submarine had been damaged, but had fired at the raider because her skipper had never seen such a target. But his torpedoes must have hit something else, hence the remains of German corpses and a massive oil-slick. The so-called experts had acted like a ship's lookout who saw only what he expected to see. It must have been another submarine. He wanted to laugh, when he recalled it was the poor chaplain who had first put the doubts about the raider's fuel supply in his mind.

It had to be that. But just because it had never been done before, nobody, not even Duffield's back-room boys had even suspected it.

God, the enemy must have been planning all this for months, and everything, even the RAF's recce reports over the Norwegian fjords, had been fooled by one ruse after another.

The door opened. 'I've brought you your shavin' gear, sir.' The steward showed his teeth. ''Ad a feelin' you might be askin' for it.'

Hemrose stared at himself in the mirror. He could still be wrong. There was nothing really solid to go on. But it was all he had. They would go right through every report and signal. If they found nothing they would do it all over again until they did.

Nobody had really considered submarines before. The Admiralty and intelligence sources had concentrated on checking lists of so-called neutrals, especially those in South American ports, where a supply ship might have been waiting for a rendezvous.

Later in the chart-room Hemrose explained his thoughts on the raider's performance.

'Hechler had that convoy on a plate. He'd knocked out the escort, and picked off the first tankers like fish in a barrel. But for the old AMC he would have polished off the whole boiling lot.'

The young navigating officer said, 'If he's damaged, he'll also need fuel.'

Hemrose nodded. 'Good thinking. When his bunkers are topped up he'll make for safe waters again – my guess is Norway.' He added grudgingly, 'Even with the Home Fleet and Force M on the alert he's the sort of captain who might just pull it off. If he sails safely into port after cutting our blockade in both directions he would do far more good for German morale at home than by wiping out that convoy.'

Godson said, 'The Germans have been using the big supply submarines in the South Atlantic for two years, I believe.'

Hemrose waited silently, seeing his hazy ideas forming into a possibility on their faces.

The first lieutenant said, 'They work to a grid system, don't they?'

Hemrose smiled. 'Check all the U-boat reports in that area, ours and the Yanks.'

Hemrose rocked back on his heels. He was already heading into disaster, so where might this additional risk take him?

'Then make a signal to *Pallas* and *Rhodesia*. I'd like to see the captains before we begin.'

Godson wilted under his stare but asked, 'And Admiralty, sir?'

'Balls to their lordships, Toby! I was given this job and I intend to see it through!' He glanced at the chaplain. 'And thanks to our warlike padre here, I think we may be on the home stretch!'

Hemrose walked out into the daylight and lifted his face to the rain.

It was hard to accept that within two hours he had risen from despair to optimism.

As he passed the forward funnel he saw the ship's crest bolted to a catwalk. Beneath it was her motto in Latin. Hemrose's red face split into a grin so that two Oerlikon gunners peered down with astonishment to watch him.

Translated, their motto was *Count your blessings*.

It was not much, but it was a start.

Leitner looked up from his littered desk and eyed Hechler for several seconds.

'You wish to see me?'

Hechler nodded. He wondered how Leitner could leave the upper bridge to spend time in his spacious quarters. The cabin was unusually chaotic, with clothes strewn about, and a life-jacket hanging on the door.

Hechler said, 'We have just buried the men who were killed, sir.'

Leitner pouted. 'Yes. I felt the ship slow down.' Some of the old edge returned to his tone. 'Not that she's exactly a greyhound of the ocean at the moment!'

'The engine-room expects the pumps will all be working at full pressure soon.' They had said that yesterday, but this time Stück seemed quite confident. 'It's B turret that worries me.'

'You? *Worry*?' Leitner put down his pen and regarded him calmly. 'After their performance with the convoy I'd have thought the whole gunnery team should be *worried*!'

It was pointless to argue, to explain that the single shell from the *Tasmania* had been a fluke shot. Anyway, Leitner seemed so preoccupied he would only have challenged that too.

Hechler said, 'The rendezvous with the supply-boat, sir. I am having second thoughts. At this reduced speed we will meet the milch-cow on her final day in the prescribed grid. After that we may not find the time to refuel before we turn for home.'

'I had considered that, Dieter.' The sudden use of his name was also unexpected. 'But we still stick to our plans. I intend to transfer the camera team to the submarine. They can make their own arrangements when she reaches Germany.' He sounded vague, almost disinterested.

'And the woman pilot?'

Leitner gave a small smile. 'Ah, yes. The lovely Erika. I am afraid she has not earned *her* release just yet.' He dragged a chart from beneath a pile of papers. 'The rendezvous is here, right?'

Hechler bent over the desk. Why go over it again? All he could see were the lines of flag-covered bodies, the rain sheeting down while he had read the burial service. Then the signal to the bridge to reduce speed, the last volley of shots, and the sea-men rolling up the empty flags for the next time. Faces and groups lingered in his mind, like little cameos of war itself. A young seaman wiping his eyes with his sleeve and trying not to show his grief at the loss of a friend. The camera crew filming the funeral, a petty officer staring at them, his eyes filled with hatred and disgust. Leitner should have been there. It was the least he could do. And he had seen the girl too, her coat collar turned up as she had gripped a stanchion below two manned anti-aircraft guns and watched him, listening to his words as he had saluted, and the pathetic bundles had splashed over the side.

Hechler had been kept busy with hardly a break. Now, in the sealed cabin it closed in like a blanket. He was dog-tired at a time when he needed to be at full alert.

Somewhere overhead one of the Arados was testing its engine.

They were off the shipping lanes, and as far as Bauer's tele-graphists had been able to determine, all enemy forces had been directed either to the convoy or further north. OKM Operations Division had been silent. It was as if the *Prinz Luitpold* had already been written off as a casualty, left to her own resources.

Hechler closed his fingers. One more cargo of fuel and he would be able to assess their immediate future. If they avoided the enemy Kröll and his artificers would repair the turret's train-ing mechanism. Otherwise all their main defences would be down aft.

Leitner did not look up from the chart, and some of his sleek hair fell forward like a loose quill. It was so unlike him that Hechler wondered if the last engagement had broken his faith.

Leitner was saying, 'Now about my boxes, hmm?'

Hechler thought of the petty officer who was still trapped. The damage control section had told him that the door was buckled, and it would have to be cut away with torches. There was an air vent, so the luckless Hammer was in no danger. Yet.

'They are working on the door, sir.'

249

Leitner did not seem to hear. 'That man had a key. He must have stolen it or made it. He is a thief, a menace to this ship, a traitor. I intend that he shall stand trial as soon as he is freed.' He raised his eyes suddenly. '*I want that door open.*' His eyes hardened. 'It can be done, *yes* or *no*?' He swung round. 'What now?'

Theil stood in the entrance, his cap dripping with rain.

'The door won't move, sir. The engine-room is supplying some heavier cutting gear –'

Leitner screamed at him, 'Don't come here with your snivelling excuses! I want the door forced open immediately! Blow it down with a limited explosion!'

Hechler stepped between them. 'It could kill Hammer, sir. In such a confined space –'

Leitner glared at him wildly. 'It will save him from the firing squad! He was spying on me, and he's not the only one! Must I repeat everything? Blow it open!'

Theil looked at Hechler, his face pleading. 'He's one of my men!'

Leitner was breathing hard. 'I have no doubt of that!'

Theil faced him. 'What exactly do you mean, sir?'

Leitner stared at him, astonished. 'Are you questioning me or my orders?'

Hechler snapped, 'I would like to remind both of you that we are in some danger.' To Theil he added, 'Wait outside. I'll deal with this matter.' As the door closed he said, 'How dare you accuse my officers of plotting against you?' He could not stop himself. 'You are supposed to offer leadership to this ship's company, not act like some sort of god!'

Leitner's jaw hung open. It was as if Hechler had struck him, or screamed some terrible curse.

Hechler continued flatly, 'I intend to fight this ship back to Germany, and to do that I need the trust of every man aboard. Respect, not fear, *sir*, is what we survive on.' He watched him coldly. 'Or we go under.'

Leitner dragged out a spotless handkerchief and slowly dabbed his lips.

'So that is your attitude?'

'It is.'

He waited, half expecting Leitner to call to the sentry and put him under arrest. A Luger lay on the table nearby. He might even drag that out and shoot him in his present unstable mood.

Leitner nodded jerkily. 'I shall remember this. Now get that door open and have that man arrested.'

Hechler stepped away from the table. Leitner had again become very calm. It was unnerving.

Leitner continued, 'Let me know when you are increasing speed to this rendezvous.' He was pointing at the chart, but his fingers were nowhere near the pencilled position. 'I shall be receiving the final instructions shortly. When I do –' He looked away. *'Leave me!'*

Hechler stepped out of the cabin and found Theil waiting.

'You think I knew, don't you?'

Theil gaped at him. 'I – I don't understand.'

'You love this ship, Viktor. I know that. In a matter of days, maybe hours, we shall be called on to fight, against odds. I shall need your loyalty then, and so will the *Prinz*.'

He looked away, unable to watch Theil's despair as he said brokenly, 'She was arrested by the Gestapo. I was not told. The house was empty.' The words were spilling from him in a torrent. 'If I hadn't read that file –'

Hechler said gently, 'It was too late to do anything when I found out about it. We were under enforced radio silence, you know that. It may not be as bad as you think –' Their eyes met and he knew it was pointless to go on. Even if the Gestapo had made a mistake, it was unlikely they would admit it. What was one more life to them?

Millions had perished. He thought of the unknown hand on the morse key at St Jorge, the men he had buried, the petty officer who had died without a mark on him. He looked around at the grey steel. They could still break through. He touched Theil's arm and this time he did not drag away. It was already too late for him.

'I am the captain of this ship, Viktor, and many people probably think I am too remote, too secure to watch minor events under my command. But I have seen and heard things. I will not allow this ship's reputation to be smeared.' His eyes were hard. 'By anyone.'

Theil touched his cap. 'I'll do what I can.' He swallowed hard. 'I wasn't certain – I –'

Hechler walked out to the open deck; it was like sharing a

terrible secret to see the tears running down Theil's cheeks. He felt suddenly sickened by it. By Leitner's inconsistent behaviour, his malice and his instability. But more by his own uncertainty. Like a man who has been given a weapon he suspects is faulty.

'You walk alone, Dieter?'

She stepped from beneath the same gun-mounting, her cheeks glowing from wind and rain.

He faced her and wanted to fold her in his arms, forget everything but this moment.

'I need to talk, Erika.' He knew some of the seamen were watching him. It was like a farewell at a railway station. Alone within a crowd. No words until it was too late to utter them.

'I know.' She gripped his arm. 'I was afraid.' She shook her head so that her damp hair bounced on the fur collar. 'No, not of war, of the fighting and the dying. But afterwards. I thought you might think it was a momentary lapse, a need which we both shared, but only for a moment.' She gripped him more tightly. 'I want you for myself.'

He smiled down at her, the other faces and figures fading into distance. 'I shall never give you up.' He turned as a messenger bustled up to them and saluted. 'From the bridge, sir. The engine-room can give full speed now.' His eyes flickered between them.

'Tell the bridge to wait. I am coming up.' He looked at the girl's eyes, hung on to what he saw, needing her to believe him, to trust him, no matter what happened.

He said, 'I love you, Erika.' Then he stepped back and saw the way she lifted her chin. It was as if they had both found a strength they had not previously recognised.

As he vanished up the ladder to the forebridge she whispered aloud, 'And I you, dearest of men.'

The deck began to tremble and she watched the wash rise up alongside as once again the bows smashed into the sea as if they despised it. She walked slowly below the high bridge structure and saw the black hole where the shell had plunged through to explode between decks. It was all so unreal to see and feel the enemy right here amongst them. She thought of Hechler's features as he had read the burial service, his strong voice raised above the laboured roar of fans, and the hiss of rain across the armour plating. She smiled sadly. *The iron pirate.* She could not see more than a day ahead, and she guessed that most of her companions felt much the same. But after this precious moment she knew she would find him again, that she could love nobody else.

The following morning, with less than an hour left of the pre-arranged rendezvous time, they made contact with the giant sub-marine. Men lined the guardrails as it surfaced, the water streaming from the casing and squat conning-tower, many of the onlookers remembering the other submarine's savage end, and wondering if this one's commander even knew about it.

Theil, megaphone in hand, watched the lines being fired across, the engineering party ready and waiting to sway the huge fuel hoses inboard and connect them to the bunkers.

He kept seeing Hechler's face, the sadness he had shown when he had confronted him about Britta.

Nothing seemed to matter any more. If they reached home there was nobody waiting for him. Anyway, Leitner would make certain he would climb no further in the navy. If they met with the enemy, he might at least save the ship.

He waved his megaphone to the boatswain's party at the guy-ropes and tackles. Either way, only Leitner could win. He stared so hard at the swaying wires and ropes between the two ill-matched hulls that his vision became blurred. Leitner had known all about Britta. He could have made a signal when they were still in safe waters, if he had wanted to help.

Theil was suddenly quite calm. He knew what he was going to do.

The pilot of the *Wiltshire*'s twin-winged Walrus was a young Wavy Navy lieutenant. Despite what other Fleet Air Arm officers said about his antiquated flying-boat he had grown extremely fond of it.

He was singing silently, his voice lost in the throaty roar of the Pegasus radial engine which hung above the cockpit like some ungainly cradle, and watching patches of blue cutting through the cloud layer, like a sea on a beach.

The three other members of his crew were peering down at the ocean, where occasionally their inelegant shadow preceded them as they tacked back and forth over a forty mile line.

Rumours had spawned in the cruiser's wardroom at a mounting

rate. Ever since it had been announced that the German's presence at St Jorge had been a clever ruse, and then that the Admiralty was ordering Hemrose to withdraw and join up with Force M. A new buzz had spread through the ship before the old one had been found true or false.

How vast the ocean looked from here, he thought. Nothing, not even a hint of land. It was a vast grey-blue desert, broken here and there by tiny white ridges, and dark troughs which from the sky seemed quite motionless.

A great ocean, with nothing ahead but the winding coastline of South America. He chuckled. And that was 500 miles away. Hemrose would have to give in soon, he thought. He had pushed his luck too far with the Admiralty this time. Old Godson would be pleased. He was scared of his own shadow.

His observer and navigator climbed up beside him and switched on his intercom.

'Time to turn in five minutes, Bob. Then one more sweep to the south and back to Father.' He peered at the endless terrain of water.

'The Old Man's not going to like it.'

The pilot eased the controls and glanced quickly at the compass. The news from Europe was amazing, advances everywhere. Only the coming of winter would slow things down now. He had been at school when the war had started, and the navy, temporary or not, was all he knew. It would probably carry on in Japan afterwards, he thought.

It was strange, but he had never dropped a bomb or fired one of their elderly Vickers machine-guns in anger. Just up and down lines of convoyed ships, or scouting like this ahead of the cruiser.

It would have been a nice thing to remember. 'What d'you reckon, Tim?'

His companion grinned. 'No chance. The Old Man's dropped a right clanger this time!'

They both laughed into their mouthpieces and then the pilot looked again and gasped, 'Christ, Tim! *It's her!*'

The old Walrus leaned over, the engine protesting shakily as he thrust the stick hard against his knee.

It was not a silhouette like the ones in their charts and manuals. It was a flaw in the sea's face, a hint of shadow, solid and somehow frightening.

254

'Quick! Back to Father!' They clung on as the Walrus tacked into a low bank of cloud with as much dignity as it could manage.

There was so much the pilot wanted to know and to recognise. He could have risked flak and worse by going nearer, but he knew what Hemrose would say if he disobeyed orders.

He felt his friend punching his shoulder and stared at him, his eyes suddenly bright with understanding pride as he shouted, 'Never mind the bloody fleet, Bob! Just remember this day! *We found the bastard!*'

Had the Germans seen them? It no longer mattered. They had indeed done what everyone else had failed to do. In all this ocean, it was a bloody miracle!

They both fell about laughing when they realised that neither of the other crew members as yet knew what had happened.

Aboard their ship Hemrose sat nodding in the moon sunlight, his cap tilted over his reddened face.

The Chief Yeoman of signals steadied his telescope and said, 'Signal from *Pallas,* sir. *In contact with your Walrus.* Message reads.' The yeoman licked his dried lips. *'Enemy in sight!'*

Hemrose slid from the chair, feeling their eyes on him. As if he had just parted the Red Sea.

'Make to squadron, Yeo. *Increase to full speed.*' He saw the yeoman watching him too, his eyes asking a question. They had been together a long time and Hemrose did not disappoint him.

'Hoist battle ensigns!'

Chapter Nineteen

Last Command

Hechler stood on the bridge wing and watched the huge submarine manoeuvring abeam. The sea seemed to flood between them, as if both vessels were stationary. Hechler knew differently, could sense the group of junior officers who had been summoned by Froebe to the bridge to study the formidable art of ship-handling. The supply-submarine had all her work cut out to maintain proper buoyancy and trim as the big hoses began to quiver like oily snakes, and the first of the precious fuel was pumped across.

Theil was with the boatswain on the maindeck, his megaphone or one hand slicing the air to control the seamen at the guy-ropes and wires.

'Revolutions seven-zero.' Hechler heard the order repeated behind him and pictured the intent group far below his feet in the armour-plated wheelhouse.

'*Stop starboard!*' He watched narrowly as the bows straightened up again, and the channel between the hulls became even.

'Slow ahead all engines.' He gripped the safety rail and leaned right over, the rain slashing across his oilskin, although he barely noticed it.

He loved to feel the might and power of the ship beneath him, as if he was holding her, as a rider will control a wilful mount. He saw a lamp blink from the conning tower and resisted the urge to smile. He knew already what the brief signal would ask.

'Signal, sir. *Request send boat with passengers.*'

'Negative. Tell the commander to break out a rubber dinghy.' It would be a lively crossing between the cruiser and the submarine even when controlled by hand-lines and tackles. He knew the camera team was already mustered by the guardrail, their cans of film safely protected in heavy bags. If he had one of their own boats lowered, the submarine might be tempted to break away and dive at the first suggestion of danger. Her commander would know this of course, but it was always worth a try.

He craned still further across the rail and saw one of the camera girls clinging to Meile, the supply officer, in a tearful embrace. Some of the sailors were grinning at them, and one hidden soul gave an ironic cheer.

Whatever happened from now on, it would be done without the benefit of a filmed record, he thought.

He said, 'Tell the wheelhouse to allow for the drag. Ease to port. Hold her there!'

The big submarine would not have a smooth passage home, he thought. All the long haul up to Iceland and around through the Denmark Strait before the ice came down. Then over to Norway, following the coastline to the narrows which guarded the way into the Baltic. What would they find when they finally reached Kiel, he wondered? It would be a prime target for the Allied air forces, and all the flak in the world could not hold out against such odds. He could picture his last visit there without effort . . .

He called sharply, '*Half astern starboard!*' He counted the seconds as the drag of one screw took effect. 'Slow ahead starboard!' He wondered if the fledgling one-stripers had noticed that his attention had drifted for those few vital seconds. He saw Theil peer up at the bridge; he of all people would know how simple it was to veer too close and grind into the supply-boat. Or to drag away, snapping lines and hoses and covering the sea with fuel.

He heard Froebe lecturing to the young officers. Hechler took a deep breath. Close thing.

A messenger called, 'Half completed, sir.' He had the engine-room handset pressed to one ear. 'Another thirty minutes.'

Hechler waved his hand without turning. There were no hoses immediately below the bridge, and he pictured the luckless petty officer, the one they called Mad Rudi, locked in his steel prison. It was still not clear how he had got there, or why, and communication between him and the working party outside was limited to a series of frustrating exchanges with hammer-taps on the heavy door.

Leitner's order to blow it open was absurd. The compartment was next to the forward flak switch-room, while beyond that was one of the great bunkers, still full and untapped.

The right gun, then the left in Turret Bruno lifted a few degrees, and the whole structure gave a drawn-out groan, as if steel were grating on steel. The turret remained motionless. Only one shell

257

had found its mark, but the effects showed no sign of improving. Kröll was fuming with anxiety and impatience and had every artificer from his department hard at work to clear the training mechanism. No, even a controlled charge to open Hammer's prison would be courting disaster. Like a man tossing a lighted cigarette into a barrel of gunpowder.

Leitner had not thought fit to discuss this further setback, but had sent Theissen, his aide, to enquire about progress.

The man obviously knew nothing of his admiral's original intention. To offload his mysterious boxes into the submarine, perhaps? If so, why bring them this far?

He heard Gudegast rumbling away in the background, pointing out the behaviour of wind and sea and their effect on two tethered hulls.

He recalled Gudegast's outburst over the old AMC. It added to the man in some way, as if he had always managed to keep his real self hidden in the past.

The boatswain walked towards the forecastle, his arm gesturing to some men with heaving lines. Brezinka knew just about everything that happened in the ship. He would certainly know the truth about Hammer.

Hechler tried not to think of the girl, how she had looked when he had blurted out his true feelings for her. He knew he would never forget. He screwed up his eyes and concentrated on the taut or slackening wires, the way that the sea was breaking over the submarine's nearest saddle-tank.

He had to see her again. Was it so hopeless that it must remain just an incident, like so many thousands in wartime?

And what of Theil? Fretting, hating, nursing his despair, which was as deep as any wound. Which would last? His love for the ship, or the inner madness that would in time destroy him?

'Radar – bridge!' The speaker made the young officers peer up with alarm.

Hechler seized the handset. 'Captain speaking.'

'Aircraft at Green one-five-oh! Moving left to right, extreme range.'

A dozen pairs of powerful glasses swivelled round and a man exclaimed, 'I saw a flash, sir!'

Hechler kept his eyes on the submarine. 'Keep watching!' He dared not hand the con to one of the others.

Froebe said, 'It's gone into some clouds, sir.' He sounded interested but nothing more. 'Dead astern now. Target moving very slowly.' He swore silently. 'Lost it again.'

The speaker intoned. 'Secondary armament stand by!'

Hechler wanted to turn, but snapped, 'Cancel that order!'

Gudegast joined him and together they stared down at the supply-boat's great whale back. The dinghy had been warped alongside and he saw one of the women being guided or dragged to the open forehatch. The sooner the passengers were safely below and the hatch slammed shut, the happier the commander would be.

Gudegast said, 'Maybe it didn't see us, sir?' He sounded doubtful.

Hechler considered it. A small aircraft, over 500 miles from land – it had to be hostile. Everyone had reported it as being very slow. He felt the dampness of sweat beneath his cap. Had it been from a carrier, it would have been swift, and soon to be joined by others.

He replied, 'It saw us all right. Might be a neutral.' He shook his head, dismissing his own assessment. 'My guess is that it's a float-plane of some kind.' He felt Gudegast sigh and added, 'I intend to assume it's from a warship, but not a carrier.'

Gudegast gave a chuckled. 'That's something, I suppose.'

Theissen appeared on the bridge companion ladder. 'I have been sent to enquire about –'

Hechler said bluntly, 'An aircraft, presumed hostile. If the Admiral wishes to know why I ordered the gun crews to stand down, please tell him that I would prefer that the enemy thinks we did *not* see him.' He watched the hoses throbbing across the lively wash of trapped water. 'I intend to complete oiling.'

As the man hurried away Gudegast asked quietly, 'What then, sir?'

Hechler was picturing the immediate chart in his mind. Soon the submarine would vanish. The ocean would be a desert again.

'Warn the first Arado to prepare for launching.' He waited for the big navigator to pass the order. 'My guess is that an enemy ship,' he hesitated, 'or *ships*, are close by. I'd say one hundred miles maximum. That plane will be going to its superior officer with the haste of hell. No radio, in case we pick him up – he'll be depending on surprise.'

259

Gudegast murmured, 'You saw all this in a few seconds, sir. I admire that very much. Gunnery patrol would have had every weapon with that range banging away in one more moment!'

Hechler smiled. 'You used to carry timber as you have often told me. I have always done this, since I was a boy. It is my life.'

'Arado ready, sir.'

Hechler said, 'See the pilot and give him a course. I want him to find the enemy and report back to me.'

Gudegast watched his profile. It would be a suicide mission. He was glad he did not have to make such decisions.

Hechler turned his attention to the other vessel. At best, the other ship would be in sight before sunset. If the enemy stood off to await reinforcements to ensure their kill, it might offer time enough to alter course, lose them in the darkness. With their far-reaching radar they had an edge on the enemy. But for it, he would never have known about that speck in the clouds, the slow-moving aircraft.

One thing was certain, no battleship or battle-cruiser had been reported in this area as yet. They were all to the north, employed with the convoys or protecting the supply lines as more and more of their troops flooded across the English Channel and into France. He bit his lip. Into Germany.

So it had to be a cruiser. He viewed his unknown adversary from every angle. If they could hold him off, or cripple him without sustaining more damage to the *Prinz*, they could still break through. Once their intentions were known, the British in particular would pull out all the stops. He remembered when the battleship *Bismarck*, the greatest warship ever built except for the trapped *Tirpitz*, had gone down with all guns firing. But it had taken the whole of the Home Fleet to find and destroy her. Revenge gave an edge to every commander, he thought. Their own sister-ship *Prinz Eugen* had slipped through the blockade then; so could they!

He heard men stand to attention and Froebe's whispered warning. Leitner moved through the bridge, his uniform soaked with rain. He stared at the submarine, his eyes listless. 'How much longer?'

'Ten minutes, sir.'

Some of the visiting one-stripers ducked as the Arado roared from the catapult and lifted above the bridge like a huge eagle on floats.

Hechler glanced quickly at the admiral. He had expected another outburst as to why the plane had been launched without his first being told.

Leitner merely grunted. 'Taking a look, eh?'

'It seems likely we'll have to increase to full speed, sir.' Hechler watched him in brief snatches while he never lost his hold over the ship. 'As soon as it's dark I shall –'

Leitner shrugged. 'The Führer will be watching us. We must not break that faith.'

He moved away and moments later, left the bridge.

Gudegast passed him on the ladder, but knew the admiral had not even seen him. He whispered to Froebe, 'What did you make of that?'

Froebe spread his big hands. 'He knows we shall fight, Josef. He feels sick about it, and so would I in his shoes.'

Gudegast eyed the captain's intent shoulders. Thank God he was in command, he thought fervently. There had to be a way out. They had done the impossible, sunk, burned and destroyed to the letter of their orders. What was there left?

He clenched and unclenched his fists. In a few moments now the submarine would slide beneath the waves and they would stand alone. He found himself hating it and all its kind. They, more than any other weapon, had brought horror and brutality to the sea. In a few months they had trodden down all the time-won lessons and the code of the brotherhood of sailors, which had once meant more than anything. It was never a perfect world, and some wars were inevitable. But that kind of cruelty would never be forgotten. He glanced up at their flag, like blood against the jagged clouds. Because of them, they were all branded the same.

'Ready to cast off, sir. Engine-room reports fuelling completed.'

Hechler straightened his back. 'Pass the word. Stand by, all lines. Warn the wheelhouse.'

He turned and glanced beyond the bridge, past the raked funnel and Leitner's command flag.

Come what may. He was ready.

'New course, zero-one-zero, sir.'

Hechler loosened his collar. The rain, thank God, was moving away.

'Full revolutions.' He stared astern, his hand to the peak of his cap as if at a salute. But there was no sign of the big supply-submarine. It was as if she had never been.

The clouds were much thinner too. Fine for the flak crews, not so good for their Arado, wherever it was.

He felt the ship trembling more urgently and pictured the engine-room dials misting over to the thrust of the three great screws. The wake was rolling away on either quarter, stiff and almost silver against the shark-coloured sea. If only –

He took a telephone from one of the boatswain's mates.

'Captain.'

It was a lieutenant with the damage-control party.

'The compartment is almost open, sir!' He sounded jubilant, as if nothing else mattered. 'Hammer is still all right.'

Hechler smiled grimly. 'Thank you. Stay with him.'

He shaded his eyes again to watch the sea which seemed to be rushing to meet them, as if he should feel some kind of impact before it parted and sliced away on either beam.

He said, 'Check Turret Bruno. I want a full report.'

As if to mock him, the left gun in that turret lifted like a tusk and then depressed again.

He heard someone say, 'There goes the admiral's crawler.' He did not have to look to know it was Bauer, the communications officer. No one seemed to like him, even less so since the incident on the island.

Hechler beckoned to Gudegast. 'Call communications and try to discover what has happened to our aircraft.' He saw Froebe watching him, gauging his own fate perhaps.

Hechler moved restlessly around the bridge. Horizon to horizon, shining and empty. It made him feel vulnerable, as if he was suddenly stripped naked.

'The admiral, sir.'

He took the handset. 'Sir?'

'I have had an important signal, Dieter.' He sounded emotional. 'Direct from our Führer. Germany is expecting great things from us –' He broke off with a curse as the intercom cut through.

'Aircraft, bearing Green four-five!' A pause, then, 'Disregard, friendly!'

Someone muttered hoarsely. 'About time too!'

Hechler held up his hand. *'Silence on the bridge!'* Apart from the wind through the halliards and superstructure it was suddenly still.

Gudegast whispered, 'Gunfire.'

Every glass was raised yet again, and even men on the gun sponsons crowded to the rails to stare at the empty sky.

Then they saw the long trail of smoke before they could identify the Arado. The smoke lifted and dipped behind the plane like a brown tail, and Hechler saw the drifting tracks of shellfire which told their own story. The pilot must have dared too much and had gone too close to the other ship, or had been trapped by her main armament.

'Stand by on deck to retrieve aircraft!'

Hechler tried not to lick his lips as he watched the Arado's desperate progress. Lower and lower, until he imagined he could see its blurred reflection on the sea's face.

He said, 'Tell damage-control what is happening. I want a side-party with scrambling nets immediately!'

It would mean reducing speed, stopping even, but he could not just leave these men to drown after what they had done.

Someone was using a hand-lamp. So they had been badly mauled, hit with flak enough to knock out their radio.

The senior signalman opened his mouth but Gudegast said, 'Signal reads, *enemy in sight to north-east*.' They were all watching him. '*One destroyer*.' He winced as the plane dived and almost hit the water before rising again like a dying bird. '*Two, repeat two enemy cruisers!*'

Froebe said tersely, 'Damage-control, sir.'

Hechler dropped his binoculars to his chest as the Arado lifted towards the sky, staggered and then exploded in a livid, orange ball of fire.

'Tell them to dismiss the side-party.'

Jaeger offered him the telephone, his face ashen.

Hechler watched the smoke as it clung to the heaving water, and pictured the fragments drifting to the ocean's floor like ashes.

'Sir?'

He had to hold the telephone away from his ear as Leitner yelled, '*Two* cruisers and a *destroyer*! So much for your reckoning, damn you!'

Hechler said sharply, 'There are people here, sir. We just lost some brave men!'

'Don't you dare to interrupt me! The Führer entrusted me with a mission!' He slammed down the handset, and Hechler looked at Gudegast with a wry smile. 'Not pleased.'

Minutes later Theil appeared on the bridge and stared wild-eyed, as if he could barely speak.

Hechler faced him, his patience almost gone. 'This had better be urgent!'

Theil swallowed hard. 'Is it true, sir? I have just been ordered to load those boxes aboard the spare Arado!'

Hechler grappled with the words, his mind still lingering on that last hopeless message. Three ships, but one only a destroyer. There was still a chance.

He said, 'Tell *me!*'

Theil recovered with considerable effort. 'The admiral's aide told me personally. I had just reported that we have forced open the compartment. The boatswain and his men did it. I sent Hammer to the sick-bay. Then I got this order!'

It was all suddenly so clear and simple that Hechler was surprised he could accept it so calmly.

'Then do it, Viktor.' He lifted the telephone from its special rack, half-expecting there would be no reply.

Leitner said, 'Under these circumstances I have no choice. Neither have you. My instructions are to fly immediately to the mainland. The fight goes on.'

Hechler saw the others staring at him, officers, seamen, young and not so young. All seemed to have the same stunned expression. Disbelief. Astonishment. Shame.

'And my orders, sir?'

Leitner shouted, 'You will take immediate steps to prevent this ship from falling into enemy hands! Close the shore and *scuttle her!*'

Gudegast murmured, 'Dear Christ!'

Hechler put down the telephone and looked at Theil. 'Load the aircraft and prepare for launching.' His voice was toneless. 'Then report to me.'

Theil stared at him despairingly. 'Not you too? You of all people!'

Hechler regarded him gravely. 'We do not have much time left.'

As Theil turned in a daze he added softly, 'No, Viktor. *Not me!*'

He was not sure if Theil heard him. He was not certain of

anything any more. He crossed to the bridge wing and watched the crane dipping over the catapult, the brightly painted Arado suddenly perched there, as if this moment was a part of destiny.

He heard her voice on the bridge ladder and said, 'No visitors!' But she knocked Jaeger's arm aside and ran towards him. *'I won't go!* Do you hear? I won't run away because of that coward!'

He caught her and held her, his eyes looking beyond her as he said, 'Slow ahead all engines.'

Then he said, 'I am ordering you to leave.' His voice was hoarse. He tried again. 'I should have guessed, Erika. A hero's return, or a hiding-place in Argentina. You will take him.' He pressed her against his body. 'I have to know that you at least are safe.'

She sobbed into his coat, her face hidden. *'No!* Don't force me!'

Hechler said, 'I need my remaining Arado. Please go now, my dearest Erika. *Please,* my men are looking to me.'

She stood back, her face very controlled despite the unheeded tears on her cheeks.

Then she said quietly, 'You'll not scuttle, Dieter? That's what you're saying?'

He did not reply directly. 'I shall never forget.'

Then he turned away. 'Escort her to the plane.'

He did not look again until she had left the bridge. He heard the Arado's engine roar into life, saw Theissen holding his cap in place, his face creased with dismay as he realised for the first time he was being left to fend for himself by the man he admired, perhaps even loved.

'Radar – bridge!' The merest pause. *'Enemy in sight!'*

Hechler barely heard the babble of instructions to the main armament. He strode to the wing and saw Theil by the catapult, then watched with surprise as Theissen was pushed up into the cockpit behind the girl.

'What the *hell* – !'

Froebe called, 'From damage-control, sir! The door to the admiral's bridge has jammed! A power failure!'

Hechler stared at the brightly painted plane, then very slowly lifted his cap high above his head.

With a coughing growl the Arado bounced from the catapult and lifted away from the ship, its wings glinting in the glare.

'Full ahead, all engines!' Hechler watched the Arado until it turned away and headed towards the western horizon.

Froebe said huskily, 'The admiral demands to speak with you, sir.'

Hechler recalled Theil's face. He alone must have cut the power from damage control to seal Leitner in his own bridge.

'Starboard twenty!' Hechler removed his oilskin and tossed it behind a flag locker.

'My respects to the admiral, but I have to fight a battle.'

When he looked again the tiny plane had vanished. And yet he could still feel her pressed against him, feel her anguish like his own when they had parted.

He said, 'We shall share our victory, but I'll never share his dishonour!'

Gudegast regarded him soberly. His one regret was that he had not yet begun the painting. Now he never would.

Hechler levelled his glasses with difficulty as the bridge shook to the vibration.

'Steady on zero-five-zero, sir.'

Hechler took the engine-room handset. 'Chief? Captain here. I need everything you can give me.'

'Can I ask?' Stück sounded faraway as if he was studying his dials.

'We are about to engage. Three ships. Do your best.' He hesitated, knowing that Stück wanted to go to his men. 'If I give the word –'

Stück voice was near again. 'I know, sir. I'll get my boys on deck, double-quick.'

Hechler turned away and plucked at the grey fisherman's jersey. It was quite absurd but he wished he had changed into a clean shirt and his best uniform. The others nearby saw him grin and were reassured. But Hechler was thinking of the little admiral. What Nelson would have done.

The speaker intoned, 'Range fourteen thousand. Bearing steady.'

Two cruisers in line abreast to offer their maximum firepower. Hechler could see them as if they were right here. The destroyer was slightly ahead; they would sight her first.

He heard Kröll's clipped tone, caught in the intercom to give another small picture of their world high above the bridge.

'Anton, Caesar and Dora will concentrate on the cruisers. Warn flak control to expect enemy aircraft, spotters, anything.'

Hechler glanced around the open bridge. He might be forced to go up to the armoured conning-tower, but he would hold out as long as possible. He had been brought up on open bridges, where he could see everything. When their lives were in the balance it was even more important that his men should see him.

Kröll again. 'Large cruiser at Green one-oh.' A brief pause. 'She's opened fire.'

Hechler found that he could watch like any spectator as the enemy salvo exploded in the sea far off the starboard bow. A leaping wall of water which seemed so slow to fall. The wind was whipping it towards them, and he could imagine that he tasted cordite. Death.

'Second ship's fired.'

Someone laughed in the background, a nervous, unstable sound, and Kröll's deputy silenced the man with a sharp obscenity.

'Main armament ready, sir!'

Hechler watched the two forward guns swing across the side, at odds with the jammed barrels of Turret Bruno. Aft, the other turrets were already lining up on Kröll's directions and bearings. Hechler jabbed the button below the screen and seconds later the six big guns lurched back on their springs, the roar and ear-splitting crashes punching at the bridge plating like giant battering rams.

More enemy salvoes fell and churned the sea into a maelstrom of leaping waterspouts and falling spray.

More seconds as the layers and trainers made their last adjustments.

'Shoot!'

The deck jumped beneath the bridge and a huge column of smoke burst over the side while patterns of falling debris were lost in seconds in their rising bow-wave.

The voice-pipes settled down into a staccato chorus, reporting, asking, pleading.

Hechler heard the taut replies from his bridge team. More like robots than men.

'Send stretcher bearers. Fire party to torpedo. TS. Report damage and casualties.'

Froebe shouted, 'One hit, sir. Under control.' He ducked as another salvo screamed over the bridge and exploded far abeam.

'*Port fifteen!*' At this speed the ship seemed to tilt right over before Hechler's calm voice brought her on course again. The din continued without a break, giant waterspouts rising and fading astern as the *Prinz Luitpold* tore towards the enemy, her own guns firing more slowly than the enemy's. Hechler knew that Kröll was marking every fall of shot, making certain that his crews concentrated on their markers and did not allow them to fall into the trap of a pell-mell battle.

'Direct hit on left ship!' Someone cheered. 'Still firing!'

A great explosion thundered alongside so that for a few moments Hechler did not know if they had received a direct hit in return. As the smoke filtered downwind he felt rain on his face, and was grateful that the clouds had returned. If they could keep up a running fight until dusk . . . He winced as two shells exploded inboard and a huge fragment of steel whirled over the bridge to plough down amongst some men at a Vierling gun. He stood back from the screen, tasting bile in his throat as he saw a seaman hacked neatly into halves before pitching down amongst the bloody remnants of his companions.

'*Another hit!*' The speaker sounded excited. 'Left ship is losing steerage way!'

Hechler wiped his face. 'Tell them to concentrate on the heavy cruiser to the right!' Kröll needed no telling, and as if to show its revived determination, Turret Bruno began to swivel round until it was trained on the same bearing as its twin.

'*Shoot!*'

All four guns recoiled together while the after-turrets followed immediately.

'*Short!*'

Hechler swung round and saw Leitner, hatless and staring, as he groped his way across the bridge. Theil must have returned the power and released him.

Leitner seemed unaware of the danger, and barely flinched as Kröll's trigger released another shattering salvo from all four turrets.

'You treacherous bastard! *You trapped me!*'

He peered around and coughed in the billowing smoke.

'I'll see you praying for death! It will be denied you!'

268

Hechler ducked as steel splinters shrieked and clattered around the bridge. *Another hit.* He tried to listen to the garbled reports, picture his men at their action stations in magazines and turrets; tending the boilers or just clinging to life.

He shouted, 'Don't lecture me! This is my ship! You are the traitor, Andreas Leitner!' He seized him violently, all caution and reserve gone in the din and thunder of gunfire. 'You were going to run like a bloody rabbit when you found you weren't your own propaganda hero after all!'

'*Captain!*' Jaeger was holding out a telephone, his face white as a thin scarlet thread ran down from his hairline.

Hechler snatched the phone. It was Gudegast.

'We should alter course now, sir.'

'Very well.' Hechler slammed it down. 'Hard a-port. Steer –' He ran to the compass repeater and wiped dust and chippings away with his sleeve. 'Steer *zero-one-zero.*' It would leave the badly damaged ship where she could not interfere and allow Kröll to concentrate on the enemy's heavy cruiser. '*Steady as you go!*' He saw a great column of water shoot up by the port quarter and felt the bridge jerk savagely as another shell slammed down near the quarterdeck. As if by magic, black, jagged holes appeared in the funnel, while severed rigging and radio wires trailed above the bridge like creepers.

'Request permission to flood Section Seven, sir?'

Hechler could imagine Theil down there with his team, watching the control panel, the blinking pattern of lights as one section after another was hit or needed help.

The main armament was trained almost directly abeam, their target hidden in smoke and distance.

Hechler dragged himself to a safety rail and squinted to clear his vision.

Small, sharp thoughts jerked through him. She would be on her way to safety. Five hundred miles was nothing to her. He wanted to shout her name. So that she would hear him. Like a last cry.

The hull shivered and flames seared out of the deck below the secondary armament. Men ran from their stations, some with extinguishers, others in panic, and one screaming with his body on fire.

'A straddle!' The voice almost broke. '*Two hits!*'

269

Hechler clambered above the rail and waited for the smoke to funnel past him. He had to hold his breath to stop himself from choking, but he must see, must know.

Then he caught a misty picture in the powerful binoculars, like a badly distorted film.

The big enemy cruiser, so high out of the water, was ablaze from stem to bridge, and both her forward turrets were knocked out, the guns either smashed or pointing impotently at the clouds.

A voice yelled, 'The pumps are holding the intake aft, sir!'

'Casualties removed and taken below!' He pictured Stroheim with bloodied fingers, his gold-rimmed glasses misting over in that crowded, pain-racked place. In his wildness he pictured the scene with music playing, Handel, from Stroheim's dusty stack of records.

A shell ploughed below the bridge and more splinters smashed through the thinner plating by the gate. Two signalmen were cut down without a sound, and Froebe clung to the gyro compass, his eyes bulging in agony as he gasped for air. There was a wound like a red star punched in his chest. Hechler reached for him, but he was dead before he hit the gratings.

Hechler yelled, 'Take his place, Jaeger!' He shook the youth's arm. 'Move yourself! We'll beat the Tommies yet!'

He saw the incredulous stare on Jaeger's face, and guessed that he must look more like a maniac than the stable captain. But it worked, and he heard Jaeger's voice as he passed another helm order, quite calm, like a complete stranger's.

Kröll's intercom croaked through the explosions. 'Both cruisers have lost way, sir. Shall I engage the destroyer? She now bears Red four-five!'

Hechler wiped his streaming face. Exertion or rain he neither knew nor cared. The destroyer would stand by her consorts; she was no longer any danger. By nightfall . . . he swung round as men ducked again and the air was torn apart by the banshee scream of falling shells.

For a split second Hechler imagined that another cruiser had got within range undetected. He knew that was impossible. Then the salvo fell across the ship in a tight straddle, the shells exploding between decks, while others brought down range-finders and the mainmast in a web of steel and flailing stays.

Hechler expected to feel pain as he struggled to the opposite side. Even as he levelled his glasses again he knew the answer. The flaw in the picture, which even Kröll's instruments had overlooked.

The destroyer had zigzagged through a smoke-screen, although there was already smoke enough from gunfire and burning ships, and had fired a full broadside into the *Prinz*. Hechler coughed painfully. Except that she was no destroyer. She was a light cruiser, which nonetheless had the fire-power to do real damage if only she could get close enough. Her two heavier consorts had seen to that.

Another scream of falling shells and this time the full salvo struck them from funnel to quarterdeck.

Hechler gripped the rail, could feel the power going from his engines as Stück fought to hold the revolutions steady.

Gudegast had appeared on the bridge and was shouting, 'Engine-room wants to reduce speed, sir!'

'*Half ahead!*' Hechler watched the two forward turrets swing round, hesitate and then fire, the shockwave ripping overhead like an express train.

There was no response from the after-turrets. The last enemy salvo had crippled them.

'*One hit!*'

The light cruiser was zigzagging back into her own smoke-screen, one yellow tongue licking around her bridge like an evil spirit. 'Tell the gunnery officer –' Hechler wiped his eyes and stared up at the control position. It was crushed, like a beer can, riddled with holes despite the thick armour.

'Transfer fire control –' He watched, sickened, as dark stains ran down Kröll's armoured cupola, as if the whole control position was bleeding. Which indeed it was.

Throughout the ship, men groped in darkness as lights were extinguished or passageways filled with choking smoke. Others clung together behind watertight doors which would now remain closed for ever.

In his sick-bay Stroheim put down a telephone and shouted, 'Start getting these men on deck!' The smoke had even penetrated down here, and spurted through doors and frames like a terrible threat.

Deeper in the hull Stück clung to his catwalk and watched his

271

men stooping and running through the oily steam, like figures in hell. The three massive shafts were still spinning but he would have to slow them still further. Was it to be now? Like this, he wondered? He felt the hull lurch as more shells exploded close by. His instinct told him they came from a different bearing, and he guessed that one of the damaged cruisers was rejoining the battle.

The two forward turrets were still firing, but more slowly under the local control of their quarters' officer.

There were fires everywhere, and not enough men to carry away the wounded, let alone the dead.

One man lay where he had fallen from a ladder, after Kröll had sent him to Turret Dora to discover the extent of the damage. Acting Petty Officer Hans Stoecker sprawled on his back, his face tightly pinched as if to protect himself from the unbroken roar of gunfire and internal explosions. Even the deck plating felt hot, and he wanted to call out for someone to help him. Each time he tried, the agony seared through him like a furnace bar, but when he attempted to move his legs he could feel nothing.

A bent-over figure slithered down beside him. It was the grey-headed petty officer, Tripz.

He made to cradle his arm under the young man's shoulder, but as a freak gust of wind drove the smoke aside he bent lower still. There was little left of Stoecker below the waist, and he tried to protect him from its horror.

He gasped, 'We did it, Hans! All that gold and jewellery! *We did it!* We'll all be rich!'

Stoecker sobbed as a single shell exploded against the bridge superstructure and sheets of steel drifted overhead like dry leaves. 'I – I – did – not – mean – to –' He clutched the other man in a pitiful embrace. His eyes blurred with agony, so that he did not see the cruel splinter which had just killed his comforter.

Stoecker lay back, the pain suddenly leaving him as he pictured his mother, and the girl called – he tried to speak her name but the effort was too much, so he died.

There were more corpses than living men on the forebridge and Hechler stared down at himself as if expecting to see blood. He was untouched, perhaps so that he should suffer the most.

Gudegast arose, shaking himself from a collapsed bank of voice-pipes, dust and paint flakes clinging to his beard as he stared around like a trapped bear.

Hechler heard Theil on the handset. 'Come up, Viktor. Tell your assistant to take over.'

He turned and saw Leitner standing in the centre of the bridge. He screamed, *'Where is Theissen?'*

'He went in the plane with your boxes!'

Hechler wondered how he could find words even to speak with him.

Leitner held out a canvas pouch and shook it wildly.

'These are mine! All that's left! Someone broke into my boxes, damn you!' He flung the pouch down in a pool of blood which was quivering to the engines' beat as if it was trying to stay alive. *'See?'*

Hechler watched as jewelled rings and pieces of gold scattered amongst the blood and buckled plating. So that was it.

He heard himself answer, 'So it was all wasted?'

'Not quite, you *bastard!'* The Luger seemed to appear in his fist like magic and Hechler knew he could not move aside in time.

All around him men were dying, or waiting to be struck down. Because of men like Leitner. He felt suddenly sickened and cheated. No wonder Leitner could never understand his ideals, his love for a ship, her loyalty.

A voice shattered the sudden stillness. *'Torpedoes to port!'*

The explosions were merged into one gigantic eruption, so that it seemed to go on and on forever.

Hechler was vaguely aware of objects crashing past him, the sounds of heavy equipment tearing adrift and thundering through the hull between decks.

His mind was cringing but all his skill and training tried to hold on, just long enough.

The light cruiser must have darted in to launch her torpedoes while her battered consorts had kept up a ragged covering fire.

He knew without hearing a single report that it was a mortal blow. Corpses were moving again, returning to life perhaps as the deck tilted over.

Gudegast hopped and limped towards him, his eyes blazing as he exclaimed, 'Thought you were done for!'

Hechler hung on to his massive shoulder. How long had he been unconscious? He could recall nothing beyond the great gout of fire as the torpedoes had exploded alongside.

The admiral lay on his side, his tongue protruding in a crude

273

grimace. One hand still held the Luger; the other was like a claw as it reached out for the scattered fragments of his fortune.

Gudegast aided the captain to the bridge chair. 'He's dead, sir.'

He watched the anguish on Hechler's profile. There was no point in adding to his pain by telling him that he had seen a bullet hole in the middle of Leitner's back. Someone must have gunned him down deliberately as he had aimed at the captain, when the torpedoes had abruptly ended all their hopes.

'The enemy's ceased fire, sir.' That was Jaeger, a bloody handkerchief pressed to his forehead.

Hechler heard the distant shouts of men on the deck below and Gudegast said, 'When I thought you were –'

Hechler held his arm. 'You ordered them to clear the lower deck?' He nodded painfully. 'Thank you, Josef. *So much.*'

Would I have done that, he wondered? Might more of my men have been made to die?

Now he would never know.

The deck gave a terrible lurch and the chart-table shattered into fragments.

Gudegast said, 'I'll pass the word, sir.'

Hechler shook his head. 'No. Let me. I must do it.'

He clung to the screen and saw the nearest enemy cruiser for the first time. Her fires were out, and her turrets were trained on the *Prinz* as she began to heel over very, very slowly.

Hechler raised his hand to the men nearest him. 'Abandon ship!' The words to wish them well choked in his emotion and he heard Gudegast mutter, 'Come on, sir. We'll still need you.'

Hechler tried to stand, but when he gripped the rail he found that he was staring not at the enemy but straight down at the littered water. Floats, broken boats, corpses, and swimmers, some of whom trod water to watch as the heavy cruiser began to roll over.

Hechler knew he had hit the sea, and that his lungs were on fire when hands seized him and dragged him into a crowded float. Someone cried, 'Here's the Captain!'

Hechler hooked his arm round Gudegast's shoulder and heard him murmur, 'Come *on*, old girl, get it over with, eh?'

It was like a great bellow of pain, an indescribable roar, as with sudden urgency the *Prinz Luitpold* lifted her motionless screws from the sea and dived.

Hechler struggled upright on the float and watched the maelstrom of flotsam, the tell-tale spread of oil.

They were still a long way from home.

But those who survived would speak for many years of the *Prinz*.

He stared up at the first, pale stars.

The Iron Pirate. The legend.

Epilogue

The train was moving very slowly as if weighed down by the packed humanity which crammed every seat and compartment. Hechler was glad he had been able to find a place by a window, although it was so gloomy beyond the misty glass he could see very little.

It was hard to believe that the journey was nearly over, that the long train was already clanking through the outskirts of Hamburg.

Prinz Luitpold had begun her life in this port. It all seemed so long ago. He glanced at his companions, mostly in army field-grey, like the rest of the train, creased, worn-out, huddled together for warmth and comfort.

It was about noon, but it could have been evening, he thought. Winter already had its grip on the countryside. He stirred uneasily as his mind explored the past like a raw wound. A year since that day in the South Atlantic when the *Prinz* had lifted her stern and had dived. So many familiar faces had gone down with her; too many.

The survivors had been gathered into the British ships, and Hechler had found himself aboard the light cruiser *Pallas*, the one which had fired the fatal salvo of torpedoes.

It was strange, but he had sensed no elation amongst the victors. It had been relief as much as anything. He had learned snatches of the final action, of the British commodore being killed by the *Prinz*'s first straddle, and the New Zealander's initiative in pressing home the attack despite an overwhelming adversary.

Hechler had been separated from his men, then from most of his officers. Some he knew had died in the cruiser's final moments. Kröll directing his guns, the taciturn Stück, dying as he had lived with his engines roaring around him when the torpedoes had burst in on him and his men.

Hechler had managed to stay with Gudegast, even after they were transferred to a fast troopship with an armed escort, to be landed eventually in the port of Liverpool.

276

He had seen young Jaeger for a while, but once in England Jaeger had been sent to an officers' prison camp somewhere in the south.

Gudegast had told him of Theil's last appearance, all that anyone had seen of him. As the ship had taken on her final list, with men pouring up from the smoke and fires between decks, several of the survivors had seen Theil returning below, as if going to his quarters. Hechler had asked if he had seemed to be in a great hurry? Perhaps he was trying to retrieve some small item of value from his cabin before he abandoned ship with all the others.

Gudegast had shaken his head. 'They said he was just walking. As if he had all the time in the world.'

A way out. Remain with the ship he loved, which was finally being taken from him. Now they would never know the truth.

Hechler thought of the months as a prisoner-of-war. He gave a faint, wry smile. *In the bag,* as his British captors termed it.

The camp had been in Scotland, a bleak, lonely place, shared mostly with embittered U-boat commanders.

Hechler had been interrogated several times, on arrival, and later by officers in civilian clothes who were described as being from Naval Intelligence.

They questioned him mostly about the incident at St Jorge, and whether he considered that as captain he was solely responsible for the shooting of the civilian mechanic. Bauer was probably the only one who knew the whole truth of that, but he had been blasted to fragments with the rest of his staff early in the engagement.

After that, nobody took much interest in him. Gudegast was good company, and when they were not walking around the wire fences and looking at the varying colours of the heather, Gudegast would be busy with his paints and sketches. He obtained all the materials he needed by offering to do portraits of the guards. It was an amicable arrangement.

Then one day Gudegast was ordered to leave for another camp in the south.

It had been a sad if unemotional farewell. They had survived too much for anything more.

He had asked Gudegast what he would try to do after the war.

The big man had plucked at his beard. 'Back to the sea. It's all I know.'

277

Before he left he had handed Hechler a small roll of canvas.

'For her,' he had said awkwardly. 'You'll meet her again, don't you fret.'

Then he had marched away with some others, and Hechler had saluted without knowing why.

After that it had been a matter of waiting and enduring. Christmas, with local children gathering outside the wire to sing carols. One of the U-boat officers had killed himself shortly afterwards. Hechler had withdrawn even further from his companions. They seemed alien; their war was not one he had shared, and he wished that Gudegast was still with him.

He often thought of the others, men like Brezinka who had survived, and the doctor Stroheim who had last been seen tying his own life-jacket to a badly wounded seaman. The quiet hero.

Then the time when the guards had fired their weapons in the air, and all the lights had been switched on.

Hechler had accepted the end of Europe's war with mixed feelings. The time seemed to drag, and yet he almost dreaded his release. He had written to Erika Franke several times at the two addresses she had left for him, but had received no reply.

His head lolled to the monotonous clank-clank-clank of the wheels and he stared through the window at some great white humps of land. He saw the khaki uniforms of British NCO's who were directing some tractors and a great army of German workers. He realised with a chill that the humps were all that was left of buildings, whole streets, now mercifully covered with the first snow of this bitter winter.

Someone said, 'Nearly there! Home sweet home!' Nobody else spoke. One man, an infantry captain, was dabbing his eyes with a soiled handkerchief, another was trying to pull his threadbare coat into position. Home? There was not much of it left.

Hechler thrust his fingers into his pocket as if to reassure himself that his pipe was still there. In his other hand he held the parcel which contained Gudegast's gift. It was a small portrait of himself, not aboard ship, but with some Scottish heather as a background. So typical of Gudegast, he thought.

He felt his stomach contract as he realised that the train was suddenly running into the station. Again there seemed to be wreckage everywhere, the platform roof blasted open like bare ribs against the dull sky.

278

He sensed a new tension all around him. Most of the soldiers had only just been released; many had come from the Russian Front, gaunt, despairing figures who rarely even spoke to each other. The train stopped with a final jerk and slowly at first, then with something like panic, the passengers spilled out on to the platform.

Here and there were signs of occupation. Station direction boards in English with regimental crests on them. The bright red caps of the military police, khaki and air force blue, voices and accents Hechler had taught himself to know while he had been *in the bag*.

He stared at the barrier beyond the mass of returning German troops. Police, service and military, a British provost marshal smoking a pipe and chatting with a friend. Further still, an unbroken wall of faces.

He came to a halt, his heart pounding. Was this freedom? Where was his courage now?

A solitary German sailor, the two ribbons whipping out from his cap in the chill breeze, dropped a package and Hechler picked it up.

'Here!'

The sailor spun round and snapped to attention.

Hechler handed him the parcel, and they both stared at one another like strangers. Then the man gave a slow grin, and reached out to shake his hand.

The saluting, like the war, was finally over for both of them.

The girl, Erika Franke, stood by one of the massive girders which supported the remains of the station roof and watched the train sigh to a halt.

It was the third one she had met this day, and her hands and feet were icy cold. Or was it the awful uncertainty? Not knowing? As each train had trundled into the station to offload its cargo of desperate, anxious servicemen she had seen the reactions of the crowd, mostly women, who waited there with her. Like her. She looked at the noticeboards which had once recorded the most punctual trains in the Reich. Now they were covered from top to bottom with photographs, some large, others no bigger than passport pictures. Addresses and names scrawled under each one. It was like a graveyard.

Now as the first hurrying figures approached the platform gates and the line of military policemen, she saw many of the same women surge forward, their pitiful pictures held out to each man in uniform.

'My son, have you seen him?' To another. 'He was in your regiment! You *must* have known my man!'

She wiped her eyes, afraid she might miss something.

A young British naval lieutenant with wavy stripes on his sleeve asked, 'You all right, Fräulein? I've got a car outside if –'

She shook her head and replied politely, 'No, thank you.'

A woman in a shabby coat with two photographs held up in front of her pushed past a red-capped policeman and asked that same question. The soldier brushed her away; he did not even look at her. He seemed embarrassed, afraid that he might recognise someone he had left in the mud with a million others.

The girl watched the other wave of figures coming through the gates. Not many sailors, this time. She would come back tomorrow.

She remembered his letters, bundled together, when she had finally returned home. It was all like a dream now, and the last flight to Argentina, an impossibility.

She recalled the moment when she had climbed down from the Arado and into a waiting launch. She had felt nothing but a sense of loss. Even when German consulate officials had opened the boxes to find them full of broken fragments of coloured glass, she had thought only of Hechler, with every minute taking him further away, perhaps to his death.

Leitner's aide had had hysterics when he had seen the broken glass. She had heard him shout the name of a petty officer called Hammer. Whoever he was, he must be a very rich man if he was still alive.

The woman with the two photographs pressed forward. 'Please, sir! Tell me, *please!* Have you seen my boys?'

The man stopped and took the photographs.

The girl felt her heart stop beating. It was Hechler. For a long moment she stared at him without moving, taking in every precious detail. The lines were deeper on either side of his mouth, and there were touches of grey beneath his cap. He was wearing that same old fisherman's jersey under his jacket. He seemed oblivious to the cold.

Hechler said quietly, 'I am sorry, my dear, I have not seen them. But don't lose hope –' He looked up and saw her and the next instant she was wrapped in his arms. He did not even see the woman staring after him, as if he had just performed a miracle.

How long they clung together, neither of them knew.

She whispered, 'It had to be the right train!' She ran her hand over him as if to reassure herself he was real. She saw the loose threads on his right breast where the Nazi eagle had once been, and looked up to see a new brightness in his blue eyes.

He said, 'I knew I'd find you, my little bird. Somehow –'

Some British sailors were waving and cheering as some of their companions boarded another train.

Hechler put his arm around her shoulders and they walked out into the drifting snow.

Once he glanced back at the station and the jubilant British sailors.

Then he squeezed her shoulders and said softly, 'Like us, they're going home.'

H.M.S. Saracen

Part One   1915

Chapter One

The Ship

In fierce short gusts the bitter north wind swept across the wide confines of Portsmouth harbour, the ranks of wavelets made by the incoming tide crumbling into white confusion at each successive blast. In the narrow entrance to the harbour itself the sea boiled in a trapped maelstrom and leapt violently against the weathered stones at the foot of the old Fort Blockhouse before being shredded by the wind and flung back into the pressing tideway. It was as if winter was still unwilling to release its grip and accept that with the coming of March it too would have to relent.

The sky was high and without colour or warmth, yet its clear emptiness seemed to turn the water below to an angry pewter which reflected against the tall sides of the moored battleships, the pitching, uneasy trots of torpedo-boat destroyers and the countless grey craft which thronged the naval anchorage and waited for the gale to ease.

There was little movement of small craft, and apart from a fat paddle-wheeled tug, with its yawing tow of loaded coal-tenders, the normally busy concourse was deserted. For although Britain was at war, and had been for seven confused months, this was Sunday forenoon, and aboard every pitching ship the church pennant was hoisted, and somewhere within each glistening hull, or hidden below the spray-dappled superstructures, some thousands of men listened automatically to the words of Peace and Love.

Richard Chesnaye ducked his head into a sharp gust of wind and pushed his way gratefully into the small green-painted hut at the top of a flight of worn stone steps which ran down to the water's edge. The hut was empty, and smelled of damp and stale cigarette smoke. Through the stained windows he could see the distorted shapes of the ships, the streaming white ensigns and the vast grey panorama of power and lordly indifference.

He was tall for his seventeen years, yet his steady grey eyes reflected some of the growing apprehension he felt as he stared across the dancing whitecaps towards his first ship. Even his new midshipman's uniform seemed to scream a contrast with the flaked walls of the hut and the worn, scrubbed benches where generations of naval officers had waited for boats to ferry them back to their ships. After a thick night ashore, perhaps, dazed, irritable, but with the dulled satisfaction always enjoyed by an unfettered sailor. Or perhaps to face a court martial. Richard Chesnaye's mouth turned down slightly. Or, like himself, to join a new world. Across that strip of water anything might be waiting. It was 1915, and the war had *not* ended in six months as the newspapers had prophesied, and as far as he could understand it was only just beginning.

He took off his cap and shook the spray absently across the floor. His hair was dark and curled rebelliously across his left forehead, helping to defeat the sensitive gravity of his features.

It was still hard to believe he was actually here and that at any moment a boat would appear, presumably at the foot of these famous King's Stairs, and carry him forward into a new way of life.

After months of training, lectures, drills and frustration he was ready. He wondered briefly what had become of all the other cadets he had known, who, as midshipmen like himself, were even now spreading throughout the Grand Fleet and beyond. He thought too of the long battle he had fought to stay level with many of those contemporaries. Not with the mysteries of seamanship and navigation, nor with the complex cult of tradition and ceremonial – as the last of a long line of naval officers Chesnaye had hardly noticed the latter – but with a tiny allowance from home he had faced the daily, even hourly, problem of keeping pace with the financially blessed and more privileged young men who fretted to complete their training and get to sea before the war ended.

Some oilskinned seamen trudged past the window, their bearded faces bowed to the wind. All at once Chesnaye wanted to call out to them, to show them he was there. One of *them*. He smiled quickly at the impulse and watched the burly figures until they were lost amongst the maze of derricks and equipment which seemed to litter the whole of Portsmouth dockyard.

As he had followed the seaman who had carried his tin trunk,

288

Chesnaye had stared at every ship, half expectantly, half fearfully, as he strode to meet his latest challenge. But H.M.S. *Saracen* was lying out in the stream, clean and untouched by the land, indifferent to the unimportant individuals who struggled to serve her.

At first Chesnaye had received his orders to join the *Saracen* with mixed feelings. As some of his friends had danced excitedly at the prospect of joining a dashing torpedo-boat destroyer or one of the hard-worked North Sea cruisers, he had stared at his appointment instructions with something like bewilderment. Unlike the bulk of the Fleet, the *Saracen* was very new, hardly older than the war itself. In addition, she was one of a fresh breed. A monitor. In every war hard experience and different conditions gave birth to new types of ships and strategies. From galleys and fire-ships to bombs and river gunboats. Wherever the tide of battle rose, so too did the requirements of the Royal Navy. After years of undisputed power and prosperity the challenge had come again, and like the waspish submarines which sheltered behind Fort Blockhouse so too the monitors were coming into their own. This war would be fought with great armies, perhaps the biggest land forces the world had ever known, but while they faced the field-grey masses on the Western Front the Navy would be stretched to the limit to sustain them. One of Chesnaye's instructors had received his questions with contempt.

'A monitor? A bastard-ship! Neither one thing nor the other!'

Chesnaye squinted his eyes to stare at the tall shape outlined against the dull slate-roofed shambles of Gosport town.

The *Saracen* was certainly an unusual-looking ship. Although she boasted nearly seven thousand tons, as much as many a cruiser, her length was little more than one of the larger destroyers. Yet if her length was puny she gave the impression of tremendous strength, even belligerence. As the instructor had also pointed out, she had been designed primarily for giving artillery support to land forces. Even a landsman would appreciate this point after only one glance. Dominating all else, and behind which the towering bridge and sturdy tripod mast looked almost incidental, two enormous fifteen-inch guns, mounted in one raised turret, pointed across the harbour like the tusks of some armoured monster. To support these great weapons the ship's designers had substituted breadth for length, and the

Saracen's ninety-foot beam added to her appearance of ponderous indestructibility.

A small black shape detached itself from the monitor's side and began to curtsy across the disordered whitecaps. The bleak light reflected dully on the picket boat's brass funnel, and Chesnaye could see a seaman already in her bows with a boathook as the sturdy little craft turned in a wide arc towards King's Stairs. They were coming for him.

Chesnaye stepped out into the wind once more, suddenly aware of hunger pangs, a sure sign of growing nervousness. The boat surged alongside the piles, the boathook already pulling at the slime-coated chains. There was an alarming clamour of bells and the boat's propeller threw up a great froth under the stern as the engine went astern.

All at once the boat was secured and Chesnaye was aware that the small midshipman who had been at the wheel, and jerking violently at the telegraph, was staring up at him, his pale eyes strained and impatient.

'Chesnaye?' His voice was shrill and added to the impression of extreme youth. 'Well, get aboard, for God's sake! No use waiting for a damned fanfare!'

Chesnaye smothered a grin and felt his way down the steep steps, the tin box grinding down dangerously against his legs.

After the spartan precision of the training ship he was used to entering and leaving boats, nevertheless he felt slightly irritated that not even one of the boat's two seamen attempted to offer him a hand.

The midshipman nodded quickly. 'Right, Morrison, let go forrard!' He jerked at the telegraph and glanced up at the dock-yard clock. 'God, three minutes adrift already!' He shouted at the seaman in the bows: 'Bear off forrard! Watch that paintwork!' But already the boat was swinging away into the tide, the hull trembling and shaking as the engine turned at full power.

The midshipman swung the brass wheel and took a quick breath. 'Sorry about the rush. My name's Pickles.' His innocent features darkened into a scowl. 'And I don't want any funny remarks!'

Chesnaye grinned and gripped the rail by the small open cockpit. 'Why the rush? Are we putting to sea immediately?'

Pickles grimaced. 'Rush? *Everything* is done like this! Right now there'll be at least two telescopes trained on this boat, and all hell will explode if I take longer than the prescribed time!'

'But suppose I had been delayed, or late?' Chesnaye watched the short figure by the wheel shiver.

'The day *you're* late you'll know the answer to that one!' Pickles laughed nervously. 'I expect you think your training days are over, eh? Well, believe me, you haven't seen anything yet!'

Chesnaye shrugged his shoulders deeper into his greatcoat and decided not to speak further. Pickles had obviously not been aboard the *Saracen* much longer than his own appointment. It was the usual game which 'old hands' played with new arrivals. Or was it? Every move which the boy made seemed charged with urgency and anxiety.

Chesnaye turned his attention to the monitor, which had suddenly loomed from indistinct distance to stark and frightening reality.

She towered above the vibrating picket boat so that he could see the twin turret as well as the battery of small four-inch guns abaft the bridge structure and all the hundred and one other details which crowded the upper deck. There was only one funnel, just aft of the great tripod mast, and a certain nakedness towards the stern, as if to compensate for the ship's great weight of armament and equipment. No black smoke belched from the funnel, and Chesnaye remembered for the first time that this ship would at least spare him the agony of coaling. The *Saracen* was modern to the last rivet, and she was oil-fired.

He glanced again at his companion. Pickles was without oilskin or bridgecoat, and the front of his shirt was grey with salt spray. Between his teeth he gripped the lanyard of a whistle which he wore about his neck, and he spoke through the cord in sharp staccato sentences as he mentally prejudged the business of getting the forty-foot steamboat alongside.

It would not be easy, either. Chesnaye decided. He had already noticed the curious way in which the monitor's hull bulged as it touched the water. All along the waterline it was swollen outwards like the ballast tanks of a submarine.

Pickles tore his eyes from the water for a moment and stared at him. 'Anti-torpedo bulges! They're an experiment!' He nodded towards the monitor's waterline. 'She's so damned slow we need 'em!' He started to smile and then checked himself. 'But you won't say I said that, will you?'

Before Chesnaye could answer he was already jerking at the bell, and the boat shuddered violently as the propeller went astern and slewed the boat dangerously into the lee of the monitor's tall side where a gleaming varnished gangway and grating hung suspended above the water. High above, silhouetted against the pale sky, a lieutenant in frock-coat and sword-belt peered down at them.

The bowman aimed at the chains and missed.

The bell jangled once more and the little boat surged ahead, the stem yawing violently in the racing tide.

Through the lanyard and his gritted teeth Pickles exclaimed, 'God Almighty!' Then in a louder voice, 'Morrison, hook on, for Pete's sake!'

The big seaman shrugged and took another swing. The hook connected, and seconds later a tugging bowline held the boat temporarily secured.

A thin voice floated from above. 'Tie up at the boom!' There was the briefest pause. 'Then report to me, *Mister* Pickles.' Another pause while Chesnaye stared at the anguish on the midshipman's face. 'A bloody *awful* exhibition!'

A seaman scurried down the gangway and picked the tin trunk from the cockpit. There was a silence but for the chafe of boat fenders and the unbroken ripple of water, and Chesnaye found himself on the great ladder and making his way upwards, towards the voice.

As his head drew level with the deck he braced himself once more, painfully aware of his heart pumping against his ribs. The quarter-deck seemed vast and vaguely hostile. In a quick glance he took in the gleaming expanse of scrubbed teak planking which curved inwards towards the rounded stern above which a giant ensign streamed stiffly in the wind. Everything looked new and perfect. Even the sideboys, whose wind-reddened faces were watching him without expression, wore white gloves, and the marine sentry, quarter-master and the rest of the gangway staff looked as if they had just been issued with fresh equipment and clothing.

Chesnaye saluted the quarterdeck and the tall, reed-thin figure of the Officer of the Day, the lieutenant whose querulous voice had already greeted his arrival.

Lieutenant Hogarth blinked his salt-reddened eyes and glared

292

at the midshipman. 'So you're Chesnaye,' he said at length. As he spoke he opened and closed his long telescope with quick nervous jerks. 'I'll have you taken to your berth and then you can report to the Commander.' He craned his thin neck towards the silent group at the gangway. 'Bosun's Mate, have this officer's gear taken below and then show him to the wardroom!' His sharp voice followed the man along the immaculate deck. 'And tell Mister Pickles I want him at the double!' Half to himself he added: 'Damned snotties! Couldn't handle a damned boat to save his damned neck!'

Chesnaye thought of the frantic dash across the harbour. 'I thought he did it rather well, sir.'

Hogarth's jaw opened and shut in time to the telescope. 'You *what*? When I require the opinion of a bloody midshipman I'll ask for it!' In a more controlled tone he added: 'I am the Gunnery Officer here. *I* am the one man in this ship who is of supreme importance!' He gestured vaguely towards the hidden guns. 'They are my responsibility. Without them this ship might well not have been built!'

Chesnaye almost laughed aloud, but controlled the mad impulse as he saw the wild sincerity in the officer's eyes. 'I see, sir,' he said carefully.

'Yes indeed!' Hogarth spoke to the quarterdeck at large. 'The primary object of the vessel is to knock hell out of the enemy. With *my* guidance we have done and will do just that!'

Chesnaye saluted and turned to follow the fast disappearing shape of the Bosun's Mate.

Hogarth added sharply, 'Do you play bridge, by the way?'

Chesnaye could not hide his grin this time, but Hogarth was fortunately staring through the telescope at a passing sloop. 'No, sir.'

'Hmmm, just as I thought. The very *bottom* of the barrel!'

As he strode uncertainly along the maindeck beneath the slim barrels of the secondary armament Chesnaye almost collided with the returning Pickles. The latter skidded to a halt, his face glistening with sweat.

'Did you meet him?'

Chesnaye nodded. There was something both endearing and pathetic about this small midshipman. 'Yes. I did. I didn't know how I was expected to react!'

293

Pickles grinned nervously. 'Mad. Quite mad. But then they're all getting like that here!'

'He was saying something about his gunnery –'

Pickles waved his grubby hands. 'Hopeless! Apart from trials and a quick shot at the Belgian coast we've not done a thing yet. Even then we missed the target! The Captain's been giving Hogarth hell!'

'I've got to report to the Commander next.'

Pickles shrugged. 'He's all right. But the Captain's straight out of Dickens! Hates everybody, especially midshipmen!'

Hogarth's voice screeched along the deck with the wind. 'Mister Pickles! At the *double*, I said!'

Chesnaye found himself two decks down, breathless and completely lost, and standing in semi-darkness beside an open steel door.

The Bosun's Mate gestured indifferently. 'Gunroom. All the young gentlemen mess in there.'

It was a small space with only one scuttle, which seemed so close to the tumbling water that it must be barely above the torpedo bulge. There was a long table with a soiled cloth, upon which two messmen were laying cutlery for the Sunday meal. Five other midshipmen's chests were stacked along one bulkhead, and there was a single piece of massive furniture which could be mistaken for either a sideboard or a bar. Apart from a few chairs and a large print of the King, the place was bare.

A messman showed his teeth. 'You'll be the new one, then, sir?' He pushed back a strand of hair from his narrow head. 'I'm Lukey, an' this 'ere is Betts. We looks after you all. Six young gentlemen, an' 'im!' He jerked his thumb towards a canvas partition which seemed to form one large tent-like cabin across the end of the mess. 'Yes, sir. Sub-Lieutenant bloody Pringle. 'E's in charge of all of you, and 'e enjoys it very much.'

Chesnaye kept his face blank. He knew it was wrong to stand and listen to a seaman openly criticising a senior officer, but he had already learned the hard way that a loyal messman was an ally indeed. So he coughed and said quickly, 'I am to report to the Commander.'

Lukey bobbed his head. 'Ah yes, sir. A real gennelman if ever there was. Commander Godden is a toff. You can't ask for 'igher than that, eh?'

'Er, quite. Where is the wardroom?'

'Right aft. All the other officers' accommodation is there. 'Cept for the warrant officers. They mess next to you.'

Chesnaye committed all these facts to memory. In a strange ship and once off the spartan lines of the upper deck it was not uncommon to get completely lost, knowing neither bows from stern, nor even which deck you were on.

Lukey rubbed his hands. 'Well, 'urry back, sir. Pork chops and roast spuds today! Nothing like Sundays on board. Bit of God, an' then a good tuck in!' He frowned unexpectedly. 'I'll bet those bloody Huns aren't gettin' grub like this!'

Chesnaye started with surprise. In the strangeness of the ship, surrounded by the unfamiliar grey paint, the whirr of fans and the gentle creak of the ship's six-thousand-odd tons of steel and machinery, he had all but forgotten the war. There just did not seem to be room for it. Pork chops, boats which ran by the clock and an Officer of the Day who looked more like a clergyman, it was all too remote for war and reality.

He turned towards the door where the seaman lounged with bored indifference. But Lukey crossed the mess in two quick steps.

'Oh, just a few things, sir.' He gave a conspiratorial wink. 'I'ope you won't take any offence, but it's better to get off on the right foot, y'see?'

Chesnaye did not, but waited mystified as Lukey continued in his peculiar rasping voice.

'Firstly, sir, you never wears a greatcoat aboard without express orders. The Captain does not believe in 'em. Says they pamper the young gentlemen, like. Next, your tin box is an officer's pattern. The Sub won't like that. *Must* 'ave regulation midshipman's chest.'

Chesnaye heard himself say, 'It belonged to my father.'

'Ah yes, sir. Very nice, I'm sure, but it won't do. I'll see if I can fix something.' He looked directly into Chesnaye's eyes. 'In this ship everything is perfect. The Captain says that's 'ow it's got to be, so that's 'ow it is. Take my tip, sir. Tread carefully, and don't ask questions.'

The Bosun's Mate said: 'The Commander'll be waitin', sir. 'E's not used to that!'

Lukey grinned. 'Off you go, sir. An' remember what I said!'

*   *   *

295

The *Saracen*'s wardroom was situated beneath the port side of the quarterdeck, and just prior to this Sunday lunch presented a scene of detached opulence mixed with one of noisy excitement. The long business of Divisions and church was over, the tense moments of inspections and cramped drills were behind for another week, and the ship's officers stood around the small oak bar, first and second drinks consumed, glasses shining in the cheerful flames from the ornamental fireplace. Large brass scuttles lined one side of the ward-room, and as the ship swung easily at her buoy the distant grey scene of Portsmouth dockyard drifted back and forth from one scuttle to the next. From the top of the tall signal tower the scare-crow arms of the semaphore wagged impatiently across the anchored warships, but these officers at least were free to ignore them.

Most of them stood in one group around the plump heavy figure of the Commander, while the remainder slumped in the well-fashioned red leather chairs, perhaps listening to the promising bustle of the stewards beyond the curtain which partly hid the long table, the shining silver and tall-backed teak chairs.

Commander Godden tilted his glass, allowing his eye to stray across the semicircle of faces around him. It was strange how no officer ever seemed to get used to the serious business of ship's ceremonial. The more senior the officer became, the more he seemed to take it to heart.

Now they were relaxed, yet at the same time excited. In their heavy dress-coats and glittering epaulettes they seemed like strangers to one another, so that their voices became louder, their gestures more extravagant.

Godden sniffed the faint aroma of roast beef and swallowed automatically. He nodded towards a hovering steward and said in his loud bass voice, 'Same again, gentlemen?' It was an invitation, and he allowed his wide mouth to lift in a grin as the glasses were raised and lowered as one.

He glanced around the spacious wardroom and felt pleased. There was something about a new ship. The fitted plum-coloured carpet, the shining gloss paint, the proud crest above the fire depicting a fierce Arab warrior with a raised scimitar; everything was glossy and full of well-being. There were only twelve ward-room officers, as some had already been taken to supplement the growing might of the Fleet, and this added little to the amount of

296

work and increased greatly to their individual comfort aboard.

Lieutenant Travis, the Navigating Officer, watched the steward shaking angostura into some of the glasses and plucked thoughtfully at his neat black beard. 'We'll soon be away, I expect?' It was a question directed at large, but meant for the Commander.

Godden winked at the ramrod figure of Major De L'Isle, whose Royal Marine's uniform fitted his massive body like a silk glove, so that some wondered how he managed to bend, let alone sit at table. 'We shall see, gentlemen! I have invited the Captain here for a drink this forenoon, so we might be told!'

De L'Isle grunted and ran a finger around the top of his tight collar. 'All this damned excitement!' The marine glared at the opposite bulkhead, his small ginger moustache bright against his florid face, the whole of which was covered with a fine web of tiny broken veins, the mark of a heavy drinker. 'One would think this was the first war the Service had been in! Lot of damned rubbish!'

The Commander took his drink and initialled the steward's chit. 'Ah, but this might be a little different. Not like China, you know, Major. Germany's damned powerful and itching for a fight!'

Lieutenant Travis frowned. 'I wonder what our next job will be?'

'Always wondering, Pilot!' Godden beamed. 'Maybe we shall have another go at the Belgian coast, eh? Give poor old Hogarth another chance to prove his worth!'

There was a quick response of laughter. Even the Chief Engineer, a grizzled and grey-haired little man called Innes, who had been standing silently on the outside of the group, seemed to come alive. 'It's no job for a ship of war!'

They all looked at him with surprise. Godden watched him with silent amusement. 'Go on, Chief. Tell us what is wrong with a monitor.'

The engineer shrugged. 'Ships are for fighting ships. Get mixed up with the damned Army and anything might happen!'

De L'Isle nodded aggressively. 'Quite right! My marines can handle any of that nonsense!'

The Navigator swirled the gin round his glass and frowned. He was a quiet, deep-thinking man and unmoved by the casual ease

297

with which his betters were dismissing the efforts of another service. 'I think it may be a mistake to think that.' He kept his dark eyes lowered. 'Jerry can fight well enough, and our sea supremacy may have to take on a completely new challenge.'

Godden grinned. 'Of what, for instance?'

Travis shrugged. 'U-boats. Even their surface ships have done well so far.'

The marine major choked. 'Bloody rubbish, Pilot! We've beaten the Jerry in every combat so far! Whipped the hides off 'em!'

'What about Coronel?' Travis met his stare angrily.

'Well, what about Coronel?' De L'Isle seemed to bristle. 'And what about the Falklands last December, and the Dogger Bank battle a couple of months ago?' He turned to the group at large, his glowing face triumphant. 'We showed them well enough!'

Travis persisted doggedly. 'What I'm saying is that it will not be an easy victory!'

Godden licked his lips. The heat of the fire, the gin and the liveliness of the conversation were having their usual effects. 'I agree with the Chief. I don't much hold with inshore fighting. Shooting at some damned target ten miles or so inland, while some fool of a soldier signals his interpretation of what you are doing!' He groped for the words. 'It's not clean, not *naval* somehow!'

A steward glided closer. 'The Captain's coming, sir.'

Godden pulled down the front of his coat and turned to face the door.

Captain Lionel Royston-Jones was slight, and at first glance even frail. Yet his small body was trim and wiry against Godden's portliness, and the bright blue eyes which darted briefly around the waiting officers were completely steady and entirely lacking in warmth.

Godden cleared his throat. 'I am glad you could accept the invitation, sir.'

The customary remark seemed to fall short and left no impression on the Captain's neat, weather-browned features. Everyone knew that a captain only entered a wardroom by invitation. Yet one look at Royston-Jones' face shattered the illusion of a favour. Who, after all, would deny a man like the Captain entrance anywhere! Royston-Jones inclined his head slightly towards the

298

Chaplain, whose dark garb, plus the outlandish habit of parting his hair dead in the centre, gave him the appearance of an anxious crow. 'Good sermon, Padre.'

The Chaplain, whose name was Nutting, rubbed his thin hands with agitation. 'Thank you, sir. Most gratifying!'

But Royston-Jones was already looking again at the Commander. 'Well, are you going to offer me a drink?' His voice was never raised, but it had a kind of crispness which made even a simple remark sound like a reprimand.

They all watched him sip his customary sherry, his pale eyes fixed on the nearest scuttle. His small figure seemed weighed down by the heavy frock-coat and gleaming epaulettes and gave him the added appearance of an officer from some bygone age. Even his hair was cut unfashionably long, with the sideburns reaching below his ears. On either cheek, too, there was a small tuft of brown hair, and these were said to have earned him the nickname of 'Monkey' on the lower deck.

At length he said calmly: 'I have just received my orders. We sail tomorrow. Seven bells of the Morning Watch. After lunch, Commander, perhaps you will be good enough to see me about final arrangements.'

Only the Chaplain dared to ask the urgent question. 'And may I be bold enough to enquire our destination, sir?' He peered at the Captain as if to see the words emerge from his mouth.

'You may, Padre.' The cold eyes moved relentlessly over the tense faces. 'And, since no more shore leave will be granted, I can be sure of some sort of security!'

There was an uneasy ripple of laughter. It was never simple to determine the Captain's humour.

'The destination will be the Mediterranean. The orders specify Gibraltar, and thence to the Eastern Mediterranean for operations against the Turks.'

Godden whistled. 'Gallipoli, by God!'

Royston-Jones pursed his lips. 'As you put it, Commander. Gallipoli.'

Immediately everyone was speaking at once, while the Captain stood like a small rock, unmoved and unmoving.

Innes ran his fingers through his grey hair. 'Well, the engine room is ready, sir.' He grinned wryly. 'No more coal to worry about!'

299

Royston-Jones touched one of the little hair tufts with a fore-finger. 'Fuel is the least of our problems.'

'But, sir, I thought the Gallipoli campaign was going to be allowed to fade out!' Travis spoke loudly in spite of the warning in Godden's eyes.

'Did you, Travis?' The blue eyes regarded him mildly. 'Perhaps their lordships have not had the benefit of your insight?'

Godden's huge bulk moved forward as if to shield the young officer's confusion. 'I think I know what Pilot meant, sir. We've been told that the squadron sent to bombard the Turkish forts along the Dardanelles and to force an entrance to the Straits was not powerful enough. There was some story too that our mine-sweepers were repulsed by gunfire and the battleships have had to make do best they can against the enemy minefields. A sort of stalemate. A good idea gone wrong.'

The Captain laid his glass very carefully on a table. 'It is a campaign, Commander, not one Lilliputian skirmish.' He spoke without emotion, yet two spots of bright colour appeared on Godden's cheeks as if he had been faced with a stream of obscenities.

'Furthermore, the object of these operations is to *capture* the Straits, and not merely to give some apparently much-needed exercise to our gunnery officers!' He continued evenly: 'With the Straits captured, Turkey is cut in two. Our ally, Russia, will have her southern ports open once more, and we will then be able to assist her in an all-out assault on Constantinople. All Turkey's arms factories are situated there. Smash their capital and their production and they will soon collapse. Germany will be without an ally, and all neutrals tempted to throw in their lot with the Kaiser will think again. In addition, the back door to Europe will be open and in our hands.'

The marine major breathed out noisily. 'My God, what a scheme!'

Royston-Jones glanced sharply at the glass in De L'Isle's hand. 'Quite so, Major. It will need *all* our attention. Also, it will mean a much greater campaign than first visualised by Mr. Churchill. Not just ships, but troops. Thousands of men and equipment must be landed and helped inland.'

Godden said quietly: 'But surely by now the Turks will have recovered from the first assaults? Won't they be dug in and ready for our troops?'

300

Royston-Jones smiled gently. 'I can see you have fully assessed the situation, Commander. That is where we come into the picture. A new weapon. A floating power of gunfire which can be brought almost to the beaches themselves. No more of this nonsense of battleships meandering back and forth under the muzzles of prepared shore-batteries. Ships too deep-hulled to get in close, or too puny to shoot more than a few miles. The *Saracen* will make history.' He looked sharply towards the shore. 'We will be well rid of the land. We will be able to concentrate on fulfilling our function before we become cluttered up with untrained men from the barracks or these wretched Reservists.' He moved towards the door. 'See that the ship is brought to security readiness immediately, Commander. You know the procedure.'

Godden nodded. 'Aye, aye, sir. We'll make a show all right!'

The slight figure stiffened. 'I am afraid that a "show", as you call it, would fall far short of what *I* have in mind!'

The door slid to and there was an empty silence.

Godden tried to grin at the others, but nothing happened. Viciously he slammed his glass on the bar and signalled for a steward.

'Bloody hell!' he said.

Richard Chesnaye settled his shoulders more comfortably within the tight confines of his hammock and stared upwards at the pipes which criss-crossed the shadowed deckhead barely inches from his face. The darkness in the stuffy gunroom was broken only by the shaded gleam of a blue police light, so that the strangeness and unfamiliarity of the place seemed to close in on him and add to his feeling of loneliness.

His first half-day in the *Saracen* had been a long one, yet so crowded with events, faces and situations that only now, in the security of his hammock, could he piece them together in his mind and go over his own impressions and reactions.

He met the Commander as expected in the wardroom, or rather on the fringe of it. Listening to the babble of conversation and laughter beyond the curtain he had found it hard to picture himself as ever being one of them. He had stared at the table beside him, laden with caps, sword-belts, even swords, where they had been dropped by the officers as they had returned from Divisions. Caps exactly like his own, but for the Commander's

301

with its leaf-encrusted peak, yet in a way so different. In the training ship there had been only two partitions. Cadets and instructors. Here in this strange ship everybody seemed slotted and packaged into divided messes, so that a sense of complete isolation existed between each one. The lieutenants and above had the wardroom, the sub-lieutenants their own mess. While the warrant officers and midshipmen, too, were subdivided again. Below them, the chief and petty officers and then the bulk of the ship's company were neatly stowed away in separate compartments, untouched by each other, yet constantly aware of status and authority.

Commander Godden had seemed pleasant enough. Jovial, full of vague encouragement, yet rather distant, as if his mind was elsewhere.

Chesnaye had returned to his own mess by a roundabout route, and met his own sort in the process of starting their Sunday meal. He had had to sit on his tin chest because there were not enough chairs, but he had not minded. He had been too busy watching and listening.

There was Beaushears, who at this moment was snoring painfully just two feet away from him, his feet whitely protruding from the end of his hammock. A tall, deceptively languid young man, with the far-seeing eyes of an adventurer, he had casually introduced the others.

'This quiet one is Bob Maintland. Plays good squash, but if you've a sister you'd better watch him!'

With a fork he had pointed to the cheerful gnome sitting opposite Chesnaye. 'Meet "Eggy" Bacon. Talks first, thinks later!'

The one addressed had merely grinned, showing a double rank of very small pointed teeth, and then turned his attention back to a tattered notebook which he was obviously studying.

Beaushears had observed: 'Better take the book off the table before the Master arrives. He can't bear anything which might distract from his fascinating conversation!' Then in his normal drawl, 'And this is "Ticky" White, so called because he is always scratching.'

White had been on duty on the quarterdeck when Chesnaye had arrived, and even now bore the red mark of his cap printed across his forehead. He was a pale uncertain-looking youth with jet-black hair and restless, very deep-set eyes. He shrugged and nodded to Chesnaye. 'I'm too tired to find a witty answer. A few hours with that maniac Hogarth drains me of human kindness!'

Beaushears smiled. 'And of course you have already met the genius of the *Saracen*, Keith Pickles.'

Chesnaye saw the small midshipman jerk out of his thoughts and look across with confusion. 'Oh, er, yes.' Pickles seemed at a loss. 'Hope you've settled in.' He had been about to add something more when the Sub-Lieutenant had entered.

Now, in the same gunroom, but in the unreal security of the hammock, Chesnaye tried to picture Pringle once more. He had the build and movement of a rugby player. Very big, glowing with health and surprisingly fast on his feet.

'Well, all sitting down!' Pringle had hurled himself into the big chair at the head of the table, his eyes already fixed on Chesnaye. 'Ah, the new boy. Good. Common practice to report to me immediately upon joining ship.' He spoke in sharp, almost breathless stacatto. 'Still, you're not to know. But in this ship ignorance is no excuse.' He snatched a spoon and dug into the soup even as the messman Lukey had placed it before him. Between noisy mouthfuls he continued in the same expressionless voice: 'Good, then let me see. What's next.' He lifted his pale eyebrows with theatrical concern. 'Ah, *yes!*' He turned to stare at Pickles.

'Another complaint about your boat-handling from Lieutenant Hogarth!' He shook his head so that the overhead light glistened on his cropped blond hair. 'Tch, tch! The honour of the gunroom soiled again!'

Chesnaye was about to grin when he realised that the others were staring stonily in front of them or busily engaged with their soup. Except Pickles. He stared at Pringle with the look of a mesmerised rabbit.

Pringle added: 'You really are hopeless, you know. We can't have our new member getting the wrong idea, now can we?' Then in a matter-of-fact tone, as if the whole matter was of no importance, 'Now what's it to be this time?' He waited, and even Chesnaye was conscious of the silence. The clatter of dishes in the small pantry had ceased, and he could imagine Lukey and Betts listening to Pickles' answer.

Pringle threw back his head. 'Take this plate away!' His voice, too, was powerful.

As Lukey flitted across the gunroom he asked: 'Now, Pickles, you've not answered? D'you want to absolve your stupidity with gloves on? If so, we can settle it immediately after grub, eh?'

Chesnaye still hardly believed what he had witnessed. A great brute like Pringle offering to take on Pickles in combat. He could have killed him with one hand and blindfolded.

Pringle had eventually nodded with apparent satisfaction. 'Right. Punishment Number Two. Immediately after lunch.'

Chesnaye twisted on to his side, his eyes wide in the darkness. Punishment Number Two had entailed a cruel and systematic beating with the leather scabbard of a midshipman's dirk.

Pickles had bent across the table opposite Pringle before Chesnaye had realised the true meaning of the punishment. Each midshipman had taken the scabbard in turn and had given Pickles three strokes across the buttocks, a total of fifteen blows.

When it was Chesnaye's turn Pringle had said evenly: 'Lay it on hard, Chesnaye. If you don't we keep going round and round again until I am satisfied!'

Chesnaye still felt the nausea of those blows, as if he himself had been beaten.

Later he had tried to speak to Pickles, but even now he was out once more in his picket boat, no doubt ferrying some of the last-minute requirements before sailing.

The monitor had her orders. The Mediterranean. It should have been the moment for which he had waited so long. Away from the land, away from home and all that it had entailed.

He tried to exclude himself from what had happened, but he could not. He tried to tell himself that Pickles was inefficient, but inwardly he knew he was no different from any other midshipman suddenly pushed into the hard system of the Navy.

Beyond the steel hull the water rippled and surged against the tough plating while overhead the sentries paced the quarterdeck and peered into the darkness of the harbour.

Tomorrow was another start. It might all be different when the ship was at sea.

He thought of Pickles' face, and wondered.

Chapter Two

No Survivors

Richard Chesnaye paused at the foot of the steel bridge ladder and stood momentarily looking up at the overcast sky. Six bells of the Morning Watch had just been struck, and already he could feel the tremor of excitement which seemed to run through the deck of the moored monitor itself. He began to climb, conscious of the darkness which still shrouded the harbour and the hard chill in the air. The wind had fallen away, and below him, just visible beyond the ship's side, he could see the flat oily current which surged into the harbour, now unbroken by whitecaps, but strong and threatening for all that.

The ship's bridge structure, pale grey against the dark clouds, seemed to overhang him like a cliff. As he climbed higher he saw the compartments and platforms alive with anonymous figures, busy and absorbed in the preparations for getting under way. Soon I will know all these faces, he thought.

The strident notes of a marine's bugle had urged the men to their stations. 'Special Sea Dutymen close up!' And now, like himself, the ship's company had fanned throughout the gently pulsating hull like small parts of a giant and intricate machine.

He reached the wide navigating bridge and slithered across the coaming into a small world of calm and orderly preparation.

From the moment the hands had been called from their hammocks Chesnaye had been on the move. In the black confusion of dawn he had followed Sub-Lieutenant Pringle's massive shape as he had strode the upper deck, pointing out all the various places of immediate importance to a new midshipman. There was so much to remember.

For entering and leaving harbour Chesnaye's place was on the navigating bridge. He had to study and assist the Officer of the Watch and generally make himself useful. At Action Stations he was also on the bridge, but would attach himself to the Signals Department and the specialists who assisted the Gunnery Officer. For, unlike normal warships, additional signalmen were required to converse with forces ashore when a bombardment was being carried out.

In harbour, apart from his divisional duties, Chesnaye was to have charge of one of the oared whalers.

Pringle had pointed to the sleek boat high in its davits and said off handedly: 'You should be able to manage that. But if Pickles does not improve you'll be getting his picket boat!'

A figure loomed out of the gloom. It was Midshipman Beaushears, who also had a station on the navigating bridge.

'You found your way, then, Dick?' His languid voice was hoarse, and Chesnaye could see his breath like steam in the damp air.

'What happens now?' Chesnaye found that he was whispering.

'Just keep quiet and get out of everyone's way!'

Chesnaye grinned and stood back from the quiet bustle of figures around him. As his eyes became more accustomed to the gloom he was able to watch every piece of the open bridge, which he knew he would soon recognise in complete darkness.

It was almost square in shape, with a raised compass platform dead in the centre. The front and sides were lined with voice-pipes which seemed to keep up an incessant chatter, and on either wing of the bridge was mounted a massive searchlight. Behind him the bridge opened into a dimly lighted charthouse where he could see Lieutenant Travis, the Navigator, leaning across a glass-topped table, a pair of brass dividers in his hands, his small beard almost skimming the chart itself.

Overhead, black and solid like an additional bridge, the great steel mass of the Upper Control Top was supported by all three legs of the tripod mast. From there Chesnaye knew that when *Saracen's* turn came to fight the gunnery staff would plot and record every shot, every hit and miss, despite what carnage might be spread below them.

Commander Godden's bulky shape moved to the forepart of the bridge. He stood on one of the newly scrubbed gratings and rested his hands on the bridge screen. His head and chest rose easily above the thin strip of canvas dodger which still glinted with a thin layer of frost, and he looked ponderously solid, like the ship beneath his straddled legs.

Without warning a sliver of grey light lanced across the harbour, a pathetic attempt to force the night to relinquish its hold.

The ship's shape seemed to harden and faces took on personality and meaning.

Chesnaye ventured a glance over the screen. Below him, like its counterpart on the other side of the bridge, the signal platform was stark against the fast-moving water. He could see the watchful signalman and the neat racks of gaily coloured bunting. A tall Yeoman of Signals was peering through his telescope towards the dockyard.

It was surprising how much bigger the ship seemed from up here. The paleness of the freshly scrubbed decks seemed to sweep away far into the distance, so that he felt strangely secure. He watched the white blobs of the seamen's bare feet and wondered how they managed to ignore the bitter cold, and saw too the last boat being swung inboard by the big power hoist. The buoy-jumpers had been picked from the lurching buoy under the monitor's bows, the cable unshackled, and now only a thin wire remained reeved through the weed-encrusted ring. The last link with the land.

Far ahead beyond the tapering muzzles of the two great guns he could faintly make out the bustling activity of the cable party, and the stringy shape of Lieutenant Hogarth, who was silhouetted against the guard-rail, his pale face turned upwards towards the bridge.

A bell jangled with sudden urgency, and a seaman reported, 'Engine room standing by, sir!'

Godden nodded absently. 'Very good.'

Flat, disinterested voices, yet Chesnaye could feel the excitement running through him like wine.

Godden peered at his watch. 'Tell the Bosun to pipe all hands for leaving harbour.' A small pause. 'Mister Beaushears. My respects to the Captain. Tell him it is ten minutes off the time to slip.'

Chesnaye watched his companion slip away and be swallowed up in the grey steel.

Another voice said, 'All dutymen closed up for leaving harbour, sir.'

Godden shrugged and said testily, 'I should bloody well hope so!'

Chesnaye could feel the freshening quiver of the gratings under his feet, and turned to watch a thickening plume of smoke thrust itself over the rim of the funnel. A brief gust of wind plucked the smoke downwards so that he coughed and dabbed at his streaming eyes. Oil or coal, funnel smoke still tasted foul, he thought.

There was a brief rustle of excitement and then silence. Without looking Chesnaye knew that the Captain had arrived. Cautiously he watched the small figure move to the front of the bridge and place himself squarely in the centre.

'Ship ready to proceed, sir.' Godden's voice sounded different. 'Very well. Sound off.'

Chesnaye heard no order passed, but below him a bugle shrilled across the dark harbour, and he could hear the slap of bare feet as the men fell into ranks for leaving harbour.

'Signal from tower, sir!' The Yeoman's harsh voice lifted easily across the screen. 'Proceed!'

Godden coughed quietly. 'I have already signalled the two tugs, sir. They are standing by.'

Royston-Jones craned his head, first to peer at the two bulky shapes which idled in the froth of their own paddles, and then to stare at his commander.

'Tugs?' His voice was quiet, but sharp enough to reach even Chesnaye. 'Since when have I required *tugs*?'

Godden said at length: 'Strong tide this morning, sir. And very poor light.' He seemed to dry up.

'I am aware of that, thank you. The Coxswain is on the wheel. He knows what to do without a whole bombardment of orders and alterations of course!'

Chesnaye bit his lip. Another bad start.

The Captain adjusted the glasses about his neck. 'Stand by!' He lifted the glasses to peer astern at the dockyard, which seemed to swing around a motionless ship. Irritably he added: 'One of the quarterdeck party is out of the rig of the day, Commander! Take his name, and deal with it!'

Chesnaye was almost fretting with suppressed excitement. How could this man bother his head with such trivial matters at a time like this? A petty officer scurried away in search of the culprit caught accidentally in the Captain's vision.

'Slow ahead together!' The bells jangled, and the bridge began to vibrate. 'Slip!'

There was a hoarse bark of orders from the fo'c'sle, and Chesnaye heard the rasp of wire as the last mooring flew through

308

the buoy-ring and was hauled aboard by the madly running seamen.

Faintly but audibly Hogarth's voice came from the bows, 'All gone forrard, sir!'

Caught in the current, the wide-hulled monitor slewed untidily in the fast water, her stern already pointing towards Gosport, her bows swinging fast across the harbour entrance.

A messenger standing near Chesnaye sucked his teeth. 'Jesus Christ!'

Royston-Jones lowered his head to one of the voice-pipes. 'Watch her head, Coxswain!'

Chesnaye knew that the coxswain of a ship was always entrusted with handling the wheel at the most important and difficult moments. Without orders he was usually left to steer his ship straight for the harbour entrance, and thus avoid the delay of repeating and passing orders.

Godden shifted uneasily. 'Still paying off, sir.'

The Captain grunted. 'Half ahead port!'

The additional power sent a wake of white froth streaming from beneath the monitor's counter, and after a few moments the blunt bows swung back towards the narrow harbour mouth.

'Slow ahead together!' Royston-Jones' right foot was tapping very quietly on the grating. 'Make a signal to our escorts to take up station in thirty minutes.'

Somewhere astern two destroyers would already be slinking after their unwieldy charge, no doubt followed with some ribald comment from their consorts.

Godden watched the pale walls of Fort Blockhouse sliding past. They looked near enough to touch, and he glanced quickly at the Captain's impassive face. It was as if he were steering close inshore deliberately. Any other warship of comparable tonnage would have scraped one of those vicious little black rocks by now. Godden watched the fast-rising tide as it surged through the glinting line of teeth below the fort.

'Fo'c'sle secured for sea, sir.'

'Very well. Fall out the hands, and stand by to exercise Action Stations. I want every man checked at his station.'

'That has been done, sir.' It was the Commander's responsibility, and Godden's voice was defiant.

'Well, do it *again*!' The Captain hoisted himself into the tall wooden chair which was bolted in the forepart of the bridge. 'And, Commander, don't forget to signal to your tugs.' There was the briefest pause. 'Otherwise they might follow me to Gibraltar!'

The third day out from Portsmouth found the *Saracen* almost across the Bay of Biscay, with the westerly tip of Spain some hundred miles on the port bow. Crossing the Bay had been uncomfortable if not actually rough. With a following sea and a stiff wind, which veered from one northern point to another, the ungainly monitor made heavy going across the endless shoulders of white rollers, when even her ninety-foot beam seemed incapable of preventing a motion so violent that at times it felt as if the ship would never right herself. The following rollers would build up beneath the rounded stern so that the quarterdeck lifted until it appeared to be level with the corkscrewing bridge, then with a violent yawing heave the whole hull would lift its flat bottom stern first over the crest and sink heavily into the next glass-sided trough. Seamen dragged themselves round the upper deck checking and re-lashing the jerking equipment and boats, while the men off watch lay wretchedly in their hammocks, eyes closed so as not to see the oilskins and loose clothing as they swung away from bulkheads, hovered for endless seconds and then canted back through another impossible angle.

Richard Chesnaye braced his shoulders against a davit and allowed the cold spray to dash across his tingling cheeks. Astern the monitor's wake hardly made a ripple, a condemnation of the painful ten knots which had been their speed since leaving England. Zig-zagging astern he could see the solitary destroyer escort rising and falling across the broken water, its fragile hull often completely hidden by clouds of bursting spray. For them it must have been much worse, he thought. To retain station on their charge the two destroyers had been made to crawl at a painstaking speed, their narrow decks and low hulls open for anything the sea could throw in their direction. One minute Chesnaye could see down the three narrow funnels, the next instant he could watch the water streaming free from the actual bilge keel as the little ship rolled like a mad thing. The second destroyer had retired with engine trouble one day out of harbour, but this one seemed doggedly determined to keep with them at all costs.

Chesnaye shaded his eyes and looked upwards at the bridge which seemed black against the harsh grey light. He could see the pale blobs of faces where the lookouts peered through their glasses, and the machine-gunners who stood by their weapons in case a periscope should suddenly appear from the creaming wavecrests.

Chesnaye bit his lip. It sounded simple enough. If a U-boat showed its periscope even for a second a well-aimed burst of fire could blind it, and force the hidden boat to the surface where it could be finished by gunfire. He looked towards the horizon and shuddered. It was small consolation to know that even U-boats were said to find this sort of weather difficult.

Nearby he could hear his party of seamen talking quietly as they climbed in and out of the slung whaler, checking gear and killing time until the next 'stand-easy.' In three days he had hardly got to know them at all. Just faces that were free and open with each other, yet when he spoke to them they froze into attentive masks. When he had been watching the hands at work on the upper deck he had wanted to intervene, if only to show them he was alive. But there was always a seasoned petty officer in the way, with a gruff, 'Leave this to me, sir,' or 'We don't do it like that in *this* ship, sir!'

A big roller creamed broken and frustrated along the weather side, the spray sluicing across the bright planking itself. Droplets of spume clung to his trousers, and he was suddenly glad that he was not prone to seasickness like some of the others.

Sub-Lieutenant Pringle had been much in evidence during the slow journey from the English Channel. Bitter, sarcastic and ever watchful for a mistake, he had approached Chesnaye the first day out, his face solemn, even sad.

'That sea-chest of yours.' He had rolled back on his heels like a boxer. 'Not regulation, y'know?'

He had then launched into a long dissertation about the importance of uniformity and discipline, and the necessity of making an example. Chesnaye had been surprised, almost shocked, to find that this first clash left him feeling neither angry nor resentful. Pringle's attitude must be an act. Even his long speeches gave the impression of planning and careful rehearsing, so that Chesnaye felt vaguely embarrassed.

He had mentioned this fact to Beaushears when they had shared

311

a Middle Watch together, but the seasoned midshipman had seemed disinterested.

'It's the system, Dick. As necessary as it is futile!' Then indifferently he had added, 'You just put up with it until it's your turn to be a Pringle!'

Chesnaye half smiled to himself. Heaven forbid!

A bugle shrilled, and as one of the seamen nearby stopped work and scampered towards the fo'c'sle for a quick smoke and a basin of tea, Chesnaye walked to the guard-rail and peered at the tilting horizon. Was it possible that they would ever reach the land mass of Europe again? It seemed impossible that hundreds of miles beyond that blue-grey line two giant armies were even now facing each other across the wire and sandbags of Flanders. Before the seamen returned to their half-hearted work hundreds of soldiers might be killed and wounded. Thousands more would perish the moment a new attack was planned.

It was a good thing to be going to the Mediterranean. It was new, clean and fresh. At home even in England the excitement of war was stifled by the daily misery of casualty lists and scarecrow figures on crutches and sticks who thronged the railway stations or waited for ambulances. The men from the battlefront had all seemed cheerful enough. The worse the wounds, the higher the spirits.

Chesnaye had mentioned this point to a nervous-looking subaltern he had met at Waterloo station. The youngster had stared at Chesnaye and then smiled coldly. 'They know they can't be sent back!' With sudden fervour he had finished. '*They're* safe now!'

Out here it was different. The ship was uncomfortable at the moment, but soon that would change. His duties were arduous and complicated and it seemed impossible to please anyone, senior or junior, yet it felt good to belong, to be a part of this ponderous Goliath.

He wondered if his mother had already written to him, and how life was proceeding in the quiet Surrey home. He tried not to think of his father. The memory of their last meeting affected him like nausea.

Being away at training, he had seen little of Commander James Chesnaye. That last night at home, with the wind rattling the small latticed windows, he had forced himself to sit quite still, to

312

watch and listen as his father rambled on about the Navy as it had been, as it should be. He lost count of the times the bottle had filled and refilled the glass at his father's elbow, but the record was stark in the man's slurred and aggrieved voice.

His father. To his wife, his son, anyone who would listen, he told the self-same story. It had been a mistake, but not his own. When his ship, the sloop *Kelpie*, had ripped open her hull on a shoal off the Chinese mainland he, Commander James Chesnaye, the vessel's captain, had been in his sea-cabin. The first lieutenant had been to blame. As the months and then years followed the court martial the blame spread. The helmsman had been unreliable, the navigating officer had borne a secret grudge, the charts had been incorrectly marked. And so it had gone on. Each time Richard Chesnaye had returned home from his cadets' training ship he had found his mother older and more subdued, and his father more definite as to the root of the disaster which had cost the Navy a ship and him a career.

This last short leave, which should have brought such promise to the home, was no better. Chesnaye, in his new midshipman's uniform and his orders in his pocket, had been confronted with the final spectacle of misery and defeat. At the very commencement of war his father had gone to the Admiralty to accept even a small command without complaint. But the Admiralty had made no offer at all. There were no familiar faces to greet him, and the records when consulted were enough to finish his small spark of embittered confidence.

As he watched the slow, mesmering pitch of water alongside, Chesnaye wondered about the truth of his own thoughts. He had wanted to believe his father, but all the time there had been the slow nagging pain of doubt in his mind. Was that why his father was so outspoken? Was it because the Admiralty had released him as painlessly as they knew how, when in fact the ill-fated *Kelpie*'s captain had been too drunk to cope with a situation for which he had been trained for twenty years?

Chesnaye thought of the tin chest which still stood in the gun-room. He had no intention of getting rid of it for Pringle or anyone else. As a boy he had watched that box arrive home from India, China, Malta and any one of the dozen stations where his father had served in the Navy. The scratched lid still bore the faint traces of the original owner's name and rank. The box had become a symbol of something he still wanted to believe.

His father had fallen silent towards the end of that last evening. His eyes had been red-rimmed as he had peered across the fire at his grave-faced son. Finally he had said, 'Never *trust* anyone, Dick!' For a moment he had been without anger, and as Chesnaye remembered that instant he could feel the emotion pricking at his eyes. 'Never trust anyone. Or you'll end up like me!'

He felt a step on the deck beside him and looked up to see Pickles watching him without expression.

Chesnaye shook the cloak of gloom from his shoulders and forced a smile. It had been pitiful to see Pickles being hounded and bullied by Sub-Lieutenant Pringle. It was equally dangerous to show such feelings. Any sign of disapproval or resentment seemed to drive Pringle to greater lengths, but always against the luckless Pickles.

'Hello, Keith, you look fed up?' Chesnaye saw Pickles' mouth turn down at the corners.

'Hell, yes. I tell you, Dick, I'm about sick of this ship, and the Navy too!'

Chesnaye looked back at the sea. Quietly he said: 'Your turn will come, Keith. Try and stick it a bit longer. Very soon the ship'll be too busy to allow Pringle much scope for his stupidity!'

Unconsciously he had spoken the last words with quiet venom, so that Pickles stared at him with surprise. 'I didn't know *you* felt like that!' His voice shook. 'He's made my life hell. I know I'm clumsy and not very good at my work, but I'm not the only one.' He glanced furtively along the spray-dappled deck. 'If you only knew the half of it.'

Chesnaye said carefully, 'If it were me I think I'd tell him to go to blazes!'

Pickles forced a grin. 'I believe you would too!' Impetuously he caught Chesnaye's sleeve. 'I'm damned glad you're aboard, Dick! You're different from the others. I'm a scholarship boy and I've not been used to their sort before. Some of them are so vain,' he floundered for the right words, 'so false. They seem to be playing some sort of game, whereas all this is terribly important to me.' He watched Chesnaye's face guardedly. 'My father has a shop in Bristol. It was hard to get me a cadetship.'

Chesnaye looked away. Hard? It must have been almost impossible.

314

Pickles continued, 'I'm the first in our family, but I expect you come from a long naval line?' When Chesnaye did not answer he added, 'And your father, is he still in the Service?'

'He's dead.'

The look of shock on Pickles' face matched the guilt which ran through Chesnaye's heart as the lie dropped so easily from him. He felt angry and ashamed with himself. Why did I say that? Was it more honourable to have a dead father than a disgraced one?

They stood in silence for a while and watched the breakers with unseeing eyes.

Pickles said at length: 'March will be over by the time we reach our destination, and the Dardanelles affair will be over. So I suppose we shall just turn round and waddle back to Portsmouth!'

Chesnaye said quickly, 'What was the bombardment like along the Belgian coast?' Something had to be done to snap them both out of the feeling of depression which seemed to hang over them like a cloud.

'Noisy.' Pickles smiled at the simplicity of his answer. 'The big fifteen-inchers pounded away about three dozen shells, and all we saw was a cloud of brown smoke beyond the woods.' He shuddered. 'When we ceased firing we heard the soldiers having a go. It went on and on. Rifles, millions of them, rattling away as if they'd never stop!' He peered up at Chesnaye's thoughtful face. 'I don't think I could stand that sort of war. It's so personal, so filthy!'

A sharp clack, clack, clack made them look up at the bridge, and Chesnaye was surprised to see the nearest searchlight flashing urgently, its bright blue beam dazzling even in the harsh daylight.

'They're signalling the destroyer!' Pickles sounded mystified as he peered astern at the pitching escort. 'That's funny, we usually use semaphore for that sort of thing.'

But Chesnaye remained stockstill, his lips moving soundlessly as he spelt out the signal. As he read the stacatto flashes he could feel his body chilling as if running with ice-water.

'There is a mine drifting dead ahead of you!' He spoke the completed signal aloud and then swung to peer at the destroyer's distorted shape. Of course, from the *Saracen's* high and reasonably steady bridge it would be possible to see a drifting mine. He stared until his eyes were running uncontrollably and he could only half see the other ship.

A brief light flashed from the distant bridge, but whether it was an acknowledgement or the beginning of a question Chesnaye never knew. There was a bright orange flash from somewhere beneath the little ship's pitching fo'c'sle and then a dull, flat explosion which rolled across the water like thunder. There was very little smoke, but in that instant the destroyer ploughed to a halt, paid off into a beam sea and began to capsize.

Chesnaye blinked and heard Pickles give a small sob. How long was it? Ten seconds? Already the frail stern was rising clear of the waves, the tiny bright screws spinning in the air like those on a toy boat.

The monitor seemed to shudder as the shock-wave punched her massive hull below the waterline, and then began to swing heavily towards the small, spray-dashed shape which rapidly grew smaller even as they watched. A bugle blared, and all at once the deserted decks were alive with running feet.

Bosun's mates urged the seamen along, their pipes twittering as they ran. 'Away first and second whalers!' The cry was taken up the full length of the ship before Chesnaye realised that he too was expected to act. His was the second whaler, and as he stumbled towards the quarter davits he could see the boat swinging clear over the water, while his five oarsmen and coxswain scrambled across the griping spar and fell into the narrow wooden hull. More cries and sharp orders, and he could see the whaler on the other side of the quarterdeck already starting to shoot down the ship's side, the rope falls screaming through the blocks like live things.

Rough hands pushed him up and over the spar, and as he fell at the coxswain's feet he heard the cry, 'Lower away!' and then the monitor's rail was above him, the waves suddenly near and frighteningly large. The boat hovered above the water while the *Saracen* still pushed herself ahead, then with the order 'Slip!' it was slipped from the falls and dropped with a sickening lurch on to the crest of a curling breaker, and immediately veered away from the parent ship on the end of its long boatrope.

Chesnaye fought to regain his breath as the hull leapt and soared beneath his feet, the first shock and panic replaced by a feeling of numbed desperation. He heard himself shout: 'Let go

316

forrard! Out oars!' and then there seemed another agonising pause while the men thrust their blades through the crutches and sat apparently glued in their places, their eyes fixed on his face. 'Give way together!' The men leaned towards him, the blades dipped, splashed at the uneven water and then sent the boat plunging into the next bank of whitecaps.

The coxswain, a leading seaman named Tobias, shouted, 'Head straight for the destroyer, sir?'

Chesnaye bit his lip hard and tried to control his shaking limbs. He had sent the whaler on a straight course to nowhere, and he glanced quickly at Tobias to see if the man was showing contempt for his stupidity. But the beetle-browed seaman's face was passive and grave.

'Yes. Thank you.'

The coxswain swung the tiller bar while Chesnaye regained his feet and tried to peer ahead across the tall, pointed white hoods. The wavecrests hid the horizon, and as the whaler dipped into each successive trough Chesnaye was conscious of the silence as the towering waves blotted out the other world, so that he was aware once more of panic, like a drowning man.

Once when he looked astern he saw only the monitor's tripod mast and upper bridge, as if the *Saracen* too was on her way to the bottom. It seemed impossible that this frail, madly pitching boat would ever regain the safety and security of its davits, or he the ordered world of the gunroom.

Tobias shouted, 'Put yer backs into it, you bastards!' He began to count, his hoarse voice carrying above the hiss and roar of the water. 'In-out! In-out!' But to Chesnaye's confused eyes it appeared as if the boat was motionless, no matter how much the men sweated and pulled on their oars. He could see the long tapering blades bending as they cut at the water, and felt the shiver and thrust of the boat's bows as each wall of spray bounded over the seamen's bent backs.

Tobias barked, 'Bows!' The man nearest the stem smartly heaved his oar inside the boat and swung himself right into the bows, his shoulders hunched as if to take on the sea itself.

Tobias said quietly, 'We're there, sir.'

The oars moved more slowly as Tobias's spatulate fingers beat their time on the tiller bar.

Chesnaye did not know how the man knew they had arrived at

the place where the destroyer had been mortally struck, but he felt no doubt. Instead he was conscious of a sense of horror and of loss.

Cutting through the glassy side of a wave like a torpedo, a broken spar, its severed wood gleaming white in the grey water, loomed dangerously towards the wallowing boat. The bowman cursed, but with a deft thrust of his boathook pushed it clear. It drifted past, a tattered ensign, waterlogged like a shroud, trailing behind it.

The men rowed carefully, their eyes unmoving as they waited for some sign or sound, but still nothing happened.

Tobias spat suddenly over the gunwhale. 'Must 'ave gone straight down. Them destroyers is pretty poor stuff. Tin an' paint. Not much more!'

Chesnaye swallowed hard. Like the bowman he had seen a single spread-eagled figure, its face and hands incredibly white, outlined momentarily against the tumbling water.

Tobias said: 'Leave 'im sir. Let 'im be!'

The sodden corpse was already sinking, dragged down by heavy sea-boots which such a short time ago had kept their owner warm. Chesnaye staggered and would have fallen but for Tobias's grip on his arm. It had to happen sooner or later in war, but this had been quite different. A silent, faceless nobody, drifting and already forgotten.

Tobias's face was very close. 'Take it easy, sir. There'll be worse before this lot's over!'

In spite of the nausea which threatened to make him vomit Chesnaye peered at the burly coxswain. But again there was neither contempt nor anger on his face, and Chesnaye realised that in that brief instant he was seeing Tobias for the first time. Not as a competent, bitter-tongued subordinate, but as a man.

The bowman said wearily: '*Saracen*'s signalling, sir! "Recall".'

Chesnaye glanced at Tobias, who merely shrugged. 'They kin see better'n us, sir. There'll be nothing left now!'

In silence the men pulled at the oars, but this time their eyes were facing the stern, where across Tobias's shoulders they could see, or imagined they could see, the frothing whirlpool which marked the destroyer's grave.

Commander Godden strode to the front of the bridge, his features strained. 'Both whalers hoisted and secured, sir.'

The Captain sat straight-backed in his chair, his eyes fixed on

318

some point along the horizon. 'Very well. Resume course and speed, and instruct all lookouts of their double importance.'

'Shall I make out a signal, sir?' Godden saw the Captain's neat hands stiffen. He added carefully, 'Another escort can be sent from Gibraltar.'

Royston-Jones turned his head, his eyes momentarily distant. 'I knew that destroyer captain well. A very promising fellow. Great pity.' Then in a sharper tone: 'No, we'll make no signals as yet. By breaking wireless silence we will invite more unwelcome attention than by continuing alone.'

'It's a risk, sir.' Godden tried to shut his mind to the sinking destroyer.

Royston-Jones shrugged irritably. 'So is polo! In any case, the responsibility rests with me, doesn't it?'

'Yes, sir.' Godden bit his lip and started to move away.

'The whalers took far too long to get away, Commander.' The voice halted him in his tracks. 'The second whaler took six minutes to clear the falls. Should be three minutes at the most. See to it!'

Hogarth, the Officer of the Watch, called, 'Resumed course and speed, sir!'

'Very well.' Royston-Jones seemed to have dismissed them.

Godden said heavily, 'Pass the word for the midshipman of the second whaler!'

Lieutenant Travis walked from the charthouse and crossed to his side. 'Pretty sudden, wasn't it?'

'Bloody mines!' Godden felt the anger boiling up inside him.

'Probably very old.' Travis sounded thoughtful. 'Maybe dropped months ago by the raider *Kap Trafalgar* on her way south.'

'Poor devils.' Godden thrust his hands deep into his pockets. 'I knew every officer in that destroyer.' He glared quickly at Royston-Jones' back. '*Not* just her captain either!'

Travis shrugged. 'That's the trouble with this regiment. Just one great family!' He glanced to the sky and moved towards the bridge ladder as Chesnaye's head appeared over the screen. 'Never mind. Here's the most junior officer aboard. He should be good enough to carry *our* burdens!'

Godden opened his mouth, and then stifled the angry retort. Travis was a queer bird. You never knew whether he was making

319

fun of his superiors. But his casual comment had struck home, and Godden was almost grateful. The Captain was always goading him, always finding fault. Travis had been right. Chesnaye had been about to take the weight of Godden's resentment.

He stared at Chesnaye's wind-reddened face. 'You were too slow,' he said at length. 'You'll have to halve the time it takes to get that boat away.'

'I see, sir.' Chesnaye looked spent.

'The power launches are useless in this weather. In any case it takes too long for the main derrick to swing 'em into the water. Whalers are best.' Godden sighed. 'But nothing would have saved those fellows, I'm afraid.'

Royston-Jones said sharply, 'Come over here!'

Chesnaye crossed to the tall chair and saluted. 'Sir?'

For a moment the Captain stared at the Midshipman, his eyes bleak and expressionless. 'Chesnaye?' The small head nodded slowly. 'Knew your father in China.' The cold eyes darted sharply at Chesnaye's. 'Commanded the *Kelpie*, eh?'

'Yes, sir.' Chesnaye could feel the bridge spinning beneath his feet.

Royston-Jones resumed staring at the horizon. 'The China Station. Now there was a place.' Some of the sharpness had gone from his tone, so that Chesnaye darted a closer look at him. 'Fleet regattas, or chasing Chinese pirates, it made no difference. No room for mistakes there, boy. A crack squadron!' The Captain's head nodded vigorously. 'A pity we're not going out there now!'

He turned in his chair, his eyes sharp and alive again. 'Well, don't stand there! Go and chase that fool Tobias and his men! Tell them you'll have their hides if they don't improve their timing!' One hand slapped sharply against the chair. '*Timing* is the thing!'

Chesnaye saluted and stepped back, conscious of the eyes all round him. 'Very good, sir!'

Royston-Jones yawned. '*Naturally*, Chesnaye!'

As Chesnaye stepped on to the top of the ladder Commander Godden patted his arm. 'Well done, lad. I think he likes you.'

His smile faded as a voice rapped: 'Too much talking on my bridge! We'll have an extra action drill before lunch to wake everyone up a bit!'

When Chesnaye reached the maindeck Sub-Lieutenant Pringle was waiting for him.

320

'Well, where the hell have *you* been?' Pringle had his big hands on his hips, and his chin was jutting with belligerence.

'To the bridge.' Chesnaye tried not to watch Pringle's eyes. Behind them it was almost possible to see the man's mind working.

'Bridge? Bloody crawling, I suppose! By God, you mids make me spew! Did a little bit of boatwork upset you?' Pringle's voice became a sneering lisp. 'Perhaps you thought you might see a bit of blood!'

Chesnaye felt the weariness soaking into his limbs. It was a game. But how sickening it was becoming! He thought of the faded corpse and gritted his teeth.

'Wait until you've seen a bit of service!' Pringle's face was getting flushed. 'You'll have something to weep about then!'

Chesnaye released his breath slowly. 'How much service have *you* seen?'

'*What* did you say?' Pringle stared at him with disbelief. 'By God, you've really asked for it now!'

Chesnaye licked his dry lips. He had committed himself. Over and over again he had warned himself about this, but it had come at the wrong time.

'Sub-Lieutenant Pringle,' he kept his voice level, 'I am not going to fight you, but if you threaten me again I am going straight to the Commander!'

Pringle's mouth opened and stayed open.

'You are my superior and I have to obey you. But as we are alone I can cheerfully tell you that in *my* opinion you are a cheat, a liar and a bully!' He stepped back, half expecting Pringle to smash him down with one of his doubled fists.

Pringle seemed unable to breathe. He spoke between short gasps, his cheeks mottled and shining. 'You'll see, Chesnaye! By God, you'll be sorry for this!'

Some seamen tramped along the nearby deck, and Pringle seemed to recover himself. 'Now get about your duties, and quick about it!'

Chesnaye touched his cap and smiled coldly. 'Yes, sir.'

Later, as he watched Tobias and his men scrubbing off the whaler's keel, he thought of the clash with Pringle and cursed himself. It would be as well to warn Pickles, just in case.

Automatically he looked astern, as if expecting to see the

321

small, faithful destroyer. The empty sea seemed to be dancing, as if to mock him.

Suddenly, in spite of Pringle and the Captain's casual remarks about his father, the *Saracen* seemed very solid and safe.

He walked towards the slung whaler and said quickly, 'D' you need any help, Tobias?'

The unnatural brightness in his tone made the leading seaman glance at him with surprise. Then Tobias gave a slow smile. Sometimes when new midshipmen found their feet they could go either way. All being well, this one might be just tolerable.

'Always do with an extra 'and, sir!'

By nightfall the *Saracen* was steaming down the Portuguese coast, and somewhere at the bottom of the Atlantic the destroyer's hull had settled for the last time and was at peace.

Chapter Three

A Girl called Helen

The sky above Gibraltar was a pale transparent blue, whilst the craggy crown of the Rock itself remained shrouded in a fine afternoon haze. A steady Atlantic breeze prevented much warmth from reaching the sheltered anchorage, but the sun was nevertheless welcome, and cast a sheen of grandeur across the straight lines of moored warships. Sheltered and dwarfed by the towering rock fortress, the town itself glittered and sparkled in countless colours which again acted as a backcloth for the grey symbols of power and reliability.

Slightly apart from the other vessels, the flagship lay in solitary splendour, the flag of Vice-Admiral fluttering cheerfully in the breeze. Across the harbour entrance the last traces of brown smoke hovered around the one moving warship, and to onlookers the last detonation of a nineteen-gun salute still seemed to echo against the weatherworn walls of the Rock.

The Vice-Admiral stepped from the small sternwalk of the battleship and entered a well-furnished stateroom. His flag-captain remained momentarily in the sunlight, his raised glasses following the slow-moving ship.

'Ugly-looking ship, sir?' The Captain reluctantly followed his superior.

The Vice-Admiral tore his eyes from the pile of signals and reference books which littered his table and looked at the other officer. 'The *Saracen* could be very useful, however.' His eyes flitted to a well-polished scuttle as the monitor's blunt bow slowly moved into view once more. On her distant fo'c'sle he could see the hands fallen in and the small cluster of figures around the bows. In spite of her unwieldy appearance there was something defiant about the *Saracen*, he thought.

'What is her captain like, sir?'

The Vice-Admiral shrugged, watching the monitor's broad hull as it glided very slowly across the glittering water. 'Royston-Jones?

An able man, to all accounts.' A small frown crossed his face. 'But *stubborn*. Damned stubborn!'

'All captains are made that way, surely, sir? The climb up the ladder is too long for a man who loses sight of his objective!'

'Maybe so. That gun salute, for instance. Did you notice?'

'Well, yes. But perhaps he overlooked the new orders about that. No salutes for the duration, that's what their lordships implied, but I daresay Royston-Jones had other things on his mind. The loss of the escort, for instance?'

The Vice-Admiral smiled wryly. 'He knew, all right. That is what worries me about him. He's one of the old school. He's always fired a salute to the Governor of the Rock in the past, and he does not see why he should alter now!'

The Captain craned his head. 'She's dropped anchor, sir.'

There was a faint splash of white beneath the monitor's fo'c'sle, and simultaneously the Jack broke out from the short staff in the bows and a new ensign appeared as if by magic from the quarter-deck.

It was as if the ship itself was alive and the tiny ant-like figures which scurried across the pale decks were superfluous. The big power derrick came to life, and almost before the vessel's bow wave had died away a launch was lowered alongside and another was being swung out ready to follow it.

The Vice-Admiral grimaced. 'He's a good captain. I'm not denying that. I imagine that by now the whole ship is working like a new clock!'

'You mean that may not be enough, sir?'

'You've seen the reports?' He gestured towards the table. 'The Dardanelles project is swelling out of all proportion. To think that a week or so ago our sailors were actually *ashore* on Turkish soil, blowing up gunsites as calm as you please!' He began to pace. 'Nothing but delays and more delays! And now they want a full-scale combined operation. Troops, landings and all the rest of it, while Johnny Turk digs himself in and prepares! By heaven, it'll be a bloody affair before we're done!'

'And now the poor *Inflexible*'s been put out of action too, sir.'

The Vice-Admiral walked to the scuttle and watched the neat launch curving towards the flagship. 'Yes. A good new battle-cruiser thrown away in a bombardment, such a damned waste! After she did such fine work in the Falklands battle too. It'll take months to do the repairs!' With sudden anger he added, 'These damned stay-at-home strategists make me sick!'

An immaculate midshipman appeared in the doorway. 'The Commander's respects, sir. The captain of *Saracen* is coming aboard.' He spoke to his captain, his over-steady eyes adding to his appearance of nervousness provoked by the other officer whose flag flew high overhead.

The Vice-Admiral waited until the young man had departed. 'Do not mention the saluting business to Royston-Jones just yet.'

'Very well, sir.' The Captain looked puzzled.

The flag-officer made up his mind. 'No. I must have his full attention. You see, it's all part of what I was saying just now. The Royal Navy is our way of life. In addition it has always been in the background of the whole Empire. Since Trafalgar we have hardly been challenged. We are accepted as the greatest sea power, the most powerful force in the world.'

The Captain tucked his cap beneath his arm and waited. 'Well, yes, sir.'

'Exactly! Now we are at war. Real war, and some of us have been on top for so long we've forgotten what it is all about! We've been *too* rich, too damned confident!' He glared at the table. 'And now we've got to face it, to pay the price. A stupid, straightforward operation which has gone to blazes and all because our top people can't agree!'

The Captain was half listening for the sound of the launch along-side, but his superior's sudden show of angry confidence in him was not to be ignored.

'Winston Churchill himself said the Fleet could "take" the Dardanelles. A good sharp knock and we could force the Straits without too much fuss, eh? Some smart chartwork and quick thinking, a useful bombardment and some new spotting aircraft,' the Vice-Admiral waved his hands, 'and the whole thing would be finished!'

'Well, sir, there is still time.'

He ignored the Captain's guarded words. 'And what did we get? A handful of obsolete battleships from the Channel Fleet and a couple of old aircraft which could hardly get off the ground! That fool Kitchener got cold feet in France and said he could not spare any troops to follow up our attack, and the government actually *believed* him!'

'The casualties have been very severe on the Western Front, sir.'

'And so they will continue to be while we've got stupid old men in charge of them! That is why we must watch ourselves too!' He looked towards the *Saracen*, which now swung easily at her cable. 'New thinking is what we want. My God, in some ways I wish we had not been so strong in the Navy.' He turned towards his captain. 'A starving man always hunts for food better than one who has been pampered and overfed!'

Later, as the pipes twittered and the marines presented arms, the Flag-Captain found a few seconds to reflect on the Vice-Admiral's words. He watched Royston-Jones' neat head lift above the rail, the hand raised to his cap, beneath which the pale, cold eyes flitted briefly across the flagship's reception party in sharp appraisal.

The Flag-Captain dropped his hand and stepped forward to welcome his opposite number. He thought irritably that it was as if Royston-Jones had come to inspect the flagship rather than receive his orders.

Royston-Jones looked along the vast decks and towering superstructure. Framed beneath the quarterdeck guns the *Saracen* looked small and deformed.

The Flag-Captain's mouth softened. It could be no joke for a senior captain to be given command of a monitor. Following the other man's gaze he said, 'Looks aren't everything, you know.'

Royston-Jones nodded vigorously. 'Quite so! Couldn't agree more!' He faced the Flag-Captain, his eyes hidden beneath his peak. 'Still, she could blow *this* relic out of the water any day, I shouldn't wonder!'

Richard Chesnaye allowed himself to be pushed along in the continuous, aimless throng which seemed to fill each and every narrow street. Although the afternoon had almost gone, it still felt warm, almost oppressive after England and the Atlantic. He had come ashore alone, and told himself it was because he wanted it this way. In fact, he knew that it was because Gibraltar was new and unfamiliar, and, as in the past, he wanted to feel his way, to hide any weakness. Pickles was on duty in his picket boat and most of the other midshipmen had headed ashore in one group to some prearranged party.

Chesnaye stared at the strange shops overloaded with garish rugs and countless ornaments and souvenirs. Already beneath his arm he was carrying a bright shawl which a beady-eyed merchant had thrust into his hands within minutes of landing. He did not care. He wanted something to send to his mother, and she would like it even though she might never wear it.

Chesnaye did not know where he was walking, and every street seemed exactly like another. All were crammed with sailors, and occasionally he caught sight of a familiar face from the *Saracen*, some already flushed with drink and full of that strange anticipation which every sailor seemed to wear like a mask when ashore.

Wearily he turned into a small, low-ceilinged café and ordered coffee. Things seemed cheap here, but all the same he would have to be careful. The café was perched on a shoulder of rock, so that he could still see part of the harbour. He toyed with the coffee and watched the moored ships and the colourful bustle below the window. There were big ugly troopships too. Their decks alive with khaki figures, the upperworks untidy with newly washed shirts and underwear. All at once he became aware of two voices behind him. The room was half empty and very carefully he turned to look at the girl whose voice broke into his tired thoughts and reminded him how few women he had seen on the Rock.

She was about his own age, suntanned, and with hair so dark that for a moment he wondered if she were Spanish. She was speaking to a young army second lieutenant, and as Chesnaye watched them he knew that they were brother and sister. The soldier wore the badges of the Royal Engineers and from his creased uniform Chesnaye guessed that he was from one of the troopships and not a garrison officer.

Once the girl looked across at Chesnaye, apparently conscious of his gaze. Her eyes were dark and very wide, and she stared at Chesnaye for several seconds. Then she spoke quietly to the soldier, who turned to look also.

Chesnaye pushed his cup aside and groped quickly for his parcel. He felt confused and furious with himself, and half expected that the others in the room would all turn to watch him leave.

The subaltern called across, 'Why don't you join us?'

It was so unexpected that Chesnaye found himself thinking of several excuses for leaving rather than accepting the invitation. Stupidly he sat down at their table and said: 'I'm sorry. It's my first visit to Gibraltar. I'm almost a tourist!'

327

The soldier laughed. 'We'd never have guessed!'

The girl frowned as Chesnaye's face showed his mounting confusion. 'Don't take any notice of my brother.' She held out a small, well-shaped hand. 'I'm Helen Driscoll, and this is Bob.'

Chesnaye tried to relax the stiffness in his body. Her handshake was warm and strong like a boy's, the skin very smooth. He said quickly, 'Do you live here?'

She smiled. 'For another few days. Our father is the Army Victualling Agent here, and we are returning to England shortly.'

'Careful, Helen, careless talk, y'know!' Her brother grinned at Chesnaye. 'This chap could be a spy!'

'Nonsense! He's far too English!' She tossed her head so that the hair which hung down her neck glimmered in the filtered sunlight. The movement reacted like pain, and Chesnaye could feel his heart beginning to pump noisily. He cursed himself for his stupidity. Tonight he would be back aboard the *Saracen* and in minutes this girl would get up and leave.

Almost too casually he asked, 'Are you under orders?' He saw the cheerful light fade in the soldier's eyes and added hastily, 'I suppose everyone who comes here is *en route* to somewhere else!'

The girl had stopped smiling, and all at once Chesnaye knew well enough why they had called him over. The soldier was from one of those troopers, and Chesnaye had already heard Commander Godden discussing their departure with the Navigator with a view to changing the *Saracen*'s anchorage. They were sailing at midnight. Eastward. That meant only one thing. The Dardanelles.

Chesnaye said awkwardly: 'Look, if you'd rather I went I'll take myself off now. I'm sorry if I was staring.' They were both looking at him. 'I suppose I'm a bit like a monk, not used to a girl like . . .' he faltered. 'Anyway, I'm sorry!'

He saw her hand on his sleeve. 'Please don't go. It was Bob's idea to call you over just to stop my worrying about him. He thought you would keep me quiet.'

Her brother did not answer but stared past Chesnaye at the darkening harbour. 'Listen!' He cocked his head as the sounds of distant bugles floated across the water.

Chesnaye nodded. 'Sunset,' he said. Somewhere out there the *Saracen*'s ensign would be slowly dipping down the staff in perfect time with all the others. It was strange, he thought. Sunset never

328

failed to move him. The slow strains of the bugle. The sense of peace of a ship at anchor.

The soldier said suddenly: 'Yes, I'm under orders. It's no secret. I suspect we are both going to the same destination?' He smiled wryly. 'Although I also suspect that you will be travelling in rather more comfort!'

The girl stood up. 'Let's get away from here.' She gestured vaguely. 'Will you come back to the house, Richard?'

The use of his name made Chesnaye start. He knew she would only be asking him to speed the agonising hours remaining before her brother had to leave, but it would be enough. It would have to be.

Chesnaye reached for his cap. 'Thank you. I would like that very much.'

Outside the sky was suddenly dark, but necklaces of lights sparkled about the base of the Rock and across the harbour the moored ships shone invitingly beneath riding lamps which reflected and multiplied in the black water.

Groups of seamen pushed their way past, faces turned to watch the young dark-haired girl and to envy the two officers whose arms she linked.

Chesnaye felt like singing. Yet the sense of sadness which his companions seemed to convey should have acted as a brake, and he knew he ought to feel ashamed of himself.

It was a short, priceless evening, the quiet house brought alive with gay, brittle conversation and laughter.

Then Chesnaye and the young subaltern took their leave, each to his separate ship.

As they stood in the doorway the girl hugged her brother and pulled his crumpled uniform into shape. Chesnaye could see her eyes shining in the lamplight and wanted to turn away.

Then she crossed to him and laid her hands on his shoulders. 'Thank you, Dick.' That was all she had said. She pulled herself up and kissed him very lightly on the mouth, and then in one movement turned away and was gone.

As the liberty boat bounced over the darkened water Chesnaye sat silent and thoughtful in the cockpit, his ears deaf to the drunken singing of the returning seamen. He tried to see the moored troopers, but it was too dark.

Next morning, when he stood quietly watching the deck parties

329

busy with hoses and scrubbers, their feet pale in the early light, he looked again. But the moorings were empty.

He thought of the girl and touched his mouth with his fingers. He would never hear Sunset played again without remembering.

'Another boat approaching, sir!' The quartermaster spoke over his shoulder with bored resignation as a small bobbing light wound its way across the dark harbour towards the anchored monitor.

Chesnaye jerked himself from his thoughts and took a quick look around him. The gangway staff were all present, and like himself were made painfully conspicuous beneath the glaring overhead lamp and the long garlands of coloured fairy-lights which had transformed the ship into a floating carnival.

The wide quarterdeck was almost completely enclosed in immaculate awnings so that the packed crowd of officers and their guests should not be bothered by the cool evening breezes, and the small orchestra which was comprised of marines from the ship's band made a bright and colourful centrepiece to the noisy, moving throng. Long tables had been rigged on either side of the deck, and a small army of stewards and marine messmen offered drinks and a wide assortment of food to the ever-changing faces before them.

Chesnaye readjusted his unfamiliar dress-jacket as the latest arrivals drew near the gangway. He had tried hard to immerse himself completely in the business of entertaining, but he was unable to fight down the strange feeling of bitterness, almost disgust. There was an air of mad gaiety, something like pagan excitement, in the ship which affected him deeply. Everything had changed yet again, even the faces which had started to become familiar seemed like strangers once more. The bright glitter of full mess dress, dazzling white shirts and bow ties, gold lace and gleaming decorations, and, above all, the alien presence of the women who crowded the quarterdeck in such noisy profusion. He had never seen women like these before. They too seemed infected by the general excitement, and as he had waited on the gangway with his weary staff he had become dazed by the profusion of bright, laughing mouths, low-cut dresses, the bold, daring eyes. The gangway quivered and another group of officers stepped into the light, casual salutes followed by noisy anticipation as they saw the crowd already assembled beyond the awnings. Like most of the other guests, the officers wore long boatcloaks lined with white

330

silk, which for Chesnaye only added to the sense of unreality he already felt.

Two women paused laughing at the top of the gangway. Chesnaye watched them warily, his face impassive as they stared round them with bright, shining eyes. One had beautiful breasts only just concealed by her flame-coloured dress, and from the corner of his eye Chesnaye could see the corporal of the gangway as he ran a hot, appraising glance over her slim body.

It seemed as if these women, like many of the others, were acting this way deliberately. They must have known the effect they were having on the stiff-backed, regimented seamen and marines around them. The sure knowledge that they were equally beyond these men's reach must have given them added confidence, he thought.

The arrival of Lieutenant Travis, the Officer of the Day, broke into his thoughts.

Travis, his neat beard making him look almost Elizabethan, swept the women before him, his words flattering, even insolent, as he piloted them into the noisy crowd which already had started to overflow from the quarterdeck.

Another boat, and yet another. Salutes, quick greetings, and then Chesnaye was alone again, immersed in his speculations. At length the flow ceased, and to Chesnaye's mind it was just as well. It seemed unlikely that the deck could hold any more. The ship's officers, once in the comfortable majority, were lost in the press. That too had been different, he thought. Usually the various grades of officer stayed apart except for matters of duty. This wild guest night had shown Chesnaye his superiors as something else again.

Commander Godden played his own part well, the busy, jovial host ably supported by the Chief Engineer, Innes, and several lieutenants.

The ship's warrant officers, hardy professional seamen, who for all their service were more strange to the wardroom and an officer's life than they were to the lower deck, kept mainly as one body, flushed, noisy, yet seemingly lacking in their younger superiors' confidence. There was Mr. Porteous, the Boatswain, his bald head crossed by one slicked wing of hair, which from a distance looked like a feather, flanked on either of his ample sides by Mr. Tweed, the Gunner, and Mr. Jay, the Gunner (T).

331

There was Holroyd, the pasty-faced Paymaster, and Mildmay, the Surgeon. The latter was a fierce, nuggety little Welshman who rarely seemed to work. Chesnaye had often seen him sitting in his Sick Bay reading while his attendants dealt cheerfully with the waiting line of bruises, cuts and other afflictions.

Even Nutting, the Chaplain, looked different. Chesnaye could just see his narrow head with its ridiculous centre parting jerking and bobbing like a bird's as he shouted at someone across Major De L'Isle's broad shoulder.

The marine, of course, was already past the danger marks of discretion. He stood very stiffly, untroubled by the pushing bodies around him, his face getting more and more flushed, so that his neck seemed to merge with his scarlet jacket. Every so often he would drop a sharp, harsh insult into the throng and watch for results. It was a game he played very often. Women, he contended, enjoyed this form of approach. They admired his strength, his obvious virility, and they only needed that extra touch of his verbal brutality to find themselves completely defenceless. Unfortunately De L'Isle's conviction in this direction seemed to be shared by no one but himself. So he drank harder, if only to bolster his own belief.

' 'Evening, Dick!' Pickles stood blinking in the bright gangway light, his uniform sparkling with droplets of spray. 'I don't think my boat will be required again for a bit. Shall I send them below for a breather?'

Chesnaye grinned. Lieutenant Travis had instructed him to make all the necessary decisions should he not be present on the gangway; it was surprising how easy the role had become.

'You do that, Keith.' He waited as the small midshipman waved to an anonymous dark figure on the maindeck. 'Kept you busy, have they?'

Pickles puffed out his cheeks. 'Like wild beasts to the fray!' He gestured towards the dark shadow of the Rock. 'Not a woman under sixty ashore tonight!'

Chesnaye's nose twitched. Pickles was reeking of beer.

'Have you had the good fortune to booze yourself, Keith?' He frowned with mock disgust. 'Never a thought for the poor watchkeepers!'

Pickles smiled unmoved. 'There is a whole gang of petty officers at the landing stage. Boat coxswains and various other skivers!

They're not too proud to remember the poor snotties!' He winked. 'However, since you are my particular blood brother, I have brought you this.' From beneath his jacket he produced with a flourish a large bottle of port.

To the watching quartermaster he said, 'Any glasses?'

The quartermaster stared at the bottle, his eyes hungry. 'Only the gangway mugs, sir!'

Pickles belched. 'Can't have that. Must have proper glasses! This happens to be vintage port. The Vice-Admiral apparently left it in his pinnace this evening!' He looked sad. 'Very careless, you will agree?' Then, in a sharper voice: 'Right, Corporal! Double away smartly and explore the underside of the awning there! Some idle drinkers always put their empty glasses on the deck so as not to waste time!'

Chesnaye smiled. It was amazing what confidence Pickles exuded with the beer under his belt. It was obvious that the men liked him too. They liked him for himself, not out of respect or necessity. They were a little sorry for him as well. Pringle's bullying was well known on the lower deck. With other midshipmen they might have said the usual, 'Well, he shouldn't have joined if he can't take a joke!' or 'What the hell does it matter, they're *all* bloody officers!' But Pickles they accepted as they would a ship's mascot.

The corporal of the gangway eyed the bottle. 'How many glasses, sir?'

Pickles grinned. 'One each, of course!'

The gangway staff brightened visibly, although Chesnaye wondered what would happen if Travis returned unexpectedly. He felt naked beneath the glaring lights, but strangely reckless.

The marine returned with an assortment of glasses, and the Admiral's vintage port was slopped into them like so much cider.

Pickles lifted his glass with obvious relish. A thin trickle of red port ran down the corner of his mouth and splattered across his shirt like blood. He said, at length, 'At least I don't have to worry about bloody Pringle!'

It was strange the way Pickles was prepared to talk about Pringle, Chesnaye thought. Not as a person, but as a disease or a strange filthy circumstance which was unavoidable.

'Good.' Chesnaye gestured towards the quarterdeck awning. 'I suppose he's enjoying himself with the other sub-lieutenants?'

Pickles darted him a sharp glance. 'You might have thought so, yes.' He eyed the glass. 'However, for a change Mister bloody Pringle is attached to the most gorgeous little piece you have ever laid eyes on!' He bobbed his head forward and mimicked Lieutenant Hogarth's high voice. 'The most alluring, quite the *most* alluring, creature aboard!'

'This I must see!' The port flowed like hot oil across Chesnaye's empty stomach. Followed by Pickles, he walked to a slit in the awning and peered across the swaying, sweating concourse.

The women looked wild and abandoned, their naked shoulders pale beneath the coloured lights and strings of gay bunting. Their escorts surged and jostled for position, but whereas Chesnaye could see Major De L'Isle's tall frame well enough, the Captain was invisible. His eye fell on Pringle's cropped blond head. He was endeavouring to dance to the muffled beat of the sweating orchestra, his broad shoulders acting like a battering ram for his partner.

Pickles grinned unfeelingly. 'That girl deserves a medal! She's keeping that ape off our backs for a bit yet!'

Chesnaye hardly heard him. As Pringle passed beneath a cluster of fairy-lights he saw the girl's upturned face. It was Helen Driscoll.

For the very first time since the *Saracen* had left home waters the sun was at last making itself felt. It seemed to enfold the ship and the water beyond, so that the air felt heavy and humid. Gone was the Atlantic grey and silver. Instead, from the clear water alongside the hull to the hazy bridge of the horizon, the sea shone in a mixture of blues both dark and fragile, while every unbroken wave and roller reflected the sun in a million glittering mirrors.

The monitor leaned slightly, as if putting her shoulder into the inviting water to test its warmth, whilst from beneath her stern the wake curved and continued to curve until the ship had altered course yet again, the other vessels astern following suit in a slow and ponderous 'follow my leader'.

Richard Chesnaye stood on one of the bridge gratings and levelled his telescope astern. He imagined he could still see the Rock's brooding outline, but could no longer be sure. There, the horizon was lost in a mirage of vapour and reflections, so that it appeared to be shrouded in steam. He steadied the glass with his elbow resting on the screen and allowing it to swing slowly over the assorted craft which had followed the monitor from Gibraltar while the town had still slept and the stars had not yet begun to fade. Like two white ghosts the tall hulls of the hospital ships cut through the water with all the elegance and grace which had made them famous less than a year ago as crack Atlantic liners, whilst astern of them three bulky colliers and an ammunition ship plodded heavily in their wake, their ugliness made apparent by the competition. On either wing of the assorted convoy a sloop moved watchfully and with the patience of a sheepdog, and far astern, her outline merely a masthead above an indistinct shadow, another sloop maintained a wary eye on the stragglers.

Chesnaye blinked as a shaft of reflected sunlight lanced up the telescope. Through the screen beneath his arm he could feel the steady, pulsating beat of the monitor's engines as the power transmitted itself to every corner and rivet of the hull. He lowered the glass and looked quickly around the upper bridge. It looked different in the bridge sunlight, and the officers and ratings in their white uniforms seemed by their contrast to have severed the last link with the other world of damp and cold.

Royston-Jones was sitting in his tall chair, his head turned to watch the manoeuvring ships. His cap was low across his forehead, but Chesnaye could see the glitter in the Captain's eyes as he followed each movement.

'Make a signal to sloop *Mystic*.' Royston-Jones' voice was sharp and seemingly out of place in the warm enclosure of the bridge. 'Maintain position four miles astern of convoy. Report presence of any other ships immediately.'

The Yeoman of Signals wrote quickly on his slate, the pencil squeaking viciously and reminding Chesnaye briefly of a far-off schoolroom.

Lieutenant Travis looked down from the compass platform and rubbed his eyes. He looked pale and tired against the clear sky, and Chesnaye wondered if he was still recovering from the week in Gibraltar.

'Course south seventy east, sir!' Travis waited, watching the Captain's foot as it tapped gently on the grating.

'Very well.' Royston-Jones did not sound very interested.

'Speed of convoy is steady at eight knots, sir.' Travis added bitterly, 'No wonder the Admiral delegated us to this lot!'

Chesnaye knew that the bulk of warships had gone on ahead, a fine picture, even without the blessing of daylight. The remaining battleships from Gibraltar, a rakish cruiser squadron and three flotillas of destroyers, their hulls almost hidden in eager bow waves, had steamed into the darkness and vanished as if wiped from a slate. The monitor was too slow to work with the Fleet, so Royston-Jones had been ordered to make his way eastwards with this small convoy. Although senior officer present, he was probably being cursed by the three sloop commanders, who must know that he was as much their responsibility as the colliers and the others. For the hospital ships, too, the slow progress must be infuriating, Chesnaye thought. They could manage twenty-three knots without too much effort, yet at eight knots they had to take their time from the slowest ships present.

Commander Godden removed his cap and wiped the band with his handkerchief. 'The hospital ships are a waste of time in my opinion. With all the troops we're mustering it will all be over in a day or two.' He looked at the Captain's shoulders. 'Before *we* get there, I shouldn't wonder!'

Royston-Jones crossed his legs and settled back in his chair. 'We will spend the forenoon at gun drills and damage control, Commander. All heads of departments will stand fast and their subordinates will take over.' He added sharply, 'Even if we are too late this time it may prove to be a long war!'

As the sun climbed higher the monitor's guns crews were led through one crisis after another. While Hogarth looked on, edgy and helpless to intervene, his assistant, a baby-faced lieutenant named Yates, sent the men sweating and cursing to obey the situations which Royston-Jones seemed to conjure up without effort. The secondary armament were divided to track and carry out mock attacks on the other ships in convoy, while the giant turret endeavoured to follow the tiny shape of the escort astern. The sloop only appeared occasionally, as it was usually hidden by the *Saracen*'s own bridge. This meant that one minute the twin fifteen-inch guns were swung round one side of the monitor's superstructure, and the next, almost before the ranges and deflections could be checked, the sloop had sidestepped daintily to the other quarter, so that the great turret had to swing through an angle of nearly two hundred and eighty degrees.

Once Hogarth, all but wringing his hands, had voiced a short protest. 'They're not *meant* for this, sir! The sort of targets they are designed for are stationary!'

Royston-Jones was unimpressed. 'Suppose the Turkish Fleet breaks out of the Straits, eh?' His eye was pitiless. 'What am I expected to do then? Send the Major and his marines to board 'em, I suppose!'

Once the training mechanism had failed in the turret, so that it stayed pointing impotently at an empty horizon while Royston-Jones barked a series of orders and complaints which became more savage as the minutes passed.

Godden, who was supposed to be 'dead' for the exercise said in a strangled voice, 'Shall I order Secure, sir?'

'No, of *course* not! Mister Chesnaye, get forrard and check what is wrong!'

Chesnaye was glad to get away even for a few moments. He had grown to hate the constant battle between the Captain and Godden, although no actual argument ever seemed to show itself. The Commander was his usual self when Royston-Jones was away, but together they seemed unable to agree about anything. Chesnaye had often imagined Godden in command, and wondered how his more humane influence and understanding would affect the ship.

Panting, he climbed the straight ladder which ran up the side of the tall circular barbette upon which the turret revolved. He could feel the sweat running down his skin and clinging to his drill tunic, and wondered if he was getting out of condition. In the training ship they had always allowed for this and had exercised the cadets without let up. Here, in spite of the complex organisation, he felt restricted and cramped. The inside of the turret was like a scene from another world. He had not entered it before, and as he blinked to accustom his eyes to the harsh glare of electric lighting he realised for the first time the ship's tremendous hitting power.

The turret was bigger than the monitor's bridge and funnel combined, and was dominated by the two giant polished breeches which gaped open and allowed the distant sunlight to reflect down the rifled perfection of the twin barrels. The white painted turret was crammed with gleaming equipment. Brass wheels, dials, voice-pipes and hoisting tackles which snaked away through circular hatches towards the bowels of the ship and the magazines. Stripped and sweating, their shining skins making them look like slaves before a mechanical altar, the gunners leaned and panted by the unmoving breeches. The gunlayers and trainers, breech

337

operators and loaders, all waited and watched the Quarters Officer, a Sub-Lieutenant Lucas, whose narrow frame was hung about with gleaming instruments like a pantomime surgeon.

He glared down from his tall stool as Chesnaye paused below him. 'Well, what the hell do you want?'

Chesnaye smiled. 'The Captain wants to know –' He never finished.

'Mother of God! What does he *expect*?' The officer peered down at his men. 'They'll all be dead before we reach Gallipoli if we keep up this pace!'

An oil-smeared petty officer appeared from nowhere. 'Fault discovered, sir.' He stared at Chesnaye as if he had come from another planet. 'Mister Tweed is fixing it now.' He added vaguely: 'A pawl in the training clutch has sheared.'

The Quarters Officer said severely, 'Mister Tweed is supposed to be "dead".' He sighed with relief. 'Still, there's no need for anyone to know!'

'What shall I tell the Captain?' Chesnaye waited, conscious of the gunners' grinning faces.

The Quarters Officer, whose father owned half of Cornwall, said stiffly: 'Report that the target returned our fire and we have sustained a direct hit. The turret is out of action!'

Chesnaye found his way back to the sunlit arena of the upper bridge and dutifully repeated the insolent message. He heard Godden catch his breath, while Hogarth looked as if he was going to be sick.

Royston-Jones nodded and rubbed his hands. 'Very well. Excellent!' He gave a sudden chuckle. 'A bright young man, that one! Uses his imagination!'

The bridge relaxed slightly. The Captain added after a moment: 'Pass the word to the Surgeon about casualties. I would like to see the Quarters Officer splintered and bandaged for, er, let me see, multiple fractures. When that has been done he can be carried to his quarters while his men are sent to Stand Easy.' He grinned with sudden delight. 'How does that suit, eh?'

Chesnaye turned away. It seemed useless to try to better Royston-Jones.

The hammocks creaked gently with each roll of the hull, but because of the lack of cool air Chesnaye felt unable to sleep. About

338

him the gunroom was in darkness, even the police light being partly obscured by a pair of underpants. He reached above his face and felt for the valve in the overhead ventilating pipe to make sure that it was directed towards him. But the air was without life and seemed to smell of oil and paint.

Chesnaye pushed his hands beneath his head and took deep breaths. He had thrown the blankets aside, and he could feel the steady stream of air across his naked body. Nearby he heard 'Ticky' White chuckling, but as he listened he realised that the other midshipman was asleep. Two days out from Gibraltar and the pace was beginning to tell. Drills, exercises and practices of every sort on top of watchkeeping duties. At first the ship's company had turned to with a will, used and trained to every whim and will of their officers. But on a placid sea, with the following ships already like part of the scenery, the enthusiasm had waned into resentful clumsiness. Things went wrong, and the harder it became to bear, the more the Captain conjured out of his imagination to drive them to the limit of endurance.

Chesnaye thought of Gibraltar, and again the feeling of loss moved inside him. It would be another week before the *Saracen* crawled to her destination, which was apparently to be Mudros, a Greek island where some of the assault forces were being assembled, and he knew that with each turn of the screws he would be blaming himself for his own handling of those short, haunting moments in Gibraltar.

The night of the big reception aboard, for instance. When he had seen Helen with Pringle he had wanted to turn his back, to hide his resentment from Pickles and cross the girl from his mind. Instead he had waited morosely by the gangway until the time had come for Helen and her father to leave. It had been difficult with the milling crowds shouting and singing around the gangway, the boats jostling for position, the women shrieking and laughing. It had been more than difficult.

He had wanted to confront her, to ask her why she had not even visited him at his place of duty, but his pride had clashed with his disappointment. When he had eventually managed to reach her she had merely looked uneasy and said, 'A very gay evening!' Then she had glanced away, her eyes sad.

He had mumbled something, but could not remember what. In any case, it did not matter when he had met Pickles that same night. Chesnaye had stumbled into the gunroom and found Pickles pressing trousers beneath a bench cushion in readiness for the morning.

Tonelessly Pickles had said, 'So it was your girl, then?'

Chesnaye had not answered, angry with himself for showing his feelings.

'It's none of my business, Dick, but . . .' Pickles turned, his eyes shaded. 'Pringle was here just now, boasting about what he'd done . . .' He faltered.

Chesnaye punched his hammock savagely. 'He was talking rubbish! They did not leave the ship together!'

'I didn't mean that, Dick. Pringle said that she was asking where *you* were, you see . . .'

Chesnaye felt uneasy. 'Well, what of it?'

Pickles fidgeted. 'Pringle pretended to be friendly, you know how he is. Then he spun her some yarn about you.' He gulped. 'That's what he was bragging about!'

'For God's sake make sense! *What* did he tell her?'

'He warned her against you. Said that you'd been boasting about the things you'd done with her . . .'

The rest of his words had been lost in the wave of fury which had engulfed Chesnaye, which still haunted him like a nightmare. Pringle had had his revenge, as he had promised. He had even managed to prevent Chesnaye from going ashore on one pretext or another, and by making a point of being meticulously correct in his behaviour had nailed down the last point in his victory.

Even now, as he lay sweating in his hammock, he could feel the anger rising within him like a flood. What was it made men like Pringle what they were? He hoarded titbits of information and used them like a sadistic blackmailer. It was obvious that he was doing the same to Pickles, although the latter strenuously denied it when Chesnaye asked him. His round face had puckered into a frightened mask and he had said: 'It's nothing, Dick! For God's sake forget it!'

The fans whirred steadily, and two decks above his head the watchkeepers peered into the velvet darkness. Chesnaye forced his eyes shut and tried to sleep. Surely his father had been wrong in his philosophy? It was futile and stupid to trust nobody.

He thought, too, about Pringle, and discovered that he was actually beginning to know the meaning of hatred.

Chapter Four

Gallipoli

The *Saracen's* broad wardroom seemed unusually crowded as the ship's officers arranged themselves in the carefully placed chairs which faced the table at the far end. The evening air was warm and heavy, and the fans which whirred from the deckhead did little to ease the drowsy stuffiness, but instead kept the infiltrating flies constantly on the move to the annoyance of the seated officers.

Outside, the darkening anchorage of Mudros was alive with launches and small craft which prowled and fluttered around the moored warships and troopers like insects, and over the whole assembly of shipping there seemed to hang an air of excited tension and eagerness.

Richard Chesnaye craned his neck to pick out each officer in turn, aware that only a chief petty officer guarded the gangway and every officer, high or low, had been assembled for what must now be a final briefing. Like the others, he was relieved, almost glad that the waiting was over. Even if he had found the time to get ashore, and his increasing duties had prevented that, Mudros seemed a dull and unprepossessing island. Crammed with troops, tented camps, ammunition dumps and makeshift field hospitals, it had wilted beneath the crushing weight of the invasion force. For two weeks the *Saracen* had lain at anchor, the sun always making the preparations harder to bear, the ship's forced immobility adding to the sense of frustration and irritation. But now, as April moved nearer its close, it looked as if the great offensive was about to begin.

Chesnaye sat tautly in his chair, his limbs stiff with expectation as he listened to the loud, indifferent voices of his superiors and the excited whispers of the other midshipmen, who like himself had been seated at the very rear of the wardroom as if to doubly indicate their lack of seniority.

He could see Travis, the Navigating Officer, Hogarth and all the other lieutenants. Pringle's glossy head was prominent among the sub-lieutenants, while Major De L'Isle jutted like a glowing pinnacle above the packed ranks of experts and professionals who made up the ship's complement of officers. The engineers, warrant officers, Surgeon, Paymaster, even the Chaplain, were crammed into the well-lighted interior.

The Captain entered without fuss or announcement, followed by Commander Godden and an unfamiliar officer in army uniform.

Royston-Jones waited beside the table until the assembled officers, who had sprung noisily to their feet, had resettled themselves, and then laid his cap carefully on a nearby chair. His cold eyes flitted briefly across the watching faces, as if to make sure that there was neither an absentee nor an interloper, then he uncovered the tall chart which up to this moment had been hanging, shrouded, on the bulkhead.

The Captain glanced at Godden, who with the soldier had seated himself on the far side of the table. 'All present?'

'Yes, sir.' Godden looked meaningly towards the sealed pantry door. 'And I've sent the stewards forrard.'

Royston-Jones gave a wry smile. 'No doubt this meeting will be common knowledge between decks whatever action we take!'

A ripple of laughter transmitted itself around the wardroom. The lower deck's telegraph system was as reliable as it was uncanny.

'However . . .' the laughter died instantly, 'I shall expect each of you to bear the importance of security in mind. This whole operation could be jeopardised by rumour, equally it might be delayed by the inability of an officer to hold his tongue!'

The officers shuffled uneasily, and Chesnaye saw that some of them held unlit pipes and cigarettes concealed in their hands. They had apparently expected the Captain to permit smoking, but as yet there was no sign of any relaxation.

Chesnaye turned his attention to the chart as Royston-Jones continued to speak. The chart showed clearly the long, sock-shaped peninsula of Gallipoli, and was dotted with small coloured counters and hostile-looking arrows.

'Gentlemen, the main Allied assault will take place forty-eight hours from tomorrow morning.' He allowed the murmurs to die. 'The main landings will be down here at the toe of the Peninsula at these three beaches, V, X and W. The Australian and New Zealand Forces are to make a separate landing to the north-west,' his brown

342

hand moved slowly up the coastline, 'and thereby divide the enemy deployment.'

Beaushears spoke from the corner of his mouth, 'We hope!'

Royston-Jones' pale eyes flickered in the overhead lights. 'The *Saracen* will assist in the latter landings, and will provide artillery support both in the assault and after the Australians have crossed the beaches and captured the surrounding heights.'

Chesnaye stared hard at the passive chart and tried to see beyond the Captain's laconic words. For days they had listened to the rumours and stories from the men of patrolling destroyers, who day and night had watched the beaches and kept an eye on the Turkish preparations. The tales they told were not reassuring. Apparently the enemy had taken full advantage of the Allied delays and, as expected by everyone aboard, had poured in soldiers by the thousand, many of whom had actually been seen and reported as throwing up massive earthworks and gun batteries, and sowing the cliffs and beaches, even the water itself, with a tangled web of barbed wire. In addition, it was well known that the Straits and surrounding areas were littered with minefields, some of which had already taken a bitter toll. In the earlier March bombardments, while *Saracen* had languished at Gibraltar, the French battleship *Bouvet* had struck a mine and turned turtle in two minutes. Within two hours the battleship *Ocean* followed her to the bottom and the crack battlecruiser *Inflexible* had been badly crippled.

Royston-Jones continued: 'The landings will be made early, but not in complete darkness, for obvious reasons. However, we must face the fact that the troops *will* in probability be advancing into point-blank fire from well-sited guns of every calibre.'

Involuntarily Chesnaye glanced at the army officer's face. It was an expressionless mask, as if he was aware that every man present was thinking the same thing.

'So our own importance, our *duty*, is plain. We must keep up a steady fire at pre-selected targets, so that the enemy is not only tied down but is also unable to harry our troops as they make their way inland.' The hand swept across the peninsula. 'This whole area is criss-crossed with gullies and ridges, any one of which could force a stalemate within days, even hours, of landing. We shall in all probability be firing at targets beyond these ridges which we cannot see. For this and other reasons I intend to land spotting teams as

343

arranged, and in co-operation with the Royal Engineers Signal Branch I shall expect an unbroken stream of information to be fed to Lieutenant Hogarth's gunners!' He stared abruptly at the Commander. 'Check each landing party personally. They might be cut off from the ship for some time.'

Chesnaye shivered at the words. With Pickles and Beaushears he was already detailed for this work. For days they had exercised with boats and men, in pitch darkness and at the height of the sun, while telescopes and watches checked every phase of the operations.

But it was good that the waiting was over. Even being chased and harried through every phase of the preparations had failed to exclude Helen Driscoll from his mind, and his feeling of helplessness had prevailed rather than faded. He had tried to tell himself that their meeting was a mere incident, something he had had to feel for the first time, but not remember. It was all useless, and the more he relived those moments at Gibraltar, the stronger his emotions became, just as his contempt and anger for Pringle had hardened.

The confined stuffiness of the wardroom was making him drowsy and he had to consciously force himself to concentrate on what the army officer was saying about the dispersal of troops, landing marks and areas of bombardment. Heads of departments were writing in their notebooks, and Godden was nodding judiciously at various points made by the tall soldier. The midshipmen had nothing to do but listen. Their work was prearranged. If the rehearsals proved to be faulty it would be too late to change anything, Chesnaye thought.

He shifted his gaze to the Captain. Even his impassive features could not hide completely the inner feelings of tension and anxiety. Royston-Jones was carefully seated, yet informal enough to create his own atmosphere of unusual excitement.

Chesnaye tried to comprehend what the Captain must be feeling. The whole ship, her company of two hundred officers and men and the mission prepared for those two massive guns, all that responsibility lay on his slight shoulders. Yet he showed little sign of true uncertainty.

Chesnaye thought, too, of his father. This might have been his command, and he wondered how he would have reacted at this moment. A pang of regret lanced through him as he recalled his father's flushed angry face.

Perhaps I should have tried to understand him more. Instead of

344

worrying about the effect on my own career? He shifted in his chair as Royston-Jones stood up impatiently and faced the company.

'There is nothing else to say at this juncture, gentlemen. The cards are down. We are committed.' He allowed his words to sink in. 'From the moment the sun rises over those beaches we will all be paying our way.'

He stepped forward, an erect figure in white against the sombre chart. Then he pointed slowly towards the ship's crest above the empty fireplace, its garish warrior's face bright in the lamplight. 'Remember the ship's motto, gentlemen.' His voice was for once without an edge, almost sad. ' "With courage and integrity, press on!" One quality is useless without the other, either for this ship or the Navy itself!' With a curt nod to the Commander he was gone.

Some officers groped for their unlit pipes and then faltered, aware of the churchlike silence which seemed to have fallen around the glittering crest.

Beaushears said quietly, 'An altar of Mars!'

But across the wardroom Nutting, the Chaplain, was not so cynical. 'May God go with us,' he said.

The army officer had gone with Godden, and Major De L'Isle clapped his massive hands across his breast and glared at the black-coated Chaplain. 'Just contain yourself, Padre!' He glared at the wardroom at large. 'I think one last damned party is indicated, what? These bloody soldiers will need too much looking after for a bit to give us much time later on!'

Beaushears winked. 'This is *our* cue to leave, Dick.' He took a last glance at the chart. 'Let's hope the whole thing doesn't get bogged down like Flanders!'

Chesnaye had a brief vision of a vast army, stale and unmoving, with the sea at its back. 'It's going to be harder than I thought.'

Beaushears shrugged. 'A noble thought. You can put it on your tombstone!'

'Steady on north eighty-five east, sir!' Travis's voice was hushed, almost lost in the *Saracen*'s sea noises as the ship crept forward at six knots.

'Very well.' Royston-Jones moved from his chair, his figure a white shadow against the grey paintwork.

Although the sea and sky still merged in darkness, the stars were

345

already pale and indistinct, and there was a faint but steady breeze as if the dawn had started to find breath.

Chesnaye shivered, but ignored the chill in his body as he peered over the port screen towards a long white line which lengthened and rippled in time to the monitor's own wash. A black, shapeless mass was moving in line abreast, and another beyond that, and another. Out there in the darkness he knew that an armada of steel was steering one fixed course, and somewhere ahead lay the barrier of the Peninsula itself. He remembered the previous afternoon and felt a lump in his throat. Because of her slow speed the monitor had sailed ahead of the main invasion fleet, and at one time had actually passed through two dawdling lines of troopships and their watchful escorts. Chesnaye knew that if he lived for ever he would never forget that moment. The sun high overhead, the clear blue sky and tall-funnelled troopers glittering above their own reflections. It had been very quiet but for the steady throb of the *Saracen*'s engines, an almost lazy, holiday atmosphere had cloaked the meaning of those double, treble rows of watching khaki figures who swarmed over every foot of the troopships' superstructures.

Something was lacking, and eventually Commander Godden had remarked: 'What a way to go to war! More like a Bank Holiday!'

Royston-Jones had been sitting in his chair, apparently dozing. His voice had been sharp and unexpected. 'Have the marine band mustered on the quarterdeck.'

Godden had stared at him. '*Now*, sir?'

'At the double, Commander! And tell the Bandmaster to go right through his repertoire until those ships are out of sight!'

It had been impressive and unreal. The fat, belligerent shape of the monitor, pale grey and shining in her new paint, with a giant ensign curling from the gaff, whilst on her scrubbed quarterdeck, paraded as if in Portsmouth barracks, the ship's band stood in a bright square, instruments glittering like jewels, sun-helmets gleaming white, watching the deft strokes of the Bandmaster's baton.

They had steamed past ship after ship, the slack, humid air suddenly coming to life with the strains of 'Hearts of Oak' and 'A Life on the Ocean Wave.'

Much later people might laugh at Royston-Jones, but Chesnaye

346

knew in his heart that anyone who had been there would have known his decision to be right.

First one ship and then another had come alive, the upper decks transformed into rippling lines of waving hands and cheering faces. The cheering went on and on, until the sea itself seemed to vibrate.

That had been yesterday. Now those same soldiers were waiting out there in the darkness, fingering their rifles, pulling in their stomach muscles.

'Fifteen minutes, sir.' Travis was crouched above the compass.

'Very well.' The Captain sounded distant, as if thinking of something else.

Lieutenant Hogarth pushed his way across the crowded bridge. He paused to peer at Chesnaye and the two other midshipmen, Beaushears and Pickles. 'Right. Nothing to do at the moment – for you that is!' He stood, his gaunt frame silhouetted against the charthouse. 'The first wave of troops is already moving up through the destroyer screen. You and your landing party will go with the second wave – got it?'

Chesnaye felt himself nodding. All at once his head seemed full of questions and doubts, his mind blank to everything he had been told.

Hogarth rubbed his hands. 'Right, then. We'll show 'em a thing or two!' But he was looking forward, as if speaking to his guns.

Even as he spoke, Chesnaye saw the tips of the two massive muzzles lift gently above the bridge screen until they were at a forty-five-degree angle. Hogarth muttered to himself and began to climb the ladder to the Upper Control Top. The ship was already at Action Stations, but the voice-pipes and handsets kept up their incessant chatter, adding to the feeling of nervous tension.

The Yeoman appeared. 'Commence general bombardment in eleven minutes, sir!'

'Very well.' The Captain climbed to his chair, his feet scraping on the grating. 'Ear-plugs, please.'

Chesnaye remembered just in time and groped for his own plugs. It would be terrible to start off with shattered eardrums.

There was a faint whirr of machinery and the great turret swivelled slightly to port. Criss-crossed along the monitor's decks the leaky hoses kept up their constant dampening, a final effort to save the planking from splintering to fragments when the bombardment started. For hours the shipwrights and stokers had been unscrewing doors, removing crockery and wooden panels, and preparing the ship for the one task for which she had been built.

'Five minutes, sir!'

Royston-Jones said: 'Let's hope the battleships know what they're doing. We don't want any of their salvoes falling short on to *us*!'

The monitor had previously passed a line of battleships steaming parallel to the invisible coast, their long guns already trained abeam, their battle ensigns making faint white blobs against the towering bridges and turrets. They would be shooting at a range of some twenty thousand yards above and beyond the wide phalanx of the advancing troops in their boats.

'Dawn's comin' up, sir!' A signalman spoke involuntarily, as if to ease his own nerves.

Chesnaye watched the pale grey and silver line with awe and surprise. It was amazing how quickly the dawn came here. But at the bottom edge, where the horizon should have been, there was a black, uneven line. The coast.

It was impossible to see the hundreds of small boats which must already be streaming towards the hidden beaches, but Chesnaye knew that they were indeed there. Whalers, cutters, pinnaces, boats of every shape and kind. Power-launches towing clusters of troop-filled boats like pods, men crammed together, sweating and silent, smelling the fear and the danger yet eager to get started.

Even the *Saracen* had sent some of her boats to help, and at least three of her midshipmen, Bacon, Maintland and 'Ticky' White, were out there with them.

Overhead the range-finders squeaked slightly as they revolved in their armoured turret, and Chesnaye heard a voice-pipe stutter: 'High explosive! Load . . . load . . . load!'

Godden said loudly, 'Leaving it to the last as usual!'

'One minute, sir!'

The young signalman by Chesnaye's side hugged his body with his arms. 'Jesus, this bloody waitin'!'

'Standing by, sir!'

'Very well.' Royston-Jones sounded calm. 'Starboard ten!'

The ship shivered and paid off into a moderate swell, her high bridge groaning. A pencil rolled from the chart table and clattered at their feet like a falling tree. Somewhere above a man coughed, and another could be heard whistling without tune.

'Zero, sir!'

'Open fire!'

Even as the order was passed, the horizon astern erupted into a jagged pattern of red and orange flashes as the hidden battleships commenced their bombardment. Seconds dragged by, and then high overhead, with the ear-searing shriek of a regiment of express trains, the first salvoes sped on their way.

Chesnaye felt the signalman gripping his sleeve, and saw the man's mouth moving. 'Gawd, sir, what a way –' But his frightened words were lost as the monitor's main armament steadied and fired. There was less sound than Chesnaye had expected, yet he was rendered deaf and stunned, as if the guns had fired beside his head. The air was sucked across the upper bridge like hot sand, and as the twin barrels were hurled back on to their recoil springs he felt the whole ship shudder and buck. It was more like being struck by a salvo than firing one.

He coughed as a cloud of acrid cordite smoke drifted across the screen. In the space of seconds it had got lighter so that he could see the lean shape of a nearby destroyer and the harder outline of the coastline ahead.

The bombardment mounted and thickened in noise and power, so that the shells screamed overhead in an unending procession. Chesnaye understood little of their effect, and only occasionally could he see the angry flash of an explosion ashore. But beyond the cliffs and hills he knew that tons and tons of high explosive were deluging down, so that the waiting Turks, if waiting they were, must be in a living hell.

'Shoot!' Again the monitor's guns bellowed and lurched backwards, and Chesnaye could imagine the Quarters Officer yelling at his gunners and listening to Hogarth's urgent orders from the Control Top.

The noise was crushing, devastating and without pity. Chesnaye lost count of time as his body and mind shook to the voice of the monitor's bombardment. Occasionally Royston-Jones ordered an alteration of course, and Lieutenant Travis, strained and ill-looking, would crouch across the binnacle, his hands shaking to the thunder of the guns.

The sun peered across the land ridge, bright and curious, an onlooker without fear. The cliffs and the dirt-brown hills beyond

349

looked suddenly close, the narrow strips of beach white crescents beneath the high rock. Like beetles the small boats were already merged with the shoreline, the progress of the soldiers marked only with occasional flashes of fire. How small and ineffective those flashes seemed compared with the monitor's guns, Chesnaye thought.

Two waterspouts rose almost alongside the *Saracen's* fo'c'sle, and Chesnaye ducked incredulously as something sped past the bridge with the sound of tearing silk.

'Enemy battery, bearing red four-five!' a lookout shouted between the gun-bursts.

Royston-Jones swung in his chair. 'Tell the Director to open fire with the secondary armament immediately!'

A rating with the handset said, 'Gunnery Officer has fixed the battery's position below the east pinnacle, sir.' Below the bridge the slim four-inch guns were already swinging shorewards.

'Very well.' The Captain seemed angry. 'Increase to half-speed, Pilot. We will close the coast and concentrate on the local batteries. That ridge is too high for the Turks to get at us once we are inshore.' He fidgeted with his glasses. 'We can hit *them*, however!'

Two more waterspouts rose alongside. Much closer.

Chesnaye flinched as the four-inch guns opened fire independently. Their voices were different. Sharp and ear-splitting, a savage whiplash.

Somehow he had not expected to be fired on himself. Up to now his thoughts had been mixed, filled with anxiety for the soldiers and uncertainty for himself. This was different. There was no sign that he could recognise along those craggy cliffs and hills, no opposite ship to plot and stalk. Merely the abbreviated scream of shells and the tall, deadly waterspouts.

The Yeoman tilted his cap as the sun lifted clear of the land and squinted at the curtain of spray as it fell abeam in the calm water. 'Quite big, too,' he said at length. 'Nine inch or bigger!' He grinned suddenly, his teeth filling his tanned face. 'Cheeky buggers!'

'Port ten!' The Captain sat hunched in his chair like a small gargoyle, his eyes following the white whirlpool which still showed the last fall of shot. The monitor swung awkwardly on her course and then steadied as another order brought her bows once more towards the beaches.

The hidden Turkish battery dropped two more shells simultaneously near the monitor's starboard beam – where the ship would have been but for Royston-Jones' sudden alteration of course.

Again the falling spray, the taste of cordite. Chesnaye stared fascinated at the leaping water, only to be knocked sideways as the *Saracen*'s big guns roared out once more. It was a wonder the turret did not tear itself clean off the ship, or that the *Saracen* remained in one piece.

Then there were no more Turkish shells, and Royston-Jones twisted round to stare up at the Control Top. Almost impishly he lifted his cap and smiled. Peering through his armoured slits, like a knight at Agincourt, Hogarth must have seen that impetuous gesture and felt a glow of satisfaction.

Royston-Jones glanced briefly at the three midshipmen. 'Away you go! Stand by to lower your boats and embark landing parties!'

Chesnaye shook himself and tore his eyes from the Captain's unblinking stare. All at once he realised that it was not over. For him it was just beginning.

A steam picket boat took the *Saracen*'s two whalers in tow until they were within half a mile of the beach and then cast them adrift. A sub-lieutenant in the power boat's sternsheets waved a megaphone and bellowed: 'Pull like hell for your landing point! It's a bit hot around here!'

As if to emphasise his words, a small shell exploded nearby and sent a wave of splinters whirring overhead.

Chesnaye gritted his teeth and peered over the oarsmen's heads. The nearest cliff, shaped like a miniature Rock of Gibraltar, hid the early sun from view and cast a deep black shadow across the two pitching whalers. 'Give way together!' His voice was surprisingly steady, and he forced himself to look at Tobias, who because of the extra passengers was squatting right aft, his legs over the tiller bar. He caught Chesnaye's eye and grinned. 'Just like a trip round Brighton pier, sir!'

Hunched in the sternsheets Lieutenant Thornton, selected by Hogarth as senior spotting officer, pawed over an assortment of leather cases which contained telescopes, handsets and other necessary gear, his face set in a scowl of concentration. Pickles was by his side, his gaze fixed on the dark shadowed cliff. The oarsmen

351

pulled hard and rhythmically, half watching the other whaler which was barely yards away.

Beaushears stood in the other boat and occasionally glanced across, his features drawn and unusually determined.

I suppose I must look like that, Chesnaye thought. We are all playing a part. More afraid of showing fear than of fear itself.

He shaded his eyes, conscious of the cool depths of the cliff's shadow as it closed about him. 'Steer over there.' He felt the tiller creak obediently.

It was too quiet, he thought. Like the sea and the sky, everything seemed shadowed and guarded by the might of the land. Faint and muffled, he could occasionally hear the sporadic rattle of small-arms and the steel whiplash of machine-guns. But they were impersonal and did not appear to belong here. Once when he glanced astern he saw the *Saracen*, her shape deformed as she turned slightly towards the headland, the long guns still probing the air, as if sniffing out a new target. Many other ships were silhouetted against the horizon, but the barrage had paused, no doubt waiting to see the effect of the troops' progress ashore.

As if reading his thoughts Pickles said breathlessly, 'It looks as if it's all over already!'

Chesnaye nodded absently. 'Watch your steering, Tobias! There are shoals of some sort ahead.' He had seen what appeared to be low, sandy rocks littered along the water's edge.

Tobias said tightly, 'Not *rocks*, sir.'

The whaler moved swiftly inshore, the last few yards vanishing in seconds. Chesnaye saw the oarsmen watching him curiously, and held his breath in an endeavour to conceal the slow sickness which was squeezing his insides like a vice.

Nearer and nearer. He could see clearly now the shoals which were strewn across the whaler's path. They moved gently in the lapping wavelets, their khaki limbs swaying and jerking as if still alive.

He heard Pickles gasp, and then as the boat cut a passage between the first of the dead soldiers the oarsmen looked too at the tangle of corpses and discarded equipment at the water's edge.

The stroke was momentarily lost, and Chesnaye choked: 'Oars! Stand by to beach!' He did not know how he had managed to give the order, nor did he recognise his own voice. The boat ground into the sand and the second whaler hit the beach close by.

A few soldiers moved along the base of the cliff, and he saw several tiny tents marked with the Red Cross already erected. But again his eyes were drawn to the waterline of dead.

Australians, New Zealanders and a few British, their faces already pale and expressionless in the salt spray. He could see the gleaming teeth of barbed wire, sewn deep in the water itself, and upon which little clusters of corpses bobbed like obscene fruit. There was blood too on the sand and all the way up the trampled beach to the foot of the cliff. A sergeant lay on his back his hands digging into his stomach, mouth wide in one last cry. His uniform was stitched from shoulder to groin with machine-gun bullets, yet equipment and bayonet were still smart and exactly in place.

Lieutenant Thornton leapt over the gunwale. 'At the double! Put out the boat anchors and run for cover!'

The men gaped from the corpses to him and then jerked into life as the sand jumped at their feet and the air echoed to the high-pitched whine of bullets.

A soldier yelled: 'Come up here, you stupid bastards! There are still snipers about!'

A bullet whacked into the boat's warm woodwork at Chesnaye's hip, and with a gasp he started up the beach. He turned to call to Lieutenant Thornton and was just in time to see him reel back, his hands clawing at his face. In fact his face had been torn away by a bullet, but blinded and screaming he staggered drunkenly in a circle while the sand spurted around him.

An Australian corporal emerged from some rocks, his bush that tilted over his eyes. Unceremoniously he pushed Chesnaye against the cliff and threw down his rifle. In three bounds he reached the naval officer, but before he could seize him Thornton dropped and rolled on to his back, his face a glistening, bright scarlet against the pale sand.

Chesnaye retched as the seamen crowded around him, Tobias carrying Thornton's leather cases.

The corporal returned and picked up his rifle. 'Of all the stupid jokers!' He pulled a cigarette from his hat and squinted up at the cliff. 'Pretty quiet landing so far, but the boys is held up in a gully over yonder.' He gestured vaguely to a small cliff path.

Beaushears sidled along the cliff and peered at Chesnaye. 'All right, Dick?' He glanced at the spread-eagled lieutenant on the open beach. 'It's up to us, then?'

Chesnaye nodded dazedly. 'I suppose so.'

'I'll set up my signal party here as arranged, Dick,' Beaushears was speaking fast as if unable to stop. 'You must take Thornton's job with the Army until *Saracen* can send a replacement.' He looked grim. 'Or do you want me to take over?'

Chesnaye shook his head. 'No. I'll go!' He wanted to scream. These stupid, formal tones. A man he had known was still bleeding barely feet away, his face a bloody pulp. An Australian was smoking a cigarette, his eyes on the distant monitor. Nothing was real any more.

Tobias said carefully: 'We'd better be off, sir. It may take some time to contact the army signals blokes.'

'Er, yes.' Chesnaye looked at Pickles' stricken face. 'Can you make it to the top?'

Pickles seemed to pull himself together. 'I'll be all right with you, Dick!'

Then they were off up the path, the soldier still leaning against the cliff, his eyes slitted as if in deep thought.

It took Chesnaye more than an hour to lead his small party of seamen to the top of the cliff path. The sun was already high in the clear sky, and every step up the dry, crumbling track brought the sweat pouring down his body, so that he repeatedly had to stop and wipe his face with his sleeve. At last he turned sharply into a deep fold of rock, the sides of the cliff rising on either side of him sheer and smooth as if the very weight of stone and boulders had split the land in two. His eyes were dazzled by the heat haze which shimmered above the barren countryside and the sparse tangle of small trees which clung desperately to the ridges above the cliff path, and he almost stumbled on to a group of soldiers who were squatting comfortably outside what appeared to be a narrow cave.

A harassed-looking subaltern rose to his feet and stared at Chesnaye and his men. 'You'll be the gunnery experts, then?' He grinned companionably and eased the weight of his revolver at his belt. 'In the nick of time too!'

Chesnaye looked around him. Just beyond the V-shaped end to the gap in the cliff he could see the rounded crest of a long ridge. It seemed quite near, yet he knew from his map that there was a deep gully between it and the coastline. And beyond that there was a higher ridge, and then another. They cut the Peninsula into a mass of valleys and gullies like a bird's eye view of a badly ploughed field, each ridge dominating the next for a watchful friend or enemy.

Already the sea had vanished, the hiss and murmur of wavelets along the beaches lost in the boom of artillery and the vicious rattle of machine-guns. Yet the dust which hovered in the humid air like smoke was tinged with salt, and a handful of angry gulls still circled and screamed above the narrow path from the shore.

The subaltern pointed towards the gap in the cliffs. 'Our chaps have pushed forward quite well. Not much resistance on the beach either, thank God!'

Chesnaye thought of the nodding corpses in the stained water. 'It looked bad to me,' he said quietly.

'Hell, no!' The Australian accent seemed strange and casual. 'My signals outfit reported that the main landings down south have had a really bad time of it! Lost hundreds in the first minutes.' He grimaced. 'Cross-fire. The Turks had the whole damn' beach zeroed in!'

Chesnaye looked across Pickles' heaving shoulders at his silent seamen. In their dusty and crumpled uniforms they seemed out of place, lost and dispirited. Chesnaye bit his lip. They had not started yet. He wondered how the dead lieutenant would have dealt with the situation. No doubt as casually and as efficiently as this young soldier.

'Can we go forward now?' Chesnaye saw Pickles stiffen at his question.

The subaltern gestured towards the squatting soldiers. 'Here, runner! Take these jolly Jacks up to the observation post.' He grinned again. 'If it's still there!'

Chesnaye waved his arm. 'Come on, lads!' He was too tired to look at them again. 'We'll rest when we get there!'

The subaltern called after them: 'Keep your heads down when you cross the first gully. There's a goddamned sniper about somewhere!'

They reached the end of the path and Chesnaye stared mesmerised at the small pile of corpses which littered the saucer-shaped arena at the opening of the gully. Not people, he thought. Just things. Khaki uniforms and discarded rifles. Heavy boots still stained from the beach, and fingers digging into the stony path as if to mark that last second of agony. Dried blood and staring

355

faces across which the flies busied themselves in their hundreds.

The runner gripped his rifle and pointed to a deep hole which had been cut into the sandy side of the rock 'Watch,' he said shortly. 'There's a fixed rifle somewhere up in that hill. The sniper fires it every so often in the hope some poor joker'll be crossing this spot. He's on to a good thing, really. It's the only path from our beach!'

There was a whiplash crack and the gravel around the hole jumped as if blasted from the inside. The bullet must have passed right through the piled corpses, for one of them turned on its side, like a sleeper who has been momentarily awakened by some unusual sound.

'Now!' The runner ducked his head and ran.

Chesnaye banged Pickles' arm. 'After him! Come on, the rest of you!'

Dazed and unsteady, the seamen scampered across the opening. Chesnaye watched them melt into the boulders beneath the rock shadow and then took a last look round. Nothing moved, yet he could feel the eyes of the nearest dead soldier watching him with fixed curiosity. Crack! The stones jumped again, and the runner called, 'Have a go for it, chum!'

Chesnaye wanted to walk calmly past the silent figures, to pass some confidence to his own small party, but as he stepped into the sun's glare he thought suddenly and clearly of that hidden marksman. Perhaps he was already shifting his rifle and even now had found Chesnaye's shoulders within his sights. He had another stark vision of his own body sprawled on top of the others, and he imagined that the corpse with the staring eyes would be glad. He ran.

Up and up they climbed, each step dislodging stones and stirring the dust. The *Saracen* seemed impossible to imagine, their mission merely a memory.

The observation post consisted only of a natural wall of boulders strewn deep into a long patch of the small, stunted trees which Chesnaye had seen from the cliff path. There was no shelter from the sun, and the stupendous view of a wide valley and the ridge beyond was swirling in a fantastic heat haze. The ridge flickered with scattered flashes as hidden marksmen crawled and out-manœuvred the enemy, whilst below him Chesnaye could see the clean scars in the hillside where soldiers had already dug their way

356

into a quickly arranged defensive trench which curved out of sight around the foot of the nearest hill.

The runner mopped his face and crouched gratefully behind the rocks. 'This is the narrowest part of the peninsula,' he said solemnly. 'That big formation of ridges to the left is Sari Bair, and over the ridge the Straits are only four miles away.' He smiled sadly. 'If we can break across this lot we'll cut the bastards in half!' He ducked instinctively as a shell droned overhead. 'Got to watch that sort,' he explained. 'Johnny Turk has got a big gun somewhere over that brown hillock. It fires shrapnel mostly. Got a lot of good cobbers this morning!' He stiffened. 'Ah, here comes your mate! I'd better be off to the command post.' With a cheerful nod he was off, his long legs taking him down the slope like a goat.

Chesnaye turned to face the young army officer with the blue and white brassard on his arm. The soldier was walking stiffly as if only just holding himself together. He looked at Chesnaye and they both stared at one another with disbelief.

Some of Chesnaye's despair seemed to melt. 'Bob Driscoll!' For a few moments he forgot his loneliness, the helpless feeling of loss, as he saw the weariness lift from the young officer's face.

They clasped hands and Driscoll said: 'Good to see you. It's been bloodly hell up here!'

Chesnaye crouched beside him as he told the seamen where to find some sort of shelter while he outlined his orders. Chesnaye felt a stab of uneasiness as he watched Driscoll's dust-stained face. The same mouth, the same grave eyes as Helen. It was unnerving.

Driscoll looked at Pickles. 'Right, then. My sappers have started to lay a wire to the beach. As soon as they've connected they'll send a morse signal to my chap here.' He gestured to a small soldier hunched over a jumble of wireless gear above which glittered a single transmitting key. 'You've got a range map of the area, but I expect we'll have to make a few alterations after the first shots.'

Chesnaye nodded, his mind clearing slightly as he collected his thoughts in time to Driscoll's calm voice. The monitor would fire from somewhere behind their spotting post, hidden by cliffs and hills, her presence only marked by the passage of her great fifteen-inch shells. It would be almost a blind shoot to start with, not much more than a compass bearing. Chesnaye and Pickles would watch and note the fall of shot and pass the alterations of range and deflection to the man with the morse key. The message would travel down the new, hastily laid wire to where Beaushears and his signalmen would be waiting at the foot of the cliffs to flag it to the watching *Saracen*.

Chesnaye swallowed hard. It sounded simple.

Driscoll was saying, 'You must be quite an important bloke, Dick!' His teeth shone in his grimed face. 'I'd have thought that your C.O.'d send someone a bit senior for this job!'

Pickles spoke for the first time. 'He was killed on the beach!' He still sounded shocked.

'Hmmm, I see.' Driscoll settled his elbow on the rocks and lifted his binoculars. 'Get your telescope rigged, Dick. You'll be able to see the Turkish battery if you watch long enough.' He winced as a shell passed overhead. 'That's a small chap. Mountain battery. The whole bloody place is alive with Turks, yet I've not seen one!' He laughed bitterly. 'Imagine that! Lost my sergeant this morning. Bang through the head. Yet we didn't see a bloody one!'

Chesnaye jammed the telescope carefully in position. In its enlarged eye the ridge seemed very near, and as he watched he saw the telltale drift of smoke as the hidden battery fired once again. On the hillside to his right the pale rocks leapt high into the air, and he imagined that he could feel the ground lurch against his crouching body.

Driscoll took off his cap and wiped his brow. 'Their shooting is improving, blast it!' He pointed at the hillside where some running soldiers had shown themselves for a few brief seconds. 'If the Turks can batter down our defences to the right of us we shall be in bad trouble. When night comes they'll try to cut down the valley and split this section in half.' He shook his head. 'Your men'll have to act like infantrymen if that happens!'

The linesman reported: 'We're through, sir! Contact with the beach signal party!'

Driscoll put on his cap. 'Well, Dick, it's all yours! Let's see what the Navy can do!'

Chesnaye peered through the telescope and watched the distant ridge. One real error and the shells would fall right on to the Australian positions below.

He gritted his teeth. 'Very well. Make a signal to *Saracen*. Commence first salvo when ready!'

His limbs seemed to grow tighter. He was committed.

Chapter Five

The Enemy

The *Saracen* shivered as the two big guns recoiled violently on their springs and the twin detonations blasted across the placid water as one. The sound was magnified and echoed by the craggy shoreline, so that the noise of the bombardment was constant and enfolded the quaking ship like a tropical storm. The two guns were angled at about forty-five degrees and pointed directly over the port rail. Already the smooth barrels were stained and blackened for several feet back from their muzzles, and the acrid cordite smoke hung over the monitor's bridge in an unmoving cloud.

Commander Godden coughed loudly into his handkerchief and then looked with distaste at the black stains on his uniform. 'How much longer, sir?'

Royston-Jones was squatting forward from his chair, elbows on the screen, his powerful glasses trained at some point along the coast. The light was beginning to fail, and there was a hint of purple shadowing across the jagged headland of Kaba Tepe. He shrugged and then jerked as the guns roared out once more.

The Yeoman moved dazedly across the bridge. His cap and shoulders were speckled with flaked paint brought down from the upper bridge by the constant gunfire and recoil. 'Signal from beach, sir. Cease fire. Turkish battery silenced and supporting infantry dispersed.'

Royston-Jones gestured impatiently. 'Very well. Cease firing and secure the guns.'

Muffled and indistinct within the great turret they could hear the tinny rattle of the 'Cease Fire' gong. The sweating, near-demented gunners would be almost too dazed to leave their stations after a day of continuous bombardment. The Quarters Officer, too, would have his work cut out to prepare the turret for immediate action if required.

Godden sighed with relief as the turret squeaked round until it was trained fore and aft, while the two guns drooped wearily to a horizontal position, their dark muzzles still smoking angrily.

'Signal from Flag, sir.' The Yeoman watched his captain warily. 'The bombarding squadron will withdraw at dusk to reinforce the southern landings. *Saracen* will maintain position in this sector until relieved or reinforced, with two destroyers in attendance. Every available effort to be made to evacuate wounded under cover of darkness.' The Yeoman looked up from his slate. 'End of signal, sir.'

Godden groaned. 'Left alone again! God, what do they think we are?' He glared round the bridge. 'What the hell are we going to do with a lot of wounded soldiers?'

Royston-Jones said flatly: 'We have a surgeon, I believe? Right, assemble all boats and prepare to carry out instructions.'

Lieutenant Travis climbed down from the compass platform and tested his legs. Gingerly he removed his ear-plugs and peered through the smoke. 'We *are* a bit vulnerable here, sir?'

Royston-Jones levered himself from the chair. 'Anchored fore and aft, you mean?'

'Well, yes, sir.'

'Quite so, Pilot.'

The ship had been virtually stationary during the bombardment, a sitting target had the Turks been able to bring a gun to bear. But protected by her own heavy fire and the close proximity of the high cliff she had remained undisturbed and wreathed in the smoke and fumes of her bombardment.

Royston-Jones shrugged. 'Nothing I can do about that. Must maintain a good position for Hogarth's sake. He did very well to all accounts.'

Travis smiled. 'So did the young snotties, sir.'

'Yes.' The Captain stretched like a small bird. 'Pity about Lieutenant Thornton. Good officer. Must write to his father. Such a waste.'

Hogarth appeared, gaunt but grinning. 'Guns secured, sir. Permission to fall out crews?'

Godden nodded, his eye on Royston-Jones. 'Very well.'

'Ah, Hogarth.' The Captain turned slowly. 'Quite a good shoot, I thought.'

Hogarth beamed. 'Eighty rounds of fifteen-inch.' He turned down his mouth. 'Mostly shrapnel, of course, but you can't have everything!'

Royston-Jones nodded gravely. 'I am sorry we hadn't enough

time to get you a more experienced spotting officer, but we were rather pressed!'

Hogarth smiled in spite of his weariness. While the whole ship had waited with frustration and anxiety for the landing party to get into position an unexpected Turkish battery had started to drop shells in the small bay, some very close to the monitor. The battery was shooting blind, but they must have known what they were after. A cheer had rippled throughout the ship when a signalman had excitedly reported contact with Midshipman Beaushears on the beach. Within a quarter of an hour the Turkish guns had fallen silent beneath a hailstorm of shrapnel and a few high-explosive shells for good measure. From that moment the *Saracen* had obediently hurled her shells inland, each salvo within minutes of the urgent signals from the beach.

Godden pulled at his lower lip. So Thornton was dead. But he wsa not the first casualty. Midshipman Maintland and his pinnace had been blasted to fragments by one stray shell from the shore even as he was returning to the ship. His crew of three had vanished also, and like a memorial the severed stem of the boat still drifted near the anchored monitor.

Pipes twittered below decks and within seconds the ship blossomed with seamen. Men who had stayed hidden and watchful behind guns and steel shutters, their ears deafened by the bombardment, scampered like children with a new-found freedom.

Royston-Jones frowned. 'Turn to both watches, Commander. Rig tackles for hoisting the wounded inboard, and have a constant guard rowed round the ship.' He yawned elaborately. 'Send for my steward. I'm going to my sea-cabin for a few moments.'

Godden fumed inwardly. That meant that he would have to stay on the bridge himself. He desperately needed to sit down, to have a drink, to think. The fierce and sudden events had left him feeling old and helpless, and the knowledge had almost unnerved him.

Hogarth was about to leave the bridge. 'Shall I signal for the shore party to return for the night?'

Godden tore his mind from his wave of self-pity. 'No. Let them bloody well stay there! It'll do 'em good!'

Hogarth showed his long teeth. 'I *say*, sir, bit savage, isn't it?'

But Godden had turned away, tired and fuddled like an

361

elephant at the end of a long charge. Already the voice-pipes were at it again, and far below the bridge the impatient, cutting voices of the petty officers could be heard mustering their men.

Hogarth shrugged and lowered himself over the screen. He paused for a moment and stared at the silent turret. It had been a triumph. From start to finish it had been a copybook bombardment. He thought of Godden's brooding face and wondered. Perhaps that generation were already too staid and steeped in peacetime routine to be able to accept this sort of warfare. Except the Captain, of course. Hogarth shook himself and continued his passage to the deck. That would be unthinkable.

The Quarters Officer, his round face blackened with powder, waited for him on the deck where seamen with hoses and scrubbers were at work removing the dirt of war. His teeth shone. 'Pretty good, eh, Guns?'

Hogarth smothered his sense of well-being and satisfaction and frowned. 'Bloody *awful*, Lucas!' He watched the other man's face lengthen. 'You'll have to do better tomorrow!'

Hogarth strode along the deck, his lips pursed in a silent whistle. It did not do to share one's laurels, he thought happily.

The tiny dugout was almost airless, so that Chesnaye awoke with the suddenness of a man suffocating in his sleep. For a few wild seconds he blinked at Robert Driscoll's bowed figure as he sat awkwardly beside a crude table of ammunition boxes, and saw that although the young soldier was staring fixedly at a worn map his eyes were empty and unfocused. The dugout measured less than eight feet by six, and the low roof, crudely supported by duck-boards and wooden props, sloped steeply at the rear, where Pickles lay in a restless bundle his head on his cap. A blanket covered the narrow entrance, and two candles, their air-starved flames short and guttering, cast weird and unnatural shadows around the hastily hewn walls. The place was crowded with ammunition cases, signals equipment and a pile of entrenching tools, and Chesnaye stared dazedly at each article in turn as understanding and memory returned to his sleep-fuddled brain.

Driscoll turned his head his eyes in shadow. 'You've been snoring for a good three hours,' he said quietly.

Chesnaye sat up, every bone protesting violently. The earth was cool and damp yet his face still tingled from the blazing

362

sunlight, and his eyes felt raw as if he had only just discarded the long spotting telescope.

He licked his dry lips. 'Have you just come in?'

Driscoll shrugged. 'An hour ago.' He fished in an open box at his feet. 'Have a drink?' He did not wait for an answer but carefully poured something into two enamel mugs. The liquid shone like amber in the candlelight. 'Brandy,' Driscoll said shortly. 'The last. From tomorrow we'll have rum like the lads. If we're lucky!'

Chesnaye swallowed a mouthful and felt the heat coursing through him. 'It's good,' he said.

'Carried it all the way from Gib.' Driscoll toyed with the empty bottle. 'God, what a long way off it seems!'

'Anything happening outside?' Chesnaye gestured with the mug towards the curtain.

'Quiet. A bloody wilderness!' He stood up, his shadow leaping across the dugout like a phantom. 'Come and take a look. I can't sleep.'

Together they ducked through the low entrance and stared up at the black hillside behind the makeshift trench. Somewhere up there the spotting post and its big boulders would be cool and deserted. But tomorrow . . . Chesnaye shuddered involuntarily.

Their feet scraped the pebbles as they walked, and occasionally Chesnaye caught sight of a dark figure huddled on the firing step, his shoulders and naked bayonet outlined against the stars. Other men lay unmoving like the dead, wrapped in greatcoats or blankets, their rifles nearby, but the war momentarily excluded from their minds.

Chesnaye had seen the stretchers going down the cliff path in the heat of the afternoon when there had been an ordered lull in the *Saracen*'s fire. Stretchers carried casually and clumsily by the Red Cross orderlies on their journey back from the vague front line. For the occupants of the stretchers were past care and beyond caring. So the living stayed in the trench and slept. Tomorrow the stretchers would take more of them away. For ever.

Chesnaye followed Driscoll as he climbed up on to the firing step near one of the sentries.

Driscoll spoke quietly, 'There's a wiring party out tonight.' His arm moved like a shadow. 'Somewhere in front of us. Nasty job. The ground's too hard for staples or digging –'

363

Chesnaye gasped as a bright blue flare erupted slightly to his left and hung in the air apparently unmoving.

'Turkish flare,' said Driscoll calmly.

The unearthly light turned the night to day, yet gave the surrounding landscape the colour and texture of something illusory. Small objects stood out starkly, whilst the hillside and the black gaping slit of trench mingled and joined as if covered by vapour.

Chesnaye felt naked and exposed as he stood on the firing step, the thin layer of sandbags barely reaching his chest. The flare glistened along the teeth of the wire and the blackened mounds which marked the edges of the day's shell craters. Out there, Chesnaye thought, men are crouching or standing, caught and mesmerised in the unblinking glare. Even the smallest movement could be fatal. The slightest moment of fear might bring instant attention from the enemy line. The flare dipped and died. Far to the right the dark sky flickered sullenly and then blossomed into a red glow. A rumble like thunder rolled around the gully and down into the deserted valley. It went on and on, so that Chesnaye found himself staring not at the glow but at the stars themselves, as if he expected to find the answer there.

'Somebody's getting it down south,' Driscoll commented. 'Night attack. It'll be our turn soon.' He stepped down into the trench and the rumble seemed to fade. 'How these Aussies can sleep!' His teeth gleamed faintly. 'They think it's a real joke to have the Navy *and* me here!'

Chesnaye smiled. 'What is your job exactly?'

'Well, apart from looking after you, I'm a jack of all trades. Communications, bit of sapping, all the usual stuff.' He sighed. 'It's a man's life in the modern Army!'

They re-entered the dugout, and Chesnaye lowered himself gingerly on to his pile of empty sandbags. 'A few more hours yet,' he said.

As he turned on to his side he heard Driscoll's voice, brittle and sharp. 'Are you in love with my sister, Dick?' Then, as Chesnaye tried to turn: 'No, don't look. Just answer.'

Chesnaye stared at the earth wall by his face. All at once he felt very calm. A girl he hardly knew, but remembered so clearly – 'Yes, Bob.'

There was a silence. The dugout vanished into darkness as the candles were extinguished, and Driscoll added quietly: 'Good. I just wanted to know.'

Chesnaye tried to laugh. 'Why did you ask?'

He heard the other man sliding into a corner of the dugout. 'I just wanted to know. Out here you need something to hold on to.'

Chesnaye lay for long afterwards, his eyes wide in the darkness, half listening to Driscoll's breathing and half to the sullen mutter of gunfire.

The first shell landed on the hillside above the trench even as the first light of dawn felt its way across the floor of the valley. Richard Chesnaye felt the dugout's floor buck beneath his back so that real pain shot through his limbs which seconds before had been relaxed in sleep. He awoke coughing and choking in a thick vapour of dust and smoke, his head reeling from the shattering explosion, as the blanket curtain across the entrance was ripped from its frame as if by an invisible hand.

The narrow confines of the trench were alive to running feet and loud cries, and even as Chesnaye struggled to his feet a second shell exploded somewhere overhead. His shocked hearing returned with startling suddenness so that he was all at once aware of a sharp, intermittent sobbing. He turned blinking in the dust to see Pickles on his hands and knees like a blinded animal, his round face wrinkled with shock and stark terror. For an instant he imagined that somehow Pickles had been hit by a splinter, but as he moved towards the scrabbling figure he heard Pickles scream: 'God, help me! I must get away!'

Chesnaye gripped his tunic and dragged him to his feet so that their faces were almost pressed together. They swayed in a struggling embrace as the dugout rocked and shivered and more explosions thundered along the side of the hill. Chesnaye felt suddenly calm and ice-cold. The sickness of fear and despair which had held him in the shock-wave of the first detonation had gone with the quickness of night, and in its place he could feel only a quiet desperation and an urgent need to get out of the quivering dugout.

A harsh Australian voice yelled above the bombardment: 'Keep down, you lot! They'll be comin' over after this!'

Pickles whimpered and pressed his head into Chesnaye's shoulder. 'I can't go on, Dick! *Please* don't make me!'

365

Chesnaye peered down at him, his racing thoughts torn between disgust and pity. He prised Pickles' fingers from his arm. 'Snap out of it, for heaven's sake! It's a bombardment. The Turks'll be coming over as soon as it drops!' He thought of Driscoll's calm words the night before. It'll be our turn next. Attack and counter-attack. The probe and the follow-up. Generals of both armies had tried it so often on the Western Front where a glut of man-power made up for their own lack of knowledge.

Pickles shrank back, small and shivering. 'I *won't* go. It's not fair!' He peered round the dust-covered floor. 'We shouldn't be here!' He stared fixedly at Chesnaye with something like hatred. 'We don't belong here at all!'

Chesnaye had a brief picture of the monitor, clean and untouched by all this disorder and sudden danger. Her guns would be helpless and impotent. Incapable of firing a single shot without the signals from the shore. From him.

He groped for his cap and then slung his telescope and leather case over his shoulder. 'We're going now, Keith,' he said quietly. 'They're depending on us.'

Without another word Pickles allowed himself to be led out into the distorted light of the trench. Dust and smoke were every-where, and the narrow, crudely hacked defences were filled with crouching khaki figures, their bodies and weapons cluttering the bottom of the trench in a dust-covered tangle. It seemed impos-sible to believe that only hours before this same place had been quiet and deserted, the only furtive movement being that of a hidden wiring party.

A tall Australian lieutenant, wild-eyed and unshaven, can-noned into Chesnaye as he peered up and behind the stone-strewn defences to the high rounded shoulder of the hill. Somewhere up there was the abandoned spotting post. Chesnaye felt his arm seized and watched the angry snapping movements of the soldier's mouth.

'You'd better get the hell out of it, sailor!' The lieutenant glanced briefly at Pickles' stricken face. 'The bastards will be having a go in a moment!' He held his breath and ducked as a shell screamed overhead and burst on the hillside.

The air seemed thick with whimpering, hissing splinters, and somewhere beyond the black smoke Chesnaye heard a chorus of unearthly screams. A loud, urgent voice called, 'Stretcher

366

bearers!' And the cry was carried on and away by other unknown, unseen men along the battered trench.

Chesnaye started as he felt sand running across his hand, and looked up to see a smoking slit in a nearby sandbag. The splinter must have missed him by inches.

He heard himself say: 'I must get up there! We're the only artillery support you've got in this sector!'

The lieutenant wiped his mouth with his hand. 'What about the rest of the Fleet?'

Chesnaye shrugged. 'Withdrawn. To support the other landing areas.'

The Australian laughed bitterly. 'Jesus, what a bloody mess!'

Nearby, a soldier was being sick while his comrades stared at him with empty, glassy eyes. They all seemed shocked and dazed by the shellfire, their faces devoid of expression.

'You'll never make it, sailor!' The Australian peered upwards, his eyes following Chesnaye's gaze. 'Johnny Turk knows what we're about. He's spraying the whole damned area with shrapnel and anything else he can get!' Angrily he added, 'I thought the Navy was supposed to have knocked out all their batteries?'

Chesnaye caught sight of Leading Seaman Tobias's tanned features at a bend in the trench and he beckoned him with sudden urgency. It was all quite clear what had to be done. In a strange voice he said: 'We're going up, Tobias. The second the barrage lifts we'll make a run for it!' He watched for some sign, but Tobias merely grunted. Chesnaye added, 'Get the rest of our men and check their rifles.'

Tobias pressed himself against the firing step as two shells tore into the hillside and sent a cascade of loose boulders clattering into the trench. A man cried out sharply, like an animal, and then fell silent. Tobias said thickly: 'Our lads won't like it, Mister Chesnaye. They're not soldiers.'

Chesnaye said savagely: 'They don't have to like it! Now go and tell them!'

He watched Tobias go, and then turned back to the lieutenant, who was crouching down and reading a signal pad which a panting runner had just delivered.

He looked up at Chesnaye's grim features. 'Worse than I thought. The Turks have overrun Hill Seventy-Five. The whole of the right flank is a bloody shambles.'

367

Chesnaye started to grope for his range map and then remembered. Hill Seventy-Five was directly on their right, the end-piece of a long ridge of narrow hills. The hill above this trench was the only one left in a commanding position now. If that fell, the way to the beach would be cut, and the enemy might roll up the flimsy defences like a carpet. He swallowed hard. 'It's as I said, then?'

The Australian eyed him with surprise. 'Well, it's been nice knowing you, kid!' He broke off, choking as an impenetrable cloud of smoke billowed round the curve in the trench. 'What th' hell?'

A brown-faced sergeant pushed his way through the crouching soldiers. His angry eyes swept across the two midshipmen and settled on his own officer. 'Bastards 'ave set the bloody gorse on fire, sir!' He waved his rifle as if it were a mere toy. 'The whole hillside is alight!'

The lieutenant shrugged. 'Accident or design, it's a cunning move. Our lads will be half blind in a second!'

Tobias appeared, followed by a bearded A.B. called Wellard. 'Ready, sir.' As if in response to his words, the barrage dropped, the echoes passing down the valley like a receding typhoon.

All at once it was very still, and Chesnaye could feel his legs quivering violently. He was almost afraid to move lest they collapsed under him. He looked at Pickles, and when he saw the naked fear on his face he felt suddenly unsure and alone.

Wellard spat into the sand at his feet. 'Not our bloody job!' He jerked his head at the rising pall of black smoke. 'Let's make for the beach now!'

Chesnaye knew that the other seamen were behind Wellard, hidden by the curve in the trench. They would be listening. Waiting. Pickles was useless, and Tobias was an impassive neutral. Either way it did not seem to matter to him.

Chesnaye felt let down and vaguely betrayed. He heard himself say sharply, 'Say "sir" when you address me, Wellard!'

The seaman plucked at his black beard and squinted at the midshipman. 'Aye, aye, *sir*!' He looked sideways at Tobias. 'Well, Hookey, don't you think it's bloody daft?'

Tobias picked up his rifle and stared at it as if for the first time. He glanced up quickly at Chesnaye's desperate face. 'Everythin' is daft 'ere, Wellard!' He gave a brief grin. 'Now do as you're bloody well told and get ready for the off!'

Chesnaye opened his mouth to speak but was almost deafened

by a shrill whistle blast at his side. The Australian officer seemed suddenly tall and remote, his features a mask of fierce determination. A bright whistle gleamed in one hand, while with the other the man groped at the flap of his holster. 'Come on, you Aussie bastards!' His voice cut across the encroaching rattle of small-arms like a saw. 'Stand to! Face your *front!*'

Obediently and dazedly, like animals, the soldiers came alive and began to scramble on to the crudely hewn firing step.

The lieutenant stood down in the trench for a while longer, his eyes darting along the bowed soldiers, the levelled rifles. 'Right, fix bayonets!' A hissing, metallic rattle rippled along the thin khaki barrier, and Chesnaye watched fascinated as the long blades were snapped into position and then vanished over the sandbagged barrier.

The lieutenant coughed in the smoke and then spun the chamber of his revolver. 'Best get going, sport. Up the hill like a Queensland rabbit, and the best of luck!'

A great sullen bellow of sound, like nothing Chesnaye had heard, echoed over the crouching heads on the firing step. He tried to place it. The baying of hounds, the thunder of surf. It was impossible to describe it.

The soldier said sharply: 'Here they come! Calling on their god to protect 'em!' He pushed his way up beside his men, the sailors already forgotten.

Chesnaye ran quickly to the rear of the trench and vaulted over the loose stones. It was now or never. A second longer and that dreadful, booming storm of voices would have held him powerless to move. As if from miles away he heard the lieutenant shout: 'One hundred yards, five rounds rapid . . . *Fire!*' The air jumped again to the savage bark of rifles, whilst from somewhere on each flank came the searching, vicious rattle of machine-guns.

Chesnaye found his feet and began to run. Behind him he sensed rather than heard the thudding footfalls of his small party. The summit of the hill seemed far away, and as he ducked behind a natural wall of boulders Chesnaye could see the advancing barrier of short angry flames where the gorse had been set alight.

The valley was hidden in smoke, yet Chesnaye could imagine the enemy already within a hundred yards of the defence line. They must be up to the wire, even across it! He heard himself cry, 'We must get there in time!'

369

A seaman started to overtake, his boots and gaiters scything through the sparse stubble with all the power he could muster. The machine-guns chattered louder, and with sudden panic Chesnaye realised that the new sounds were coming from the flank, from the other hill. Hoarsely he yelled: 'Down! Get *down!*'

The seaman who had passed him peered back, his teeth bared with the determination of his own efforts to reach shelter. 'Get down yerself!' He turned to run on, but was plucked from his feet as the machine-gun found him. The corpse rolled down the hillside, followed and flayed by the hidden gun. The running man changed to a corpse even as the others watched. From a man to a rolling thing. From a recognisable, breathing companion to a tattered, scarlet bundle.

Tobias wriggled to Chesnaye's side. 'They've got us pinned down, sir.'

Chesnaye shut his ears to the sounds behind him, the bark and rattle of guns, the harsh, desperate voices and the clatter of rifle bolts. He must think. He had to decide. Like a wind the machine-gun fanned the air above his head, and he heard his men cursing and praying as they dug their fingers into the hillside.

Chesnaye could feel the early sunlight already warm against his neck, and saw a small beetle scurrying across the ground near his cheek.

He looked at the dirt on his hands and the scratches on the skin where he had torn at the loose stones to get clear of the trench. Perhaps the others were right. It was a futile gesture which had already cost a seaman's life. But he remembered the soldiers who were fighting for their lives with the blind desperation of all front-line troops. Not knowing what was happening or even why they were there. For all they knew, the whole front might have collapsed, with the enemy already encircling them for final destruction. He shook his head as if to clear his tortured mind.

Eventually he said: 'We'll work our way round the side of that small rise in the ground, Tobias. Once there we'll be under cover for a bit. Then we'll take the last hundred yards in short stages. He gripped the other man's sleeve. 'But we can't hang about!'

The journey to the top was a nightmare. By a twist of fate it was the smoke from the burning hillside which saved them. The enemy machine-gunners fired long bursts through the drifting black cloud, but it was difficult for them to range their sights on

370

the long slope, and so, gasping and sweating, the two midshipmen and five seamen found themselves once again in the spotting post. The cleft in the rock was scarred and disfigured by shellfire, and the wall of boulders was scattered amidst the black score marks of the Turkish barrage.

There were three soldiers waiting by the sandbagged wireless position. One was dead, one was white-faced and wounded in both legs, whilst the third sat by the wireless smoking a cigarette. The latter nodded companionably. ' 'Mornin', gentlemen! I suppose you're ready to start?'

It was nearly half an hour before Chesnaye could plot some idea of the change in the enemy positions and from which direction the main assault was being directed. The smoke eddied and swam across the valley, trapped and demented, its colours changing to the flicker of countless rifles, and later to the brightly flashing grenades. Once there was a brief gap in the smoke, and Chesnaye lost valuable seconds as he stared mesmerised at the battle which raged below.

For the first time he saw the enemy. Not as individuals, but as a vast surging throng, colourless and without apparent shape. It broke across the narrow strip of wire, while the chattering machine-guns mowed down rank after rank, and left the scattered remnants hanging on the gleaming barbs, twisting and kicking. Still they came on, until the soldiers below could no longer fire, but leapt from their trenches to meet them on the parapets face to face. Chesnaye saw the madly struggling throng sway back and forth, while the flash of bayonets brought colour to the shrill cries and desperate movements of the battle.

Chesnaye caught his breath as a body of Turkish infantry overflowed the trench and began to run madly up the side of the hill itself. Another machine-gun came into play, and with systematic care cut the small figures to shreds and left them scattered around the body of the dead seaman. Chesnaye also saw the Australian lieutenant, hatless and with his revolver held like a club, fighting astride a pile of corpses, while dark-faced Turks closed in from every side. Even as reinforcements surged along the shattered trench Chesnaye saw the flash of yet another bayonet and watched sickened as the lieutenant screamed and fell clutching his stomach.

Behind him he heard the army wireless operator say, 'Contact with the beach party, sir!'

371

He had already scribbled the signal and range orders on his pad, and blindly he passed it to the man's eager hand.

How could he be sure he had done the right thing? There was no way of knowing in this confusion. Lieutenant Thornton would have known, but he was dead. Where was Robert Driscoll? He would have known too. Chesnaye peered through the smoke as the morse key began to stammer. Driscoll was probably down there, dead with the others in that bloody carnage, where terror was making men fight like wild beasts. It had all seemed so easy. An order. An alteration perhaps, but then the big guns would do the work cleanly and impartially. That was not war at all. *This* was real. Where you could see your enemy first as a living mass which came on in spite of everything until it was broken into individuals and flesh and blood. Until it was too close even for bullets, and you could feel his desperate breath on your face even as you twisted and struggled to drive home your bayonet.

The Turkish assault faltered and swayed back from the trench. In an instant the Australian infantry were at them once more. Down the slope from the parapet the battle-crazed Australians surged in pursuit, only to be met by a savage cross-fire of well-sited machine-guns. As officers fell they were replaced by sergeants. Within an hour the sergeants were dead and junior corporals found themselves in command.

At the head of the valley, where Turkish reinforcements waited for the order to advance, the sky was bright and clear of smoke. It looked at peace and beyond reach through Chesnaye's telescope. Then a wind seemed to ruffle the hillsides and the end of the valley appeared to fade within a shadow. Chesnaye watched the sudden change with cold satisfaction. The *Saracen's* first salvo had landed.

Tobias rolled on to his side and looked at the sky as the big shells sighed overhead. 'Just in time,' he said at length. He glanced quickly at Chesnaye's drawn face. 'You've done a nice job, sir.'

Chesnaye did not speak. He looked down at the shell-battered defences, the scattered corpses where here and there a hand or a foot still moved as if its owner believed in the right to survive. A bugle blared, and the Australians fell back, some still shooting, others dragging wounded comrades behind them. He could see the white brassards and red crosses moving up the line, the limp

372

stretchers with their telltale scarlet stains. He saw it all with the patient horror of a man looking at some terrible panorama of death. Men without arms or faces, men who ran in circles blinded and lost, and others who whimpered like idiots until led away. Even the dead were without dignity, he thought. Ripped and torn, grinning and grimacing, broken and forgotten, their blood mingled with that of the enemy.

Chesnaye retched and leaned his head against a sun-warmed boulder.

A runner panted up the hill, his jacket soaked in sweat. 'Cease fire, sir!' He handed Chesnaye a grimy signal. 'Message from Brigade.' He glanced at the dead soldier without curiosity. 'This section will re-group and reinforcements are already movin' up!' He removed the bayonet from his rifle and stooped to wipe it on the gorse at Chesnaye's feet.

Chesnaye noticed for the first time that the blade was patterned with bright red droplets. He stared, fascinated at the soldier's lined face. 'How was it?'

The man took a cigarette gratefully from Tobias and sucked in slowly. As he breathed out his limbs began to quiver, and Tobias turned away as if ashamed to watch.

The soldier wiped his eyes with his cuff. 'Christ, it was awful. Lost me two mates, y'see.' He stared blindly at the bayonet. 'It was just a bloody slaughter!' He swallowed hard and then said harshly, 'Thanks fer the fag.'

They watched him go, loping down the hillside. A small individual who for a brief instant had detached himself from the mass.

The Australians counter-attacked in the late afternoon. The *Saracen*, this time supported by a far-off battleship and two destroyers, laid down a barrage which held the Turks in hiding until it was too late to stem their advance. By nightfall the enemy had lost Hill Seventy-Five and a mile and a half of the valley. Between dawn and sunset three thousand dead and wounded marked the rate of advance, but when the stars showed themselves above the highest ridge the new line was established.

Chesnaye followed his men down the hillside, his jacket open to the waist, the night air cold across his damp skin. He did not turn his head as he passed the shadowy shapes which littered the ground and lay inside the broken trench itself.

373

He was ordered to return to the beach and find his way back to the monitor. He still found it hard to believe that there was to be a break in this new world of noise and suffering.

A figure loomed from the darkness and a groping hand found his. Chesnaye swayed and heard Driscoll's voice say: 'I'm glad you made it, Dick! You did damned well!'

Even on the beach amongst the groaning lines of wounded which seemed to stretch into the infinity of the night Chesnaye could still feel the warmth of that handshake, and understood how the soldier with the reddened bayonet must have felt when he had lost his friends. His thoughts were becoming jumbled and confused, and he felt Tobias's hard hand at his elbow.

'You all right, sir?' The man's face seemed to swim against the stars.

Tobias added: 'I can see a boat comin', sir. That'll be fer us!'

He spoke with the fervent hope of a man lost in an unfamiliar world, but as the cutter moved smartly inshore and the rowers tossed their oars, Chesnaye was suddenly reluctant to leave.

He fell into the boat, and the last thing he heard before exhaustion claimed him was the voice of one of his remaining seamen.

'Move over there, lads! Let 'im sleep!' Then in a voice tinged with awe: 'Proper little tiger is Mister Chesnaye! You should 'ave *seen* 'im!'

Chapter Six

Driftwood

Richard Chesnaye shielded his eyes from the sun's glare and peered astern. Like the purple back of a basking whale the island of Mudros was already merging with the shimmering horizon, its shape distorted by the heat haze. The sun was high overhead, and on the monitor's upper deck there seemed to be no cover at all in spite of the narrow awnings, so that Chesnaye's small working party toiled half-heartedly, their paint-brushes hardly moving across the shield of one of the small quick-firing guns below the tall funnel. Soon they would be released from the pretence of working and go below to their stuffy messdeck and the tempting tot of watered rum. Then, lunch over, they would once more be kept active for a few hours while the ship moved slowly and ponderously along her set course. Back to the Peninsula. Back to the bombardments and the mounting frustrations.

Chesnaye winched as a shaft of sunlight seared his neck like a flame. The ship was so slow, so completely airless that every movement was an effort. It seemed incredible to believe that it was less than three weeks since he had left the darkened beach and found his way back to the *Saracen*. They had weighed anchor almost at once and returned to Mudros, and there unloaded the wretched cargo of wounded soldiers. Some had died on the way, and the Captain had buried them at sea. April had given way to May, and the probing sun left no room for corpses in an overcrowded ship of war.

Chesnaye could not remember when he had enjoyed a full night's rest. There always seemed to be some crisis or other. Loading stores and ammunition from the ubiquitous lighters, the decks of which still bore the dark stains of wounded men, and then out again at dawn to take the monitor alongside the deep-bellied oiler to replenish the half-empty tanks.

Tempers became frayed, seamen overstayed their miserable shore-leaves, and were punished with the same weary resignation which had made them rebel in the first place.

The monitor had returned briefly to the Peninsula and had carried out two minor bombardments in conjunction with a battleship and some destroyers. No spotting party had been landed, but Chesnaye had stood on the upper bridge, his plugged ears conscious of the angry barrage, yet his mind constantly with the other world beyond the glittering shoreline and craggy hills. He imagined the tiny, antlike soldiers and the persistent probing and attacking which was going on beyond the range of his telescope. He remembered that last run up the hillside when the seaman had been cut down by the machine-gun. When he had pressed his face into the ground and seen the small beetle scurrying through the sand. Now distance had made the armies into insects, but this time he could understand their suffering.

The *Saracen* had waddled back to Mudros and disgorged another three hundred broken bodies, taken on more stores and was returning once more.

It seemed incredible to understand that the daring and desperate attack on the Dardanelles had been forced to a bloody stalemate. Day after day ships of the Fleet patrolled the slender Peninsula, like dogs worrying an aged deer, yet nothing happened to break the deadlock. Eighteen battleships, twelve cruisers, twenty destroyers and eight submarines, plus an armada of auxiliaries had pressed home attacks, blockaded, and covered innumerable landings, yet still the well-defended Turks held their own, and hit back again and again.

In the midst of it all the *Saracen*, unlovely and unloved, moved alone. Too slow to work with the destroyers, and too ungainly to keep with the battleships, she wandered from one allotted task to the next. Even the ship's company sensed their situation, and the Captain had ordered that no matter what else happened they were to be kept busy at all times and the ship maintained at a level of peacetime discipline.

There had been one break in the ship's misfortune, however. Mail had awaited the *Saracen* in Mudros, and Chesnaye had received two letters from his mother. His father was apparently ill, brought on by his mounting depression and his inability to return to active duty. Between the lighter comments his mother made about the weather and the state of the garden Chesnaye could sense her despair, and he was reminded of the great distance which separated him from his home. He had written a carefully worded reply, and even more thoughtfully had sent a letter to Helen. He had used the Gibraltar address, and wondered if it would ever reach her. Already he was regretting the impulse. Afraid she would not answer. More afraid of what her reply might be.

A bugle blared 'Up Spirits!' In a moment the sickly smell of rum would float along the spotless decks and the seamen would stir themselves like old cavalry horses at the sound of a trumpet.

Chesnaye yawned. 'Right, start securing that paint.'

The seamen did not even glance at him. They were lost in their own thoughts.

Soon it would be time, too, to return to the gunroom, to Lukey's rasping patter as he served another unsuitable meal of hot stew or leathery beef. Pringle would be sitting, glowing with health and vigour, at the head of the table, eating with obvious relish, while the midshipmen sat immersed in thought or hoping that their over-lord would fall down dead. There was more room in the small mess now. With Maintland killed, and the overhanging threat of more action, the midshipmen seemed to draw further apart, a situation encouraged by Pringle, who took every opportunity to remark on Maintland's absence, as if to watch their reactions, or perhaps, as Chesnaye suspected, to show them how hardened and unmoved he was himself.

But the most changed member of the mess was Pickles. Morose and stiff-faced, he had borne Pringle's taunts without flinching, as if he had completely withdrawn into himself. Once Pringle had remarked loudly that he had heard some story that a certain snotty had lost his nerve ashore on the Peninsula and had broken down in front of the men. Pringle had yawned elaborately and added, 'Just the thing one might expect from a poor type with no breeding!'

Chesnaye had tried to ignore the constant friction in the gun-room, but it was beginning to wear him down. He noticed that Pringle was careful to be polite to him in front of the others, and had once seen the flash of anger in Pickles' eyes.

To Pringle it was just a game. But it could not last under these conditions.

Almost guiltily he heard Pringle's voice at his side. 'What the hell are these loafers doing? Who gave you permission to pack up your gear?' Pringle's question was directed at the bearded A.B. Wellard.

The seaman stiffened. 'Mister Chesnaye, sir.'

377

Pringle showed his teeth. 'Well?' He looked at Chesnaye without expression.

Chesnaye shrugged wearily. 'They were finished. There's only a minute or so to go.'

Pringle turned back to the watching men. 'Never take advantage of an inexperienced officer! Now take the lids off those paint tins and get back to work!'

'We've finished!' Wellard glared from beneath his shaggy brows.

A bugle blared sharply, but Pringle tapped the side of his nose with his finger and said pleasantly: 'Well you can do fifteen minutes' extra work to make up for your laziness. *Now get to it!*'

He stood aside and said quietly to Chesnaye: 'They're an idle lot of swine. You've got to keep them at it *all* the time.'

'I don't agree.' Chesnaye's cheeks were still smarting from Pringle's behaviour in front of his own men.

'Well, of course *you* wouldn't!' Pringle rocked back on his heels. 'You think that by being slack with 'em you'll win their hearts. Imagine you'll be their little idol, eh?' His face darkened. 'Remember what I said. They're the scum of the earth, and only understand firmness and discipline!'

Chesnaye felt the heat beating across his neck. 'I think I'll make up my own mind about that, if you don't object?'

Pringle paused as he turned to leave, his eyes red and angry. 'I *thought* so! Like father like son, eh? No wonder your old man got the bloody sack!'

The world seemed to explode around Chesnaye, and he was only half aware of the suddenly watchful seamen, the sun on his neck and the rasp of Pringle's words. He was conscious too of the pain in his knuckles and the jarring shock which travelled up his right arm.

His vision cleared just as quickly, and he found himself staring down at Pringle's upturned face. Pringle was holding his mouth, and his fingers were bright red with blood.

The seaman Wellard put down his brush and said flatly: 'Christ! 'E's 'it the sod!'

Captain Lionel Royston-Jones bit his lower lip to control the rising irritation he always felt when watching Holroyd, the Paymaster, at work. The latter was perched on the edge of one of the

Captain's pale green chairs in the spacious day-cabin below the monitor's quarterdeck, and as usual was nervously absorbed in the endless matter of ship's business. Royston-Jones stared slowly round his wide cabin, crossing his legs as he did so to force himself to relax. All forenoon he had made himself listen to Holroyd, the session interrupted at irregular intervals by the various heads of departments as the *Saracen* moved slowly towards the enemy coast. Soon it would be time to leave these comfortable quarters once more and return to the spartan restrictions of bridge and sea-cabin, but for the moment it was good to get away from the others and the pressing problems of command.

Here at least he felt almost remote from the rest of the ship, his comfortable chair placed barely feet from the ship's stern. The sea noises were indistinct and muffled, and even the regular bugle-calls were far off and impersonal. Royston-Jones scowled as if to dismiss the hint of sentiment, and Holroyd, a bald, worried little man, happening to glance at his captain at that particular moment, wilted accordingly.

Royston-Jones let his pale eyes drift towards one of the cabin's gleaming brass scuttles. The deep blue of the horizon line mounted the circular scuttle, paused, and then receded with the same patient slowness, while the hidden sun played across the sea's numberless mirrors and threw a dancing pattern across the cabin's low deckhead, where a wide-bladed fan revolved to give an impression of coolness.

An original oil-painting of King George made a tasteful patch of colour against the white bulkhead, and beyond a nearby door the Captain knew that MacKay, his personal steward, would be hovering and waiting for the bell. It was getting near time for a sherry. A quiet lunch, and then – Royston-Jones looked up irritated again as Holroyd gave his nervous cough and handed some papers across for signature.

'All complete, sir.' The little man blinked and watched anxiously as the Captain began to read. He never signed anything without reading it at least twice, and this fact did little to help the Paymaster's fading confidence.

'This war will be bogged down with paper before long!' Royston-Jones reached for his pen which stood exactly upright in a silver inkstand fashioned in the shape of a dolphin. On the stand's base a well-polished inscription stated: 'Presented to

Sub-Lieutenant Lionel Royston-Jones, H.M.S. *Jury* 1893, Singapore Fleet Regatta.'

The private thoughts of sherry and seclusion vanished as Royston-Jones suddenly remembered that Commander Godden was waiting to see him. He toyed with the idea of keeping him waiting a little longer, but then decided against it. Almost savagely he wrote his signature on six documents and replaced the pen. Holroyd scrambled to his feet, his face filled with obvious relief. Royston-Jones almost smiled when he imagined what the Paymaster would think or say if he knew that his captain was so short-sighted that most of the documents were a meaningless blur. For reading Royston-Jones wore a pair of narrow, steel-rimmed glasses, but few had seen them. MacKay, his steward, was used to finding his master in the privacy of the day-cabin, glasses perched on nose, a favourite book of Shakespeare plays on his crossed legs. MacKay kept the secret well. For that reason he had been with the Captain for many years.

Royston-Jones jabbed the pantry bell, and added as an after-thought, 'Some of those victualling returns look a bit casual, Holroyd.' He watched the panic mounting with cold satisfaction. 'Check them again yourself.'

'Aye, aye, sir.' The wretched man almost bowed himself out of the cabin.

MacKay appeared with a tiny silver tray. On it was a decanter, one glass and a dog-like arrowroot biscuit.

Royston-Jones sighed. 'Get another glass, and ask the Commander to step in.'

What was wrong this time? he wondered. Some wretched non-sense about a split awning, or a petty officer sick with piles. What a small man Godden seemed to carry about inside that great body. Royston-Jones detested unnecessary size, and overweight officers were a particular hate of his. Perhaps that was why he never had got off to a good start with Godden. He knew it was more than that but even so . . .

Godden entered the cabin and waited in silence until MacKay had glided back to his pantry.

Royston-Jones felt his foot beginning to tap. Sharply he said, 'Put your cap down and have a sherry.'

'If you don't mind, sir,' Godden looked grim, 'this is rather serious.'

'Yes, I *do* mind.' Royston-Jones sipped at his sherry and then banged the glass down. It was all spoilt. 'Well, spit it out, man!'

'I think we have a court martial on our hands, sir.' He swallowed. 'Sub-Lieutenant Pringle has been assaulted!'

The Captain said slowly, 'And the rating responsible?'

'It was an officer, sir. Midshipman Chesnaye!'

Royston-Jones stood up and walked to the nearest scuttle. For a moment longer he watched the handful of white gulls which still followed the ship's slow course. Wheeling and dipping they added to the impression that the *Saracen* was unmoving.

'I see.' Over his shoulder he asked, 'And what have you done about it, may I ask?'

'I have sent Chesnaye to his quarters. Pringle is outside. I would have brought him earlier, sir, but his lip was still bleeding.'

Half to himself Royston-Jones said coldly, 'I would have guessed that Pringle's mouth would be implicated!' He swung round. 'This is very serious, you realise that, don't you?' He waited, the absurdity and at the same time the danger of the situation making his cheeks burn with two small spots of colour. '*Well*?' He saw Godden jump as his voice echoed round the cabin. 'Is that all?'

'I thought you should know, sir –' Godden's face looked shiny with sweat.

'You did, did you?' The long-pent-up anger was coursing through Royston-Jones like fire. For a little while longer he would give way to it. 'If there had been no war, Commander, you would have been happier, I expect? The usual sickening round of events, regattas, fleet balls, admiral's inspections which end in a sea of gin and broken reputations. I can just imagine it!'

'That's not fair, sir!' Godden was quivering with sudden rage.

'Don't you dare to interrupt! It's a pity you can't show the same energy for your duty as you display in righteous indignation!' He took a few quick paces. 'The Commander's work in a ship is to present that ship as a working concern to his captain. You are not even near that standard. You are a passenger and almost a liability!'

Godden's face was white. 'Now look here, sir! How could I have prevented this trouble?'

The Captain's eyes glittered in a shaft of yellow sunlight. '*This* trouble! I have carried you through trouble of one sort or another since you came aboard! I have your measure now! You want *me* to act over this so-called assault so that you can sink back into your old role of jovial dependability, the friendly buffer between the downtrodden wardroom and the tyrannical captain, right?' He screwed up his face to watch Godden's reactions. 'I am telling you now, I am sick of your side-stepping! And I will not tolerate it!'

Godden did not speak, but looked as if he was going to be sick.

Almost as calmly Royston-Jones said: 'This is war. Nothing like it has ever struck the Royal Navy before. We have been unchallenged, untouched, for over a hundred years, and now the battle is joined. All of us have been trained for war by men who have known only peace and frivolous security.' He waved his hand with sudden bitterness. 'Take this ship, *my* ship. She is entirely new, a fresh weapon in a strange war. And why do you suppose I got command, eh? I will tell you. Because some pompous popinjays at the Admiralty are afraid that the *Saracen* will be a white elephant, a failure. So they must have a scapegoat, just in case!' He tapped his breast. 'Me! A good captain with a blameless record, so that the ship can be given every chance of success. But also a man without connections or influence, one who is expendable.' He gave a small smile. 'Your expression has changed, Commander! From guilt to anger, and from anger to shocked disbelief. Well, I'll not continue along these lines. There is work to be done.' He fixed Godden with a cold stare, unwinking and devoid of pity. 'But I can assure you that I intend this ship to succeed if I have to run her ashore to prove her worth!'

Weakly Godden said, 'And Chesnaye, sir?'

Completely controlled and calm, Royston-Jones turned the arrowroot biscuit between his neat fingers. 'Ah yes, Chesnaye.' Very quietly, 'What do you suggest?'

Shocked and miserable at the assault, Godden's words tumbled out in a confused heap. 'Well, sir, Pringle's a bit of a bully, I know that. But Chesnaye struck him, and there was one seaman at least who witnessed it!'

One word. 'Who?'

'Able Seaman Wellard.'

'Ah, that bearded oaf.' He nodded, the man's face registering like a faded photograph. 'Good boxer. Won a cup for the ship, I believe?'

'Yes, sir.'

'And you think that Pringle's majesty should be upheld?'

382

'Well, I'm sorry for the midshipman, sir, but we all had to go through it in our time.'

'That doesn't make it right, Commander. However, it must be stopped, you are correct there at least. Find out the reason for the assault –'

Godden interrupted quickly, 'Pringle made some remark about Chesnaye's father –'

'What?' Royston-Jones stared at Godden with amazement. 'Why didn't you say so?'

'Well, sir, I mean – it was true what he said –'

'I can imagine.' The Captain turned back to the quiet sea beyond the scuttle. 'I knew Chesnaye's father. He was a good officer. Perhaps *he* was a scapegoat too. But that does not alter the fact that young Chesnaye is now the only officer with battle experience of spotting ashore.' He laughed sharply and without humour. 'Laughable, isn't it? A young midshipman, a mere boy, and a valuable asset already!' He rubbed his palms together. 'And as for Wellard seeing the incident, I will leave him to you. But this war is getting to be a complex and serious affair. I will not jeopardise the use and safety of my ship because Able Seaman Wellard has had his illusions shattered. I doubt very much if he has *ever* respected a piece of gold lace!'

'I see, sir.' Godden's voice sounded strangled. 'And Chesnaye?'

'I will see both officers separately. In the Dog Watches sometime today. You arrange it. It will give them time to fret a little!'

'Anything more, sir?'

Royston-Jones picked up the glass and rolled its slender stem between his fingers. 'Oh, one thing, yes. We have been ordered to carry out a landing and a bombardment, south of the Anzac beaches.'

'Who are we supporting, sir?'

Royston-Jones waited a little longer. 'We will be alone, Commander!' He turned to watch the effect of his words. 'Quite alone. It seems that one or more U-boats have been making their way through the Mediterranean in this direction for some time. Their lordships in all their wisdom have decided to withdraw the battleship *Queen Elizabeth* and certain other units as soon as the Germans get too near.' He allowed the sherry to moisten his lower lip. 'So everybody else can apparently go hang!'

*   *   *

Lieutenant Hogarth, the Gunnery Officer, lifted his powerful night glasses and took a long look across the *Saracen*'s blunt bows. From the upper bridge he had an uninterrupted view of the whole ship, and although it was well past midnight, with the Middle Watch settled and composed at their stations, the sky seemed to lack depth, so that it merged with the sea in a transparent, vapourous obscurity. Untroubled by wind, the sea's surface around the labouring ship was flat and glittering in long oily swells, whilst around the monitor's rounded stern only a hint of froth broke the pattern and betrayed the power of the thrashing screws below.

Hogarth ran his eye quickly around the bridge to ensure that the lookouts were indeed doing their job. Somewhere on the maindeck Sub-Lieutenant Pringle, his assistant, was doing his rounds and would soon join him, his restlessness breaking the quiet of the watch.

He stiffened as a figure detached itself from the chartroom and glided to the front of the bridge. It was not the Captain, but Travis, the Navigator. Hogarth relaxed.

'Can't you sleep, Pilot?'

'Just checking my charts.'

They both spoke in a semi-whisper, their voices merging with the creaking of steel and spars. At night the ship always seemed to be more powerful, more overbearing.

Hogarth yawned elaborately. 'Ship's company all tucked up for the night. Just the poor bloody watchkeepers alive!' He peered at his companion. 'We'll be up to the coast before dawn then?'

'Running, or rather *crawling* to schedule!' Travis sounded bitter. 'I'll be glad when we get started.'

Hogarth nodded, and adjusted his meticulous mind to the problems the next day would offer him. 'A quick bombardment, rush in the landing parties, and then rapid fire on the enemy's flank. Sounds easy, eh?'

'I'm sick of it all!' Travis gripped the screen with frustration. 'The whole operation is going rotten on us!'

'Well, I would rather be in the old Keppel's Head in Pompey *naturally*, but as we are involved I don't see what we can do about it!' Hogarth shifted uneasily. Travis was too much of a thinker. That was bad.

Travis shrugged. 'It's better for you. You are so wrapped up with your damned gunnery you don't have time to contemplate the rest of the business. *I* on the other hand have had to sit and listen at every conference the Old Man has attended. God! The people at Whitehall must be raving mad!'

'How d'you mean?' Hogarth did not really care, but he was interested in Travis's sudden display of emotion.

'Well, you know that Fisher has resigned from First Sea Lord?' He did not wait for a reply. 'And Churchill is being hauled over the coals about the hold-ups and disasters out here?'

'What of it?'

'It means in simple language that the powers-that-be have lost interest in a quick victory. For all we know they may have written off the whole operation already!'

'Oh for God's sake!' Hogarth broke off as a telephone buzzed in the darkness by his elbow. In a strained voice he said into the mouthpiece, 'Upper bridge, Officer of the Watch speaking.'

Far below Pringle's voice replied: 'Rounds completed. All correct, sir.'

'Very well.' He dropped the handset and said absently, 'I think this assault business is much more serious.'

Travis turned away. 'You would!'

'There's no need to be like that, old man.'

Travis moved closer and tried again. 'Look, just think about what I've been saying. If the Gallipoli landings have been a waste of time, we should know about it. You can't just leave a whole army to rot away and do nothing!'

'I have always done my duty and nothing more,' Hogarth answered stiffly.

He sounded so hurt and pompous that Travis laughed, his teeth white against his beard. 'Well done, Guns! Spoken like a true gentleman!'

Hogarth did not smile. 'No, seriously, I feel very strongly about that. We must maintain our standards even in war. I think the Captain was wrong to ignore Chesnaye's behaviour, even if Pringle *is* a fool.'

'He's that, all right!'

'But he must be upheld. The Commander is quite right in his resentment.'

'Oh, has he spoken to you about it, then?' Travis sounded interested.

'A little. He's pretty fed-up, actually.'

'Too bad. But in the meantime we've got a very nasty job on our hands at daybreak.'

'Oh *that*!' Hogarth sounded scornful. 'We'll manage the bloody Turks well enough, you see!'

Pringle appeared in the gloom and moved to one side of the bridge.

Travis said quietly but unfeelingly, 'How's your jaw, Sub?'

'I'd rather not talk about it.' Pringle sounded furious.

'Well, I think you asked for it!' Travis turned his back. 'I'm going to snatch an hour's sleep, Guns. Call me if the ship capsizes!'

He disappeared from the bridge and Hogarth was left with his thoughts. Travis was probably right, he thought. Few campaigns ever succeeded unless they got off to a good start. It was true that the more modern and useful ships were being withdrawn with unseemly haste, and even the *Saracen*'s future role was uncertain. Still, very soon they would be too occupied for conjecture. At first light his big guns would be needed again, and Major De L'Isle's mad marines would be hitting the shore for the first time. It would be quite a party. But suppose Travis was right too about Whitehall? To be killed in battle was one thing. To die for no purpose was another entirely.

Sub-Lieutenant Pringle, on the other hand, was not thinking of battle or the shortcomings of this campaign. He could still hardly believe the deliberate cruelty of the Captain's words when he had seen him in his cabin. Pringle had been so sure of his ground, so outraged at the deliberate affront to his position, that he had almost expected Royston-Jones to compliment him on his self-control. Instead, the Captain had gathered force and momentum like a small hurricane, his words stripping away Pringle's composure like the skin from his bones. He still felt the echoes of the little man's last words ringing in his ears.

'Remember this, Pringle! In war the demands will soon outgrow the supplies. Young and junior regular officers will be worth their weight in gold. Even this ship will have to take on Reserve officers and untrained ratings as soon as we return to Base, and every professional, no matter how inferior in rank and ability, will have his work cut out to make the simplest routine run smoothly!' The Captain had paused to run his cold eyes over

386

the sweating officer. 'Even you will probably have a command of some sort within a couple of years, *if* you are careful! But I *will* not have you behaving in this irresponsible manner, do you hear? You insulted this midshipman and he reacted in the only way he knew at that time. He has lived under strain and in no little danger for some weeks, doing a job for which a much more responsible officer had been selected. I will not tolerate any such behaviour in future!'

Pringle still cursed himself for his own inability to justify himself. He had only managed a throaty and servile, 'I'm sorry, sir.'

The Captain had dismissed him with a few more terse sentences, ending with: 'I think you might have promise if only you can think a little less about yourself and a lot more of your duty. You will have that chance tomorrow when we reach the enemy coast. When the main landing is carried out you will take charge of the seamen employed ashore, is that understood?' The cold eyes flickered with something like menace. 'Be warned, Pringle. The light of forgiveness is short in its duration!'

He had not seen Chesnaye since his interview with Royston-Jones and he wondered how he had fared. The Captain had probably buttered him up instead of putting him under arrest, he thought savagely. They were all the same. All trying to get at him, just because he was better than they!

A voice shattered the silence. 'Driftwood on the starboard beam, sir!'

Hogarth strode to the screen and peered into the darkness. A few pieces of waterlogged timber bobbed down the monitor's bulging flank and vanished astern. It was odd how all sorts of driftwood and wreckage meandered around the coast, he thought. An endless journey in tideless waters.

He watched a faint red glow far on the monitor's beam where a momentary flash of sparks betrayed their escorting destroyer. No doubt her stokers were busy with the never-ending misery of fire-trimming. Thank God the *Saracen* was oil-burning. That at least was some comfort.

He said wearily: 'I'm just going to check our position, Sub. Take over.'

Pringle moved to the front of the bridge, his blood running hot as he relived each separate humiliation.

Almost bored, the port lookout's voice interrupted, 'Object fine on the port bow, sir!'

Pringle, caught off guard, snapped. 'Well, what is it, man?'

A pause. 'A piece o' driftwood, I think, sir.' The lookout sounded aggrieved at being asked an unfair question.

'Well, keep your eyes open for important things, damn you! *Not* this everlasting bloody driftwood!'

The man answered sulkily, 'Aye, aye, sir.'

Pringle breathed out hard and groped for his glasses. Damned useless fools, the lot of them. He trained his glasses across the port side of the gently corkscrewing bows. The white arrowhead of the bow wave, the undulating water, and then . . . he started aghast at the shining black shape with its vicious horns which moved so calmly and deliberately towards the monitor's hull.

The frantic orders were torn from his throat. 'Hard a-starboard! Mine dead on the port bow!'

He was almost knocked from his feet as Hogarth flung himself at the voice-pipe.

'Belay that order! Port fifteen!' Viciously over his shoulder he added to Pringle, 'You'd swing the stern right across it, you idiot!' Then he ran to the screen, his lanky frame bowed to watch for the small deadly object. He punched at a gaping petty officer. 'Clear lower decks! Jump to it!'

The mine curtsied past the bridge even as the monitor swung ponderously in response to the rudder. Once it seemed to brush against the massive anti-torpedo bulge, but a freak of current thrust it away, so that a watching seaman sobbed with relief.

A marine bugler sent the alarm call frantically across the sleeping ship, whilst messengers and bosun's mates scampered down ladders and hatches, pipes shrilling, voices raised in hoarse urgency. 'Clear lower deck! Close all watertight doors and scuttles!'

Captain Royston-Jones was on the bridge even before the bugler had drawn breath, but as he crossed to Hogarth's side another freak current encircled the drifting mine and cradled it inwards towards the *Saracen*'s stern. Another few feet and it would have vanished in the ship's white wake. Gently it bumped against the rough plating, the motion making the horns gyrate almost gaily . . . until one of them made contact and broke.

Richard Chesnaye could hardly remember how he came to be on the upper bridge. The previous minutes had been merged into a desperate scramble made worse by the blare of a bugle and the insane twittering of pipes. One second he had been lying in his hammock, the next he had been running barefoot for the nearest ladder, clad only in drill trousers with his jacket somehow wedged beneath his arm.

Then there had been the explosion. For one long moment the whole hull had quivered like an oil-drum struck with a masssive hammer. Running men had faltered or fallen with the shock, that had been followed at once by a long-drawn-out shuddering which had seemingly gripped the ship from stem to stern. Every piece of loose gear had cascaded on to the dazed men, and as they had started running once more the hull had been plunged into darkness, so that Chesnaye was suddenly reminded of the two decks he must scale before he reached the open air.

On deck the packed ranks of stumbling figures had fanned out in every direction, while harsh voices called names and repeated orders, goading them on, stopping them from thinking. Chesnaye had been conscious of the smell of seared paintwork and the fact that the engines were stopped.

He reached the bridge, breathless, and suddenly cold. As he fumbled with his jacket he heard Royston-Jones say sharply, 'A complete muster of all hands, and then tell the Bosun to have the boats swung out and to check all rafts.'

A voice said, 'Port whaler destroyed, sir.'

'Very well.' The Captain added, 'Tell me the moment a report comes in from either the damage-control party or the engine room.'

Chesnaye was aware of the great pall of smoke which hovered over the after part of the ship and the sluggish movement of the hull itself.

Lieutenant Travis, who was by the wheelhouse voice-pipe, reported: 'Wheel not answering, sir. Way off ship.'

The Captain nodded. 'Hmm. Stopped engines in time, I think. You acted promptly, Guns.'

Another voice. 'Damage Control reporting from aft, sir!'

Royston-Jones walked quickly to the proffered handset. 'Well?'

Muffled by depth and distance, a voice he recognised as the Commander's reached his ear. 'After steering compartment and lower storeroom flooded, sir. Fire party dealing with outbreak in secondary paint store. All watertight doors holding and secure.'

'Very good.'

Chesnaye strained his ear for some expression or hint in the Captain's tone, but there was nothing to show his inner thoughts.

There were said to be many hundreds of drifting mines in the area, but it seemed incredible, even impossible, that one had reached the *Saracen*.

A voice-pipe squeaked, and Royston-Jones bent his head to listen. 'Captain here!'

Far below, in the gleaming jungle of brass and powered steel, Innes, the Chief Engineer, adjusted his words for that other world of open sea and fresh air. 'The pumps are all working well, sir, but I'm afraid I can't let you use the port engine.'

Royston-Jones remained crouched by the speaking-tube, his eyes half closed as he translated Innes's brief words into their full meaning. 'The shaft tube is badly damaged, then?' He waited, forcing himself to keep his voice level.

'Can't tell for sure, sir. My lads are clearing away the mess, then they'll be able to get a better picture. My immediate guess is that the port screw is badly damaged too, might even have lost a blade.' Then, more firmly: 'Either way, it's a dockyard job, sir. We're lucky the mine didn't blow the guts out of the stern!'

'Lucky, Chief? It depends which way you look at it!' He snapped down the tube and stood up.

Travis, who had been waiting nearby, reported quietly: 'Damage Control have extinguished the fire, sir. And the intake of water has been contained.'

Chesnaye listened intently and tried to fit the terse pieces of information into the pattern of the ship. The monitor seemed too large, too vital, to be affected, yet she was noticeably heavier aft, and without power was yawing heavily in the small cross-swell.

When he had climbed wearily into his hammock Chesnaye had been unable to think of anything but his short interview with the Captain. His words had been harsh, cutting, but, Chesnaye knew, well chosen. Now all that was momentarily forgotten and the events which led to that interview made small and petty by comparison with this new disaster. He was more conscious of the weight of the Captain's immediate problems than he was of any sense of danger. The little man who now stood amidst chaos and disorder, whose mind was their only weapon, whose wrong word could only add to the ship's misfortune.

'Signal from escort, sir!'

390

'Well?' The Captain did not look up.

'Request instructions, sir. Will prepare to take you in tow at daybreak. Request permission to signal for further assistance. Signal ends, sir.'

Beaushears, who had appeared unseen at Chesnaye's elbow, whispered, 'That's the end of the landing, then!'

Chesnaye did not hear him, but watched fascinated as the Captain turned yet again to speak to Mildmay, the Surgeon.

'Ten casualties, sir.' The Surgeon sounded brisk and fully awake. 'Also one man missing. Probably lost overboard.'

'Who was that?' Royston-Jones sounded distant.

'An Ordinary Seaman named Colt.'

'Hmmm, yes. Fo'c'sleman. Bad luck.'

Chesnaye breathed out slowly. How in heaven's name did the Captain find time to remember a mere face at such a moment?

The Captain said sharply: 'Signal to escort to resume station. Negative her requests. I intend to continue at reduced speed on remaining screw.'

'But, sir –' Travis interrupted and then faltered.

The white figure moved slightly. 'Yes, Pilot?'

'Well, sir, I don't mean to question your judgement, but our orders are exact. We have to be in position before daylight, otherwise the enemy shore batteries will have our measure before we can cope with them! On one screw we can make a bare three knots!' His voice gained strength. 'We shall be a sitting target!'

'Quite so. Unfortunately we have no choice. Without us there is no support for the troops in that sector. They are relying on our attack on the enemy flank.'

Travis said tightly, 'We may not be in much shape to help anyone, sir!'

Royston-Jones seemed to have forgotten him. 'Pipe all hands to prepare ship for action. Then see that they have a good breakfast before dawn. I want the ship smart and efficient before that time!'

Commander Godden climbed into the bridge, his face streaked with smoke stains. 'She's two feet down by the stern, sir. It's not possible to rig collision mats, and in any case the frames are well buckled as far as I can make out in this light. When we get to the nearest dockyard we can assess the damage better.'

'I quite agree.' Royston-Jones sounded quite calm. 'However, we have this small operation to complete first. I shall want to

391

speak to all heads of departments in one hour, particularly to the Major of Marines. We are one whaler short, I understand, so the boats will be hard-worked when the time comes. Perhaps you will arrange to have the larger rafts ready for lowering. I think they could be safely towed ashore under present conditions with some of the marines aboard?'

Godden sounded as if he had misunderstood. 'You are surely not suggesting that we go through with it, sir?'

'I will put your lack of respect down to strain, Commander. However, I should add that we are now committed. I have no intention of letting the disbelievers cast their scorn at this ship or her company. I thought I had already made that quite clear? If not, then let me only add that I expect every man aboard to, er . . .' He faltered, so that Chesnaye was conscious of the tension amongst the small group of officers. But the Captain smiled and continued, 'I *was* going to say "do his duty", but I realise that another distinguished officer has already said it rather better, and under more inspiring circumstances!'

Below in the shuttered wheelhouse Chief Petty Officer Ashburton, the Coxswain, leaned on the polished wheel and cocked his head as a gust of uncontrolled laughter swept down the bell-mounted voice-pipe. The starboard telegraph swung to 'Slow-Ahead', but still the laughter persisted. The Coxswain turned his eyes to the binnacle and said just loud enough for the mystified telegraphsmen to hear: 'Listen to 'em! Bloody officers! All bloody mad!'

392

Chapter Seven

Pickles

Richard Chesnaye walked slowly forward along the monitor's broad fo'c'sle deck between the massive anchor cables and halted only when he stood hard against the jackstaff in the very bows of the ship. It was quiet, the sluggish bow wave hardly gurgling as the slow-moving hull thrust itself towards the long purple strip of land which lined the horizon. There was no warmth in the low sun, and although the clear bright sky hinted of the heat to come, Chesnaye's limbs felt stiff and weary from the night's exertions and his face a mask of tiredness. He looked back at the *Saracen's* bridge which seemed to hang between the two long guns, and up at the topmast which shimmered like burnished gold in the growing power of the sunlight. The bridge was faceless, yet he knew that many eyes were watching the gentle shore as it grew from the blue and silver sea and basked beneath the empty sky. From his lonely position he could see the black smoke stains on her upperworks and bridge and the splintered deck planking which had been sandwiched by the mine's blast. The *Saracen* moved like an injured beast, almost crabwise, as her ungainly bulk fought against the thrust of one screw and the sweating exertions of the helmsman. He turned his back on the ship and leaned forward against the jackstaff. By so doing he could exclude the ship's indignity and pain, and as he watched the low-lying shapes of the two destroyer escorts which were already racing ahead of their charge he felt as if he alone was drifting towards that hateful strip of prized land.

He had been ordered to make a last check of the fo'c'sle, but a flint-eyed petty officer had made sure that there was nothing left for him to do. The ship was ready and waiting. It had received its first wound, but was already sniffing out the enemy in the manner of any injured beast.

Boats were slung out or ready and waiting beneath the big power derrick. Major De L'Isle's marines were, he knew, mustered in sections athwart the quarterdeck, their bodies deformed

393

by packs and rifles, entrenching tools and water-bottles. He peered at his watch. It was time to return to the others. To put on his mask and hide his apprehension.

Leading Seaman Tobias, hung about with webbing and bayonet, saluted him as he strode beneath the shadow of the bridge. 'Our party mustered, sir.'

'Good. See that they stay under cover until we leave the ship.'

Tobias squinted towards the bows. 'It's very quiet, sir.'

Chesnaye knew that he meant the shore, but his own thoughts returned to the feeling of loneliness and loss he had felt when the dawn had laid the sea bare.

Wiped away as if they had never been. The battleships and cruisers, the darting shapes of a hundred smaller craft. The majesty of the world's mightiest fleet gone in the twinkling of an eye.

What must the stranded troops be thinking? he wondered. Their ever-sure armada, the grey shield which every Briton had grown up to expect as a right had slunk away, vanished. Chesnaye tried to accept the reasons, but he could not swallow the feeling of hurt and loss. Of course, there were U-boats in the vicinity, but surely they must have been foreseen? Apparently not.

It was said that a battleship had already fallen to a U-boat's torpedoes off the very beaches which he had seen the Australian and New Zealanders take with his own eyes. Perhaps the Turks were unaware of the monitor's approach, or even indifferent. This part of the coast was separated from those other landings by that same jutting headland some miles to the north-east. The Allied forces in the south were even further away. A lonely, slab-sided coastline with a jumbled mass of hills and gullies beyond. No wonder the Turks were confident.

He imagined the thousands of soldiers to the north waiting for the *Saracen*'s bombardment of the enemy's flank. The relieving of the pressure just long enough for another small advance. He shut his eyes and saw again the wire and the minute running figures. Even in his nostrils he imagined he could scent the sickening smell of burned flesh and offal. The refuse of a battlefield.

Able Seaman Wellard slouched towards them and clumsily banged his rifle on the deck. He glanced at Chesnaye and then pursed his lips in a silent whistle.

Tobias tucked his thumbs in his belt and nodded towards the

394

distant destroyers. 'They're getting pretty near, sir.'

Chesnaye did not answer. The monitor was about six miles from the land. The two escorts were getting dangerously close inshore.

As if in answer to his thoughts, two orange flashes glowed briefly against the purple hills, and seconds later the nearest destroyer was bracketed by twin waterspouts which seemed to hang for a long time before falling back as broken spray.

' 'Ere we go, then!' Wellard loosened his rifle-sling and glanced towards the bridge. 'I 'ope the Skipper knows what 'e's about!'

Chesnaye took a last searching look at Tobias's impassive features and then started to climb the long steel ladder to the upper bridge. Tobias would not break. He was no leader, but he was reliable.

The bridge was surprisingly calm and quiet. Each officer seemed to be looking through his binoculars, and every rating stood by voice-pipe and telephone.

The Captain was sitting in his chair, elbows on the screen, cap tilted against the slowly climbing sun. Over his shoulder he said, 'Hoist battle ensigns.'

Chesnaye felt a lump in his throat as he watched the giant ensigns mounting masts and ensign staff alike. The challenge was being accepted. It seemed wrong that the sea was so empty. No one to watch, to applaud. Even to pity.

He remembered the cheering troopships when they had first sailed for this place. The ranks of waving khaki. Now there was no one. Except the hidden enemy.

'The destroyers have opened fire, sir!' Travis looked down at the Captain's slight shoulders. Across the still water they could all hear the sharp crack of the vicious four-inch guns, although the harsh sunlight and mounting haze hid the results of their work.

The big turret groaned slightly and the twin guns lifted a few inches. Behind that massive armour the Quarters Officer and his men would be straining every nerve and muscle, knowing that this time it was vital for everything to work like a precise clock. A misfire, an accident, and the monitor's role would be ended, and the men who served her wiped out.

A handset buzzed, 'Twelve thousand yards, sir!'

'Very good.' Nothing more.

Beaushears said thickly, 'They've started to make smoke!'

Sure enough the two small destroyers were weaving across the monitor's bows, parallel with the beachless coast, whilst from their squat funnels billowed a languid pall of black, greasy smoke. It hung across the water, shutting out the sun and darkening the smiling seascape like a curtain.

Chesnaye could feel his nails biting into his palms as he watched the destroyers' efforts and matched them against the *Saracen*'s slow and painful progress. They were nearer the coast now, but there was still a long way to go. He stiffened as he caught sight of more waterspouts beyond the smokescreen. More this time. Maybe six or seven.

Above the bridge the gunnery team would be watching too. Calculating and waiting. It could not be much longer.

The Captain spoke. 'Prepare to lower boats.'

The order was passed, and below the bridge Chesnaye could see the frantic efforts to get the big cumbersome launches slung out over the side.

Royston-Jones added testily: 'Pulling boats first. They can be taken in tow with the rafts.' He shifted briefly in his chair and glanced at the watching midshipmen. 'Well, off you go.' He waited as they saluted. 'And good luck.'

Chesnaye could feel his stomach muscles tight against his belt as he pushed his way through the marines who were milling excitedly around the davits. Half the night they had practised this manœuvre, but already the situation looked tangled and near disaster.

Commander Godden stood by the rail, his face grim as he watched the first boat squeaking down the falls. It hit the water and was soon drifting clear of the crawling monitor. Rafts, lowered over the side for once heedles of paintwork, were immediately taken in tow by the whaler, and as the power boats were lowered alongside, momentarily pinioned to allow more men to scramble aboard, Chesnaye suddenly realised the enormity of their task.

He caught sight of Tobias and then Pickles in their allotted places beside Major De L'Isle, and he felt himself scrambling with the desperation of the men he had just been watching like an onlooker.

The Major of Marines was standing up in the launch, his face scarlet as he yelled at his Colour Sergeant, who was in another boat. 'Keep those men quiet, d'you hear? God damn your eyes if I hear another word!' He flopped down on the thwart beside Chesnaye and banged his short leather-covered stick against his boot. 'Let them save their energy, that's what I say!'

Spouting smoke and fumes, the power boats gathered up the cutters and whalers with their attendant rafts into three separate tows. At a signal from De L'Isle they formed into lines and turned towards the shore, some of the men cheering and shouting in spite of the threats from the N.C.O.s.

The boats gathered way, so that the *Saracen*'s jagged shape seemed to grow small and indistinct in minutes. Only the three great ensigns stood out clear and bright, while the ragged hole left by the mine was already lost in the haze.

There was a great whistling roar, and for a few seconds Chesnaye thought that the *Saracen* had opened fire. As he twisted his head to watch he saw a blinding light burst alongside the monitor's low hull, so bright that he winced and shut his eyes. But not before he had seen the tall topmast quiver and then plunge over the side. The blast of the explosion fanned across the flat water and deluged the small boats in noise, so that most of the men could only gape as the falling mast slithered into the sea followed by its attendant tangle of rigging and men.

De L'Isle was the first to recover his wits. 'A big 'un, I should say. Fourteen-inch at least!'

Chesnaye's heart sank. No wonder the Turks were confident about this part of their coast. With a well-sited gun of that calibre, and with their target silhouetted against an empty sea, it was just a matter of time.

He dug his fingers into the boat's warm gunwale and gritted his teeth as another fountain of water burst abreast the monitor's bridge. Still she did not return fire, and Chesnaye could feel himself almost weeping at the ugly ship's slow progress.

De L'Isle sniffed and moved his holster on his belt. 'At least the bloody Turks won't be expecting us to arrive like this, what?'

Chesnaye turned with difficulty amidst the close press of bodies and looked at Pickles. He was surprised to see that the young midshipman was apparently calm, or was he resigned? He tried to grin at him, but his jaws felt stiff and enlarged.

Pickles moistened his lips and then reached across a seaman's bent shoulders to touch his hand. His lips moved very slowly,

397

and Chesnaye realised he was trying to tell him something. The scream of the next shell made further words impossible, so he merely squeezed Pickles' hand and then turned back to watch the boats and the nearness of the smokescreen. But his hand, long after he had released Pickles', was still ice cold from the contact.

The beach at the foot of the tall brown cliffs was smaller than it had first appeared, and consisted not of sand but of broken stones and rubble washed or blown down over the centuries to form a narrow, treacherous slope. It shelved steeply and immediately into deep water which surged in the cliff's black shadow in a constant, angry maelstrom of short, steep waves. Singly and in pairs the boats staggered and lurched against the loose stones while the packed men leapt and stumbled ashore, their heavy packs and rifles adding to the confusion. All about them, wafted by a freak offshore breeze, the remnants of the destroyers' smoke screen made some of them cough, others curse noisily as they peered anxiously for their comrades and correct positions on the beach. The sun was much higher, but beneath the tall, threatening cliff face the air seemed tinged with ice, so that some of the sweating marines were shivering and stamping their feet.

Keith Pickles felt the water draining from his trouser legs and stepped unsteadily towards the brown crumbling wall where Major De L'Isle and half of his men were already examining the means of reaching the top of this natural barrier. Pickles again tried to examine his inner feelings, to face some thought or idea which he could recognise, but nothing came. He felt light-headed, as if he was gliding from one phase to the next as in a dream. Time and distance had shortened, so that the long and agonising passage through the oily smoke to this shore now seemed the same length as climbing from the pitching launch or adjusting his belt and revolver.

He turned to watch as a section of marines led by Lieutenant Keats, De L'Isle's willowy second-in-command, moved briskly around a short spur of rock and began to scramble up the cliff face. Like mountaineers, they were silhouetted darkly against the pale colours and hues of the next bay, far beyond this overcast place, their bent bodies like bronze sculptures on a memorial.

He heard De L'Isle bark to no one in particular: 'Damn' fine landing! Not a man lost! Must have caught John Turk with his breeches dangling, what?'

398

Some of his men laughed shortly and nervously, as if they were out of breath. Pickles watched them narrowly and saw the way they were fingering their rifles and peering up at the moving section of marines. Nervous, afraid even.

Pringle's voice was here, too, loud and blustering as he yelled at the wallowing boats: 'Stand off the beach! Wait for further orders!' It was odd, but Pickles was able to listen and calculate Pringle's words without nervousness. The shouted orders seemed empty and meaningless, extra and unnecessary. It was strange he had never realised that so much of Pringle's world was pure show. Perhaps he was afraid too? He watched the man's flushed and angry face and wondered.

De L'Isle waved his leather stick. 'Close up! Lively there!'

Obediently the officers and N.C.O.s drew round him, their expressions mixed and cautious.

De L'Isle was speaking fast and sharply. 'Right. No time to lose. Second section move off to the left. Sergeant Barnes!'

The tall Colour Sergeant, who looked as if he had just prepared himself for an admiral's inspection, stiffened to attention on the loose stones. 'Sir!'

'You take 'em off at the trot right away. You know the picture, but things may be different once we get over this ridge. The Turks'll not be expecting our little lot, but it won't take 'em long to move up a force of some sort.' His bulbous eyes flashed meaningly. 'Your orders and *mine* are to hold off any local attack until the spotting team have homed the guns on the enemy's flank.' He spoke to the group at large. 'That fourteen-inch gun which is trying to knock hell out of the poor old ship is probably intended for our lads up the coast. That, and any other battery, must be wiped out, and quick.'

The Colour Sergeant was well over six feet tall and as broad as a door. His big-boned face was decorated with a ginger upturned moustache which gave him the appearance of one of Wellington's grenadiers, and he looked entirely calm and unmoved as he listened to his superior. At a nod from the Major he swung round and slung his rifle across his shoulder, his hard eyes already searching out his own particular section of marines. As they moved clear Pickles heard the sergeant say angrily: 'Keep your distances! Don't huddle together like a lot of bloody matelots!' Then they were gone.

The Major grunted approvingly. 'First things first. Don't fancy having some damned Turk bouncing grenades on us while we're chatting, what?'

Less laughter this time. Pickles realised that the beach already seemed larger, and the landing force which had been made important by its density now appeared small and insignificant as it broke up into little groups.

De L'Isle glanced at the officers. 'Ready, you three?'

Pringle cleared his throat. 'I'll stop here and supervise the shore party of seamen.'

The Major laughed unpleasantly. 'Like Jesus you will, boy! You get up to the ridge with the two snotties an' double quick!'

Pickles felt his heart thumping with sudden excitement. He turned to look at Chesnaye, but the latter's face was grave and expressionless.

Pringle seemed shocked. 'My orders are to stay here, sir!'

'Damn your orders! I'm in command here!' He leaned forward, his polished boots creaking. 'I've been in more campaigns and trouble spots than you've had pork chops! The men may think this is a picnic, but *I* don't. It may happen that once we top the cliff we'll be for it. If that happens, half our party might get wiped out, *see*?' He turned his heavy frame, his mind apparently busy on other things. 'In any case, you're more experienced. So do your job!'

Pringle did not look at the two midshipmen. Through his teeth he muttered, 'Come on, then, and no shirking, Pickles!' But there was no bite in his voice. It was as if he was someone else.

There was a sudden stammer of machine-gun fire from the extreme right, followed immediately by shouts and a ragged rifle volley.

De L'Isle was cursing quietly. He waved his stick and said, 'Corporal, get your men up this cliff, right here!' He stabbed angrily at the crumbling mould. 'Come on, lad! It won't bite you!' He waited impatiently as the first men began to climb, and then said to Pringle: 'You too. We might as well get started!'

Pickles felt the grit and stones falling on his shoulders as he followed the heavy-booted marines towards the pale, bright sky, but he was entirely absorbed in his new thoughts. He felt hot and cold in turns, and once when he looked down at the handful of seamen left on the beach he felt like laughing aloud. It was as if every doubt and agony had left his mind at once. Just knowing

400

that he was going to be killed seemed to make it much easier to bear. Before, in that earlier landing, it had been different. There had been a small chance of survival, a tiny hope perhaps. It had made living and thinking a nightmare. Even his life aboard the *Saracen* had been a mere building up for this moment. Now there was no turning back, and the future was suddenly mercifully plain and exact.

Once when he rested in a hanging pattern of gorse he turned to look for the monitor. Small and pale, the ship was still shrouded in smoke. He could not tell what the smoke represented. Her own guns or the enemy's, or just the vapour from the screen left by the two small ships which darted along the coast. One of the destroyers appeared to be on fire, but her guns still flashed and her bow wave spoke of her tremendous speed and grace.

Pickles watched the *Saracen* as if seeing it for the first time. It could have been so different. Or could it? For once he could question his constant defence without a tremor. Pringle had brought an edge to his misery, but there had been his own stupid pride and ignorance too. It had all been so wonderful at first. Home on leave before joining the ship. The uniform, the admiring glances from all the girls he had once known and played with in the road outside his father's shop. He seemed to have grown to a man while they still appeared gawky and pigtailed. He remembered too the dark sweet-smelling parlour at the back of the shop where his early life had revolved. The mantelpiece crowded with silver-framed photographs of relatives, singly or in groups, of dogs and cats, and all the other faces which had made up the Pickles family past.

His father, short and fat, with a lick of hair plastered across his forehead. He had been proud, too, but more cautious. Perhaps he had known what lay ahead of his son in his new career.

'They might seem different to you, Keith,' he had said on more than one occasion. 'You know, posh homes and plenty of cash. I've had to work for what I've got here, and I was hopin' you'd join me one day in the shop.'

Pickles remembered now how he had felt embarrassment at the way his father had always dropped his g's. But he had been right. All the way. Try as he might, Pickles had met this strange barrier at every stage. He had helped to make it worse by fighting back, by trying to play a part he had never known. He had run short of money two weeks after joining the *Saracen*, at a time when the new ship was open for one party and celebration after another. He had borrowed ten pounds from a tailor in Portsmouth. Once in debt he had increased his misery until the small tailor had come to the ship to press his demands. It might have been better if the man had gone to the Commander, but instead he had approached Pringle, who with a show of hurt pride had paid the man and sent him packing. From that moment he had made Pickles' life a nightmare. He had piled one humiliation after another on him, each time with some sneer or jibe at his upbringing and background. The other midshipmen in the gunroom stayed silent and watchful. Taking no sides. They, too, obviously agreed with Pringle.

Then Chesnaye had joined the ship, and a small glimmer of hope had returned to Pickles' heart. It was rumoured that Chesnaye was under a cloud because his father had failed in some way, that he too was from a poor family. He had felt something like love when the tall, grave-faced Chesnaye had stood up for him against Pringle, but even this had been soured by jealousy when Pickles had seen that the other midshipmen had accepted the newcomer in spite of his alleged faults. He was one of them. He belonged whatever he did.

There was a sudden clatter of feet to his right, and he craned his head to watch the first section of marines reappear on the top of a wedge-sided fall of rock. They were already a hundred yards away, but he could detect the sudden urgency and desperation in their movements.

A burst of machine-gun first sent the pale dust dancing once more, and three marines skidded down the rock face their bodies torn and bloodied. The young marine lieutenant, Keats, seeing his men falter and hang back from the sun-dappled ridge, leapt forward, waving his stick. 'Come on, lads! Forward, marines!' He staggered and fell at once as the next burst smashed into his crouched body.

De L'Isle raised his binoculars and dug his elbows into the slope. 'God! What a mess!' In a louder voice he shouted: 'Round to the left, men! Get that Lewis gun mounted and spray the slope!'

More marines ducked and ran forward. Some made it, others fell writhing before the unseen death which sang and whistled in the dusty air.

In twos and threes De L'Isle's party reached the top of the cliff

402

and flopped down amongst a long line of smooth boulders. The Lewis gun began to chatter, and some of the men shouted encouragement to the section which was pinned down on the right.

De L'Isle was breathing heavily as he rested his binoculars on a piece of sun-warmed rock. To Pringle he said sharply: 'No need for you to bother about us. Get your party across this gully and up on to that ridge there.'

Pickles listened and moved up alongside the sweating marines to peer at the long, dark-sided ridge which lined the other side of a deep gully. It was slab-shaped with a tall pinnacle at one end, like the steeple of a petrified church. He saw too a small, stone-walled hut, roofless and deserted, at the foot of the pinnacle, perched on the ridge, as if forgotten for many years. He heard De L'Isle say: 'Make for that. Once up there you'll get a good view over the ridge and across the valley beyond.'

Pickles turned his head and looked at the rolling panorama of hills and cheerless ragged ridges which undulated away to the south where the high arrogant peak of Achi Baba still dominated the Peninsula. A barren, arid, unwanted place, he thought. Gorse, a few sparse trees and the ever-moving dust. Somewhere to the north the troops were waiting. But did it matter? Did anything count in this cruel land?

A bullet whimpered overhead and passed away over the sea behind him. He shivered and drew his head deeper into his shoulders. A sniper? They were said to be everywhere. On every hill and ridge. No man could move in the open and live. He stared at the dark ridge again. Yet we have to get there, he thought. Three officers and three seamen.

The Colour Sergeant called from what seemed a great distance, 'Ready, sir!'

Major De L'Isle wiped the sweat from his eyes. 'Must clear those batteries before noon,' he said absently. Then, as if having come to a decision, he blew sharply on his whistle and lumbered to his feet. As the Lewis gun sprayed the slope beyond the cliff edge the ragged line of marines rose from cover and began to run forward. Slowly at first, and then when nothing happened faster and more wildly. There were a few unexpected rifle shots from the foot of the ridge, and three more marines cried out and fell face down in their own blood. Even more unexpectedly, as if from the rock itself, a handful of blue-grey figures rose directly in

403

the centre of the small advance, their alien uniforms and dark faces suddenly very clear and close.

The marines faltered, but De L'Isle waved his stick and screamed: 'Get them! *Get them!*' The words seemed to be wrung from his very heart.

Two of the Turkish soldiers dropped to their knees and began to fire their long rifles as fast as they could reload.

Pickles realised that the strange real enemy was directly in his path, but he could not stop himself from running, nor could he draw his revolver. Faster, faster. The rifle muzzles spurted yellow flame directly in his eyes. A marine, yelling like a fiend, screamed and clutched his stomach as a bullet smashed him down, but another marine reached the seemingly paralysed Turk and drove his bayonet deep into this throat. The Turk gurgled and rolled on to his face. With a sob the frantic marine turned and swung the bayonet again, the full force of his body pinioning the writhing man on the ground like an insect.

From the flank Colour Sergeant Barnes bellowed: 'Just give 'im two inches! Don't make a bloody meal of it!'

The battle-crazed marine faltered as he withdrew the reddened bayonet and blinked dazedly towards the parade-ground voice, then obedient and happy he staggered after the rest, the Turk already forgotten beside the bodies of the others.

Like savage, desperate animals the marines fell into the position vacated by the small enemy outpost, fear temporarily forgotten as lust and hatred dispersed itself in a frenzy of preparations.

Grenades banged on the right, and another ragged cheer announced the end of the hidden machine-gun. De L'Isle said unevenly, 'It's a start, anyway!'

A big shell sighed overhead, and then another. In the far distance beyond the ridge two green puffs of lyddite smoke blossomed and hung unmoving against the dull hills. The monitor had fired at last. Two vague, unchartered shots to give the enemy something to think about.

The marines settled down amongst the rocks and readjusted their sights. Sergeant Barnes strode briskly towards Major De L'Isle and saluted. 'Fifteen killed, sir. Ten wounded.' His pale eyes watched the Major's face with something like affection. 'I'm afraid one of the young gentlemen 'as bin 'it too, sir,'

Pickles, who had been fighting to regain his breath, jerked

upright at the words. All the things Chesnaye had said and done, all the pent-up fears and wants of the past weeks roared into his brain as Barnes added sadly, 'Must 'ave got 'it just as we reached 'ere, sir.' Pickles stood up and began to run back across the open ground.

A wounded marine cried out: 'Help me, fer Christ's sake! Me eyes, I'm blind!' As Pickles dashed past he screamed again: 'Come 'ere, you bastards! Don't leave me!' Another marine, dead and cold-eyed, lay with his torn shoulder already alive with blue flies, his mouth half open as if in rebuke.

A bullet snickered past Pickles' head, but he ran on, deaf to it and the shouts of the marines. Perhaps this was how it was meant to end. He tucked in his head and ran even faster.

Richard Chesnaye forced himself to lie quite still until his mind was able to break through the enveloping pain, and only then did he try to move. Very gingerly he took his weight on his hands and pushed himself slowly into a siting position. The sudden movement made him cry out, and with something like terror he forced himself to look at the long dark stain which was soaking his right thigh and staining the dry stones at his side. His throat felt raw with sudden thirst, and as he stared round the small, saucer-shaped depression into which he had fallen he was aware for the first time of the complete stillness and sense of loneliness. Gritting his teeth against the pain, he twisted his head to look around him, his eyes taking in the clear empty sky and the unmoving bent grass which crested the edges of the depression, and the clump of faded yellow balsam. He stared dazedly and uncomprehending for several seconds at the brown, claw-like hand which hung over the grass by his head, its wrist lined with dark dried blood upon which the flies were already at work.

He tried to concentrate, to recall the exact moment when he had been singled out from the frantic, noisy dash across that vague open ground and had been thrown down by the savage, white-hot blow. He lifted his wrist and then sighed with despair as he stared at his broken watch. Hours or minutes? The high unshielded sun gave him no clue. He stiffened as a distant rattle of machine-gun fire echoed through the dusty grass. They were not all dead, then. As if to settle his disordered thoughts a pain-racked voice, cracked and unrecognisable, cried out and then

405

died before he could judge its distance. His ears began to pick out other sounds too. The far-off rumble of heavy guns, the background to some other battle.

He fell back again on the warm earth, his eyes closed against the glare. His brain told him to make just one more effort to move, but something else held him back. The pain washed over him, and in his mind he saw a sudden picture of his father framed against the deep green of the English lawn and the worn, leather-bound books along the wall of his room. He flinched as a spent bullet thudded into the ground by his side, and tried to think more clearly. Was the ship still off the coast or even afloat? With sudden clarity he remembered the small knot of Turkish soldiers and the flash of bayonets just before he had fallen. He recalled, too, that he had been keeping his mind blank when it had happened, yet unable to tear his eyes from the desperate, spurting rifles which blocked his way. Perhaps the dead hand which gripped so fervently at the grass by his head belonged to one of those soldiers? In any case it could not be long before others arrived. He felt his stomach muscles tighten as he imagined the figures tall against the sky on the edge of his hiding place, the agonising moment of discovery. And then the bayonets.

Another burst of firing cut through the lazy air, and it was followed immediately by distant shouts and more firing. Through the ground at his back he felt the sudden thud of running feet, and he imagined he could hear quick, desperate breathing as the running man drew nearer.

It was then that he realised just how desperately he wanted to live, and the approaching, hidden terror made him roll on to his side, his bloodied fingers groping frantically for his revolver. Whimpering and cursing, he tugged at the holster, the agony in his thigh adding to his sense of urgency. Just as he succeeded in freeing the flap a shadow blotted out the sun, and he tightened his body into one agonised ball, unable to look round, but waiting for the murderous thrust of steel.

As if in a dream he heard Pickles say: 'Thank God, Dick! Here, let me have a look!'

Chesnaye allowed himself to be rolled on his back, still only half believing what he saw. Pickles, breathless but engrossed, his round face screwed in set concentration as he tore open the side of the dripping trousers. More pain when his hands found the place,

406

but a quick reassuring grin when the warm snugness of a bandage and dressing cut off the probing sun and the eager flies.

Pickles sat on his haunches. 'I don't know much about these things, Dick, but the bullet seems to have missed the bone.' He grinned widely, as if the realisation of what he had achieved had suddenly reached him. 'I *knew* I'd find you if I ran far enough!'

A shell passed overhead, and Pickles said: 'We must get out of here. The rest of our chaps are about a hundred yards further on, by the ridge.'

Chesnaye felt the relief coursing through him like brandy. 'I'm ready when you are!'

Pickles sat upright and wrinkled his nose like a dog. For a long moment he stared at the dead Turk and then said: 'Seems a bit quieter. We'll chance it.'

Together they crawled over the lip of the depression, their faces brushed by the grass and ageless gorse. Chesnaye kept his right arm across Pickles' shoulder, and dragging his damaged leg between them the two midshipmen pulled themselves towards the ridge which had now lost its shadow and shone in the sunlight like brown coral.

They paused for a brief rest and Chesnaye said slowly, 'There's a lot to do, Keith.'

Pickles grinned. 'You can say that again! We've not started yet, and, quite frankly, I think it'll be up to *us* again!'

Chesnaye stared at him which open wonder. Then he gave Pickles' shoulder a quick squeeze. 'Thank you, Keith. I'll not forget.'

Pickles sighed as three marines charged from cover and hauled them to safety behind a slab of broken rock. Dusting the grit from his trousers he said flatly, 'I'm not sure that *I* will either!'

Major De L'Isle greeted Chesnaye with a savage grin. 'Well done, lad. We'll be needing you as soon as my orderly can patch you up. Think you can make it up to the top?' He beamed as Chesnaye nodded vaguely, but then turned on a scowl for Pickles' benefit. 'By God, you should have been shot for what you did! You're raving bloody mad, did you know that?'

Pickles stood in the centre of an admiring circle of staring marines and felt the prickle of real happiness for the first time since he had stepped aboard the *Saracen*. He looked down at Chesnaye's drawn face and said, 'I suppose I've got used to running!'

Chapter Eight

The Pinnacle

The distant hills danced like a mirage in the twin lenses of Chesnaye's field-glasses so that it took him precious minutes to refocus them and assess what he saw. Each second added to the pain in his leg, which in spite of the dressing felt raw and torn, and the more he looked through his glasses, the more hopeless seemed the task. It was quiet on top of the ridge. Quiet and with very little cover. The three naval officers and three seamen had crawled back and forth over an area which measured about fifty yards by twenty and represented the highest part of the ridge. Highest, that is, but for the tall, bleak pinnacle.

It was funny how clearly he could think about the job in hand. Chesnaye moved the glasses slightly and watched two faint shellbursts to the north. Perhaps the concentration was the only thing holding back the nausea and agony, or the sense of defeat.

He tried again. Everything seemed to come back to the pinnacle. The ridge was good enough to pinpoint the enemy bombardment area, but then again was invisible to the ship. The pinnacle was the monitor's aiming mark, a known object on chart and gunnery grid-maps. It glimmered in the bright sunlight, smooth and unlovely. It was about sixty feet high with a deep cleft just below the top. His heart quickened and he looked sideways at Sub-Lieutenant Pringle, who was squatting tensely behind some boulders his back against the wall of the derelict hut. His sun-reddened face was worried and brooding.

Chesnaye cleared his throat. 'We'd better send a runner back to the beach with the first signal.' He spoke through tight lips intolerant of Pringle's silence, which was even more unnerving than his noisy protests when the party had landed. 'What d'you say?'

Pringle jerked himself from his thoughts. His eyes flashed with some of his old arrogance. 'What's the hurry? We're probably wasting our time, anyway!'

Pickles said quickly, 'Shall I go?'

Chesnaye wrote on his pad and handed the folded signal to one of the seamen. 'No, Keith. You and I are going up the old rock needle here.'

Pickles looked up and grimaced. 'Ouch!' Then with a look of concern. 'Can you make it? I would have thought *he* could go!' He spoke loudly enough for Pringle to hear.

'Now that's enough from you!' Pringle leapt to his feet, his face working furiously. 'Just because you've been doing some petty heroics you think you're something, eh?' His face twisted with anger. 'Well, *I* know a few things about you! By God, I'm sick of the lot of you!'

Chesnaye nodded to the gaping seaman, who tore his eyes from the gesticulating Pringle and began to climb over the side of the ridge. Below him the marines in their prepared positions watched him descend with interest.

With the whiplash crack Chesnaye had heard before, the sniper's rifle sent the birds wheeling from the ridge in screaming protest. The seaman hung for a moment longer, his eyes on the pinnacle above him, and then plummeted down the side of the ridge.

The hillsides re-echoed again to the rattle of the Lewis gun as the marines swept the silent rocks in a miniature dust-storm in a vain effort to find the hidden marksman. Then there was silence once more.

Chesnaye bit his lip with sudden determination. 'Here, give me a hand, Keith.' Slinging his glasses round his neck he walked to the foot of the pointing rock and began to climb up towards the small cleft. Each move was agony, but his mind was too occupied with the urgency of his task and the fact that he had just sent a man to his death for nothing.

Pringle's nerve snapped as the two midshipmen turned away from him. He shook his fists in the air and yelled: 'What the hell is happening? For God's sake let's get out of here!'

Pickles paused ahead of Chesnaye and held out his hand to help him. 'I know how he feels,' he said hoarsely, 'and that makes a change!'

Chesnaye forced himself to grin, and dragged himself further up the steep edges of hot stone. Once there and I'm done for, he thought. He could feel the blood beginning to pump through the bandage, and his right foot seemed to be dead.

He heard another crack, and a bullet smacked hard against the

409

pinnacle, hurling small splinters against his hands. With a sob Pickles pulled him unceremoniously into the cleft and a tiny, wonderful patch of shade.

Chesnaye had difficulty in controlling his mouth as Pickles upended his water-bottle to allow a little lukewarm water to moisten his parched lips. He nodded, grateful, not trusting words. He watched Pickles with something like apprehension as he stowed away the bottle and busied himself with making Chesnaye comfortable. How much longer could they both last? he wondered. If he died what would Pickles do? It was suddenly terribly important that Pickles should be spared any more of this nightmare.

Pickles pointed with surprise. 'Look, Dick! The ship!'

Sure enough, the *Saracen* was visible, listing and shrouded in smoke.

'She's in much closer.' Pickles leaned out to watch, but jerked back as another bullet whipped against the rock and ricocheted away over the ridge with an insane shriek. 'God, they're after *us*!'

Chesnaye twisted round on the tiny space and levelled his glasses.

Pickles tore his eyes from the ship and pulled the long Very pistol from his belt. 'Ready?'

Chesnaye nodded grimly. It had been arranged that if the exact bearings and ranges could not be sent by signal then a blind shoot would be carried out.

Pickles snapped a cartridge into the breech and then said quietly, 'God, there are Turks on that hill.'

Chesnaye turned in time to see sunlight flash momentarily on metal and the quick movement of men amongst the rocks on the nearest hillside. They're going to try and stop us, he thought dully.

The Very pistol coughed and sent its light soaring high over the ridge. Like a green eye it hung apparently motionless in the clear sky, and some of the marines cheered.

'Watch the ship!' Chesnaye rested on his elbows and concentrated on the brown elbow of hills some four miles distant where the main Turkish support lines were said to be.

Behind him Pickles said excitedly, 'Now!'

Subdued by the sea-cliff and the side of the ridge, the monitor's voice was none the less impressive. Chesnaye waited, the sweat

410

running into his eyes as he counted away the seconds. His heart
sank as twin clouds of white smoke erupted above the slumbering
hills. The monitor was firing shrapnel first. It was easier to see.
He groaned: 'God, they're miles out! They're almost firing on to
our lines!'

Pickles leaned over the side of the cleft and shouted down to
Pringle: 'You must get a runner back to the beach and send a
signal! It's an overshoot!'

Pringle stared up at them, his eyes red. 'No one can get through!
There are snipers all round us!'

From below came a sudden burst of firing from the marines and
the sound of Major De L'Isle's whistle. Chesnaye closed his eyes
and tried to clear his reeling mind. The monitor would wait for
another flare and then open the real bombardment. Or would it
wait? He tried to imagine the battered ship with the impatient,
desperate gunners crouching beneath the sun-heated armour.
They might not wait, and it was not unknown for ships to drop
shells on their own men. But not a ship like the *Saracen*. Each of
her giant shells weighed nearly a ton. He shook himself angrily. It
did not bear thinking about. Tightly he said: 'Tell Pringle to get
up here and have a look! He must be made to realise what's
happening!'

Pringle did not even listen. He covered his head with his hands
and ran into the roofless hut.

One of the seamen ran from cover on the far side of the ridge,
his face angry. ' 'Ere, come back, sir!' But instead of an answer he
received a bullet in the throat and fell back writhing on the rocks,
the dust around him brightly speckled with his blood.

Chesnaye felt sick. 'Here, give me a hand up.'

Pickles reached out, his face mystified, until he saw Chesnaye's
leg buckled under him. Chesnaye lay on his back, his eyes still on
his objective. Pickles followed his gaze and then stood up, his
face suddenly white. 'I'm ready. I'll make that signal.'

Chesnaye wrote shakily on his pad, the figures and bearings
dancing as if through a mist. It had to be done. It was the only
way. He felt a wave of fury run through him as he thought of
Pringle hiding below in the stone hut. 'Here, Keith.' He handed
him the pad. 'Just semaphore the first four sets of figures. They
will have to do!'

A voice called up from below: 'The Major's compliments, sir,

411

but can you get a move on? The bastards are trying to get between us an' the cliffs!'

But Chesnaye did not answer. There was a lot he wanted to say, but nothing came. Instead he gripped Pickles' hand. 'Be careful, Keith!'

With a quick grin Pickles leapt from the cleft and began to climb with the ease and agility of a monkey. Pieces of rock splintered around him as snipers on the hillside became aware of the small dark figure that was making for the very top of the pinnacle.

Chesnaye lay back, his eyes fixed on Pickles' body as he reached the end of his climb. For a second he peered down at Chesnaye and then, turning his back on the enemy hills, he commenced to wave his arms towards the distant, toylike ship.

Still the rifles cracked, but as the big searchlight on the *Saracen*'s bridge flashed an acknowledgement Pickles began to send his message. Chesnaye could picture the activity in the big turret, the gleaming shells being rammed home, the creak of elevating gear as the twin barrels lifted on to their target.

'Finished!' Pickles threw his cap in the air and yelled, 'They're going to open fire now!'

Then he fell. Without a cry or protest he rolled down the steep slope and crumpled across Chesnaye, who could only stare horrified at the widening patch of scarlet across his chest. Pickles' eyes were still wide from excitement, but without recognition or understanding. With a sob Chesnaye pulled him against his own body, aware again of the colds hands and that last insane eagerness.

Overhead, the great shells winged on their way to roar and thunder across the enemy lines, to destroy guns and stores, and the men who waited for the attack.

But Chesnaye did not notice. He watched his dead friend and the bright red stain which was still spreading. He remembered that night at Gibraltar, when it had all begun. Pickles with his shirt sprinkled with port. So eager to please.

It still seemed impossible to believe what had happened. Yet the sigh of the monitor's shells told him it was true. Once again Pickles had surprised them all.

'Signal from tug *Crusader*, sir.' The Yeoman of Signals paused and coughed uneasily. For a moment he thought that the Captain was asleep in his chair on the deserted bridge, but even as he looked

412

Royston-Jones turned his head very slightly and gave a faint gesture with his hand. 'Will be alongside in half an hour. Will you be ready to slip?' The Yeoman followed the Captain's gaze towards the tall-sided hospital ship which was anchored two cables away. White and graceful, she looked invulnerable against the low hills and straggling trees of the Mudros foreshore. 'Signal ends, sir.'

'Thank you, Yeoman. Tell them affirmative.' Royston-Jones held himself stiffly in his chair until the Yeoman had clattered down the ladder to the signal bridge, and then allowed his narrow shoulders to sag. There was so much waiting to be done, yet his mind and brain rebelled against even leaving the bridge. The sun was harsh across his smoke-stained uniform, and the humid air was filled with the smells of scorched paintwork and burned cordite. It seemed impossible that the ship was so still, that the great guns, blackened and blistered with continuous firing, were silent in their turret. Without looking over the screen he knew the seamen were busy on the upper deck, still using their hoses and scrubbers to clean away the filth and dirt of the bombardment and the destruction. He stiffened as a string of bunting broke out from the hospital ship's mainyard. She was getting ready to sail. It did not take much imagination to picture the pain and misery which was outwardly hidden by that white hull, he thought.

Almost unwillingly he stood up and walked to the rear of the bridge. Very gently he ran his hand across the scarred teak rail and looked up at the tall funnel pitted with shell splinters, blackened by smoke. Down towards the maindeck where only hours before the hands had been busy removing the empty shell-cases from around the secondary armament and gathering the shattered remains of boats and hatches, and mopping away the dark stains from the once smooth deck planking. The ship still listed to port, but she was quite motionless, as if resting. Shortly they would be weighing anchor once more, but this time in the care of some grubby tug which would take them on the long haul to Alexandria. And then? Royston-Jones shook himself as the weariness and inner misery closed over him once again.

There was a quiet step on the gratings nearby, and he turned quickly as if to cover his thoughts.

Lieutenant Hogarth saluted and glanced momentarily towards the splintered topmast above the bridge. 'I have reorganised the

413

watches, sir. The Bosun has given orders for the fo'c'sle party to fall in in fifteen minutes.'

Royston-Jones blinked. It seemed strange for Hogarth to be speaking about the ship's organisation instead of his beloved guns. It should have been Godden, but, of course, he was already in that hospital ship, a shattered arm his passport to another world. 'Very good.' He forced himself to look at Hogarth's concerned face. 'Anything else?'

Hogarth shut his mind to the scenes he had witnessed for so many long hours. The shell-holes and broken plates. Armour twisted into the fantastic shapes of wet cardboard, everything battered and smashed into a shambles. It did not seem as if the ship would ever be the same again.

He cleared his throat. 'I think you should go aft to your quarters for a while, sir,' he said carefully. 'I have instructed your steward to get a meal for you.' As the Captain did not reply he added more firmly, 'You have done more than enough, sir!'

Royston-Jones made a small sound. It could have been a laugh or a sob. 'You are talking like a commander already, Hogarth!' He placed his hands on the screen, as if to feel the reactions of his battle-torn ship. It was quite still. He sighed. 'There were moments when I thought we should never see Mudros again. Or anywhere else, for that matter!'

They stared in silence as the big hospital ship's anchor cable began to shorten and a small cloud of steam rose from her capstan.

If he closed his eyes for one moment he knew that he would not sleep. They were all worried about him, but he knew that food and rest were not the answer. If he faltered for an instant and allowed himself to relax he knew it would all come back. The bombardment and the havoc wrought by the Turkish guns would be a mere backcloth to what had happened later. The returning boats, barely half filled, and then mostly with wounded men.

He could torture himself by remembering Major De L'Isle's empty face as he had climbed to the bridge to make his report. The bridge, with its pitted plating and dead men, an unrecognisable place.

Royston-Jones had sat quite still in his chair, almost afraid to look at the marine's features as he retold the efforts and the final retreat of the landing party.

De L'Isle had said of Sub-Lieutenant Pringle, 'He was shot

414

during the final Turkish attack.' Then, 'He was shot in the back, sir.'

Pringle's death had formed a background to the rest of that heartbreaking report. Somehow it seemed to sum up their brave but pathetic efforts, to mark the whole episode with shame.

Over half the landing force had been killed, and many of the remainder wounded. Some had died well, others had ended their moments in the madness and bitterness of men who had been cheated and betrayed.

Royston-Jones listened unmoving to De L'Isle's account of Pickles' death, and wondered how much more he could stand.

De L'Isle's harsh voice had been unsteady. 'Colour Sergeant Barnes had to go up for the two snotties in the end, sir. Chesnaye was in such a bad way we thought he was past hope. But even then he put up a fight.'

Royston-Jones' mind had been too dulled to realise what he meant. 'Fight?'

'He wouldn't leave young Pickles, sir. He hung on to his body and refused to leave without him!' De L'Isle's reserve had suddenly fallen away. 'My God, I was proud of them! *All* of them!'

Now it was over, and soon the *Saracen* would be crossing the open sea once more. Perhaps then he would be able to tell De L'Isle and the others. Tell them of the signal he had received to mark the end of what might now be classed as a mere episode.

So far only Godden knew, and he would no doubt make use of its contents once his own personal pain was sufficiently dimmed for him to remember beyond those moments of united suffering and valour.

The attack, the suffering, the slaughter, had been for nothing. At the very last moment the Army had not made its attack.

As Pickles died on a bare rock pinnacle, and Chesnaye fought his own battles against pain and grief, even while Pringle received a bullet from some unknown marksman as he ran terror-stricken from the enemy; while all these things and many more were happening, and the *Saracen* changed from a sparkling symbol to a battered and listing hulk as she pressed home her attack, the soldiers stood in their trenches and listened. Some were grateful, others were ashamed. All wondered at the circumstances which allowed such things to happen.

Royston-Jones had not left his bridge since the anchor had

415

dropped. He knew he was afraid of what he might see and of what he might find in the eyes of his men. For nothing, he thought. It was all for nothing.

De L'Isle had faltered as he had been about to leave the bridge. 'What shall I say in my report about Pringle?' He had seemed at a loss. 'I don't see why the others should have their names slurred because of him!'

He had replied: 'Say that he died of his wounds. That is enough.'

Hogarth's voice cut into his wretchedness, 'The hospital ship has weighed, sir.'

Like a white ghost the ex-liner began to glide between the moored ships. Royston-Jones saw, too, the tug's ungainly shape hovering nearby. 'Tell Lieutenant Travis to come to the bridge,' he said to a messenger.

The young seaman only stared at him until Hogarth gestured quickly for him to leave. Quietly he said, 'Travis was killed, sir.'

The Captain rubbed his dry hands across his face. 'Oh yes. Thank you.' He turned, caught off guard again as a ripple of cheering floated across the glistening water. 'What is that?'

Hogarth said: 'The hospital ship, sir. The men on her upper deck are cheering the old *Saracen*!'

Royston-Jones blinked and rubbed his eyes. 'They are cheering *us*?'

'Yes, sir.' Hogarth watched sadly as the little figure in soiled uniform and scorched cap looked round him as if lost in bewilderment.

Then with something like his old vigour he climbed on to the screen and held his cap high above his head. As his arm tired he changed his cap from hand to hand, his eyes blinded by the sun.

Long after the hospital ship's wash had been smoothed from the quiet anchorage he still stood and saluted his men, and a memory.

Unlike the engines of a warship, those of the hospital ship seemed far away and remote, so that the gentle tremor which had started almost unnoticeably was more of a sensation, like something in the mind.

Chesnaye cursed the weakness in his body and tried once more to lift himself in the narrow, spotless-sheeted bunk. He had no

416

idea what part of the ship he was in, nor did he care. From what he could see in the vast compartment he deduced that the whole vessel was crammed with wounded like himself, regimented and lined up in enamelled bunks, bandaged, splintered and drugged for the voyage to England. Above his head a large fan purred discreetly, and the long rectangular port which opened on to the sunlit anchorage seemed to accentuate his new status, his sense of not belonging. By straining every muscle and ignoring the fire in his thigh he could lift his head far enough to see the tapering topmasts of an achored cruiser, her commissioning pennant limp in the scorching heat, her tall funnels devoid of smoke. And, beyond, the rounded hills which now seemed alien and hostile.

Another gentle vibration rattled the enamel dishes on his small bunk-side table, and very faintly he could hear the shout of orders and the brief scurry of feet on the big ship's spacious upper deck. Soon they would be leaving Mudros and the Mediterranean, perhaps for ever.

He fell back, biting his lip to stem the feeling of anguish and misery. Like unfinished pictures in his mind the memories of the Peninsula, with its record of pain and death, flooded through him. Those last moments were still hazy and obscure, and again he wondered if time would clear away the mist, or if in fact he would lose the reminders altogether.

He closed his eyes tightly as Pickles' face came back to him. The empty loneliness of that rock pinnacle and the triumphant crack of snipers' rifles. Nothing seemed to go beyond that, but for his own weak but desperate struggle with Sergeant Barnes, who had somehow climbed into that terrible place and had carried him to safety. There were a few madly distorted recollections of running marines, their mouths and eyes working in frenzy or fear, rifles glowing with heat as they fired and fired again at the invisible enemy. Then there was one final picture, stark and terribly clear.

He had seen Leading Seaman Tobias running towards him as he lay helpless in a tiny gully, the man's face suddenly alight with pleasure. Tobias's expression had changed to one of disbelief as Pringle had burst from cover and had run blindly towards the path to the beach. Chesnaye still wondered how many of the others who had lived had seen what he and Tobias had then witnessed. Able Seaman Wellard, bleeding from several wounds, had staggered to his feet from a small pile of rocks, his teeth bared

417

in his beard from the agony that movement must have cost him. As more bullets whipped and cracked about him he lifted his rifle, the final effort making him cry out like some trapped animal, and then he had fired. As Pringle's running figure had fallen, Wellard had thrown down his rifle and stood quite still. Then, with a final glance towards the gentle sea he had limped away, back towards the enemy lines. He had not been seen again.

Chesnaye realised that morphia must have claimed his reeling mind for some long hours after that moment. When he had opened his eyes again he had been aboard the *Saracen*, and there was no more gunfire, no scent of smoke and scorched bracken in his nostrils; just the pain and the sense of near breakdown to keep the memories alive.

The Captain had visited him, but it now seemed like part of a dream, with Royston-Jones' figure hovering against a background of red mist. Beaushears, too, had found a moment, and had patiently answered Chesnaye's desperate, wandering questions.

Now, as some of the mist cleared, he could piece together what he had been told. Of the faces he had known in the *Saracen* who were now dead, or scattered somewhere in this ship like himself. Of Lieutenant Travis who had lost a leg but stayed on the bridge until he had died. Of Nutting, the Padre, who had gone mad as he had crawled from one corpse to the next, his gabbled prayers meaningless in a world for which he had never been trained. And of Commander Godden, who despite his wound seemed happier and more relaxed than he had ever been.

Beaushears had said bitterly: 'He's glad to be out of it! He must think the Captain acted wrongly.' He had shrugged, suddenly old and weary. 'To think I once thought him a better man than the Captain!'

Chesnaye remembered, too, what Major De L'Isle had said when he had paid one of his visits to his wounded marines. 'It could have been a great campaign, boy!' He had peered round the shellscarred wardroom which was being used as an additional sick bay, his red face sad and disillusioned. 'It was devised by a genius, but it was left to bloody fools to carry out!'

Perhaps that was a suitable epitaph.

There was a step on the deck beside the bunk, and Chesnaye opened his eyes. For several moments he stared at the soldier who leaned on his stick and peered down at him.

418

Robert Driscoll took a deep breath and shifted his bandaged leg to a more careful position. Very carefully he said, 'I knew I'd find you if I looked long enough, Dick.'

They watched each other without speaking. Driscoll looked thin and much older, his uniform hanging on him like the rags on a scarecrow. After a while he added, 'We can go and see Helen together now, eh?'

As the hospital ship shortened her cable, Driscoll perched himself on Chesnaye's bunk, and each allowed his thoughts to drift back to the distant Peninsula and all that it would mean to them for as long as they lived.

Driscoll's sudden appearance had brought a faint warmth to Chesnaye's heart, but sadness too with the memory it had conjured up. Again it was of Pickles, when he had come to look for him. 'I knew I'd find you if I ran far enough!' Perhaps he was still up there in that cleft of rock, his eyes wide and empty of pain.

There was the sound of cheering, and Chesnaye roused himself from the drowsiness which always seemed to be ready to close in. With sudden desperation he gasped: 'Help me, Bob! Hold me up!'

His eyes eagerly sought the bottom edge of the big open port as Driscoll's arm lifted his shoulders from the bunk. For a moment he thought the other ship was moving, and then with something like numbness he realised that it was the hospital ship which was gathering way and already gliding towards the end of the anchorage.

He had to blink rapidly to clear his eyes so as not to miss even the smallest detail of that scarred but so familiar shape which passed slowly across his vision.

The high, ugly bridge and tripod mast, the big, ungainly turret, and those splintered decks which had once gleamed so white and new. In his mind's eye he could see the three battle ensigns, and hear the cheering soldiers on the laden troopships.

Driscoll said quietly, 'I've got my binoculars here, Dick?'

Chesnaye struggled upright and shook his head. The *Saracen* was already a world away, but the sudden pain of separation was almost too much. He wanted to find the strength to cheer with the others, but nothing came.

Almost to himself he replied: 'No, I want to see her just as she is. Or perhaps as she was.'

The hospital ship altered course, and the small picture of the blackened listing ship changed to one of the open sea.

419

Robert Driscoll stood up and glanced down the long lines of silent bunks. Perhaps, he thought, if someone like Chesnaye could feel as he did it had not all been a waste of time.

Limping heavily, he moved across to the open port, feeling as he did so that first easy pitch to the vessel's deck as she met the first swell of the open sea. He leaned out over the crisp water and drew several deep breaths.

He tried to sum it all up with a few thoughts, but he could only think of it as a farewell to something lost. The brooding shape of Achi Baba, the trenches and the wire. The true comradeship of fear and pride, the dirt and the ignorance of what lay in store.

He turned his back on the sea and looked towards Chesnaye's white face, and wondered.

Part Two   1941

Chapter One

The Captain

April in the Mediterranean, the month when Malta should have been at its best, with the night air cool and clear after the heat of the day. But this was April 1941, and the unusually low clouds which hung above the battered island and hid the stars were slashed and torn in a mad galaxy of colours as the nightly air raid got under way and mounted in steady force.

Occasionally above the crash of anti-aircraft fire and the rumble of collapsing buildings could be heard the steady, unbroken beat of aircraft engines. Dozens or hundreds, it was difficult to assess. The sound was without break, without change. It was a constant threat, a mockery against the blind barrage which seemed to rip the night apart.

From the naval anchorage the long streams of gay tracers crept away into the sky, whilst from inland the heavier guns hurled their shells to explode beyond the clouds so that their underbellies seemed to be alight.

Streets which had been clear and busy during the sunlight had become narrow valleys between walls of rubble and scorched timber, beneath which men and women cowered and waited, whilst in the chaos around them the despairing troops and workers searched out the feeble cries and felt for the imprisoned hands.

It was like a mad storm of forked lightning, every night a repetition, but for the fact that each one was just a little worse than the one which had preceded it.

The Night Operations Officer in one of the many naval underground strongpoints gritted his teeth as a fresh, muffled rumble made the naked light bulb dance on its flex and brought down another layer of dust to join that which already covered filing cabinets, desks and occupants in a grey film. The tarnished lace on his jacket proclaimed him to be a lieutenant-commander, but his tired and strained face, which twisted with each distant explosion, seemed too old for his rank.

Through a massive door he could hear the constant jingle of

telephones and the clatter of a teleprinter. Signals, demands, orders and chaos. It never let up. His eye fell on a week-old paper from England. The headline referred proudly to Malta as 'the gallant island fortress'. 'The thorn in Italy's soft underbelly!' Another roar, and the lights flickered momentarily.

A petty officer crunched through the dust and placed a chipped cup and saucer on the officer's desk. 'Char, sir.' He glanced incuriously at the flaking walls and said, 'Good thing we're down here, sir?'

The Operations Officer picked up the cup and watched the tea's surface quivering in his hand. Bitterly he replied: 'Built by galley slaves hundreds of years ago. *They* at least had the right idea!'

A rating poked his head round the door. 'Stick of bombs across Parlatoria Wharf, sir.'

The officer looked at the floor. 'Again? I hope to God the destroyers there are all right.' Almost viciously he added, 'Let me know more as soon as you can!'

The petty officer walked to the operations board which covered one of the walls and ran his finger down the pencilled list of ships' names. 'With raids day *and* night it'll be hard for the ships to take on fuel, sir.'

'Unless we get some help and some fighter planes there won't be any damned fuel! What the hell do they expect of us?' He glared at the man's worn features. 'Do they want us to go and fight them with pikes or something?' He broke off as the other door opened slightly. 'What th' hell d'you want?'

The petty officer stiffened and cleared his throat noisily, his eyes taking in the shadowy shape of the newcomer with both experience and immediate caution. He had seen the feeble light from the corridor shine briefly on the four gold stripes, and he tried to cover his superior's surprise by saying hastily, 'Can I get *you* a cup of tea, sir?'

Captain Richard Chesnaye limped into the centre of the room so that the naked bulb shone directly above his head and made his dark hair appear glossy and fresh, although in fact he had not slept for two days. He sat down in a vacant chair and looked calmly at the other officer's dazed face. He said: 'My name is Chesnaye. I believe I was expected yesterday, but the convoy was attacked.' He saw the man jump as the floor quivered to another explosion. 'So if possible I should like to join my ship at once.'

424

The Operations Officer passed his hand across his face and turned wearily to his desk. He forced himself to leaf through a pile of papers while he reassembled his thoughts. A year ago, perhaps even a month, and he would have jumped with horror at the thought of being caught off guard by a full captain. Now it did not seem to matter. The whole world was falling around them. It was just a matter of time. The enemy bombers which were destroying Malta and preventing sleep, or even rest, were flying from a mere fifty miles away. How could an island right on the enemy's doorstep, with a mere handful of clapped-out fighters, expect to survive?

He glanced quickly across his desk at the newcomer. He noticed that one of the gold stripes was brighter than the other three and that he was wearing several decorations which he could not recognise in the poor light. His mind began to recover. This captain was yet another sign of what was happening to the country and the Royal Navy.

With Britain standing alone against the combined weight of Germany and Italy every experienced officer was seemingly being promoted overnight. At the other end of the scale even yatchtsmen with brief weekend sailing their only background had been pitchforked into the battle as temporary Reserve Officers. There was no time for training now, and few with experience to pave the way. Yet from the look of this stranger's newly added gold stripe he guessed he had only just been promoted, and that pointed clearly enough to the fact that he was yet another officer who had been 'beached' between the wars and so lost way in the struggle for advancement and promotion. He noticed, too, the small tense lines at the corners of the captain's mouth. As if he was forcing himself to appear calm with constant effort. He had a grave, intelligent face, and his figure was slim, even youthful. And yet . . . he shook his head and tried to clear his starved mind. A month ago he would have had every appointment and fact at his fingertips. He groped through the pile of papers. 'Which ship, sir?'

Richard Chesnaye watched him without expression. He had seen that look on faces enough to know what the man was thinking. 'I am taking command of *Saracen*,' he said.

The Operations Officer sat down heavily and felt his inner resentment change to something like pity. It was slowly coming back to him now. In his mind's eye he could even see the signals which had referred to this man Chesnaye who was coming from England to assume command of the *Saracen*. He had seen the elderly monitor alongside the wharf only that forenoon. She must be over twenty-five years old, he thought. She was something of a joke at the Base, or had been until joking had gone out of fashion. She was an ugly, antiquated-looking ship, her disproportionate shape made even more peculiar by her garish dazzle paint which had been introduced to foil the prowling submarines. As a colleague had remarked at the time, 'Like a poor old spinster in a party frock!'

Her previous captain had just returned to England following a court martial. He had taken the old ship to the North African coast to lend support to the hard-pressed troops who, even now, were falling back across Libya, leaving positions and bases which they had won so bravely months before. The monitor had 'fired short', and several hundred British soldiers had been killed and wounded. On top of that the *Saracen* had run aground and had only been towed clear within minutes of the dive-bombers smelling her out. It might have been better if they had got to her first.

Too lightly he said, 'I expect you know all about her, sir?'

'My first ship.' He repeated the words in his mind. My first ship. What a lot they implied. But no one could understand what they meant to him at that moment.

Chesnaye added half to himself. 'Yes, I know a great deal about her.'

He shifted in his chair as the ache in his thigh returned. A few more hours and he would be aboard. All the waiting and the yearning were nearly over.

What would she be like now? Perhaps like himself. Unsure, even unwanted.

Some of the old anger and defensive bitterness moved within him. Sharply he said, 'I should like to get to her at once.'

The Operations Officer nodded. 'I'll see what I can do do. She's out on a buoy at the moment.' He smiled. 'I'm sorry I can't give you the full formality, sir. I expect you're thinking it's rather different from peacetime?' He bit his lip as the words dropped out. That was a stupid thing to say. This captain was like so many others. He must have spent many of the peacetime years lost and miserable without the Service which so unexpectedly had been denied them. He had seen them at Fleet Reviews and Open Days

426

at the dockyards. Eager, keen-eyed, yet so pathetically on the outside.

He saw the shutters drop behind Chesnaye's grey eyes. Hastily he muttered, 'I'll put through a call, provided the line's still in place!'

Chesnaye forced himself to sit back in the chair, to ignore the officer's short, staccato words on the dusty telephone. The man was sorry for him, and confused too. It no longer mattered. It had hurt at first, but not any more. As if to reassure himself he touched the lace on his sleeve, and felt the excitement welling inside him.

The other officer dropped the telephone and looked uneasy. 'No boats running tonight, sir. Very heavy raid up top. It gets worse all the time.' As if to make the unwanted conversation last he added: 'They fly over in daylight and machine-gun the place too. St. Paul's Bay, the outlying villages, everywhere!'

'When can I get across, then?' Unwittingly Chesnaye dropped his guard and leaned forward.

'First light, sir.' He glanced at the petty officer. 'We could give you a bunk here if you'd prefer not to go over to the quarters? It's not much, but'll be on hand.' He dropped his eyes as Chesnaye's face flooded with obvious relief.

'Thank you. I'd like that.' Chesnaye stood up and grimaced.

The petty officer held open the door and reached for a torch. 'Hurt your leg, sir?'

Chesnaye paused in the doorway and regarded him slowly. 'A long time ago. But it helps to keep my memory intact!'

The door closed behind him and the Operations Officer stretched his arms above his head.

A rating called urgently, 'Number Seven fuel tank ablaze, sir!'

The officer shook himself. 'Bloody hell!' He reached for his telephone.

Lieutenant-Commander John Erskine, the *Saracen*'s First Lieutenant, ran his fingers through his long fair hair and sat back in his swivel chair. His tiny office was lined with shelves loaded with ledgers and files, and the hanging desk covered with signals awaiting his attention. It was early morning, and the sun which filtered through the one thick scuttle was as yet without warmth. Erksine had breakfasted alone in the still deserted wardroom which smelled of drink and tobacco from the previous night. He

427

had persuaded himself that he wanted an early start to allow himself time to clear the mounting pile of paperwork, although he knew well enough that the real reason was quite different.

The other officers would be watching him, gauging his mood and reactions to the events which had so suddenly changed his small world. He was twenty-eight years old, with a clear-cut open face entirely devoid of pretension, but at this moment was filled with gloom. He had been in the old monitor for nine months, almost since the day Italy had cast caution to the wind and joined with Germany in a combined attack on Britain. During that time he had watched the change creep over the ships and men of the Mediterranean Fleet, once the most efficient and powerful force of its kind in the world, but now stretched to and beyond the limit even of safety. It had all been so clear cut at first. In peacetime they had exercised with extravagant enthusiasm under every condition conceived by an over-confident Admiralty. Always with the knowledge that the other great navy, the French, was ready to close any gaps and make the Mediterranean the one sure buffer below Europe's long coastline.

Without apprehension they had watched the rebirth of Germany's sea-power and skill, and with amusement the preparations with which the Italians had followed their partner's every move. It was still hard to fathom what had gone wrong. The swift, lightning war in France, followed by Dunkirk and the complete collapse of England's European allies. Only the Greeks tagged along the end of the line now, and even they were receiving the first probes from a confident Wehrmacht. In the Mediterranean the Navy had managed to retain its old appearances of calm superiority, up to the last few months, that is. Ships of the Fleet had followed the Army's triumphant advances along the North African coast, where one crushing defeat after another had scattered the Italian troops to the winds and filled the prison compounds to overflowing. Now the tide was turning even there. With Europe safely under lock-and-key and the remains of the British Expeditionary Force flung back across the English Channel, the German Army was able to look around, to estimate the extent of her enemy's remaining positions. Apparently disgusted with Italy's efforts, the Wehrmacht had joined the battle. In spite of the hard-pressed naval patrols, German troops were being ferried across to Africa, and aircraft of every kind were making their appearance in the clear and smiling skies.

In the *Saracen*, too, the new strain had shown itself very clearly. From a new complement of officers the strength had shrunk and changed. New, untrained faces appeared each month. The straight lace of the regulars was replaced by the wavy lace of the R.N.V.R. and the intertwined braid of the R.N.R. Erskine had been irritated by his appointment to such an ancient ship, although it was the rule rather than the exception now. The Mediterranean Fleet, once filled with the cream of the destroyer flotillas and the proudest cruisers, was now supported and reinforced with the strangest collection of craft ever assembled. Ex-China river gunboats, flat-bottomed and unsteady even in a slight breeze, cruised along the African coast and grimly exchanged shots with modern E-boats and screaming dive-bombers. Paddle steamers, once the joy of day-excursionists on their trips from Dover to Calais, swept mines, patrolled the boom-gates and tried to do the hundred and one tasks for which they had never been designed. So the old monitor was just another symbol of events.

Erskine was a calm, capable officer, and despite his lack of outward emotion looked forward to a command of his own. He knew his work in this worn-out old ship would serve him well when that time came. So too his contact with the new Navy, the reservists and the seamen who daily poured out from distant training barracks, would make him more confident when his chance came.

The previous captain had been too old, too long in retirement, for the breathtaking savagery of the Mediterranean war. But what he had lacked in foresight and preparedness he had made up in Erskine's estimation in his dignity and complete courage. He still remembered the look on the old man's face after the court martial. It was the expression of a dead man. In wartime anything could happen. Men died as easily from caution as from eagerness and as quickly from over-confidence as from cowardice.

The fact remained that the ship had disgraced herself, and not only the Captain would take the blame. Once it might have been different, but now with every ship and man stretched to the limit there were no acceptable excuses. Responsibility and personal liability grew as resources shrank, and in the cold, dispassionate arena of the court-martial room who could see beyond the bare facts?

There was a gentle tap at the door, and Erskine looked up to see

Lieutenant McGowan, the Gunnery Officer, watching him with his sad, deepset eyes.

'Good morning, sir.' McGowan's voice was formal, but he gave a quick smile as Erskine waved him to a chair. He peered round at the piles of paper. 'What a war!'

Erskine tapped his pencil against his teeth and waited. McGowan was the only other regular officer aboard, apart from a midshipman and a couple of grizzled warrant officers, but apart from that fact he was also a close friend.

McGowan said slowly: 'Bad raid last night. A destroyer over in Sliema copped it, I believe. *And* the ruddy tanker they escorted all the way from Alex!'

Erskine watched the sun's rays strengthening against the sombre grey paint. 'We might get it again before we sail.' He frowned. 'When we've mustered the hands get the cable party to rig a slip wire to the buoy. If pushed we can break the cable and get away in a hurry.'

McGowan showed his teeth in a mock grin. 'Hurry? What, this ship?'

'Now look, James, let's not get started on your pet moan. This is our ship. We must do our best.' He cocked his head to listen to the sluice of water and brooms across the upper deck. 'It'll be Colours in ten minutes, so get cracking!' He forced a smile. 'You are O.O.D., I presume?'

McGowan stood up and reached for his cap. 'I wouldn't have stayed aboard otherwise, my friend! A nice booze-up followed by the exotic charm of a dusky filly, is more the way my mind is going these nights!' He suddenly became serious. 'I just wanted you to know I think it's a bloody shame about your getting saddled with this ship. First the bombardment going wrong, and then the old fool running her on the putty, that was all bad enough. I don't see why you should have to stagnate here when you're a natural for command of a destroyer!'

Erskine dropped his eyes. 'That will do, James.' His voice was flat.

McGowan snorted: 'I suppose the new skipper'll be even worse! One bloody deadbeat after another. Even a good ship couldn't be expected to survive this!'

Erskine looked up his eyes flashing. 'That will *do*! You know damn well you shouldn't talk like this, and I won't have it!' He watched the surprise on his friend's face and added quietly: 'I depend on your support. Any sort of talk like that and there's no saying what might spread through the ship.'

McGowan adjusted his cap and said stubbornly, 'I still think it's a shame, even if I'm not allowed to say it!'

Erskine looked back at the signals as a bugle blared overhead. 'Go to hell!'

McGowan grinned wearily. 'Aye, *aye*, sir!'

Erskine threw down his pencil and stood up. As he leaned against the rough metal and idly watched the clear water below the scuttle he listened to the bugle as it sounded for morning Colours. Opposite the monitor's buoy he could see three destroyers and an anti-aircraft cruiser moored together. As he watched he saw their ensigns slowly mounting the staffs, as the *Saracen*'s was doing at that moment above the quarterdeck.

He looked past the other ships towards the unmoving pall of brown smoke which hovered across Valletta. Over there people had died in the twinkling of an eye. Women, children, it made no odds to death's impartiality. But so long as the White Ensign was hoisted every morning there was still a chance, a glimmer of hope. He smiled in spite of his complete weariness. I sound like a bloody politician, he thought.

He turned as a messenger tapped at the door. 'Yes?'

'Signal, sir.' He handed over a sealed envelope with the flimsy sheet of paper. 'And sailing orders, sir.'

Erskine darted a quick look at the man's wooden expression. On the lower deck sailing orders were a constant topic of conjecture. But today this rating had placed the signal in priority. It was unnatural. 'What does the signal say, Bunts?'

The man grimaced. 'New captain is comin' aboard in ten minutes, sir!'

Erskine stared at him, his normal reserve momentarily forgotten. 'What?'

'In fact, sir, there's a launch waitin' at the jetty *now*.' He spoke with the satisfaction of a man who has seen a superior caught off guard.

Erskine snatched his cap and jammed it on his head. One damned thing after another, he thought bitterly. McGowan was probably right. Troubles had a habit of breeding very rapidly.

'My compliments to the O.O.D. Tell him I require his presence

431

on the quarterdeck immediately!' He took a last glance at the disordered office, his mouth curving with sudden resentment. 'And pass the word for the Chief Bosun's Mate.'

The man hurried away, and Erskine followed him more slowly. Of course, it would have to be like this. Night liberty-men not yet returned, the ship a shambles from the night's air raid and the Duty Watch only just recovering from a hurried breakfast.

On the broad quarterdeck he felt the first promise of the day's warmth, and unconsciously he ran his finger round the inside of his collar.

Chief Petty Officer Craig, a massive, wintry-eyed pensioner, saluted and tucked his list of working-parties beneath his arm. 'You want me, sir?'

'Yes, Chief Bosun's Mate. The new captain'll be aboard in a few moments.' He saw with faint satisfaction that the tanned face of the Chief Petty Officer was unmoved by his terse announcement. 'Fall in the side party and stand by the gangway.' Erskine ran his eye quickly along the hose-littered deck. 'And for God's sake get this potmess cleared up!'

Craig saluted and marched purposefully away, his mouth snapping open and shut like a trap as he called out a string of names.

Gayler, one of the monitor's midshipmen, saluted and cleared his throat. 'Boat shoving off from the jetty, sir!' He was fresh from Dartmouth and very conscious of himself. 'It looks like a fine day, sir.'

You don't know the half of it, thought Erskine. Aloud he snapped: 'Man the side! Stand by to receive the Captain!'

The pinnace squeaked gently against the jetty's rubber fenders, and as he looked down the flight of stone steps Chesnaye saw that his personal gear had already been stowed in the boat's cockpit. A seaman stood at the bow and stern, and the coxswain waited loosely beside the brass wheel. As the boat pitched, a shaft of sunlight glanced off Chesnaye's metal trunk, and just for a brief instant he felt the old emotion touch his eyes. The years seemed to fall away. It could have been Portsmouth harbour with Pickles, a boy like himself, waiting impatiently to take him to the ship. So much had happened, yet so little. It was the same ship. As if she had waited all these years. Unfamiliar in her dazzle paint, but unmistakable. She had lost her tall topmast, and her maindeck

432

sprouted several Oerlikons and other automatic weapons instead of the old twelve-pounders. Yet she was the same. The ship which had stayed with his thoughts over time itself. Once or twice he had seen her since those terrible days at Gallipoli. At Portsmouth he had once watched her waddling out to sea past the misty outline of the Isle of Wight, and again in Rosyth, paid-off and neglected. She had steamed her way back to the Mediterranean, and on to China. From Hong Kong to Spain to evacuate refugees from the Civil War, and then across the endless water to Ceylon as a training ship for cadets. Back into Reserve again, and then called once more to serve, like himself.

Chesnaye shifted his weight to the other leg and cursed the pain in his thigh. Like his memory of the *Saracen*, the old wound had been his constant companion. He turned his head to look at the other warships moored nearby. Commanded by officers younger and junior to himself, they reminded him again that he had only held one command in his life. That had been a small sloop just after the Great War. A short, uneventful commission to break the endless monotony of shore appointments, junior posts in large ships and the final misery of his discharge from the Service. Many others had been 'axed' from the reduced Navy, but each case was individual. Some had been grateful, after being entered into the Navy by their parents at the age of twelve, to a service they had always hated. Others had been defiant, unwilling to accept the injustice, and had wasted precious time and money in a flare of effort to prove their worth in other fields. Chicken farms, the Civil Service, even the Church, had received and rejected them. Men like Chesnaye had been too dazed, too shocked, to act foolishly. They readapted themselves more slowly, licked their wounds and tried again.

For nearly ten years he had wandered alone from one country to the next, working without complaint at whatever job took his eye. He had no ties. Both his parents were dead. His father during the final months of that first, far-off war, and his long-suffering mother in the influenza epidemic which followed it. Chesnaye first tried to return to the sea. He joined the Norwegian Antarctic whaling fleet, and for several years worked as a deck officer in the filth and noise of the factory-ship. His old wound reacted sharply, and he moved on to New Zealand, where with his carefully saved capital he bought a half-share in a farm-appliance firm. Business improved, but as world affairs deteriorated, and the clouds gathered above Munich, Chesnaye quietly said his goodbyes to his astonished partner and started back for home.

He was constantly dogged by the picture of his father as he had remembered him before the first war. He was determined that he would never lose his pride and suffer the final misery of complete rejection by the Service he had always loved. Chesnaye had never forgotten the Navy. He did not have to buy a bungalow in Southsea, to walk the promenade and watch the distant grey shapes slipping down-channel, and to stand moist-eyed at the sound of a barracks' bugle. The Service was part of him. It never left him, no matter what he attempted. And to symbolise that trust and understanding the memory of the ugly monitor had acted as a prop. He knew, too, that unlike his father, he would accept the position of Officer of the Watch on Southend pier if necessary; but he had accepted the post of Training Commander in one of the new intake establishments with equal calmness. It was a start.

But the waiting had been harder than he had anticipated. The first excitement of training and guiding the endless procession of civilian sailors – office boys, labourers, milkmen and others – wore off as he again felt the yearning and the want.

He had almost laughed when he had seen the expression on the face of his captain when that gentleman had told him of his new appointment. The old man had been apologetic and then angry. 'An old ship like that indeed! By God, Richard, you're more use to me here!' He had waved his veined hand across the expanse of the establishment, glittering with painted white stones, flagmast and immaculate sentries. Months before, it had been a holiday camp, but through the old captain's eyes it had shone like a battleship.

Now he was here. The waiting and the suspense forgotten. LIke an unwanted burden the years seemed to slide from his shoulders.

A voice interrupted his thoughts. 'I say, any chance of a lift out to the *Saracen*?'

Chesnaye swung round, irritated at being caught dreaming as well as with the casual form of address. He saw a dishevelled officer, whose wide pale eyes were peering at him as if their owner were more used to hiding behind powerful spectacles. On his crumpled sleeve he wore two wavy stripes, between which ran a line of bright scarlet.

Chesnaye nodded. 'Yes, I am going in her direction.'

434

The officer beamed, his youthful face creasing with pleasure. 'Oh, jolly good!' He held out his hand. 'I'm Wickersley, the *Saracen*'s doctor, actually.' He chuckled disarmingly. 'I suppose I've got a cheek really. A tiny voice of caution warns me that you are *rather* senior!'

Chesnaye felt his taut muscles relaxing. 'Captain Chesnaye.'

'Oh, splendid.' Wickersley looked down at the waiting boat. 'I'm not really genned up on the ranks yet. I've only been in the Andrew a month. I was at St. Matthew's, y'know!' He gestured towards the smoke-covered houses behind him. 'Been over there all night keeping the jolly old hand in!'

They went down the steps, and Chesnaye automatically stepped aside to allow the junior officer to enter the boat first, as was customary. But the Doctor shook his head cheerfully. 'Oh no, sir! After *you*!'

The coxswain dropped his salute and eyed the interloper balefully. He had expected the grave-eyed captain to blast the Doctor skywards as he bloody well deserved. Instead . . . ah well – he shook his head sadly. It was a different Navy now. 'Shove off, forrard!' he yelled. The little boat swung into the stream and turned towards the mass of shipping.

Spray danced across the pinnace's canopy as it lifted gaily on the sparkling water. Chesnaye staggered and put out his hand to steady himself against the motion. On the long voyage from England he had noticed how unprepared he had become for all the mannerisms and tests of seaboard life. The restless sea, the daily routine, all seemed vaguely strange and unnerving. The convoy had slipped through Gibraltar Straits and had been attacked soon afterwards. Appalled, Chesnaye had watched ship after ship blasted to fragments by the enemy bombers which appeared to fill the sky. The destroyer escort in which he had been a passenger was commanded by an Australian who had done little to hide his irritation at Chesnaye's constant presence on his bridge. Once he had snapped: 'Jesus, Captain, you'll get enough of this later on! Why don't you get your head down?' But Chesnaye had found the Australian accent somehow reassuring, as it reminded him of the life in New Zealand. He wondered how that captain had fared in the night's air raid.

He instantly dismissed the convoy and everything else from his

435

thoughts as he watched the sharpening shape of the monitor. Eagerly, hungrily, his eyes darted up and down her length, as if afraid to miss some scar or mark, as a mother will look at a grown-up son. She was older, but the same. There were streaks of rust around her hawse-pipe and more than one dent along her bulging hull, but nothing that he could not put right.

The Doctor spoke from the cockpit. 'I'd like to ask you aboard for a noggin, but it's a bit early.'

The boat drew nearer, and Chesnaye saw the familiar scurry and frantic preparations which culminated in a rigid knot of figures at the head of the long varnished gangway.

His eyes misted, and over the years he heard Lieutenant Hogarth's high-pitched voice screaming down threats to the flustered Pickles. And later when Pickles had warned him of the Captain. 'He hates everybody, especially midshipmen!'

Is that how they are thinking of me? he wondered.

The boat lost way and idled towards the gangway, the polished boathook poised and ready.

Wickersley called, 'Jolly decent of you to drop me here!'

Chesnaye looked down at him, knowing that he was glad he had had company for those last few agonising yards. 'Actually, I'm coming aboard myself!'

The Doctor's eyes widened. 'Oh?' Then, as the realisation flooded his mind, '*Oh!*'

Chesnaye straightened his back and stepped on to the gangway. He tried not to count the wide, well-worn steps, his mind blank to all else but the whirl of events which had at last overtaken him. His head lifted above the deck, and his brain only half registered the line of tanned faces, the raised hands, and then the shrill twitter of pipes which washed across him like floodwater. A few mumbled words, more salutes, a guard presenting arms and the flash of a sword.

One face seemed to swim out of the mist. A calm, youthful voice said the words he had waited so long to hear.

'Welcome aboard, sir!' He was back.

Chapter Two

Out of the Sun

Lieutenant Malcolm Norris, R.N.V.R., walked nervously to the front of the bridge and stared for several seconds into the darkness. The four hours of the Middle Watch had all but dragged to their close, and now that it was almost time to be relieved the same old feeling of nervous anticipation was making his heart thump against his ribs.

It was still very dark, with the stars high and bright against a cloudless sky and reflected in the black oily water which slopped and gurgled against the ship's labouring hull as the monitor plodded slowly towards the invisible horizon. A steady south-west breeze made the ship rock uncomfortably, so that every piece of metal in the bridge structure groaned in regular protest, yet its clammy breath brought no life to the men on watch, but made them move continuously as they peered into the darkness.

Norris cleared his throat and jumped at the noise the sound brought to the silence around him. He still could not believe that he was Officer of the Watch, for four hours in sole charge of the ship and the safety of every man aboard. For the four months he had been aboard he had been assistant to Lieutenant Fox, the Navigating Officer, and had shared the Middle Watch without complaint. Fox was a hard-bitten professional seaman from the Merchant Navy, who until the outbreak of war had been First Mate of a banana boat. He was an uncouth, outspoken man who frequently gave vent to criticism of his straight-laced companions and all the Royal Navy stood for. As the months passed and the ship took on more amateur officers like Norris, Fox's criticism and complaints gave way to contempt and finally long periods of silence, broken only occasionally by a string of fierce swearing and rage when an error of seamanship or navigation offended his watchful attention. If nothing else, Norris conceded, Fox was a first-rate seaman, and when you shared a watch with him you had nothing to worry about. Norris had been content to dream and dwell in the brave world of his imagination, and carry out the minor jobs of the night's most hated watch.

He realised now only too well that he should have made more use of his time. Overnight everything had altered. The watches had been changed around because Erskine, the senior watch-keeper, had been taken off the rota in order to assist the new captain during his takeover period. In a flash Norris found himself in charge of the watch, and, even worse, had been given Harbridge, the Gunner (T), as his assistant. Harbridge was a squat, vindictive little warrant officer of the old school. He had worked his way slowly and steadily from the spartan misery of an orphans' home to the undreamed power of his one thin stripe of gold lace. The journey had covered many years, through a boys' training ship, destroyers, cruisers, naval barracks and practically every other type of ship or establishment which flew the White Ensign. He had become used and hardened to harsh discipline, and had never expected anything else. Accordingly, he treated his subordinates with the same lack of feeling and understanding, and had never altered his own rigid standards of efficiency.

Norris knew all this about his companion, and had felt the man's bitter resentment the moment he had joined the wardroom. Norris had been a teacher in a London secondary school. Apart from a few evenings a week at lectures given by a fierce-eyed instructor at the local drill-ship, he knew little of the Navy. All he knew was that he loved and admired everything about it. The war had been the one final opening previously denied him. After an uneventful few months aboard an old cruiser which spent most of its time anchored in the Firth of Forth, Norris had been sent to a gunnery course at Whale Island. The shouting, noise and robot-like drill had appealed to him instantly, and although he had finished the course not far from the bottom of the list, the impression of the gunnery school had been marked on his mind like a battle honour. He had gone on leave and revisited the old school. How small and untidy it had seemed after Whale Island. The sticky paper across the windows as a safeguard against bomb-blast, the brown glazed tiles and the rain-dappled playground. Most of the children had been evacuated for the duration, but to the remainder, and the members of the dingy staff-room, Norris had tried to pass on the new-found glory and happiness which he had found in his new life.

When he had been appointed to the monitor Norris had outwardly expressed indignation and dismay. Inwardly, however, he was satisfied. The ship seemed big and safe. There always seemed to be another officer or a competent petty officer close by when a small crisis arose. In a destroyer it might have been different, but as it was Norris found himself in his present position with hardly an idea of how he got there.

Joyce, his wife, had been scornful whenever he had dared to mention his inner doubts to her. 'Don't you let them push you around, Malc!' He hated the way she abbrieviated his name, just as he did her sharp South London accent. 'You're as good as they are, and don't you forget it!'

In his mind's eye Norris saw himself sitting in the wardroom as he had so often in the last four months. Outwardly attentive and bright-eyed, he had carefully watched and listened to the men who shared his steel world, and had tried to pick the ones he should follow, even copy, and those he should avoid.

John Erskine was his secret hero. Calm, handsome and so very sure of himself. The senior member of the mess, a Dartmouth officer, all the things which Joyce would have warned him about, yet the very accomplishments which would have made her purr should they have come in her direction. Norris liked the way the ratings respected Erskine yet never took advantage of his casual manner. He saw himself like that. Well, *one* day.

He disliked his immediate superior, the Gunnery Officer. McGowan always seemed to be watching him, just as Fox had once watched him on the bridge. It was more curiosity than concern, he thought, and this irritated him very much. He also avoided Tregarth, the Chief Engineer, and Robbins, his assistant. They were both ex-Merchant Navy like Fox, and kept very much to themselves. He quite liked Wickersley, the Doctor, but the man's cheerful indifference to ceremonial and tradition marked him as a man too dangerous to befriend seriously. The latest example of the Doctor's unreliability had caused a wave of laughter in the wardroom the previous day. He had actually come aboard with the new captain, apparently after cadging a ride in the boat, and even offering the Captain a drink in his own ship!

Harbridge's harsh voice cut into his thoughts. 'Watch yer course, Quartermaster! You're wandering about like a ruptured duck!'

Norris swallowed hard with disgust. He heard Harbridge slam

down the mouth of the wheelhouse speaking-tube and stump to the rear of the bridge, the sound of his footsteps sounding like an additional rebuke. Norris knew that he should have checked the compass and warned the helmsman himself. On the other hand, Harbridge might have warned him.

A bosun's mate appeared in the gloom. 'Fifteen minutes to go, sir.'

'Very well. Call the Starboard Watch.' He tried to avoid listening to his own stiff, unnatural voice as he passed his orders. It was like Joyce, he thought. When she spoke to the headmaster, or met some of the awful school governors, Norris could hardly recognise her voice then. At home she changed back again, but in front of what she called 'our sort' she used her mock-B.B.C. accent.

Harbridge said suddenly, 'Bloody helmsman's half asleep again!'

'I shall deal with him later.' Then, in an effort to break the ice, 'Still, he's not been an A.B. long.'

Harbridge sniffed loudly. 'Not the only one either!'

Norris sighed and turned away. The watch was almost done. He had managed it on his own. After this he could meet Harbridge's eyes across the table without embarrassment.

The whirr of a telephone at his elbow made him start violently. He jammed it to his ear, his eyes screwed with concentration. 'Officer of the Watch.' He waited, his heart pounding once more. Probably some fool asking for a time check.

From the other end of the ship came a frantic voice: 'Man overboard, sir! Starboard side, aft!'

The handset dropped from Norris's fingers. For several more seconds he could only stare at the bridge screen, his mind blank, his eyes refusing to recognise even the familiar objects nearby. With each agonising second the monitor's big screws pushed her further and further away from that anonymous man who had brought Norris to the fringe of complete panic.

Harbridge said, 'What's up, then?'

'Man overboard.' Norris answered in a small voice, like a boy replying to his form master. Helplessly he twisted his head to stare at the swaying bridge, the great tower of steel which he suddenly did not know how to control.

'For Christ's sake!' Harbridge almost fell in his eagerness to reach the voice-pipe. 'Stop engines!' Then, as a bosun's mate scurried

440

into view: 'Away seaboat's crew! Man overboard!' He then turned and stared fixedly at Norris's white face. 'You useless bastard!' He was shaking with sudden anger, but from across the darkened bridge Norris had the impression that he was grinning.

Richard Chesnaye rolled on to his side in the narrow bunk and turned his back on the glare from his desk lamp. He tried not to look at his watch, but knew nevertheless that he had been in the tiny sea-cabin for nearly three hours without once closing his eyes. Through the door and beyond the charthouse he could hear the faint shuffling footsteps of the watchkeepers on the upper bridge and the regular creak of the steering mechanism as the Quarter-master endeavoured to keep the slow-moving *Saracen* on her course away from Malta.

Chesnaye had had to force himself to leave the bridge. It had been almost a physical effort, but he knew that when daylight came the ship would still be less than a hundred miles from Malta, well within range of enemy aircraft as well as all the other menaces.

He rubbed his sore eyes and marvelled at the amount of ship's correspondence he had read and absorbed during the night watches. Piece by piece he had built up a picture of the men and equipment which filled the ship like machinery and made it work badly or well. During his one day in Malta he had toured every quarter of the monitor, and made a point of being seen by as many people as possible. He had spoken to all his senior ratings, and some of the new ones as well. Before lunch he had visited the ward-room and had confronted his officers. He was not sure what he had been expecting, but the meeting had left him feeling more than a little uneasy. He had known that the wardroom was comprised mainly of new and untried officers, but there was something more, an air of nervous cynicism, which seemed to border on contempt. Chesnaye did not care what they thought of him. Every captain had to prove himself. But much of their casual attitude seemed directed towards the ship. The respectful but distant interview had been interspersed with 'What does it matter?' and 'What can you expect in a ship like this?' When an air-raid warning had sounded it had come as something like a relief.

Erskine had followed him around the ship, full of information and quick suggestions which he was careful not to offer as advice. Chesnaye would have felt better if Erskine had been more out-

441

spoken, even critical, but he was careful not to commit himself. It was well known that any ship could be under a cloud after her captain's court martial, but with Erskine it seemed to go much deeper. The memory of Commander Godden kept returning like an old nightmare, and the way that he had secretly undermined the *Saracen's* first captain. The monitor no longer even warranted a commander. There was this matter of the sailing orders, for instance. Chesnaye frowned as he remembered Erskine's reactions.

The ship was to proceed to Alexandria, escorted part of the way by one A/S trawler. It was incredible how short of minor war vessels the Fleet had become. In Alexandria she was to take on 'military stores' in accordance with so-and-so signals. When he had questioned Erskine about the stores he had replied with a shrug: 'Oh, we do any old thing! Hump stores, petrol, bully beef, anything the Senior Officer thinks fit!' He had spoken with such fierce bitterness that Chesnaye had looked at him with sudden anger.

'What do you mean by that?'

'Nobody cares about the *Saracen*, sir. She's old, clapped out, like half the ships we've got here!' He had waved his arm vaguely. 'Now we're putting the Army into Greece to help out there. That'll mean ships to support them, and more work for the rest of us.'

'We shall just have to manage.'

Erskine had given a small smile. 'Yes, sir.'

'You don't like this ship, do you?' Chesnaye had felt the old agitation once more.

'I'm used to it. That's about all. She's slow, out-of-date, badly equipped and manned. Her main armament is so worn out by practice use in peacetime that the barrels are almost smooth-bores! No wonder we dropped shells on those poor pongos!'

Chesnaye afterwards cursed himself for allowing himself to be drawn. He was tired and worn out after his journey and the excitement of joining the ship. Otherwise he might have been more guarded. 'When I first joined *Saracen* it was an honour to be selected. She was brand-new then, a different kind of weapon. But there were old ships in the Fleet as well, even older than she is now. The job had to be done. *Any* job.' He had regarded the other man coldly. 'And if our orders are to hump stores, then we will be better at it than any *other* ship, d'you understand?'

442

Erskine had stiffened, his face suddenly a mask. 'I think I do, sir.'

Chesnaye rolled on to his back and stared up at the deckhead. Of course he didn't understand. But I should have told him. *Made* him! A ship was what you made of her. It had always been true. It had not changed.

He thought again of his officers. Very mixed. Two or three strong characters who could make or break any ship. He started once more to mentally sort them into categories. Tregarth was a good man. Not much to say. But in his round Cornish voice, coupled with a hard handshake, he had told Chesnaye that when the time came he could rely on the engine room giving its best.

That's when Fox, the Navigator, had interrupted. 'We've got two speeds here. Dead slow and stop!'

Fox would have to be watched. Independent, and very stubborn. McGowan, the Gunnery Officer, seemed competent enough. A dead pattern of a regular officer. Like a hundred others, he thought. Reliable, but not much imagination. Then there was Norris, the officer on watch on the other side of the door at this moment. He could go either way. If only he could relax and concentrate on his job. Chesnaye had kept away from the bridge during the Middle Watch in order to give Norris a chance to assert himself. The watch was quiet enough. It might be of some use.

The junior officers were all R.N.V.R., except Midshipman Gayler and the two warrant officers. They would behave and react according to the example set by their superiors. How *I* behave.

Of course, it was a disappointment to be relegated to a kind of store-ship. There was no hiding the bitterness and hurt he felt in his own heart. But, as Erskine had rightly pointed out, the line would be stretched even thinner, and there was no saying what might happen in the next months, even weeks.

The Fleet had scored a tremendous victory over the Italians off Cape Matapan only a fortnight earlier, when in a brilliant night action they had routed and decimated a force of powerful, modern cruisers without the loss of a single man.

But the land battle was something else. After a breath-taking advance along the North African coast they were now being forced to fall back. It was said that even Tobruk, the one hard-fought port of any true importance, was in danger of being retaken.

The Army, too, had problems, it seemed. With more and more troops and aircraft being withdrawn from the desert to help the beleaguered Greeks, and the Germans arriving daily to support the disgraced Italians, it would get a damned sight worse unless some sort of miracle happened.

Chesnaye thought of his officers' attentive faces and felt vaguely angry. They were amused, even scornful, he thought.

He sat up suddenly and stared round the little cabin. How many captains have sat here wondering about their officers? How many reputations have been formed or lost? Like Royston-Jones planning to hurl his untried ship into a battle already decided, or his most recent predecessor, out of touch but determined, who had ended his command in failure and disgrace.

He felt cold all over, and was conscious of the numbness in his leg. 'Not me,' he whispered. 'Not *me!*'

Outside a telephone buzzed impatiently. He peered at his watch. Ten minutes to eight bells. There was the sound of running feet, muffled shouts and the sudden jangle of engine-room telegraphs. With a shudder the engines' steady vibrations stopped, and as Chesnaye jumped to the deck and tugged on his leather wellingtons his mind began to click into place. He had wondered how he would react when the time came. It had been a long while since he had been tried. But the time was now. Perhaps they had overtaken the little trawler escort in the darkness and were about to run her down. He realised that his breathing was faster and his hand was shaking as he groped urgently for the door.

It was all over in minutes. He was grateful that he had been awake and that the darkness hid the anxiety on his face. He heard himself say: 'Resume course and speed. Secure the seaboat.'

And as Lieutenant Norris started again to stutter what had happened he barked: 'Make a signal to escorting trawler. Tell them to make a sweep astern for the missing man immediately!' Then to the bridge at large, 'Who was he, by the way?'

Harbridge answered. 'O'Leary, sir. One of the boat-lowerers. He was skylarkin' on watch and slipped on the guard-rail!'

'I see.' Chesnaye had a brief picture of a cheerful seaman suddenly thrown into nothingness. From a safe, well-worn deck to a nightmare of black water and cruel stars. 'He should be wearing a lifebelt and safety-light. The trawler might spot him.'

Erskine was suddenly at his side, his face made boyish by his dishevelled hair. 'Are you not waiting, sir?'

Chesnaye shut out the intruding picture of the terrified drowning

444

seaman, who could probably still see the monitor's fading shape above the water-crests. God! 'We are not. I will not endanger the ship for one man.' He forced himself to look at Erskine's shocked face. 'I am far more concerned about the apparent lack of control and discipline. I shall want a full report from the Officer of the Watch tomorrow morning.' He turned slightly. 'And, Norris?'

'Sir?' Small voice. Shaken. Unsure.

'Never stop the ship unless absolutely necessary. This area is alive with submarines and heaven knows what else. There are risks and *risks*.'

Harbridge said sullenly, 'Another minute an' I could've had the seaboat lowered, sir!'

'Then you can thank your stars you did not find that minute, Mr. Harbridge. I would have ensured it to be your last order!'

He forced himself to look across the screen as a dark shape with a towering white bow wave steamed down the *Saracen*'s beam. The trawler's signal lamp flashed briefly, and then she was gone. Below his feet Chesnaye felt the deck vibrating again. The monitor stopped her yawing and began to gather way.

Lieutenant McGowan appeared at the bridge ladder. His loud, cutting greeting, 'Morning Watchkeepers greet you all!' faded away as he assessed the grimness of the little group around the Captain.

Chesnaye nodded curtly. 'Carry on!' Then he walked slowly to the sea-cabin and closed the door behind him.

McGowan spread his hands and peered at Norris. 'What happened for God's sake?'

Norris half sobbed: 'Man overboard. The Captain left him to drown!'

Harbridge said, 'I can see we're going to get on fine, I *don't* think!'

The watch changed, and McGowan stood looking at Erskine, who had still not moved. 'Try to keep a sense of proportion, John.' McGowan resisted the temptation to peer astern for the searching trawler. 'It's hard luck, but we'll have to get over it.'

Erskine was staring at the closed door, his fists clenched. 'I've met some in my time. But, by God, this one is a callous bastard!'

Beyond the door the man who had so easily smashed the calm of the Middle Watch sat on the edge of his bunk, his hands clasped across his stomach as he fought back the wave of nausea which threatened to engulf him.

Ten minutes earlier he had been wondering what opportunity would offer itself to enable him to start the new pattern. Now he had made that start, but the cost was tearing him in two.

Lieutenant Roger Fox stood back from the chart table to allow the Captain more light. He waited in silence as Chesnaye pored over the worn chart and watched as he traced the faint pencilled lines of the ship's course, the neat cross bearings, times and distances which he knew were faultless.

Chesnaye straightened his back and stared thoughtfully across the open bridge to the straight silver line of the horizon. The first morning at sea was clear and bright, and the sun already hot across the steel plating and newly scrubbed gratings. The Forenoon Watch had just taken over, and he saw that Fox still had a trace of egg at the corner of his thin mouth.

'Another six and a half days to Alexandria.' Chesnaye was thinking aloud. He had been unable to sleep, and the hoped-for freshness of the new day still eluded him. 'It's a long way, Pilot.'

'Hmm. Six knots is about the best she can manage nowadays.' Fox shrugged. 'Poor old cow!'

Chesnaye eyed him sharply. 'You've not been used to slow passages?'

The Navigator grinned. 'Hell no, sir. Running fresh fruit to catch the market was a quick man's game!'

Chesnaye walked on to the bridge and immediately felt the sun across his shoulders. A round-faced sub-lieutenant was standing in the front of the bridge, his glasses trained straight across the bows. Chesnaye knew from the young man's stiff and alert stance that he was only bluffing and was very conscious of his captain's presence.

'Good morning, Sub. You are Bouverie, I take it?'

The officer lowered his glasses and saluted. 'Yes, sir.'

Chesnaye saw that upon closer inspection he was older than he had first appeared. That was the trouble with these Reserve officers. You could never judge age by rank. Bouverie's boyish features were only a first impression. His eyes, squinting against the reflected glare, were steady and shrewd. His voice, too, was controlled and almost offhand.

Bouverie reported as an afterthought, 'Course oh-nine-five, sir.'

'Quite so.'

Chesnaye stepped on to the gratings and peered across the screen. On the port bow he could see the small trawler pushing through the flat water without effort, her spindly funnel trailing a fine wisp of greasy smoke.

Bouverie said quietly, 'They picked up the body of our chap, sir.'

Chesnaye stiffened. He had already been told about the dead seaman, but he was conscious of the casual way Bouverie was introducing the subject.

'Yes, I know.'

'No lifebelt, sir.' A small pause. 'Hell of a way to die.'

'It always is.'

Chesnaye walked to the tall wooden chair in the corner of the bridge. Ignoring Bouverie's curious glance, he ran his hand across the well-worn arms, remembering in an instant the small hunched figure of Royston-Jones with his cap tilted across his birdlike face. The same chair. Like the small sea-cabin, a place for thought and contemplation.

'I gather this is your first ship, sir?' Bouverie spoke respectfully, but as if expecting an answer.

Chesnaye ignored the question. 'How long have you been in the Service, Sub?'

'One year, almost to a day, sir.'

'And before that?'

'I am a barrister, sir.'

Chesnaye smiled to himself. Am a barrister, he thought. Not *was*. That accounted for much in the man's apparent ease and confidence. In the old Navy it had been so simple to get a man's measure. Rank and family background had usually sufficed to weigh a man's worth and prophesy his future, Provided there were no unfortunate interruptions, he added grimly.

'Do you like this life?'

Bouverie looked at him with open surprise. 'I really hadn't thought, sir. But it is better than the Army, I suppose.'

Chesnaye sat down in the chair and took a deep breath. No, you could never tell from first appearances any more.

'Aircraft bearing Red one-one-oh! Angle of sight two-oh!'

Chesnaye swivelled in his chair as Fox bounded across the bridge and stabbed at the small red button below the screen. The gurgling scream of klaxons echoed below decks, followed immediately by the rush of feet as the men poured through hatches into the

447

sunlight. Chesnaye had to grip the arms of the chair to control the rising edge of excitement which was making his heart pound so painfully. He knew it had to come, but out here in the bright sunlight and placid sea it did not seem right or even real.

He lifted his glasses and moved them slowly across the port quarter. Once as he searched for the intruders his glasses moved across the *Saracen* herself, so that some of his men's faces sprang into gigantic focus, distorted and inhuman. He saw too the slim barrels of the Oerlikons already probing skywards and the short stubby ones of the two-pounder pompoms as the gunners whipped off the canvas screens.

Then he saw them. Tiny silver specks, apparently unmoving, like fragments of ice above the glittering water.

He heard Fox say, 'Ship at Action Stations, sir!'

'Very good, Pilot. Increase to maximum revolutions.'

The Yeoman of Signals, a bearded Scot named Laidlaw, peered round the steel lockers at the rear of the bridge. 'Escort requests instructions, sir?'

'Take up station in line ahead.'

He half listened to the clatter of the lamp as the signal flashed across the calm sea. There was no point in the trawler being impeded by the slower monitor. The enemy would be after the *Saracen*. The trawler could wait.

The mounting revolutions transmitted themselves through the tall chair, so that he imagined the ship was shivering. As he was doing. The sudden stark prospect of losing the *Saracen* had momentarily pushed everything else from his racing thoughts.

'Six aircraft, sir! Dive-bombers!'

Chesnaye gritted his teeth and turned to watch McGowan, who with handset in fist was watching the aircraft through his glasses. His voice was sharp, edgy. 'Stand by . . . short-range weapons!' He looked across at Chesnaye, but did not seem to see him. In his mind's eye he would be seeing his plan of anti-aircraft guns throughout the ship, each unit an individual weapon, every crew dependent upon its own ability and experience. In their huge turret the two big fifteen-inch guns still pointed imperiously across the blunt bows. They had no part in this type of warfare, and their size seemed to emphasise the ship's unnatural element.

Chesnaye watched the six small aircraft climbing higher and higher, their shapes drawing apart in the lenses of his glasses as

448

they turned in a wide half-circle and swam across the pale blue sky. Higher and higher, and faster as they flashed along the monitor's beam. Well out of effective range. Marking their target. Drawing ahead, until in a moment of near panic Chesnaye imagined they were going for the trawler, after all. He blinked as the sunlight lanced down the glasses and made his eyes stream. Of course, they were getting the sun behind them to blind the gunners. Also, most of the monitor's A.A. guns were abaft the beam, they were taking the minimum risks.

'They're turning, sir!' A nearby bridge lookout was shouting at the top of his voice, although Chesnaye was almost touching him.

Chesnaye said sharply, 'Open fire when your guns bear!'

The first aircraft began to dive. Silhouetted against the sun like a black crucifix, it plunged steeply towards the labouring monitor. It seemed to be flying straight down the forestay, as if drawn inevitably to the bridge itself.

Again Chesnaye heard the unearthly scream as the bat-shaped bomber hurled itself into its dive. The sound he had heard in that Malta convoy. A prelude to death and destruction. But this time it was his ship. They were after *Saracen*!

In sudden anger he barked, 'Starboard twenty!'

Shaking at her full speed of seven knots, the monitor wheeled heavily in obedience to the repeated order. The ship's port side swung to face the screaming bomber, and in those frantic seconds opened up with everything she had. The bridge structure shook and vibrated as pompoms and Oerlikons and then the long four-inch guns joined in frantic chorus. All at once the narrowing distance between ship and bomber became pitted with brown shell-bursts, the empty sky savagely crossed with gay tracers.

Chesnaye forced himself to watch as the big bomb detached itself from the aircraft which now seemed to fill the sky itself.

He did not even recognise his own voice any more. 'Midships!'

The bomb seemed to be falling very slowly, so that he had time to notice that the small trawler had joined in the fray, her puny guns lost in the roar of the *Saracen*'s own defences.

The dive-bomber, having released its load, pulled out of its nerve-tearing plunge, the scream changing to a throbbing roar as the pilot pulled his plane out and over the swinging ship. For another moment Chesnaye saw the spread of wings, the black

449

crosses, even the leather-helmeted head of a man who was trying to kill him.

The tracers whipped across the trailing wings, but the bomber was past and already turning away.

The monitor shuddered, and a few shreds of salt spray dropped into the bridge. Chesnaye swallowed hard, his mouth dry. The bomb had missed, he had not even heard it explode.

'Here comes the next one!'

Again the inferno of gunfire and savage bursts, the scream of that merciless siren, and then the roar of the bomb. Another miss. Chesnaye found that he was getting angrier with each attack.

'The bombers are splitting up, sir!' Bouverie sounded steady but different from the young man of ten minutes earlier.

'Three aside.' Chesnaye watched them with hatred. 'I am going to swing the ship . . . now!' In the same breath he barked. 'Hard a-port!'

Leaning heavily the old ship began to pivot, the distant trawler swinging across the bows as if airborne. Instead of a semi-defenceless wedge, the diving pilots saw the lengthening shape of the *Saracen* swinging across their paths. As they dived she continued to swing, a wild surging froth beneath her fat stern as one engine was flung full astern to bring her about. Too late the airmen realised that their ponderous adversary was not just turning to avoid the next bomb. Before, she had side-stepped each attack and hit back as best she could. The airmen had split up to take care of this irritating manœuvre. One section to make the ship turn, the second section to catch her out. But this time the ship did not steady on course. With her protesting engines and rudder threatening to tear themselves adrift, and aided by her shallow draught, the *Saracen* curtsied round until every gun in the ship was brought to bear.

The first bomber staggered and fell sideways, its grace lost in an instant. Trailing black smoke, it dived over the heeling bridge and ricocheted across the water in a trail of fiery fragments. The leader of the second attack pressed on and down, he was committed, he could not reverse *his* engine. The tracers knitted and joined in a vortex of fire, so that the forepart of the aircraft seemed to disintegrate even as it plunged towards its target. With one blinding flash it vanished, while the clear water below was pockmarked with falling wreckage.

450

One bomb fell almost alongside the ship's anti-torpedo bulge, a shattering detonation which would have stove in the hull of a light cruiser with little effort. *Saracen* shook herself and steamed unscathed through the falling spray, her guns still chattering defiance.

Then the sky was empty. As suddenly as they had arrived the survivors of the would-be assassins planed towards the horizon, their engines fading and futile.

'Bring her round on course, Pilot!' Chesnaye kept his face towards the sea. 'Resume cruising speed, and fall out Action Stations.'

Fox's voice was husky. 'Aye, aye, sir!'

Chesnaye rubbed his palm along the screen. She had done it! Together they had shown them all, doubters and bloody Germans alike!

Erskine appeared at his elbow. His face was streaked with smoke from the guns he had been directing from aft. 'No damage or casualties, sir.'

'Good.' Chesnaye turned to see the watchful surprise on Erskine's features. 'I thought the port Oerlikons were a little slow in coming to grips. Have a word with Guns about it, will you?'

'I will, sir.' Erskine seemed at a loss for words.

Chesnaye rubbed his hands. Two bombers shot down. Not bad.

Below on the signal bridge he heard an anonymous voice say: 'Handled the old cow like a bleedin' destroyer! I thought we'd bloody well 'ad it!'

Another voice, loud with obvious relief: 'What's the use, Ginger? No bastard'll ever believe you when you tell 'em!'

Chesnaye smiled. His body felt weak and shaking, and he could taste the nearness of vomit at the back of his throat. But he smiled.

Fox stepped back from the voice-pipe and watched him narrowly. The other officers had been quick to voice their opinions of the new captain, but he had been slower to make up his mind. He had served with too many eccentric or difficult skippers to do otherwise. This one was in a class apart, he thought. He actually *believed* in this ship. Whereas for some of the others she was a penance or a stepping-stone for something better, for Richard Chesnaye it was the ultimate reward. It was incredible, slightly unnerving. But as he watched Chesnaye's hand moving almost lovingly along the bridge screen, Fox knew he was right.

* * *

John Erskine pushed the pile of opened letters away from him across the wardroom table and groped for a cigarette from the tin at his elbow. It was empty. He gave an exasperated sigh and looked over at Wickersley, who was apparently engrossed in one of the letters.

'Cigarette, Doc? My duty-frees have run out.'

Wickersley pushed an unopened tin towards him without taking his eyes from the letter. Eventually he said, 'Bloody amazing some of the things our people write to their wives.'

Erskine blew out a stream of smoke. 'You're supposed to be censoring those things. Doc. Not bloody well passing judgement!'

Wickersley looked up and grinned. 'All the same, they do make me feel as if I've been living a very sheltered life!'

Somewhere beyond the wardroom a tannoy speaker crackled. 'All the Starboard Watch! Starboard Watch to Defence Stations!'

Erskine glanced at the salt-streaked scuttle. Eight bells, evening drawing in, but still clear and bright. The horizon line mounted the scuttle, hovered motionless, and then receded with timeless conformity. The Port Watch would be coming from their stations to face greasy plates of bangers and beans, washed down with unspeakably sweetened tea. If they were very lucky the duty cooks would have skimmed the cockroaches off the surface beforehand.

In one corner of the wardroom Harbridge and Joslin, the Gunner, dozed in chairs like two Toby jugs, while at a writing desk Sub-Lieutenant Philpott, the Paymaster, was busy writing to his parents.

'How are you getting on with the Old Man?' Wickersley stamped the letter and reached for the cigarette tin.

'All right.' Erskine spoke guardedly. 'Why?'

'Oh, just wondered.' The Doctor waved the smoke away from his face. 'Seems quite a chap to me!'

Quite a chap. Erskine wondered how the Captain really did appear to one as uninvolved as the Doctor. 'Yes. But I don't feel I have his measure as yet.'

'He's got a lot on his mind.'

Haven't we all? Erskine thought of the three days which had dragged remorselessly after the monitor's wake. Two more bombing attacks. Constant vigilance, with the hands almost asleep at their posts. The ship's company was working watch and watch. Four hours on, and four off, not allowing for the constant

452

calls to Action Stations and the normal work which had to be carried out no matter what happened. Painting, scraping, repairs and endless maintenance, with tempers and nerves becoming frayed and torn with each turn of the screws. All the time the Captain seemed to be watching him. He never actually complained about the way Erskine was running the ship, but a hint here, a suggestion there, made him wonder just what standard Chesnaye had in mind. He seemed to make no allowance for the ship's tiredness, her unsuitability, and the general pressures which were wearing down the whole Fleet, let alone this one old ship.

Wickersley was watching him. 'His leg seems to bother him. I might ask if I can have a look at it some time.'

Erskine smiled in spite of his preoccupied thoughts. 'You do that. He'll have you for breakfast!'

'He got it in the First World War, I gather. Odd really.'

'What is? Quite a few blokes got cut up then!'

'No, I mean it's strange the way he looks.' He eyed Erskine musingly 'He's over ten years older than you, yet you look about the same age. Don't you think that's odd?'

Erskine laughed. 'It's a bloody wonder I don't look like his father, the things which I've got on *my* mind!'

Ballard, the senior steward, emerged from the pantry. 'We'd like to lay the table for dinner now, sir?' He eyed the letters bleakly. 'Er, could you . . .?'

Erskine nodded. 'I'll move.' He looked at his watch. 'I've lost my appetite.'

Wickersley rubbed his hands as some more figures drifted wearily into the wardroom. 'I think a noggin is indicated.'

Erskine shook his head. 'I never drink at sea, Doc.'

'Your loss, my friend!' Wickersley waved to a steward. 'Large pink Plymouth!' He beamed at Lieutenant Norris, who had just slumped down in one of the battered armchairs. 'What about you, old sport?'

Norris looked pasty-faced and crumpled from sleep. 'A large one, please.'

Erskine paused and looked down at him. 'Watch it, Malcolm,' he said quietly. 'You've got another Middle Watch in four hours.'

Norris flushed. 'I can manage, thank you.'

Erskine shrugged and walked to the scuttle. The sea was getting furrowed with deep shadows, and the sky lost its warmth. Three

453

more days and they would be back in Alexandria. Then what? A place full of bustling activity alongside fear and indecision. Orders would be waiting for them, and then they would be off to sea once more.

And somewhere in the middle of all this there was Ann. Even now she might be in her tiny apartment above the harbour, watching the ships, and waiting for him. Or helping at the hospital. She might even be laughing over a drink with some other naval officer.

Ann Curzon, tall, slim, so completely desirable. Erskine remembered vividly that first night when they had had a little too much to drink, and they had made love with such fierceness in that same apartment.

Yet he knew so little about her, or what had made her leave England to join this mad world of uncertainty and chaos. She was only twenty-three, yet in so many ways seemed more mature than he. She always appeared to be laughing at him, thrusting away his caution and reserve with her own happiness. Yet he had the deeper feeling that she could be easily hurt.

How had it all started? He thought of her wide, clear eyes, and the way her short, sun-bleached hair tossed when she laughed at something he said. Now he would have to choose. Perhaps it would be easier than he imagined. He pressed his head against the cool glass to compose himself. The radio began to blare with another sentimental song. Vera Lynn. 'There'll be bluebirds over the white cliffs of Dover . . .' Somebody started to whistle. The clink of glasses. Small talk and age-worn jokes while the officers waited for dinner. Without looking round, Erskine knew what was happening. The exact picture, the exact moment.

The long tablecloth, now soiled and stained, the worn chairs, and the much-used wardroom silver. The officers sitting and standing around, legs straddled to the gentle heave of the deck, the eyes swinging occasionally to the pantry hatch. As if they did not know what was coming. As if some superb meal was to be expected, instead of tinned sausages and dehydrated potatoes.

He toyed with the idea of going to the bridge, and imagined Chesnaye sitting in the tall chair, his face in shadow. It was a strong face, he thought. But it was almost impossible to tell what he was thinking. Like Fox, Erskine was used to conforming to the ways of various captains. To all their little mannerisms and foibles. But Chesnaye gave away nothing. He seemed completely controlled,

454

impassive. And yet there was so much more to him than Erskine could understand.

The way he handled the ship, for instance. Calmly enough, and yet with a quiet desperation, as if he were afraid he was going to fail in some way. When the ship had left harbour Chesnaye had watched every detail, from the very moment the hands had been called for getting under way, from the second the slip-wire had been let go. He seemed to nurse the ship, as if at the slightest display of temperament from the old monitor he would feel that he and not this twenty-five-year-old relic had made a mistake.

At first Erskine had assumed it was because Chesnaye was unsure of his own ability after his enforced absence from active duty. After what he had seen when the bombers had made their attacks he knew differently. Even from aft he had seen the effort and cunning Chesnaye had used to elude the ruthless Stukas. Astern the ship's wake had curved and waved, and the deck beneath his feet had seemed to buck as the engines had been put this way and then that.

He shook his head. It can't go on. It can't last. Sooner or later Chesnaye was going to discover that he and the ship were only essential because of a general shortage. If he puts a foot wrong he'll be finished for good, he thought.

He looked again at the sea. Whatever else happens, I must not get involved again. He spoke the words inwardly like a prayer. Sentiment is one thing, but if I give way now I will never get another chance. He thought again of Chesnaye's face that first day when he had assumed command. Desperate, hungry, even grateful. *I* could be like him, he thought. When this war's over they'll soon forget. There'll be plenty of Chesnayes again. Thrown out, unwanted.

Ballard coughed at his elbow. 'Permission to lower deadlight, sir? We'd better darken the wardroom before we start dinner.'

Erskine turned away from the circle of sea and sky without comment. Yes, he thought savagely, let us get on with the game. Calm and cool. Cheerful and offhand about everything. Who the bloody hell are we fooling!

Chapter Three

Face from the Past

John Erskine held up his hand to shield his eyes from the light which seemed to be burning into his brain. One moment he had been deep in an exhausted sleep, and the next he was struggling in his bunk, his body still shaking from the messenger's violent tugging.

'What is it, man?' Erskine peered beyond the torch at the seaman's shadowy shape. His brain still rebelled, and every muscle called out to him to fall back on the bunk. He was still partly under the impression that he was dreaming. His mind cleared with startling suddenness as he realised that the reassuring beat of the ship's full power was muted and feeble.

'Captain's compliments, sir. 'E wants you on the bridge at once.'

Erskine fell out of his bunk and switched on the small table lamp. No wonder he was tired. He had only been off his feet for a few hours. The Morning Watch had not even been called yet.

Being careful to keep his voice normal, he asked. 'What's happening up top?'

The seaman was looking round the cramped and untidy cabin with open interest. Perhaps he had expected something better for the ship's second-in-command. 'Stopped the port engine, sir. Trouble in the shaft, I think.'

Erskine's mind began to work again. That's all we need, he thought. One bloody engine. 'Tell the Captain I'm on my way.'

He followed the man briskly on to the upper deck, blinking his eyes in the deep darkness. By the time he had climbed to the upper bridge, past the dozing gunners and peering lookouts, his mind had been further cleared by the crisp night air, and only the soreness of his eyes and the kiln-dryness in his throat reminded him of his complete fatigue. He groped his way to the forepart of the bridge, where he could just discern the Captain's tall figure against the screen.

'Good morning, John.' Chesnaye's voice was calm enough, but

more abrupt than usual. 'Bit of bother in the engine room.'

'Bad, sir?' Erskine tried to gauge Chesnaye's mood.

'More of a nuisance really. The Chief has been up to tell me that a bearing is running hot. Might be a blocked pipe.' He laughed shortly. 'He was very insistent that I stop that screw to give his men a chance to look round.' He added bitterly: 'It's an after bearing. A bit tricky to get at. Still, it might have been worse, I suppose.'

Erskine nodded. If they didn't stop the shaft it might seize up completely for lack of oil. There could be no dodging the bombers with only one screw, he thought. His tiredness made him suddenly angry and despairing. All Chesnaye's desperate manœuvring had done this. If only this was a thirty-knot destroyer, he thought. One screw or two, you always had a few thousand horsepower up your sleeve then!

He said, 'Shall I call the men to quarters, sir?'

'No, let half of 'em get their sleep. They need it.'

Chesnaye had spoken unconsciously, but his words brought the sudden realisation to Erskine that the Captain had been on the bridge almost continuously since the ship had slipped her buoy in Malta.

Erskine asked: 'Can I relieve you for a bit, sir? The ship'll hardly make headway in this sea.'

'I'm all right. I just wanted to put you in the picture.'

Erskine leaned against the cool plates and looked at the black sea. 'Very quiet, sir.' A slight breeze fanned his face and rattled the signal halyards overhead.

Chesnaye grunted. His arm moved like a dark shadow towards the starboard beam. 'Tobruk's over there. Less than a hundred miles away. I wonder how the Army are managing?'

Erskine stared at him. The Captain was concerned about his ship, yet he found time to worry about the nameless men in the desert. The ship trembled beneath his shoes, and he felt thankful that he were here and not lying out on the sand and rocks, waiting for the dawn to uncover the advancing enemy.

'You're not married, are you, John?'

The question was so sudden that Erskine was momentarily confused.

'No, sir. That is, not yet.'

'Thought about it?'

457

Erskine had a fleeting picture of Ann's face and felt even more unsure of himself. 'Not really, sir. In wartime it's hard to make such a decision.'

Chesnaye was tapping the stem of his unlit pipe against his teeth, and might have been studying him but for the darkness. 'You don't want to think like that, John.' Then with unexpected vehemence, 'No, it's a chance that does not come very often.'

There was a metallic clatter from aft, and Erskine heard Chesnaye curse under his breath.

Somewhere in the darkness Harbridge, the Gunner (T), said stiffly, 'The stokers are 'avin' a go, sir!'

'Bloody row!' Chesnaye took off his cap and ran his fingers across his hair.

'It's a big job. But Tregarth will be as quick as he can. He's a good Chief, sir.' Erskine waited for Chesnaye to answer and added: 'To go back to what we were saying, sir. About marriage. I was wondering why you haven't done so if what you say . . .' He faltered as Chesnaye took a step towards him.

'Let us keep our minds on the job in hand, eh?' Chesnaye's tone was cold, like a slap in the face. 'I suggest you take a turn around the decks to see that the men are aware of what is happening. We still have the A/S trawler with us, but I want a good lookout kept!'

Erskine stepped back, stifling his resentment and his surprise. 'Aye, aye, sir.'

As Erskine walked past the tall, warm shape of the funnel where the Morning Watch was being mustered, he bumped into the lanky figure of McGowan.

' 'Morning, John, is all well in the world?'

Erskine bit back the angry words which seemed to be bursting from his lips and replied shortly: 'Bit of a flap on. Nothing the Captain can't handle, apparently.'

McGowan watched him go and wondered. He heard his petty officer say throatily: 'Two volunteers for a nice cushy job! 'Oo are they ter be, then?'

Two voices called assent from the anonymous swaying ranks of duffel-coated seamen.

'Right,' said the P.O. 'Bates an' Maddison. Get aft an' clear the blockage in the officers' 'eades.'

The men groaned, while their comrades sniggered with unsympathetic delight.

McGowan said severely, 'Now is that the way to get volunteers, P.O.?'

The hardened regular rubbed his hands and grinned. 'A volunteer is a bloke wot's misunderstood the question, sir. Either that or 'e's as green as grass. But the officers' 'eads 'ave got to be cleaned afore you gentlemen gets up in the mornin'!'

'Er, quite. Carry on, P.O.'

The men shuffled away into the darkness, and McGowan started to climb towards the bridge.

For the rest of the night the ship pushed her way at a snail's pace, while down below, right aft and beneath the waterline, Tregarth and his mechanics worked and sweated to trace the one tiny injury which was making every man aboard apprehensive and irritable.

Morning passed, and with it came a stiff north-east wind which whipped the flat water first into a mass of dancing whitecaps and soon changed the whole sea to a pitching panorama of long, steep rollers. The *Saracen* slowed even more, until eventually it was only possible to retain steerage-way. The monitor took the mounting sea with obvious dislike. The long diagonal swells cruised rapidly to hit her below the port bow, each jagged crest crumbling beneath the force of the wind, so that the men off watch felt the surging power of water thunder against the hull like a roll of drums, and then waited as the ship staggered and heaved herself bodily over and down into the waiting troughs, and so to the next onslaught. On watch it was even worse. The gunners, signalmen and lookouts were always in danger of losing their footing and handholds. Equipment and ammunition rattled and banged, men cursed as their boots skidded on the heaving decks, and their eyes and binoculars were blinded by the long streamers of shredded spray which seemed to cruise over the hull and superstructure like birds of prey.

In the near distance the trawler pitched and yawed, showing first her bilge and then her open bridge, upon which her watchkeepers in shining oilskins clung like seals on a rock.

Chesnaye forced himself to stay in his chair. Occasionally, when off guard, his eyes strayed to the engine-room telephone. The handset was temptingly near, but he knew it was futile and a waste of time to call Tregarth to speak to him. He was doing his best. That had to suffice.

'Your oilskin, sir!' A bosun's mate was holding it out to him, so that Chesnaye realised with sudden shock that his uniform was dripping from the spray and blown spume. He nodded with a brief smile and pulled it across his shoulders. As he leaned forward in his chair to tuck the coat behind him he caught a glimpse of Erskine and the Chief Bosun's Mate, followed somewhat reluctantly by a small party of seamen, making their rounds of the fo'c'sle and anchor cables. He noticed how the men's bodies stood at nearly a forty-five-degree angle as the wide deck canted against the weight of water which piled up beneath the bows. Spray burst across the guard-rail and drenched the groping men, and Chesnaye saw Erskine turn to shout something, his collar flapping in the vicious wind.

Chesnaye sat back and thought about his conversation with Erskine during the night. I was wrong to speak to him like that. Stupid, and cowardly.

He was glad he had been unable to see Erskine's face when it had happened. But even that was small comfort. How was he to know about Helen? Chesnaye cursed himself once more. By bringing up the subject of marriage in the first place, *he* and not Erskine was to blame.

He ducked his head as more water deluged across the screen and ran down his stubbled face and through the soggy protection of the towel he had wrapped around his neck.

The Mediterranean. Calm and inviting. Or wild and irresponsible. It had all happened here, he thought. Meeting Helen Driscoll in Gibraltar. The Dardanelles and the misery which followed. He remembered the long journey back to England in the hospital ship. So full of hope in spite of his feeling of loss and despair. Robert Driscoll had never left his side, and even afterwards in that Sussex hospital he had visited him often.

But the rest of the dream had never materialised. Helen Driscoll had stayed in Gibraltar, and had been there when the *Saracen* had eventually dropped anchor *en route* for home waters and the final battle for France.

Even now, after all these years, Chesnaye could not accept what had happened so easily. He knew he had no rights, no first call or demands over her. Nevertheless, he had felt real pain when Robert Driscoll had met him with the news.

Helen had become engaged to Mark Beaushears, once midshipman of the *Saracen*'s unhappy gunroom, then acting lieutenant and *en route* with the monitor for a new ship. An up-and-coming young officer, they had said, and Chesnaye had written to him to wish him luck. He had written the letter while the misery was fresh in his heart and the hatred very real in his mind.

In all parts of the world and on many occasions he had told himself: If only she had waited. Why Beaushears? But he had known well enough that it was just another delusion which, like the *Saracen*'s memory, never left him.

Lieutenant Fox lurched across the bridge and saluted. 'Signal, sir. Priority. Small convoy being attacked. Request immediate assistance!'

Chesnaye pushed himself off the chair and limped towards the charthouse. 'Is there more of it?'

'Yes, sir. Still coming in on W/T. Two Italian cruisers and some destroyers have dropped on the convoy from Piraeus. The bloody Eye-ties must have pushed down the Greek coast during the night.'

He watched Chesnaye's eyes flicker from the signal pad to the chart, and the almost desperate speed with which he moved the parallel rulers and dividers. He knew well enough what Chesnaye was thinking. Crete to the north, the Libyan coast to the south. The small convoy must have skirted the island of Crete on the mainland side to keep as covered as possible from surface attack. Then it had turned south with the intention of wheeling eastwards to Port Said. It was one of the many urgently needed convoys of supplies for the British troops in Greece. The enemy were obviously aware of the importance of every ship in the sea. They intended to finish off this convoy, and only the *Saracen* by a stroke of fate was in a position to help them. That is, she *would* have been in a position to help them, thought Fox grimly as he watched the anguish on Chesnaye's face.

The dividers clicked across the chart once more, as if Chesnaye had not trusted his first impression. Slowly he said, 'But for this breakdown we would have been right amongst them.'

Fox glanced at his personal log. 'Yes, sir. We would probably have sighted the convoy wing escort at eleven hundred.' He sucked his teeth. 'Bloody bad luck!'

In a strange voice Chesnaye snapped: 'Bring her about, Pilot. Lay off a new course to intercept.' He hurried past the astonished

461

Fox. 'Bosun's Mate! Get the First Lieutenant for me at once!' His mind was in a complete whirl as he picked up the engine-room handset. 'Captain speaking. Get me the Chief!'

At that moment Erskine pushed his way into the charthouse his eyebrows raised questioningly as he saw Fox's troubled face.

Fox shrugged and gestured towards the signal pad. 'Local convoy under cruiser attack. They're requesting assistance.'

Chesnaye's voice came from the bridge, sharp and urgent, 'Have you got that new course yet, Pilot?'

Fox picked up his logbook and looked hard at Erskine. 'I'm a seaman and that's all.' He turned slowly towards the open door. 'You tell the Skipper what it's all about. Frankly, I haven't got the heart!'

'What the hell are you saying?' Erskine rubbed his wind-reddened face. 'Why are we changing course?'

Fox sighed deeply. 'He thinks we should be there to give assistance. We would have been but for the bloody engines. I must say *I'm* not sorry, I don't fancy mixing it with some brand-new cruisers, Wops or not!'

He walked briskly on to the bridge, his solid body swaying easily to the ship's heavy rolls. A moment later Erskine heard his voice, flat and calm once more. 'Port fifteen. Steady. Steer oh-four-five.'

Erskine swallowed hard and followed him into the wind. The ship was leaning heavily, her bows corkscrewing as she laboured round into the teeth of the gale.

Chesnaye looked past him, his eyes distant, as if his mind was somewhere else. 'Ah, John, here you are. The Chief has patched up the trouble at last. I am just ringing down for maximum revs.' Suddenly his grey eyes focused directly on Erskine's face. 'The W/T office are letting me have a regular report of the situation. I – I can't understand it. The convoy has called for air support, and nothing has happened!'

Erskine looked away. 'There isn't any, sir. It's been like that for months.' He turned slightly to watch the disbelief change to helpless anger.

Chesnaye waved his hand across the plunging white rollers. 'But good God, man! This is an emergency! There are valuable ships out there! Ships and *men!*'

You poor bastard, thought Erskine dully. 'Every available

aircraft is in the desert, or Greece. If you're caught on your own, that's just too bad!'

'Signal, sir.' Laidlaw, the Yeoman, had appeared on the bridge, his beard glistening with diamonds of spray. He faced Erskine as Chesnaye read through the lines of neat, pencilled information.

Erskine watched Chesnaye's lips moving as he read in silence. He noticed that the Captain's hand was shaking. Erskine knew that this was a crucial moment, but for once he felt unable to cope with it. The shock and open despair on Chesnaye's face robbed him of controlled thought.

'They're relying on us.' The words were wrung from Chesnaye's mouth. 'The Second Inshore Squadron are on way to help the convoy. We are to engage the enemy until our cruisers arrive!'

A telegraph jangled, and moments later the bridge began to throb and quiver in response to the revived engines.

'We'll not be in time, sir.' Erskine hated himself as he saw the effect of his words. 'They've a head start on us.'

Fox called: 'Signal, sir. Convoy's scattering.'

Sub-Lieutenant Bouverie, who until this moment had been watching in silence, said: 'A bit too late, I imagine. These Italian cruisers are damn' fast.'

Chesnaye crumpled the signal flimsy into a ball, his eyes furious. 'Hold your tongue! What the hell do you know about it?'

'I beg your pardon, sir. I just thought –'

Chesnaye did not seem to hear him. 'You can't imagine what it's like. Waiting for help. Seeing your friends die around you and not able to do anything!'

'Maximum revolutions, sir!'

Chesnaye nodded. 'Have the main armament cleared for action.'

Erskine wanted to leave the bridge. To get away from the suspense and the feeling of helplessness. The Captain had proved himself so capable, so brilliant at handling the ship under the air attacks, that it had never occurred to him he was totally unaware of the true situation which faced every British ship in the Mediterranean.

He heard Chesnaye ask in a more controlled tone, 'What escorts do they have?'

'Two destroyers and an old sloop, sir.' Fox was holding his

463

logbook like a bible. 'They can't spare much else at present.'

The big turret creaked slightly and the left gun dipped a few degrees. Within the massive steel hive the gunners were already testing the controls, preparing their cumbersome charges for battle. Not a stationary target ashore or a straggling collection of troops and installations, but the cream of the Duce's navy. Thirty-knot cruisers, most likely, each one a floating arsenal.

Chesnaye folded his hands across the screen and rested his chin on them. He could feel the hull's convulsions and hear the clatter of feet on bridge ladders as messengers raced to and fro and men hurried to their stations. Behind him nobody spoke but to relay an order or to answer one of the voice-pipes.

Damn them, he thought savagely. Bouverie with his immature and fatuous remarks. What did he know? They were not involved, so they did not care. One man was lost overboard because of his own carelessness and stupidity, and the ship almost went into mourning because their captain did not stop. In submarine-patrolled waters they had expected him to offer the ship as a sitting target. But now that hundreds of lives and precious ships were being smashed and killed beyond the horizon they just did not see reason for alarm or interest!

What was worse was the way Erskine accepted the Navy's new vulnerability. Chesnaye remembered his own feeling of loss and betrayal that morning off the Gallipoli Peninsula when the *Saracen* had moved in for her final bombardment. The supporting fleet gone. The sea empty. The men in the convoy must feel like that. Their only hope was the *Saracen*, and she was to be denied them.

He pounded the screen with slow, desperate beats. Come on, old lady! Give me all you've got. Faster . . . faster!

Only twenty miles to go, and but for the driving spray and gale they might even have been able to see something. But the sea was grey with anger, and the wind showed no sign of easing. Instead it hurled itself like a barricade across the ship's thrusting stem, cutting away the speed under remorseless pressure.

Fox looked across from the charthouse towards the Captain's stooped shoulders. 'No further signals, sir.' He caught Erskine's anxious stare. 'I guess it's all over,' he added quietly.

Erskine waited for Chesnaye to resume his old course and speed. There was nothing to be gained now. The small convoy must have been decimated, like others would be before this was all over. Chesnaye was only offering his own ship as a target and deck, nothing more.

Two more hours dragged by. Hardly a man moved on the upper deck, and the voices of the men on watch were hushed and rare.

The wind slackened, veered round and dropped away as if it had never been. The hazy clouds rolled aside and the sun moved in to greet them. Humid at first, and then with its old penetrating brilliance, so that the grey shadows fled from the sea and the wave crests gave way to deep swells of glittering blue and silver.

Once the engine room asked permission to reduce speed, but Chesnaye said shortly, 'Not yet.'

Erskine could not take his eyes off him. He is waiting for something to happen, he thought uneasily.

The watches changed. Men relieved went to their messes to eat, but without their usual noisy gaiety. Even the rum was issued without comment, and the men drank their watered tots with their eyes upwards towards the bridge, where the dark outline of the Captain's head and shoulders stayed rigidly like a carving on the front of a church.

'Smoke, sir! Bearing Red two-zero!'

Every glass was swivelled and then steadied to watch.

Slowly, remorsefully, like a reaper in a field, the monitor pounded her way across the inviting water. Without a wind the sea parted to allow the *Saracen* easy access, as if eager for her to see the spoils.

Chesnaye said at last, 'Slow ahead.'

From the corner of his eye he saw the seamen off watch lining the guard-rails, their faces turned towards the smoke.

There was little of the ship to be seen. It had been a sizeable freighter, and it lay on its beam, only a fire-rusted shell to show where the hull had once been. The eddying bow wave from the monitor's blunt stem pushed gently against the dying ship and made the littered surface of the water between the two vessels surge with sudden life.

Chesnaye heard a man cry out, and saw a white flash as a hand pointed involuntarily at the flotsam of war.

Broken planks and blackened hatch covers. A headless corpse trailing scarlet weed in the clear water, an unused life-jacket found, too late.

The sinking freighter coughed deep in its shattered insides and plunged hissing into a maelstrom which mercifully sucked down some of the grisly relics also.

Far on the port beam the little trawler was picking her way through more wreckage, like a terrier in a slaughterhouse.

A patch of oil a mile wide parted next across the monitor's bows. Then there was more debris, much of it human.

Erskine felt sick. When he looked sideways at Chesnaye's face he saw that it was impassive, almost expressionless.

Chesnaye said quietly, 'If only we had been here in time.'

Then over his shoulder he said in a strange, cruel tone: 'Well, Sub, what do you think of all this, eh? We *were* too late for these chaps; you were right!'

A dead rating bobbed past the monitor's anti-torpedo bulge, and a seaman on lookout said in a strangled voice: 'God! One of *our* chaps!'

The guard-rail quivered as the lines of watching men leaned to look at the lonely, passing figure. At last the diaster was no longer anonymous and indistinct. The corpse was in naval uniform. Even the red badges on its sleeve were clear and mocking.

Chesnaye stood up, his feet thudding on the grating. 'Bring her back to her old course, Pilot!' He glanced only briefly at Erskine. 'Make a signal to C.-in-C., John. Repeated Second Inshore Squadron.' He looked up at the flapping commissioning pennant at the masthead. 'Convoy destroyed. No survivors.'

'Aye, aye, sir. Anything else?'

Chesnaye was filling his pipe with short, angry thrusts. 'There's a lot I'd like to tell them at the Admiralty. But it will keep for the moment!'

Erskine wanted to help, to make the Captain understand, and he tried to find the right words.

Before he could speak Chesnaye said: 'Get those gawping men off the upper deck, or find them something to do! Like a bloody circus!'

Erskine was suddenly grateful for the bite in Chesnaye's voice, even though they both knew it was merely acting.

Lieutenant Malcolm Norris stood high on the port gratings, his hands clasped tightly behind his back. From his lofty position he could just see over the Captain's shoulder and beyond the screen where, transfixed between the two big guns, the monitor's bows moved very slowly towards the long strip of land.

He could see Erskine and some of the fo'c'sle party already moving around the cables, making a last check before entering harbour.

He heard Fox say quietly: 'Starboard ten. Midships.' The Navigating Officer's buttons rasped against metal as he bent over the compass and swung the pelorus on to another fix. 'Steer one seven-five.'

Norris bit his lip. Fox was so calm, so ice cold when he was working. The halyards squeaked and a string of flags soared upwards to the yard. Through the shore haze, beyond the long, low-lying breakwater, a signal lamp blinked rapidly, and Norris heard Laidlaw goading his signalmen into further action.

But as Officer of the Watch Norris had little to do. The *Saracen* was at last arriving in Alexandria and the Captain and Fox were conning the ship over the last half-mile.

Norris felt the sweat running down his spine, but did not relax his vigilant position. It was like everything else he did. He did not dare drop his guard for a second. Speaking, thinking, passing orders, each action had to be vetted.

He watched the busy harbour life opening up across the ship's bows. Nodding buoys, weird Arab sailing craft poised like bats on their own reflections, an outward-bound sloop gathering way as it passed the harbour limit.

As the sloop drew abeam the trill of pipes echoed across the flat water.

The monitor's tannoy barked: 'Attention on the upper deck! Face to starboard and salute!'

The bosun's mates, already in a small line on the *Saracen*'s upper bridge, raised their pipes. C.P.O. Craig snapped, 'Sound!'

Again the twittering, shrill and ear-splitting as the senior ship returned the sloop's mark of respect.

Craig watched the other ship with slitted, critical eyes. 'Carry on!'

The Yeoman called hoarsely: 'Signal from Flag, sir! Anchor as ordered!'

Chesnaye grunted, his eyes fixed on the shimmering anchorage. Like a pewter lake, he thought. Cruisers, destroyers and supply ships. Bobbing derricks, squealing cranes, dust and busy preparation.

467

At the head of a line of moored cruisers was the *Aureus*, the flagship. Every glass would be watching the monitor's approach. Every eye critical, perhaps amused. He heard the rasp in his voice as he ordered, 'Slow ahead both!'

He heard, too, Norris stammer as he repeated the order down the voice-pipe. He was obviously worried and strained. Like me, thought Chesnaye, with sudden bitterness. He wondered what Norris had thought about the shambles left by the Italian cruisers. Probably thinks I took the ship there just to frighten everybody.

Somewhere deep in his brain a voice persisted. Why did you go there? You knew it was too late! Was it to prove something to yourself?

'Time to take her round, sir!' Fox's voice startled him. A prickle of alarm made him stiffen in his chair.

Dreaming again. Too tired. Can't think clearly any more.

'Very good. Port fifteen.'

More shouted orders. 'Port Watch fall in for entering harbour! First part forrard! Second part aft!'

The decks blossomed with scampering figures, unfamiliar in correct uniform and without the well-used duffel-coats and balaclavas. Chesnaye's aching mind began to drift again. There should have been a marine guard and band on the quarterdeck. It would have made all the difference.

He gritted his teeth. Those days were gone. No marines. Just an old ship, with God-knows-what job ahead. 'Midships!'

'Coming on to bearing now, sir!' Fox sounded alert.

Chesnaye stood up and stepped on to the forward grating. The monitor moved slowly past a destroyer which glittered like a yacht from beneath its impeccable awnings. More piping, and tiny, antlike figures stiffening in salute.

'Half a cable, sir!'

'Stop engines!' Chesnaye shielded his eyes and peered down at the fo'c'sle. Erskine was standing right in the bows, his face towards him across the length of the foredeck. A signalman stood at his side ready to break out the Jack on the staff the moment the anchor went plummeting down. The cable party stood in various stances, like athletes waiting for the gun. Eyes on the massive, treacherous cable and the brake which would halt its welcome sound.

468

Still the monitor glided forward. Almost graceful in the clear water.

'Coming up now, sir!' Fox was busy checking bearings again.

Chesnaye lifted his arm, and saw the rating with the big hammer brace himself above the slip, the only force now holding the anchor. Chesnaye felt elated but unsteady. It was a combination of exhaustion and over-eagerness, so that he felt he had to speak, to break the unbearable waiting. 'The flagship looks smart enough.' He even forced himself to smile as he said it.

Fox grunted. 'The Flag Officer of the Second Inshore Squadron is rather particular!' The air on the bridge was light-hearted, even gay.

Suddenly Chesnaye realised that he had been so preoccupied during the last harrowing days he did not even know who his new senior officer was to be. Not that it mattered now. The time he had been apart from the Navy had cut all his old connections. 'What is the Admiral's name, Pilot?'

Fox frowned, his gaze on the open water ahead of the bows. The Skipper was cutting it fine. From the corner of his eye he could see the empty tanker, high and ungainly, backing stern first across the narrowing anchorage. Absently he replied, 'Vice-Admiral Beaushears, sir.'

Chesnaye staggered as if struck a blow. It couldn't be! Not now, out here? He looked round like a trapped animal, his mind reeling.

Fox's voice, controlled but sharp, cut into his tortured thoughts. 'Let go, sir! Let *go*!'

Almost in a trance Chesnaye dropped his arm, and from forrard came the sharp click, followed immediately by the rumble of cable as the anchor roared from its rust-steaked hawsepipe.

Fox was now up on the grating, his eyes anxious. 'Are you all right, sir?'

Chesnaye swallowed hard and nodded. 'Yes!' Over his shoulder he called, 'Slow astern together!'

Norris, an imaginative man at any time, had watched the little drama mesmerised like a rabbit. He repeated the last order and heard the Coxswain's voice answer him up the voice-pipe. Slowly the monitor moved astern, paying out her cable along the bottom of the anchorage. But Norris was unable to take his eyes from Chesnaye's square shoulders and the anxious Fox at his side.

Later in his cabin he would be able to think about it more clearly. Norris knew that something really big had happened. With this vital knowledge, once he had unravelled it, he would make those smug bastards in the wardroom really sit up and notice him!

'Stop engines!'

Norris watched as the stern-moving tanker floundered across the bows, its half-bared screw thrashing the water in a snow-white froth. Norris held his breath. He was quite sure Chesnaye had not even seen the other ship. But for Fox's quick action there might even have been a collision.

Chesnaye turned towards him, so that with sudden terror Norris thought he had been thinking aloud. 'Ring off main engines!' He brushed past Norris and walked into his sea-cabin.

Norris was quivering with excitement, his past fears moment-arily forgotten. 'Did you *see* that?' He waited impatiently as Fox stopped rolling a chart and peered across at the gleaming white buildings and tall minarets. 'Did you see the Captain's face?'

Fox cleared his throat and picked up the chart. For a moment he looked hard at Norris's flushed features. 'Nice place, Alex. Think I'll take a run ashore tomorrow!' Then he was gone.

Satisfied, the *Saracen* swung at her anchor while the cable and side parties dismissed and hurried below to escape the sun. On the maindeck Mr. Joslin, the Gunner, was supervising the rigging of an awning, while McGowan and Sub-Lieutenant Bouverie watched over the boats as they were dropped in the water alongside.

From the flagdeck the signalmen eyed the shore and the flag-ship, but in the wheelhouse the wheel and telegraphs stood unattended and already forgotten.

Norris still paced the empty upper bridge, ignoring the sun on his neck as he tried to fathom out the enormity of his knowledge. He felt a new man. The ship was safe in harbour, and there was the strength of other ships and men nearby. Already he had forgotten that but for the Captain the *Saracen* would be lying even more quietly on the bed of the Mediterranean, while on some distant airfield the Stuka pilots would be celebrating, instead of mourning their dead comrades.

Norris thought of his wife. 'You're as good as they are!' He grinned. For once she had been right.

*　　　*　　　*

470

Chesnaye followed the flagship's captain down the quarterdeck ladder and into the cool shade below. His stomach felt uneasy, and he wished now he had made time to take a good meal before leaving the *Saracen* prior to attending for his interview with the man whose flag flew high on the *Aureus*'s tapering masthead.

The two captains passed down a narrow passageway, the sides of which were so well painted that they shone like polished glass. Chesnaye darted a quick glance at his opposite number and wondered how he got on with Vice-Admiral Sir Mark Beaushears. Captain Colquhoun had met him at the gangway, his tanned face set in an automatic smile of welcome. He was pleasant enough, but Chesnaye had the impression that he was a much-harassed man. It could not be pleasant to have a flag officer for ever breathing down your shoulder, he thought.

Chesnaye noted the smart marine sentry outside the Admiral's quarters, and waited with mounting curiosity and apprehension as Colquhoun tucked his cap beneath his arm and stepped over the coaming. Chesnaye followed him, aware of the soft carpet beneath his shoes and the air of quiet well-being the stateroom seemed to exude.

There were two men present. A tall, languid flag-lieutenant rose slowly to his feet, glanced at Chesnaye and then turned to watch his superior.

Vice-Admiral Sir Mark Beaushears was only a year older than Chesnaye, but time and ambition had been hard on his outward appearance. He still appeared cool and relaxed, but his tall figure was markedly stooped, and his once-athletic body was marred by a definite paunch. His hair had receded, too, so that the high forehead gave him a new expression of watchful deliberation, and he appeared to be summing up Chesnaye from the moment he stepped into the cabin. Only his eyes were the same, Chesnaye thought. Veiled, giving nothing away.

Beaushears waved his hand to a chair in front of the well-turned desk. Again Chesnaye had the distinct impression that everything had been carefully planned beforehand and the chair had been placed in position like a stage prop.

He sat down and folded his hands in his lap. He ticked off each item in his mind. No handshake. Only the briefest hint of a smile. Beaushears said evenly: 'It's been a long time. I watched you dropping anchor earlier and wondered if you had changed much.'

Chesnaye waited for him to dismiss the other officers. Colquhoun was looking stiff and uneasy, and the young flag-lieutenant faintly amused. He is going to keep them here, he thought. As a sort of barrier. He is afraid of old acquaintanceships and memories.

This new knowledge did nothing to comfort him, but instead made him vaguely angry. In a formal tone he began: 'I have submitted my report about the voyage from Malta. I was very sorry I was unable to help that convoy.' He toyed with the idea of mentioning the bombers *Saracen* had shot down, but he knew Beaushears was well aware of the facts. Let him bring it up first, he thought with irritation.

'Yes, a great pity. Still, if, as you say, you were unavoidably detained, there's nothing more to be said, is there?'

Chesnaye stiffened in his chair, his fingers laced together with painful fierceness. What did he mean?

Aloud he said, 'I did my best, sir.'

Beaushears leaned back in his chair. 'You lost a man overboard too?'

'It's all in the report.' Chesnaye could feel the colour rising to his cheeks. 'It was the only decision.'

'Yes.' Beaushears pressed a small button. 'The sun is well over the yardarm. A drink will do us good.' Almost casually he said, 'I thought for one small moment that you were going to overshoot the anchorage when you came into harbour.' He smiled for the first time. 'She's not a fleet destroyer, y'know!'

The flag-lieutenant showed his perfect teeth. Like a cat, Chesnaye thought.

A petty officer steward brought in a tray and glasses and busied himself pouring iced pink gins. No one was asked what he wanted, and Chesnaye had the idea that was the way the flagship was run under Beaushears. The gin was, however, a small but welcome distraction.

He drank deeply and signalled with sudden recklessness to the steward. 'Another!' He saw the man dart a brief glance at Beaushears and then pour the drink. Chesnaye smiled grimly to himself. A good master/servant atmosphere.

Beaushears cleared his throat impatiently. 'Well, now that you are here you'd better be put in the picture.' He turned to the lieutenant. 'Over to you, Harmsworth.'

The flag-lieutenant tapped a bulky envelope with his finger. 'It's all in here, Captain. You will be *attached* to this squadron until further notice.'

Chesnaye noticed the slight emphasis. *Saracen* was to be with but not *of* Beaushears' squadron.

Harmsworth continued in the same bored tones: 'You will find all the relevant information concerning the military situation in Libya up-to-date as far as it goes. You will start loading supplies and stores in the forenoon tomorrow. The Maintenance Commander has all the details ashore and will arrange for lighterage, etcetera. Your first destination will be west of Tobruk. The Army is getting in a bit of a flap down there.'

Chesnaye looked at Beaushears. 'Will Tobruk he held?'

Beaushears shrugged. 'Unlikely, I should think. The enemy will probably bypass it and take it at leisure. We shall then have to evacuate the marooned troops with whatever we have available.' He gestured towards the open scuttle. 'Jerry has got his eye fixed on Alexandria. After all, he's less than three hundred miles away at this moment!'

Chesnaye twisted uneasily in his chair. My God, is it really as bad as that? He said, 'Can't they stop him?'

Beaushears glanced at his slim gold watch. 'They have a plan. But they intend to fall back and re-group. Present a fixed front outside the Alexandria perimeter. The Staff chaps say that with the sea on one side and the Qattara Depression on the other the Army will be able to make a good show. It will make up in some ways for lack of air cover.'

Chesnaye remembered the mass of shipping in the harbour. 'And what of *our* support, sir?'

Harmsworth interrupted smoothly. 'Mostly for Greece. We're really giving a bit of weight in that direction!' He seemed pleased, as if personally responsible.

Chesnaye felt light-headed and suddenly reckless. He had been made to feel like a small boy by Beaushears in front of the others. He had expected it would be like that. He had thought about this meeting from the moment Fox had dropped his bombshell as the *Saracen* crossed the anchorage.

Beaushears had always been aloof and cool, even as a midshipman. Now he was something more, and although he acted in a detached and formal manner, Chesnaye thought he could

473

detect a deeper meaning to his behaviour. His remarks had been double-edged, as if he had implied that Chesnaye could have done more.

Chesnaye felt the sweat forming on his forehead. Perhaps he had even suggested that the *Saracen* had deliberately held back from the convoy? That *he* had been afraid for the ship and himself! Even losing the man overboard could be misconstrued as an unwillingness to stop, even cowardice! He felt the glass shaking in his hand.

'I think Greece is a waste of time!' Chesnaye's voice was not loud, but from the other officers' expressions he got the impression he had just shouted an obscenity.

Beaushears controlled his features and said calmly, 'Please go on.'

Chesnaye shrugged. 'Have you forgotten the Dardanelles fiasco?' He saw Colquhoun and Harmsworth exchanging awkward glances but he no longer cared. The fact was that behind Beaushears' manner, his ability to offend without the slightest trace of personal embarrassment, was something which had stayed with him over the years. He had probably wanted to meet Chesnaye, but for quite a different reason. He had no doubt expected a changed Chesnaye. Humble, even ashamed, of the circumstances which had parted him from the Navy and now given him command of the oldest ship in the Fleet. Then there was Helen . . . Chesnaye checked his racing thoughts. 'Anyone can see we can't hold Greece, let alone use it as a springboard into Europe! If it's another proud gesture, then it's going to be a damned costly one!'

Beaushears eyed him coldly. 'I think otherwise, Chesnaye. However, it is hardly your concern. You are here to command your ship in the best way you know.' He was watching Chesnaye with sudden intentness. 'She's not much of a catch, but we can't be choosers. I need every vessel I can lay my hands on!' Carefully he added: 'When you reach the Libyan destination you may find that the enemy has overrun our people already. You'll get no support from Tobruk, which is the nearest strongpoint. You will be on your own.'

Chesnaye looked at the carpet. For a split second he had a picture of the bullet-scarred pinnacle and Keith Pickles dead in his arms. 'It won't be the first time!' He looked up to see that the shot had gone home. Beaushears face was no longer calm. He looked almost guilty.

Harmsworth said hurriedly, 'Another gin, sir?'

Chesnaye took the drink and touched his glass with the tip of his tongue. If they expect me to crawl they are going to get a surprise, he thought.

Beaushears had composed himself again. In a flat voice he said, 'In your assignment you may have to sacrifice your ship!'

Chesnaye started as if struck in the face. Lose *Saracen*? He felt the cabin closing in on him. 'What do you mean?'

Beaushears stood up, the sunlight reflecting on his thick gold lace. Without waiting further he attacked. 'She's an old ship! Useful at the moment, but expendable! If you are pinned down, and the enemy catch you inshore, you must sink the *Saracen* before they get their hands on the supplies!' His voice grew louder and sharper. 'This is a mobile, fast-moving war! Tanks and armoured columns, and *not* like the Dardanelles at all! No front line, poor communications, with each day making the maps obsolete!' He turned suddenly, his eyes flashing. 'Both sides need fuel and supplies like life-blood!'

Chesnaye imagined the *Saracen* going down under his own hand, and felt the pain in his heart like fire. 'I'll manage!' His voice was thick and unsteady.

'You *must*!' He eyed Chesnaye slowly, his face calm again. 'I know you of old. Sentimental and unrealistic.' He waved his hand. 'Don't bother to argue. I wasn't going to say this, but you opened the batting! The Navy's changed. You either keep up with events or you go to the wall! We've got amateurs, failures, has-beens and every sort of man who's ever breathed. There's no room for sentiment any more!'

'So I see, sir.' Chesnaye rose to his feet.

Beaushears forced a tight smile. 'Keep out of trouble, Chesnaye. Don't try to act as if your ship is a battlecruiser! Just do your job, and use discretion.'

Chesnaye turned to leave. Before he could stop himself he had asked, 'How is Helen?

Beaushears dropped a hand to his desk as if to steady himself. He looked towards the scuttle, his face hidden. 'Lady Helen is well, thank you.'

Chesnaye felt the gin raw and hot in his throat. So he had been right. After all these years Beaushears was still jealous. It was incredible. He was successful, he had even stolen the girl Chesnaye had loved, yet he was still dissatisfied.

Harmsworth looked confused, the fierce exchange of words between his admiral and the tall, grave-eyed captain had been beyond his experience. He said, 'I – I'll see you over the side, sir.'

Chesnaye regarded him coldly. 'Captain Colquhoun can do that, thank you!'

On the sun-dried quarterdeck he looked down at the *Saracen*'s pinnace as it moved in towards the gangway. Beside the Admiral's barge and the cruiser's other smart boats it looked outdated and worn, but he noted with quiet satisfaction that the boat's crew were smart and alert, boathooks poised and ready. He felt a pang in his throat as he saw, too, the small midshipman who stood in the sternsheets shading his eyes as he looked for his captain.

Damn Beaushears, he thought savagely. I did not want it this way, but if he expects me to grovel – he jerked from his thoughts as the flagship's captain held out his hand.

'Goodbye, Chesnaye. I hope we meet again soon.' He eyed Chesnaye with sudden warmth. 'A remarkable interview.'

Chesnaye grinned, feeling the recklessness once more.

Colquhoun looked up at the Vice-Admiral's flag, now limp in the dipping sun. 'I don't think that fool Harmsworth will sleep for a week!'

The two men separated, the pipes trilled, and then Chesnaye was in his pinnace, with *Saracen*'s outline ahead of him like a challenge.

Chapter Four

Tobruk

The air in the small sea-cabin abaft the *Saracen's* bridge was already thick and stifling, and the blue tobacco smoke hung in an unmoving cloud above the heads of the waiting officers. The door opened and Lieutenant McGowan forced himself round its edge and eased his shoulders against the steel bulkhead. Chesnaye sat on his bunk, his legs out straight beneath the littered table.

By his side Erskine was squatting on a chair, his eyes thoughtful as he checked each cramped figure. 'All present, sir.'

'Right.' Chesnaye eyed the others impassively, his features a mask for his inner thoughts. The head of every department was present, even Tregarth, his face pasty and moist from the engine room's humid breath, and Chesnaye could tell from their expressions that they were wondering at his unexpected summons.

He waited a while longer until McGowan had lighted a cigarette, and then tapped the chart which lay across the table. 'A change of plans, gentlemen.' Their eyes followed his hand across the straggling Libyan coastline. 'The enemy have pushed on rather faster than expected, and our proposed landing area has been overrun.' He had already explained this to Erskine before the others had arrived, and even now sensed the man's opposition to his words. 'Tobruk, on the other hand, has been bypassed by the Afrika Korps, so our people there will need everything they can get. Every sort of supply will have to be carried by sea. For that reason I intend to unload our stores there!'

It all sounded so cold, so easy, that he wanted to laugh. He remembered Beaushears' face when he had described the mission. He had known the impossibility of the task. He *must* have known.

Tregarth said imperturbably, 'Well, at least Tobruk's a tiny bit nearer!'

Erskine added half to himself, 'It's a damned long way back!'

Chesnaye scraped a match along a box and puffed at his pipe. It gave him time to think about the new developments. It had taken nearly two days to load these military stores in Alexandria. The Commander-in-Chief had made it clear that with Tobruk under constant pressure it was almost impossible to get into the port except with the cover of darkness. Now the place was bypassed, and no one seemed to know exactly where the nearest enemy units were. *Saracen* would be a sitting target the moment she was uncovered by daylight, and with her decks covered by drums of petrol and cases of ammunition.

It had taken three more days to make the trip from Alexandria, keeping well clear of the coast and skirting local convoy routes. By some miracle they had managed to avoid detection, and had only once sighted an enemy aircraft in the far distance. The aircrew must have been looking in the wrong direction, he thought.

But now – he looked up as Fox said thoughtfully: 'Is it really essential for us to go in, sir? I mean, according to the signals received, the Army is being supplied by smaller, faster ships than ours. A quick turn-round, and off to sea seems to be the order of the day.'

Chesnaye fought back the desire to yawn. The stuffy atmosphere and quiet watchfulness of his officers added to his feeling of complete weariness. Fox was right, of course. Beaushears had said, 'Use your discretion.' A trite, well-used phrase which had spelled disaster to many a captain. If you were right, others took the credit. But if you made the wrong decision you took the consequences alone.

Erskine seemed to make up his mind. 'I think it is a bad risk, sir.'

The others shifted uncomfortably. Fox, hard-faced and watchful, McGowan biting his lip and eyeing his friend with obvious agreement.

Chesnaye looked at Tregarth. Nothing there. The Chief would do as he was expected. In the engine room only the machinery meant anything to him. Above, in the clean open world of sea and sky, other decisions might be called for, but they did not affect him.

Wickersley, the Doctor, looked fresh-faced and bright, the only man present who never stood a watch or missed his sleep. He would be busy enough soon if things turned out badly.

Chesnaye said calmly, 'I don't see that we have any choice, Number One.'

Erskine tightened his jaw. 'We'll be close inshore for two or three days, sir. It could be fatal.'

Chesnaye shrugged lightly. 'It could.'

They all fell silent, so that the throb of engines intruded into the cramped cabin and they could hear the scrape of feet from the bridge and the creak of the steering gear.

A lonely, darkened ship, Chesnaye thought. Steering beneath an arch of bright stars which reflected so clearly on the flat sea.

He shifted irritably. 'Lay off the new course, Pilot. We'll close Tobruk tomorrow at dusk.' He eyed the Navigating Officer bleakly. 'Make a double check on recognition signals. I don't want a salvo from our own troops!'

Fox nodded. He at least did not appear surprised at Chesnaye's decision.

Erskine repeated, 'It's a bad risk, sir.'

'It's a bad piece of organisation, John. The men who should be in the desert are in Greece at this moment!'

Erskine looked at him with surprise. 'But, sir, surely that is entirely different? That risk is justified!'

Chesnaye heard an intake of breath from McGowan, but remained surprisingly calm. He tapped the sheaf of signals. 'The British forces in Greece are already falling back, John.' He remembered the smug confidence on Beaushears' face and felt suddenly sorry for Erskine and all those others who had never known the bitterness of defeat and betrayal. 'In a matter of weeks there'll be another Dunkirk in Greece.' He had almost said Gallipoli. The signals had briefly reported the quick change of strength, the savage enemy advance through Greece and Yugoslavia. The British Army was falling back so rapidly that already tons of arms and equipment had fallen into German hands.

Chesnaye shuddered when he imagined the waiting ships, unprotected by air cover, which were expected to ferry the surviving forces to the island of Crete. And what then? How could they be expected even to hold that? What in God's name were the harebrained strategists in Whitehall thinking when they ordered such a hopeless gesture? He could feel the old anger beginning to boil inside him.

'You have heard my decision.' He spoke to the group at large, but his words were directed at Erskine. 'In times like these morale is of the utmost importance. The men at Tobruk do not question

479

their orders. It is our duty,' he faltered, 'no, our honour, to give them every support!'

Erskine stood up, his eyes dull. 'You can rely on the ship, sir.'

Chesnaye scraped his pipe, his features towards the chart. 'Good. For a small moment I was beginning to wonder!'

Wickersley stepped forward, darting a quick glance from Erskine to the seated captain. 'Perhaps I could be of some use to the army medical chaps, sir?'

His bright, eager voice seemed to break the tension, and Chesnaye looked up at him with a small, curious smile. 'Yes, Doc. We can take aboard as many wounded as we can, and then you can get some practice in!'

Tregarth laughed throatily. 'Better them than me!'

The officers collected their notebooks and caps and shuffled towards the door.

Erskine was the last to leave. 'If we fail, sir, you could lose the ship!' His eyes were hidden by shadow. 'It's happened to others.'

Chesnaye regarded him slowly. 'If I ran for home without trying, John, I should lose something more!'

Long after Erskine had departed Chesnaye sat staring emptily at the soiled chart. Everything was repeating itself. Only time had moved on. Like Tobruk, he had been bypassed and overlooked but now the stage was set. He had committed himself, the ship and two hundred men to uncertainty, even disaster.

The ship wallowed heavily as the wheel was put over. Fox was already setting her on her course. How did *Saracen* feel about it? he wondered. Right from birth she had never been offered a fair and balanced fight. Now he was doing this to her. Another uneven struggle. Another gesture.

Fox slid open the door and peered into the yellow lamplight. 'On course, sir. One-nine-five.'

Fox was looking at the pile of signals, and Chesnaye could imagine what was running through his mind. There was nothing to say that the *Saracen*'s stores were to be run into Tobruk. Not in so many words. Chesnaye was to use his direction. He was to weigh up the situation as he found it. By which time, of course, it would be too late for alternatives. It was a heartless position for a man who commanded a ship too slow to run away.

'Very well, Pilot. Thank you.' Chesnaye looked up sharply, aware of the despair which had crept into his voice.

But Fox grinned, unperturbed by his captain's tired and strained features. 'It's a damned sight harder than running bananas, sir!'

'Steady on course. Closing at two thousand yards.'

Erskine nodded. 'Very good.' Fox's voice was calm and unruffled, like a cricket commentator's, he thought. He wiped a drip of spray from his night-glasses and swung them once more across the screen. The monitor's fo'c'sle was like a pale wedge on the dark rippling water as the *Saracen* crawled at reduced speed towards the shoreline. Voices were hushed, and he was conscious of the metallic creaks around him and the distant ping of the echosounder. Across the bows lay the shore. With macabre regularity the night sky rippled with dull red and yellow flashes, like distant lightning, he thought. With each threatening glow he could see the undulating shoulders of the land mass below, where men and guns crouched and waited.

The ship trembled, and he heard a man curse as an ammunition belt jangled sharply against the steel plates. The monitor's crew was at Action Stations, and had been for several hours. During the Dog Watches they had first sighted the faint purple smudge along the horizon. As the daylight had faded, and the stars had picked out the clear sky, the ship had felt her way slowly and purposefully towards the coast, every man waiting for discovery and the touch of battle. Nothing happened, and the slow minutes dragged into hours. The same pace. The same sounds. But there was a new smell in the cool air. The scent of land. The smell of dust and smoke.

'Starboard ten. Steady. Steer one-seven-five.' A hushed order, and an uneasy movement of feet on the gratings.

Erskine tried to relax his taut stomach muscles. His whole body felt cramped and strained. Why was this time so different? he wondered.

He heard Chesnaye say evenly, 'Looks like a fair bit of activity in the desert tonight?'

Just words, thought Erskine. He's worried. He could find no consolation in the fact.

It was amazing the way things changed in war, even for individuals. In Alexandria Erskine had reported to the flagship to discuss some arrangements concerning the coming voyage. Quite by chance, it seemed, he had met the Vice-Admiral himself.

Beaushears had insisted that he take drinks with him in his quarters, and, flattered, Erskine had accepted. Now, in the darkness, it all looked different. As he relived those friendly, casual moments it almost seemed as if Beaushears had been questioning him, as if the meeting had not been by chance at all. He had not asked direct questions about Chesnaye, yet he was rarely absent from the conversation. Beaushears had shattered Erskine's normal reserve and caution by announcing casually, 'You'll know in a few days' time, but I'd like to be the first to tell you the good news.' Beaushears had smiled, and waited for a few more seconds. 'I think you'll be getting a very pleasant surprise shortly. I happen to know that you are earmarked for a command in the very near future.' He had watched the surprise changing to pleasure on Erskine's face. 'A destroyer, as a matter of fact.'

There had been more drinks, which, added to the heat, had made Erskine dazed and openly overjoyed. He could not believe it was happening to him, after the confusion and slurs of *Saracen's* behaviour and the threat to his own career.

Beaushears had chatted amiably and at great length. 'We need your sort, Erskine. The Navy has got mixed up, slack. We have to put up with every sort of misfit imaginable, but, then, I don't have to tell you that, eh?' They had both laughed, although Erskine was only half listening.

Beaushears had continued: 'I wouldn't like to see your career damaged in any way because of a superior officer's ambition or pigheadedness. It would not be *right*. I can be blunt with you. I know your record and your family. There was a time when we didn't mention such things, but things have changed. One man's behaviour reflects on all those around him. Either way, as local commander I want to know what is happening in the ships under my control. Incidents, actions by my captains, can give me a clearcut picture of the over-all efficiency, if you see what I mean?'

He had questioned Erskine about the *Saracen's* inability to help the stricken convoy, even about the man lost overboard. Beaushears had ended by saying offhandedly, 'I daresay you might have acted differently were you in command, eh?'

Erskine had been confused, and tried to reassemble his thoughts. He still could not recall exactly if he had given the Vice-Admiral the impression that he disapproved of Chesnaye's actions or whether Beaushears had put the words into his mouth.

482

In any case, he was glad to leave the flagship, to get back to his cabin and think about the piece of news Beaushears had given him. A command at last. The waiting and marking time were over. Soon the *Saracen* and all she represented would be a thing of the past. Like the disinterested wardroom and the endless, futile tasks the ship was called to perform.

A new ship would mean another change, too. He would have to return to England, and a new life which must exclude Ann. He stirred uneasily at the thought. Perhaps she would understand. Maybe she had guessed that their lightning affair would not last. In spite of his insistence, he could not console himself, or remove the vague feeling of guilt. Inwardly he knew that it had been his indecision and not duty which had stopped him going ashore to tell her the news.

'Ah, there it is!' He heard Chesnaye's voice very close.

A faint blue lamp stabbed across the water.

'Make the reply, Yeoman!' Chesnaye turned in his chair. 'The M.L. is here to guide us in.' He sounded fully awake and relaxed, although Erskine knew how rarely he slept.

The motor launch's low shape cut across the bows and then straightened on course, a faint sternlamp glittering to guide the monitor's helmsman. From inland came the muted rumble of artillery, followed by tiny white peardrops in the sky. Very lights. Erskine shivered. This operation had to be all right. If anything went badly this time, Beaushears would be quick to change his mind about his appointment.

He heard Fox grunt with alarm as a bulky freighter loomed out of the darkness and seemed to hang over the monitor's port rail.

But Chesnaye said calmly: 'A wreck. That M.L. skipper certainly knows his harbour in the dark!'

Sure enough, the little launch glided between scattered wrecks, leading the cumbersome monitor like a dog with a blind man.

Chesnaye peered at the luminous dial of his watch. 'Right, John. Get forrard and prepare to let go. We'll be up to the anchorage in two minutes or so.' His teeth shone in the darkness. 'Probably find we're in the middle of a blasted sand-dune when the sun comes up!'

Erskine grunted and heaved himself over the side of the bridge. He's actually enjoying himself, he thought. Still doesn't realise what it's all about.

483

He reached the fo'c'sle breathless and nervous, and two minutes later the *Saracen*'s anchor crashed into the sand and shingle of Tobruk harbour.

Within half an hour of dropping the anchor *Saracen* was required to move again. Guided by briefly flashing handlamps and her own power boats, she sidled blindly and warily nearer the shattered remains of a crumbling stone jetty. Another listing wreck barred her passage, and with more hushed and urgent orders she moved alongside the broken ship and was secured for final unloading. Using the wreck as a quay, and aided by three battered landing craft as well as her own boats, the monitor began to unload.

Hours passed and the labour continued without pause. From nowhere, and with hardly a word being spoken, came a horde of unshaven, tattered soldiers, who handled the drums and cases with the practised ease of men who have become accustomed to anything. Occasionally their faces showed themselves in the cold glare of a drifting flare, but otherwise they remained a busy, desperate collection of shadows.

Lieutenant Norris was stationed aboard the wrecked ship with a working party of some thirty seamen. At first he tried to assist, even speed, the unloading, but his orders seemed superfluous, and he himself inevitably got entangled with a knot of scurrying figures.

Sub-Lieutenant Bouverie was with him, as well as the young midshipman Danebury. That suited Norris, they were both his juniors, and both were amateurs like himself.

Once he tried to start a conversation with an army lieutenant who appeared briefly on the wreck's listing foredeck. Norris said with elaborate coolness: 'Hell of a job getting here. Gets harder all the time!'

The soldier had stopped dead in his tracks. 'Hard? You must be bloody well joking! Christ, I'd give my right arm to live your cushy life!' He had vanished before Norris could recover his dignity.

Out of curiosity he climbed a rusting ladder and found the comparatively undamaged charthouse. He lit a cigarette and was just settling himself on a small swivel chair when Bouverie clattered up the ladder and joined him.

Norris peered at him through the gloom. 'Everything all right,

Sub?' He disliked Bouverie's casual manner, his complete ease with his betters. In his other life he had always feared men of Bouverie's calibre, their acceptance of things he was denied, the vague references to a world he could never join.

'Going like a bomb.' Bouverie squatted on a table and craned his neck to look through the shattered windows towards the *Saracen*'s dark outline. 'The Skipper seems to know what he's up to. I wouldn't care to con a ship alongside in pitch darkness!'

Norris forced a yawn. 'When you've had a bit more experience you'll get the hang of it.'

'Really?' Bouverie's voice gave nothing away. 'I would have thought otherwise.'

'What's the snotty doing?' Norris curbed his annoyance with an effort. He knew Bouverie was laughing at him again.

'Oh, just keeping an eye on things. He's got a good P.O. with him. He'll be better without us breathing down his neck.'

'Damned snotties!' Norris drew heavily on the cigarette so that his face glowed red in the darkness. 'Think they know it all!'

'He seems a nice enough lad to me. A bit quiet, but then he was at school only a few months ago.'

Norris grunted irritably. 'How some of these people get commissions I'll never know.'

'I've wondered about some.' Bouverie changed the subject as Norris peered at him more closely. 'Dawn'll be up soon. Things might get lively then.'

'Now don't get windy, Sub!' Norris sounded angry. 'It'll be the Captain's fault if anything goes wrong!'

'I'm not *windy*, as you put it. Not yet, anyway. I've not had a lot of experience of the Andrew as yet, but if I have to learn there's no captain I'd rather have as a teacher.'

'He choked *you* off a while back!' Norris felt that the conversation was getting out of hand. This knowledge only made him angrier. 'I suppose you think because you've had a soft upbringing he'll take you under his wing!'

Bouverie smiled. 'You really are being rather offensive, you know! Why the enormous chip on the shoulder?'

Norris choked. 'What the hell d'you mean?'

'Well, just that you seem to think the whole damned world owes you something. I'd have thought you'd have settled down very well in the Navy.'

485

'I will!' Norris was confused. 'I mean, I have! I didn't ask to be sent to this old relic. In fact, I think someone had it in for me. Some of these regulars can never forgive the fact that *we* can earn a better living outside!'

'Teaching, for instance?'

'Damn you!' Norris was standing. 'Yes, teaching, if you put it like that!'

Bouverie nodded solemnly. 'A very rewarding task, I should imagine. A kind of challenge.'

'You don't know what it's like!' Norris was completely lost now. 'You've had an easy life, and now that you've found your way here you seem to expect the rest of us to carry you!'

Bouverie laughed quietly. 'As a lowly sub what choice do I have?'

There was a scrape of feet, and Norris swung round to face Danebury, the midshipman. 'Well? What are you skulking up here for?'

Danebury was a slight, fragile-looking youth, with pale eyes and a wide, girlish mouth. Strangely enough, he was well liked by the ship's company, who seemed to think that he needed protecting rather than respecting.

'All the petrol is clear, sir.' He shifted from one foot to the other. 'The hands are starting on the ammunition now.'

'Well, what d'you expect me to do? Give you a bloody medal?' Norris was shouting. 'Get down to the foredeck and try to set an example!'

The boy fled, and Norris felt a little better.

Bouverie stood up and brushed at his jacket. 'You really are a little bastard, Norris!'

He turned to go, and Norris yelled: 'How dare you speak to me like that? Stand *still* when I'm addressing you!'

'There are no witnesses, Norris, so forget it!' Bouverie's drawling voice had gained a sudden edge. 'I've watched you for weeks. You don't seem to know what you want to get from life, and really it's rather sad. I don't know why you worry so much about your station in life, when in fact you don't seem to belong anywhere!'

Then he was gone, and for several minutes Norris could only choke and gasp for breath. He felt halfway to tears, yet his anger refused to be quenched. How dare that bloody ex-barrister, with

486

his casual references to Eton, his maddeningly offhand treatment of superior officers, speak to him as he had just done? When we get out of this place I'll wipe that smirk off his stupid face!

He was still muttering to himself when hours later the first greyness of dawn touched the desert, and in their distant emplacements the German gunners rubbed the too-brief sleep from their eyes and turned their attemtion to the battered harbour.

Chesnaye watched the paling edge of the eastern horizon and rubbed his face briskly with his palms. Sleep seemed to be dragging him down, and he knew that if he did not resist the temptation to sit on the bridge chair he was done for. He heard a petty officer reporting to Fox: 'The ammunition is unloaded, sir. We've got all hands on the other stores now.'

Fox sounded entirely spent. 'Very well. Get the Buffer's party to shift that tinned food from aft first. It'll give the stretcher bearers more room to breathe when they haul the wounded aboard.'

Chesnaye leaned against the cool plating. 'Has the Doc got everything sorted out down there?'

'Yes, sir. There are two hundred wounded expected, mostly stretcher cases. They're going in the wardroom, the petty officers' quarters and the forrard messdeck. We'll keep the lower decks clear of wounded for the moment. I imagine one lot of ladders is enough to navigate if you've got a few splinters in your guts!'

Chesnaye smiled. 'I agree. I hope we can give them a quiet passage.'

'Me too.' Fox sniffed the air. 'Half an hour and we'll be kind of naked out here!'

Chesnaye rose on his toes and peered down at the wreck alongside. Already he could see the ship's outline more clearly, and the antlike activity back and forth across the upper deck. He felt the dryness in his throat and tried to control the urge to go below and hurry the men along.

It was not enough to get rid of the petrol and the ammunition. There was still the ship, and the real danger which lay beyond the dawn light.

'Have hands stationed at all wires and springs, Pilot. And make sure the Chief is kept informed of the exact position, so that he can crack on speed at short notice.'

'I've done that, sir.'

487

'Good. This must be a bloody awful place to defend.'

Fox grunted. 'Brings back a few memories does it, sir?'

'A few. I never expected I should see this sort of warfare again.'

'Too little too late.' Fox was yawning in spite of his efforts to stop himself. 'Always the bloody same!'

The hull shuddered slightly as a landing craft came along the unoccupied side. There was the clatter of a derrick and some fierce shouting.

White against the black water and dull steel Chesnaye could see the patchwork of bandages and could sense the suffering. With a sudden impulse he swung himself on to the ladder and began to descend. 'Take over, Pilot. I'll not be far away.'

He joined Erskine by the guard-rail and watched in silence as the wounded soldiers were swayed aboard. Many willing hands reached out to steady them, to ease the pain on the last journey.

A harassed medical orderly, his steel helmet dented and scarred, held up his hand. ' 'Ere, stop lowerin'. Let this one down 'ere!' Skilfully the seamen manipulated the guys so that the pinioned soldier could be laid on the deck. The orderly knelt down, his fingers busy with the bandages. Half to himself he said: 'Shouldn't 'ave sent 'im. 'E's done for.' He stood up as another batch of wounded were heaved over the rail, and then turned quickly towards Chesnaye. ' 'Ere, mate! Keep an eye on this bloke for a tick!'

Erskine stepped forward to speak, but Chesnaye shook his head. 'All right, John, you can forget the protocol!' Then he stooped down and peered at the soldier's face, which suddenly seemed so small and shrunken. The man stared with fixed glassy eyes at Chesnaye's oak-leaved cap, so that for a few seconds he appeared to be dead. Then his hand moved from the stretcher and reached out vaguely.

'Where am I?'

Chesnaye took the soldier's hand in his own. It was ice cold. Like Pickles' hand had been. 'It's all right. You're safe now.'

The soldier coughed weakly. 'The Navy. The bloody Navy. Never thought I'd see you lot again.'

Chesnaye watched the man's life ebbing away with each feeble pump of his heart. Who was this anonymous man? What had his sacrifice meant?

The soldier spoke with sudden clarity, 'It'll be all green in Dorset now, I expect?'

Chesnaye nodded, unable to speak.

'A real picture. I wanted so much to . . .' Then his hand tightened on Chesnaye's and he was dead.

A petty officer said harshly, 'Two more boats comin' alongside, sir!'

Erskine looked swiftly at Chesnaye's kneeling figure. 'Shall we tell them to stand off, sir. We should give ourselves more sea room!'

'Carry on with the loading, John.' Chesnaye stood up and walked back towards the bridge. 'We'll slip when we've taken on the last available man!'

Erskine watched him go, his mind torn apart with emotions. All at once he felt that he hated the unsteady, groaning figures who were coming aboard with such maddening slowness. Each man represented precious minutes. Each minute brought more light to the harbour and the desert beyond.

He found, too, that he hated Chesnaye for refusing to listen. For that and many other reasons which he could no longer define. He had become a symbol, an outlet for all his pent-up anxieties. Yet he knew, too, that all this was inevitable, just as he understood with sudden clarity that he was afraid.

Daylight showed the vast undulating rollers of the desert and the pitiful shambles which had once been a dusty and untroubled town. The harbour itself was littered with wrecks, some only marked by a solitary masthead, others by listing bridges and bombscarred superstructures.

With the pale light came the first bombardment, probing and slow at first, and then with the fierceness of a tornado. There were few good houses left to fall, so that the screaming highexplosives ploughed into the rubble and churned the torn remains into a living ferment.

Alongside the wreck the *Saracen* still lay imprisoned by her mooring wires, her decks littered with broken packing cases and discarded equipment. One landing craft was alongside, and the tired seamen worked in a living chain to carry or guide the last of the wounded aboard.

Erskine ducked involuntarily as a shell exploded in the centre of the harbour and sent a stream of splinters whining overhead. The landing craft sidled clear, her hold for once empty.

Erskine broke into a run, but skidded to a halt as the tannoy speaker blared, 'Clear the upper deck, stand by to slip!' He stared uncomprehendingly as the big turret began to swing slightly to starboard, the twin guns lifting with purposeful menace. Erskine could not believe his eyes. Surely Chesnaye was not going to open fire! The enemy did not know of the *Saracen*'s presence as yet, otherwise he would soon have called upon his dive-bombers. Yet Chesnaye intended to betray his presence, to throw away those last vital moments. He had ordered the upper deck cleared so that the guns could blast away the moment the monitor was under way. The last of the seamen were already leaping from the wreck alongside, and Erskine could see the men by the mooring wires already slackening off and getting ready to slip.

A trail of dark smoke blossomed from the funnel, and beneath his feet Erskine could feel the impatient rumble of engines. From the bridge a voice echoed through a megaphone, 'Get those men aboard!' The last of the seamen from the wreck looked up, startled, and then jumped for the guard-rails.

Erskine climbed rapidly to the bridge where Chesnaye was hanging impatiently over the screen a megaphone in his hand. 'All working parties aboard, sir. Boats hoisted and secure. Ready to proceed.' The words dropped from Erskine's mouth as he watched Chesnaye signalling vigorously to the side party.

'Good. Let go aft. Slow ahead port!' Chesnaye walked briskly to the front of the bridge to watch as the monitor moved cautiously ahead and nudged her weight against the one spring which held her to the wreck. Using one engine the *Saracen* pushed until the wire was bar-taut, until her stern began to swing slowly away from the listing ship.

'Stop port! Let go forrard!' Chesnaye's red-rimmed eyes were feverishly bright.

A rating with a handset looked across at him. 'All gone forrard, sir!'

Chesnaye seemed to force himself to stand quietly in the forefront of the bridge, his shoulders squared against the bright blue sky. 'Slow astern together!'

Very slowly the monitor gathered way, her rounded stern pushing through the oil and scum which covered the harbour in a fine web. Overhead the director squeaked on its mounting as McGowan and his plotters adjusted their sights and weighed up their target.

490

Chesnaye said coldly, 'When we pass the last wreck we can open fire.'

Erskine felt unsteady. So that was why they were leaving sternfirst. Chesnaye had every intention of using the guns to best advantage. He seemed to have thrown reason to the winds.

Chesnaye peered astern, his cap tilted to shut out the mocking glare from the water. The turret was still swinging, the guns rising towards the sun. He forced himself to watch the ship's slow passage between two sunken ships, his mouth a tight line. 'Starboard ten. Midships!' He held his breath as the monitor's fat flank almost brushed a forlorn mast which still had a tattered flag trailing across the unmoving water. Soon now. He could still feel the soldier's cold hand and he moved his fingers with sudden anger.

A light stabbed from amongst the shattered town, like sunlight reflecting from a telescope. He heard a signalman spelling out the signal, and then Laidlaw called, 'They say "good luck", sir!' The light flashed again, even as a brown shell-burst exploded beneath a last defiant minaret. 'And "Many thanks"!'

Chesnaye kept his eyes on the stone breakwater. 'Tell them "It was all part of the service!" '

Surprisingly, a man laughed, and another lifted his cap to wave at the long line of sun-dappled ruins.

The breakwater sidled past, and a small wave-crest surged eagerly beneath the *Saracen's* counter.

Chesnaye lifted his glasses and looked towards the shell-bursts and listened to the distant chatter of machine-guns. Something stirred inside him like an old memory, and he found that he was momentarily able to forget the ship's nakedness and the open sea which awaited him.

He turned and met Erskine's stare and the watchful silence which seemed to hang over the bridge.

Almost challengingly he said, 'Stop engines.' And as the rumble died away, 'Open fire!'

Chapter Five

Stuka

In spite of the steady breeze the air was without life, and seemed almost too hot to breathe. The watchkeepers stood listless and heavy, each man careful to keep his body clear of the steel plates and shimmering guns as the sun ground down on their solitary ship. A fine blue haze hid the horizon and added to the sense of complete isolation, and a million tiny mirrors danced on the flat water to add further to the discomfort of the lookouts.

Chesnaye slumped in his chair, forcing himself to remain still as a thin stream of sweat moved down his spine. His clothes felt rough and sodden, so that even taking a breath became sheer discomfort.

The bridge throbbed to the tune of the two engines which in spite of all else maintained a steady six and a half knots, and made the small bow wave gurgle cheerfully around the ship's stem. On the decks nothing moved, although Chesnaye knew without looking that the ship's company was at Action Stations. Men were relieved in small batches to enjoy brief respite in the messdecks, or to help tend the long lines of army wounded. Between decks there was a smell of pain, so that the seamen were soon back on deck, as if uneasy at what they had seen.

Chesnaye glanced at his watch. Five hours since the short bombardment and their departure from Tobruk. It still seemed incredible that nothing more had happened. The shoreline had faded into the morning mist and the sun had risen high as if to pin them down on this pitiless sea. But nothing happened.

At first he had been almost unable to remain still under the mounting tension. Now, with each cheerful turn of the screws, he found a few moments to hope. In spite of Erskine's doubt and open resentment, the watchful eyes of the others and the very real fear of his own abilities, Chesnaye could feel a glimmer of pleasure, even pride.

A bosun's mate placed an enamel mug at his elbow. 'Lemon juice, sir.' Chesnaye nodded and sipped it gratefully. His eyes felt raw and gummed with fatigue, and any distraction, no matter how small, helped to hold him together.

As he sipped at the already warm liquid he glanced at the bridge party. The Officer of the Watch, Fox, and his assistant, Sub-Lieutenant Bouverie, were standing elbow to elbow on the central gratings, their reddened faces turned to either bow as they took occasional sweeps of the horizon with their glasses. Two bosun's mates and a messenger stood at the rear by the charthouse entrance, eyes heavy and listless, waiting like terriers to pass the word of their master. Just to the rear of the bridge Chesnaye could see the slim Oerlikon barrels pointing skywards, the gunners already strapped in position, their half-naked bodies deeply tanned and immune to the probing rays.

McGowan would be at his station, keeping a watchful eye on the ship's defences, while his mind was no doubt still thinking of the short attack on the German positions.

It had been quick, savage and breathtaking. While the *Saracen* pitched easily on the small harbour swell the calm morning air had been torn apart by her massive onslaught. To the German gunners beyond the battered town it must have been even more of a shock. Used to fighting artillery duels with guns of their own calibre, and confident that the Tobruk fortress was almost ready to capitulate, the sudden thunder from the harbour must have seemed unreal. Unreal perhaps until the great fifteen-inch shells had begun to fall around them. McGowan and his gunnery team had very little to go on, but with methodical determination he had laid down a barrage some five miles wide, his heart jumping as each gun hurled itself back on its worn springs.

Then, with smoke still streaming from the two long guns, the monitor had swung about and steamed towards the open sea.

That was five hours earlier. Five hours. Chesnaye rubbed his eyes and drained the last few drips from the enamel mug.

There was a rustle of movement behind him. Fox said, 'Signal, sir!'

Chesnaye felt his stomach muscles contract, but forced his voice to remain steady. 'Read it.'

'From C.-in-C. Italian minelayer reported in vicinity. Believed north of Bardia and heading west. Minelayer is damaged and will try to reach first available harbour. Must be sunk or held until other forces available. There are two escorts.' Fox took a breath.

'There are a few alleged positions, sir, but that is the crux of the signal.'

Chesnaye ran his tongue along the back of his teeth. Once again the *Saracen* was to forget her own immediate problems. By the moving of a small pin or flag on some distant chart she had been drawn into the over-all plan of campaign. A few seconds before he had been thinking only of getting back to Alexandria without loss. Now, in a stammer of morse, he had another picture in his aching mind.

A minelayer. No doubt one of those fast cruiser-type ships which had been playing havoc around Malta, Crete and every piece of British-held shoreline in the Mediterranean. In hours a ship like that could lay a deadly field which if undetected would send many good craft to the bottom. Even if discovered at once, a minefield was still a menace. It had to be swept, and during that slow and painful business nothing could be allowed to move in that area. This particular minelayer had apparently been caught, probably by one of the few aircraft available for coastal patrol. Damaged, her speed might be severely cut, and her captain would think only of getting back to safety.

Chesnaye stood up, and felt a shaft of pain lance through his cramped thigh. He tried not to limp as he led the way to the charthouse, and then he waited as Fox laid off the possible position and course of the enemy ships.

Chesnaye leaned forward and squinted at the converging lines. 'Not bad.' He prodded the chart with the dividers. 'If I were the Italian captain I would not keep too close to the coast. Yesterday *we* were none too sure of the enemy positions in the desert. If this minelayer has been in the Eastern Mediterranean on operations her captain'll be no better informed than we were!' He tapped the chart thoughtfully. 'Probably keep about twenty miles off. But will follow the coast just in case of surface attack.' He was thinking aloud, while Fox watched him with open interest. 'He'll know that Tobruk is closed as far as we are concerned. His only danger will be from behind him, from Alex, or from a patrol further north. The first is obviously the only likely one, as we'll not be able to spare anything from the Greek campaign.'

Fox said: 'That's what the signal meant, I expect? The "other forces available" must be pursuing him from Alex?'

Chesnaye tightened his jaw. The Second Inshore Squadron, no

doubt. Beaushears so determined to catch this sly interloper in his own area that he had even called in the *Saracen*. He smiled, but added in a calm voice: 'Yes, Pilot, the Italian gentlemen will not expect a ship of our size right ahead of him! Lay off course to intercept, and send for the First Lieutenant.' He walked back into the sunlight, his fingers tightly laced behind his back. This would make up for their inability to help the convoy, for the hints and sneers which he and the ship had been made to endure.

He turned to see Erskine's flushed face already on the bridge. In short, terse sentences he explained the position and what he intended to do. Erskine listened without speaking, his eyes fixed on some point above his Captain's right shoulder.

Chesnaye concluded: 'Two or three rounds from the main armament should do the trick, even at extreme range. If she's carrying mines she'll go up like a Brock's Benefit, but in any case she'll be no problem.'

Erskine asked quietly, 'And the escorts, sir?'

'Well, they say there are two. They can't amount to much, though.'

'Why do you say that, sir?' Erskine looked mystified.

'It's hardly likely we'd have been told about the damaged minelayer if the escorts were bigger and more important, is it?'

'Well, no, sir.' Erskine was dazed by the change of events. As his tired mind cleared, he found a growing excitement. This enemy ship coming out of the blue was a gift indeed. The monitor could pound it to pulp even if the other vessel was four times as fast and ten times as manœuvrable. It was as if Providence had decided to make an offering to relieve the fear and apprehension of Tobruk.

Erskine had hardly spoken to the Captain since the monitor had left the smoking harbour. He had looked for some light of triumph or contempt on Chesnaye's face, but it was impassive as always, giving nothing of the inner man away.

But this new venture would make all the difference. Erskine could even feel the news transmitting itself through the ship as he stood on the bridge with Chesnaye. The infallible system which carried information from man to man faster than any telegraph.

There was a cheer from aft, and Chesnaye remarked, 'Our people want another crack at the enemy, it seems!' He spoke evenly, but for a few seconds Erskine saw through the mask to the almost boyish excitement beyond.

Erskine received his orders in silence, and then as Chesnaye began to move away he said quickly, 'I want to apologise, sir.'

Chesnaye turned, his eyes alert. 'For what?'

'Tobruk. I didn't think the risk was worth making.' He stumbled miserably over each word. 'I was wrong. This minelayer will put us one up again!'

He saw Chesnaye's mouth soften slightly. 'We've not sunk it yet, John!' But although Chesnaye's voice was gruff he was obviously pleased.

Erskine looked across at Fox. 'We'll be up to her in less than an hour, eh?'

The Navigator grinned and nodded towards the Captain's back. 'I hope so, for *my* sake!'

Erskine climbed on to the ladder. Chesnaye was right. This ship was alive. Nothing had changed, but for the vague news of an enemy ship and the consequences of possible danger. Yet the ship stirred and came to life in a way Erskine had never seen before.

As the hands of the bridge clock embraced for noon the mine-layer was sighted. The powerful range-finder above the bridge fastened on the tiny speck which hovered just below the rim of the horizon, and McGowan informed the Captain.

Almost simultaneously, Able Seaman Rix, anti-aircraft look-out on the starboard wing of the bridge, yelled: 'Aircraft! Bearing Green four-five!'

The klaxons screamed their warning, and once more the *Saracen*'s men faced outwards and waited.

Lieutenant Max Eucken licked his lips and tried to retain the taste of the coffee he had been drinking only half an hour earlier. In spite of the tremendous heat which glared through the long perspex cockpit cover Eucken was able to remain completely relaxed, and his eyes hardly wavered as he stared ahead through the silvery arc of the Stuka's propeller. Without looking he knew that the other six aircraft were formed on either flank in a tight arrowhead for-mation, just as he could picture the face of each pilot, as well as the exact capability of every man under his command.

Below him the sea shone like a sheet of bright blue glass, and around him the sky was clear and inviting. Eucken was twenty-two years old, and at that very moment extremely contented.

It was amazing what a difference it made to a man's life the

496

moment he was airborne, he thought. All the irritating faults and stipulations of the dusty airstrip were forgotten as soon as the wheels left the makeshift runway. Up here a man was king. Master of his own and others' destinies.

Voices crackled in his earphones, but he was able to ignore them. The other pilots were like himself. Excited and eager. Discipline and instant obedience could be switched on at a second's notice with the precision of a bombsight. For the moment the pilots could be left alone, trusted to keep formation and good lookout.

Behind him, at the rear of the long cockpit, Steuer, the rear-gunner, hunched over his weapons like an untidy sack. A bovine, unimaginative man, but completely reliable. He did as he was told, and trusted his pilot. Those qualities were quite enough by Eucken's standards.

He pulled in his stomach muscles and felt the sweat trickling down beneath the waistband of his shorts. Apart from these he was clad only in flying helmet and sandals, and he flexed his arms with sensuous pleasure, pleased with his own reflection in the oil-smeared perspex. His body was an even golden-brown, and the hairs on his forearms were bleached almost silver from the strange hermit existence in the desert.

He twisted his head to look at the three Stukas on his port quarter. Rising and falling gently like leaves in the wind, they appeared to be hovering against the pale sky, their wide-straddled fixed undercarriages poised like the claws of hunting hawks, which indeed they were. The nearest pilot raised his hand, and Eucken acknowledged him with a brief wave. That was Bredt, the only man apart from Steuer who had been with him since France and the big break-through.

To Eucken each phase of his war was interesting, provided it did not remain the same. He needed excitement, and enjoyed each aspect of it as some men relished sexual pleasure. He had lived long enough and had taken too many risks to believe in fear. He had forgotten its meaning soon after the first solo flight, and almost certainly following his first individual action in France. He could still remember that first time, perhaps more clearly than some of the things which had happened quite recently. The long, straight roads choked and overflowing with streaming French refugees. While the Wehrmacht battered its way through a crumbling and decadent French Army and the British Expeditionary Force

497

scattered towards Dunkirk, Eucken and his quadron helped to sow the seeds of confusion and panic behind the front. Jammed roads meant chaos and a break in supplies. The Stukas dived and screamed on the terror-stricken columns, their bombs carving bloody craters in the helpless victims below. As each bomber whined out of its dive the rear-gunner would take his toll too, the stammering machine-guns mowing down the trapped people like corn. Men, women, children, horses and cattle swept across the windshield in a crazed panorama from hell.

And so it went on. Victory after victory, until France was contained and the Stukas were sent further afield in search of prey.

Eucken rarely thought of his comrades in the other services. He disliked the Navy for its hidebound and arrogant ways. The U-boat Service was the only real attack weapon they had. The rest of the Navy seemed badly organised and not used to its fullest advantage. Neither did the Army appeal to him. Their sort of warfare conjured up pictures of a bygone age, as told to him by his father. Squalor, lice, ignorance and stagnation.

No, the air was the thing. And of all the planes which flew for Germany, the Stuka had struck the greatest blow. He could almost sense the great armour-piercing bomb which was slung a few feet beneath him. Soon he would be rid of it, and another ship would be on the bottom of that glistening water.

He had been lounging in the mess-tent beside the desert airstrip when the news had been received. Army Intelligence had reported a sudden and devastating bombardment from the sea off Tobruk. The enemy ship had escaped it seemed, and now there were cries for recriminations.

How like the Army! he thought with contempt. Always wanted the Luftwaffe to do its dirty work. And then, of course, there was this Italian minelayer. That, too, was somehow typical. How much better it would have been if the British had been Germany's allies. Together they could have stamped on all these sub-standard nations. But as the Führer had already explained, the British had been misled by Jews and Communists. They would just have to pay for their mistakes.

His handsome features crinkled in a small frown as Bredt's sharp voice cut into his ears. 'There it is! Dead ahead!' Eucken gave himself a small rebuke for allowing his mind to wander and so allow

498

another to make the first sighting report. He leaned forward, his clear eyes reaching out ahead of his formation.

At first he thought the ship was stationary, and then almost in the same second he imagined that the strange-looking vessel had already been attacked. She looked ungainly, her superstructure unevenly spaced, so that at first glance he thought she had lost part of her stern. But as he drew nearer, and the vessel's outline hardened through the haze, he realised that this was indeed the one they were looking for. From the approach angle the monitor's shape was not unlike a tailor's steam iron, and from her small wash he guessed that she was doing less than eight knots. It would be a copybook attack. The one they had executed so often in these waters.

He felt quite happy at the prospect. Perhaps it was because this was to be another new experience. The monitor was quite big, although he had no way of gauging its actual potential and value in over-all strategy.

Calmly he gave his orders and settled himself more comfortably in his harness. It would soon be over. There would probably be more decorations after this. Personally he did not care very much, but he knew that his parents would be pleased. It would make up in some way for his two brothers who had already died for the Fatherland. One in France, on the flank of the Maginot Line, the other in Holland, when his scoutcar had run over a mine. Strangely enough, he could hardly remember what they looked like.

The Stuka wagged its wings as the air suddenly blossomed with brown shell-bursts. The Tommies were evidently awake. Eucken smiled gently. Let them make the most of it. It would be a long swim for the survivors. About forty miles, at a guess.

The joke amused him, and he was still smiling as the port wing of bombers, led by Leutnant Bredt, curved away and plummeted down towards the toylike ship. More shell-bursts, but the three Stukas flashed throught them unscathed.

The other three Stukas were climbing to the right for a cross-attack, while Eucken idled along the same course, his keen eyes on the drama below.

Another voice shouted, 'I can see the minelayer!'

Sure enough, the limping Italian ship was also appearing on the scene. Eucken grinned. The more, the merrier.

A nerve jumped in his cheek as the first Stuka exploded in direct line with the monitor. Impassively he watched as the remnants of Bredt's aircraft were scattered across the calm sea in little white feathers of spray. The second Stuka was diving. Tracers lifted to greet it. The plane quivered then dropped into a full dive. All at once smoke poured from its wings and it continued to dive straight for the water. Eucken imagined he could hear the thunderous explosion as the Stuka's bomb exploded on impact. Bomb, aircraft and crew vanished in a bright orange flash well clear of the defiant monitor.

Eucken could feel his hands shaking with sudden rage. It was *his* fault. He had been over-confident.

His voice grated over the stuttering intercom: 'Keep clear! This is Red Leader! I am attacking!'

He heard the engine swell into a ferocious roar as he gunned the Stuka into a sidestepping dive. He saw the third attacker falter and pull away, a thin smoke trail streaming behind it. Down, down, faster and faster; until it seemed as if the wings would tear themselves free. Aloud he said, 'Don't forget to give them a long burst as I pull out, Steuer!' Behind him he heard the gunner grunt assent. Steuer never saw anything until the aircraft was out of its dive. It was a lonely job.

Eucken forgot Steuer, the Squadron and everything else as he used every ounce of skill and cunning on his approach. Behind his goggles his eyes were slitted with concentration as he hurled the bomber towards the strange ship. Already it had grown in size. It filled the windshield, and he could see the white caps on its upper bridge like tiny flowers on a grey rock.

Steady now! Ach . . . here come the tracers. Deceptively lazy the red lines climbed to criss-cross over the bomber's path. He watched his sighting mark, his breath almost stopped. Now! The Stuka fell into its final dive, the unearthly scream enclosing Eucken's mind like a drug.

Faster and faster! The aircraft was rocking madly from side to side, and he felt the thud and rip of metal against the fuselage. Above in the clear sky his comrades would be watching and waiting their turn.

Everything seemed enclosed in those tiny final seconds of attack. Eucken could see himself in his mind's eye, the black aircraft almost vertical as it plunged down. Its proud yellow stripes and squadron badge below the cockpit, a wolf with a ship between its jaws.

Almost time. The moment! He pressed the release button and pulled the Stuka out of its headlong plunge even as the monitor's tapering top mast swept to meet him. The plane jumped as the bomb left its rack, and Eucken wished that he could watch it strike home, as he knew it would.

There was one abbreviated explosion, and the Stuka fell over on to its side. All at once the tense but orderly world of the cockpit had exploded about him.

There was fire all around him, and he could hear someone screaming like a tortured animal Automatically he flexed his arms to adjust the controls, but dumbly realised that only his brain was working, his limbs were frozen and useless.

The bright sun – which should have been at his back – was suddenly below him. First there was the sky and then the sea. The aircraft was revolving with gathering force as it plunged towards the blue water.

The pain came simultaneously with the realisation. But it was all too late. With glazed eyes Max Eucken, aged twenty-two, watched the sea tearing to meet him. He could see the windshield being sprayed with his own blood, just as he could hear himself screaming. But he felt completely detached, and was still staring when the black Stuka hit the water.

To drop the bomb which struck the *Saracen* the Stuka pilot had planned his approach with great care. With a slight curve he had dived across the ship's port quarter, almost brushing the main topmast, so that the few who saw him imagined for a moment that the screaming aircraft was going to plunge into the mouth of the funnel itself. While the bomber banked and began to haul itself out of its steep dive, the single, gleaming bomb detached itself and plummeted straight for the crowded bridge.

Then several things happened simultaneously. As the Stuka displayed its striped underbelly the monitor's Oerlikon gunners, who had been keeping up a steady fire since the first enemy attack, saw their opportunity. Even as the aircraft began to regain height the fuselage sparkled in a long, unbroken line of small shell-bursts. The Stuka staggered, picked up again, and then began to spin out of control while the Oerlikons still hammered home their deadly blows. No one saw the German actually hit the water, for in that tiny instant the ship seemed to jump bodily as the bomb exploded.

501

It was well aimed, and in the seconds which passed to the sounds of blast and destruction it should have sent the ship on its way to the bottom to join the remains of the shattered aircraft. With the speed of light the bomb struck the front of the bridge superstructure with the sound of a giant hammer and ricocheted forward and down until it sliced into the rear of the tall barbette upon which the ship's great gun-turret was mounted. That first change of direction saved the *Saracen* from the mortal blow. It guided the bomb clear of the small area of thinly armoured deck between the turret and the bridge, and instead sent it smashing its way at a forty-five-degree angle towards the empty lower messdeck where it exploded. Had the bomb struck the area intended, it would have cleaved straight down through two decks and on to the keel itself. Fuel and ammunition would have made an inferno to cover the inrush of water, and would have made escape impossible for many of the ship's company. As it was, the bomb was turned aside, to spend itself like a crazed beast before exploding in the monitor's steel bowels.

But in those agonising seconds, and in the long minutes which followed, there were few who really knew what had happened. Each man wondered and feared for his own safety, and many verged on the edge of panic.

Tending to the army wounded in the forward messdeck, Surgeon Lieutenant Wickersley felt the bomb strike the ship, and sat frozen on the deck as he listened to the thing tearing its way through the toughened steel with the noise of a bandsaw. The explosion lifted him from his trance, and as the long space filled with dust and drifting smoke he found with sudden surprise that he was able to ignore the unknown danger and turn, instead, to the bandaged figures which lay trapped and helpless around him. His assistants, made up of cooks, stewards and writers, and many others of the men who were not actually employed in fighting the ship, were staring at him, suddenly dependent and waiting.

Wickersley stood up and brushed some flaked paintwork from his hair. He gave his orders in a calm voice, inwardly grateful that now the moment had arrived he had beaten his fear and was ready to cope with the work for which he had been trained.

High above the bridge in the encased world of the control tower Lieutenant Norris had been sitting hunched and fascinated beside McGowan, the Control Officer. The small armoured nerve centre of the ship's gunpower had suddenly vibrated to the scream of the diving Stuka, so that even the stammer of Oerlikons and the deeper bark of pompoms seemed muted by comparison. Still Norris had been unable to accept that the moment had arrived. Not until the shadow of the screaming aircraft had enveloped the open bridge below him, and a dark streak had flashed down across his vision towards the figure of the Captain himself, did Norris fully realise his very real danger. He wanted to turn away, or bury his face in the back of the rating at the training mechanism, but he was quite unable to close his eyes to the impossible sight of the bomb grinding across the front of the bridge in a shower of sparks to disappear somewhere at the foot of the massive turret. The explosion came after what seemed an age of waiting, and then it was as if it had come from another bomb altogether. Far away, muffled and sullen, it seemed to be in the very bowels of the ship. The air was filled with black smoke which fanned by the breeze billowed back over the bridge until the lonely control tower was lost and isolated in an impenetrable cloud. McGowan's face looked grey, but his voice was toneless as he spoke quickly to his handset. The four ratings glanced quickly at their officers and then settled back again on their stools. If they were near terror they gave no sign as far as Norris could see, even though their small refuge and the tripod mast beneath still thrummed like some maniac instrument.

Until the bombers were sighted Norris had been watching the slow approach of the enemy minelayer. As Spotting Officer he had been mentally rehearsing his duties, even looking forward to the moment when the guns would begin to pound the injured enemy to fragments. His task would be to guide the groping guns directly on to their target, a feeling which at a safe range gave him the satisfaction of immeasurable power.

McGowan was saying sharply: 'Exploded in lower messdeck! The damage control party is on its way!'

For something to say, Norris asked weakly, 'Is the turret safe?'

McGowan shrugged and looked at Norris for the first time. 'Quarters Officer reports several injuries. Concussion mostly!' He laughed harshly, as if unable to understand that he was alive. 'The other bombers have buggered off!'

Erskine was already making his way below to the roaring inferno of fire and black smoke. Around him men fought with

503

hoses and extinguishers to control the feelers of flame, while others dealt with the menace beyond the glowing watertight doors. Messengers came and went, while Erskine passed his orders almost in a daze. He still did not know the full extent of the damage, but what he had seen was bad enough.

A petty officer and two seamen who had been pulped to a purple mess by the force of the explosion. An Oerlikon gun complete with gunner and magazine which had been torn from its mounting and hurled over the port rail with the ease of a child's toy. A nameless rating, stripped naked by blast, who had dashed past him screaming, his body flayed by foot-long wood splinters from the deck at the base of the turret.

The Chief Bosun's Mate said in his ear: 'We'll soon 'ave the fire in 'and, sir! Must get some of the wounded moved a bit sharpish afore they get roasted!'

Erskine shook himself. 'Yes. Very well, Buffer, you get your men on to it.' He broke off, coughing as more smoke funnelled its way through the avenue of shattered mess tables, shredded clothing and smashed crockery.

The Chief Bosun's Mate wiped his sweating face and gestured towards a pin-up which still remained seductively in position above a smouldering locker. 'I couldn't even manage 'er at the moment, sir!'

Erskine tried to smile, but his jaws felt fixed and taut. With a groan he began to retrace his steps as another messenger ran towards him through the smoke. I must report to the bridge. His brain rebelled, but he forced himself to concentrate, the effort making him sway.

There was so much to do. And there was still the minelayer to be pinned down and sunk.

'Here, sir! Let me help you!'

Chesnaye felt Fox's hand beneath his elbow and staggered to his feet. His head felt as if it was splitting in half, and as the smoke billowed over the lip of the bridge he knew he was near to collapse. It was as if the bomb had been aimed at him. He had actually seen it, a dark smudge against the bright sky, before it struck the steel behind him and hurled him to the deck with its searing shock-wave. Everyone seemed to be shouting, and each voice-pipe and telephone was demanding attention.

'Bombers making off, sir!' Fox was still holding his arm, his dark face tight with concern. 'Damage reports coming in now.'

Chesnaye nodded vaguely and limped to the forward screen. Broken glass crunched beneath his shoes, and he felt a cold hand on his heart as he looked down at the deck below. The teak planking had been jack-knifed by the explosion, and from the jagged tear in the foot of the barbette he saw the unbroken spiral of black smoke. There were mixed cries and shouted orders, and he could see the stretcher bearers already groping their way towards the ship's wound.

He must not think of it. The others would do their job. He had to control the ship. To find the enemy.

He blinked his streaming eyes. 'Alter course two points to starboard.' Must get this damned smoke clear of the bridge.

He stared for several seconds at the raw scar on the edge of the steel left by the bomb. It must have missed me by inches, he thought. A few feet this way and the wheelhouse would have been knocked out. A bit further forward and the turret might have been wrecked.

Fox said, 'Eight of our people killed, sir. One missing.'

'Thank you.' Missing? That must have been the Oerlikon gunner.

Fox was holding a handset. 'The Gunnery Officer, sir.'

Chesnaye took the handset, his eyes still on the clouds of smoke. With the slight alteration of course the ship was being kept clear. 'Give me the target range, Guns.' He felt some of the tension draining from him. They had survived again. They had been attacked, but had hit back in spite of the enemy's determination.

'Range is ten thousand yards, sir.' McGowan sounded strained. 'I should like to clear the turret, sir.'

Chesnaye's mind snapped back to the immediate problems 'Clear the turret? The Quarters Officer has reported no serious damage!'

McGowan said flatly: 'He has just reported to me, sir. The bomb passed through the working chamber below the turntable compartment and has sheared off a section of the lower roller path.'

Chesnaye tried to drive the sense of unreality from his brain. 'D'you mean the turret won't train?'

'That's right, sir. The guns are quite intact and fully operational. But the turret cannot be moved.'

Chesnaye felt as if the bridge was closing in on him. A strong eddy of wind cleared the smoke from the fo'c'sle, and for a few

505

moments he was able to see the black silhouette of the Italian ship fine on the port bow. The minelayer's shape was already lengthening. She was sheering away.

Controlling his voice with an effort, Chesnaye said, 'If we can't use the training gear, what about operating the turret by hand?'

McGowan sounded almost gentle. 'No, sir. Until the shore artificers can fix the roler path the turret is fixed.'

'Very well. Keep me informed.' Blindly he handed the receiver to Fox and walked to the front of the bridge.

Like an additional mockery he heard a messenger repeat: 'Fire under control, sir! Damage Control report no damage to hull.'

The density of smoke faded, and Chesnaye lifted his glasses to stare again at the distant minelayer. He could see the ship quite clearly and the two trawler-type escorts which hovered on either beam. The Italian captain must be wondering what was happening. A powerful ship, its tall turret so easy to see with binoculars, had suddenly appeared in his path. Death and destruction must have seemed inevitable. Even the timely entrance of seven dive-bombers had failed to remove this new and threatening shape.

But now, as the Italian coaxed the last ounce of steam from the damaged engines and altered course away from the enemy, he must have become aware of something even stranger. Those great guns remained stiff and unmoving. As the bearing changed, the guns stayed pointing impotently at some point far astern.

Chesnaye said at length, 'Ask McGowan if we can try a sighting shot if I swing the ship by engines alone.'

He waited, aware that every man on the bridge was avoiding his eye.

Fox said quietly: 'Negative, sir. It could do the turret irreparable damage, and in any case it would be almost impossible to get a close shot under these circumstances.' Fox looked past Chesnaye and followed the enemy ship with hatred in his eyes. 'Goddamn, she was so near too!'

Chesnaye walked to his chair. Without looking, he knew that Erskine had joined the others behind him. At length he said: 'Fall out Action Stations. Resume course for Base.'

He heard Fox swear, and then stiffened as McGowan joined him on the bridge. McGowan said: 'I'm sorry, sir.'

Chesnaye could not tear his eyes from the smudge of smoke

which marked the place where the minelayer had dipped over the horizon. 'So am *I*, Guns.'

From far away he heard Erskine's voice. 'There will have to be a signal, sir.'

Damn you! Chesnaye knew that Erskine was watching him, waiting for him to crack. To admit his mistakes.

Coldly he replied: 'Make a signal, then. We are returning to Base. Lost contact with enemy.'

Erskine persisted, his voice heavy, 'You could add that we have been damaged and require escort, sir?'

Chesnaye half turned, his eyes bitter. 'That's how you would do it, I suppose? Well, I don't need any damned excuses for my ship!'

A shutter fell across Erskine's troubled features. 'Very well, sir. I'll have the signal sent off now.'

Chesnaye stared ahead over the bows. Yes, you do that. Get ready to save yourself when I am being crucified!

Later in the charthouse McGowan said softly: 'Well, it was only a Wop minelayer. We were lucky to get away with the bloody bombing!'

Fox stared at him and then shrugged. 'It's not just a Wop minelayer to the Skipper. It was a chance for him and the old ship. In the eyes of your bloody admiral he's made a cock of it, an' that's all there is to it!'

McGowan frowned. 'I don't see it that way at all.'

'That's what is wrong with you regulars! You don't see anything beyond K.R.s and A.I.s. It explains why you're so bloody callous with each other!' With sudden rage Fox slammed down his ruler and stamped back on to the bridge.

Why should *I* care? he thought angrily. They're all the damned same! Why get involved with something which has always been the same, and probably always will?

He felt his eyes drawn to the Captain's shoulders and knew he was deceiving himself. Nothing could ever be quite the same in future.

Chapter Six

Ann

'Ship secure, sir!' Erskine saluted formally and waited as Chesnaye stared down at the long, dusty jetty. Already parties of *Saracen*'s seamen were running out the long brows, watched incuriously by the drivers of the silent convoy of khaki ambulances which had been waiting for the ship to come alongside the wharf.

Alexandria was much the same as usual. Anchored ships, dust and the over-all heat haze. But it was Sunday morning, and in spite of the threatening news from the Western Desert, and the painful withdrawals from Greece, the vessels of the Mediterranean Fleet which were lucky enough to be in harbour were observing the ceremonial of the Day of Rest. Church pennants fluttered from ship's yards, and from a towering battleship which had once seen service at Jutland came the strains of a marine band. 'For those in peril on the sea . . .' Bared heads, best uniforms, and here and there the flutter of a sailor's collar, although there seemed to be no breeze.

Only the *Saracen* provided movement and an alien air of untidiness. Two tall cranes had squeaked along their miniature railway and now stood poised like ungainly herons as they inspected their prey. The ship's own derricks clattered into life and began to swing some of the more seriously wounded troops ashore, and Erskine could see Wickersley and his two sick-berth attendants conferring with some of the army medical orderlies on the jetty.

The engines had fallen silent, and groups of unemployed seamen were moving wearily around the upper deck as if seeing the scars and damage for the first time.

Erskine waited. He had nothing planned any more. He felt uneasy and unsure, as if he was on the brink of a new phase in his life. His orders might already be on their way to the ship. This time tomorrow he could be *en route* for England. Involuntarily he glanced towards the white houses above the harbour and wondered if Ann was already watching the ship and waiting for him. This time there could be no excuses. He would have to try to explain to her. The ship would need a good deal of attention from the repair workers, and even with speed and priorities the work would take more than a week, perhaps longer. In that time he would have to make a decision.

Chesnaye said, 'Keep both watches at work until midday and then pipe Make-and-Mend.'

'Shore leave, too, sir?' Erskine turned to look at the Captain's tired, stubbled face and tried to keep his own mind from becoming involved with Chesnaye's problems.

'Yes. There'll be little done today if I know the authorities here. Just keep the duty part of the watch aboard. The rest have earned a breather. They've done well.'

Erskine said suddenly, 'I thought we might have a wardroom party while we're here, sir?' He was almost surprised to hear his own suggestion. Deep down he knew it was just another excuse. Surrounded by familiar faces it might be easier to explain to Ann. 'We could get a few friends from the Base, some of the nurses and so on?'

Chesnaye nodded, his thoughts far away. 'You arrange it if you want to.'

'Anything else, sir?'

'Yes. Get the hands out of working rig as soon as possible. There's no reason for the ship's company to look like a lot of pirates.'

Erskine sighed. Across the water on the battleship he could see the lines of white-clad seamen, the flash of sunlight on the band's polished instruments. By comparison the *Saracen* looked a wreck. Smoke-stained and battered, with her splintered deck and gashed turret adding to the appearance of shabbiness.

Chesnaye looked around the bridge and said, 'I'm going to my quarters to complete my reports.'

'I'll keep an eye on things.' Erskine hated this game with words. The Navy made it so easy. Question and answer. Challenge and password. In this manner you could speak to superior and subordinate for months and yet say nothing.

There was a slight cough, and Fox appeared at the head of the bridge ladder. 'Signal from Flag, sir.' He held out the pad, his eyes anxious.

Chesnaye did not take the pad. 'For the captain of *Saracen* to report on board the flagship forthwith?' He smiled briefly at Fox's discomfort. 'I was expecting it.' He seemed to square his shoulders. 'Tell my steward to lay out a clean uniform while I take a shave and shower. I expect the Admiral can wait a little longer!' There was no bitterness in his tone, in fact there was nothing at all.

Fox stood aside to let him pass and then said to Erskine, 'The signal requires a report from *you* too, Number One!'

Erskine started from his troubled thoughts. 'Me?' Fox's stare made him feel uneasy.

'The Admiral apparently requires your statement for some reason or other. It seems he was rather keen on catching that damned minelayer!'

Erskine looked away. So there was to be no escape, no easy way even from this. Beaushears wanted him to stab Chesnaye in the back. With sudden anger he kicked at the gratings. Well, Chesnaye had acted incorrectly. He should have kept clear of Tobruk once he had found that the original landing point was unusable. He had risked the ship to get rid of the stores, and by his bombardment had drawn attention to the ship's position. His action had cost the ship the chance of sinking the minelayer. It might cost Chesnaye much more.

Fox said quietly, 'What will you say?'

'That's my affair!' Erskine avoided Fox's hard eyes. 'It's unfair that I should be involved in this business at all!'

'So you intend to walk out on us, eh?' Fox stood his ground.

'What the hell are you talking about?'

'You think that getting promotion is suddenly so god-damned important that you can act like a bloody judge!' Fox's eyes were flashing dangerously. 'I know you can log me for speaking like this, but someone's got to tell you!'

Erskine felt the colour rushing to his face. 'What d'you know about it? After this war's over you'll run back to your damned banana boat! I'm in the Navy for a *career*!'

Fox threw the signal pad on to an ammunition locker. 'It may have escaped your notice, but we've not won the bloody war yet! And the way we're going, it now seems almost unlikely!' He stared at Erskine with calm distaste. 'When we *have* won you can throw men like Chesnaye back on the beach and men like me

510

back to earning a living from the sea. Until that happy time just remember that it's the Chesnayes of this world who can save us, *if* they're given a chance!' He turned to leave. 'They're the only poor bastards who *don't* think of the future!'

Erskine knew he should have stopped Fox's outburst, but he had been incapable of doing anything. It had been like a scourge, a necessary punishment. Or perhaps it was because Fox was the most unlikely officer aboard to show such emotion.

He shook himself and moved to the rear of the bridge where Pike, the Master-at-Arms, was waiting with a little procession of defaulters. It never stopped, Erskine told himself wearily, peace or war, whatever you had to torment your inner self, routine must still be observed.

He straightened his cap. 'Very well, Master. Let's get it over with!'

Compared with the arctic brightness of the street outside the narrow window, the room seemed dim and somehow smaller than Erskine had remembered it. He sat heavily on the sagging sofa his hands hanging between his knees, his eyes on the girl's back as she stood silhouetted against the white-fronted building opposite.

Over her shoulder she said quietly, 'Well, that's it, then, isn't it?' Her voice was low and even, and it seemed to stir yet another memory in Erskine, like the return of an old pain.

'I thought I ought to tell you right away, Ann. It seemed only fair.' Already he was regretting that he was here, yet at the same time unable to stop his mind responding to her presence.

Ann Curzon was tall and slim, and Erskine noticed with another pang that she was barefoot on the tiled floor. She had remembered that he had once remarked about her being his own height. She had been waiting for him. Expecting him. Even the small, overcrowded room looked friendly and pleased with itself, as if Ann had taken special pains for his visit. She turned and looked down at him. She was wearing a plain white blouse and narrow green skirt which accentuated the perfect shape of her body.

Erskine could not see beyond the shadows which hid her eyes and said: 'I hope you'll be able to come aboard the *Saracen* this evening. It'll probably be the last time we'll all be together.'

511

The girl walked slowly to a small table and ran her fingers across the unopened wine which stood with its attendant glasses. Erskine noted the rich tan of her bare legs and the way the fringe of hair across her forehead had become bleached by the sun. The old yearning stirred inside him, and he added tightly, 'We knew this might happen, Ann.'

She sat down on a stool and picked up a packet of cigarettes. 'Did we?' Then she smiled, as if at some inner memory. 'I suppose *I* must have known.'

Erskine felt sick. Of this situation, of himself. Of what he had done.

As if reading his thoughts she said. 'Why did you have to tell that story about your captain?'

Erskine started. 'It was the truth as I saw it.' Being suddenly on the defensive made him confused.

'As *you* saw it!' She blew out a stream of smoke. 'I expect the Admiral was pleased with you.'

'I wish I'd not told you about it. I thought it might explain –'

She cut him short. 'You came because you thought it was your duty. Just as you felt you should inform the Admiral that in your opinion your captain is incapable of doing his job!' Her wide eyes flashed with anger. 'Result? Exit captain and enter John Erskine, the Admiral's friend!'

Erskine jumped to his feet. He felt betrayed, as if the ground had suddenly been dragged from beneath him. 'That's unfair! I was asked what I thought. I told him!'

'I'll bet!' She was also on her feet, and as Erskine watched she walked quickly to the window. Across the street the carpet trader still sat outside his small shop surrounded by his dusty rugs, which hung from the flaking walls like battle flags.

Erskine tried again. 'Look, Ann, I didn't want it to be like this. I didn't want to talk about the ship, but about us.' He stood behind her and put his hands on her shoulders. 'I'll have to go to England, and after that I don't know what might happen.' He felt the moist warmth of her shoulders through the thin blouse and tried to pull her against him. He felt her stiffen, and saw the quick tilt of her head.

She slipped from his grasp and turned to face him. 'You've a short memory, John. It was here in this room, remember? Down there on the floor!'

He started to step back, but her voice held him. 'Don't you like to face it, John? Doesn't it fit in with your scheme of things?'

'I can only say that I'm sorry. I know it doesn't help.'

Her lips parted in a small smile. 'No, it doesn't.'

Then, in an almost matter-of-fact voice, she added, 'I'm leaving here, too.'

Erskine answered quickly, relieved to change the subject, 'Oh, where are you going?'

'To Malta.'

Erskine, who had been stealing a quick glance at his watch, stared at her with surprise. 'Malta? Like hell you are!'

'You have no control of my life any more, John. If you ever did. As you know, I've been some use at the hospital. I could do something over there too.'

'They'll never allow it!' Erskine was surprised to find out how much the news had unsettled him.

'They already have. The Red Cross can do any damn' thing!' She eyed him calmly. 'Even your admiral couldn't stop me!'

Erskine reached for his cap. 'Look, Ann, I must go back to the ship. There's a lot to do.' He knew he had to see her again, to make it right with her. 'I mean this, Ann. Could you come aboard tonight?'

Surprisingly she replied: 'I wouldn't miss it for the world. I think I shall get drunk!'

He reached out and held her arm. It was warm and very smooth. All at once the old memories came crowding back. That evening ashore, the laughter and the friendly jibes from the others. Then being alone, here, with Ann. The quick, breathless movements, and the eager pressure of her flesh against his. He squeezed her arm. 'It doesn't have to be like this, Ann.'

She looked directly at his face. 'Perhaps we were lovers, John. But apparently we were not in love.' She withdrew her arm and touched it with her fingertips, her eyes distant. 'You want to go, John, but because of your code you want to go with my blessing.' She shrugged. 'Well, you've got it, now for God's sake leave me to think.'

He moved quickly to the door. An unnerving thought crossed his mind and he said, 'You'll be all right?'

Without looking up, she answered, 'I'll not cut my throat, if that's what you mean!'

Then he was out in the street and almost running towards the harbour. But the freedom he had anticipated still eluded him, and the guilt which he had tried to hold at bay enclosed like a sea-fog.

He slowed his pace, his face creased in thought. He had done the only thing possible, both with Ann and with the ship. Yet just being with her again had reopened the wound, and even as he walked away from the quiet street he could feel the old yearning and desire. How had she really taken this news? Did she even care? He was still deep in thought when he reached the jetty and the jagged outline of the *Saracen*.

Chesnaye left his littered desk and walked slowly to the open scuttle. The sun was already low and threw a dark shadow of the monitor's superstructure across the harbour's placid water. He loosened his jacket and peered down at a small harbour launch which was carrying a noisy party of libertymen from one of the anchored destroyers. He had always liked to watch the life of a busy port, but now it did not seem to matter. Behind him the desk waited with its pile of reports, requisitions and stores demands. The hundred and one things which every captain was expected to deal with the moment his ship nestled alongside. Normally Chesnaye enjoyed this task. From his aloof over-all position of command it brought him in regular contact with all the small details which made the ship a working machine. Even the pathetic signals about unfaithful wives, bombed-out homes and relatives killed in action helped to preserve his sense of humanity and understanding of the men who served him. Mere faces had become personalities, and abilities no longer had to be judged by record papers or the badges on a rating's sleeve.

Now that was soon to be finished. As a fresh wave of despair passed over him he began to move quickly and aimlessly about the wide, shabby stateroom, with its heavy furniture and frayed carpet. When Chesnaye had returned from his brief visit to the flagship he had thrown himself into the waiting correspondence as if by doing so he could blot out the misery which Beaushears had so coldly thrown at him. Now Paymaster Sub-Lieutenant Philpott and the Chief Writer had departed, and he was unable to keep his wretchedness at bay. The interview with the Admiral had been much as he had expected. After being kept waiting for the best part of an hour he had been ushered into Beaushears' quarters by the same elegant flag-lieutenant. But this time Beaushears had seen him alone, his face stiff and yet somehow eager as he slammed home one point after another.

'I warned you, Chesnaye.' Beaushears had started to pace, as if he had been working himself into a rage for some time. 'But you still think you know best! I've had a dozen reports to do concerning this minelayer business, and I'm about sick of it!'

Chesnaye had kept his voice under control with effort. 'My orders gave me a certain latitude, sir. I landed my stores and the Army were very grateful.'

Beaushears waved his hand impatiently. 'I've received a signal about that *and* the bombardment you took upon yourself to supply!' He seemed beside himself. 'Naturally the Army were pleased! What do they know about our situation? We're snowed under with work, and, in case you're interested, we're even shorter of ships and men than we were before!'

Chesnaye spoke carefully: 'The Greek campaign was a waste of time. I implied as much when I was here before!' He could feel his reserves of patience draining away. Days and nights on the bridge without sleep were taking their toll. In any case, Beaushears had obviously made up his mind without much goading. 'I understand we lost twenty-three ships in one day, and two hospital ships to boot. I'm not surprised the Admiralty are worried!'

Beaushears had stopped his pacing and had stared at him with sudden calm. 'Look, Chesnaye, you seem to misunderstand why you are here! I didn't call you to this ship to ask your opinions of world strategy or how to run my squadron. You were given a task, straightforward and uncomplicated. Not to mince words, you made a complete muck of it. If it hadn't been for that stupid bombardment you would have been clear away and in a position to stop the minelayer. It's the convoy all over again. You just cannot bring yourself to understand that your job is not to decide policy but to obey orders, in this instance *my* orders!'

Outside the curtained doorway Chesnaye had heard the distant laughter of the flagship's officers as they gathered for their pre-lunch gins in the wardroom. Always after Sunday Divisions the occasion seemed gayer and more exuberant, like a first-night of a dramatic society where the players have brought off a performance without muffing their lines.

515

It had painfully reminded him of the day he had joined the *Saracen* for the first time in Portsmouth. A callow youth, nervous, but hiding behind a mask of impassive calm, as he was before Beaushears. At that far-off time the monitor's officers had also been recovering from Divisions. In his mind's eye Chesnaye recalled the scene like a picture from an old book. The heavy epaulettes and frock-coats, but otherwise the same Navy. The thought and realisation made him angry again. Of course, that was the fault with the Navy, with the whole fighting machine. The men who were the professionals were in fact only amateurs. They ignored experience, and carried on with their same outworn ideas.

Coldly he had replied, 'The *Saracen's* first task is to supply support for land forces –'

Beaushears' interruption had been loud and final. 'Not any more! She's little more than a store-ship as far as I'm concerned! With the enemy putting on the pressure throughout the Mediterranean it now seems even that role is unsuitable!' Beaushears had forced himself to sit down. 'Your orders will explain what you have to do. *Saracen* will sail when repairs are completed, probably within seven days, and proceed to Malta. The island is near collapse because of lack of supplies, and we are going to push a fast convoy from here in the hope that some of the ships get there. Force "H" will be faking a dummy run from Gibraltar to divide enemy forces, and everything will be done to get the ships through. *Saracen* will sail early, and our convoy should overtake you a day or so before you reach Malta. You can supply extra anti-aircraft cover, and my squadron will screen the convoy from surface attack.' Beaushears had dropped his eyes. 'At Malta *Saracen* can continue to supply A.A. cover for the harbour and act as a base ship for personnel, etcetera. If she avoids being sunk she might still be of some use.'

Chesnaye could still feel the shock of those words. 'You mean she'll not be required for sea again, sir? Not *wanted*?'

'That is exactly what I mean. You have two hundred trained ratings aboard. Most of them will be needed for other ships as replacements. Your second-in-command has been offered a ship of his own, and most of your other officers will no doubt be willing to leave as early as they can.'

Chesnaye had a mental picture of the *Saracen* tied alongside

516

the bombed shambles of Malta's dockyard as the island received one air raid after another. Destroyers and cruisers had already fallen to the attacks. The old monitor would survive for an even shorter period.

In a strangled voice he had asked, 'Will I be retained in command?'

Beaushears had regarded him directly for the first time. 'That will be up to your new flag officer. But I have stated in my report that I consider the maintenance of a full captain aboard to be unnecessary. The ship will be a floating gun battery. Any junior officer should be able to do that job! No, Chesnaye, your place is at home. Go back to training men for the Navy. Your ideas are out of touch. Perhaps later,' he had shrugged indifferently, 'but now we have an immediate job to do.'

It had taken every once of Chesnaye's control to stop from openly pleading. Looking back, it seemed as if that was what Beaushears had expected. There had been a long silence, and then Beaushears had said, 'You would have said the same if the roles were reversed.'

Chesnaye had stood up, his face pale. 'Your seniority gives you the right to express that opinion, sir. It still gives me the right to repudiate it!'

Chesnaye glanced at his watch. The interview had only taken place a few hours ago. The wounded troops had been landed just that morning. It all seemed so long past that Chesnaye felt confused. He needed sleep, and he had not found the time to eat, yet he knew that he could not give in or leave himself open to his despair. In a moment or two his steward would be fussing around him and getting his uniform ready for the wardroom party. The thought almost made him give in to the flood of emotion which pressed so hard on his reason.

No wonder Erskine had wanted a party. *He* had already known the outcome of the interview with Beaushears. To think that Beaushears could use his position to destroy him through a subordinate officer. It did not matter what Erskine had said. There was no open accusation of negligence, so, as usual, the Admiral had it all on his side.

Chesnaye thought of the pseudo-training establishments with their painted stones and pompous instructors. In a fit of anger he told himself he should have stayed in New Zealand, and then he looked again at the shabby stateroom and seemed to see beyond and through the length of the ship herself.

Sailing day was still a week away. Anything might happen before that. But even as he tried to restore his belief he knew that he was deluding himself.

If he had been given command of any other ship this would never have happened. But he did not want another command. The *Saracen* was not just a ship, nor had she ever been.

He was staring at the open scuttle when the steward entered and began to lay out his uniform.

The *Saracen's* wardroom had been cleared of unnecessary furniture and fittings for the party, but was nevertheless crammed to overflowing with noisy, perspiring visitors. Mostly officers and officials from the Base, with a sprinkling from other wardrooms of nearby ships. Older, more senior, officers looked unnaturally gay in their mess-jackets, whilst the reservists stood or slumped in white drill which was already crumpled and stained in the close, smoke-thickened atmosphere. There were women, too. Mostly nurses, with a handful of Wren officers, the wives of government officials and a few others who had merely arrived with their escorts.

Wickersley leaned back in a canvas chair, one arm resting on the side of the long makeshift bar, behind which the stewards ladled ice into pink gins and refilled glasses as fast as they were able. He glanced at his companions and swallowed some more gin. From his short experience of the Navy these parties all seemed the same. All you needed was a ship. There was always an unlimited number of people waiting to be invited. Mostly shorebased people who never turned their backs on a chance of getting hold of some duty-free booze. Wickersley laughed at the idea and groped vaguely for another glass.

Must be getting tight already, he thought. It was always the same. You drank too much to stave off the boredom of speaking to people you did not know and would not see again, and then you were too far gone to care. With one ear he could hear Fox speaking to Tregarth, the Chief Engineer. They had both been drinking steadily, their faces set and fixed with the grim determination of men who do not intend to give away their exact state of intoxication.

518

'Lot of bloody rot, Chief!' Fox sounded angry. 'It's as good as paying off the old ship!'

Tregarth grunted, 'Wouldn't last five minutes in the Union Castle!'

Wickersley wondered what would not last five minutes but he knew what Tregarth was angry about. Just before the first guests had arrived the Captain had met all the officers in the wardroom and told them of the new arrangements. Wickersley had watched him fixedly, looking for some sign of the man's inner feelings.

Only when Bouverie had said unexpectedly, 'Well, I think it's a damned shame, sir!' had Chesnaye dropped his guard. He had regarded the ex-barrister for several seconds and then, 'It is, Sub.' Wickersley thought that was the end of it, but something seemed to be driving Chesnaye on, as if he could no longer bear the strain of his secret. 'As a matter of fact I love this ship. To some of you that may seem strange.' He looked round the flag-decorated wardroom, his eyes suddenly wretched. 'Given a chance we would have done something worth while together.'

Wickersley still wondered about the use of 'we'. Did he mean the whole ship's company, or just ship and captain?

Anyway, it was all decided. Wickersley tasted the neat gin on his tongue and ran his finger around his tight collar. But he knew what Chesnaye felt. From the moment Wickersley had opened his letters from home he had understood, perhaps for the first time, what loneliness meant, and Chesnaye certainly knew that.

Wickersley's wife had written a neat, concise letter. She always wrote like that, just as she lived. Neat, well thought out, nothing wasted.

He felt the anger surging through his drink-clouded mind. She had told him in the shortest possible style that she had left him. Just like that. There was no hint of who the other man was, except that 'he is a friend of yours'. So that was that.

'Jesus!' Wickersley banged down the glass and the others stared at him. Even Norris, who had been watching an elderly officer dancing pressed against a slim nurse, looked surprised.

Fox said: 'What's eating you, Doc? Been at the pills again?'

Wickersley shrugged and signalled to a steward. 'Something like that!' What was the point of spreading it around? It could not help him now. He caught sight of Erskine approaching their small group with his hand resting lightly on the elbow of a tall, very attractive girl.

Erskine stood looking down at the others, his face smiling but unsure. 'This is Ann Curzon.' He made the introductions as they got to their feet. 'They're the core of the wardroom!'

In spite of his anger and misery Wickersley's keen senses told him that the atmosphere was strained. Fox was looking at Erskine as if he was a complete stranger, and the girl seemed too bright, too casual, like someone playing a part, he thought.

Rudely Wickersley interrupted the stilted conversation, 'Well, Ann, how about having a drink with the poor old doctor?'

She smiled, and it was then that he noticed the slight redness around her eyes. That bastard Erskine, he thought vaguely.

'Yes, I'd like that.'

She moved towards him, but Erskine said quickly, 'There are one or two more people you should meet, Ann.'

'Come with me.' Wickersley took her arm, an idea forming in his reeling mind.

He almost pushed the girl out of the small semicircle, and then Erskine tried to bar his path. 'I think you've had a bit too much to drink, Doc!'

Wickersley weighed up the facts with elaborate care. The girl was very willing to leave Erskine. She was not putting on an act now. He leaned across to Erskine and said in his ear, 'Go and get stuffed!' Then with a fixed smile on his streaming face he guided the girl through the swaying dancers and towards the quarter-deck ladder.

'It's cooler on deck,' he said. 'Much nicer.'

Erskine had mentioned this girl once or twice. Like a possession, he thought. Now, if half the rumours were right, he was getting rid of her too. 'I apologise for my haste, Ann. But, as you see, I've had a hard day.'

The quarterdeck was deserted but for an anonymous couple huddled right aft below the ensign staff. Side awnings had been rigged to protect any strollers from the cool harbour breeze and to contain the glare of light from the wardroom hatch. Wickersley led the girl to a gap in the awnings and pointed across the glittering water.

'A bit of air does the patient good, y'know!'

Her teeth gleamed in the purple half-light. 'Thank you for

pulling me out of that crowd. I was beginning to wonder why I came at all!'

Wickersley fumbled for his cigarettes. We are all playing parts, he thought. Each hiding some inner worry from the next and thinking it doesn't show.

She took the proffered cigarette and waited as he clicked his lighter. 'I'm not usually like this,' he said after a moment, 'but things have been a bit hectic here lately.' And, by the way, my wife has run off with a good friend of mine, he wanted to add. 'It's like a calm *after* a storm.'

He felt her start and turn to the footsteps which thudded across the deck planking.

Erskine loomed out of the darkness, his mess-jacket gleaming like a ghost. 'Now what the *hell* are you playing at?'

Wickersley was not sure which one of them was being addressed, but the irritated rasp in Erskine's tone was the final straw. 'Go away!'

'You're drunk!' Erskine seemed twice his normal size in Wickersley's misty vision. 'D'you think this is the way to behave in front of my guest?'

The Doctor shrugged. 'I'm past caring what you think.'

The girl threw her cigarette over the rail. 'Really, John, don't be so stuffy! Anyway, I'm not your guest. I'm not your anything any more!'

Erskine seemed to recoil. 'So that's the way of it. Drop one, grab another!'

She turned her face away, and Wickersley said thickly, 'If you don't shove off I'm going to forget my oath and smash that arrogant face in!'

There was a quiet footfall by the hatch and Chesnaye stood motionless against the pale awning.

The other three stood like statues. Erskine with hands on his hips, jaw jutting forward, Wickersley, whose fists were already raised but frozen in mid-air. Only the girl seemed real. She had half turned and was watching Chesnaye's tall figure as if to gauge the power he seemed to hold over the others.

Chesnaye said evenly: 'There are guests below, Number One. There seems to be a preponderance of ship's officers up here.'

Erskine said, 'I was dealing with the Doctor, sir, he –'

Wickersley interrupted calmly, 'I was just going to knock his head off.'

There was a pause and Chesnaye continued, 'When I was a midshipman I once knocked a senior officer to the deck!' Surprisingly he chuckled. 'It did me a power of good!' Then, as the other officers gaped at him: 'Now go below and behave yourselves. If anybody in this ship has a right to beat somebody's brains out I think I have already proved myself eligible by my early example!'

Erskine sounded confused. 'Yes, sir.' Without another word he walked to the ladder.

Wickersley decided it was time for another drink. A large one. It had been a remarkably simple feat, really. Get the girl on deck *and* Erskine, and the Captain was bound to follow.

Chesnaye was completely alone, but unlike any other man aboard he could not share his emptiness. This Ann Curzon might make him forget, even for an evening. The near disaster had been worth it. Erskine needed a good hiding anyway.

Wickersley bowed to the girl and then said: 'Permission to fall out, sir? Perhaps you would take over my duties as escort?'

Chesnaye grinned. 'Go below before you fall over.'

They watched Wickersley stagger towards the ladder, neither aware of his inner misery, but on the deserted deck each suddenly conscious of one another.

'It's a beautiful view from here.'

The night air was almost cold as it fanned across the upper bridge, but the girl did not seem to notice it. She stood on the port gratings, her body pale against the grey steel, her arms wide as she rested them on the broken screen.

Chesnaye stood in the centre of the deserted bridge, his mind unable to associate this girl's presence with what had gone before. The ship was quite still and he could no longer hear the raucous beat of the wardroom gramophone, nor the almost hysterical gaiety from the remaining visitors. Overhead, the stars were large and very low, and it was quite impossible to imagine what had been enacted above this very place. The screaming bombers and the last desperate attack by that fanatical pilot.

Without even returning to the wardroom party Chesnaye and the girl had moved slowly along the deserted upper deck.

Sometimes Chesnaye had talked, answered her questions, and other times they had both found a strange contentment in silence and looking across the darkened harbour.

She said, 'I still can't believe that the Germans may be here soon.' Her arm moved above the screen. 'Their ships where ours are now.'

'I don't think it will happen.' Chesnaye climbed on to the gratings, again conscious of her nearness, the scent of her body. 'Necessity makes our people achieve remarkable things.'

She shivered and he said quickly, 'Would you like to go down?'

'Not yet.' She half turned, and he sensed the sadness in her voice. 'I may not get another chance. It's been wonderful.'

Chesnaye asked, 'What made you come out here in the first place?'

She shrugged. 'I was in Malta when the war started. On holiday. I got sort of involved with things, and no one seemed to mind.' Some hair blew across her cheek as she said dreamily: 'I couldn't go back to England after that. My parents wanted me to, but I felt I belong here.'

'Where is *home*?' Chesnaye felt that he wanted every last scrap of information about her. He could no longer explain his desire, nor the hopelessness of it.

She chuckled. 'Surbiton. Exotic, isn't it?'

'And now you want to go back to Malta?'

'I *am* going.' She touched the cold metal below her. 'I work with the Red Cross, although God knows how it happened. I'm really very squeamish!'

Somewhere below a pipe shrilled and a metallic voice intoned: 'Duty fire party fall in! Men under punishment to muster!'

She was facing him now, her eyes like dark pools in her face. 'You're not a bit as I imagined you would be. You're not even like the others.'

Chesnaye grinned. 'I haven't got two heads!'

'No, I'm not joking. Perhaps it's because you've been away from the Navy for all that time. New Zealand, everything. Some of the others in your position are so – so pompous, does that sound silly?'

'It's a compliment.'

'And the way you are about this ship. I've been listening to you for hours. I could go on listening, and that's not like me at all!

523

John is quite different. He always worries about something he can't even see.'

'He's a good officer.' Chesnaye no longer knew what to say.

She shrugged impatiently. 'So is Goering, I expect!'

'I think I know what you mean.' He looked past her at the flapping signal halyards. 'You must put every ounce of energy into a ship. Whatever ship it may be at the time. Otherwise it's just a pile of metal and spare parts!'

There was a movement of people on the deck below, and Chesnaye knew that the last of the visitors were leaving. He could feel another sensation of loss already, and he knew he was unable to prevent it.

She said quietly: 'I came here prepared to hate everything. But I don't remember when I've been so happy.' She laughed, but sounded unsure and suddenly nervous. 'That just proves what a weird creature I am!'

She turned to step from the gratings, but the heel of her shoe caught in one of the small holes and she fell heavily against him. For another long moment they stayed quite still, and Chesnaye could feel his heart pounding uncontrollably against her warm body.

In a breathless voice she said, 'If this was a film they would say I planned that fall!'

He felt her hair against his cheek and with sudden desperation pulled her tightly to him. She did not resist but stayed motionless, her breast pressed against his heart.

Her voice seemed to come from far away. 'Why didn't this happen earlier?'

Chesnaye held her bare arms and guided her across the bridge. There were so many things he wanted to say, so many fears to share. She was not for him. It was her natural reaction to Erskine's behaviour. In any case she was nearly twenty years younger. She was going away. He might never see her again, even if she wanted to after tonight.

But instead he said, 'Can I see you?'

She turned lightly in his hands, and he could see the brightness of her eyes. Like tears, he thought.

'I *want* to see you!' She tried to laugh. 'Do you think you can tear yourself from the ship for a while?'

If anyone else had said that Chesnaye knew he would have

524

reacted differently. But they both stood on the empty bridge, smiling through the darkness like conspirators.

Quickly she said, 'I'll give you my address before I go.'

'If I'm delayed –'

She cut him short. 'I'll still be waiting.' She reached out and touched his hand. 'You just *get* there somehow!'

Below on the quarterdeck Wickersley watched them pass. He was near complete oblivion but not quite there. His eyes drooped, and when he opened them again the girl had vanished. The Captain was standing over him, and Wickersley realised for the first time that he must have fallen to the deck.

Through the mist he had built up to stave off the misery of that letter he nevertheless heard Chesnaye say quietly, 'You may be unconscious now, Doc, but you'll never know what you've done for me.' Then the Doctor felt strong hands under his armpits and allowed himself to be carried down to an all-enveloping darkness.

Chapter Seven

Convoy

Chesnaye finished tamping down his pipe and reached for his matches. The reflected glare from the shimmering sea was so intense in the noon sun that he was wearing sun-glasses, and his white drill tunic, although freshly laundered, felt clammy against his skin. He drew in on the pipe and watched the blue smoke hover uncertainly across the baking bridge.

Lieutenant Norris, red-cheeked and perspiring freely, moved to the front of the bridge and saluted. 'Afternoon Watch closed up at Defence Stations, sir. Course two-seven-five, steady at six knots.'

'Very well.' Chesnaye eased his limbs more comfortably on the hard chair and stared absently at the empty horizon. Four and a half days out from Alexandria, six hundred miles of empty sea.

Norris sounded strained, he thought. It was strange how he changed once the ship was at sea again. In harbour he had been a different man. Whenever his duties permitted he had been ashore and usually returned on board slightly the worse for drink.

He heard Harbridge, the Gunner (T), say: 'Take the slack off them halyards, Bunts! Like a bloody Naafi boat!'

Chesnaye swung round in his chair and levelled his glasses astern. As he did so he saw the watchkeepers avert their eyes and become engrossed in their duties. It was all as usual.

His glasses settled on their one faithful companion. Squat, purposeful and seemingly out of place, H.M. Rescue Tug *Goliath* was keeping in perfect station about half a mile astern. Her bulky hull was garish in dazzle paint with the additional adornment of a giant bow wave which was as false as her appearance. Sometime tomorrow the fast convoy from Alexandria would overtake the *Saracen* and her consort and consolidate in readiness for action. The rescue tug would be busy enough then. A friendly scavenger to remind every ship in the convoy of its constant peril.

On the fo'c'sle Chesnaye could see Mr. Joslin supervising a working party by the anchor cables, and other seamen were busy scraping and painting one of the capstans. Chesnaye bit on his pipe and refused to accept the everyday task as a waste of time. Whatever else happened, *Saracen* would not look uncared for when she entered Malta.

Erskine appeared with his usual quietness. 'We've just decoded that signal, sir. It's all over in Crete.'

Chesnaye did not look at him, but stared hard at the friendly water and the cloudless sky beyond the bows. 'I see.' So the British Army had pulled out of yet another impossible position. How was it that everything seemed so peaceful and quiet when only two hundred miles away that bloodied island would be the scene of so much suffering and despair? Where would the next blow fall?

Erskine had stepped back and was speaking quietly to Norris. He had given no sign or hint of his inner feelings, but Chesnaye guessed that he was watching him more closely than ever. Since that night of the mess party and the events which had followed so surprisingly quickly.

The *Saracen* had been in Alexandria exactly seven days. Each morning brought a flood of repair workers aboard until it seemed as if the monitor was the last ship they expected to work on. For the British at least.

Chesnaye could still remember Erskine's face on the first morning as the rivet guns began to crackle and stutter overhead. Chesnaye had signed a few letters and initialled several orders, and had then said: 'I am going ashore this afternoon. You can take control of the working parties for the moment.' A pause. 'Continue to give as much shore leave as possible to our people, and go easy on the libertymen when they come off.' There had been a long string of defaulters that morning for drunkenness and so forth. 'It does everyone good to let off steam once in a while.'

Erskine had said quickly, 'Where can you be reached in an emergency, sir?'

The two men had looked at each other in silence for a few seconds, and then Chesnaye had said, 'I'll leave the address with my writer.' But he knew that Erskine was well aware of his destination.

He had found the narrow street above the harbour easily enough. It was off the mainstream of wandering sailors and hurrying townsfolk. Even the inevitable traders and hawkers were few, while the bustle of the harbour was forgotten. Only the Mediterranean itself showed between the buildings in a hard blue line.

He was not sure what he had expected to find. Surprise or embarrassment. A polite but awkward visit soon to be ended. Even when he reached the shaded door he felt on the edge of panic and uncertainty. There was nothing hesitant about her welcome, and he could still clearly remember the pleasure in her eyes as she guided him into the shady half-light of the small room.

'You *are* prompt!' She took his cap and then stood back with her hands on her hips. She was wearing a tan-coloured dress which seemed to accentuate her beauty and momentarily made Chesnaye marvel at Erskine's stupidity.

'This really *is* grand!' She was laughing again, like an exuberant child, he thought. 'Entertaining a full captain!' Chesnaye was sitting on the sagging sofa, and she stopped to touch the lace bars of his shoulder straps. 'But I simply can't call you Captain. Do you mind Dick? Or would you prefer Richard?'

He had forced a frown. 'Only my close friends are allowed Dick!'

She had jumped to her feet, her hands already reaching for the bottle of chilled wine. 'Watch out then, Dick! I may become more than a friend!'

And so it had continued. The small room had been full of laughter, quick changes of mood with each newly gained piece of understanding.

When the evening shadows had crossed the dusty street they had gone out. First to an overcrowded club where naval officers had outnumbered everyone else and many curious glances had been cast at the slim tanned girl and the tall captain. They had tried to dance on the stifling floor, and Chesnaye marvelled at the fact that his thigh no longer seemed to have any effect, as if a truce had been called.

After a while she said gravely, 'You hate it here, don't you?'

He had looked at her anxiously. 'Why d'you say that?'

'All these people. You must be tired of seeing them.'

So they had gone to the outskirts of the town, to a low-roofed café with a blaring radiogram. There were a few servicemen, mostly soldiers. But three seamen were about to leave as Chesnaye entered, his head ducking below the beams, and he stood aside as the white-clad trio lurched towards the street.

He suddenly realised that they were three of the *Saracen*'s men. They stared first at him, then at the girl. The sight of their captain in this sort of place seemed to unnerve them.

One, an able seaman named Devlin, started to salute and then said, ' 'Evenin', sir; 'evenin', miss!' He had been unable to stop his huge grin. 'I thought the officers went to all the posh places, sir?'

Chesnaye felt sudden warmth for these three tipsy seamen. At sea they were little cogs he hardly saw. Names on a muster sheet, requestmen or defaulters perhaps. Now they were just men like himself.

One of the seamen said, 'No wonder we can't find any decent girls, sir!' and stared at Chesnaye's companion with open admiration.

Chesnaye coughed. 'One of the advantages of seniority, lads!' They had gone off laughing into the night, and Chesnaye had felt foolishly happy.

The far end of the café was lined with booths. The impassive-faced Turkish head waiter had guided them towards it with the air of a foreign ambassador, when suddenly, as Chesnaye had passed abreast of one of the booths, two soldiers had lurched upright and blocked his progress. For a moment he thought there was going to be trouble of some sort. He recognised the Australian bush hat and wondered if the soldiers took exception to his presence for some reason. Then he noticed that both men were wounded. One leaned on sticks, the other had his arm strapped across his chest. Behind them, still propped in the booth, was another soldier, whose bandaged eyes were turned towards the small group and whose hands were already reaching out in an unspoken question.

The biggest Australian, a corporal, said loudly, 'You'll not remember me?' He did not wait for a reply, but turned to the girl and took her hands in his big paws without further delay. 'I hope you have a very pleasant evening, miss. You happen to be with the best goddamned Pommie I have ever met!'

Chesnaye stared from one man to the other. 'I don't quite follow?'

The second soldier grinned and moved his strapped arm carefully. 'You brought us back from Tobruk, Cap'n. But for your bloody guts we'd by lying out there in the muck right this minute!'

He held out his good hand. 'Here, take this, I want to be able to tell my folks I shook your hand!'

The blind soldier was now on his feet. 'We'll be off for home soon, Captain. I didn't see a thing after that ruddy mortar shell, but me mates told me what you did!' His voice shook. 'You didn't have to take us off, did you? You just bloody well did it!'

Chesnaye turned his face away with confusion. 'Thank you!'

The corporal waved his arm. 'Let's make a night of it!'

But the second soldier grinned and winked at the girl. 'Leave 'em be, you flamin' wombat! The Captain's got other things to attend to!'

They were still calling out cheerfully as Chesnaye almost pushed the girl into the end booth.

The waiter lit the candle on the table and went to get some wine. When Chesnaye had recovered sufficiently to meet her gaze he was astonished to see that her eyes were brimming with tears.

'What's the matter, Ann?'

But she reached across the small table and gripped his sleeve hard. 'Don't ask me, not yet!' Then she shook her head, smiling in spite of the tears across her cheeks. 'I know what those men meant. You really are a wonderful person!'

The small sea-cabin behind the bridge seemed stuffy and humid, and after a quick glance at his desk Chesnaye unscrewed the deadlight and opened the scuttle. There was a good moon, and the black restless water came to life in its cold stare, and the horizon shone with a million tiny lights like some gay, uncaring shoreline.

He propped open the cabin door to encourage even the slightest breath of air, and half listened to Fox's voice from the compass platform as he patiently explained the mysteries of the stars to the two midshipmen. If anything, Fox seemed to be more interested in his duties now that leaving the ship was inevitable.

Chesnaye peeled off his jacket and allowed the air to explore his skin. Feet scraped on a ladder, and he could hear the faint strains of a mouth-organ from one of the four-inch gun positions below the bridge. The patient waiting, the sadness and the calm resignation of war.

He loosened his belt and lowered himself on to the bunk. It was peaceful, even relaxing. Automatically his hand moved to touch the scar on his thigh, but instead of pain the simple action reawakened another memory like the discovery of some precious souvenir.

Without closing his eyes he could see every yard of that walk home from the café with Ann, stepping across the bars of moonlight between the sleeping houses with serious concentration. They had not spoken much, and Chesnaye was again aware of the danger of words, and was almost afraid to break the strange spell which seemed to hold them together.

They had reached the house, and Chesnaye had half expected to find some urgent message waiting to jerk him back to reality, but there was nothing. The tiny room was quiet, and she had been humming softly as she lit the one small table lamp.

'I suppose I had better make my way to the ship?' Chesnaye had stared ruefully around him, as if rediscovering the birthplace of his new happiness. 'I don't know if I can go now.'

She did not answer, but left the room to return almost immediately with two glasses of brandy. 'The last,' she announced gravely.

They sat on the old sofa, their glasses untouched, their eyes unseeing on the opposite wall and the shuttered window. Chesnaye felt lost, even desperate. Tomorrow the carpet trader would be squatting in the dust outside, while he would be cherishing a memory and sinking back into the endless and futureless routine.

She nestled her head against his shoulder and kicked off her sandals. For a moment she said nothing, then: 'It's been wonderful. It really has.'

'I know. I never believed it possible.'

'It's always possible. With the right person.' She twisted slightly so that he could feel her breath on his cheek. 'I'm so afraid.'

He encircled her shoulders in one quick movement, his eyes searching. 'Of what? Tell me, Ann!'

Her mouth quivered in a half-smile. 'Of smashing something. Of losing the only thing which really matters now.'

Chesnaye held her very tightly and smoothed the hair from her cheek. He could feel her quivering with each movement, and felt the forgotten pain returning to his heart.

531

'I don't want you to go, Dick. Not now. Not ever.' She had lowered her head against his chest as if unable to meet his eyes. 'There is so little time. We cannot waste it!' With sudden vehemence she said, 'You understand, don't you?'

A glass rolled unnoticed as Chesnaye pulled her to him. He could feel the desperate urgency of her kiss, and felt himself swimming in an uncontrolled desire.

With a jerk she freed herself and moved behind the sofa. Then with slow deliberation she pulled the dress over her head and threw her small shadows of underwear into the corner of the room. She walked across the room and knelt against Chesnaye's knees. He was still staring at her, wanting her, yet unwilling to break the spell.

'You see, you can't go now?' She looked up at him, her eyes misty.

Chesnaye could still feel the intensity of their love and the perfection of her body.

Afterwards, in an even smaller room, he had lain pressed beside her in the narrow bed below an open window. In the filtered moonlight he propped himself on one elbow to look down at her relaxed body and the deep shadows below her breasts and across the silky smoothness of her thighs. It was at that moment she had reached out and touched the scar which he had carried through the years. Her eyes were still closed, but he could see the quick movement of her breasts as the contact reawakened desire.

Down, down . . . that other world which excluded all else but the love of two persons. Once she cried out, but their mouths found each other to stifle the delicious pain, and her hands locked behind his back to complete their bond.

When the first faint light of dawn cut through the narrow street Chesnaye prised himself away and knelt beside the bed to look at her face. It was relaxed and still, like a painting, and he wanted more than anything to hold her just once more.

He passed through the other room and paused to pick her clothes from the floor and switch off the lamp which had been left unnoticed. Down the hill, through the gates guarded by drowsy sentries, and out on to the long wide jetty which had hardly changed since Roman soldiers had mounted a similar watch. The fresh, early scent from the sea, the querulous gulls nodding and grumbling on the dockside sheds as the solitary figure passed. Then the *Saracen* and the startled Quartermaster springing to life at the head of the gangway.

The decks felt damp and friendly, and in the pale light the tired ship looked almost beautiful.

He thrust his hands behind his head and stared up at the deck-head. How quickly those seven days had passed, and how wretched had been the parting. *Saracen* had been required to slip and proceed to sea under cover of darkness. On that last day he had spent only an hour with Ann Curzon, an hour of brimming happiness verging on despair.

To leave her was bad enough, without the growing suspense of the convoy. It seemed as if she should still be in her little room above the harbour and not at this moment lying in some over-crowded cabin aboard a darkened, hurrying ship.

Chesnaye was beginning to fret again, and with an impatient movement swung himself off the bunk. Slinging his jacket across his bare shoulders like a cape, he walked quietly on to the bridge his unlit pipe in his mouth.

The two midshipmen were just going below, their lesson completed. 'Learnt anything?' They both stopped startled as they recognised their captain half dressed and dishevelled.

Danebury said seriously, 'It's all very difficult, sir.'

Fox was standing by the compass, his hair ruffling slightly in the weak breeze. 'Too many classroom ideas in their heads, sir.'

'You'll soon put that right, eh, Pilot?' Chesnaye grinned. 'The Navy's never been very keen on matchbox navigation!'

'*Their* loss, sir!' Fox was unperturbed.

Chesnaye wandered around the bridge, his eyes slowly becoming accustomed to the distorted moonglow. The ship had little motion, and it did not need much imagination to conjure up a picture of Ann standing by the screen, her body poised like a statue. He touched the screen, smooth and unmarked from the repair yard.

In Malta they could pick up the threads again. They *must*.

She had wanted to walk with him to the harbour gates, but he had persuaded her against it.

'You'll soon be the Captain again!' She had held him at arm's length, her eyes bright and wistful. 'You're my life now, Dick. I need you so much.'

He had pulled her close so that she should not see the pain on his face. 'And I you.'

'I know. Just being together has been wonderful. But it's not enough. Not now. Not ever.'

A step grated behind him and he heard Fox handing over the watch. Midnight already. A shiver ran through him as he thought of what tomorrow would bring.

Sharply he said, 'Have you got the signal about the convoy decoded yet, Pilot?'

Fox sounded wary. 'In the charthouse, sir. The First Lieutenant has been working on the order of advance so that we can adjust the plot. There won't be much time after tomorrow, sir.'

'Right. I'll take a look.'

Back into the stuffiness, where the fresh charts and notebooks were lined up like surgical instruments. A new list of ships and their positions in convoy was pinned alongside the chart table. Quickly Chesnaye scanned the list. There was still a chance that Ann's ship might not have sailed for some reason. His gaze faltered. Third ship in the starboard column, *Cape Cod*, it *had* sailed. His finger was resting on the vessel's name, and Fox remarked casually, 'That one'll be just about on our beam if the Admiral sticks to his sailing orders.'

Chesnaye wondered briefly if Erskine knew the girl would be aboard that ship. If so he must have had bitter thoughts when he was decoding the signal.

Fox yawned. 'I'm going to turn in unless you need me for anything?'

'Nothing at the moment, Pilot.' Chesnaye sounded far away.

'We might get through without a scratch, sir.' Fox was watching him closely. 'I'm not too worried.'

Chesnaye gave a small smile. 'Well, you keep that way.' Bombers, submarines, even E-boats, might already be groping through the darkness.

Fox turned to leave. 'Radio room reports all quiet, sir. Might be a good sign.'

'When the jungle falls silent, Pilot, *that's* the time to watch out!'

Chesnaye walked back under the stars and watched the tug *Goliath* as she pushed her black bulk across the moon's silver path. If only a storm would blow up. Anything would be better than this. He could easily imagine a U-boat commander watching the *Saracen's* shape in his cross-wires, or even the torpedoes skimming through the water at this very moment.

On one of the Oerlikon platforms a gunner laughed, and Chesnaye heard the rattle of cocoa mugs. Every man is my responsibility, he thought. But tomorrow I shall be helpless and have the agony of an onlooker. He gripped the screen and strained his eyes into the darkness. Oh, Ann, take care! I shall be so near to you tomorrow, yet so helpless!

In the deserted wardroom Fox paused to pick up a tattered copy of *Men Only* before going to his cabin. Then he saw the Doctor dozing in one of the deep armchairs a cup of cold coffee still by his elbow.

'Aren't you going to bed, Doc?'

Wickersley rubbed his eyes. 'I suppose so. What's it like up top?'

Fox looked round the wardroom. 'Quiet. I think the Skipper's worrying about tomorrow. But the way I see it this ship'll be the safest in the convoy. The bastards will be after the fat loaded merchantmen!'

Wickersley levered himself upright and peered at his watch. 'I think he's worried about losing something other than the ship,' he said quietly.

Fox watched him go and then gave a shrug. With his magazine under his arm he groped his way down the passage to his cabin. Poor, trusting merchant ships, he thought. In peacetime it was either depression or cut-throat competition. In war it was sheer bloody murder.

He was wondering what Wickersley had meant when he fell suddenly asleep, the magazine on his chest like a dead warrior's scroll.

Chesnaye awoke with a start, aware that someone had touched his arm.

McGowan was waiting at a respectful distance. 'Convoy sighted, sir!' He watched as Chesnaye licked his dry lips and got slowly from his chair. 'Wing escort has just made the recognition signal.'

Chesnaye nodded vaguely and walked stiffly to the rear of the bridge. The sun was blazing hot, and seemed to strike up at him with every step. It almost brought physical pain to look seawards, to the tiny grey shape which had just lifted above the horizon. He steadied his glasses. The indistinct black crucifix of the newcomer's superstructure and the white slash of bow wave below. A powerful destroyer tearing ahead of the convoy, searching and listening for any lurking U-boat. A pinpoint of diamond-bright light flickered over the miles of shining water.

The Yeoman raised his telescope, his lips moving as his signal-man wrote down each letter. He said a moment later: 'Signal from escort, sir. Convoy will take up station as ordered.'

'Very well.' What else was there to say? Others would call the tune. The convoy could only wait.

Like cautious and newly trained beasts the fourteen escorted merchantmen ponderously obeyed the impatient signal lamps and the jaunty hoists of bunting. It took half an hour to satisfy the flagship. Eventually there were two parallel lines of six supply ships, each line a mile apart. In the centre of the convoy the two most vulnerable vessels, an ammunition ship and a well-loaded oiler steamed ahead and astern of the *Saracen* to be given maximum protection by the monitor's anti-aircraft guns.

Far out on either beam of the columns four destroyers and two elderly sloops slowly fanned into their positions for the final drive towards Malta. Then at reduced speed the convoy settled down and awaited the Admiral's ultimate inspection. From right astern the cruiser *Aureus* steamed briskly through the length of the procession, her high bridge glittering with trained binoculars, her yards alive with soaring signal flags. She was a sleek-looking ship. A product of the early thirties, she was a craft to be proud of. Even her dazzle paint could not hide the outlines of power and speed. Her four twin turrets, as well as her secondary armament, were already manned and cocked skywards.

Chesnaye watched her pass, but lowered his glasses as Beaushears' sun-reddened face leapt into the lenses. Even at that distance he could see the searching, irritable expression beneath the multi-oak-leaved cap, and was not surprised to see the big signal lamp begin to stutter almost immediately.

The Yeoman said: 'From Flag, sir. Keep correct distance from *Corinth Star.*'

Chesnaye nodded. 'Thank you, Laidlaw.' Then to Fox, 'Fall back two inches from the ammunition ship, Pilot!'

Fox grinned. 'Aye, aye, sir!'

The flagship continued on its lordly way, and finally reduced speed with an impressive display of white froth when in position ahead of the convoy.

Sub-Lieutenant Bouverie sighed. 'Do you ever have the feeling you are being watched?'

A telephone buzzed, and Fox said, 'Screening squadron on station, sir.'

'Very well.' Chesnaye eased himself from the chair and walked quickly to the chart table which had been clipped in position on the bridge. Beaushears' four cruisers were steaming somewhere below the horizon, ready to give support and to head off any intrepid intrusions by enemy warships.

Chesnaye took a quick glance astern. Only occasionally visible beyond the rusty bulk of a Greek freighter he could see the squat outline of the rescue tug. She at least would probably escape any enemy attention.

McGowan hurried past on his way to the Director, a sheaf of papers under his arm. 'I've just been round the A.A. guns, sir. All cleared away and manned.'

'Good. You can use the crew of the fifteen-inch turret to relieve the gunners at regular intervals. I don't want them dropping off to sleep in this heat.'

McGowan tried not to look pained. 'I've attended to that, sir.'

Chesnaye walked back to the front of the bridge, but to the starboard side. Bouverie stepped aside to leave room for him, but watched curiously as his captain began to study the nearest freighter with apparent care.

The *Cape Cod* was a fairly new ship, her hull low in the water, and the wide upper decks also crammed with heavy crates and additional stores for the besieged island.

Bouverie said: 'She looks overloaded, sir. Wouldn't like to be in her if she gets a packet!'

'Be so good as to attend to your duties, Sub!' Chesnaye did not even notice the harshness in his own voice or the look of surprise on Bouverie's face. From the compass platform Fox glanced down at them and sensed the sudden tension.

Bouverie climbed up beside him and said in a bewildered tone, 'What's got into *him*?'

Fox felt suddenly uneasy, but answered unfeelingly: 'Do as he says! This isn't the bloody Old Bailey, y'know!'

Chesnaye moved his glasses carefully over the labouring freighter, across the upper bridge where a bearded captain was speaking to his mate and two seamen were fitting drums on a pair of Lewis guns. Then down past the black funnel and along the boatdeck. He stiffened. Beside one of the swan-necked davits he saw a small knot of figures. Two or three men in khaki and then four women. Three of the latter were nurses in uniform, but the fourth, in khaki slacks and grey shirt, whose hair rippled carelessly in the warm breeze was Ann.

She was shading her eyes with one hand and staring across the strip of surging water between the two ships, and seemed to be looking directly at him. He lowered the glasses to wipe one of the lens and felt a tinge of disappointment as the clear picture shrunk to the reality of distance. Forgetting the men behind him, he stepped up on to a locker and with his binoculars to his eyes began to wave his cap slowly above his head.

From the compass platform Fox took a quick look around the bridge to make sure that everyone was occupied, and then raised his own glasses. It did not take him long to find the small group of figures and the laughing girl who was pointing and waving towards the *Saracen*. So that was it, he thought. Chesnaye's sharpness earlier had made him suspect something else. He would not have blamed Chesnaye for being rattled and uncertain with Beaushears breathing down his neck, and knowing that whatever happened with this convoy his command was soon to be ended.

But this was something else again. He dropped his glasses hastily as Chesnaye stepped down from the locker. The girl; Chesnaye's complete change of manner while the ship had been undergoing repairs; it all added up. He caught Chesnaye's eye and wanted to share his inner happiness. But the Captain looked through him, his eyes distant and suddenly troubled. Fox sighed. So near and yet so far. He could guess what Chesnaye must be thinking.

Bouverie said suddenly: 'Signal, sir. One U-boat reported in vicinity.'

A string of bunting broke out from the flagship's yard, and Laidlaw said flatly, 'Alter course signal, sir.'

Slowly the signal was seen and acknowledged along the lines of ships. As the distant flags vanished, the slow-moving vessels wheeled heavily on to the new course. It didn't do much good because the enemy was probably well informed of both the convoy and its destination. But Beaushears obviously intended to play the game to its bitter end.

'Steady on two-seven-nine, sir.'

Chesnaye started to refill his pipe, the movements jerky and tense. 'Very good. Check the U-boat's alleged position, Pilot. There may be more soon.'

He jammed his pipe between his teeth and then forgot it. With the other ships all around the pace seemed even slower. Only the slosh of mingled bow waves and an occasional down-draught of funnel smoke gave any hint of movement.

Laidlaw interrupted his thoughts once more. 'Destroyer *Scimitar* reports aircraft bearing Green four-five, sir. Possibly a Focke-Wulf. Out of gun range and appears to be circling.'

Chesnaye forced himself to light his pipe. It needed all his concentration to stop his hand from shaking. So the enemy was showing his hand. As in the Atlantic, the big Focke-Wulf was merely a searcher and a shadower. He would already be reporting back, homing other forces on to the convoy. 'He may not see anything.' Chesnaye cursed himself for his empty words. Unlike the Atlantic, where weather was often the best ally, this flat, innocent sea was as ideal for a spotting aircraft as some giant plotting table.

He lifted his glasses. The destroyer which had made the signal was the leading escort on the starboard wing. It was almost lost in a bank of haze, but Chesnaye could see the tell-tale signal flags and the faint movement of her guns as they impotently tracked the invisible intruder.

Fox said imperturbably, 'Sunset in four hours, sir.'

'Good.' Was it really as late as that? It seemed incredible when each minute dragged with such painful slowness.

Erskine crossed the bridge, his eyes hidden by sun-glasses. 'I've checked with the supply officer, sir. He'll feed the men in four batches. Bag meals will be sent up to the guns first.'

'Good idea.' Chesnaye saw Erskine glance quickly towards the nearby freighter. 'You can relieve me for the night watches, John. I want to try to snatch a few hours' rest. I have a feeling it's going to be a busy day tomorrow.'

Erskine tore his eyes from the *Cape Cod*. 'She looks very vulnerable, sir.'

Chesnaye replied coldly, 'They all are.' For a moment he could find no words beyond the necessities of duty. 'But we'll give a warm reception to anyone who comes sniffing around!'

Erskine licked his lips. 'I'd like to see you privately, if I may, sir? There's something I'd like to get off my chest.' He removed his sun-glasses, and Chesnaye could see the deep shadows under his eyes. 'I want you to hear my side of the story!'

'I see.' Chesnaye looked at him calmly and found that it did not seem to matter what Erskine had said or done. 'It'll keep. But one day, John, when you understand the loneliness of command, I hope you can learn something from all this –'

He broke off as Fox said sharply: 'Urgent signal, sir. Intelligence reports heavy surface units at sea approx. one hundred and fifty miles east of Syracuse. No further details yet.'

Chesnaye climbed on to his chair and glanced towards the freighter. 'No further are necessary, I should think!'

So there were to be no slip-ups, after all. The enemy was ready and warned. Somehow, somewhere, there was to be a killing ground. He shifted his binoculars to the flagship. All at once she seemed to have become smaller and more vulnerable.

Over his shoulder he said, 'If you want to do something useful, John, go and tell the Chief Telegraphist to play some records over the tannoy!'

Erskine stared at him. 'Now, sir? And our talk?'

'That can wait. I want our people to be relaxed when the time comes.'

So as the sun dipped towards the horizon haze, and the watchful escorts listened and watched for the hidden enemy, the Saracen ploughed steadily through the centre of the convoy, her speakers blaring music, the feet of her gunners tapping, as they were carried forward towards the prearranged settlement.

Chapter Eight

Don't Look Back!

In the comparative quiet of the Morning Watch the shock-wave of the torpedo explosion was magnified beyond reason.

Chesnaye slipped and fell from his bunk even as the dying echoes sighed against the monitor's hull, and for a moment he imagined that he had been allowed to oversleep and that dawn was already upon the convoy. The sea-cabin door had been pushed open by the unseen hand of blast, and through it the upper bridge seemed to be shimmering in distorted sunlight.

Even as a bosun's mate crashed through the door, his voice calling for the Captain, Chesnaye realised with sudden chill that the light was that of a burning ship.

Voice-pipes were clamouring for attention, and Chesnaye could hear Fox barking instructions to the helmsman.

Erskine said hoarsely: 'There, sir! On the port quarter! It was the old Greek!'

Chesnaye shaded his eyes from the bright red glare and the tall curtain of spluttering sparks which mounted with every second above the ship's black shape. Already she had fallen out of station and had lost her identity.

A creaming white line cut across the dark water, above which Chesnaye could faintly see the rakish shape of a searching destroyer. There was a dull crack, followed in a few seconds by the snowbright glare of a starshell.

Severl voices cried as one: 'There it is!'

Chesnaye tore his night-glasses from the leather case and peered at the pencil-slim silhouette outlined beneath the motionless flare. He bit his lip and took a quick look at the other ships. The U-boat must have been temporarily misled by the convoy's alteration of course. To avoid losing a target altogether, its commander had chased after the convoy and made his attack on the surface. Even now the submarine was turning away, while the destroyer increased speed to engage.

A lookout called: 'Torpedo passing on the port beam!'

541

A faint, ruler-straight line lengthened across the *Saracen*'s bow wave and vanished into open water. Chesnaye breathed again. The U-boat must have fired a full salvo, but had found only one target.

'She's diving, sir!' Every eye watched as the shadowy hull hid itself in an upflung surge of foam and froth

Fox said thickly: 'The Greek's capsizing! Poor bastards!'

In a smaller voice Bouverie asked, 'Can't we do something?'

Harshly Chesnaye snapped: 'Keep station! Tell the lookouts to watch the other ships. If the convoy breaks now they're done for!'

Inwardly he felt a kind of agony as he watched the dying ship. The tug *Goliath* was clearly outlined against the searing flames, but was held at bay by the force of the blaze. Chesnaye could even see the Greek's hull changing from black to glowing pink as the fire tore at her inside. Every ship in the convoy gleamed and shimmered in the reflected fires, like paintings come alive.

Then the blazing ship dipped her bows and with startling suddenness began to dive. The hissing roar of exploding boilers merged with the triumphant inrush of water and the tearing crash of steel as the engine tore itself free from its bed and smashed through the white-hot bulkheads. Like a candle extinguished she was gone, and only the drooping starshell showed the end of the drama.

Once more the *Saracen*'s hull boomed and reverberated to magnified explosions as the destroyer's depth-charges thundered down. Tall pyramids of spray marked each charge, and as the destroyer finished her attack, one patch of torn white water showed clearly the shining hull of the U-boat as it was blown to the surface. Like a beast gone mad the destroyer slewed round, every rivet and plate groaning as her forty thousand horsepower and a full rudder threw her over.

Above the crash of gunfire and hoarse bellow of orders they all heard the solid crunch of tearing steel as the destroyer's knife-like stem bit into the wallowing hull. Then she was through and over, while the broken U-boat writhed in a great bubbling cascade of black oil.

The victorious destroyer, her bows crumpled like cardboard, ploughed to a halt, her narrow shape rocking gently in the life blood of her victim.

Some of the *Saracen*'s men cheered. It was a cruel, desperate sound, and Chesnaye said sharply: 'Keep those men quiet! Tell them to watch their front!'

Someone else on the bridge started to say excitedly, 'That's one less of the bastards!'

But Fox added dourly: 'One less escort, too! She'll be no more use for a month or so!'

The escorts increased speed and dashed around the merchant ships like watchful dogs. As if for greater protection the two leading freighters had turned slightly inwards, and the milling vessels astern of them followed suit. It took over an hour to restore order and establish discipline. By that time the dawn had found the convoy once more, and when the sun climbed free of the brightening water it showed clearly the shortened line of ships, and of the destroyer there was no sign. She was already limping back to Alexandria. Beaushears could not spare another ship to accompany her, so she must make the lonely voyage unaided.

Chesnaye slumped in his chair, his mind still filled with the reddened picture of the burning ship. There were no survivors. But the other ships still headed westward and no one looked back. Close the ranks. Do not stop for anyone or anything. When it's your turn you must accept it.

Chesnaye swore aloud, and Fox looked across at him. 'Sir?'

'Nothing, Pilot!' Chesnaye watched the *Cape Cod*'s crew washing down the boatdeck with hoses. 'Not a damned thing!'

Just before noon the first bombers appeared high in the clear sky. This time they were not Stukas but twin-engined Italian aircraft which cruised in six neat arrowheads with such calm indifference that it almost seemed as if they would pass over and ignore the convoy completely.

The *Saracen* stirred into readiness, the gunners almost glad that the tension of waiting was over at last.

Chesnaye wiped his streaming eyes with the back of his hand and ran his gaze briefly over the monitor's defences. The four-inch guns were already tracking the tiny silver specks, and he could hear the clatter of the breech blocks as the first shells were slammed home.

'They're splitting up, sir!'

Chesnaye lifted his glasses again. Yes, the small flights of bombers were separating, and half of them seemed to be diving in a shallow sweep towards the escorts on the starboard wing of the slow-moving merchantmen. Chesnaye wondered briefly what would happen if the ammunition ship received the first salvo. Surely no one in the near vicinity could escape the blast? Her crew too must be thinking just that.

'Signal from Flag, sir! Retain station. Stand by for alteration of course.'

Fox said to Bouverie, 'Fat lot of good that'll do!'

'Three aircraft Green four-five! Angle of sight two-oh!'

Chesnaye kept his ear tuned to the flat, dispassionate voices from the voice-pipes, and watched the approaching aircraft with narrowed eyes. In spite of being prepared, he tensed automatically as two of the destroyers opened fire. The small brown shell-bursts mushroomed across the bright sky and seemed to drift past the purposeful intruders.

'Aircraft closing! Two hundred and fifty knots!'

A sudden burst of gunfire from astern of the convoy told Chesnaye that the other bombers were trying to draw the escort's firepower from the approaching trio. It was a good attack, he thought coldly. They would cross the convoy's line of advance at forty-five degrees, and would gain a bit of protection from the *Aureus*'s firepower by diving above the ammunition ship.

A gong jangled below the bridge, and in the momentary silence which followed Chesnaye heard McGowan's voice distorted by his microphone. 'Commence, commence, commence!'

The four-inch guns spat out orange flame and hurled themselves back on their mountings. Their ear-piercing cracks seemed to penetrate the innermost membranes of the men's ears, and more than one seaman cried out with pain. The guns swung like oiled rods and fired again. The barrage was thickening, and the air was already pock-marked with their mingled shell-bursts. Even some of the merchantmen had joined in with their ancient twelve-pounders.

Still the bombers came on, their cockpit covers glinting in the sunlight, their engines lost in the barrage.

Chesnaye watched the range falling away. Half a mile, and the three planes swept over the first zig-zagging escort. At last they were in range of the short-range weapons, and before the jangle of bells had died away the pompoms and Oerlikons clattered into life. Darker shell-bursts, long pale lines of tracer, it seemed impossible for anything to live in it.

One of the bombers swung out of line and dived whining over the flagship, a straight black smoke-trail marking its passing. The *Aureus*'s gunners pounced on the unexpected prize and followed it down, the savage tracers cutting away the fusilage like skin from bones, even as two small parachutes blossomed in the smoke-stained sky.

'Bombs falling, sir!'

Not a single one this time. As the leading aircraft swept over the convoy's centre Chesnaye saw the glittering stick fall with apparent carelessness from her belly.

The sound of the barrage changed, like thunder deflected by a sudden wind, as half of *Saracen*'s armament swung astern to cover the oiler from another attack from aft. Three bombers had side-stepped the screening barrage and were already large and stark in the madly vibrating gun-sights.

Chesnaye felt his mouth go dry as the falling bombs gathered momentum and shrieked towards the ammunition ship. He felt his chest jar against the screen as the bombs exploded. The ammunition ship still steamed ahead, her stained hull neatly bracketed by the hundred-foot columns of water. But the remaining bomber was overhead and the next salvo was already falling.

'Alter course, sir!'

Chesnaye shook himself as the air split apart to the screeching roar of bombs. They had missed again, but he could hear the whiplash crack of splinters as they slashed at the passing ships. Too damn' near.

Laidlaw reported calmly, 'Signal close up, sir!'

Chesnaye watched the ammunition ship ahead of the monitor's bows, and waited.

'Down, sir!' The small flag hoist disappeared from the flag-ship's yard, and obediently the convoy plodded round after her curving wake.

'Christ, a hit!' The words were torn from Bouverie's throat, and Chesnaye stared past him at the sternmost ship on the starboard column. In the middle of her turn the bomb had caught her right behind the bridge. Boats, mainmast and half of her superstructure flew skywards, and from the smoking crater Chesnaye could see the first licking tongues of flame. The freighter staggered like a

545

wounded animal and began to swing inwards, her bows almost pointing at the oiler. A collision now would be fatal.

Chesnaye snapped, 'Signal her to keep station!'

Laidlaw nodded, and seconds later the big projector began to clatter.

Three more aircraft were attacking from port, but Chesnaye ignored the fanatical clatter of automatic weapons and continued to watch the freighter. Her upper deck was well ablaze, and some of the crated deck cargo was also alight. But through the swirling smoke came an answering signal.

Laidlaw said in an awed tone, 'She says, "Mind your own bloody business", sir!'

Chesnaye smiled tightly as he saw the freighter's battered stem feel its way back on course. 'If they can talk like that they're all right!'

Fox said, 'That was close!' A long line of bomb-bursts churned the sea skywards in tall white waterspouts, and once more the air echoed to the whining splinters.

The four-inch gun immediately below the starboard wing of the bridge fell silent, and a voice yelled stridently: 'Still! Misfire!' A few moments later the voice came again, harsh with relief, 'Carry on!'

The whole convoy was now covered with drifting smoke, and all around men were coughing in the acrid fumes of burned paint and cordite.

Bouverie pointed over the screen as something surged sluggishly in the monitor's bow wave and grated along her fat reinforced bulge. 'Who bagged that?' It was a half-submerged bomber, its fire-blackened body already sinking out of sight. Pinned like some sort of insect, the pilot was still moving his arms and staring up at them as the hull thrust him down and back into the racing screws.

'The freighter's got the fire under control, sir!'

Chesnaye nodded and looked carefully down the line of ships. In the thick smoke it was hard to see anything, let alone the circling bombers.

There was a sullen roar from far astern, and moments later Fox said thickly: 'One of the escorts, sir. The sloop *Gorgon* has turned turtle. Direct hit.'

Another warship gone, and two hundred miles to go. Chesnaye

546

mopped his face. His cheek muscles felt numb and his head ached from the constant gunfire.

The bombers had had a sharp reception. Four were shot down in twenty minutes, and the final flight of aircraft were apparently unwilling to press home their attack. Instead they climbed rapidly towards the sun and released their bombs at random.

The cunning and bravery of the other pilots were unrewarded but for the sinking of one poorly protected sloop. The bombs which fell from five thousand feet, with their bomb-aimers not even bothering to take note of the results, straddled the port column and cut deep into the heart of the leading freighter. Like some hideous steel flower the whole ship heaved and opened outwards, the sea and sky suddenly filled with flying wreckage. Chesnaye felt the hot breath of the explosions across his streaming face, and stared in horror as the big freighter began to career across the tightly bunched ships.

More inner explosions began to tear the ship apart, and derricks and bridge sagged together into the burning crater which had once been the foredeck.

'She's out of control, sir!' Fox sounded taut. 'She'll be up to us in a moment!'

Chesnaye watched, holding his breath as the burning ship floundered pathetically towards the ammunition ship. The gap narrowed, until it was almost hidden by the eagerly licking tongues of flame.

'Missed her!' Fox changed his tone. 'Now it's our turn!'

Chesnaye watched the ship, feeling the sweat pouring down his neck and chest. The smoke stung his eyes, and he could no longer see the other leading ships.

'Starboard fifteen!' He tried to see some movement against the freighter's waterline, but smoke and fire hid it from view. It was not possible even to gauge her speed through the churned water. 'Midships!' Steady now, let her get nearer. God, she's almost on top of us!

Behind him he could hear someone whimpering like a child. Too much swing on her. 'Port ten!' The monitor's hull quivered and swung very slightly towards the other ship, to allow her room to brush past.

Faintly through the fog of smoke he could hear Erskine's strident voice, 'Stand by, fire parties!'

The men on the upper bridge fell back as the wall of fire drifted down the monitor's side, and there was a hurried clatter of metal while the Oerlikon gunners ripped off their loaded magazines and pulled them clear of the searing heat.

The freighter was an old three-island type with high poop and fo'c'sle. Her rusted bows and heavy anchors almost brushed the *Saracen*'s bridge as she moved past, but Chesnaye's eye were fixed on the tiny group of figures which was poised directly on the fo'c'sle head. Four men, one already crumpled in the heat but held out of reach of the flames by his comrades, men without hope on a burning island. Already the ship was beginning to fall away, and Chesnaye could see the sea exploring the buckled remains of her afterdeck.

One of the stranded seamen reached out as if to touch the monitor's bulk, his face suddenly clear and stark to every watching man.

Bouverie cried: 'Can't we help, sir? Lower a boat?'

But Chesnaye did not answer. What was the use of words?

There was a tiny cry, and when Chesnaye looked again there were only three figures on the fo'c'sle head. One must have jumped. Chesnaye willed the others to follow suit. The *Goliath* might find them, even in this.

The two who were still standing seemed about to jump when one of them looked down at the man who lay helpless on the deck. As the *Saracen* pulled clear they were still standing like statues outlined against the advancing fire, and then they were lost, and mercifully hidden in the smoke.

Bouverie was biting his knuckles. 'Oh my God! Did you see that?'

'No damage, sir!' Erskine was on the bridge again, his eyes white in his smoke-blackened face. He seemed to notice Bouverie's attitude of misery and despair as a man will recognise some sort of enemy. 'Get a grip on yourself, Sub!'

Chesnaye watched Fox bringing the ship back on course. 'He's been doing well, Number One!' he said quietly.

'But it's bad for the men, sir,' Erskine persisted, as if repeating an old lesson. 'Some of these reservists are sent to sea with nothing more than a brief idea of what's happening.'

Chesnaye dabbed his eyes and stared at him coldly. 'You must learn not to measure a man's worth by the amount of lace on his sleeve!'

The cease-fire gongs sounded cheerfully through the smoke, and he added, 'Go round the guns and tell them "Well done".'

He forgot Erskine as a stronger breeze pushed the smoke bank back across the convoy. Two merchantmen gone, and the escort depleted by an equal number. The enemy's wounds were unimportant. You could only gauge your loss against their successes.

When the smoke had rolled far astern the sky was again empty. There was even a slight breeze to fan the sweating faces of the men throughout the convoy. But the prowling Focke-Wulf was still nearby, and Chesnaye wondered what fresh hell lay in store across the deceptive horizon.

An hour later he was no longer in doubt.

He sat on his tall chair, an empty tea mug still grasped in his fingers, his eyes on the sun-dappled shape of the *Cape Cod*. Ann was somewhere within that overloaded hull. Sleeping perhaps after the fury of the air attack, or even watching him from some vantage point above the decks. The big freighter was leading the starboard column now, and seemed desperately far away.

'Signal, sir.' Fox was there again. 'Priority.'

'Well, spit it out!'

Fox said evenly: 'Four heavy enemy units fifty miles to northeast of convoy. Appear to be shadowing.'

Chesnaye sat upright in his chair, his tiredness forgotten. 'Waiting for night, more likely!'

Fox stood by the chart, his hands almost gentle as he spanned the pencilled lines with his dividers.

Chesnaye looked across the port quarter, noticing as he did so the small, silver-edged splinter hole in the funnel. It must have been hit during the attack. He frowned and concentrated on the new threat. Four units. Cruisers most likely. He strained his aching mind and felt vaguely uneasy. There was something wrong, but he could not sort his ideas into order. He crossed to the chart and stared at Fox's calculations.

'Fifty miles, eh?' He rubbed his chin and felt the stubble against his palm.

'That's what it says, sir. But you know these Intelligence reports!'

'Hmm.' Chesnaye looked up as a signal lamp began to clatter on the flag deck. 'What's happening now?'

Fox shrugged as if unconcerned. 'I expect the Admiral has some ideas about all this.'

Chesnaye waited impatiently as the signalman finished his writing. He re-read the brief message twice before he understood what he had missed in his first summing-up. Beaushears intended to call up his own four cruisers which were screening the convoy and smash into the enemy ships without delay. He read the signal aloud and heard Fox say: 'Best bloody thing for them! They won't be expecting it!'

Chesnaye paced to the chart again. There was something wrong. What could it be? Beaushears was taking the correct action. And yet . . . 'Get me the first signals about that Italian force which was reported yesterday.' As Fox hurried into the charthouse Chesnaye said to Laidlaw: 'Make a signal to Flag, Yeoman! Reference yesterday's signal –' He broke off as Laidlaw's eyebrows lifted almost imperceptibly. 'I've not time to find the damned time of origin!' He lifted his gaze to the distant flagship as he continued slowly, 'Enemy surface units may be different from those earlier reported.'

Fox was breathing heavily at his side, 'I don't quite understand, sir?'

Chesnaye made sure that Laidlaw was sending the signal and then walked back to the chart table. 'Yesterday's signal referred to a major enemy group one hundred and fifty miles east of Syracuse.' He tapped the chart in time to his words. 'Now we get a signal that they are fifty miles to the north-east of us.'

Fox sounded puzzled. 'They could do it, sir. Allowing for these positions being correct, and the fact that the Eye-tie ships can steam pretty fast. They *could* just do it.'

'Unlikely. The convoy has made umpteen alterations of course since leaving Alex. Tomorrow would be the earliest hope of making contact.'

'Well, what do you think, sir?' Fox stared at him. 'One of the signals is wrong?'

'No. I think there are two enemy groups, Pilot!' Chesnaye's voice was cold. 'And if the Admiral detaches the cruiser screen, the way will be open!'

Fox was still staring at him as the Yeoman called: 'Signal from Flag, sir. Disregard previous Intelligence sighting report. Inshore squadron will proceed immediately and engage!' The Yeoman cleared his throat and looked uncomfortable. '. . . and, sir, the signal adds: "Don't be frightened. *Aureus* will stay in company." End of signal, sir.'

550

Chesnaye clenched his fists as a wave of fury swept through him. Of all the bloody stupid fools!

'Quite a sense of humour, I don't think!' Fox sounded indignant.

Laidlaw was still standing unhappily on the gratings. He seemed to feel the Admiral's insulting signal as if it had been addressed to him. 'Any reply, sir?'

'No, Yeoman. Nothing.' Chesnaye had difficulty in keeping the anger from his voice. How Beaushears must be grinning on his bridge, and probably sharing the joke with Captain Colquhoun and the others. Practically every ship in the convoy must have read the signal.

Chesnaye forced himself to stand still for several minutes until his mind cleared. It was easy to see Beaushears' point of view, of course, but then again how was it possible to question a senior officer's judgement without appearing to show insubordination?

Chesnaye stared round the convoy with despair. Even without seeing the shadowing cruisers of Beaushears' squadron it had been a comfort to know they were there. He banged his fists together. How typical of Beaushears to send them tearing away at the first hint of a prize. All he thought about was his own prestige. With the enemy ships driven off or sunk there would be no limit to his reward.

The worst of it was he was probably right in his assumption about the Intelligence reports. Nevertheless, his first duty was to the convoy. Nothing else mattered.

He stared half-blinded at the sun. Still eight hours before night hid the slow-moving ships. Even then it was never safe.

The afternoon dragged by, and as the sun moved with such painful slowness towards the horizon the next blow fell.

The first hint of danger was the shriek of a destroyer's siren on the starboard wing, followed by that ship's rapid alteration of course away from the convoy.

'Torpedoes running to starboard!' There could be no exact bearing from the tired lookouts, for the torpedoes, some seven or eight of them, swept across the line of advance in a widespread, many-fingered fan.

No doubt a U-boat had fired the salvo, all her bow tubes at once, after taking up a carefully planned position slightly ahead of the advancing ships.

551

Like tired troops the ships swung to starboard in response to the Admiral's urgent signal, and pointed their ragged lines at the glittering white tracks which sliced amongst them with breathtaking speed. Two torpedoes struck home, the rest passed between the ships and flashed harmlessly to the open waters beyond.

One old freighter was loaded with steel frames and building materials for the Malta defences. She received the death blow deep in the boiler room, and lifted only slightly with a muffled bellow of pain. She broke in two and sank out of sight almost before her consorts had completed the turn. Only a few pieces of flotsam littered the spreading oil-slick, but not a single survivor.

The second victim was luckier. The torpedo exploded twenty feet from her stem and sheared off the bows like a butcher carving meat. She too was well-laden, but before the forward bulkhead collapsed her master had time to stop engines and call away the boats. But even she went to the bottom in only seven minutes.

The three destroyers dropped depth-charges and searched the placid water without result. They did not even make a contact with their probing Asdics, and after an hour the Admiral called them back and re-formed the convoy.

Goliath signalled briefly. 'Have twenty survivors aboard' and then fell silent.

As darkness mercifully closed over the ten remaining merchantmen and their depleted escort, the crews no longer felt like rest. Like Chesnaye they seemed to sense that their ordeal had only been a beginning, a casual probe by an enemy who was prepared to wait.

Chesnaye watched the bosun's mates going their rounds of the guns with their massive fannys of cocoa and enamel mugs. Corned-beef sandwiches of stale bread, and meat which had been tinned many years ago.

The cruel injustice seemed the more bitter when Chesnaye compared the convoy's planning and management with that other war of so long ago. Then the generals had used their infantry just as today's strategists used these ships. No one even expected half of the convoy to survive. They might have allowed for only two ships to reach Malta. The others were the justifiable odds, the expendable fodder of war.

Chesnaye recalled with sickening clarity the soldiers at

Gallipoli, their shoulders hunched beneath packs and equipment, walking, some just staggering, into the wire and the stammering machine-guns. Far away from such madness the planners moved their coloured flags and markers, and played soldiers with reality and blood.

His head suddenly touched the vibrating screen, and he jerked himself awake with almost vicious determination. 'What time is sun-up?' His question fell across the bridge like a rebuke.

Fox answered slowly, 'Well, with this visibility it'll be light at eight bells, sir.'

'Very well.' Chesnaye settled himself more comfortably in the chair. We'll see who's right when daylight comes. He stared ahead at the cruiser's graceful upperworks. Suddenly he found himself dreading the dawn, and all that it might hold.

Chapter Nine

Make this Signal

Lieutenant Fox bent over the bridge chart table and carefully blew some funnel soot from his pencilled calculations. When he straightened his back he looked again at the blood-red curve of the sun as it lifted slowly above the horizon astern. The forward part of the monitor was still in black shadow, but like the other ships in convoy and the surrounding water itself, the *Saracen*'s super-structure and guns were shining like dull and unused bronze.

I've rarely seen a dawn like this, he thought. Fiery, menacing. Aloud he said casually, 'Looks like another scorcher today!'

A messenger paused in his task of gathering the night's enamel mugs and battered plates to stare with open amazement at his cap-tain. Chesnaye was standing just outside the charthouse, stripped to the waist, apparently wholly intent on shaving. He was using a tiny mirror and was busily scraping away several days of stubble as if it were the most natural thing in the world. The messenger caught the eye of a bosun's mate, who merely shrugged. It seemed to sum up the complete uncertainty of officers in general.

Sub-Lieutenant Bouverie stepped down from the compass and said flatly, 'All ships on station, sir.'

Fox watched the young officer with narrowed eyes. It was quite obvious that Bouverie had still not recovered from yesterday's impartial slaughter. He looked and sounded completely exhausted.

Whereas the ship's company were relieved in batches from their posts, the officers remained at their Action Stations. The lucky ones snatched an odd hour's rest from time to time, others used every ounce of cunning and willpower to restrain their drooping eyelids and sagging bodies.

Fox wondered how long they could all stand it. Another hot day ahead. And probably it was all for nothing. He had sensed the mood of resentment which had passed through the ship when at sunset they had all heard the distant bugle from the flagship. *Aureus*'s men were even now still at Defence Stations. Half the men on watch, the others sleeping like dead men. While we . . . he shook his head angrily, shutting out his dulled thoughts.

Instead he looked at Chesnaye. In the bold red-gold light his lean, hard body looked youthful and alert. Perhaps that was why he was taking the trouble to shave instead of sleeping in his chair? He must be dead on his feet. Held together with sheer determination.

Erskine walked across the bridge carrying his cap. He glanced first at the chart and then at the compass. To no one in particular he remarked, 'We might get a clear run today.'

Nobody answered. Fox felt almost sorry for Erskine. It was amazing the way he had changed. Perhaps we all have?

High above the monitor's outmoded superstructure Lieutenant Norris tried to ease the cramp which repeatedly returned to his legs. The confined shell of the Control Top was filled with the strange glare, and being the highest vantage point in the ship, and for that matter throughout the convoy, Norris had been aware of the dawn for some time. Close at his side but on a slightly higher stool sat McGowan in his position as Control Officer. His neat, plain features were completely relaxed in sleep, and his fingers were laced together in his lap.

At regular intervals the small tower revolved, first on one beam and then in a full one hundred and eighty degrees to the other, as the rating at the training controls rotated their little eyrie to allow the giant telescopes and range-finder to peer to and beyond the horizon. Of course, the sea was empty. It was just as Norris had expected, and the constant image of his comfortable bunk reawakened the irritation in him like a bad tooth.

The training mechanism squeaked and began to move again. The slight motion and the smell of sweat and oil all around made Norris swallow hard. Even with all the observation shutters pinned back it was a foul place, he thought. His stool was now pointing across the starboard beam, and through an open slit he could feel the hint of warmth on his right cheek. God! Another day in here. The fans were useless, and soon it would be like an oven.

He leaned his elbows on the telephone rest and peered down at the nearest merchantman. She seemed far below, her decks still deserted. Lucky bastards, he thought savagely. Once when he had first joined the ship, watchkeeping had been almost enjoyable. With Fox to cover his mistakes he had been able to lose himself in

555

his imagination. He often saw himself as in a film, and thought of what those dowdy creatures in the school staff room would think if they had been lucky enough to see him too.

'Ship, sir!' He realised with a start that the Control Top was motionless and the rating at the big telescope by his knees was stiff in his stool like a gun-dog.

Norris released the catch on his own spotting telescope and pressed his eyes to the sight. High above the monitor's decks, in the centre of the quiet convoy, Norris and the seaman watched the tiny black flaw on the gleaming horizon line.

He felt a sharp movement at his side, and McGowan was as wide awake as he had been fast asleep a second before. He too crouched to look, his fingers moving deftly on his sighting controls.

Norris knew what McGowan was doing without pausing to look at him. As the light hardened across his lenses he stared with fixed concentration at the far off ship. He heard McGowan say sharply: 'Two more ships. One on either side of the first.' Then in a more normal tone: 'Disregard those. Concentrate on the centre one.'

How typical of McGowan's sort, thought Norris. He could see the second pair of ships as indistinct smudges in the morning haze, but they could very likely be cruisers. The centre vessel was much smaller. Surely he was wasting valuable time? Querulously he said, 'She's a small cruiser, Guns, or even just a destroyer, don't you think?'

There was a faint smudge of smoke, too, which seemed to link the three strangers together in a flimsy canopy made golden in the sunlight.

McGowan ignored him and snatched the handset. 'Director . . . Forebridge!' Then a second later, 'Call the Captain to the phone!' Over his shoulder he said with a faint grin: 'Keep watching, my friend. Just watch your *destroyer* grow!'

Norris flushed, aware of the stiff backs of the ratings sitting below his legs. Damn McGowan!

He peered again through his sights, and then as he watched felt his heart falter, as if it would stop altogether. McGowan was speaking in terse, short sentences, but in Norris's curdled brain the words meant nothing.

The centre ship, at first so small and delicate in the lenses, had indeed grown. Even as he stared it seemed to heighten with every

556

passing second. What he had taken for a destroyer's bridge was merely an armoured fire-control position, and as the ships moved to meet the convoy more and more of the central warship crawled up and over the horizon, as if it was rising out of the sea itself. Bridge upon bridge, and even the massive triple turrets could not be masked by distance. Norris bit back a gasp of terror. It was a battleship!

He had seen battleships before. Usually in harbour, or at naval reviews. They always appeared so safe, so impressively permanent like the legend of the Royal Navy and all it stood for. But they had never seemed as warlike or as real as other ships, and now . . . He dashed the sweat from his eyes as McGowan's voice broke into his jumbled thoughts.

'Yes, sir. Battleship and two cruisers.' He broke off as a rating said abruptly, 'Two more ships astern of the cruisers, sir.' McGowan nodded and continued evenly: 'Two more cruisers, sir. The whole squadron is on the same bearing of Green eight-five. Still at extreme distance of thirty thousand yards. I'll start reading the ranges in five minutes.' He slammed down the handset and reached for his headphones and mouthpiece. Catching Norris's wide-eyed stare he said, 'I think the Captain was *expecting* visitors!'

Surgeon-Lieutenant Wickersley rubbed his eyes and stared at the nearest freighter. It looked as if it was covered in a skin of fine gold, he thought, and in the dawn light the old merchantman took on a kind of majesty. Wickersley swallowed hard to clear the stale taste from his throat. He had been asleep in the Sick Bay but had decided to get up and take a breath of fresh air. His sickberth attendants were still snoring. They were like himself in that their lack of duties made them the most envied men aboard. Apart from the Captain's steward that is. He was answerable to nobody but the Captain, and was known to drink heavily from anything which took his fancy.

Wickersley climbed the cool steel ladders to the upper bridge and felt some of the night's muzziness clearing from his dull brain. He was almost ashamed of the amount of gin he had consumed in the privacy of his quarters. It was odd to think of the advice and warnings he had given to others, the sad contempt he had felt for them. Because of that letter he had almost joined their ranks.

Almost. He reached the bridge and was instantly aware of its alien and tense atmosphere.

Chesnaye was standing by the voice-pipes and speaking rapidly into a handset. Fox was watching the flagship through his glasses, and Bouverie leant across the chart, watched by Erskine.

Chesnaye dropped the handset and saw Wickersley for the first time. His drill-jacket was open to the waist and his hair was dishevelled. By contrast his smooth cheeks and cold, alert eyes seemed to belong to someone else. 'Hello, Doc. Come to referee?'

He turned away as a voice-pipe squeaked, 'Main armament closed up!'

Wickersley's brain was completely clear now. Main armament? He joined the Yeoman who was looking at his young signalman on the flag deck below. 'What's up, Yeo?'

Laidlaw plucked at his beard. 'Battleship and four Eye-tie cruisers on the starboard beam. They're heading this way it seems!'

Wickersley peered towards the open water beyond one of the wallowing freighters as if he expected to see the enemy for himself.

The Yeoman added, 'They're about fourteen miles off at present, sir.'

As if to back up his words they heard the magnified voice of the range-taker. 'Range two-eight-five!'

Bouverie looked up. 'Flagship's signalling, sir!'

A shaded lamp flickered along the lines of ships. 'Alter course, sir! Steer two-two-five!'

Chesnaye sounded cool. 'Follow the next ahead, Pilot.'

'We might miss them, d'you think?' Wickersley found he was whispering.

Fox lowered his glasses and grinned. 'If we take our shoes off!'

Lifting a spare pair of glasses from their rack, Wickersley climbed on to a grating and peered vaguely across the lightening water. It was all glare, and gold mirrors. The sea was flat, yet alive with a million tiny movements and reflections. As far as he could see the convoy had the sea to itself. He felt suddenly frustrated and out of place. 'Seems quiet enough!'

Chesnaye was crossing the bridge and paused at his side. 'The Admiral intends to steer away from the enemy. There's always a chance, of course.' He did not sound as if he believed it. 'It's a *Littorio*-class battleship. One of the new ones. Nine fifteen-inch guns, thirty knots.'

'*Aureus*'s turning, sir.'

They watched the sleek cruiser fall away and begin to steam slowly round the convoy to place herself between the ships and the invisible enemy.

'How far can they shoot, sir?' Wickersley was watching Chesnaye's calm, unblinking eyes.

'They'll be in range at twenty thousand. Effective shooting at ten thousand yards in this early haze.' He shrugged. 'After that it's anyone's guess.'

'Range two-eight-oh!'

Wickersley half listened to the regular, patient reports and the repeated orders. It was unreal and unnerving. Everything was just the same. The columns of ships, the monitor's steady engine beat, the bright, empty sky. Yet somewhere over the horizon, steaming at full speed, was a terrible force which his mind could not contemplate. A battleship, a floating steel town of guns and armour, as well as four cruisers. Against them would be one cruiser, three destroyers and a sloop. And the *Saracen*. He stared round with sudden despair. The *Saracen*. Even at the mention of the battleship's speed his heart had sunk. Thirty knots against six and a half. The monitor would not even be able to join battle. With the merchantmen she would be made to wait like a patient animal outside the slaughterhouse.

All at once Wickersley felt the anger boiling inside him, driving out the misery and self-pity which had been his companions for so many days. 'Have we just got to damned well sit here and take it?'

Chesnaye eyed him calmly. 'We'll have to wait and see.'

'Range two-seven-oh!'

Fox crossed the bridge. 'The bearing's changed, sir. They're after us.'

Chesnaye nodded as if his mind was elsewhere. 'Yes.'

Fox glanced at the Doctor and shrugged. He knew that he had wanted the Captain to produce some miracle, to reassure him. Just as he was certain that there was no miracle now.

Chesnaye turned his back on all of them and watched the *Aureus* as she swung round in a tight turn to take up station on the convoy's starboard flank. Her four turrets were already trained on her quarter, and he could see the tiny figures filling her bridge. He wondered briefly what Beaushears was thinking at this very moment. As far as he was concerned he was alone. The trap was sprung.

559

There was no time for the 'If onlys' and the 'perhapses', this was now.

He heard a lookout say involuntarily, 'Christ it's gettin' bright!' as if the man was willing back the sun.

'Range two-six-oh!'

Twenty-six thousand yards. Thirteen miles. Chesnaye levelled his glasses and stared for several seconds at the faint black shapes which were already lifting above the blue and gold line.

Chesnaye felt his fingers buttoning his jacket, as if the agonising wait was too much for them. He had to control and regularise his breathing to stop his anxiety joining the white-hot anger which he felt for Beaushears and everything which he had known was going to happen. He could even foretell Beaushears' next move. He would wait until the enemy was within range and then go in to the attack. A brave, useless gesture. The battleship would pound him to pieces before his little six-inch guns could even splash her paintwork. There was no hope of air cover, and the supporting cruisers of Beaushears' squadron would take a day to find the convoy. By that time . . .

'Signal from Flag, sir. Maintain courses and speed!'

Chesnaye did not turn round. The signal made him feel sick. It was as if Beaushears was issuing signals merely for something to do. Perhaps his nerve had gone and he was unable to think beyond his normal routine.

Chesnaye concentrated on adjusting his mind yet again. It was just possible that *Aureus* could hold off the attacking ships long enough. The merchantmen still had the destroyers and one sloop. If they could hold out for another day, and increase speed, there might be time to get help from Malta. Submarines perhaps?

'Range two-double-oh!'

A ripple of orange flashes mingled with the sunlight, and Chesnaye found himself gripping the screen with sudden doubt.

'The enemy's opened fire, sir!'

Every eye on the bridge watched the flagship, a slender outline above her glittering reflection.

With the sound of tearing silk the first salvo came screaming down from above. It seemed to take minutes; to some the wait was like an hour, but there were cries of surprise and horror as the first six waterspouts rose with magnificent and terrible splendour not around the flagship, but across the starboard line of merchantmen.

Chesnaye could only stare with disbelief as the nearest merchant-

560

man received a direct hit from one of the great fifteen-inch shells full on her maindeck. The blast was like a thunderclap, and the great searing tongue of flame seemed to cut the ship in two.

The battleship had turned on an almost parallel course, so that her third turret could be brought to bear, and within seconds the next salvo was on its way. The stricken freighter seemed to topple over as some internal explosion rocked the hull and brought the bridge tottering into the great flaming crater left by the shell.

The flagship turned towards the enemy, the froth mounting beneath her counter as she increased to maximum speed. Beaushears had expected to be the target, to die doing his duty. But the Italian commander had no intention of being side-tracked by any noble gestures. He was after the convoy. The convoy would go first.

The Yeoman ducked as a tall column of water rose less than half a cable from the *Saracen*'s bows. 'Signal from Flag, sir! *Scatter!*'

Chesnaye tasted the salt spray hurled by the explosion, and stared at the signal flags on the *Aureus*'s yard. *Scatter*. Beaushears had taken the only solution he knew. Every ship for itself. Instead of being destroyed together, they would be sunk one at a time by the speedy cruisers.

Fox said sharply, 'The *Cape Cod*'s been hit!'

Chesnaye spun round as if he had been struck. The big freighter had never faltered, had never lost station even under attack. Now as he watched he saw the smoke pouring uncontrollably from her foredeck, and realised with sudden shock that the front of her tall bridge had gone completely. *Cape Cod* was momentarily hidden by another three tall columns of water. Each falling shell threw up a waterspout some hundred feet in the air. Even the noise of their falling made his ears sing.

Fox said: 'Their steering's gone, sir. They're trying to steer from aft!'

A lookout called, 'Direct hit on the destroyer *Brigadier*, sir!'

Chesnaye tore his eyes from the burning freighter and the tiny figures which were running aft to the emergency steering position. One of the escorts was already sinking, her stern high in the water like the arm of a drowning man.

Through his teeth he barked: 'Request to re-form convoy! Make that signal to Flag, Yeoman!'

They must keep together. It was their only chance.

Fox threw up his hands to shade his eyes as the flagship's upperworks burst apart with one deafening roar. Her control top and upper bridge seemed to slide sideways, and even the main topmast, with Beaushears' own flag still flying, staggered over the great pall of black and yellow smoke which surged to meet it.

Laidlaw, who had been about to flash the signal himself, lowered the lamp and stared at the cruiser, which in a second had changed its shape and form to a blazing hulk. The *Aureus* slewed round, the smoke blown across her impotent guns which had still not fired.

Fox lowered his hands. 'My God!' He seemed at a complete loss. 'God all-bloody Mighty!'

Chesnaye stepped to the centre of the bridge, the *Cape Cod* was burning fiercely, the flames glittering across the water like the dawn sun. But she was afloat. If only they had more time. Like a stranger he stared round his shocked bridge. Laidlaw with the signal lamp hanging from his fingers. Fox, who could not drag his eyes from the battered cruiser, and Bouverie, who seemed like a man under drugs.

In a strained voice Chesnaye heard himself say: 'Make a signal to escorts. Reassemble convoy forthwith and proceed on course at maximum speed.'

He felt his legs shake as he crossed to the front of the bridge. Dear God, let Ann be safe. She *has* to be safe!

He closed his mind again. 'Starboard twenty!' It was a second or two before Fox repeated the order or realised what it implied.

Then as the wheel went down and the bows began to swing, Chesnaye said sharply: 'Tell the Chief I want maximum revolutions! I want this ship to go as she did at Gallipoli!'

Laidlaw returned, shaking his head like a dog. 'Signal executed, sir!'

'Good. Now, Yeoman, you can do one more thing this morning.'

'Sir?' Laidlaw's tired eyes were watching the merchantmen careering across the monitor's bows as the *Saracen* continued to turn.

Chesnaye paused, his glassed levelled on the far off shapes. 'Midships! Steady!' He glanced briefly at Laidlaw again. 'Hoist battle ensigns!'

Above and below the bridge, gunners, signalmen and lookouts watched with awe and shock as the big ensigns broke out from gaff and yard. Even down in the engine room Lieutenant-Commander (E) Tregarth and his assistant sensed the new flood of power which pulsated through the old ship like fire. Tregarth watched the dials and wiped his hands across his white overalls. 'Glad I'm down here,' was his only comment, and that was lost in the roar of *Saracen's* machinery.

Vice-Admiral Sir Mark Beaushears clenched his teeth and bit back the agonising pain. He shook his head from side to side, still unable to speak lest the waiting scream escaped from his lips. The arm behind his shoulders lowered him again to the deck, and Beaushears stared fixedly at the bright star-shaped area of blue sky which shone through the jagged hole above him. The bridge was a shambles, and above all there was an ear-splitting hiss of escaping steam. If he closed his eyes Beaushears imagined he could see himself as a young midshipman beside his tearful mother at Waterloo station. He had hated her coming with him to the train. There were other midshipmen all around him, watching, and passing knowing smiles. Over all there had been that nerveshaking sound of steam from the engines in the station, which had made the parting even more difficult.

A shadow crossed the patch of sky, and he stared vaguely at Captain Colquhoun, who was watching him as if from far away. Beaushears tried to move again. 'Harmsworth! Where the devil's my flag-lieutenant?'

Colquhoun looked at the ship's surgeon, who was still trying to support the Admiral's shoulders as he struggled weakly on the littered bridge. The surgeon shook his head briefly, and the Captain guessed that nothing could be done.

Around and below the bridge the air was filled with shouts and the clatter of running feet. Colquhoun wanted to dash out into the smoke and sunlight. His ship, his precious *Aureus*, was listing badly, and a thousand things were needed. He glanced unwillingly at the pulped corpse below the voice-pipes. Harmsworth was still grinning, his teeth white against the flayed skin.

Beaushears said thickly, 'What's happening, Colquhoun?'

The Captain listened to the steam and felt the wretched shuddering of the ship beneath him. 'Direct hit, sir. Steering's gone. I'm going to try to –'

He broke off as an officer, his cheek torn apart in a long gash, staggered into the bridge and shouted: 'Sir! The *Saracen*'s going past!' He reeled against the torn plates as if shocked by his own words. 'The old girl's closing the enemy!'

Colquhoun stood up and walked quickly to the screen. Flotsam from his own ship floated around in the calm water, and he could see the smoke from the *Aureus*'s wounds streaming astern towards the scattered convoy. But for a few moments longer he forgot his own duties and stared fixedly at the monitor.

She was less than a quarter of a mile away, and seemed to be leaning forward as she thrust her blunt bows deep into the blue water, the plume of funnel smoke adding to the impression of desperate effort and urgency. He saw the great battle ensigns, and the two massive guns swinging slowly on their barbettes, their muzzles pointing protectively across his own stricken ship.

Behind him he heard Beaushears croak: 'What *is* it? What is that madman doing?'

Colquhoun said: 'It *is* the *Saracen*. She's going to tackle the bastards alone!'

Beaushears contracted his muscles against the pain. It was almost as if the shell splinters were gouging his chest wide open. 'Tell me, Colquhoun! Describe it!' Each word was agony.

The Captain winced as three waterspouts rose alongside the monitor. 'The enemy have found her!' He banged the screen with mounting excitement. 'By God, she's going to open fire!' As he spoke the two long guns belched fire and brown smoke, and the air seemed to shiver from the force of the twin detonations.

Beaushears fell back, suddenly quiet. So Chesnaye had been right, after all. He had thought it all out, just as he did at the Dardanelles. He closed his eyes and saw with sudden clarity the boats crammed with marines and Major De L'Isle waving his walking stick. The *Saracen*'s spotting officer falling dead on the beach, and Chesnaye saying '*I'll* go!' Now he was steaming past. The pictures were becoming mixed and disjointed. He could see the trim, clean-painted monitor with ensigns streaming, but Royston-Jones was the officer in command. Faintly he muttered: 'Chesnaye'll do something today! He's mad enough for anything!' Then in a stronger voice he called: 'Helen! For God's sake!'

The Doctor stood up. 'He's dead, sir.'

'Come over here, Doc!' Colquhoun seemed to have forgotten his

564

admiral. 'Take a good look. You'll never see the like again in a lifetime!'

The Doctor clung to the screen as the monitor's guns lurched back once again. The flagship had swung slightly in the gentle swell, so that he could see the *Saracen* steaming away at right angles. Over and beyond her queer tripod mast he saw the battle-ship for the first time. It seemed to fill the horizon, flanked on either beam by two cruisers. Every gun on the battleship was firing, and the water ahead and on either side of the monitor was pitted with rising waterspouts or torn curtains of falling spray. The enemy cruisers were silent, and Colquhoun said. 'They can't reach the *Saracen* yet. The battleship is sharing the kill with nobody!' Then, as if the strain was too much for him, he took off his cap and waved it wildly in the air. 'What d'you think of *that*!' When he tore himself away to tend to his own ship, the Doctor saw that the Captain's eyes were streaming.

Lieutenant Norris drew his head into his shoulders as the monitor opened fire. He wanted to tear his eyes from his telescopic sight, but the sight of the battleship held him as if paralysed. He saw the two pinnacles of silver water leap across the great ship's outline and had to lick his parched lips before he could speak. 'Short! Up eight hundred!' The lights flickered and a small bell rang in the fume-filled Control Top.

McGowan sat hunched on his stool his eyes on his own sight, his lips moving as he spoke into his microphone. At the other end of the communicating wires, hidden within the swivelling turret, Lloyd, the Quarters Officer, and his crew of fifty men sweated and fed the smoking breeches.

'Sights on!'

'Shoot!'

As the switches were made yet again the whole ship seemed to lurch with the recoil. The Control Top felt as if it would tear itself from the tripod mast and hurl itself into the sea.

Norris gulped as his vision momentarily misted with spray. He felt the sudden shock-wave like a body blow and ducked away from the sights as a sheet of flame rose from the monitor's bows.

McGowan punched his arm and snarled: 'Keep watch! Report the fall!'

Shaking and sick, Norris pressed his forehead to the rubber pad.

He was just in time to see the small white feathers rise beyond the other terrifying ship. He could hardly speak at all now. 'Over! Down two hundred!'

McGowan was shouting orders with wild excitement. He seemed completely absorbed, almost unaware of the danger and the fact that an enemy shell had exploded within feet of the *Saracen*'s stem. At last the old monitor had made herself felt. The next salvo might make an impression. Victory was impossible. But they would show the bastards.

At that very instant the air was sucked from the Control Top, and Norris jack-knifed in a fit of coughing. He felt the shudder of a hit on the monitor's hull, and with his eyes closed against the hot smoke he pushed open one of the steel shutters, retching and moaning as he sucked at the fresh air from that other world.

The rating with the headset shouted wildly, his eyes red-rimmed with smoke, 'Sight set, sir!'

A bell rang urgently, but Norris could not stop himself from coughing.

He half turned to see what had happened to McGowan's control, but stared instead at the Gunnery Officer's bent frame and the long, unending stream of blood which coursed down the back of his stool. His telescopic sight was fractured and must have deflected a flying splinter from the last shell. Sobbing hysterically, Norris reached over and seized McGowan's jacket. 'For Christ's sake speak to me!'

The bell rang again, and the rating said sharply. 'He's had it, sir!' As if to emphasise the horror he gestured to the flecks of scarlet which had sprayed across the switches. 'Straight through the guts!'

'Oh my God!' Norris rocked back on his stool as the ship quivered yet again. The mast vibrated to the fall of broken plating, and in the far distance he heard the crackle of flames.

A telephone buzzed and the rating said urgently: 'Sir! It's the Captain!'

Norris took the handset, his eyes still fixed on McGowan's pale, piercing stare. It was over. He was alone. He felt as if he was already dead himself, instead of McGowan. All four of the seamen who completed the control-team had turned in their seats to watch him. Even McGowan was watching him.

He felt an all-consuming madness hovering in the corner of his mind, so that the tiny steel space seemed to be closing in, crushing him.

566

Suddenly, out of the horror and mounting insanity came a voice. Norris clutched the handset and stared at it, his face changing to an expression of pathetic submission. Almost gratefully he listened to Chesnaye's calm, even caressing, voice. After a while he nodded, oblivious of the watching seamen, even of McGowan.

'Yes, sir,' he said. 'I shall do my best.'

He dropped the handset and lowered his head to the sights. In a strange, robot-like tone he murmured: 'Continue tracking! Standby!'

Lieutenant-Commander John Erskine stood loosely in the centre of the damage-control base, a small enclosed compartment below the aft shelter deck. On one bulkhead was a plan of the ship showing every watertight compartment, magazine, store-space and the thousand smaller corners which had been crammed into the monitor's hull. Four ratings sat at the switchboard, their lips moving into chest-mouthpieces as they answered calls from other parts of the ship.

Craig, the Chief Bosun's Mate, said unhurriedly, 'Fire in the starboard four-inch battery, sir!'

Erskine forced his mind to concentrate on the plan, and tried to imagine his small parties of stokers and seamen who were already dealing with the first shell damage.

Craig nodded to one of the telephonists. 'Send Benson's party at the double!'

The deck bounced beneath their feet like a steel springboard. From the cracks around the sealed door came small wisps of smoke, like steam being forced from an overheated engine.

'Direct hit aft, sir!' The rating sounded hoarse. 'Tiller flat flooded!'

Erskine ran his fingers through his hair. 'Very well. Report any other damage!' He wanted to leave this enclosed prison, to help the damage-control parties, anything but stand here and supervise the ship's funeral rites.

Craig said, 'Must be hell up top, sir?'

How true, Erskine thought wildly. The monitor would be destroyed piecemeal. The great fifteen-inch shells from a modern, fast-moving battleship could gnaw away even the heaviest armoured ship in minutes once the range had been found. He staggered as the deck canted suddenly beneath him. The wheel was going over again. Chesnaye must be doing everything possible to avoid those terrible waterspouts. Erskine remembered the numbing shock he had endured when he had seen the flagship struck by just one shell. And every dragging minute brought the two antagonists closer together.

Midshipman Gayler pushed open the door, a grubby rag pressed to his mouth. He was covered in dirt and his uniform was dripping with water. 'Four-inch battery well alight, sir!' He seemed calm enough, Erskine thought, but his youth probably saved him from the agony of experience. 'Mister Joslin wants to flood the battery's magazine!' Gayler blinked rapidly as two more thunderous explosions shook the compartment and brought the paint flakes cascading over their heads.

Erskine swallowed hard. Flood the magazine? It would take all of twenty minutes. But if they waited? He snatched up the bridge telephone.

Far away, his voice punctuated by explosions and the tearing roar of passing shells, Fox answered his questions. 'Range down to twelve thousand yards! Still closing!'

Erskine said: 'Permission to flood starboard magazine? We've a bad fire there!'

A fit of coughing. 'I can bloody well see it!' A pause, complete silence as Fox covered the telephone with his hand, and then, 'The Captain says flood!' Click. Erskine stared at the dead handset, then nodded to Craig.

'Have the valves opened. Watch the table and get ready to order a counter-flooding to port. We must keep her at correct trim. Guns will need that at least for his fire-control!'

Gayler looked up from wiping his face. 'Lieutenant McGowan's dead, sir.'

Erskine turned away. My God! Outside this prison friends and familiar faces were being wiped away as if from a slate. Tightly: 'I'm going aft to supervise the quarterdeck party. Report any major damage to the bridge!' Then he was through the door, blundering through the mad world of tearing noise and billowing, blinding smoke. Voices called all around him, and he could hear the ring of axes, the desperate voices of men working in semi-darkness. A man yelled, 'Stretcher party *here!*' And there was an inhuman sound of groaning and bubbling.

Another voice: 'Keep still, Fred! I'll get help!'

568

A great explosion almost alongside and a tidal wave of shredded water which tasted of cordite swept across the decks.

A petty officer cannoned into Erskine and stared at him wildeyed. 'Lost three men, sir. There are seven more right aft. Smashed ter bits.' He peered through the smoke. 'It won't be long now, sir!'

Erskine pushed past him and felt his way further aft. There were several bodies scattered amongst the wreckage, their limbs and entrails mingling with the fire party's hoses. In the middle of the carnage Wickersley was squatting beside a wounded seaman, his face grimy but intent as he forced morphia into the man's arm. He glanced up. 'Busy day!'

Erskine felt suddenly ashamed. Even the Doctor seemed to have forgotten everything else but the immediate present. His own hopes for the future, a command, a fresh start, meant nothing now. He had misjudged everything, just as he had lost his real opportunity with Ann. She had died already without a doubt. Carried down in a blazing ship, as he would be too. He felt his limbs beginning to shake in sharp, uncontrollable spasms.

Wickersley was on his feet, waving impatiently to two cowering stretcher bearers. 'I wish I felt as cool as you look, Number One!' Wickersley wiped his mouth with the back of his hand. 'No wonder you're always carping about we reservists!' He laughed and picked up his satchel. 'Well, see you around!' Then he was gone, swallowed up by the smoke.

Erskine stared after him and wondered. The Doctor's words seemed to steady him, to sober his wretched thoughts.

A messenger skidded to a halt beside him. 'Can you come, sir? Control report damage and casualties in the T/S!'

He started to run, but Erskine said: 'Walk, lad! We don't want to start a panic.'

The seaman saw his smile and felt reassured. There might still be hope.

Together they walked towards the bank of smoke with its depraved scarlet centre.

Chesnaye ducked as the blasted water spattered over the bridge screen. Each shell-burst seemed to punch his body like a steel fist, and every direct hit drove him to a kind of inner frenzy. The water boiled and seethed on either beam, like devils' whirlpools.

That last salvo had been a perfect straddle. 'Port twenty!' He prayed that the armoured wheelhouse was still unscathed. He felt the ship beginning to swing, and saw the big turret turn slightly to compensate for the alteration of course. Thank God he had been able to calm Norris after that first hit. He watched narrowly as more shells whimpered overhead. Not so heavy this time?

Fox said sharply, 'The cruisers have opened fire, sir!'

Chesnaye felt his heart plunge. They had to hit the battleship before the combined gunfire of the enemy blasted the *Saracen* bodily out of the water. They *had* to! Dazedly he ordered, 'Midships!'

The turret shivered as another two shells roared away into the smoke. He steadied his shaking body against the screen and tried to clear his thoughts. All around him men were shouting and passing orders. Occasionally a voice-pipe fell silent, only to be reopened by some different, frightened voice as a man stepped into the place left by killed and wounded. It could not last. Then the enemy would still destroy the convoy after all.

Another salvo. More spray, and at least two thudding blows into the monitor's battered hull. 'Starboard ten!'

At the back of his mind Chesnaye could still feel the agony he had endured when Laidlaw had reported: '*Cape Cod*'s gone, sir! She's rolled over!'

Even the overpowering menace of the battleship's winking guns could not lessen that final anguish.

There was a sharp crack behind him as more splinters whined over the bridge. As he turned he saw Fox stagger and fall beside the compass, his teeth bared in pain.

Bouverie fell on his knees beside him, his eyes searching but helpless. Fox spoke betweeen his teeth, his agonised gaze fixed on Bouverie's face. 'Get away from me, you maniac!' He moved his hands across his waist where the scarlet stain was spreading with each painful breath. 'Get up on that compass, you bloody lawyer! And try to remember what I've taught you!'

He even grinned as Bouverie staggered to his feet and climbed on to the compass platform. Then he looked up at Chesnaye who had knelt beside him. 'He'll do, sir! He won't let you down!' His hard, uncompromising features seemed to soften, and he lowered his forehead against Chesnaye's shoulder. 'Don't reproach yourself, Skipper! You were right!' Then his head lolled to one side.

Chesnaye stood up, his face ashen. 'Report damage!'

They were all dying. And for what?

He crossed to the bridge sight and pressed his head against the worn pad. The careering battleship leapt into life in the lenses, her three turrets smoking as the gunners reloaded. His feet tingled as another shell ploughed along the *Saracen*'s deck and exploded below an Oerlikon mounting, blasting the gunners to oblivion. The enemy cruisers were increasing speed, dashing in to complete the kill.

Chesnaye stared with dull disbelief as the battleship's forward turret opened skywards in one long orange flash.

Chesnaye snatched the control handset, only to hear Norris screaming like a maniac: 'A hit! Jesus Christ, a bloody *hit*!'

One of the monitor's shells, dropping with the speed of hundreds of feet a second, had found a target. The great, armour-piercing mass of screaming explosive had punctured the flat surface of the ship's 'A' turret even as the gunners had been reloading. Three fifteen-inch shells had been about to enter three smoking breeches. The Italian gunnery officer had been confident that they would be the final death blow to the shell-blasted wreck which had been crawling and staggering towards the ship, and which had defied every explosion.

The *Saracen*'s shell and the three Italian ones joined together in one mighty chorus, which was heard in the convoy and by the trapped and dying men in the *Saracen*'s hull. The battleship's turret was lifted bodily from its barbette, and in going severely buckled the neighbouring 'B' turret, so that it too was rendered harmless.

The cruisers continued to fire. The nearest one was already sweeping round in a tight arc to cut its way past the maddened *Saracen*.

Chesnaye lowered his glasses and heard the puny cracks from the port four-inch battery. Pin-pricks against the cruiser. But whatever else happened now, his ship, his *Saracen*, had struck home.

He thought distantly of Royston-Jones' small monkey face. His grave, unwavering pride in the ship. 'With courage and integrity, press on!'

Bouverie called: 'Fire gaining hold aft, sir! They want to flood the compartment!'

Chesnaye answered wearily, 'Very well.'

The monitor was already sluggish and hardly answering his constant wheel orders. As soon as the battleship had recovered its wits the other big turret would be brought to bear again. There would be no mercy now.

Chesnaye turned his back on the enemy and looked back at his ship. The tripod mast was only supported by its stays, the whole structure sagging against the rear of the bridge. The funnel leaked smoke from hundreds of splinter holes, and through the fog of battle Chesnaye caught glimpses of the upper deck. It was pitted with massive craters, some of which glittered with black water. The ship was slowly being torn apart. Dead and dying men lay everywhere. Even his own uniform was spattered with blood from a cut across his scalp.

Yet the old girl was hanging on. With a schoolmaster, half crazy with terror, gauging each shot and guiding the monitor's guns on to their target. A barrister at the compass, white-faced, but strangely determined as his legs still straddled Fox's crumpled body.

And what of me? He ran his eye across the smashed and torn ship. I brought them all to *this*.

The bridge shook, and a signalman screamed as a splinter tore away his arm. Chesnaye heard Wickersley's voice through the bedlam, and watched as the first-aid party clambered over the buckled metal to get at the victims.

The cruisers were on either beam, but Norris still obeyed Chesnaye's last order. Keep firing at the battleship. Keep hitting her no matter what else happens.

A seamen was staggering down the port waist carrying a limp, spread-eagled figure. Chesnaye watched the man's groping footsteps with chilled fascination. He was carrying Danebury, the small midshipman. The man passed into safety behind the bridge, and Chesnaye had to shake himself to clear away the nightmare. The dead midshipman. Back across the years. It was like an additional, cruel taunt.

Bouverie was sobbing: 'Sir! Sir!'

Chesnaye turned slowly, afraid of what he might see.

Bouverie half fell as he groped his way towards him. He held Chesnaye's hands, all else forgotten but what he had just seen.

'Sir! They're pulling *away*! They've had enough!'

Dazed, Chesnaye lifted his glasses for the hundredth time. The battleship's shape looked quite different. She was end on, a mounting froth at her stern. Like unwilling hounds the cruisers fired their last shots and then closed protectively around their leader. They too would have a difficult passage home now.

He nodded vaguely and touched Bouverie's arm. He could find no words. They were all round him. Wickersley, quiet and concerned, Bouverie, grinning like a schoolboy. Even Fox looked as if he was smiling.

Below he could hear cheering. Faint at first, then stronger, unquenchable, like the old ship herself.

Chesnaye saw Erskine too. He looked older. Changed. He felt his hand in his and heard him say, 'I'm *sorry*, sir!'

Sorry? For what? For Ann perhaps. For the poor, battered ship, or for himself? It did not matter which any more.

'Signal from destroyer escort, sir!' Laidlaw's beard was singed but still jaunty. 'Request instructions?'

Chesnaye felt his way to the front of the bridge. Through the mist across his eyes he could still see the fast-disappearing shapes of the enemy ships. He felt the heat-blistered steel. We did it.

The Yeoman added excitedly, 'Escort reports return of our cruiser squadron, sir!' The lights still stammered. 'They request instructions?'

Chesnaye said in a tired voice, 'Tell the Senior Officer!'

Laidlaw said thickly, '*You* are the Senior Officer now, sir!'

Chesnaye nodded. 'Very well.' They were all looking at him.

Laidlaw unconsciously left the most important item till last. 'Tug *Goliath* reports all survivors of *Cape Cod* safe on board.' He sounded puzzled. 'They keep repeating, sir. *All* survivors safe?'

Chesnaye turned away from them, and Erskine said, 'Thank you, Yeoman.' Then in a loud, clear voice he continued: 'Make this signal. To Commander-in-Chief, repeated Inshore Squadron.' He paused, his eyes fixed on Chesnaye's bowed shoulders. Then he looked across at Wickersley, and together they stood behind him.

The Captain was resting his head on the screen, as if he was speaking with the ship.

Erskine continued, 'His Majesty's Ship *Saracen* and convoy will enter harbour as ordered.'

Epilogue

Dr. Robert Wickersley walked slowly from the club dining room and crossed to the library. It was cool in the club after the exhaust-filled streets, and the London traffic was entirely cut off by the stout old walls and ancient furniture.

The library was fortunately empty, but for one of the brass-buttoned servants who immediately crossed to a corner chair and pulled a small table beside it.

'Good evenin', sir. Your usual?'

'Yes, thank you, Arthur.' Wickersley sank down in the chair and reached again for the evening paper. He no longer felt the weariness of a long day in his surgery, nor the irritation of delving into the case histories of people who had too much time and too much money to know the meaning of real illness.

With something like shock he noticed that his hand was shaking as he opened the paper at the middle page where his efficient secretary had ringed a small item near the bottom.

He had read it several times already, even in the heavy traffic as Matthews had guided the powerful Bentley skilfully towards the club. All through dinner he had thought of nothing else, yet he had been afraid to allow his mind to explore its full impact, as a surgeon falters before the moment to begin an operation.

Now he was alone. He read the item of news very slowly.

The death was reported last night of Captain Richard Chesnaye, Victoria Cross, Royal Navy (Retired), who died at his Hampshire home of a heart attack whilst watching television. Captain Chesnaye won his V.C. during the last war when defending a convoy to Malta against superior enemy forces. He leaves a widow and one son.

Wickersley folded the paper across his lap and stared unseeingly at the glass which had quietly appeared at his elbow. Twenty-three years ago. Yet in the cool silence of the library it seemed like yesterday. Like now.

574

Were we really like that? One figure remained fixed in his drifting thoughts. He could see Chesnaye's face outlined against the smoke and flames, and seemed to hear his voice.

Suddenly Wickersley was on his feet and groping through the neatly laid lines of papers and magazines. He found the *Radio Times* and thumbed back to the previous night's programmes. His heart was thumping painfully, but he knew somehow that he would find the answer there.

There it was, another small item near the bottom of the page.

Tonight viewers will see a short film from the Pacific of Britain's latest air-to-surface nuclear missile. The film, presented with the co-operation of the United States Navy, will show the missile being homed on to a moored target ship. The vessel used was an old British hulk, once named Saracen.

Wickersley sat down in his chair and stared emptily at the shadows.

So, even at the end, they had been together.